MARK TWAIN was born Samuel
Langhorne Clemens in Florida, Missouri, in 1835, and
died at Redding, Connecticut, in 1910. In his person
and in his pursuits he was a man of extraordinary contrasts. Although he left school at twelve when his father
died, he was eventually awarded honorary degrees from
Yale University, the University of Missouri, and Oxford
University. His career encompassed such varied occupations as printer, Mississippi riverboat pilot, journal-
ist, travel writer, and publisher. He made fortunes
from his writing but toward the end of his life he had
to resort to lecture tours to pay his debts. He was hot-
tempered, profane, and sentimental—and also pessi-
mistic, cynical, and tortured by self-doubt. His nostal-
gia for the past helped produce some of his best books.
He lives in American letters as a great artist, the writer
whom William Dean Howells called "the Lincoln of
our literature."

THE PRINCE AND THE PAUPER

A tale for young people of all ages

—————— AND ——————

A CONNECTICUT YANKEE IN KING ARTHUR'S COURT

by Mark Twain

Introduction by Marcus Cunliffe

Ⓒ

A SIGNET CLASSIC

NEW AMERICAN LIBRARY

TIMES MIRROR
New York and Scarborough, Ontario

SIGNET CLASSIC TRADEMARK REG. U.S. PAT. OFF. AND FOREIGN COUNTRIES
REGISTERED TRADEMARK—MARCA REGISTRADA
HECHO EN CHICAGO, U.S.A.

SIGNET, SIGNET CLASSICS, MENTOR, PLUME, MERIDIAN AND NAL
BOOKS are published *in the United States* by
The New American Library, Inc.,
1633 Broadway, New York, New York 10019,
in Canada by The New American Library of Canada Limited,
81 Mack Avenue, Scarborough, Ontario M1L 1M8

First Printing (Double Signet Classic Edition), March, 1982

1   2   3   4   5   6   7   8   9

PRINTED IN THE UNITED STATES OF AMERICA

Mark Twain and his "English" Novels

Samuel L. Clemens (or "see *Mark Twain*," as indexes and encyclopedias shunt us to the more famous pen name) was born in 1835 and died in 1910. It is generally felt that Twain's best work was done in his fourth and fifth decades, ranging from *The Adventures of Tom Sawyer* (1876) to *The Tragedy of Pudd'nhead Wilson* (1894), with *Life on the Mississippi* (1883) and *Huckleberry Finn* (1884) probably the summit of his achievement. Sam Clemens quit Hannibal, Missouri, before he was a grown man, and later on went back there only to gather notes for the autobiographical *Life on the Mississippi*. By then he was a well-established resident of New England, living in Hartford, Connecticut, in prosperous proximity to such other celebrities as Harriet Beecher Stowe. However, it is also generally assumed that Twain was a profoundly *American* writer, drawing his truest inspiration from the great Mississippi valley of boyhood and youth—the realm of his remembered, inmost heartland.

If this is so, how are we to deal with what might be called his two "English" novels? *The Prince and the Pauper* was published in December 1881. *A Connecticut Yankee in King Arthur's Court* came out eight years after, at the end of 1889. They thus belong chronologically to Twain's most productive period. Do they belong in more important respects? In any case, are they a closely related pair? Several answers—not necessarily congruent one with another—have been offered by critics and biographers. These can be summarized; then a few more may be added.

The first sort of argument is that the further Twain departed from America, in time, space, and theme, the less sure his touch. *The Prince and the Pauper* and *A Connecticut Yankee* were set not merely in England but in the past, one in the mid-16th century and the other in a semi-mythical Arthurian kingdom of around 600 A.D. Twain liked to read about the past, whether in the Waverley novels of Sir Walter Scott, the diary of Samuel Pepys, or Thomas Carlyle's fulminations on *The French Revolution*. He boned up on English history, looking for local color and for clues to how people actually spoke. But he was not a historian by instinct. Precise accuracy was unimportant to him. Sometimes he attributed to one era behavior he knew of in connection with a different period. He defended himself by arguing that if the behavior (usually brutal) were a feature of a later, supposedly more civilized time, then it was reasonable to infer that such conduct existed earlier.

At any rate, Twain scholars are apt to brush aside *The Prince and the Pauper*. They may grant that the novel is tighter in construction and more consistent in tone than much of Twain's fiction, including *A Connecticut Yankee*. Otherwise they tend to classify it with *The Personal Recollections of Joan of Arc* (1896), Twain's subsequent venture into historical romance, as irrelevant to his deepest concerns. *The Prince and the Pauper* is in this view not "American," or is too obliquely so to carry conviction. We are told that Twain yielded to Hartford neighbors who begged him to put his talents to higher use than mere slapstick. He did indeed endeavor to present a reasonably authentic picture of the England of Henry VIII and Henry's heir, Edward VI, imparting (in the slightly coy claim of the subtitle) moral lessons for "young people of all ages." The publication date fitted in with the Christmas-gift season. The "historical" narrative style Twain concocted was almost free from Americanisms. He considered publishing the book anonymously; and a reviewer in the *Atlantic Monthly,* in fact, remarked that "not even a critical expert" would attribute *The Prince and the Pauper* to Mark Twain "if his name were withheld from the title page." Twain did do this with *Joan of Arc,* introducing it as a *Harper's* magazine serial with his own authorship concealed—as if to deny an essential identity.

The *Connecticut Yankee* has been far more thoroughly worked over by critics, yet often with the intent to account for the book's uncertainty of touch. Back in 1889 the London *Spectator* disparaged the novel as "coarse and clumsy." An Edinburgh newspaper said it was "a 'lecture' in dispraise of monarchical institutions and religious establishments, and in praise of Yankee cuteness and Wall Street chicanery as compared to the simple fidelity . . . of the knightly ideal." Though such dismissals have been commoner in Britain than in the United States, we can trace a recurrent notion that when Twain strayed too far from home, literarily, he lost his way.

A second approach is to maintain that while the *Yankee* is a considerably more interesting work, both novels fit perfectly well into the Twain canon. *The Prince and the Pauper* can, for example, be show to reveal the author's lifelong fascination with doubles, twins, and reversed identities. The accidental exchange of roles between the boy-prince, England's future king Edward VI, and Tom Canty, a lad from a London slum, anticipates the switching in *Pudd'nhead Wilson* of a light-hued slave baby and a white infant. The reversal of fortunes that exposes Edward, Prince of Wales, to rags, to hunger, and to danger, likewise anticipates the plight in *A Connecticut Yankee* of King Arthur, sold into slavery through error when he accompanies Hank Morgan on an incognito tour of his domain. "Boss" Morgan, former superintendent of the Colt arms factory in Hartford, is projected back into medieval England. Twain portrays him as the quintessential American—irreverent, laconic, shrewd, and versatile. He may start out as a New England Yankee; yet as the book goes on, Morgan's skills reach out to embrace the West also: he proves to be a good horseman, a dead shot, and an expert with a lariat.

So *A Connecticut Yankee* can be thought of as a novel about Twain's America rather than about medieval England. That was the interpretation put forward by Twain's close friend, the critic-novelist William Dean Howells, reviewing *A Connecticut Yankee* with almost uncritical amity. Twain, "our arch-humorist," in Howell's words, transcended mere humor. "At every moment the scene amuses, but it is all the time an object lesson in democracy. It makes us glad of our republic and our epoch; but it does not flatter us into a fond content with them"—for, Howells suggested, the noble of King Arthur's day was shown to be basically identical to the exploitative entrepreneur of nineteenth-century Britain or America. Certainly the parallels with his modern world were specified, to Twain's hearty approval, in the illustrations supplied by the American artist Dan Beard for the first edition. (Tennyson, the poet laureate, and author of the Arthurian *Idylls of the King*, appeared as the wizard Merlin. The American "robber baron" Jay Gould was caricatured as a medieval slavemaster.)

Much of this commentary is concerned with the complexities of Clemens/Twain. Twain biographers Henry Nash Smith and Justin Kaplan have analyzed Twain's increasing difficulty in completing any book. *The Prince and the Pauper* was four interrupted years in the making. *A Connecticut Yankee* involved a still more distracted struggle. Twain was preoccupied with the Paige typesetting machine, on which he staked his and his wife's resources in the expectation that the perfected invention would revolutionize printing and bring him a vast fortune. The Paige machine, however, remained intricately imperfect. Its failure bankrupted Twain, forcing him to sell his Hartford home and live abroad in Europe during most of the 1890s. Hence, some biographers surmise, the gradual turn in *A Connecticut Yankee* from pride in nineteenth-century know-how to the grim finale of "The Battle of the Sand Belt." Twenty-five thousand knights perish in vain assaults upon an electrified defense system manned by a handful of "Boss" Morgan's technicians; but the Boss and his followers are themselves trapped and doomed inside their cave. The dream of glorious modernity goes awry. So did the author's own fantasy of becoming a tycoon—greater than Jay Gould, on a par with the multimillionaire Andrew Carnegie, with whom Twain was delighted to be on first-name terms.

Justin Kaplan detects an additional link between the novel and its creator's experiences. In 1887, Twain dropped work on it temporarily to deliver a comic-confessional lecture to some Civil War veterans. "The Private History of a Campaign that Failed" was Twain's version of how, for a few weeks in 1861, he and some Missouri acquaintances had formed a rebel or Confederate unit: a Tom Sawyerish prank, except that Sam Clemens was by then twenty-five years old, and that the gang shot an isolated stranger they mistook for the vanguard of a Union attack. In the lecture, Twain facetiously referred to the killing as "the only battle in the history of the world where the opposing force was *utterly exterminated. . . .*" Having then decided to quit the war, seceding from the seceders, he in hindsight called his decision wise, the United States being the "sole country nameable in history or tradition where a man *is* a man and manhood the only royalty." The democratic ethos is obviously a major element in *A Connecticut Yankee*. In the book, Twain's farcical-horrible "battle" memory is reversed, becoming a conflict between the modern Union and the feudal Confederacy of aristocracy and church.

The blend of criticism and biography has been a conspicuous feature of Twain scholarship. Not surprisingly: his writing is, to a degree, unusual among authors, personal in tone and at least implicitly autobiographical. Twain's unevenness, his abrupt shifts of plot, the jump from joke to sobriety, and from one level of humor to another, prompt us to seek explanations in the contrarieties of Clemens the man.

For instance, it is tempting to see his ambivalent judgments on rulers and ruled, elites and mobs, as signs of an innate dualism. Clemens/Twain was descended on one side of the family from the Lambtons—Earls of Durham, who even up to his day professed a strong attachment to visions of medieval chivalry. On the other side, he claimed descent from a regicide judge: a man associated with sending King Charles I to the scaffold in 1649.

This dualism has been charted by Howard G. Baetzhold (*Mark Twain and John Bull: The British Connection*) as an alternating dislike of and admiration for Great Britain, with admiration eventually coming out on top. Twain's final visit to England, to receive an honorary doctorate from Oxford University, was for him a marvelous accolade; and it brought his Atlantic crossings to a grand total of thirty-one. The figure is a reminder that he was an enthusiastic traveler and that he often turned toward England. He stayed for several months in 1872, and again twice in 1873-74. He toured the Continent in 1878-79, winding up with another English visit.

During the 1870s Twain was on the whole an emphatic anglophile. What he cherished, and what he missed in his own country, was the honest efficiency of government, local and national, and the enduring appeal of tradition. During the 1873 visit he told an American friend, with lyric wistfulness, of his emotion in glimpsing Admiral Nelson's *Victory*—"that colossal & superb old ship, all beflagged . . . & her old historical signal flying at her masthead once more. . . . God knows I wish we had some of England's reverence for the old & great."

Not long afterward, in 1875, Twain contributed an anonymous satire, "The Curious Republic of Gondour," to the *Atlantic Monthly*. The essay amounted to a condemnation of American-type universal suffrage, and a definite preference for a society graded through education and traditional wealth, like that of Britain. In his imaginary paradise of Gondour, every citizen had one basic vote. But a person could receive up to nine votes; the additions were reckoned on an ascending scale of educational attainment plus affluence. In a letter of 1877, Twain, probably without any tinge of irony, asserted that "Republican Government, with a sharply restricted suffrage, is just as good as a Constitutional monarchy with a virtuous & powerful aristocracy; but with an unrestricted suffrage it ought to . . . perish because it is founded in wrong & it is weak & bad & tyrannical."

By 1881, when he finished *The Prince and the Pauper*, Twain's estimate of republican democracy was more favorable, at least by the negative gauge of Reformation England. Edward, as prince and monarch, hitherto utterly ignorant of the miseries of the poor, begins to learn only when thrown among beggars and thieves. The lesson takes a while to sink in: "carve me this rabble to rags!" is his imperious cry on being rescued from a mob. Still, Edward does eventually realize that "kings should go to school to their own laws. . . , and so learn mercy." All ends happily enough. Tom Canty the pauper, and other worthy persons are properly rewarded for their loyal services. Though Edward VI died after only a few years on the throne, Twain concedes that his reign was "singularly merciful for those harsh times." Edward's courage is never in doubt; nor are his innate intelligence and decency.

Anglophilia, we are told, gave way during the 1880s to irritability and then to fury. One stimulus was *The People's History of the English Aristocracy,* a book sent to Twain in 1887 by its radical English author, George Standring. Standring edited a magazine called *The Republican,* and insisted that hereditary privilege was a fatal impediment to the development of democracy in Britain. The same argument colored *Triumphant Democracy* (1886), a hymn of praise to America by the Scottish-born magnate Andrew Carnegie. Twain, thanking Carnegie for the book in 1890, misnamed it "The Triumphant Republic," and claimed it "helped to fire me up" for the writing of *A Connecticut Yankee.*

Twain's pendulum swing toward anglophobia, if that is what it was, can also be inferred from his touchy response to various pronouncements by the distinguished English critic Matthew Arnold, who, unlike Howells, was not Twain's chum. In various articles and lectures of the 1880s, Arnold decided that the United States was not distinguished, or "interesting." Americans lacked reverence: a deficiency manifest in their "addiction to the 'funny man.'" Twain had at the outset conceived *A Connecticut Yankee* as a light, deliberately anachronistic burlesque, poking fun at outworn chivalric and superstitious modes: in short, an up-to-date equivalent of Cervantes' *Don Quixote.* This approach is still evident in the opening chapters, and intermittently thereafter.

But Twain's anger, fueled by other books like W.E.H. Lecky's *History of European Morals,* then impels him to denounce the past from the vantage point of modern America. Countering "reverence" with caustic irreverence, he adopts the unsophisticated Yankee mechanic Hank Morgan as his spokesman. Twain-as-Morgan heaps abuse upon "king, nobility and gentry, idle, unproductive, acquainted mainly with the arts of wasting and destroying, and of no . . . use or value in any rationally constructed world." They are abetted in his tale by a priesthood (mostly symbolized by Merlin) that is both credulous and unscrupulous: a Twainian composite, embodying his prejudices against Roman Catholicism as well as the established Church of England, not to mention Mormonism and Christian Science.

His principal conscious target was privileged, supercilious, parochially narrow England, his principal intended contrast an America of vigorous freemen. Scholars offer various theories to account for his renewed politeness toward England. How could such an outright republican find himself paying lavish tribute to Queen Victoria—a unique monarch, he said, surpassing the virtuous young Edward VI in her dedication to "lofty ideals"—on the occasion of her Diamond Jubilee in 1897?

One argument is that with old age Twain became more radical and more focused, that his new targets—Russia's Tsarist régime, the horrors perpetrated in the Congo by Leopold of the Belgians—made the offenses supposedly committed by a Matthew Arnold appear negligible. This thesis can be restated to stress Twain's mounting pessimism—a deterministic bias so bleak that almost all human activities, virtuous or otherwise, shrank into microscopic insignificance. Twain's final, posthumous novel, *The Mysterious Stranger* (1916), is also "historical" in that it is set in medieval Austria. Its message, however, is that human history is neither comic nor tragic, neither progressive nor reactionary, but fundamentally unreal.

Pieces of evidence can be produced in support of all the above propositions. There is no doubt, for instance, that as he grew older Mark Twain wavered in his ideas as to the role of humor. Was "fun" mainly a method of amusing, and so winning a mass audience? He obviously cared a great deal about the techniques of comedy, spoken and written: the deadpan delivery, the seeming *non sequitur*, the exact timing of the "clincher." On the other hand, he sought to justify himself, oxymoronically, as a serious entertainer, maintaining that his brand of humor, at least, was inherently humanitarian and reformist. Howells put the point by remarking that except for political humorists, notably J.R. Lowell, American funny men before Twain "chose the wrong side. . . ; they were on the side of slavery, of drunkenness, and of irreligion; the friends of civilization were their prey; their spirit was thoroughly vulgar and base."

Twain commentators have contended that Twain's temperament, and his circle of friends, imposed impossible strains. Certainly we cannot help noticing his lapses into sentimentality, especially in writing about women and children. There is also Twain the entrepreneur—an aspect that led him to attribute to the superintendent-mechanic, Hank Morgan, talents and ambitions (e.g. running a stock exchange) more appropriate to the banking magnate J.P. Morgan. This was the Twain who from time to time announced his imminent retirement from the drudgery of authorship, on the calculation that he could live off royalties and investments.

However valid these explanations, more remains to be said, emphasizing the cultural context rather than his own idiosyncratic biography. Howells was correct in believing that Twain signaled the arrival of some new force in literature, which had to do with mood, style, versatility in genre, and breadth of appeal. One of the puzzles in Twain's story is how by the early 1870s he was able to gain recognition, at home and in Europe, as an important man of letters. At that stage Twain's *curriculum vitae* included little more than the "Celebrated Jumping Frog" story, popularity as a platform humorist, and *The Innocents Abroad* (1869). The record itself is not big enough to account for his astonishing reception in the Anglo-American literary realm. The popularity came, I think, because he filled a gap—the need hitherto met by W.M. Thackeray and Charles Dickens, who died in 1863 and 1870 respectively. Thackeray and Dickens both began as humorists (with comic pseudonyms), yet evolved into more serious art. Both were versatile, and prolific. Both lectured, Dickens with especial histrionic flair. In 1846 both brought out travel narratives, Thackeray the *Notes of a Journey from Cornhill to Grand Cairo* and Dickens the *Pictures from Italy,* which combined solemn art appreciation with passages of facetious swagger. Both, as professional authors, produced for the Christmas market. Both tried their hand at historical novels (Thackeray's *Henry Esmond,* Dickens' *A Tale of Two Cities*). And, to repeat, both died in mid-career, leaving a vacuum that no one else seemed quite equipped to fill. By default, in came the American claimant, Samuel Langhorne Clemens, AKA Mark Twain.

The parallels with Twain are intriguing. And he, of course, wrote a play and a novel entitled *The American Claimant* (1892), probably inspired by the case of the Tichborne Claimant, an English real-life drama of the early 1870s which Twain had followed with avid interest. The claimant to the Tichborne family fortune was deemed to be a fraud, and so was Colonel Sellers, the American "heir" of Twain's story. At no conscious level, however, did he think that he had stepped into someone else's shoes, or that he was inferior in quality. We do know that Twain said he had never been able to laugh at *Pickwick Papers,* the book that brought early fame to

Dickens. Moreover, he came to detest his onetime friend Bret Harte, and counted among Harte's faults a tendency to plagiarize, from Dickens. In 1879, too, he was bruised by a clipping from a London newspaper which preferred Harte's humor as "more English and less thoroughly Yankee" than Twain's, and added that the crude lack of reverence in *Innocents Abroad* would prevent such humor from ever reaching the heights occupied by Dickens and Thackeray.

Consciously or not, Mark Twain did achieve an Anglo-American renown almost as great as that of Sir Walter Scott, more popularly based than that of the gentlemanly Thackeray, and possibly equivalent to that of the spectacularly self-made entertainer-moralist Dickens. Scott was the only one of the three Twain publicly denigrated—and this (from *Life on the Mississippi*) mainly in the guise of an indictment of the false chivalry of the American South, which he blamed on an excessive appetite for reading Scott's romances. Twain studied Scott, however, in preparation for his own ventures into historical fiction; and there is clear evidence that he felt such an endeavor was fitting for important authors on the plane of Scott, Thackeray, Dickens, and perhaps another prolific, well-known British novelist, Bulwer Lytton.

In other words, Twain regarded historical fiction as a genuine challenge. It sold well, on both sides of the Atlantic (and with both of which authors as famous as Dickens and Twain must win approval: hence the passionate interest of both men to improve international copyright protection). Some of this work was designed for the increasingly numerous juvenile market. Twain himself admitted that he had picked up notions for *The Prince and the Pauper* from Charlotte M. Yonge, whose tales of English history for young folks included *The Little Duke* and *The Prince and the Page*. He convinced himself that his own book had stimulated Frances Hodgson Burnett to write her best-selling *Little Lord Fauntleroy* (1886). Twain's *Prince and the Pauper* was intended to sell, to readers of all ages and as many countries as possible (not surprisingly, he was eager to be published in other languages). But on some higher plane, *The Prince* like *Joan of Arc* and (more confusedly) *A Connecticut Yankee*, was visualized by Twain not as a hasty commercial offering, but as a demonstration of his full literary armament.

Despite mock-humorous disclaimers, Twain felt he could speak to a worldwide audience, as Dickens had done. In part this was because of the universality of humor. In part it derived from his own unvarying certainty: that the best English was now being written by Americans, and that the very best came from his pen. We should add that, hostile reviewers aside, a multitude of people agreed with him.

Twain devoted an extraordinary intensity of effort to denouncing the stylistic errors of *bêtes noires* such as Matthew Arnold and James Fenimore Cooper, as if their literary sins were forms of moral depravity. To be made an Oxford D.Litt., in 1907, was almost to suggest that the republic of letters was better understood as a kingdom. "King" was in fact the nickname given to Twain by his court of intimates in these last years.

This is not to say he was ultimately an anglophile. On the contrary: he resented the overlordship of English literature, and exulted in the belief that the Americans had taken "the bulk of the shares" in the "joint stock company" of their common language, with himself the chief speculator in cornering the market. He felt the process was an Americanizing one, but also that slang or hyperbole were by no means the only American modes. Pure diction and universal/historical material were available to every master of the British or American culture.

In the process, Twain was a prominent figure, but only one of several; and like them he was influenced by more than purely personal concerns. In a literary sense it is doubtful whether any author directly "influenced" him. He was entitled to take pride in his wayward originality. Nevertheless, a quite considerable quantity of novels and stories in the Anglo-American literary domain are close enough to his to show that certain problems, plots, and so on were in the common air. Some of these are often mentioned: for instance, the dual personality theme in Robert Louis Stevenson's *Dr. Jekyll and Mr. Hyde* (1886). Another much-read novel, Rider Haggard's *King Solomon's Mines* (1885) anticipates Hank Morgan: Haggard's hero, in peril among savages, overawes them through foreknowledge that a solar eclipse is about to occur. The exchange of roles in *The Prince and the Pauper* can be compared to F. Anstey's comic English novel *Vice Versa* (1882), in which a wretched schoolboy is delighted to change places with his father Mr. Bultitude, a pompous businessman. In 1889, the same year as *A Connecticut Yankee*, another American humorist, the whimsical Frank Stockton, published *The Great War Syndicate*, an ingenious fantasy of future technological combat.

One other fascinating anticipation deserves attention. Several novels by Edward Bulwer Lytton were in Twain's Hartford library, among them *The Last of the Barons* (1843). It deals with the fifteenth-century Earl of Warwick, the "Kingmaker," at whose castle the story of Hank Morgan is introduced. Warwick is a brave leader, though finally killed in battle, and for his day unusually open-minded. A subplot involves a scientist-inventor named Adam Warner. Warner at one moment applies his intelligence to improving the design of the primitive cannon of the period. His main task however is to perfect his "Eureka" machine, a kind of steam engine. When Warner explains the project to the Earl, Warwick is worried that if actually put into service the machine would "turn this bold land of yeomanry and manhood into one community of griping traders and sickly artisans. *Mort Dieu!* we are over-commerced as it is. . . ." Even so, the Earl is sensible enough to grasp that "if thou canst succeed in making the elements do the work of man with equal precision, but with far greater force and rapidity, thou must multiply eventually, and, by multiplying, cheapen all the products of industry; that thou must give to this country the market of the world—and that thine would be the true alchemy that turneth all to gold." The Kingmaker determines to encourage the inventor, for the good of mankind, and above all, of England. He warns his assembly not to accuse Adam of black magic: "For ye wot well that the commons, from ignorance, would impute all to witchcraft that passeth their understanding."

But there is a cleric-villain, Friar Bungey, as envious, ignorant, bigoted, and vicious as Twain's Merlin. Bungey contrives the destruction of the "Eureka" machine and a painful death for the hapless inventor.

Did Twain read *The Last of the Barons?* Did the tale lodge in his subconscious, surfacing when he began the saga of Hank Morgan? We cannot tell and perhaps it does not greatly matter. What is important to grasp is that in the last third of the nineteenth century, dozens of authors, British and American and some from other countries, drew eclectically upon a large available stock of genres and motifs. Some, including R.L. Stevenson and Rudyard Kipling, went beyond Twain in at least one respect: they were fluent versifiers where he had to content himself with notebook doggerel. Some, such as Stockton and Jerome K. Jerome, never quite broke out of the limiting conventions of middlebrow entertainment. Some engaged themselves in the relatively new field of detective fiction. Several—Jules Verne, Edward Bellamy, H.G. Wells—addressed themselves to what has become known as "futurology."

Several others looked back, often to Tudor or Plantagenet England. A few hinted at burlesque, perhaps remembering the absurd fiasco of the Eglinton Tournament of 1839—a romantic pageant in Scotland, washed out by rain. Most, though, were more or less in earnest. The American Charles Major, for example, sold many thousand copies of his historical romance *When Knighthood Was in Flower* (1898). It and similar novels prompted Howells to complain that in current literature "nothing of late has been heard but the din of arms, the horrid tumult of the swashbuckler swashing on his buckler." William Morris (e.g. *A Dream of John Bull*, 1888) was among those who resorted to the past in order to create fables of an alternative future.

The more ambitious a writer, the more diversely experimental as a rule, and often the more restless. Bulwer Lytton had a go at almost everything, even a novel of the future *(The Coming Race)*. Arthur Conan Doyle, unhappy at being confined to the exploits of Sherlock Holmes, ventured both into historical fiction and into stories of ultramodern combat.

Mark Twain was shaped by this Anglo-American milieu. He also helped to shape it, being more gifted and no more erratic than a number of his contemporaries. As an American, who had indeed started out as a "funny man," he was perhaps under exceptional pressure to prove himself entitled to equal Thackeray and Dickens. We may still feel that his very best work was located in the Mississippi Valley. But he *was* versatile. He wished to prove himself so. He did genuinely share the complex enthusiasm of his age for historical romance. He had, he told Howells, felt "jubilant" in the writing of *The Prince and the Pauper*—at ease, confident in his power to bring the past alive in the present. Mark Twain's forays into English and European history were in his own estimation as justified as, perhaps finer than, all his other writings. If we do not altogether share this view, it merits sympathetic consideration. And, whatever our reservations as to Twain's skill at historical pastiche, a glance at the efforts of other authors in the same vein helps to bring out his decisive superiority. What he could have done if he had set out to dissect the "literary offences" of *When Knighthood was in Flower* or of *The Last of the Barons!*

—Marcus Cunliffe
George Washington University

THE PRINCE
AND THE
PAUPER

A tale for
young people of all ages

A NOTE ON THE TEXT

The Signet Classic text of *The Prince and the Pauper* is reprinted from the first edition, which was published in 1882 by James R. Osgood and Company, Boston. Spelling and punctuation have been brought into conformity with current American usage.

To

those good-mannered and agreeable children

Susie and Clara Clemens

this book

is affectionately inscribed

by their father

The quality of mercy . . . .
                    is twice bless'd;
It blesseth him that gives, and him that takes;
'Tis mightiest in the mightiest: it becomes
The thronèd monarch better than his crown.
                             Merchant of Venice

CONTENTS

PREFACE

I will set down a tale as it was told to me by one who had it of his father, which latter had it of *his* father, this last having in like manner had it of *his* father, and so on, back and still back, three hundred years and more, the fathers transmitting it to the sons and so preserving it. It may be history, it may be only a legend, a tradition. It may have happened, it may not have happened; but it *could* have happened. It may be that the wise and the learned believed it in the old days; it may be that only the unlearned and the simple loved it and credited it.

FROM THE NATIONAL MANUSCRIPTS PRESERVED BY THE BRITISH GOVERNMENT

[Facsimile of a handwritten letter in sixteenth-century script; text largely illegible.]

HUGH LATIMER, *Bishop of Worcester, to* LORD CROM-
WELL, *on the birth of the* PRINCE OF WALES
(*afterward* EDWARD VI)

FROM THE NATIONAL MANUSCRIPTS PRESERVED BY
THE BRITISH GOVERNMENT

Ryght honorable, *Salutem in Christo Jesu,* and Syr here
ys no lesse joynge and rejossynge in thes partees for the
byrth of our prynce, hoom we hungurde for so longe, then
ther was (I trow), *inter vicinos* att the byrth of S. I.
Baptyste, as thys berer, Master Erance, can telle you. Gode
gyffe us alle grace, to yelde dew thankes to our Lorde Gode,
Gode of Inglonde, for verely He hathe shoyd Hym selff
Gode of Inglonde, or rather an Inglyssh Gode, yf we
consydyr and pondyr welle alle Hys procedynges with us
from tyme to tyme. He hath overcumme alle our yllnesse
with Hys excedynge goodnesse, so that we ar now moor
then compellyd to serve Hym, seke Hys glory, promott Hys
wurde, yf the Devylle of alle Devylles be natt in us. We
have now the stooppe of vayne trustes ande the stey of
vayne expectations; lett us alle pray for hys preservatione.
Ande I for my partt wylle wyssh that hys Grace allways
have, and evyn now from the begynynge, Governares,
Instructores and offyceres of ryght jugmente, *ne optimum
ingenium non optimâ educatione depravetur.*

Butt whatt a grett fowlle am I! So, whatt devotione
shoyth many tymys butt lytelle dyscretione! Ande thus the
Gode of Inglonde be ever with you in alle your procedynges.

The 19 of October.

Youres, H. L. B. of Wurcestere, now att Hartlebury.

Yf you wolde excytt thys berere to be moore hartye ayen
the abuse of ymagry or mor forwarde to promotte the
veryte, ytt myght doo goode. Natt that ytt came of me, butt
of your selffe, &c.

(*Addressed*) To the Ryght Honorable Loorde P. Sealle
hys synguler gode Lorde.

1 THE BIRTH OF THE PRINCE AND THE PAUPER

In the ancient city of London, on a certain autumn day in the second quarter of the sixteenth century, a boy was born to a poor family of the name of Canty, who did not want him. On the same day another English child was born to a rich family of the name of Tudor, who did want him. All England wanted him too. England had so longed for him, and hoped for him, and prayed God for him that now that he was really come, the people went nearly mad for joy. Mere acquaintances hugged and kissed each other and cried. Everybody took a holiday, and high and low, rich and poor, feasted and danced and sang, and got very mellow; and they kept this up for days and nights together. By day London was a sight to see, with gay banners waving from every balcony and house-top and splendid pageants marching along. By night it was again a sight to see, with its great bonfires at every corner and its troops of revelers making merry around them. There was no talk in all of England but of the new baby, Edward Tudor, Prince of Wales, who lay lapped in silks and satins, unconscious of all this fuss, and not knowing that great lords and ladies were tending him and watching over him—and not caring either. But there was no talk about the other baby, Tom Canty, lapped in his poor rags, except among the family of paupers whom he had just come to trouble with his presence.

2 TOM'S EARLY LIFE

Let us skip a number of years.

London was fifteen hundred years old, and was a great town—for that day. It had a hundred thousand inhabitants—some think double as many. The streets were very narrow, and crooked, and dirty, especially in that part where Tom Canty lived, which was not far from London Bridge. The houses were of wood, with the second story projecting over the first, and the third sticking its elbows out beyond the second. The higher the houses grew, the broader they grew. They were skeletons of strong crisscross beams, with solid material between coated with plaster. The beams were painted red or blue or black, according to the owner's taste, and this gave the houses a very picturesque look. The windows were small, glazed with little diamond-shaped panes, and they opened outward on hinges like doors.

The house which Tom's father lived in was up a foul little pocket called Offal Court, out of Pudding Lane. It was small, decayed, and rickety, but it was packed full of wretchedly poor families. Canty's tribe occupied a room on the third floor. The mother and father had a sort of bedstead in the corner; but Tom, his grandmother, and his two sisters, Bet and Nan, were not restricted—they had all the floor to themselves and might sleep where they chose. There were the remains of a blanket or two and some bundles of ancient and dirty straw, but these could not rightly be called beds, for they were not organized; they were kicked into a general pile mornings, and selections made from the mass at night for service.

Bet and Nan were fifteen years old—twins. They were

goodhearted girls, unclean, clothed in rags, and profoundly ignorant. Their mother was like them. But the father
and the grandmother were a couple of fiends. They got
drunk whenever they could; then they fought each other or
anybody else who came in the way; they cursed and swore
always, drunk or sober; John Canty was a thief, and his
mother a beggar. They made beggars of the children but
failed to make thieves of them. Among, but not of, the
dreadful rabble that inhabited the house was a good old
priest whom the king had turned out of house and home
with a pension of a few farthings, and he used to get
the children aside and teach them right ways secretly.
Father Andrew also taught Tom a little Latin and how
to read and write, and would have done the same with
the girls, but they were afraid of the jeers of their friends,
who could not have endured such a queer accomplishment
in them.

All Offal Court was just such another hive as Canty's
house. Drunkenness, riot, and brawling were the order
there every night and nearly all night long. Broken heads
were as common as hunger in that place. Yet little Tom
was not unhappy. He had a hard time of it, but did not
know it. It was the sort of time that all the Offal Court
boys had; therefore he supposed it was the correct and
comfortable thing. When he came home empty-handed at
night, he knew his father would curse him and thrash him
first, and that when he was done the awful grandmother
would do it all over again and improve on it, and that
away in the night his starving mother would slip to him
stealthily with any miserable scrap or crust she had
been able to save for him by going hungry herself, notwithstanding she was often caught in that sort of treason
and soundly beaten for it by her husband.

No, Tom's life went along well enough, especially in
summer. He only begged just enough to save himself, for
the laws against mendicancy were stringent and the
penalties heavy; so he put in a good deal of his time
listening to good Father Andrew's charming old tales
and legends about giants and fairies, dwarfs and genii,
and enchanted castles, and gorgeous kings and princes. His
head grew to be full of these wonderful things, and many
a night as he lay in the dark on his scant and offensive
straw, tired, hungry, and smarting from a thrashing, he

unleashed his imagination and soon forgot his aches and pains in delicious picturings to himself of the charmed life of a petted prince in a regal palace. One desire came in time to haunt him day and night: it was to see a real prince, with his own eyes. He spoke of it once to some of his Offal Court comrades, but they jeered him and scoffed him so unmercifully that he was glad to keep his dream to himself after that.

He often read the priest's old books and got him to explain and enlarge upon them. His dreamings and readings worked certain changes in him by and by. His dream people were so fine that he grew to lament his shabby clothing and his dirt and to wish to be clean and better clad. He went on playing in the mud just the same, and enjoying it too; but instead of splashing around in the Thames solely for the fun of it, he began to find an added value in it because of the washings and cleansings it afforded.

Tom could always find something going on around the Maypole in Cheapside and at the fairs; and now and then he and the rest of London had a chance to see a military parade when some famous unfortunate was carried prisoner to the Tower by land or boat. One summer's day he saw poor Anne Askew and three men burned at the stake in Smithfield and heard an ex-bishop preach a sermon to them which did not interest him. Yes, Tom's life was varied and pleasant enough on the whole.

By and by Tom's reading and dreaming about princely life wrought such a strong effect upon him that he began to *act* the prince, unconsciously. His speech and manners became curiously ceremonious and courtly, to the vast admiration and amusement of his intimates. But Tom's influence among these young people began to grow now day by day, and in time he came to be looked up to by them, with a sort of wondering awe, as a superior being. He seemed to know so much! And he could do and say such marvelous things! And withal, he was so deep and wise! Tom's remarks and Tom's performances were reported by the boys to their elders; and these also presently began to discuss Tom Canty and to regard him as a most gifted and extraordinary creature. Full-grown people brought their perplexities to Tom for solution and were often astonished at the wit and wisdom of his decisions. In fact he was become a hero to all who knew him except his own family—these only saw nothing in him.

Privately, after a while, Tom organized a royal court! He was the prince; his special comrades were guards, chamberlains, equerries, lords- and ladies-in-waiting, and the royal family. Daily the mock prince was received with elaborate ceremonials borrowed by Tom from his romantic readings; daily the great affairs of the mimic kingdom were discussed in the royal council; and daily his mimic highness issued decrees to his imaginary armies, navies, and viceroyalties.

After which, he would go forth in his rags and beg a few farthings, eat his poor crust, take his customary cuffs and abuse, and then stretch himself upon his handful of foul straw and resume his empty grandeurs in his dreams.

And still his desire to look just once upon a real prince in the flesh grew upon him, day by day, and week by week, until at last it absorbed all other desires and became the one passion of his life.

One January day, on his usual begging tour, he tramped despondently up and down the region round about Mincing Lane and Little East Cheap, hour after hour, barefooted and cold, looking in at cookshop windows and longing for the dreadful pork pies and other deadly inventions displayed there; for to him these were dainties fit for the angels; that is, judging by the smell they were, for it had never been his good luck to own and eat one. There was a cold drizzle of rain; the atmosphere was murky; it was a melancholy day. At night Tom reached home so wet and tired and hungry that it was not possible for his father and grandmother to observe his forlorn condition and not be moved—after their fashion; wherefore they gave him a brisk cuffing at once and sent him to bed. For a long time his pain and hunger and the swearing and fighting going on in the building kept him awake; but at last his thoughts drifted away to far, romantic lands, and he fell asleep in the company of jeweled and gilded princelings who lived in vast palaces and had servants salaaming before them or flying to execute their orders. And then as usual, he dreamed that *he* was a princeling himself.

All night long the glories of his royal estate shone upon him: he moved among great lords and ladies in a blaze of light, breathing perfumes, drinking in delicious music, and answering the reverent obeisances of the glittering throng as it parted to make way for him, with here a smile and there a nod of his princely head.

And when he awoke in the morning and looked upon the wretchedness about him, his dream had had its usual effect: it had intensified the sordidness of his surroundings a thousandfold. Then came bitterness, and heartbreak, and tears.

3 TOM'S MEETING WITH THE PRINCE

Tom got up hungry, and sauntered hungry away, but with his thoughts busy with the shadowy splendors of his night's dreams. He wandered here and there in the city, hardly noticing where he was going or what was happening around him. People jostled him, and some gave him rough speech; but it was all lost on the musing boy. By and by he found himself at Temple Bar, the farthest from home he had ever traveled in that direction. He stopped and considered a moment, then fell into his imaginings again, and passed on outside the walls of London. The Strand had ceased to be a country road then and regarded itself as a street, but by a strained construction; for though there was a tolerably compact row of houses on one side of it, there were only some scattering great buildings on the other, these being palaces of rich nobles, with ample and beautiful grounds stretching to the river—grounds that are now closely packed with grim acres of brick and stone.

Tom discovered Charing Village presently and rested himself at the beautiful cross built there by a bereaved king of earlier days; then idled down a quiet, lovely road past the great cardinal's stately palace, toward a far more mighty and majestic palace beyond—Westminster. Tom stared in glad wonder at the vast pile of masonry, the wide-spreading wings, the frowning bastions and turrets, the huge stone gateway, with its gilded bars and its magnificent array of colossal granite lions, and the other signs and symbols of English royalty. Was the desire of his soul to be satisfied at last? Here indeed was a king's palace. Might he not hope to see a prince now, a prince of flesh and blood, if heaven were willing?

At each side of the gilded gate stood a living statue, that is to say, an erect and stately and motionless man-at-arms clad from head to heel in shining steel armor. At a respectful distance were many country folk and people from the city waiting for any chance glimpse of royalty that might offer. Splendid carriages with splendid people in them and splendid servants outside were arriving and departing by several other noble gateways that pierced the royal enclosure.

Poor little Tom, in his rags, approached and was moving slow and timidly past the sentinels, with a beating heart and a rising hope, when all at once he caught sight through the golden bars of a spectacle that almost made him shout for joy. Within was a comely boy, tanned and brown with sturdy outdoor sports and exercises, whose clothing was all of lovely silks and satins, shining with jewels—at his hip a little jeweled sword and dagger, dainty buskins on his feet, with red heels, and on his head a jaunty crimson cap with drooping plumes fastened with a great sparkling gem. Several gorgeous gentlemen stood near—his servants, without a doubt. Oh! He was a prince —a prince, a living prince, a real prince—without the shadow of a question; and the prayer of the pauper-boy's heart was answered at last.

Tom's breath came quick and short with excitement, and his eyes grew big with wonder and delight. Everything gave way in his mind instantly to one desire: that was to get close to the prince and have a good, devouring look at him. Before he knew what he was about, he had his face against the gate bars. The next instant one of the soldiers snatched him rudely away and sent him spinning among the gaping crowd of country gawks and London idlers.

The soldier said, "Mind thy manners, thou young beggar!"

The crowd jeered and laughed, but the young prince sprang to the gate with his face flushed and his eyes flashing with indignation and cried out, "How darst thou use a poor lad like that! How darst thou use the king my father's meanest subject so! Open the gates and let him in!"

You should have seen that fickle crowd snatch off their hats then. You should have heard them cheer and shout, "Long live the Prince of Wales!"

The soldiers presented arms with their halberds, opened

the gates, and presented again as the little Prince of Poverty passed in, in his fluttering rags, to join hands with the Prince of Limitless Plenty.

Edward Tudor said, "Thou lookest tired and hungry: thou'st been treated ill. Come with me."

Half a dozen attendants sprang forward to—I don't know what; interfere, no doubt. But they were waved aside with a right royal gesture, and they stopped stock-still where they were, like so many statues. Edward took Tom to a rich apartment in the palace, which he called his cabinet. By his command a repast was brought such as Tom had never encountered before except in books. The prince, with princely delicacy and breeding, sent away the servants so that his humble guest might not be embarrassed by their critical presence; then he sat nearby and asked questions while Tom ate.

"What is thy name, lad?"

"Tom Canty, an' it please thee, sir."

" 'Tis an odd one. Where dost live?"

"In the city, please thee, sir. Offal Court, out of Pudding Lane."

"Offal Court! Truly 'tis another odd one. Hast parents?"

"Parents have I, sir, and a grandam likewise that is but indifferently precious to me—God forgive me if it be offense to say it—also twin sisters, Nan and Bet."

"Then is thy grandam not over kind to thee, I take it."

"Neither to any other is she, so please your Worship. She hath a wicked heart and worketh evil all her days."

"Doth she mistreat thee?"

"There be times that she stayeth her hand, being asleep or overcome with drink; but when she hath her judgment clear again, she maketh it up to me with goodly beatings."

A fierce look came into the little prince's eyes, and he cried out, "What! Beatings?"

"Oh, indeed, yes, please you, sir."

"*Beatings!* And thou so frail and little. Hark ye; before the night come she shall hie her to the Tower. The king my father——"

"In sooth, you forget, sir, her low degree. The Tower is for the great alone."

"True, indeed. I had not thought of that. I will consider of her punishment. Is thy father kind to thee?"

"Not more than Gammer Canty, sir."

"Fathers be alike, mayhap. Mine hath not a doll's temper. He smiteth with a heavy hand, yet spareth me; he spareth me not always with his tongue, though, sooth to say. How doth thy mother use thee?"

"She is good, sir, and giveth me neither sorrow nor pain of any sort. And Nan and Bet are like to her in this."

"How old be these?"

"Fifteen, an' it please you, sir."

"The lady Elizabeth, my sister, is fourteen, and the lady Jane Grey, my cousin, is of mine own age, and comely and gracious withal; but my sister the lady Mary, with her gloomy mien and— Look you; do thy sisters forbid their servants to smile, lest the sin destroy their souls?"

"They? Oh, dost think, sir, that *they* have servants?"

The little prince contemplated the little pauper gravely a moment, then said, "And prithee, why not? Who helpeth them undress at night? Who attireth them when they rise?"

"None, sir. Wouldst have them take off their garment and sleep without—like beasts?"

"Their garment! Have they but one?"

"Ah, good your Worship, what would they do with more? Truly they have not two bodies each."

"It is a quaint and marvelous thought! Thy pardon, I had not meant to laugh. But thy good Nan and thy Bet shall have raiment and lackeys enow, and that soon too; my cofferer shall look to it. No, thank me not; 'tis nothing. Thou speakest well; thou hast an easy grace in it. Art learned?"

"I know not if I am or not, sir. The good priest that is called Father Andrew taught me, of his kindness, from his books."

"Knowst thou the Latin?"

"But scantly, sir, I doubt."

"Learn it, lad; 'tis hard only at first. The Greek is harder; but neither these nor any tongues else, I think, are hard to the lady Elizabeth and my cousin. Thou shouldst hear those damsels at it! But tell me of thy Offal Court. Hast thou a pleasant life there?"

"In truth, yes, so please you, sir, save when one is hungry. There be Punch-and-Judy shows, and monkeys —oh, such antic creatures, and so bravely dressed!—and there be plays wherein they that play do shout and fight till all are slain, and 'tis so fine to see, and costeth but a farthing, albeit 'tis main hard to get the farthing, please your Worship."

"Tell me more."

"We lads of Offal Court do strive against each other with the cudgel, like to the fashion of the 'prentices, sometimes."

The prince's eyes flashed. Said he, "Marry, that would not I mislike. Tell me more."

"We strive in races, sir, to see who of us shall be fleetest."

"That I would like also. Speak on."

"In summer, sir, we wade and swim in the canals and in the river, and each doth duck his neighbor, and spatter him with water, and dive and shout and tumble and——"

" 'Twould be worth my father's kingdom but to enjoy it once! Prithee go on."

"We dance and sing about the Maypole in Cheapside; we play in the sand, each covering his neighbor up; and times we make mud pastry—oh, the lovely mud, it hath not its like for delightfulness in all the world!—we do fairly wallow in the mud, sir, saving your worship's presence."

"Oh, prithee say no more; 'tis glorious! If that I could but clothe me in raiment like to thine, and strip my feet, and revel in the mud once, just once, with none to rebuke me or forbid, meseemeth I could forgo the crown!"

"And if that I could clothe me once, sweet sir, as thou art clad, just once——"

"Oho, wouldst like it? Then so shall it be. Doff thy rags and don these splendors, lad! It is a brief happiness, but will be not less keen for that. We will have it while we may, and change again before any come to molest."

A few minutes later the little Prince of Wales was garlanded with Tom's fluttering odds and ends, and the little Prince of Pauperdom was tricked out in the gaudy plumage of royalty. The two went and stood side by side before a great mirror, and lo, a miracle: there did not seem to have been any change made! They stared at each other, then at the glass, then at each other again. At last the puzzled princeling said, "What dost thou make of this?"

"Ah, good your worship, require me not to answer. It is not meet that one of my degree should utter the thing."

"Then will *I* utter it. Thou hast the same hair, the same eyes, the same voice and manner, the same form and stature, the same face and countenance that I bear. Fared we forth naked, there is none could say which was you, and which the Prince of Wales. And now that I am clothed as thou wert clothed, it seemeth I should be able the more nearly to feel as thou didst when the brute soldier— Hark ye, is not this a bruise upon your hand?"

"Yes; but it is a slight thing, and your Worship knoweth that the poor man-at-arms——"

"Peace! It was a shameful thing and a cruel!" cried the little prince, stamping his bare foot. "If the king— Stir not a step till I come again! It is a command!"

In a moment he had snatched up and put away an article of national importance that lay upon a table, and was out at the door and flying through the palace grounds in his bannered rags, with a hot face and glowing eyes. As soon as he reached the great gate, he seized the bars and tried to shake them, shouting, "Open! Unbar the gates!"

The soldier that had maltreated Tom obeyed promptly; and as the prince burst through the portal, half smothered with royal wrath, the soldier fetched him a sounding box on the ear that sent him whirling to the roadway and said, "Take that, thou beggar's spawn, for what thou got'st me from his Highness!"

The crowd roared with laughter. The prince picked himself out of the mud and made fiercely at the sentry, shouting, "I am the Prince of Wales, my person is sacred; and thou shalt hang for laying thy hand upon me!"

The soldier brought his halberd to a present arms and said mockingly, "I salute your gracious Highness." Then angrily, "Be off, thou crazy rubbish!"

Here the jeering crowd closed around the poor little prince and hustled him far down the road, hooting him and shouting, "Way for his royal Highness! Way for the Prince of Wales!"

4 THE PRINCE'S TROUBLES BEGIN

After hours of persistent pursuit and persecution, the little prince was at last deserted by the rabble and left to himself. As long as he had been able to rage against the mob, and threaten it royally, and royally utter commands that were good stuff to laugh at, he was very entertaining; but when weariness finally forced him to be silent, he was no longer of use to his tormentors and they sought amusement elsewhere. He looked about him now but could not recognize the locality. He was within the city of London—that was all he knew. He moved on aimlessly, and in a little while the houses thinned and the passersby were infrequent. He bathed his bleeding feet in the brook which flowed then where Farrington Street now is, rested a few moments, then passed on, and presently came upon a great space with only a few scattered houses in it and a prodigious church. He recognized this church. Scaffoldings were about everywhere, and swarms of workmen, for it was undergoing elaborate repairs. The prince took heart at once; he felt that his troubles were at an end now. He said to himself, "It is the ancient Grey Friars' Church, which the king my father hath taken from the monks and given for a home forever for poor and forsaken children, and new-named it Christ's Church. Right gladly will they serve the son of him who hath done so generously by them, and the more that that son is himself as poor and as forlorn as any that be sheltered here this day, or ever shall be."

He was soon in the midst of a crowd of boys who were running, jumping, playing at ball and leapfrog, and otherwise disporting themselves, and right noisily too. They were all dressed alike, and in the fashion which in that day prevailed among servingmen and 'prentices *—that is to say, each had on the crown of his head a flat black cap about the size of a saucer, which was not useful as a

* See Note 1 at end of volume.

covering, it being of such scanty dimensions; neither was it ornamental; from beneath it the hair fell, unparted, to the middle of the forehead, and was cropped straight around; a clerical band at the neck; a blue gown that fitted closely and hung as low as the knees or lower; full sleeves; a broad red belt; bright-yellow stockings, gartered above the knees; low shoes with large metal buckles. It was a sufficiently ugly costume.

The boys stopped their play and flocked about the prince, who said with native dignity, "Good lads, say to your master that Edward, Prince of Wales, desireth speech with him."

A great shout went up at this, and one rude fellow said, "Marry, art thou his Grace's messenger, beggar?"

The prince's face flushed with anger, and his ready hand flew to his hip, but there was nothing there. There was a storm of laughter, and one boy said, "Didst mark that? He fancied he had a sword—belike he is the prince himself."

This sally brought more laughter. Poor Edward drew himself up proudly and said, "I am the prince, and it ill beseemeth you that feed upon the king my father's bounty to use me so."

This was vastly enjoyed, as the laughter testified. The youth who had first spoken shouted to his comrades, "Ho, swine, slaves, pensioners of his Grace's princely father, where be your manners? Down on your marrow-bones, all of ye, and do reverence to his kingly port and royal rags!"

With boisterous mirth they dropped upon their knees in a body and did mock homage to their prey. The prince spurned the nearest boy with his foot and said fiercely, "Take thou that till the morrow come and I build thee a gibbet!"

Ah, but this was not a joke; this was going beyond fun. The laughter ceased on the instant, and fury took its place. A dozen shouted, "Hale him forth! To the horse-pond, to the horsepond! Where be the dogs? Ho, there, Lion! Ho, Fangs!"

Then followed such a thing as England had never seen before—the sacred person of the heir to the throne rudely buffeted by plebeian hands and set upon and torn by dogs.

As night drew to a close that day, the prince found himself far down in the close-built portion of the city. His body was bruised, his hands were bleeding, and his rags were all besmirched with mud. He wandered on and on, and grew more and more bewildered, and so tired and faint he could hardly drag one foot after the other. He had ceased to ask questions of anyone, since they brought him only insult instead of information. He kept muttering to himself, "Offal Court—that is the name; if I can but find it before my strength is wholly spent and I drop, then am I saved, for his people will take me to the palace and prove that I am none of theirs, but the true prince, and I shall have mine own again." And now and then his mind reverted to his treatment by those rude Christ's Hospital boys, and he said, "When I am king, they shall not have bread and shelter only, but also teachings out of books, for a full belly is little worth where the mind is starved, and the heart. I will keep this diligently in my remembrance, that this day's lesson be not lost upon me, and my people suffer thereby; for learning softeneth the heart and breedeth gentleness and charity." *

The lights began to twinkle, it came on to rain, the wind rose, and a raw and gusty night set in. The houseless prince, the homeless heir to the throne of England, still moved on, drifting deeper into the maze of squalid alleys where the swarming hives of poverty and misery were massed together.

Suddenly a great drunken ruffian collared him and said, "Out to this time of night again, and hast not brought a farthing home, I warrant me! If it be so, an' I do not break all the bones in thy lean body, then am I not John Canty, but some other."

The prince twisted himself loose, unconsciously brushed his profaned shoulder, and eagerly said, "Oh, art *his* father, truly? Sweet heaven grant it be so; then wilt thou fetch him away and restore me!"

"*His* father? I know not what thou meanst; I but know I am *thy* father, as thou shalt soon have cause to——"

"Oh, jest not, palter not, delay not! I am worn, I am wounded, I can bear no more. Take me to the king my father, and he will make thee rich beyond thy wildest dreams. Believe me, man, believe me! I speak no

* See Note 2 at end of volume.

lie, but only the truth! Put forth thy hand and save me!
I am indeed the Prince of Wales!"

The man stared down, stupefied, upon the lad, then
shook his head and muttered, "Gone stark mad as any
Tom o' Bedlam!"—then collared him once more and
said with a coarse laugh and an oath, "But mad or no mad,
I and thy Gammer Canty will soon find where the soft
places in thy bones lie, or I'm no true man!"

With this he dragged the frantic and struggling prince
away and disappeared up a front court followed by a
delighted and noisy swarm of human vermin.

5 TOM AS A PATRICIAN

Tom Canty, left alone in the prince's cabinet, made good use of his opportunity. He turned himself this way and that before the great mirror, admiring his finery; then walked away, imitating the prince's highbred carriage, and still observing results in the glass. Next he drew the beautiful sword and bowed, kissing the blade and laying it across his breast as he had seen a noble knight do, by way of salute to the lieutenant of the Tower, five or six weeks before, when delivering the great lords of Norfolk and Surrey into his hands for captivity. Tom played with the jeweled dagger that hung upon his thigh; he examined the costly and exquisite ornaments of the room; he tried each of the sumptuous chairs and thought how proud he would be if the Offal Court herd could only peep in and see him in his grandeur. He wondered if they would believe the marvelous tale he should tell when he got home or if they would shake their heads and say his overtaxed imagination had at last upset his reason.

At the end of half an hour it suddenly occurred to him that the prince was gone a long time; then right away he began to feel lonely; very soon he fell to listening and longing, and ceased to toy with the pretty things about him; he grew uneasy, then restless, then distressed. Suppose someone should come and catch him in the prince's clothes, and the prince not there to explain. Might they not hang him at once and inquire into his case afterward? He had heard that the great were prompt about small matters. His fears rose higher and higher, and trembling, he softly opened the door to the antechamber, resolved to fly and seek the prince, and through him, protection and release. Six gorgeous gentlemen servants and two young pages of high degree, clothed like butterflies, sprung to their feet and bowed low before him. He stepped quickly back and shut the door. He said, "Oh, they mock at me! They will go and tell. Oh! Why came I here to cast away my life?"

He walked up and down the floor, filled with nameless fears, listening, starting at every trifling sound. Presently the door swung open and a silken page said, "The lady Jane Grey."

The door closed, and a sweet young girl, richly clad, bounded toward him. But she stopped suddenly and said in a distressed voice, "Oh, what aileth thee, my lord?"

Tom's breath was nearly failing him, but he made shift to stammer out, "Ah, be merciful, thou! In sooth I am no lord, but only poor Tom Canty of Offal Court in the city. Prithee let me see the prince, and he will of his grace restore to me my rags and let me hence unhurt. Oh, be thou merciful and save me!"

By this time the boy was on his knees and supplicating with his eyes and uplifted hands as well as with his tongue. The young girl seemed horror-stricken. She cried out, "Oh, my lord, on thy knees? And to *me!*"

Then she fled away in fright; and Tom, smitten with despair, sank down, murmuring, "There is no help, there is no hope. Now will they come and take me."

Whilst he lay there benumbed with terror, dreadful tidings were speeding through the palace. The whisper, for it was whispered always, flew from menial to menial, from lord to lady, down all the long corridors, from story to story, from saloon to saloon, "The prince hath gone mad, the prince hath gone mad!" Soon every saloon, every marble hall, had its group of glittering lords and ladies and other groups of dazzling lesser folk, talking earnestly together in whispers, and every face had in it dismay. Presently a splendid official came marching by these groups, making solemn proclamation, "In the name of the king! Let none list to this false and foolish matter, upon pain of death, nor discuss the same, nor carry it abroad. In the name of the king!"

The whisperings ceased as suddenly as if the whisperers had been stricken dumb.

Soon there was a general buzz along the corridors of, "The prince! See, the prince comes!"

Poor Tom came slowly walking past the low-bowing

groups, trying to bow in return, and meekly gazing upon his strange surroundings with bewildered and pathetic eyes. Great nobles walked upon each side of him, making him lean upon them, and so steady his steps. Behind him followed the court physicians and some servants.

Presently Tom found himself in a noble apartment of the palace and heard the door close behind him. Around him stood those who had come with him. Before him, at a little distance, reclined a very large and very fat man with a wide, pulpy face and a stern expression. His large head was very gray; and his whiskers, which he wore only around his face, like a frame, were gray also. His clothing was of rich stuff, but old and slightly frayed in places. One of his swollen legs had a pillow under it and was wrapped in bandages. There was silence now, and there was no head there but was bent in reverence, except this man's. This stern-countenanced invalid was the dread Henry VIII. He said—and his face grew gentle as he began to speak—"How now, my lord Edward, my prince? Hast been minded to cozen me, the good king thy father, who loveth thee and kindly useth thee, with a sorry jest?"

Poor Tom was listening, as well as his dazed faculties would let him, to the beginning of this speech; but when the words "me, the good king" fell upon his ear, his face blanched and he dropped as instantly upon his knees as if a shot had brought him there. Lifting up his hands, he exclaimed, "Thou the *king?* Then am I undone indeed!"

This speech seemed to stun the king. His eyes wandered from face to face aimlessly, then rested, bewildered, upon the boy before him. Then he said in a tone of deep disappointment, "Alack, I had believed the rumor disproportioned to the truth, but I fear me 'tis not so." He breathed a heavy sigh and said in a gentle voice, "Come to thy father, child; thou art not well."

Tom was assisted to his feet, and approached the Majesty of England, humble and trembling. The king took the frightened face between his hands and gazed earnestly and lovingly into it awhile, as if seeking some grateful sign of returning reason there, then pressed the curly head against his breast and patted it tenderly. Presently he said, "Dost not know thy father, child? Break not mine old heart; say thou knowst me. Thou *dost* know me, dost thou not?"

"Yea, thou art my dread lord the king, whom God preserve!"

"True, true—that is well—be comforted, tremble not so; there is none here would hurt thee; there is none here but loves thee. Thou art better now; thy ill dream passeth; is't not so? And thou knowest thyself now also; is't not so? Thou wilt not miscall thyself again, as they say thou didst a little while agone?"

"I pray thee of thy Grace believe me, I did but speak the truth, most dread lord, for I am the meanest among thy subjects, being a pauper born, and 'tis by a sore mischance and accident I am here, albeit I was therein nothing blameful. I am but young to die, and thou canst save me with one little word. Oh, speak it, sir!"

"Die? Talk not so, sweet prince; peace, peace, to thy troubled heart; thou shalt not die!"

Tom dropped upon his knees with a glad cry, "God requite thy mercy, O my king, and save thee long to bless thy land!" Then springing up, he turned a joyful face toward the two lords-in-waiting and exclaimed, "Thou heardst it! I am not to die; the king hath said it!" There was no movement, save that all bowed with grave respect; but no one spoke. He hesitated, a little confused, then turned timidly toward the king, saying, "I may go now?"

"Go? Surely, if thou desirest. But why not tarrry yet a little? Whither wouldst go?"

Tom dropped his eyes and answered humbly, "Peradventure I mistook; but I did think me free, and so was I moved to seek again the kennel where I was born and bred to misery, yet which harboreth my mother and my sisters, and so is home to me; whereas these pomps and splendors whereunto I am not used— Oh, please you, sir, to let me go!"

The king was silent and thoughtful awhile, and his face betrayed a growing distress and uneasiness. Presently he said, with something of hope in his voice, "Perchance he is but mad upon this one strain and hath his wits unmarred as toucheth other matter. God send it may be so! We will make trial."

Then he asked Tom a question in Latin, and Tom

answered him lamely in the same tongue. The king was delighted, and showed it. The lords and doctors manifested their gratification also. The king said, " 'Twas not according to his schooling and ability, but sheweth that his mind is but diseased, not stricken fatally. How say you, sir?"

The physician addressed bowed low and replied, "It jumpeth with mine own conviction, sire, that thou hast divined aright."

The king looked pleased with this encouragement, coming as it did from so excellent authority, and continued with good heart, "Now mark ye all; we will try him further."

He put a question to Tom in French. Tom stood silent a moment, embarrassed by having so many eyes centered upon him, then said diffidently, "I have no knowledge of this tongue, so please your majesty."

The king fell back upon his couch. The attendants flew to his assistance; but he put them aside and said, "Trouble me not—it is nothing but a scurvy faintness. Raise me! There, 'tis sufficient. Come hither, child; there, rest thy poor troubled head upon thy father's heart and be at peace. Thou'lt soon be well; 'tis but a passing fantasy. Fear thou not; thou'lt soon be well." Then he turned toward the company; his gentle manner changed, and baleful lightnings began to play from his eyes. He said, "List ye all! This my son is mad, but it is not permanent. Overstudy hath done this, and somewhat too much of confinement. Away with his books and teachers! See ye to it. Pleasure him with sports, beguile him in wholesome ways, so that his health come again." He raised himself higher still and went on with energy, "He is mad, but he is my son and England's heir, and mad or sane, still shall he reign! And hear ye further, and proclaim it: whoso speaketh of this his distemper worketh against the peace and order of these realms and shall to the gallows! Give me to drink—I burn: this sorrow sappeth my strength. There, take away the cup. Support me. There, that is well. Mad, is he? Were he a thousand times mad, yet is he Prince of Wales, and I the king will confirm it. This very morrow shall he be installed in his princely dignity in due and ancient form. Take instant order for it, my lord Hertford."

One of the nobles knelt at the royal couch and said,
"The king's majesty knoweth that the Hereditary Great
Marshall of England lieth attainted in the Tower. It were
not meet that one attainted——"

"Peace! Insult not mine ears with his hated name. Is
this man to live forever? Am I to be balked of my will? Is
the prince to tarry uninstalled because, forsooth, the realm
lacketh an earl marshal free of treasonable taint to invest
him with his honors? No, by the splendor of God! Warn
my Parliament to bring me Norfolk's doom before the sun
rise again, else shall they answer for it grievously!" *

Lord Hertford said, "The king's will is law," and rising,
returned to his former place.

Gradually the wrath faded out of the old king's face,
and he said, "Kiss me, my prince. There. What fearest
thou? Am I not thy loving father?"

"Thou art good to me that am unworthy, O mighty
and gracious lord; that in truth I know. But—but—it
grieveth me to think of him that is to die, and——"

"Ah, 'tis like thee, 'tis like thee! I know thy heart is
still the same, even though thy mind hath suffered hurt, for
thou wert ever of a gentle spirit. But this duke standeth
between thee and thine honors; I will have another in
his stead that shall bring no taint to his great office.
Comfort thee, my prince; trouble not thy poor head
with this matter."

"But is it not I that speed him hence, my liege? How
long might he not live, but for me?"

"Take no thought of him, my prince; he is not worthy.
Kiss me once again and go to thy trifles and amusements,
for my malady distresseth me. I am aweary and would
rest. Go with thine uncle Hertford and thy people, and
come again when my body is refreshed."

Tom, heavyhearted, was conducted from the presence,
for this last sentence was a deathblow to the hope he had
cherished that now he would be set free. Once more he
heard the buzz of low voices exclaiming, "The prince, the
prince comes!"

His spirits sank lower and lower as he moved between
the glittering files of bowing courtiers, for he recognized
that he was indeed a captive now and might remain for-

* See Note 3 at end of volume.

ever shut up in this gilded cage, a forlorn and friendless prince, except God in his mercy take pity on him and set him free.

And turn where he would, he seemed to see floating in the air the severed head and the remembered face of the great Duke of Norfolk, the eyes fixed on him reproachfully.

His old dreams had been so pleasant, but this reality was so dreary!

6 TOM RECEIVES INSTRUCTIONS

Tom was conducted to the principal apartment of a noble suite and made to sit down, a thing which he was loath to do since there were elderly men and men of high degree about him. He begged them to be seated also, but they only bowed their thanks or murmured them and remained standing. He would have insisted, but his "uncle" the Earl of Hertford whispered in his ear, "Prithee, insist not, my lord; it is not meet that they sit in thy presence."

The lord St. John was announced, and after making obeisance to Tom, he said, "I come upon the king's errand, concerning a matter which requireth privacy. Will it please your royal Highness to dismiss all that attend you here, save my lord the Earl of Hertford?"

Observing that Tom did not seem to know how to proceed, Hertford whispered him to make a sign with his hand and not trouble himself to speak unless he chose. When the waiting gentlemen had retired, Lord St. John said, "His Majesty commandeth that for due and weighty reasons of state, the prince's grace shall hide his infirmity in all ways that be within his power till it be passed and he be as he was before. To wit, that he shall deny to none that he is the true prince and heir to England's greatness; that he shall uphold his princely dignity and shall receive, without word or sign of protest, that reverence and observance which unto it do appertain of right and ancient usage; that he shall cease to speak to any of that lowly birth and life his malady hath conjured out of the unwholesome imaginings of o'erwrought fancy; that he shall strive with diligence to bring unto his memory again those faces which he was wont to know—and where he faileth he shall hold his peace, neither betraying by semblance of surprise or other sign that he hath forgot; that upon occasions of state, whensoever any matter shall perplex him as to the thing he should do or the utterance he should make, he shall show nought of unrest to the curious that look on, but take advice in that matter of the lord Hertford or my humble self, which are commanded of the king to be upon this service and close at call till this commandment be dissolved. Thus saith the king's majesty, who sendeth greeting to your royal Highness and prayeth that God will of his mercy quickly heal you and have you now and ever in his holy keeping."

The lord St. John made reverence and stood aside. Tom replied resignedly, "The king hath said it. None may palter with the king's command or fit it to his ease, where it doth chafe, with deft evasions. The king shall be obeyed."

Lord Hertford said, "Touching the king's majesty's ordainment concerning books and such like serious matters, it may peradventure please your Highness to ease your time with lightsome entertainment, lest you go wearied to the banquet and suffer harm thereby."

Tom's face showed inquiring surprise, and a blush followed when he saw Lord St. John's eyes bent sorrowfully upon him. His lordship said, "Thy memory still wrongeth thee, and thou hast shown surprise; but suffer it not to trouble thee, for 'tis a matter that will not bide, but depart with thy mending malady. My lord of Hertford speaketh of the city's banquet which the king's majesty did promise, some two months flown, your Highness should attend. Thou recallest it now?"

"It grieves me to confess it had indeed escaped me," said Tom in a hesitating voice, and blushed again.

At this moment the lady Elizabeth and the lady Jane Grey were announced. The two lords exchanged significant glances, and Hertford stepped quickly toward the door. As the young girls passed him, he said in a low voice, "I pray ye, ladies, seem not to observe his humors nor show surprise when his memory doth lapse, it will grieve you to note how it doth stick at every trifle."

Meantime Lord St. John was saying in Tom's ear, "Please you, sir, keep diligently in mind his Majesty's desire. Remember all thou canst, *seem* to remember all else. Let them not perceive that thou art much changed from thy wont, for thou knowest how tenderly thy old play-fellows bear thee in their hearts and how 'twould grieve them. Art willing, sir, that I remain? And thine uncle?"

Tom signified assent with a gesture and a murmured word, for he was already learning, and in his simple heart was resolved to acquit himself as best he might, according to the king's command.

In spite of every precaution, the conversation among the young people became a little embarrassing at times. More than once, in truth, Tom was near to breaking down and confessing himself unequal to his tremendous part; but the tact of the princess Elizabeth saved him, or a word from one or the other of the vigilant lords, thrown in apparently by chance, had the same happy effect. Once the little lady Jane turned to Tom and dismayed him with this question, "Hast paid thy duty to the queen's majesty today, my lord?"

Tom hesitated, looked distressed, and was about to stammer out something at hazard when Lord St. John took the word and answered for him with the easy grace of a courtier accustomed to encounter delicate difficulties and to be ready for them, "He hath indeed, madam, and she did greatly hearten him, as touching his Majesty's condition; is it not so, your Highness?"

Tom mumbled something that stood for assent, but felt that he was getting upon dangerous ground. Somewhat later it was mentioned that Tom was to study no more at present, whereupon her little ladyship exclaimed, " 'Tis a pity, 'tis such a pity! Thou wert proceeding bravely. But bide thy time in patience; it will not be for long. Thou'lt yet be graced with learning like thy father, and make thy tongue master of as many languages as his, good my prince."

"My father!" cried Tom, off his guard for the moment. "I trow he cannot speak his own so that any but the swine that wallow in the sties may tell his meaning; and as for learning of any sort soever——"

He looked up and encountered a solemn warning in my lord St. John's eyes.

He stopped, blushed, then continued low and sadly, "Ah, my malady persecuteth me again, and my mind wandereth. I meant the king's grace no irreverence."

"We know it, sir," said the princess Elizabeth, taking her "brother's" hand between her two palms, respectfully but caressingly; "trouble not thyself as to that. The fault is none of thine, but thy distemper's."

"Thou'rt a gentle comforter, sweet lady," said Tom gratefully, "and my heart moveth me to thank thee for't, an' I may be so bold."

Once the giddy little lady Jane fired a simple Greek phrase at Tom. The princess Elizabeth's quick eye saw by the serene blankness of the target's front that the shaft was overshot, so she tranquilly delivered a return volley of sounding Greek on Tom's behalf and then straightway changed the talk to other matters.

Time wore on pleasantly, and likewise smoothly, on the whole. Snags and sandbars grew less and less frequent, and Tom grew more and more at his ease, seeing that all were so lovingly bent upon helping him and overlooking his mistakes. When it came out that the little ladies were to accompany him to the Lord Mayor's banquet in the evening, his heart gave a bound of relief and delight, for he felt that he should not be friendless now among that multitude of strangers, whereas an hour earlier the idea of their going with him would have been an insupportable terror to him.

Tom's guardian angels, the two lords, had had less comfort in the interview than the other parties to it. They felt much as if they were piloting a great ship through a dangerous channel; they were on the alert constantly, and found their office no child's play. Wherefore, at last, when the ladies' visit was drawing to a close and the lord Guilford Dudley was announced, they not only felt that their charge had been sufficiently taxed for the present, but also that they themselves were not in the best condition to take their ship back and make their anxious voyage all over again. So they respectfully advised Tom to excuse himself, which he was very glad to do, although a slight shade of disappointment might have been observed upon my lady Jane's face when she heard the splendid stripling denied admittance.

There was a pause now, a sort of waiting silence which Tom could not understand. He glanced at Lord Hertford, who gave him a sign, but he failed to understand that also. The ready Elizabeth came to the rescue with her usual easy grace. She made reverence and said, "Have we leave of the prince's grace my brother to go?"

Tom said, "Indeed your ladyships can have whatsoever of me they will for the asking; yet would I rather give them any other thing that in my poor power lieth than leave to take the light and blessing of their presence hence. Give ye good den, and God be with ye!" Then he smiled inwardly at the thought; " 'Tis not for nought I have dwelt but among princes in my reading and taught my tongue some slight trick of their broidered and gracious speech withal!"

When the illustrious maidens were gone, Tom turned wearily to his keepers and said, "May it please your lordships to grant me leave to go into some corner and rest me?"

Lord Hertford said, "So please your Highness, it is for you to command, it is for us to obey. That thou shouldst rest is indeed a needful thing, since thou must journey to the city presently."

He touched a bell, and a page appeared, who was ordered to desire the presence of Sir William Herbert. This gentleman came straightway and conducted Tom to an inner apartment. Tom's first movement there was to reach for a cup of water; but a silk-and-velvet servitor seized it, dropped upon one knee, and offered it to him on a golden salver.

Next the tired captive sat down and was going to take off his buskins, timidly asking leave with his eye, but another silk-and-velvet discomforter went down upon his knees and took the office from him. He made two or three further efforts to help himself, but being promptly forestalled each time, he finally gave up with a sigh of resignation and a murmured, "Beshrew me but I marvel they do not require to breathe for me also!" Slippered and wrapped in a sumptuous robe, he laid himself down at last to rest, but not to sleep, for his head was too full of thoughts and the room too full of people. He could not dismiss the former, so they stayed; he did not know enough to dismiss the latter, so they stayed also, to his vast regret —and theirs.

Tom's departure had left his two noble guardians alone. They mused awhile, with much headshaking and walking the floor; then Lord St. John said, "Plainly, what dost thou think?"

"Plainly, then, this. The king is near his end, my nephew is mad, mad will mount the throne, and mad remain. God protect England, since she will need it!"

"Verily it promiseth so, indeed. But—have you no misgivings as to—as to——"

The speaker hesitated and finally stopped. He evidently felt that he was upon delicate ground. Lord Hertford stopped before him, looked into his face with a clear, frank eye, and said, "Speak on; there is none to hear but me. Misgivings as to what?"

"I am full loath to word the thing that is in my mind, and thou so near to him in blood, my lord. But craving pardon if I do offend, seemeth it not strange that madness could so change his port and manner! Not but that his port and speech are princely still, but that they *differ* in one unweighty trifle or another from what his custom was aforetime. Seemeth it not strange that madness should filch from his memory his father's very lineaments; the customs and observances that are his due from such as be about him; and, leaving him his Latin, strip him of his Greek and French? My Lord, be not offended, but ease my mind of its disquiet and receive my grateful thanks. It haunteth me, his saying he was not the prince, and so——"

"Peace, my lord, thou utterest treason! Hast forgot the king's command? Remember I am party to thy crime if I but listen."

St. John paled and hastened to say, "I was in fault, I do confess it. Betray me not, grant me this grace out of thy courtesy, and I will neither think nor speak of this thing more. Deal not hardly with me, sir, else am I ruined."

"I am content, my lord. So thou offend not again, here or in the ears of others, it shall be as though thou hadst not spoken. But thou needst not have misgivings. He is my sister's son; are not his voice, his face, his form, familiar to me from his cradle? Madness can do all the odd conflicting things thou seest in him, and more. Dost not recall how that the old baron Marley, being mad, forgot the favor of his own countenance that he had known for sixty years, and held it was another's; nay, even claimed he was the son of Mary Magdalene and that his head was made of Spanish glass; and sooth to say, he suffered none to touch it, lest by mischance some heedless hand might shiver it. Give thy misgivings easement, good my lord. This is the very prince, I know him well—and soon will be thy king; it may advantage thee to bear this in mind and more dwell upon it than the other."

After some further talk, in which the lord St. John covered up his mistake as well as he could by repeated protests that his faith was thoroughly grounded now and could not be assailed by doubts again, the lord Hertford relieved his fellow keeper and sat down to keep watch and ward alone. He was soon deep in meditation. And evidently the longer he thought, the more he was bothered. By and by he began to pace the floor and mutter.

"Tush, he *must* be the prince! Will any he in all the land maintain there can be two, not of one blood and birth, so marvelously twinned? And even were it so, 'twere yet a stranger miracle that chance should cast the one into the other's place. Nay, 'tis folly, folly, folly!"

Presently he said, "Now were he impostor and called himself prince, look you *that* would be natural; that would be reasonable. But lived ever an impostor yet who, being called prince by the king, prince by the court, prince by all, *denied* his dignity and pleaded against his exaltation? *No!* By the soul of St. Swithin, no! This is the true prince, gone mad!"

7 TOM'S FIRST ROYAL DINNER

Somewhat after one in the afternoon, Tom resignedly underwent the ordeal of being dressed for dinner. He found himself as finely clothed as before, but everything different, everything changed, from his ruff to his stockings. He was presently conducted with much state to a spacious and ornate apartment, where a table was already set for one. Its furniture was all of massy gold, and beautified with designs which well-nigh made it priceless, since they were the work of Benvenuto. The room was half filled with noble servitors. A chaplain said grace, and Tom was about to fall to, for hunger had long been constitutional with him, but was interrupted by my lord the Earl of Berkeley, who fastened a napkin about his neck, for the great post of Diaperers to the Princes of Wales was hereditary in this nobleman's family. Tom's cupbearer was present and forestalled all his attempts to help himself to wine. The Taster to his Highness the Prince of Wales was there also, prepared to taste any suspicious dish upon requirement and run the risk of being poisoned. He was only an ornamental appendage at this time and was seldom called upon to exercise his function; but there had been times, not many generations past, when the office of taster had its perils and was not a grandeur to be desired. Why they did not use a dog or a plumber seems strange, but all the ways of royalty are strange. My lord D'Arcy, First Groom of the Chamber, was there to do goodness knows what; but there he was—let that suffice. The Lord Chief Butler was there and stood behind Tom's chair, overseeing the solemnities under command of the Lord Great Steward and the Lord Head Cook, who stood near. Tom had three hundred and eighty-four servants beside these, but they were not all in that room, of course, nor the quarter of them; neither was Tom aware yet that they existed.

All those that were present had been well drilled within the hour to remember that the prince was temporarily out of his head and to be careful to show no surprise at his vagaries. These "vagaries" were soon on exhibition before them, but they only moved their compassion and their sorrow, not their mirth. It was a heavy affliction to them to see the beloved prince so stricken.

Poor Tom ate with his fingers mainly, but no one smiled at it or even seemed to observe it. He inspected his napkin curiously and with deep interest, for it was of a very dainty and beautiful fabric; then said with simplicity, "Prithee take it away, lest in mine unheedfulness it be soiled."

The Hereditary Diaperer took it away with reverent manner and without word or protest of any sort.

Tom examined the turnips and the lettuce with interest, and asked what they were and if they were to be eaten, for it was only recently that men had begun to raise these things in England in place of importing them as luxuries from Holland.* His question was answered with grave respect, and no surprise manifested. When he had finished his dessert, he filled his pockets with nuts; but nobody appeared to be aware of it or disturbed by it. But the next moment he was himself disturbed by it and showed discomposure, for this was the only service he had been permitted to do with his own hands during the meal, and he did not doubt that he had done a most improper and unprincely thing. At that moment the muscles of his nose began to twitch, and the end of that organ to lift and wrinkle. This continued, and Tom began to evince a growing distress. He looked appealingly, first at one and then another of the lords about him, and tears came into his eyes. They sprang forward with dismay in their faces and begged to know his trouble. Tom said with genuine anguish, "I crave your indulgence; my nose itcheth cruelly. What is the custom and usage in this emergence? Prithee speed, for 'tis but a little time that I can bear it."

None smiled, but all were sore perplexed and looked one to the other in deep tribulation for counsel. But be-

* See Note 4 at end of volume.

hold, here was a dead wall, and nothing in English history
to tell how to get over it. The Master of Ceremonies was
not present; there was no one who felt safe to venture
upon this uncharted sea or risk the attempt to solve this
solemn problem. Alas! There was no Hereditary Scratch-
er. Meantime the tears had overflowed their banks and
begun to trickle down Tom's cheeks. His twitching nose
was pleading more urgently than ever for relief. At last
nature broke down the barriers of etiquette: Tom lifted
up an inward prayer for pardon if he was doing wrong
and brought relief to the burdened hearts of his court by
scratching his nose himself.

His meal being ended, a lord came and held before him
a broad, shallow, golden dish with fragrant rose water
in it to cleanse his mouth and fingers with; and my lord
the Hereditary Diaperer stood by with a napkin for his
use. Tom gazed at the dish a puzzled moment or two,
then raised it to his lips and gravely took a draft. Then
he returned it to the waiting lord and said, "Nay, it likes
me not, my lord; it hath a pretty flavor, but it wanteth
strength."

This new eccentricity of the prince's ruined mind made
all the hearts about him ache, but the sad sight moved
none to merriment.

Tom's next unconscious blunder was to get up and
leave the table just when the chaplain had taken his stand
behind his chair, and with uplifted hands and closed, uplifted eyes was in the act of beginning the blessing. Still
nobody seemed to perceive that the prince had done a
thing unusual.

By his own request, our small friend was now conducted to his private cabinet and left there alone to his
own devices. Hanging upon hooks in the oaken wainscot-
ing were the several pieces of a suit of shining steel armor,
covered all over with beautiful designs exquisitely inlaid
in gold. This martial panoply belonged to the true prince,
a recent present from Madam Parr, the queen. Tom put
on the greaves, the gauntlets, the plumed helmet, and such
other pieces as he could don without assistance, and for
a while was minded to call for help and complete the matter, but bethought him of the nuts he had brought away
from dinner and the joy it would be to eat them with no

crowd to eye him and no Grand Hereditaries to pester him with undesired services; so he restored the pretty things to their several places and soon was cracking nuts and feeling almost naturally happy for the first time since God for his sins had made him a prince. When the nuts were all gone, he stumbled upon some inviting books in a closet, among them one about the etiquette of the English court. This was a prize. He lay down upon a sumptuous divan and proceeded to instruct himself with honest zeal. Let us leave him there for the present.

8 THE QUESTION OF THE SEAL

About five o'clock Henry VIII awoke out of an unrefreshing nap and muttered to himself, "Troublous dreams, troublous dreams! Mine end is now at hand; so say these warnings, and my failing pulses do confirm it." Presently a wicked light flamed up in his eye, and he muttered, "Yet will not I die till *he* go before."

His attendants perceiving that he was awake, one of them asked his pleasure concerning the Lord Chancellor, who was waiting without.

"Admit him, admit him!" exclaimed the king eagerly.

The Lord Chancellor entered and knelt by the king's couch, saying, "I have given order, and according to the king's command, the peers of the realm, in their robes, do now stand at the bar of the House, where, having confirmed the Duke of Norfolk's doom, they humbly wait his Majesty's further pleasure in the matter."

The king's face lit up with a fierce joy. Said he, "Lift me up! In mine own person will I go before my Parliament, and with mine own hand will I seal the warrant that rids me of——"

His voice failed, an ashen pallor swept the flush from his cheeks, and the attendants eased him back upon his pillows and hurriedly assisted him with restoratives. Presently he said sorrowfully, "Alack, how have I longed for this sweet hour! And lo, too late it cometh, and I am robbed of this so coveted chance. But speed ye, speed ye! Let others do this happy office sith 'tis denied to me. I put my Great Seal in commission; choose thou the lords that shall compose it, and get ye to your work. Speed ye, man! Before the sun shall rise and set again, bring me his head, that I may see it."

"According to the king's command, so shall it be.

Will't please your Majesty to order that the Seal be now restored to me, so that I may forth upon the business?"

"The Seal? Who keepeth the Seal but thou?"

"Please your Majesty, you did take it from me two days since, saying it should no more do its office till your own royal hand should use it upon the Duke of Norfolk's warrant."

"Why, so in sooth I did; I do remember it. What did I with it? I am very feeble. So oft these days doth my memory play the traitor with me. 'Tis strange, strange—"

The king dropped into inarticulate mumblings, shaking his gray head weakly from time to time and gropingly trying to recollect what he had done with the Seal.

At last my lord Hertford ventured to kneel and offer information, "Sire, if that I may be so bold, here be several that do remember with me how that you gave the Great Seal into the hands of his Highness the Prince of Wales to keep against the day that——"

"True, most true!" interrupted the king. "Fetch it! Go; time flieth!"

Lord Hertford flew to Tom, but returned to the king before very long troubled and empty-handed. He delivered himself to this effect: "It grieveth me, my lord the king, to bear so heavy and unwelcome tidings; but it is the will of God that the prince's affliction abideth still, and he cannot recall to mind that he received the Seal. So came I quickly to report, thinking it were waste of precious time and little worth withal that any should attempt to search the long array of chambers and saloons that belong unto his royal High——"

A groan from the king interrupted my lord at this point. After a little while his Majesty said, with a deep sadness in his tone, "Trouble him no more, poor child. The hand of God lieth heavy upon him, and my heart goeth out in loving compassion for him, and sorrow that I may not bear his burden on mine own old trouble-weighted shoulders, and so bring him peace."

He closed his eyes, fell to mumbling, and presently was silent. After a time he opened his eyes again and gazed vacantly around until his glance rested upon the kneeling Lord Chancellor. Instantly his face flushed with wrath: "What, thou here yet! By the glory of God, an' thou gettest not about that traitor's business, thy miter shall have holiday the morrow for lack of a head to grace withal!"

The trembling Chancellor answered, "Good your Majesty, I cry you mercy! I but waited for the Seal."

"Man, hast lost thy wits? The small Seal which aforetime I was wont to take with me abroad lieth in my treasury. And since the Great Seal hath flown away, shall not it suffice? Hast lost thy wits? Begone! And hark ye; come no more till thou do bring his head."

The poor Chancellor was not long in removing himself from this dangerous vicinity, nor did the commission waste time in giving the royal assent to the work of the slavish Parliament and appointing the morrow for the beheading of the premier peer of England, the luckless Duke of Norfolk.*

* See Note 5 at end of volume.

9 THE RIVER PAGEANT

At nine in the evening the whole vast river-front of the palace was blazing with light. The river itself, as far as the eye could reach citywards, was so thickly covered with watermen's boats and with pleasure barges, all fringed with colored lanterns and gently agitated by the waves, that it resembled a glowing and limitless garden of flowers stirred to soft motion by summer winds. The grand terrace of stone steps leading down to the water, spacious enough to mass the army of a German principality upon, was a picture to see, with its ranks of royal halberdiers in polished armor and its troops of brilliantly costumed servitors flitting up and down, and to and fro, in the hurry of preparation.

Presently a command was given, and immediately all living creatures vanished from the steps. Now the air was heavy with the hush of suspense and expectancy. As far as one's vision could carry, he might see the myriads of people in the boats rise up, and shade their eyes from the glare of lanterns and torches, and gaze toward the palace.

A file of forty or fifty state barges drew up to the steps. They were richly gilt, and their lofty prows and sterns were elaborately carved. Some of them were decorated with banners and streamers, some with cloth of gold and arras embroidered with coats of arms, others with silken flags that had numberless little silver bells fastened to them which shook out tiny showers of joyous music whenever the breezes fluttered them; others of yet higher pretensions, since they belonged to nobles in the prince's immediate service, had their sides picturesquely fenced with shields gorgeously emblazoned with armorial bearings. Each state barge was towed by a tender. Besides the rowers, these tenders carried each a number of men-at-arms in glossy helmet and breastplate, and a company of musicians.

The advance guard of the expected procession now appeared in the great gateway, a troop of halberdiers. They were dressed in striped hose of black and tawny, velvet caps graced at the sides with silver roses, and doublets of murrey-and-blue cloth embroidered on the front and back with the three feathers, the prince's blazon, woven in gold. Their halberd staves were covered with crimson velvet, fastened with gilt nails, and ornamented with gold tassels. Filing off on the right and left, they formed two long lines, extending from the gateway of the palace to the water's edge. A thick, rayed cloth, or carpet, was then unfolded and laid down between them by attendants in the gold-and-crimson liveries of the prince. This done, a flourish of trumpets resounded from within. A lively prelude arose from the musicians on the water, and two ushers with white wands marched with a slow and stately pace from the portal. They were followed by an officer bearing the civic mace, after whom came another carrying the city's sword; then several sergeants of the city guard, in their full accouterments and with badges on their sleeves; then the garter king-at-arms, in his tabard; then several knights of the bath, each with a white lace on his sleeve; then their esquires; then the judges, in their robes of scarlet and coifs; then the lord High Chancellor of England, in a robe of scarlet, open before and purfled with miniver; then a deputation of aldermen, in their scarlet cloaks; and then the heads of the different civic companies, in their robes of state. Now came twelve French gentlemen, in splendid habiliments, consisting of pourpoints of white damask barred with gold, short mantles of crimson velvet lined with violet taffeta, and carnation-colored *hauts-de-chausses*, and took their way down the steps. They were of the suite of the French ambassador, and were followed by twelve cavaliers of the suite of the Spanish ambassador, clothed in black velvet unrelieved by any ornament. Following these came several great English nobles with their attendants.

There was a flourish of trumpets within; and the prince's uncle, the future great Duke of Somerset, emerged from the gateway arrayed in a doublet of black cloth of gold and a cloak of crimson satin flowered with gold and ribanded with nets of silver. He turned, doffed his plumed cap, bent his body in a low reverence, and began to step backward, bowing at each step. A prolonged trumpet blast followed, and a proclamation, "Way for the high and mighty, the lord Edward, Prince of Wales!" High aloft on the palace walls a long line of red tongues of flame leaped forth with a thundercrash; the massed world on the river burst into a mighty roar of welcome; and Tom Canty, the cause and hero of it all, stepped into view and slightly bowed his princely head.

He was magnificently habited in a doublet of white satin, with a frontpiece of purple cloth of tissue, powdered with diamonds, and edged with ermine. Over this he wore a mantle of white cloth of gold pounced with the triple-feather crest, lined with blue satin, set with pearls and precious stones, and fastened with a clasp of brilliants. About his neck hung the Order of the Garter and several princely foreign orders, and wherever light fell upon him jewels responded with a blinding flash. O Tom Canty, born in a hovel, bred in the gutters of London, familiar with rags and dirt and misery, what a spectacle is this!

10 THE PRINCE IN THE TOILS

We left John Canty dragging the rightful prince into Offal Court, with a noisy and delighted mob at his heels. There was but one person in it who offered a pleading word for the captive, and he was not heeded; he was hardly even heard, so great was the turmoil. The prince continued to struggle for freedom and to rage against the treatment he was suffering, until John Canty lost what little patience was left in him and raised his oaken cudgel in a sudden fury over the prince's head. The single pleader for the lad sprang to stop the man's arm, and the blow descended upon his own wrist. Canty roared out, "Thou'lt meddle, wilt thou? Then have thy reward."

His cudgel crashed down upon the meddler's head; there was a groan, a dim form sank to the ground among the feet of the crowd, and the next moment it lay there in the dark alone. The mob pressed on, their enjoyment nothing disturbed by this episode.

Presently the prince found himself in John Canty's abode, with the door closed against the outsiders. By the vague light of a tallow candle which was thrust into a bottle he made out the main features of the loathsome den and also the occupants of it. Two frowzy girls and a middle-aged woman cowered against the wall in one corner with the aspect of animals habituated to harsh usage and expecting and dreading it now. From another corner stole a withered hag with streaming gray hair and malignant eyes. John Canty said to this one, "Tarry! There's fine mummeries here. Mar them not till thou'st enjoyed them; then let thy hand be heavy as thou wilt. Stand forth, lad. Now say thy foolery again, an' thou'st not forgot it. Name thy name. Who art thou?"

The insulted blood mounted to the little prince's cheek

once more, and he lifted a steady and indignant gaze to
the man's face and said, " 'Tis but ill breeding in such as
thou to command me to speak. I tell thee now, as I told
thee before, I am Edward, Prince of Wales, and none
other."

The stunning surprise of this reply nailed the hag's feet
to the floor where she stood, and almost took her breath.
She stared at the prince in stupid amazement, which so
amused her ruffianly son that he burst into a roar of
laughter. But the effect upon Tom Canty's mother and
sisters was different. Their dread of bodily injury gave
way at once to distress of a different sort. They ran forward
with woe and dismay in their faces, exclaiming, "O poor
Tom, poor lad!"

The mother fell on her knees before the prince, put her
hands upon his shoulders, and gazed yearningly into his
face through her rising tears. Then she said, "O my poor
boy! Thy foolish reading hath wrought its woeful work at
last and ta'en thy wit away. Ah! Why didst thou cleave to
it when I so warned thee 'gainst it? Thou'st broke thy
mother's heart."

The prince looked into her face and said gently, "Thy
son is well and hath not lost his wits, good dame. Comfort
thee; let me to the palace where he is, and straightway will
the king my father restore him to thee."

"The king thy father! O my child! Unsay these words
that be freighted with death for thee and ruin for all that be
near to thee. Shake off this gruesome dream. Call back
thy poor wandering memory. Look upon me. Am not I
thy mother that bore thee and loveth thee?"

The prince shook his head and reluctantly said, "God
knoweth I am loath to grieve thy heart, but truly have I
never looked upon thy face before."

The woman sank back to a sitting posture on the floor,
and covering her eyes with her hands, gave way to heart-
broken sobs and wailings.

"Let the show go on!" shouted Canty. "What, Nan!
What, Bet! Mannerless wenches! Will ye stand in the
prince's presence? Upon your knees, ye pauper scum, and
do him reverence!"

He followed this with another horselaugh. The girls
began to plead timidly for their brother, and Nan said,

"An' thou wilt but let him to bed, Father, rest and sleep will heal his madness; prithee, do."

"Do, Father," said Bet; "he is more worn than is his wont. Tomorrow will he be himself again, and will beg with diligence, and come not empty home again."

This remark sobered the father's joviality and brought his mind to business. He turned angrily upon the prince and said, "The morrow must we pay two pennies to him that owns this hole; two pennies, mark ye—all this money for a half year's rent, else out of this we go. Show what thou'st gathered with thy lazy begging."

The prince said, "Offend me not with thy sordid matters. I tell thee again I am the king's son."

A sounding blow upon the prince's shoulder from Canty's broad palm sent him staggering into goodwife Canty's arms, who clasped him to her breast and sheltered him from a pelting rain of cuffs and slaps by interposing her own person. The frightened girls retreated to their corner, but the grandmother stepped eagerly forward to assist her son. The prince sprang away from Mrs. Canty, exclaiming, "Thou shalt not suffer for me, madam. Let these swine do their will upon me alone."

This speech infuriated the swine to such a degree that they set about their work without waste of time. Between them they belabored the boy right soundly, and then gave the girls and their mother a beating for showing sympathy for the victim.

"Now," said Canty, "to bed, all of ye. The entertainment has tired me."

The light was put out, and the family retired. As soon as the snorings of the head of the house and his mother showed that they were asleep, the young girls crept to where the prince lay and covered him tenderly from the cold with straw and rags; and their mother crept to him also, and stroked his hair, and cried over him, whispering broken words of comfort and compassion in his ear the while. She had saved a morsel for him to eat also, but the boy's pains had swept away all appetite, at least for black and tasteless crusts. He was touched by her brave and costly defense of him and by her commiseration, and he thanked her in very noble and princely words, and begged her to go to her sleep and try to forget her sorrows. And he added that the king his father would not let her loyal kindness and devotion go unrewarded. This return to his "madness" broke her heart anew, and she strained him to her breast again and again and then went back, drowned in tears, to her bed.

As she lay thinking and mourning, the suggestion began to creep into her mind that there was an undefinable something about this boy that was lacking in Tom Canty, mad or sane. She could not describe it, she could not tell just what it was, and yet her sharp mother instinct seemed to detect it and perceive it. What if the boy were really not her son after all? Oh, absurd! She almost smiled at the idea, spite of her griefs and troubles. No matter, she found that it was an idea that would not "down," but persisted in haunting her. It pursued her, it harassed her, it clung to her, and refused to be put away or ignored. At last she perceived that there was not going to be any peace for her until she should devise a test that should prove, clearly and without question, whether this lad was her son or not, and so banish these wearing and worrying doubts. Ah yes, this was plainly the right way out of the difficulty; therefore she set her wits to work at once to contrive that test. But it was an easier thing to propose than to accomplish. She turned over in her mind one promising test after another, but was obliged to relinquish them all: none of them were absolutely sure, absolutely perfect; and an imperfect one could not satisfy her. Evidently she was racking her head in vain; it seemed manifest that she must give the matter up. While this depressing thought was passing through her mind, her ear caught the regular breathing of the boy, and she knew he had fallen asleep. And while she listened, the measured breathing was broken by a soft, startled cry, such as one utters in a troubled dream. This chance occurrence furnished her instantly with a plan worth all her labored tests combined. She at once set herself feverishly but noiselessly to work to relight her candle, muttering to herself, "Had I but seen him *then,* I should have known! Since that day, when he was little, that the powder burst in his face, he hath never been startled of a sudden out of his dreams or out of his thinkings, but he hath cast his hand before his eyes, even as he did that day; and not as others would do it, with the palm inward, but always with the palm turned outward. I have seen it a hundred times, and it hath never varied nor ever failed. Yes, I shall soon know now!"

By this time she had crept to the slumbering boy's side with the candle, shaded, in her hand. She bent heedfully and warily over him, scarcely breathing in her suppressed excitement, and suddenly flashed the light in his face and struck the floor by his ear with her knuckles. The sleeper's eyes sprung wide open, and he cast a startled stare about him, but he made no special movement with his hands.

The poor woman was smitten almost helpless with surprise and grief, but she contrived to hide her emotions and to soothe the boy to sleep again; then she crept apart and communed miserably with herself upon the disastrous result of her experiment. She tried to believe that her Tom's madness had banished this habitual gesture of his, but she could not do it. "No," she said, "his *hands* are not mad; they could not unlearn so old a habit in so brief a time. Oh, this is a heavy day for me!"

Still, hope was as stubborn now as doubt had been before; she could not bring herself to accept the verdict of the test; she must try the thing again: the failure must have been only an accident; so she startled the boy out of his sleep a second and a third time, at intervals, with the same result which had marked the first test; then she dragged herself to bed and fell sorrowfully asleep, saying, "But I cannot give him up. Oh, no, I cannot, I cannot; he *must* be my boy!"

The poor mother's interruptions having ceased and the prince's pains having gradually lost their power to disturb him, utter weariness at last sealed his eyes in a profound and restful sleep. Hour after hour slipped away, and still he slept like the dead. Thus four or five hours passed. Then his stupor began to lighten. Presently while half asleep and half awake, he murmured, "Sir William!"

After a moment, "Ho, Sir William Herbert! Hie thee hither, and list to the strangest dream that ever. Sir William! Dost hear? Man, I did think me changed to a pauper, and— Ho there! Guards! Sir William! What! Is there no groom of the chamber in waiting? Alack, it shall go hard with——"

"What aileth thee?" asked a whisper near him. "Who art thou calling?"

"Sir William Herbert. Who art thou?"

"I? Who should I be but thy sister Nan? Oh, Tom, I had forgot! Thou'rt mad yet; poor lad thou'rt mad yet; would I had never woke to know it again! But prithee master thy tongue, lest we be all beaten till we die!"

The startled prince sprang partly up, but a sharp reminder from his stiffened bruises brought him to himself, and he sunk back among his foul straw with a moan and the ejaculation, "Alas, it was no dream then!"

In a moment all the heavy sorrow and misery which sleep had banished were upon him again, and he realized that he was no longer a petted prince in a palace with the adoring eyes of a nation upon him, but a pauper, an outcast, clothed in rags, prisoner in a den fit only for beasts, and consorting with beggars and thieves.

In the midst of his grief he began to be conscious of hilarious noises and shoutings, apparently but a block or two away. The next moment there were several sharp raps at the door; John Canty ceased from snoring and said, "Who knocketh? What wilt thou?"

A voice answered, "Knowst thou who it was thou laid thy cudgel on?"

"No. Neither know I, nor care."

"Belike thou'lt change thy note eftsoons. An' thou would save thy neck, nothing but flight may stead thee. The man is this moment delivering up the ghost. 'Tis the priest Father Andrew!"

"God-a-mercy!" exclaimed Canty. He roused his family and hoarsely commanded, "Up with ye all and fly, or bide where ye are and perish!"

Scarcely five minutes later the Canty household were in the street and flying for their lives. John Canty held the prince by the wrist and hurried him along the dark way, giving him this caution in a low voice, "Mind thy tongue, thou mad fool, and speak not our name. I will choose me a new name speedily to throw the law's dogs off the scent. Mind thy tongue, I tell thee!" He growled these words to the rest of the family: "If it so chance that we be separated, let each make for London Bridge; whoso findeth himself as far as the last linen-draper's shop on the bridge, let him tarry there till the others be come; then will we flee into Southwark together."

At this moment the party burst suddenly out of darkness into light, and not only into light, but into the midst of a multitude of singing, dancing, and shouting people massed together on the river frontage. There was a line of bonfires stretching as far as one could see, up and down the Thames; London Bridge was illuminated; Southwark Bridge likewise; the entire river was aglow with the flash and sheen of colored lights; and constant explosions of fireworks filled the skies with an intricate commingling of shooting splendors and a thick rain of dazzling sparks that almost turned night into day; everywhere were crowds of revelers; all London seemed to be at large.

John Canty delivered himself of a furious curse and commanded a retreat, but it was too late. He and his tribe were swallowed up in that swarming hive of humanity and hopelessly separated from each other in an instant. We are not considering that the prince was one of his tribe; Canty still kept his grip upon him. The prince's heart was beating high with hopes of escape now. A burly waterman, considerably exalted with liquor, found himself rudely shoved by Canty in his efforts to plow through the crowd; he laid his great hand on Canty's shoulder and said, "Nay, whither so fast, friend? Dost canker thy soul with sordid business when all that be leal men and true make holiday?"

"Mine affairs are mine own; they concern thee not," answered Canty roughly; "take away thy hand and let me pass."

"Sith that is thy humor, thou'lt *not* pass till thou'st drunk to the Prince of Wales, I tell thee that," said the waterman, barring the way resolutely.

"Give me the cup, then, and make speed, make speed!"

Other revelers were interested by this time. They cried out, "The loving cup, the loving cup! Make the sour knave drink the loving cup, else will we feed him to the fishes."

So a huge loving cup was brought; the waterman, grasping it by one of its handles, and with his other hand bearing up the end of an imaginary napkin, presented it in due and ancient form to Canty, who had to grasp the opposite handle with one of his hands and take off the lid with the other, according to ancient custom.* This left the prince hand-free for a second of course. He wasted no time, but

* See Note 6 at end of volume.

dived among the forest of legs about him and disappeared. In another moment he could not have been harder to find under that tossing sea of life if its billows had been the Atlantic's and he a lost sixpence.

He very soon realized this fact and straightway busied himself about his own affairs without further thought of John Canty. He quickly realized another thing too. To wit, that a spurious Prince of Wales was being feasted by the city in his stead. He easily concluded that the pauper lad, Tom Canty, had deliberately taken advantage of his stupendous opportunity and become a usurper.

Therefore there was but one course to pursue—find his way to the Guildhall, make himself known, and denounce the impostor. He also made up his mind that Tom should be allowed a reasonable time for spiritual preparation and then be hanged, drawn, and quartered according to the law and usage of the day in cases of high treason.

11 AT GUILDHALL

The royal barge, attended by its gorgeous fleet, took its stately way down the Thames through the wilderness of illuminated boats. The air was laden with music; the river banks were beruffled with joy flames; the distant city lay in a soft luminous glow from its countless invisible bonfires; above it rose many a slender spire into the sky, encrusted with sparkling lights, wherefore in their remoteness they seemed like jeweled lances thrust aloft; as the fleet swept along, it was greeted from the banks with a continuous hoarse roar of cheers and the ceaseless flash and boom of artillery.

To Tom Canty, half buried in his silken cushions, these sounds and this spectacle were a wonder unspeakably sublime and astonishing. To his little friends at his side, the princess Elizabeth and the lady Jane Grey, they were nothing.

Arrived at the Dowgate, the fleet was towed up the limpid Walbrook (whose channel has now been for two centuries buried out of sight under acres of buildings) to Bucklersbury, past houses and under bridges populous with merrymakers and brilliantly lighted, and at last came to a halt in a basin where now is Barge Yard, in the center of the ancient city of London. Tom disembarked, and he and his gallant procession crossed Cheapside and made a short march through the Old Jewry and Basinghall street to the Guildhall.

Tom and his little ladies were received with due ceremony by the Lord Mayor and the Fathers of the City, in their gold chains and scarlet robes of state, and conducted to a rich canopy of estate at the head of the great hall, preceded by heralds making proclamation, and by the mace and the city sword. The lords and ladies who were

to attend upon Tom and his two small friends took their
places behind their chairs.

At a lower table the court grandees and other guests
of noble degree were seated with the magnates of the
city; the commoners took places at a multitude of tables
on the main floor of the hall. From their lofty vantage
ground the giants Gog and Magog, the ancient guardians
of the city, contemplated the spectacle below them with
eyes grown familiar to it in forgotten generations. There
was a bugle blast and a proclamation, and a fat butler
appeared in a high perch in the leftward wall, followed
by his servitors bearing with impressive solemnity a royal
Baron of Beef, smoking hot and ready for the knife.

After grace, Tom (being instructed) rose—and the
whole house with him—and drank from a portly golden
loving cup with the princess Elizabeth; from her it passed
to the lady Jane and then traversed the general assemblage. So the banquet began.

By midnight the revelry was at its height. Now came
one of those picturesque spectacles so admired in that old
day. A description of it is still extant in the quaint wording of a chronicler who witnessed it:

"Space being made, presently entered a baron and an
earl appareled after the Turkish fashion in long robes of
bawdkin powdered with gold, hats on their heads of
crimson velvet, with great rolls of gold, girded with two
swords called scimitars hanging by great bawdricks of
gold. Next came yet another baron and another earl, in
two long gowns of yellow satin, traversed with white satin,
and in every bend of white was a bend of crimson satin,
after the fashion of Russia, with furred hats of gray on
their heads, either of them having an hatchet in their
hands and boots with pikes" (points a foot long), "turned
up. And after them came a knight, then the Lord High
Admiral, and with him five nobles, in doublets of crimson velvet, voyded low on the back and before to the
cannell-bone, laced on the breasts with chains of silver;
and over that, short cloaks of crimson satin, and on their
heads hats after the dancers' fashion, with pheasants'
feathers in them. These were appareled after the fashion
of Prussia. The torchbearers, which were about an hundred, were appareled in crimson satin and green, like
Moors, their faces black. Next came in a *mommarye*.

Then the minstrels, which were disguised, danced; and the lords and ladies did wildly dance also, that it was a pleasure to behold."

And while Tom, in his high seat, was gazing upon this "wild" dancing, lost in admiration of the dazzling commingling of kaleidoscopic colors which the whirling turmoil of gaudy figures below him presented, the ragged but real little Prince of Wales was proclaiming his rights and his wrongs, denouncing the impostor, and clamoring for admission at the gates of Guildhall! The crowd enjoyed this episode prodigiously and pressed forward and craned their necks to see the small rioter. Presently they began to taunt him and mock at him, purposely to goad him to a higher and still more entertaining fury. Tears of mortification sprung to his eyes, but he stood his ground and defied the mob right royally. Other taunts followed, added mockings stung him, and he exclaimed, "I tell ye again, you pack of unmannerly curs, I am the Prince of Wales! And all forlorn and friendless as I be, with none to give me word of grace or help me in my need, yet will not I be driven from my ground, but will maintain it!"

"Though thou be prince or no prince, 'tis all one; thou be'st a gallant lad, and not friendless neither! Here stand I by thy side to prove it; and mind I tell thee thou mightst have a worser friend than Miles Hendon and yet not tire thy legs with seeking. Rest thy small jaw, my child; I talk the language of these base kennel-rats like to a very native."

The speaker was a sort of Don Caesar de Bazan in dress, aspect, and bearing. He was tall, trim-built, muscular. His doublet and trunks were of rich material, but faded and threadbare, and their gold-lace adornments were sadly tarnished; his ruff was rumpled and damaged; the plume in his slouched hat was broken and had a bedraggled and disreputable look; at his side he wore a long rapier in a rusty iron sheath; his swaggering carriage marked him at once as a ruffler of the camp. The speech of this fantastic figure was received with an explosion of jeers and laughter. Some cried, " 'Tis another prince in disguise!" " 'Ware thy tongue, friend; belike he is dangerous!" "Marry, he looketh it; mark his eye!" "Pluck the lad from him; to the horsepond wi' the cub!"

Instantly a hand was laid upon the prince, under the

impulse of this happy thought; as instantly the stranger's
long sword was out and the meddler went to the earth
under a sounding thump with the flat of it. The next moment a score of voices shouted, "Kill the dog! Kill him!
Kill him!" And the mob closed in on the warrior, who
backed himself against a wall and began to lay about him
with his long weapon like a madman. His victims sprawled
this way and that, but the mobtide poured over their
prostrate forms and dashed itself against the champion
with undiminished fury. His moments seemed numbered,
his destruction certain, when suddenly a trumpet blast
sounded, a voice shouted, "Way for the king's messenger!"
and a troop of horsemen came charging down upon the
mob, who fled out of harm's reach as fast as their legs
could carry them. The bold stranger caught up the prince
in his arms and was soon far away from danger and the
multitude.

Return we within the Guildhall. Suddenly, high above
the jubilant roar and thunder of the revel, broke the
clear peal of a bugle note. There was instant silence, a
deep hush; then a single voice rose—that of the messenger
from the palace—and began to pipe forth a proclamation,
the whole multitude standing, listening.

The closing words, solemnly pronounced, were, "The
king is dead!"

The great assemblage bent their heads upon their
breasts with one accord, remained so in profound silence
a few moments; then all sunk upon their knees in a body,
stretched out their hands toward Tom; and a mighty
shout burst forth that seemed to shake the building,
"Long live the king!"

Poor Tom's dazed eyes wandered abroad over this
stupefying spectacle and finally rested dreamily upon the
kneeling princesses beside him a moment, then upon the
Earl of Hertford. A sudden purpose dawned in his face.
He said in a low tone at Lord Hertford's ear, "Answer
me truly, on thy faith and honor! Uttered I here a command, the which none but a king might hold privilege
and prerogative to utter, would such commandment be
obeyed, and none rise up to say me nay?"

"None, my liege, in all these realms. In thy person
bides the majesty of England. Thou art the king; thy
word is law."

Tom responded in a strong, earnest voice, and with great animation, "Then shall the king's law be law of mercy from this day, and never more be law of blood! Up from thy knees and away! To the Tower and say the king decrees the Duke of Norfolk shall not die!" *

The words were caught up and carried eagerly from lip to lip far and wide over the hall, and as Hertford hurried from the presence, another prodigious shout burst forth, "The reign of blood is ended! Long live Edward, King of England!"

* See Note 7 at end of volume.

12 THE PRINCE AND HIS DELIVERER

       As soon as Miles Hendon and the little prince were clear of the mob, they struck down through back lanes and alleys toward the river. Their way was unobstructed until they approached London Bridge; then they plowed into the multitude again, Hendon keeping a fast grip upon the prince's—no, the king's—wrist. The tremendous news was already abroad, and the boy learned it from a thousand voices at once— "The king is dead!" The tidings struck a chill to the heart of the poor little waif and sent a shudder through his frame. He realized the greatness of his loss and was filled with a bitter grief, for the grim tyrant who had been such a terror to others had always been gentle with him. The tears sprung to his eyes and blurred all objects. For an instant he felt himself the most forlorn, outcast, and forsaken of God's creatures; then another cry shook the night with its far-reaching thunder, "Long live King Edward the Sixth!" And this made his eyes kindle and thrilled him with pride to his finger's ends. "Ah," he thought, "how grand and strange it seems—I AM KING!"

Our friends threaded their way slowly through the throngs upon the bridge. This structure, which had stood for six hundred years and had been a noisy and populous thoroughfare all that time, was a curious affair, for a closely packed rank of stores and shops, with family quarters overhead, stretched along both sides of it, from one bank of the river to the other. The bridge was a sort of town to itself; it had its inn, its beer houses, its bakeries, its haberdasheries, its food markets, its manufacturing industries, and even its church. It looked upon the two neighbors which it linked together—London and Southwark—as being well enough as suburbs, but not otherwise particularly important. It was a close corporation, so to speak; it was a narrow town, of a single street a fifth of a mile long; its population was but a village population, and everybody in it knew all his fellow townsmen intimately and had known their fathers and mothers before them—and all their little family affairs into the bargain. It had its aristocracy, of course—its fine old families of butchers, and bakers, and what-not, who had occupied the same old premises for five or six hundred years and knew the great history of the bridge from beginning to end, and all its strange legends, and who always talked bridgy talk, and thought bridgy thoughts, and lied in a long, level, direct, substantial bridgy way. It was just the sort of population to be narrow and ignorant and self-conceited. Children were born on the bridge, were reared there, grew to old age and finally died without ever having set a foot upon any part of the world but London Bridge alone. Such people would naturally imagine that the mighty and interminable procession which moved through its street night and day, with its confused roar of shouts and cries, its neighings and bellowings and bleatings and its muffled thunder-tramp, was the one great thing in this world, and themselves somehow the proprietors of it. And so they were, in effect; at least they could exhibit it from their windows, and did—for a consideration—whenever a returning king or hero gave it a fleeting splendor, for there was no place like it for affording a long, straight, uninterrupted view of marching columns.

Men born and reared upon the bridge found life unendurably dull and inane elsewhere. History tells of one of these who left the bridge at the age of seventy-one and retired to the country. But he could only fret and toss in his bed; he could not go to sleep, the deep stillness was so painful, so awful, so oppressive. When he was worn out with it at last, he fled back to his old home, a lean and haggard specter, and fell peacefully to rest and pleasant dreams under the lulling music of the lashing waters and the boom and crash and thunder of London Bridge.

In the times of which we are writing, the bridge furnished "object lessons" in English history for its children, namely, the livid and decaying heads of renowned men impaled upon iron spikes atop of its gateways. But we digress.

Hendon's lodgings were in the little inn on the bridge. As he neared the door with his small friend, a rough voice said, "So, thou'rt come at last! Thou'lt not escape again, I warrant thee; and if pounding thy bones to a pudding can teach thee somewhat, thou'lt not keep us waiting another time, mayhap." And John Canty put out his hand to seize the boy.

Miles Hendon stepped in the way and said, "Not too fast, friend. Thou art needlessly rough, methinks. What is the lad to thee?"

"If it be any business of thine to make and meddle in others' affairs, he is my son."

" 'Tis a lie!" cried the little king hotly.

"Boldly said, and I believe thee, whether thy small headpiece be sound or cracked, my boy. But whether this scurvy ruffian be thy father or no, 'tis all one; he shall not have thee to beat thee and abuse, according to his threat, so thou prefer to bide with me."

"I do, I do—I know him not, I loathe him, and will die before I will go with him."

"Then 'tis settled, and there is nought more to say."

"We will see as to that!" exclaimed John Canty, striding past Hendon to get at the boy. "By force shall he——"

"If thou do but touch him, thou animated offal, I will spit thee like a goose!" said Hendon, barring the way and laying his hand upon his sword hilt. Canty drew back. "Now mark ye," continued Hendon, "I took this lad under my protection when a mob of such as thou would have mishandled him, mayhap killed him; dost imagine I will desert him now to a worser fate? For whether thou art his father or no—and sooth to say, I think it is a lie —a decent swift death were better for such a lad than life in such brute hands as thine. So go thy ways, and set quick about it, for I like not much bandying of words, being not overpatient in my nature."

John Canty moved off, muttering threats and curses, and was swallowed from sight in the crowd. Hendon ascended three flights of stairs to his room, with his charge, after ordering a meal to be sent thither. It was a poor apartment, with a shabby bed and some odds and ends of old furniture in it, and was vaguely lighted by a couple of sickly candles. The little king dragged himself to the bed and lay down upon it, almost exhausted with hunger and fatigue. He had been on his feet a good part of a day and a night, for it was now two or three o'clock in the morning, and had eaten nothing meantime. He murmured drowsily, "Prithee call me when the table is spread," and sunk into a deep sleep immediately.

A smile twinkled in Hendon's eye, and he said to himself, "By the mass, the little beggar takes to one's quarters and usurps one's bed with as natural and easy a grace as if he owned them—with never a by-your-leave or so-please-it-you, or anything of the sort. In his diseased ravings he called himself the Prince of Wales, and bravely doth he keep up the character. Poor little friendless rat, doubtless his mind has been disordered with ill usage. Well, I will be his friend; I have saved him, and it draweth me strongly to him; already I love the bold-tongued little rascal. How soldierlike he faced the smutty rabble and flung back his high defiance! And what a comely, sweet, and gentle face he hath, now that sleep hath conjured away its troubles and its griefs. I will teach him, I will cure his malady; yea, I will be his elder brother, and care for him and watch over him; and whoso would shame him or do him hurt may order his shroud, for though I be burnt for it he shall need it!"

He bent over the boy and contemplated him with kind and pitying interest, tapping the young cheek tenderly and smoothing back the tangled curls with his great brown hand. A slight shiver passed over the boy's form. Hendon muttered, "See, now, how like a man it was to let him lie here uncovered and fill his body with deadly rheums. Now what shall I do? 'Twill wake him to take him up and put him within the bed, and he sorely needeth sleep."

He looked about for extra covering, but finding none, doffed his doublet and wrapped the lad in it, saying, "I am used to nipping air and scant apparel; 'tis little I shall mind the cold"; then walked up and down the room to keep his blood in motion, soliloquizing as before. "His injured mind persuades him he is Prince of Wales; 'twill be odd to have a Prince of Wales still with us, now that he that *was* the prince is prince no more, but king—for this poor mind is set upon the one fantasy and will not reason out that now it should cast by the prince and call itself the king. If my father liveth still, after these seven years that I have heard nought from home in my foreign dungeon, he will welcome the poor lad and give him generous shelter for my sake; so will my good elder brother, Arthur; my other brother, Hugh—but I will crack his crown, an' *he* interfere, the fox-hearted, ill-conditioned animal! Yes, thither will we fare—and straightway too."

A servant entered with a smoking meal, disposed it upon a small deal table, placed the chairs, and took his departure, leaving such cheap lodgers as these to wait upon themselves. The door slammed after him, and the noise woke the boy, who sprung to a sitting posture and shot a glad glance about him; then a grieved look came into his face and he murmured to himself with a deep sigh, "Alack, it was but a dream, woe is me." Next he noticed Miles Hendon's doublet—glanced from that to Hendon, comprehended the sacrifice that had been made for him, and said gently, "Thou art good to me; yes, thou art very good to me. Take it and put it on; I shall not need it more."

Then he got up and walked to the washstand in the corner, and stood there, waiting. Hendon said in a cheery voice, "We'll have a right hearty sup and bite now, for everything is savory and smoking hot, and that and thy nap together will make thee a little man again, never fear!"

The boy made no answer, but bent a steady look that was filled with grave surprise and also somewhat touched with impatience upon the tall knight of the sword. Hendon was puzzled and said, ""What's amiss?"

"Good sir, I would wash me."

"Oh, is that all! Ask no permission of Miles Hendon for aught thou cravest. Make thyself perfectly free here, and welcome, with all that are his belongings."

Still the boy stood, and moved not; more, he tapped the floor once or twice with his small impatient foot. Hendon was wholly perplexed. Said he, "Bless us, what is it?"

"Prithee pour the water, and make not so many words!"

Hendon, suppressing a horselaugh and saying to himself, "By all the saints, but this is admirable!" stepped briskly forward and did the small insolent's bidding; then stood by in a sort of stupefaction until the command, "Come, the towel!" woke him sharply up. He took up a towel from under the boy's nose and handed it to him without comment. He now proceeded to comfort his own face with a wash, and while he was at it his adopted child seated himself at the table and prepared to fall to. Hendon dispatched his ablutions with alacrity, then drew back the other chair and was about to place himself at table when the boy said indignantly, "Forbear! Wouldst sit in the presence of the king?"

This blow staggered Hendon to his foundations. He muttered to himself, "Lo, the poor thing's madness is up with the time! It hath changed with the great change that is come to the realm, and now in fancy is he *king!* Good lack, I must humor the conceit too—there is no other way—faith, he would order me to the Tower, else!"

And pleased with this jest, he removed the chair from the table, took his stand behind the king, and proceeded to wait upon him in the courtliest way he was capable of.

While the king ate, the rigor of his royal dignity relaxed a little, and with his growing contentment came a desire to talk. He said, "I think thou callest thyself Miles Hendon, if I heard thee aright?"

"Yes, sire," Miles replied; then observed to himself, "If I *must* humor the poor lad's madness, I must sire him, I must majesty him, I must not go by halves, I must stick at nothing that belongeth to the part I play, else shall I play it ill and work evil to this charitable and kindly cause."

The king warmed his heart with a second glass of wine and said, "I would know thee—tell me thy story. Thou hast a gallant way with thee, and a noble—art nobly born?"

"We are of the tail of the nobility, good your Majesty. My father is a baronet—one of the smaller lords, by knight service *—Sir Richard Hendon, of Hendon Hall, by Monk's Holm, in Kent."

"The name has escaped my memory. Go on—tell me thy story."

" 'Tis not much, your Majesty, yet perchance it may beguile a short half hour for want of a better. My father,

* He refers to the order of baronets, or baronettes—the *barones minores*, as distinct from the parliamentary barons—not, it need hardly be said, the baronets of later creation.

Sir Richard, is very rich and of a most generous nature. My mother died whilst I was yet a boy. I have two brothers: Arthur, my elder, with a soul like to his father's; and Hugh, younger than I, a mean spirit, covetous, treacherous, vicious, underhanded—a reptile. Such was he from the cradle; such was he ten years past, when I last saw him—a ripe rascal at nineteen, I being twenty then and Arthur twenty-two. There is none other of us but the lady Edith, my cousin—she was sixteen then—beautiful, gentle, good, the daughter of an earl, the last of her race, heiress of a great fortune and a lapsed title. My father was her guardian. I loved her and she loved me, but she was betrothed to Arthur from the cradle, and Sir Richard would not suffer the contract to be broken. Arthur loved another maid and bade us be of good cheer and hold fast to the hope that delay and luck together would some day give success to our several causes. Hugh loved the lady Edith's fortune, though in truth he said it was herself he loved; but then 'twas his way, alway, to say the one thing and mean the other. But he lost his arts upon the girl; he could deceive my father, but none else. My father loved him best of us all and trusted and believed him, for he was the youngest child and others hated him—these qualities being in all ages sufficient to win a parent's dearest love; and he had a smooth persuasive tongue, with an admirable gift of lying—and these be qualities which do mightily assist a blind affection to cozen itself. I was wild—in troth I might go yet farther and say *very* wild, though 'twas a wildness of an innocent sort, since it hurt none but me, brought shame to none, nor loss, nor had in it any taint of crime or baseness or what might not beseem mine honorable degree.

"Yet did my brother Hugh turn these faults to good account, he seeing that our brother Arthur's health was but indifferent, and hoping the worst might work him profit were I swept out of the path— But 'twere a long tale, good my liege, and little worth the telling. Briefly, then, this brother did deftly magnify my faults and make them crimes, ending his base work with finding a silken ladder in mine apartments—conveyed thither by his own means—and did convince my father by this and suborned evidence of servants and other lying knaves that I was

minded to carry off my Edith and marry her in rank
defiance of his will.

"Three years of banishment from home and England
might make a soldier and a man of me, my father said,
and teach me some degree of wisdom. I fought out my
long probation in the continental wars, tasting sumptu-
ously of hard knocks, privation, and adventure; but in
my last battle I was taken captive, and during the seven
years that have waxed and waned since then, a foreign
dungeon hath harbored me. Through wit and courage
I won to the free air at last and fled hither straight, and
am but just arrived, right poor in purse and raiment, and
poorer still in knowledge of what these dull seven years
have wrought at Hendon Hall, its people and belongings.
So please you, sir, my meager tale is told."

"Thou hast been shamefully abused!" said the little
king with a flashing eye. "But I will right thee—by the
cross will I! The king hath said it."

Then, fired by the story of Miles's wrongs, he loosed his
tongue and poured the history of his own recent misfortunes into the ears of his astonished listener.

When he had finished, Miles said to himself, "Lo, what
an imagination he hath! Verily this is no common mind,
else, crazed or sane, it could not weave so straight and
gaudy a tale as this out of the airy nothings wherewith
it hath wrought this curious romaunt. Poor ruined little
head, it shall not lack friend or shelter whilst I bide with
the living. He shall never leave my side; he shall be my
pet, my little comrade. And he shall be cured! Aye, made
whole and sound; then will he make himself a name; and
proud shall I be to say, 'Yes, he is mine—I took him, a
homeless little ragamuffin, but I saw what was in him,
and I said his name would be heard some day—behold
him, observe him—was I right?' "

The king spoke in a thoughtful, measured voice, "Thou
didst save me injury and shame, perchance my life, and
so my crown. Such service demandeth rich reward. Name
thy desire, and so it be within the compass of my royal
power, it is thine."

This fantastic suggestion startled Hendon out of his
reverie. He was about to thank the king and put the matter aside with saying he had only done his duty and desired no reward, but a wiser thought came into his head,

and he asked leave to be silent a few moments and consider the gracious offer—an idea which the king gravely approved, remarking that it was best to be not too hasty with a thing of such great import.

Miles reflected during some moments, then said to himself, "Yes, that is the thing to do; by any other means it were impossible to get at it, and certes, this hour's experience has taught me 'twould be most wearing and inconvenient to continue as it is. Yes, I will propose it; 'twas a happy accident that I did not throw the chance away." Then he dropped upon one knee and said, "My poor service went not beyond the limit of a subject's simple duty and therefore hath no merit, but since your Majesty is pleased to hold it worthy some reward, I take heart of grace to make petition to this effect. Near four hundred years ago, as your Grace knoweth, there being ill blood betwixt John, king of England, and the king of France, it was decreed that two champions should fight together in the lists and so settle the dispute by what is called the arbitrament of God. These two kings, and the Spanish king, being assembled to witness and judge the conflict, the French champion appeared; but so redoubtable was he that our English knights refused to measure weapons with him. So the matter, which was a weighty one, was like to go against the English monarch by default. Now in the Tower lay the lord De Courcy, the mightiest arm in England, stripped of his honors and possessions, and wasting with long captivity. Appeal was made to him; he gave assent and came forth arrayed for battle; but no sooner did the Frenchman glimpse his huge frame and hear his famous name but he fled away, and the French king's cause was lost. King John restored De Courcy's titles and possessions and said, 'Name thy wish and thou shalt have it, though it cost me half my kingdom'; whereat De Courcy, kneeling, as I do now, made answer, 'This, then, I ask, my liege; that I and my successors may have and hold the privilege of remaining covered in the presence of the kings of England, henceforth while the throne shall last.' The boon was granted, as your Majesty knoweth; and there hath been no time these four hundred years that that line has failed of an heir; and so, even unto this day, the head of that ancient house still weareth his hat or helm before the king's majesty, without let or hindrance, and this none other may do.* Invoking this precedent in aid of my prayer, I beseech the king to grant to me but this one grace and privilege—to my more than sufficient reward—and none other, to wit: that I and my heirs forever may *sit* in the presence of the Majesty of England!"

"Rise, Sir Miles Hendon, knight," said the king gravely, giving the accolade with Hendon's sword; "rise, and seat thyself. Thy petition is granted. Whilst England remains, and the crown continues, the privilege shall not lapse."

His Majesty walked apart, musing, and Hendon dropped into a chair at table, observing to himself, " 'Twas a brave thought and hath wrought me a mighty deliverance; my legs are grievously wearied. An' I had not thought of that, I must have had to stand for weeks, till my poor lad's wits are cured." After a little, he went on, "And so I am become a knight of the Kingdom of Dreams and Shadows! A most odd and strange position truly for one so matter-of-fact as I. I will not laugh—no, God forbid, for this thing which is so substanceless to me is *real* to him. And to me also, in one way, it is not a falsity, for it reflects with truth the sweet and generous spirit that is in him." After a pause: "Ah, what if he should call me by my fine title before folk! There'd be a merry contrast betwixt my glory and my raiment! But no matter; let him call me what he will, so it please him, I shall be content."

* The lords of Kingsale, descendants of De Courcy, still enjoy this curious privilege.

13 THE DISAPPEARANCE OF THE PRINCE

A heavy drowsiness presently fell upon the two comrades. The king said, "Remove these rags," meaning his clothing.

Hendon disappareled the boy without dissent or remark, tucked him up in bed, then glanced about the room, saying to himself ruefully, "He hath taken my bed again, as before; marry, what shall *I* do?"

The little king observed his perplexity and dissipated it with a word. He said sleepily, "Thou wilt sleep athwart the door and guard it." In a moment more he was out of his troubles, in a deep slumber.

"Dear heart, he should have been born a king!" muttered Hendon admiringly. "He playeth the part to a marvel."

Then he stretched himself across the door, on the floor, saying contentedly, "I have lodged worse for seven years; 'twould be but ill gratitude to Him above to find fault with this."

He dropped asleep as the dawn appeared. Toward noon he rose, uncovered his unconscious ward—a section at a time—and took his measure with a string. The king awoke just as he had completed his work, complained of the cold, and asked what he was doing.

"'Tis done now, my liege," said Hendon; "I have a bit of business outside, but will presently return; sleep thou again—thou needest it. There—let me cover thy head also—thou'lt be warm the sooner."

The king was back in dreamland before this speech was ended. Miles slipped softly out and slipped as softly in again in the course of thirty or forty minutes, with a complete secondhand suit of boy's clothing, of cheap material and showing signs of wear, but tidy and suited to the season of the year. He seated himself and began to

overhaul his purchase, mumbling to himself, "A longer
purse would have got a better sort, but when one has not
the long purse one must be content with what a short one
may do:

> " 'There was a woman in our town
>   In our town did dwell—'

"He stirred, methinks. I must sing in a less thunderous
key; 'tis not good to mar his sleep, with this journey before him and he so wearied out, poor chap. This garment
—'tis well enough—a stitch here and another there will set
it aright. This other is better, albeit a stitch or two will
not come amiss in it likewise. *These* be very good and
sound, and will keep his small feet warm and dry—an
odd new thing to him, belike, since he has doubtless
been used to foot it bare, winters and summers the same.
Would thread were bread, seeing one getteth a year's
sufficiently for a farthing, and such a brave big needle
without cost, for mere love. Now shall I have the demon's
own time to thread it!"

And so he had. He did as men have always done, and
probably always will do, to the end of time—held the
needle still and tried to thrust the thread through the
eye, which is the opposite of a woman's way. Time and
time again the thread missed the mark, going sometimes
on one side of the needle, sometimes on the other,
sometimes doubling up against the shaft; but he was
patient, having been through these experiences before
when he was soldiering. He succeeded at last and took up
the garment that had lain waiting meantime across his
lap and began his work.

"The inn is paid—the breakfast that is to come, included—and there is wherewithal left to buy a couple
of donkeys and meet our little costs for the two or three
days betwixt this and the plenty that awaits us at Hendon
Hall:

> " 'She loved her hus—'

"Body o' me! I have driven the needle under my nail!
It matters little—'tis not a novelty—yet 'tis not a convenience neither. We shall be merry there, little one, never
doubt it! Thy troubles will vanish, there, and likewise
thy sad distemper:

" 'She loved her husband dearilee,
   But another man—'

"These be noble large stitches!"—holding the garment up and viewing it admiringly. "They have a grandeur and a majesty that do cause these small stingy ones of the tailorman to look mightily paltry and plebeian:

" 'She loved her husband dearilee,
   But another man he loved she—'

"Marry, 'tis done—a goodly piece of work, too, and wrought with expedition. Now will I wake him, apparel him, pour for him, feed him, and then will we hie us to the mart by the Tabard Inn in Southwark and—be pleased to rise, my liege!—he answereth not—what ho, my liege! —of a truth must I profane his sacred person with a touch, sith his slumber is deaf to speech. What!"

He threw back the covers; the boy was gone!

He stared about him in speechless astonishment for a moment, noticed for the first time that his ward's ragged raiment was also missing; then he began to rage and storm and shout for the innkeeper. At that moment a servant entered with the breakfast.

"Explain, thou limb of Satan, or thy time is come!" roared the man of war, and made so savage a spring toward the waiter that this latter could not find his tongue for the instant, for fright and surprise. "Where is the boy?"

In disjointed and trembling syllables the man gave the information desired.

"You were hardly gone from the place, your worship, when a youth came running and said it was your worship's will that the boy come to you straight, at the bridge end on the Southwark side. I brought him hither, and when he woke the lad and gave his message, the lad did grumble some little for being disturbed 'so early,' as he called it, but straightway trussed on his rags and went with the youth, only saying it had been better manners that your worship came yourself, not sent a stranger; and so——'

"And so thou'rt a fool: a fool, and easily cozened;

hang all thy breed! Yet mayhap no hurt is done. Possibly no harm is meant the boy. I will go fetch him. Make the table ready. Stay! The coverings of the bed were disposed as if one lay beneath them; happened that by accident?"

"I know not, good your worship. I saw the youth meddle with them—he that came for the boy."

"Thousand deaths! 'Twas done to deceive me—'tis plain 'twas done to gain time. Hark ye! Was that youth alone?"

"All alone, your worship."

"Art sure?"

"Sure, your worship."

"Collect thy scattered wits—bethink thee—take time, man."

After a moment's thought the servant said, "When he came, none came with him; but now I remember me that as the two stepped into the throng of the bridge, a ruffian-looking man plunged out from some near place; and just as he was joining them——"

"What *then?* Out with it!" thundered the impatient Hendon, interrupting.

"Just then the crowd lapped them up and closed them in, and I saw no more, being called by my master, who was in a rage because a joint that the scrivener had ordered was forgot, though I take all the saints to witness that to blame *me* for that miscarriage were like holding the unborn babe to judgment for sins com——"

"Out of my sight, idiot! Thy prating drives me mad! Hold! Whither art flying? Canst not bide still an instant? Went they toward Southwark?"

"Even so, your worship; for, as I said before, as to the detestable joint, the babe unborn is no whit more blameless than——"

"Art here *yet!* And prating still? Vanish, lest I throttle thee!" The servitor vanished. Hendon followed after him, passed him, and plunged down the stairs two steps at a stride, muttering, " 'Tis that scurvy villain that claimed he was his son. I have lost thee, my poor little mad master —it is a bitter thought—and I had come to love thee so! No! By book and bell, *not* lost! Not lost, for I will ransack the land till I find thee again. Poor child, yonder is his breakfast and mine, but I have no hunger now; so let the rats have it. Speed, speed! That is the word!" As he wormed his swift way through the noisy multitudes upon the bridge, he several times said to himself, clinging to the thought, as if it were a particularly pleasing one, "He grumbled, but he *went*—he went, yes, because he thought Miles Hendon asked it, sweet lad—he would ne'er have done it for another, I know it well."

14

Toward daylight of the same morning, Tom Canty stirred out of a heavy sleep and opened his eyes in the dark. He lay silent a few moments, trying to analyze his confused thoughts and impressions and get some sort of meaning out of them; then suddenly he burst out in a rapturous but guarded voice, "I see it all, I see it all! Now God be thanked, I am indeed awake at last! Come, joy! Vanish, sorrow! Ho, Nan! Bet! Kick off your straw and hie ye hither to my side, till I do pour into your unbelieving ears the wildest madcap dream that ever the spirits of night did conjure up to astonish the soul of man withal! Ho, Nan, I say! Bet!"

A dim form appeared at his side, and a voice said, "Wilt deign to deliver thy commands?"

"Commands? Oh, woe is me, I know thy voice! Speak, thou—who am I?"

"Thou? In sooth, yesternight wert thou the prince of Wales; today art thou my most gracious liege, Edward, king of England."

Tom buried his head among his pillows, murmuring plaintively, "Alack, it was no dream! Go to thy rest, sweet sir; leave me to my sorrows."

Tom slept again, and after a time he had this pleasant dream. He thought it was summer and he was playing all alone in the fair meadow called Goodman's Fields, when a dwarf only a foot high, with long red whiskers and a humped back, appeared to him suddenly and said, "Dig, by that stump." He did so and found twelve bright new pennies—wonderful riches! Yet this was not the best of it, for the dwarf said, "I know thee. Thou art a good lad and a deserving; thy distresses shall end, for the day of thy reward is come. Dig here every seventh day, and thou shalt find always the same treasure, twelve bright new pennies. Tell none—keep the secret." Then the dwarf vanished, and Tom flew to Offal Court with his prize, saying to himself, "Every night will I give my father a penny; he will think I begged it, it will glad his heart, and I shall no more be beaten. One penny every week the good priest that teacheth me shall have; Mother, Nan, and Bet the other four. We be done with hunger and rags now, done with fears and frets and savage usage."

In his dream he reached his sordid home all out of breath, but with eyes dancing with grateful enthusiasm, cast four of his pennies into his mother's lap, and cried out, "They are for thee! All of them, every one! For thee and Nan and Bet—and honestly come by, not begged nor stolen!"

The happy and astonished mother strained him to her breast and exclaimed, "It waxeth late; may it please your Majesty to rise?"

Ah, that was not the answer he was expecting. The dream had snapped asunder—he was awake.

He opened his eyes; the richly clad First Lord of the Bedchamber was kneeling by his couch. The gladness of the lying dream faded away; the poor boy recognized that he was still a captive and a king. The room was filled with courtiers clothed in purple mantles—the mourning color—and with noble servants of the monarch. Tom sat up in bed and gazed out from the heavy silken curtains upon this fine company.

The weighty business of dressing began, and one courtier after another knelt and paid his court and offered to the little king his condolences upon his heavy loss whilst the dressing proceeded. In the beginning, a shirt was taken up by the Chief Equerry-in-Waiting, who passed it to the First Lord of the Buckhounds, who passed it to the Second Gentleman of the Bedchamber, who passed it to the Head Ranger of Windsor Forest, who passed it to the Third Groom of the Stole, who passed it to the Chancellor Royal of the Duchy of Lancaster, who passed it to the Master of the Wardrobe, who passed it to Norroy King-at-Arms, who passed it to the Constable of the Tower, who passed it to the Chief Steward of the Household, who passed it to the Hereditary Grand Diaperer, who passed it to the Lord High Admiral of England, who passed it to the Archbishop of Canterbury, who passed it to the First Lord of the Bedchamber, who took what was left of it and put it on Tom. Poor little wondering chap, it reminded him of passing buckets at a fire.

Each garment in its turn had to go through this slow and solemn process; consequently Tom grew very weary of the ceremony, so weary that he felt an almost gushing gratefulness when he at last saw his long silken hose begin the journey down the line and knew that the end of the matter was drawing near. But he exulted too soon. The First Lord of the Bedchamber received the hose and was about to encase Tom's legs in them when a sudden flush invaded his face and he hurriedly hustled the things back into the hands of the Archbishop of Canterbury with an astounded look and a whispered, "See, my lord!"— pointing to a something connected with the hose. The Archbishop paled, then flushed, and passed the hose to the Lord High Admiral, whispering, "See, my lord!" The admiral passed the hose to the Hereditary Grand Diaperer and had hardly breath enough in his body to ejaculate, "See, my lord!" The hose drifted backward along the line, to the Chief Steward of the Household, the Constable of the Tower, Norroy King-at-Arms, the Master of the Wardrobe, the Chancellor Royal of the Duchy of Lancaster, the Third Groom of the Stole, the Head Ranger of Windsor Forest, the Second Gentleman of the Bedchamber, the First Lord of the Buckhounds, accompanied always with that amazed and frightened "See! see!"—till they finally reached the hands of the Chief Equerry-in-Waiting, who gazed a moment, then hoarsely whispered, "Body of my life, a tag gone from a trusspoint! To the Tower with the Head Keeper of the King's Hose!"—after which he leaned upon the shoulder of the First Lord of the Buckhounds to regather his vanished strength whilst fresh hose, without any damaged strings to them, were brought.

But all things must have an end, and so in time Tom Canty was in a condition to get out of the bed. The proper official poured water, the proper official engineered the washing, the proper official stood by with a towel, and by and by Tom got safely through the purifying stage and was ready for the services of the Hairdresser Royal. When he at length emerged from this master's hands, he was a gracious figure and as pretty as a girl in his mantle and trunks of purple satin and purple-plumed cap. He now moved in state toward his breakfast room through the midst of the courtly assemblage; and as he passed, these fell back, leaving his way free, and dropped upon their knees.

After breakfast he was conducted, with regal ceremony, attended by his great officers and his guard of fifty Gentlemen Pensioners bearing gilt battle axes, to the throne room, where he proceeded to transact business of state. His "uncle," Lord Hertford, took his stand by the throne to assist the royal mind with wise counsel.

The body of illustrious men named by the late king as his executors appeared to ask Tom's approval of certain acts of theirs—rather a form, and yet not wholly a form, since there was no Protector as yet. The Archbishop of Canterbury made report of the decree of the Council of Executors concerning the obsequies of his late most illustrious Majesty and finished by reading the signatures of the executors, to wit: the Archbishop of Canterbury, the Lord Chancellor of England, William Lord St. John, John Lord Russell, Edward Earl of Hertford, John Viscount Lisle, Cuthbert Bishop of Durham—

Tom was not listening; an earlier clause of the document was puzzling him. At this point he turned and whispered to Lord Hertford, "What day did he say the burial hath been appointed for?"

"The sixteenth of the coming month, my liege."

" 'Tis a strange folly. Will he keep?"

Poor chap, he was still new to the customs of royalty; he was used to seeing the forlorn dead of Offal Court hustled out of the way with a very different sort of expedition. However, the lord Hertford set his mind at rest with a word or two.

A secretary of state presented an order of the council appointing the morrow at eleven for the reception of the foreign ambassadors, and desired the king's assent.

Tom turned an inquiring look toward Hertford, who whispered, "Your Majesty will signify consent. They come to testify their royal masters' sense of the heavy calamity which hath visited your Grace and the realm of England."

Tom did as he was bidden. Another secretary be-

gan to read a preamble concerning the expenses of the
late king's household, which had amounted to £28,000
during the preceding six months—a sum so vast that it
made Tom Canty gasp; he gasped again when the fact
appeared that £20,000 of this money were still owing
and unpaid,* and once more when it appeared that the
king's coffers were about empty and his twelve hundred
servants much embarrassed for lack of the wages due
them. Tom spoke out with lively apprehension, "We be
going to the dogs, 'tis plain. 'Tis meet and necessary
that we take a smaller house and set the servants at large,
sith they be of no value but to make delay, and trouble
one with offices that harass the spirit and shame the
soul, they misbecoming any but a doll, that hath nor
brains nor hands to help itself withal. I remember me of
a small house that standeth over against the fish market,
by Billingsgate——"

A sharp pressure upon Tom's arm stopped his foolish
tongue and sent a blush to his face; but no countenance
there betrayed any sign that this strange speech had
been remarked or given concern.

A secretary made report that forasmuch as the late
king had provided in his will for conferring the ducal
degree upon the Earl of Hertford and raising his brother,
Sir Thomas Seymour, to the peerage, and likewise Hertford's son to an earldom, together with similar aggrandize-
ments to other great servants of the Crown, the council
had resolved to hold a sitting on the sixteenth of February
for the delivering and confirming of these honors; and
that meantime, the late king not having granted in writing
estates suitable to the support of these dignities, the
council, knowing his private wishes in that regard, had
thought proper to grant to Seymour "£500 lands," and
to Hertford's son "800 pound lands and 300 pound of
the next bishop's lands which should fall vacant,"* his
present Majesty being willing.

Tom was about to blurt out something about the propriety of paying the late king's debts first before squan-
dering all this money, but a timely touch upon his arm
from the thoughtful Hertford saved him this indiscretion,
wherefore he gave the royal assent, without spoken comment but with much inward discomfort. While he sat

* Hume.

reflecting a moment over the ease with which he was doing strange and glittering miracles, a happy thought shot into his mind: why not make his mother Duchess of Offal Court and give her an estate? But a sorrowful thought swept it instantly away: he was only a king in name, these grave veterans and great nobles were his masters; to them his mother was only the creature of a diseased mind; they would simply listen to his project with unbelieving ears, then send for the doctor.

The dull work went tediously on. Petitions were read, and proclamations, patents, and all manner of wordy, repetitious, and wearisome papers relating to the public business; and at last Tom sighed pathetically and murmured to himself, "In what have I offended, that the good God should take me away from the fields and the free air and the sunshine to shut me up here and make me a king and afflict me so?" Then his poor muddled head nodded awhile and presently drooped to his shoulder, and the business of the empire came to a standstill for want of that august factor the ratifying power. Silence ensued around the slumbering child, and the sages of the realm ceased from their deliberations.

During the forenoon Tom had an enjoyable hour, by permission of his keepers, Hertford and St. John, with the lady Elizabeth and the little lady Jane Grey, though the spirits of the princesses were rather subdued by the mighty stroke that had fallen upon the royal house; and at the end of the visit his "elder sister"—afterwards the "Bloody Mary" of history—chilled him with a solemn interview which had but one merit in his eyes, its brevity. He had a few moments to himself, and then a slim lad of about twelve years of age was admitted to his presence, whose clothing, except his snowy ruff and the laces about his wrists, was of black—doublet, hose and all. He bore no badge of mourning but a knot of purple ribbon on his shoulder. He advanced hesitatingly with head bowed and bare and dropped upon one knee in front of Tom. Tom sat still and contemplated him soberly a moment. Then he said, "Rise, lad. Who art thou? What wouldst have?"

The boy rose and stood at graceful ease, but with an aspect of concern in his face. He said "Of a surety thou must remember me, my lord. I am thy whipping boy."

"My *whipping* boy?"

"The same, your Grace. I am Humphrey—Humphrey Marlow."

Tom perceived that here was someone whom his keepers ought to have posted him about. The situation was delicate. What should he do? Pretend he knew this lad, and then betray by his every utterance that he had never heard of him before? No, that would not do. An idea came to his relief: accidents like this might be likely to happen with some frequency now that business urgencies would often call Hertford and St. John from his side, they being members of the council of executors; therefore perhaps it would be well to strike out a plan himself to meet the requirements of such emergencies. Yes, that would be a wise course; he would practice on this boy, and see what sort of success he might achieve. So he stroked his brow perplexedly a moment or two and presently said, "Now I seem to remember thee somewhat, but my wit is clogged and dim with suffering—"

"Alack, my poor master!" ejaculated the whipping boy with feeling, adding to himself, "In truth 'tis as they said —his mind is gone; alas, poor soul! But misfortune catch me, how am I forgetting! They said one must not seem to observe that aught is wrong with him."

" 'Tis strange how my memory doth wanton with me these days," said Tom. "But mind it not—I mend apace— a little clue doth often serve to bring me back again the things and names which had escaped me. [And not they only, forsooth, but e'en such as I ne'er heard before—as this lad shall see.] Give thy business speech."

" 'Tis matter of small weight, my liege, yet will I touch upon it an' it please your Grace. Two days gone by, when your Majesty faulted thrice in your Greek in the morning lessons—dost remember it?"

"Y-e-s—methinks I do. [It is not much of a lie— an' I had meddled with the Greek at all, I had not faulted simply thrice, but forty times.] Yes, I do recall it now; go on."

"The master, being wroth with what he termed such slovenly and doltish work, did promise that he would soundly whip me for it, and——"

"Whip *thee!*" said Tom, astonished out of his presence of mind. "Why should he whip *thee* for faults of mine?"

"Ah, your Grace forgetteth again. He always scourgeth me when thou dost fail in thy lessons."

"True, true—I had forgot. Thou teachest me in private; then if I fail, he argueth that thy office was lamely done, and——"

"Oh, my liege, what words are these? I, the humblest of thy servants, presume to teach *thee?*"

"Then where is thy blame? What riddle is this? Am I in truth gone mad, or is it thou? Explain—speak out."

"But good your Majesty, there's nought that needeth simplifying. None may visit the sacred person of the Prince of Wales with blows, wherefore when he faulteth, 'tis I that take them; and meet it is and right, for that it is mine office and my livelihood."*

Tom stared at the tranquil boy, observing to himself, "Lo, it is a wonderful thing—a most strange and curious trade; I marvel they have not hired a boy to take my combings and my dressings for me—would heaven they would!—an' they will do this thing, I will take my lashings in mine own person, giving God thanks for the change." Then he said aloud, "And hast thou been beaten, poor friend, according to the promise?"

"No, good your Majesty, my punishment was appointed for this day, and peradventure it may be annulled as unbefitting the season of mourning that is come upon us; I know not, and so have made bold to come hither and remind your Grace about your gracious promise to intercede in my behalf——"

"With the master? To save thee thy whipping?"

"Ah, thou dost remember!"

"My memory mendeth, thou seest. Set thy mind at ease; thy back shall go unscathed; I will see to it."

"Oh, thanks, my good lord!" cried the boy, dropping upon his knee again. "Mayhap I have ventured far enow; and yet——"

Seeing Master Humphrey hesitate, Tom encouraged him to go on, saying he was "in the granting mood."

"Then will I speak it out, for it lieth near my heart. Sith thou art no more Prince of Wales, but king, thou canst order matters as thou wilt, with none to say thee nay; wherefore it is not in reason that thou wilt longer

* See Note 8 at end of volume.

vex thyself with dreary studies, but wilt burn thy books
and turn thy mind to things less irksome. Then am I
ruined, and mine orphan sisters with me!"

"Ruined? Prithee how?"

"My back is my bread, O my gracious liege! If it go
idle, I starve. An' thou cease from study, mine office
is gone, thou'lt need no whipping boy. Do not turn me
away!"

Tom was touched with this pathetic distress. He said,
with a right royal burst of generosity, "Discomfort thyself
no further, lad. Thine office shall be permanent in
thee and thy line forever." Then he struck the boy a
light blow on the shoulder with the flat of his sword,
exclaiming, "Rise, Humphrey Marlow, Hereditary Grand
Whipping Boy to the royal house of England! Banish
sorrow; I will betake me to my books again and study
so ill that they must in justice treble thy wage, so mightily
shall the business of thine office be augmented."

The grateful Humphrey responded fervidly, "Thanks, O
most noble master; this princely lavishness doth far sur-
pass my most distempered dreams of fortune. Now shall
I be happy all my days, and all the house of Marlow
after me."

Tom had wit enough to perceive that here was a lad who
could be useful to him. He encouraged Humphrey to talk,
and he was nothing loath. He was delighted to believe
that he was helping in Tom's "cure," for always, as soon
as he had finished calling back to Tom's diseased mind
the various particulars of his experiences and adventures
in the royal schoolroom and elsewhere about the palace,
he noticed that Tom was then able to "recall" the circumstances quite clearly. At the end of an hour Tom found
himself well freighted with very valuable information concerning personages and matters pertaining to the court, so
he resolved to draw instruction from this source daily,
and to this end he would give order to admit Humphrey
to the royal closet whenever he might come, provided the
majesty of England was not engaged with other people.
Humphrey had hardly been dismissed when my lord Hertford arrived with more trouble for Tom.

He said that the lords of the council, fearing that some
overwrought report of the king's damaged health might

have leaked out and got abroad, they deemed it wise and best that his Majesty should begin to dine in public after a day or two—his wholesome complexion and vigorous step, assisted by a carefully guarded repose of manner and ease and grace of demeanor, would more surely quiet the general pulse, in case any evil rumors *had* gone about, than any other scheme that could be devised.

Then the earl proceeded very delicately to instruct Tom as to the observances proper to the stately occasion, under the rather thin disguise of "reminding" him concerning things already known to him; but to his vast gratification it turned out that Tom needed very little help in this line: he had been making use of Humphrey in that direction, for Humphrey had mentioned that within a few days he was to begin to dine in public, having gathered it from the swift-winged gossip of the court. Tom kept these facts to himself, however.

Seeing the royal memory so improved, the earl ventured to apply a few tests to it, in an apparently casual way, to find out how far its amendment had progressed. The results were happy, here and there, in spots—spots where Humphrey's tracks remained; and on the whole my lord was greatly pleased and encouraged. So encouraged was he, indeed, that he spoke up and said in a quite hopeful voice, "Now am I persuaded that if your Majesty will but tax your memory yet a little further, it will resolve the puzzle of the Great Seal—a loss which was of moment yesterday, although of none today, since its term of service ended with our late lord's life. May it please your Grace to make the trial?"

Tom was at sea—a Great Seal was a something which he was totally unacquainted with. After a moment's hesitation he looked up innocently and asked, "What was it like, my lord?"

The earl started, almost imperceptibly, muttering to himself, "Alack, his wits are flown again! It was ill wisdom to lead him on to strain them." Then he deftly turned the talk to other matters, with the purpose of sweeping the unlucky Seal out of Tom's thoughts—a purpose which easily succeeded.

15 TOM AS KING

The next day the foreign ambassadors came, with their gorgeous trains; and Tom, throned in awful state, received them. The splendors of the scene delighted his eye and fired his imagination at first, but the audience was long and dreary, and so were most of the addresses; wherefore, what began as a pleasure grew into weariness and homesickness by and by. Tom said the words which Hertford put into his mouth from time to time and tried hard to acquit himself satisfactorily, but he was too new to such things and too ill at ease to accomplish more than a tolerable success. He looked sufficently like a king, but he was ill able to feel like one. He was cordially glad when the ceremony was ended.

The larger part of his day was "wasted"—as he termed it in his own mind—in labors pertaining to his royal office. Even the two hours devoted to certain princely pastimes and recreations were rather a burden to him than otherwise, they were so fettered by restrictions and ceremonious observances. However, he had a private hour with his whipping boy, which he counted clear gain, since he got both entertainment and needful information out of it.

The third day of Tom Canty's kingship came and went much as the others had done, but there was a lifting of his cloud in one way: he felt less uncomfortable than at first; he was getting a little used to his circumstances and surroundings; his chains still galled, but not all the time; he found that the presence and homage of the great afflicted and embarrassed him less and less sharply with every hour that drifted over his head.

But for one single dread, he could have seen the fourth day approach without serious distress—the dining in public; it was to begin that day. There were greater matters in the program, for on that day he would have to preside at a council which would take his views and commands concerning the policy to be pursued toward various foreign nations scattered far and near over the great globe; on that day too, Hertford would be formally chosen to the grand office of Lord Protector; other things of note were appointed for that fourth day also, but to Tom they were all insignificant compared with the ordeal of dining all by himself with a multitude of curious eyes fastened upon him and a multitude of mouths whispering comments upon his performance—and upon his mistakes, if he should be so unlucky as to make any.

Still, nothing could stop that fourth day, and so it came. It found poor Tom low-spirited and absentminded, and this mood continued; he could not shake it off. The ordinary duties of the morning dragged upon his hands and wearied him. Once more he felt the sense of captivity heavy upon him.

Late in the forenoon he was in a large audience chamber, conversing with the Earl of Hertford and dully awaiting the striking of the hour appointed for a visit of ceremony from a considerable number of great officials and courtiers.

After a little while Tom, who had wandered to a window and become interested in the life and movement of the great highway beyond the palace gates—and not idly interested, but longing with all his heart to take part in person in its stir and freedom—saw the van of a hooting and shouting mob of disorderly men, women, and children of the lowest and poorest degree approaching from up the road.

"I would I knew what 'tis about!" he exclaimed with all a boy's curiosity in such happenings.

"Thou art the king!" solemnly responded the earl with a reverence. "Have I your Grace's leave to act?"

"Oh, blithely, yes! Oh, gladly, yes!" exclaimed Tom excitedly, adding to himself with a lively sense of satisfaction, "In truth, being a king is not all dreariness; it hath its compensations and conveniences."

The earl called a page and sent him to the captain of the guard with the order, "Let the mob be halted, and inquiry made concerning the occasion of its movement. By the king's command!"

A few seconds later a long rank of the royal guards,

cased in flashing steel, filed out at the gates and formed across the highway in front of the multitude. A messenger returned to report that the crowd were following a man, a woman, and a young girl to execution for crimes committed against the peace and dignity of the realm.

Death—and a violent death—for these poor unfortunates! The thought wrung Tom's heartstrings. The spirit of compassion took control of him, to the exclusion of all other considerations: he never thought of the offended laws or of the grief or loss which these three criminals had inflicted upon their victims, he could think of nothing but the scaffold and the grisly fate hanging over the heads of the condemned. His concern made him even forget for the moment that he was but the false shadow of a king, not the substance; and before he knew it he had blurted out the command, "Bring them here!"

Then he blushed scarlet, and a sort of apology sprung to his lips; but observing that his order had wrought no sort of surprise in the earl or the waiting page, he suppressed the words he was about to utter. The page, in the most matter-of-fact way, made a profound obeisance and retired backwards out of the room to deliver the command. Tom experienced a glow of pride and a renewed sense of the compensating advantages of the kingly office. He said to himself, "Truly it is like what I was used to feel when I read the old priest's tales and did imagine mine own self a prince, giving law and command to all, saying, 'Do this, do that,' whilst none durst offer let or hindrance to my will."

Now the doors swung open; one high-sounding title after another was announced, the personages owning them followed, and the place was quickly half filled with noble folk and finery. But Tom was hardly conscious of the presence of these people, so wrought up was he and so intensely absorbed in that other and more interesting matter. He seated himself absently in his chair of state and turned his eyes upon the door with manifestations of impatient expectancy, seeing which, the company forebore to trouble him and fell to chatting a mixture of public business and court gossip one with another.

In a little while the measured tread of military men was heard approaching, and the culprits entered the presence in charge of an undersheriff and escorted by a detail of the king's guard. The civil officer knelt before Tom, then stood aside; the three doomed persons knelt also and remained so; the guard took position behind Tom's chair. Tom scanned the prisoners curiously. Something about the dress or appearance of the man had stirred a vague memory in him. "Methinks I have seen this man ere now, but the when or the where fail me—" Such was Tom's thought. Just then the man glanced quickly up, and quickly dropped his face again, not being able to endure the awful port of sovereignty; but the one full glimpse of the face which Tom got was sufficient. He said to himself, "Now is the matter clear; this is the stranger that plucked Giles Witt out of the Thames and saved his life that windy, bitter, first day of the new year—a brave good deed; pity he hath been doing baser ones and got himself in this sad case. I have not forgot the day, neither the hour; by reason that an hour after, upon the stroke of eleven, I did get a hiding by the hand of Gammer Canty which was of so goodly and admired severity that all that went before or followed after it were but fondlings and caresses by comparison."

Tom now ordered that the woman and the girl be removed from the presence for a little time, then addressed himself to the undersheriff, saying, "Good sir, what is this man's offense?"

The officer knelt and answered, "So please your Majesty, he hath taken the life of a subject by poison."

Tom's compassion for the prisoner and admiration of him as the daring rescuer of a drowning boy experienced a most damaging shock.

"The thing was proven upon him?" he asked.

"Most clearly, sire."

Tom sighed and said, "Take him away—he hath earned his death. 'Tis a pity, for he was a brave heart—na—na, I mean he hath the *look* of it!"

The prisoner clasped his hands together with sudden energy and wrung them despairingly, at the same time appealing imploringly to the "king" in broken and terrified phrases, "O my lord the king, an' thou canst pity the lost, have pity upon me! I am innocent—neither hath that wherewith I am charged been more than but lamely proved—yet I speak not of that; the judgment is gone forth against me and may not suffer alteration; yet in mine extremity I beg a boon, for my doom is more than I can bear. A grace, a grace, my lord the king! In thy royal compassion grant my prayer; give commandment that I be hanged!"

Tom was amazed. This was not the outcome he had looked for.

"Odds my life, a strange *boon!* Was it not the fate intended thee?"

"O good my liege, not so! It is ordered that I be *boiled alive!*"

The hideous surprise of these words almost made Tom spring from his chair. As soon as he could recover his wits he cried out, "Have thy wish, poor soul! An' thou had poisoned a hundred men thou shouldst not suffer so miserable a death."

The prisoner bowed his face to the ground and burst into passionate expressions of gratitude, ending with, "If ever thou shouldst know misfortune—which God forefend!—may thy goodness to me this day be remembered and requited!"

Tom turned to the Earl of Hertford and said, "My lord, is it believable that there was warrant for this man's ferocious doom?"

"It is the law, your Grace—for poisoners. In Germany coiners be boiled to death in *oil*—not cast in of a sudden, but by a rope let down into the oil by degrees, and slowly; first the feet, then the legs, then——"

"Oh, prithee no more, my lord; I cannot bear it!" cried Tom, covering his eyes with his hands to shut out the picture. "I beseech your good lordship that order be taken to change this law. Oh, let no more poor creatures be visited with its tortures."

The earl's face showed profound gratification, for he was a man of merciful and generous impulses—a thing not very common with his class in that fierce age. He said, "These your Grace's noble words have sealed its doom. History will remember it to the honor of your royal house."

The undersheriff was about to remove his prisoner; Tom gave him a sign to wait; then he said, "Good sir, I would look into this matter further. The man has said his deed was but lamely proved. Tell me what thou knowest."

"If the king's grace please, it did appear upon the trial

that this man entered into a house in the hamlet of Islington where one lay sick—three witnesses say it was at ten of the clock in the morning and two say it was some minutes later—the sick man being alone at the time, and sleeping; and presently the man came forth again and went his way. The sick man died within the hour, being torn with spasms and retchings."

"Did any see the poison given? Was poison found?"

"Marry, no, my liege."

"Then how doth one know there was poison given at all?"

"Please your Majesty, the doctors testified that none die with such symptoms but by poison."

Weighty evidence, this—in that simple age. Tom recognized its formidable nature and said, "The doctor knoweth his trade; belike they were right. The matter hath an ill look for this poor man."

"Yet was not this all, your Majesty; there is more and worse. Many testified that a witch, since gone from the village, none know whither, did foretell, and speak it privately in their ears, that the sick man *would die by poison,* and more, that a stranger would give it—a stranger with brown hair and clothed in a worn and common garb; and surely this prisoner doth answer woundily to the bill. Please your Majesty to give the circumstance that solemn weight which is its due, seeing it was *foretold.*"

This was an argument of tremendous force in that superstitious day. Tom felt that the thing was settled; if evidence was worth anything, this poor fellow's guilt was proved. Still he offered the prisoner a chance, saying, "If thou canst say aught in thy behalf, speak."

"Nought that will avail, my king. I am innocent, yet cannot I make it appear. I have no friends, else might I show that I was not in Islington that day; so also might I show that at that hour they name I was above a league away, seeing I was at Wapping Old Stairs; yea more, my king, for I could show that whilst they say I was *taking* life, I was *saving* it. A drowning boy——"

"Peace! Sheriff, name the day the deed was done!"

"At ten in the morning, or some minutes later, the first day of the new year, most illustrious——"

"Let the prisoner go free; it is the king's will!"

Another blush followed this unregal outburst, and he

covered his indecorum as well as he could by adding, "It enrageth me that a man should be hanged upon such idle, harebrained evidence!"

A low buzz of admiration swept through the assemblage. It was not admiration of the decree that had been delivered by Tom, for the propriety or expediency of pardoning a convicted poisoner was a thing which few there would have felt justified in either admitting or admiring—no, the admiration was for the intelligence and spirit which Tom had displayed. Some of the low-voiced remarks were to this effect: "This is no mad king; he hath his wits sound." "How sanely he put his questions; how like his former natural self was this abrupt, imperious disposal of the matter!" "God be thanked his infirmity is spent! This is no weakling, but a king. He hath borne himself like to his own father."

The air being filled with applause, Tom's ear necessarily caught a little of it. The effect which this had upon him was to put him greatly at his ease and also to charge his system with very gratifying sensations.

However, his juvenile curiosity soon rose superior to these pleasant thoughts and feelings; he was eager to know what sort of deadly mischief the woman and the little girl could have been about; so, by his command the two terrified and sobbing creatures were brought before him.

"What is it that these have done?" he inquired of the sheriff.

"Please your Majesty, a black crime is charged upon them, and clearly proven; wherefore the judges have decreed, according to the law, that they be hanged. They sold themselves to the devil; such is their crime."

Tom shuddered. He had been taught to abhor people who did this wicked thing. Still, he was not going to deny himself the pleasure of feeding his curiosity, for all that; so he asked, "Where was this done? And when?"

"On a midnight, in December, in a ruined church, your Majesty."

Tom shuddered again.

"Who was there present?"

"Only these two, your Grace—and *that other*."

"Have these confessed?"

"Nay, not so, sire; they do deny it."

"Then prithee, how was it known?"

"Certain witnesses did see them wending thither, good your Majesty; this bred the suspicion, and dire effects have since confirmed and justified it. In particular, it is in evidence that through the wicked power so obtained, they did invoke and bring about a storm that wasted all the region round about. Above forty witnesses have proved the storm; and sooth one might have had a thousand, for all had reason to remember it, sith all had suffered by it."

"Certes this is a serious matter." Tom turned this dark piece of scoundrelism over in his mind awhile, then asked, "Suffered the woman also by the storm?"

Several old heads among the assemblage nodded their recognition of the wisdom of this question. The sheriff, however, saw nothing consequential in the inquiry; he answered with simple directness, "Indeed did she, your Majesty, and most righteously, as all aver. Her habitation was swept away, and herself and child left shelterless."

"Methinks the power to do herself so ill a turn was dearly bought. She had been cheated had she paid but a farthing for it; that she paid her soul, and her child's, argueth that she is mad; if she is mad she knoweth not what she doth, therefore sinneth not."

The elderly heads nodded recognition of Tom's wisdom once more, and one individual murmured, "An' the king be mad himself, according to report, then is it a madness of a sort that would improve the sanity of some I wot of, if by the gentle providence of God they could but catch it."

"What age hath the child?" asked Tom.

"Nine years, please your Majesty."

"By the law of England may a child enter into covenant and sell itself, my lord?" asked Tom, turning to a learned judge.

"The law doth not permit a child to make or meddle in any weighty matter, good my liege, holding that its callow wit unfitteth it to cope with the riper wit and evil schemings of them that are its elders. The *devil* may buy a child if he so choose, and the child agree thereto, but not an Englishman; in this latter case the contract would be null and void."

"It seemeth a rude, unchristian thing, and ill-contrived, that English law denieth privileges to Englishmen, to waste them on the devil!" cried Tom with honest heat.

This novel view of the matter excited many smiles, and was stored away in many heads to be repeated about the court as evidence of Tom's originality as well as progress toward mental health.

The elder culprit had ceased from sobbing and was hanging upon Tom's words with an excited interest and a growing hope. Tom noticed this, and it strongly inclined his sympathies toward her in her perilous and unfriended situation. Presently he asked, "How wrought they to bring the storm?"

"By pulling off their stockings, sire."

This astonished Tom and also fired his curiosity to fever heat. He said eagerly, "It is wonderful! Hath it always this dread effect?"

"Always, my liege, at least if the woman desire it and utter the needful words, either in her mind or with her tongue."

Tom turned to the woman and said with impetuous zeal, "Exert thy power; I would see a storm!"

There was a sudden paling of cheeks in the superstitious assemblage, and a general though unexpressed desire to get out of the place, all of which was lost upon Tom, who was dead to everything but the proposed cataclysm. Seeing a puzzled and astonished look in the woman's face, he added excitedly, "Never fear; thou shalt be blameless. More, thou shalt go free; none shall touch thee. Exert thy power."

"Oh, my lord the king, I have it not; I have been falsely accused."

"Thy fears stay thee. Be of good heart; thou shalt suffer no harm. Make a storm; it mattereth not how small a one —I require nought great or harmful, but indeed prefer the opposite; do this and thy life is spared; thou shalt go out free, with thy child, bearing the king's pardon, and safe from hurt or malice from any in the realm."

The woman prostrated herself and protested with tears that she had no power to do the miracle, else she would gladly win her child's life alone and be content to lose her own, if by obedience to the king's command so precious a grace might be acquired.

Tom urged; the woman still adhered to her declarations. Finally he said, "I think the woman hath said true. An' *my* mother were in her place and gifted with the devil's functions, she had not stayed a moment to call her storms and lay the whole land in ruins if the saving of my forfeit life were the price she got! It is argument that other mothers are made in like mold. Thou art free, goodwife —thou and thy child—for I do think thee innocent. *Now* thou'st nought to fear, being pardoned, pull off thy stockings! An' thou canst make me a storm, thou shalt be rich!"

The redeemed creature was loud in her gratitude and proceeded to obey, whilst Tom looked on with eager expectancy, a little marred by apprehension, the courtiers at the same time manifesting decided discomfort and uneasiness. The woman stripped her own feet and her little girl's also, and plainly did her best to reward the king's generosity with an earthquake, but it was all a failure and a disappointment.

Tom sighed and said, "There, good soul, trouble thyself no further; thy power is departed out of thee. Go thy way in peace; and if it return to thee at any time, forget me not, but fetch me a storm."*

* See Notes to Chapter 15 at end of volume.

16 THE STATE DINNER

The dinner hour drew near, yet strangely enough the thought brought but slight discomfort to Tom, and hardly any terror. The morning's experiences had wonderfully built up his confidence; the poor little ash-cat was already more wonted to his strange garret after four days' habit than a mature person could have become in a full month. A child's facility in accommodating itself to circumstances was never more strikingly illustrated.

Let us privileged ones hurry to the great banqueting room and have a glance at matters there whilst Tom is being made ready for the imposing occasion. It is a spacious apartment, with gilded pillars and pilasters, and pictured walls and ceilings. At the door stand tall guards, as rigid as statues, dressed in rich and picturesque costumes, and bearing halberds. In a high gallery which runs all around the place is a band of musicians and a packed company of citizens of both sexes in brilliant attire. In the center of the room, upon a raised platform, is Tom's table. Now let the ancient chronicler speak:

"A gentleman enters the room bearing a rod, and along with him another bearing a tablecloth, which, after they have both kneeled three times with the utmost veneration, he spreads upon the table, and after kneeling again they both retire; then come two others, one with the rod again, the other with a salt cellar, a plate, and bread; when they have kneeled as the others had done and placed what was brought upon the table, they too retire with the same ceremonies performed by the first; at last come two nobles, richly clothed, one bearing a tasting knife, who, after prostrating themselves three times in the most graceful manner, approach and rub the table with bread and salt with as much awe as if the king had been present."*

---

* Leigh Hunt's *The Town*, p. 408, quotation from an earlier tourist.

So end the solemn preliminaries. Now, far down the echoing corridors we hear a bugle blast and the indistinct cry, "Place for the king! Way for the king's most excellent majesty!" These sounds are momently repeated—they grow nearer and nearer—and presently, almost in our faces, the martial note peals and the cry rings out, "Way for the king!" At this instant the shining pageant appears and files in at the door with a measured march. Let the chronicler speak again:

"First come gentlemen, barons, earls, knights of the Garter, all richly dressed and bareheaded; next comes the Chancellor, between two, one of which carries the royal scepter, the other the Sword of State in a red scabbard studded with golden fleurs-de-lis, the point upwards; next comes the king himself, whom, upon his appearing, twelve trumpets and many drums salute with a great burst of welcome, whilst all in the galleries rise in their places, crying, 'God save the king!' After him come nobles attached to his person, and on his right and left march his guard of honor, his fifty gentlemen pensioners, with gilt battle-axes."

This was all fine and pleasant. Tom's pulse beat high, and a glad light was in his eyes. He bore himself right gracefully, and all the more so because he was not thinking of how he was doing it, his mind being charmed and occupied with the blithe sights and sounds about him; and besides, nobody can be very ungraceful in nicely fitting beautiful clothes after he has grown a little used to them, especially if he is for the moment unconscious of them. Tom remembered his instructions and acknowledged his greeting with a slight inclination of his plumed head and a courteous, "I thank ye, my good people."

He seated himself at table without removing his cap, and did it without the least embarrassment, for to eat with one's cap on was the one solitary royal custom upon which the kings and the Cantys met upon common ground, neither party having any advantage over the other in the matter of old familiarity with it. The pageant broke up and grouped itself picturesquely, and remained bareheaded.

Now, to the sound of gay music, the yeomen of the guard entered, "the tallest and mightiest men in England, they being carefully selected in this regard." But we will let the chronicler tell about it:

"The yeomen of the guard entered, bareheaded, clothed in scarlet, with golden roses upon their backs; and these went and came, bringing in each turn a course of dishes, served in plate. These dishes were received by a gentleman in the same order they were brought, and placed upon the table, while the taster gave to each guard a mouthful to eat of the particular dish he had brought, for fear of any poison."

Tom made a good dinner, notwithstanding he was conscious that hundreds of eyes followed each morsel to his mouth and watched him eat it with an interest which could not have been more intense if it had been a deadly explosive and was expected to blow him up and scatter him all about the place. He was careful not to hurry, and equally careful not to do anything whatever for himself, but wait till the proper official knelt down and did it for him. He got through without a mistake—flawless and precious triumph.

When the meal was over at last and he marched away in the midst of his bright pageant, with the happy noises in his ears of blaring bugles, rolling drums, and thundering acclamations, he felt that if he had seen the worst of dining in public, it was an ordeal which he would be glad to endure several times a day if by that means he could but buy himself free from some of the more formidable requirements of his royal office.

17 FOO-FOO THE FIRST

Miles Hendon hurried along toward the Southwark end of the bridge, keeping a sharp lookout for the persons he sought and hoping and expecting to overtake them presently. He was disappointed in this, however. By asking questions, he was enabled to track them part of the way through Southwark; then all traces ceased, and he was perplexed as to how to proceed. Still, he continued his efforts as best he could during the rest of the day. Nightfall found him leg-weary, half famished, and his desire as far from accomplishment as ever; so he supped at the Tabard Inn and went to bed, resolved to make an early start in the morning and give the town an exhaustive search. As he lay thinking and planning, he presently began to reason thus: The boy would escape from the ruffian, his reputed father, if possible; would he go back to London and seek his former haunts? No, he would not do that; he would avoid recapture. What, then, would he do? Never having had a friend in the world or a protector until he met Miles Hendon, he would naturally try to find that friend again, provided the effort did not require him to go toward London and danger. He would strike for Hendon Hall, that is what he would do, for he knew Hendon was homeward bound and there he might expect to find him. Yes, the case was plain to Hendon—he must lose no more time in Southwark, but move at once through Kent, toward Monk's Holm, searching the wood and inquiring as he went. Let us return to the vanished little king now.

The ruffian whom the waiter at the inn on the bridge saw "about to join" the youth and the king did not exactly join them, but fell in close behind them and followed their steps. He said nothing. His left arm was in a sling, and he wore a large green patch over his left eye; he limped slightly and used an oaken staff as a support. The youth led the king a crooked course through Southwark, and by and by struck into the high road beyond. The king was irritated now and said he would stop here—it was Hendon's place to come to him, not his to go to Hendon. He would not endure such insolence; he would stop where he was. The youth said, "Thou'lt tarry here, and thy friend lying wounded in the wood yonder? So be it then."

The king's manner changed at once. He cried out, "Wounded? And who hath dared to do it? But that is apart; lead on, lead on! Faster, sirrah! Art shod with lead? Wounded, is he? Now though the doer of it be a duke's son, he shall rue it!"

It was some distance to the wood, but the space was speedily traversed. The youth looked about him, discovered a bough sticking in the ground, with a small bit of rag tied to it, then led the way into the forest, watching for similar boughs and finding them at intervals: they were evidently guides to the point he was aiming at. By and by an open place was reached, where were the charred remains of a farmhouse, and near them a barn which was falling to ruin and decay. There was no sign of life anywhere, and utter silence prevailed. The youth entered the barn, the king following eagerly upon his heels. No one there! The king shot a surprised and suspicious glance at the youth and asked, "Where is he?"

A mocking laugh was his answer. The king was in a rage in a moment; he seized a billet of wood and was in the act of charging upon the youth when another mocking laugh fell upon his ear. It was from the lame ruffian who had been following at a distance. The king turned and said angrily, "Who art thou? What is thy business here?"

"Leave thy foolery," said the man, "and quiet thyself. My disguise is none so good that thou canst pretend thou knowest not thy father through it."

"Thou art not my father. I know thee not. I am the king. If thou hast hid my servant, find him for me, or thou shalt sup sorrow for what thou hast done."

John Canty replied in a stern and measured voice, "It is plain thou art mad, and I am loath to punish thee; but if thou provoke me, I must. Thy prating doth no harm here, where there are no ears that need to mind thy follies,

yet is it well to practice thy tongue to wary speech, that
it may do no hurt when our quarters change. I have
done a murder and may not tarry at home; neither shalt
thou, seeing I need thy service. My name is changed, for
wise reasons; it is Hobbs—John Hobbs; thine is Jack;
charge thy memory accordingly. Now then, speak. Where
is thy mother? Where are thy sisters? They came not to
the place appointed; knowest thou whither they went?"

The king answered sullenly, "Trouble me not with these
riddles. My mother is dead; my sisters are in the palace."

The youth nearby burst into a derisive laugh, and the
king would have assaulted him, but Canty—or Hobbs,
as he now called himself—prevented him, and said,
"Peace, Hugo, vex him not; his mind is astray, and thy
ways fret him. Sit thee down, Jack, and quiet thyself;
thou shalt have a morsel to eat, anon."

Hobbs and Hugo fell to talking together in low voices,
and the king removed himself as far as he could from
their disagreeable company. He withdrew into the twilight of the farther end of the barn, where he found the
earthen floor bedded a foot deep with straw. He lay down
here, drew straw over himself in lieu of blankets, and was
soon absorbed in thinking. He had many griefs, but
the minor ones were swept almost into forgetfulness by the
supreme one, the loss of his father. To the rest of the
world the name of Henry VIII brought a shiver and suggested an ogre whose nostrils breathed destruction and
whose hand dealt scourgings and death; but to this boy
the name brought only sensations of pleasure, the figure
it invoked wore a countenance that was all gentleness and
affection. He called to mind a long succession of loving
passages between his father and himself and dwelt fondly
upon them, his unstinted tears attesting how deep and
real was the grief that possessed his heart. As the afternoon wasted away, the lad, wearied with his troubles,
sunk gradually into a tranquil and healing slumber.

After a considerable time—he could not tell how long
—his senses struggled to a half consciousness, and as he
lay with closed eyes vaguely wondering where he was
and what had been happening, he noted a murmurous
sound, the sullen beating of rain upon the roof. A snug
sense of comfort stole over him, which was rudely broken
the next moment by a chorus of piping cackles and coarse

laughter. It startled him disagreeably, and he unmuffled his head to see whence this interruption proceeded. A grim and unsightly picture met his eye. A bright fire was burning in the middle of the floor at the other end of the barn; and around it, and lit weirdly up by the red glare, lolled and sprawled the motliest company of tattered gutter scum and ruffians, of both sexes, he had ever read or dreamed of. There were huge, stalwart men, brown with exposure, long-haired, and clothed in fantastic rags; there were middle-sized youths of truculent countenance, and similarly clad; there were blind mendicants with patched or bandaged eyes, crippled ones with wooden legs and crutches; there was a villain-looking peddler with his pack, a knife-grinder, a tinker, and a barber-surgeon with the implements of their trades; some of the females were hardly grown girls, some were at prime, some were old and wrinkled hags, and all were loud, brazen, foul-mouthed; and all soiled and slatternly; there were three sore-faced babies; there were a couple of starveling curs, with strings about their necks, whose office was to lead the blind.

The night was come, the gang had just finished feasting, an orgy was beginning, the can of liquor was passing from mouth to mouth. A general cry broke forth, "A song! A song from the Bat and Dick Dot-and-Go-One!"

One of the blind men got up and made ready by casting aside the patches that sheltered his excellent eyes and the pathetic placard which recited the cause of his calamity. Dot-and-Go-One disencumbered himself of his timber leg and took his place, upon sound and healthy limbs, beside his fellow rascal; then they roared out a rollicking ditty, and were reenforced by the whole crew at the end of each stanza in a rousing chous. By the time the last stanza was reached, the half-drunken enthusiasm had risen to such a pitch that everybody joined in and sang it clear through from the beginning, producing a volume of villainous sound that made the rafters quake. These were the inspiring words:

> Bien Darkmans then, Bouse Mort and Ken,
> The bien Coves bings awast,
> On Chates to trine by Rome Coves dine
> For his long lib at last.

Bing'd out bien Morts and toure, and toure,
Bing out of the Rome vile bine,
And toure the Cove that cloy'd your duds,
Upon the Chates to trine. *

Conversation followed; not in the thieves' dialect of the song, for that was only used in talk when unfriendly ears might be listening. In the course of it, it appeared that "John Hobbs" was not altogether a new recruit, but had trained in the gang at some former time. His later history was called for, and when he said he had "accidentally" killed a man, considerable satisfaction was expressed; when he added that the man was a priest, he was roundly applauded and had to take a drink with everybody. Old acquaintances welcomed him joyously, and new ones were proud to shake him by the hand. He was asked why he had "tarried away so many months." He answered, "London is better than the country, and safer these late years, the laws be so bitter and so diligently enforced. An' I had not had that accident, I had stayed there. I had resolved to stay and never more venture countrywards, but the accident has ended that."

He inquired how many persons the gang numbered now. The "Ruffler," or chief, answered, "Five and twenty sturdy budges, bulks, files, clapperdogeons and maunders, counting the dells and doxies and other morts.** Most are here; the rest are wandering eastward along the winter lay. We follow at dawn."

"I do not see the Wen among the honest folk about me. Where may he be?"

"Poor lad, his diet is brimstone now, and over hot for a delicate taste. He was killed in a brawl, somewhere about midsummer."

"I sorrow to hear that; the Wen was a capable man, and brave."

"That was he, truly. Black Bess, his dell, is of us yet, but absent on the eastward tramp; a fine lass, of nice ways and orderly conduct, none ever seeing her drunk above four days in the seven."

"She was ever strict—I remember it well—a goodly

* From *The English Rogue;* London, 1665.
** Canting terms for various kinds of thieves, beggars, and vagabonds and their female companions.

wench and worthy all commendation. Her mother was more free and less particular, a troublesome and ugly tempered beldame, but furnished with a wit above the common."

"We lost her through it. Her gift of palmistry and other sorts of fortune-telling begot for her at last a witch's name and fame. The law roasted her to death at a slow fire. It did touch me to a sort of tenderness to see the gallant way she met her lot—cursing and reviling all the crowd that gaped and gazed around her, whilst the flames licked upward toward her face and catched her thin locks and crackled about her old gray head. Cursing them, said I? Cursing them! Why, an' thou shouldst live a thousand years thou'dst never hear so masterful a cursing. Alack, her art died with her. There be base and weakling imitations left, but no true blasphemy."

The Ruffler sighed; the listeners sighed in sympathy; a general depression fell upon the company for a moment, for even hardened outcasts like these are not wholly dead to sentiment, but are able to feel a fleeting sense of loss and affliction at wide intervals and under peculiarly favoring circumstances—as in cases like to this, for instance, when genius and culture depart and leave no heir. However, a deep drink all round soon restored the spirits of the mourners.

"Have any others of our friends fared hardly?" asked Hobbs.

"Some—yes. Particularly newcomers, such as small husbandmen turned shiftless and hungry upon the world because their farms were taken from them to be changed to sheep ranges. They begged, and were whipped at the cart's tail, naked from the girdle up, till the blood ran, then set in the stocks to be pelted; they begged again, were whipped again, and deprived of an ear; they begged a third time—poor devils, what else could they do?—and were branded on the cheek with a red-hot iron, then sold for slaves; they ran away, were hunted down, and hanged. 'Tis a brief tale, and quickly told. Others of us have fared less hardly. Stand forth, Yokel, Burns, and Hodge—show your adornments!"

These stood up and stripped away some of their rags, exposing their backs, crisscrossed with ropy old welts left by the lash; one turned up his hair and showed the place

where a left ear had once been; another showed a brand
upon his shoulder—the letter V—and a mutilated ear; the
third said, "I am Yokel, once a farmer and prosperous,
with loving wife and kids, now am I somewhat different in
estate and calling, and the wife and kids are gone; mayhap
they are in heaven, mayhap in—in the other place; but
the kindly God be thanked, they bide no more in *England!*
My good old blameless mother strove to earn bread by
nursing the sick; one of these died, the doctors knew not
how, so my mother was burnt for a witch, whilst my babes
looked on and wailed. English law! Up, all, with your cups!
Now altogether and with a cheer! Drink to the merciful
English law that delivered *her* from the English hell!
Thank you, mates, one and all. I begged, from house to
house—I and the wife—bearing with us the hungry kids;
but it was crime to be hungry in England, so they stripped
us and lashed us through three towns. Drink ye all again
to the merciful English law! For its lash drank deep of my
Mary's blood and its blessed deliverance came quick. She
lies there, in the potter's field, safe from all harms. And
the kids—well, whilst the law lashed me from town to
town, they starved. Drink lads—only a drop—a drop to
the poor kids, that never did any creature harm. I begged
again—begged for a crust, and got the stocks and lost an
ear—see, here bides the stump; I begged again, and here
is the stump of the other to keep me minded of it. And still
I begged again, and was sold for a slave—here on my
cheek under this stain, if I washed it off, ye might see the
red S the branding iron left there! A *slave!* Do ye understand that word! An English *slave!* That is he that stands
before ye. I have run from my master, and when I am
found—the heavy curse of heaven fall on the law of the
land that hath commanded it!—I shall hang!" *

A ringing voice came through the murky air, "Thou
shalt *not!* And this day the end of that law is come!"

All turned and saw the fantastic figure of the little king
approaching hurriedly; as it emerged into the light and was
clearly revealed, a general explosion of inquiries broke out:
"Who is it? *What* is it? Who art thou, manikin?"

The boy stood unconfused in the midst of all those
surprised and questioning eyes and answered with princely
dignity, "I am Edward, king of England."

* See Note 10 at end of volume.

A wild burst of laughter followed, partly of derision and partly of delight in the excellence of the joke. The king was stung. He said sharply, "Ye mannerless vagrants, is this your recognition of the royal boon I have promised?"

He said more, with angry voice and excited gesture, but it was lost in a whirlwind of laughter and mocking exclamations. "John Hobbs" made several attempts to make himself heard above the din, and at last succeeded, saying, "Mates, he is my son, a dreamer, a fool, and stark mad; mind him not—he thinketh he *is* the king."

"I *am* the king," said Edward, turning toward him, "as thou shalt know to thy cost, in good time. Thou hast confessed a murder—thou shalt swing for it."

"*Thou'lt* betray me? *Thou?* An' I get my hands upon thee—"

"Tut-tut!" said the burly Ruffler, interposing in time to save the king, and emphasizing this service by knocking Hobbs down with his fist. "Hast respect for neither king *nor* Rufflers? An' thou insult my presence so again, I'll hang thee up myself." Then he said to his Majesty, "Thou must make no threats against thy mates, lad; and thou must guard thy tongue from saying evil of them elsewhere. *Be* king, if it please thy mad humor, but be not harmful in it. Sink the title thou hast uttered—'tis treason; we be bad men in some few trifling ways, but none among us is so base as to be traitor to his king; we be loving and loyal hearts in that regard. Note if I speak truth. Now, all together: 'Long Live Edward, king of England!' "

"Long live Edward, king of England!"

The response came with such a thundergust from the motley crew that the crazy building vibrated to the sound. The little king's face lighted with pleasure for an instant, and he slightly inclined his head and said with grave simplicity, "I thank you, my good people."

This unexpected result threw the company into convulsions of merriment. When something like quiet was presently come again, the Ruffler said firmly but with an accent of good nature, "Drop it, boy; 'tis not wise nor well. Humor thy fancy if thou must, but choose some other title."

A tinker shrieked out a suggestion, "Foo-foo the First, king of the Mooncalves!"

The title "took" at once, every throat responded, and a roaring shout went up of "Long live Foo-foo the First, king of the Mooncalves!" followed by hootings, catcalls, and peals of laughter.

"Hale him forth and crown him!"

"Robe him!"

"Scepter him!"

"Throne him!"

These and twenty other cries broke out at once; and almost before the poor little victim could draw a breath he was crowned with a tin basin, robed in a tattered blanket, throned upon a barrel, and sceptered with the tinker's soldering iron. Then all flung themselves upon their knees about him and sent up a chorus of ironical wailings and mocking supplications, whilst they swabbed their eyes with their soiled and ragged sleeves and aprons: "Be gracious to us, O sweet king!" "Trample not upon thy beseeching worms, O noble Majesty!" "Pity thy slaves, and comfort them with a royal kick!" "Cheer us and warm us with thy gracious rays, O flaming sun of sovereignty!" "Sanctify the ground with the touch of thy foot, that we may eat the dirt and be ennobled!" "Deign to spit upon us, O sire, that our children's children may tell of thy princely condescension, and be proud and happy forever!"

But the humorous tinker made the "hit" of the evening and carried off the honors. Kneeling, he pretended to kiss the king's foot, and was indignantly spurned; whereupon he went about begging for a rag to paste over the place upon his face which had been touched by the foot, saying it must be preserved from contact with the vulgar air and that he should make his fortune by going to the highway and exposing it to view at the rate of a hundred shillings a sight. He made himself so killingly funny that he was the envy and admiration of the whole mangy rabble.

Tears of shame and indignation stood in the little monarch's eyes; and the thought in his heart was, "Had I offered them a deep wrong they could not be more cruel; yet have I proffered nought but to do them a kindness, and it is thus they use me for it!"

The troop of vagabonds turned out at early dawn and set forward on their march. There was a lowering sky overhead, sloppy ground underfoot, and a winter chill in the air. All gaiety was gone from the company; some were sullen and silent, some were irritable and petulant, none were gentle-humored, all were thirsty.

The Ruffler put "Jack" in Hugo's charge, with some brief instructions, and commanded John Canty to keep away from him and let him alone; he also warned Hugo not to be too rough with the lad.

After a while the weather grew milder and the clouds lifted somewhat. The troop ceased to shiver, and their spirits began to improve. They grew more and more cheerful and finally began to chaff each other and insult passengers along the highway. This showed that they were awaking to an appreciation of life and its joys once more. The dread in which their sort was held was apparent in the fact that everybody gave them the road and took their ribald insolences meekly, without venturing to talk back. They snatched linen from the hedges occasionally, in full view of the owners, who made no protest but only seemed grateful that they did not take the hedges too.

By and by they invaded a small farmhouse and made themselves at home while the trembling farmer and his people swept the larder clean to furnish a breakfast for them. They chucked the housewife and her daughters under the chin whilst receiving the food from their hands, and made coarse jests about them, accompanied with insulting epithets and bursts of horselaughter. They threw bones and vegetables at the farmer and his sons, kept them dodging all the time, and applauded uproariously when a good hit was made. They ended by buttering the head of one of the daughters who resented some of their familiar-

ities. When they took their leave they threatened to come
back and burn the house over the heads of the family if
any report of their doings got to the ears of the authorities.

About noon, after a long and heavy tramp, the gang
came to a halt behind a hedge on the outskirts of a
considerable village. An hour was allowed for rest, then the
crew scattered themselves abroad to enter the village at
different points to ply their various trades.

"Jack" was sent with Hugo. They wandered hither and
thither for some time, Hugo watching for opportunities
to do a stroke of business but finding none; so he finally
said, "I see nought to steal; it is a paltry place. Wherefore
we will beg."

"*We,* forsooth! Follow thy trade—it befits thee. But *I*
will not beg."

"Thou'lt not beg!" exclaimed Hugo, eyeing the king
with surprise. "Prithee, since when hast thou reformed?"

"What dost thou mean?"

"Mean? Hast thou not begged the streets of London all
thy life?"

"I? Thou idiot!"

"Spare thy compliments—thy stock will last longer.
Thy father says thou hast begged all thy days. Mayhap
he lied. Peradventure you will even make so bold as to
say he lied," scoffed Hugo.

"Him *you* call my father? Yes, he lied."

"Come, play not thy merry game of madman so far,
mate; use it for thy amusement, not thy hurt. An' I tell
him this, he will scorch thee finely for it."

"Save thyself the trouble. I will tell him."

"I like thy spirit, I do in truth; but I do not admire thy
judgment. Bone-rackings and bastings be plenty enow in
this life without going out of one's way to invite them. But
a truce to these matters; *I* believe your father. I doubt
not he can lie; I doubt not he *doth* lie upon occasion, for
the best of us do that; but there is no occasion here. A
wise man does not waste so good a commodity as lying
for nought. But come; sith it is thy humor to give over
begging, wherewithal shall we busy ourselves? With rob-
bing kitchens?"

The king said impatiently, "Have done with this folly;
you weary me!"

Hugo replied with temper, "Now harkee, mate; you will

not beg, you will not rob; so be it. But I will tell you what you *will* do. You will play decoy whilst *I* beg. Refuse, an' you think you may venture!"

The king was about to reply contemptuously when Hugo said, interrupting, "Peace! Here comes one with a kindly face. Now will I fall down in a fit. When the stranger runs to me, set you up a wail and fall upon your knees, seeming to weep; then cry out as all the devils of misery were in your belly and say, 'Oh, sir, it is my poor afflicted brother, and we be friendless; o' God's name cast through your merciful eyes one pitiful look upon a sick, forsaken, and most miserable wretch; bestow one little penny out of thy riches upon one smitten of God and ready to perish!' And mind you, keep you *on* wailing, and abate not till we bilk him of his penny, else shall you rue it."

Then immediately Hugo began to moan, and groan, and roll his eyes, and reel and totter about; and when the stranger was close at hand, down he sprawled before him, with a shriek, and began to writhe and wallow in the dirt, in seeming agony.

"Oh dear, oh dear!" cried the benevolent stranger. "Oh, poor soul, poor soul, how he doth suffer! There, let me help thee up."

"Oh, noble sir, forbear, and God love you for a princely gentleman—but it giveth me cruel pain to touch me when I am taken so. My brother there will tell your worship how I am racked with anguish when these fits be upon me. A penny, dear sir, a penny to buy a little food; then leave me to my sorrows."

"A penny! Thou shalt have three, thou hapless creature"—and he fumbled in his pocket with nervous haste and got them out. "There, poor lad, take them, and most welcome. Now come hither, my boy, and help me carry thy stricken brother to yon house, where——"

"I am not his brother," said the king, interrupting.

"What! Not his brother?"

"Oh, hear him!" groaned Hugo, then privately ground his teeth. "He denies his own brother—and he with one foot in the grave!"

"Boy, thou art indeed hard of heart if this is thy brother. For shame! And he scarce able to move hand or foot. If he is not thy brother, who is he then?"

"A beggar and a thief! He has got your money and has picked your pocket likewise. An' thou wouldst do a healing miracle, lay thy staff over his shoulders, and trust Providence for the rest."

But Hugo did not tarry for the miracle. In a moment he was up and off like the wind, the gentleman following after and raising the hue and cry lustily as he went. The king, breathing deep gratitude to heaven for his own release, fled in the opposite direction and did not slacken his pace until he was out of harm's reach. He took the first road that offered and soon put the village behind him. He hurried along as briskly as he could during several hours, keeping a nervous watch over his shoulder for pursuit; but his fears left him at last, and a grateful sense of security took their place. He recognized now that he was hungry, and also very tired. So he halted at a farmhouse, but when he was about to speak he was cut short and driven rudely away. His clothes were against him.

He wandered on, wounded and indignant, and was resolved to put himself in the way of like treatment no more. But hunger is pride's master; so as the evening drew near, he made an attempt at another farmhouse, but here he fared worse than before, for he was called hard names and was promised arrest as a vagrant except he moved on promptly.

The night came on, chilly and overcast; and still the footsore monarch labored slowly on. He was obliged to keep moving, for every time he sat down to rest he was soon penetrated to the bone with the cold. All his sensations and experiences as he moved through the solemn gloom and the empty vastness of the night were new and strange to him. At intervals he heard voices approach, pass by, and fade into silence; and as he saw nothing more of the bodies they belonged to than a sort of formless drifting blur, there was something spectral and uncanny about it all that made him shudder. Occasionally he caught the twinkle of a light—always far away apparently, almost in another world; if he heard the tinkle of a sheep's bell, it was vague, distant, indistinct; the muffled lowing of the herds floated to him on the night wind in vanishing cadences, a mournful sound; now and then came the complaining howl of a dog over viewless expanses of field and forest; all sounds were remote; they made the little king feel that all life and activity were far removed from him and that he stood solitary, companionless, in the center of a measureless solitude.

He stumbled along through the gruesome fascinations of this new experience, startled occasionally by the soft rustling of the dry leaves overhead, so like human whispers they seemed to sound; and by and by he came suddenly upon the freckled light of a tin lantern near at hand. He stepped back into the shadows and waited. The lantern stood by the open door of a barn. The king waited some time; there was no sound, and nobody stirring. He got so cold, standing still, and the hospitable barn looked so enticing that at last he resolved to risk everything and enter. He started swiftly and stealthily, and just as he was crossing the threshold he heard voices behind him. He darted behind a cask within the barn and stooped down. Two farm laborers came in, bringing the lantern with them, and fell to work, talking meanwhile. Whilst they moved about with the light, the king made good use of his eyes and took the bearings of what seemed to be a good-sized stall at the further end of the place, purposing to grope his way to it when he should be left to himself. He also noted the position of a pile of horse blankets, midway of the route, with the intent to levy upon them for the service of the Crown of England for one night.

By and by the men finished and went away, fastening the door behind them and taking the lantern with them. The shivering king made for the blankets with as good speed as the darkness would allow, gathered them up, and then groped his way safely to the stall. Of two of the blankets he made a bed, then covered himself with the remaining two. He was a glad monarch now, though the blankets were old and thin and not quite warm enough, and besides, gave out a pungent horsey odor that was almost suffocatingly powerful.

Although the king was hungry and chilly, he was also so tired and so drowsy that these latter influences soon began to get the advantage of the former, and he presently dozed off into a state of semiconsciousness. Then, just as he was on the point of losing himself wholly, he distinctly felt something touching him! He was broad awake in a moment, and gasping for breath. The cold horror of that mysterious touch in the dark almost made his heart stand still. He lay motionless and listened, scarcely breathing. But nothing stirred, and there was no sound. He continued to listen and wait during what seemed a long time, but still nothing stirred, and there was no sound. So he began to drop into a drowse once more at last; and all at once he felt that mysterious touch again! It was a grisly thing, this light touch from this noiseless and invisible presence; it made the boy sick with ghostly fears. What should he do? That was the question, but he did not know how to answer it. Should he leave these reasonably comfortable quarters and fly from this inscrutable horror? But fly whither? He could not get out of the barn, and the idea of scurrying blindly hither and thither in the dark within the captivity of the four walls, with this phantom gliding after him and visiting him with that soft, hideous touch upon cheek or shoulder at every turn, was intolerable. But to stay where he was and endure this living death all night? Was that better? No. What, then, was there left to do? Ah, there was but one course; he knew it well—he must put out his hand and find that thing!

It was easy to think this, but it was hard to brace himself up to try it. Three times he stretched his hand a little way out into the dark, gingerly, and snatched it suddenly back, with a gasp—not because it had encountered anything, but because he had felt so sure it was just *going* to. But the fourth time, he groped a little further, and his hand lightly swept against something soft and warm. This petrified him, nearly, with fright: his mind was in such a state that he could imagine the thing to be nothing else than a corpse newly dead and still warm. He thought he would rather die than touch it again. But he thought this false thought because he did not know the immortal strength of human curiosity. In no long time his hand was tremblingly groping again—against his judgment, and without his consent, but groping persistently on just the same. It encountered a bunch of long hair; he shuddered, but followed up the hair and found what seemed to be a warm rope; followed up the rope and found an innocent calf! For the rope was not a rope at all, but a calf's tail.

The king was cordially ashamed of himself for having gotten all that fright and misery out of so paltry a matter as a slumbering calf; but he need not have felt so about it, for it was not the calf that frightened him but a dreadful nonexistent something which the calf stood for; and any other boy in those old superstitious times would have acted and suffered just as he had done.

The king was not only delighted to find that the creature was only a calf, but delighted to have the calf's company, for he had been feeling so lonesome and friendless that the company and comradeship of even this humble animal was welcome. And he had been so buffeted, so rudely entreated by his own kind, that it was a real comfort to him to feel that he was at last in the society of a fellow creature that had at least a soft heart and a gentle spirit, whatever loftier attributes might be lacking. So he resolved to waive rank and make friends with the calf.

While stroking its sleek warm back——for it lay near him and within easy reach——it occurred to him that this calf might be utilized in more ways than one. Whereupon he rearranged his bed, spreading it down close to the calf; then he cuddled himself up to the calf's back, drew the covers up over himself and his friend, and in a minute or two was as warm and comfortable as he had ever been in the downy couches of the regal palace of Westminister.

Pleasant thoughts came at once; life took on a cheerfuller seeming. He was free of the bonds of servitude and crime, free of the companionship of base and brutal outlaws; he was warm, he was sheltered; in a word, he was happy. The night wind was rising; it swept by in fitful gusts that made the old barn quake and rattle; then its forces died down at intervals and went moaning and wailing around corners and projections; but it was all music to the king, now that he was snug and comfortable: let it blow and rage, let it batter and bang, let it moan and wail, he minded it not, he only enjoyed it. He merely snuggled the closer to his friend, in a luxury of warm contentment, and drifted blissfully out of consciousness into a deep and dreamless sleep that was full of serenity and peace. The distant dogs howled, the melancholy kine complained, and the winds went on raging, whilst furious sheets of rain drove along the roof; but the Majesty of England slept on, undisturbed, and the calf did the same, it being a simple creature and not easily troubled by storms or embarrassed by sleeping with a king.

19 THE PRINCE WITH THE PEASANTS

When the king awoke in the early morning, he found that a wet but thoughtful rat had crept into the place during the night and made a cozy bed for itself in his bosom. Being disturbed now, it scampered away. The boy smiled and said, "Poor fool, why so fearful? I am as forlorn as thou. 'Twould be a shame in me to hurt the helpless, who am myself so helpless. Moreover, I owe you thanks for a good omen; for when a king has fallen so low that the very rats do make a bed of him, it surely meaneth that his fortunes be upon the turn, since it is plain he can no lower go."

He got up and stepped out of the stall, and just then he heard the sound of children's voices. The barn door opened and a couple of little girls came in. As soon as they saw him their talking and laughing ceased, and they stopped and stood still, gazing at him with strong curiosity; they presently began to whisper together, then they approached nearer, and stopped again to gaze and whisper. By and by they gathered courage and began to discuss him aloud. One said, "He hath a comely face."

The other added, "And pretty hair."

"But is ill-clothed enow."

"And how starved he looketh."

They came still nearer, sidling shyly around and about him, examining him minutely from all points as if he were some strange new kind of animal, but warily and watchfully the while, as if they half feared he might be a sort of animal that would bite upon occasion. Finally they halted before him, holding each other's hands for protection, and took a good satisfying stare with their innocent eyes; then one of them plucked up all her courage and inquired with honest directness, "Who are thou, boy?"

"I am the king," was the grave answer.

The children gave a little start, and their eyes spread themselves wide open and remained so during a speechless half minute. Then curiosity broke the silence, "The *king?* What king?"

"The king of England."

The children looked at each other, then at him, then at each other again—wonderingly, perplexedly; then one said, "Didst hear him, Margery? He saith he is the king. Can that be true?"

"How can it be else but true, Prissy? Would he say a lie? For look you, Prissy, an' it were not true, it *would* be a lie. It surely would be. Now think on't. For all things that be not true be lies; thou canst make nought else out of it."

It was a good tight argument, without a leak in it anywhere; and it left Prissy's half doubts not a leg to stand on. She considered a moment, then put the king upon his honor with the simple remark, "If thou art truly the king, then I believe thee."

"I am truly the king."

This settled the matter. His Majesty's royalty was accepted without further question or discussion, and the two little girls began at once to inquire into how he came to be where he was, and how he came to be so unroyally clad, and whither he was bound, and all about his affairs. It was a mighty relief to him to pour out his troubles where they would not be scoffed at or doubted, so he told his tale with feeling, forgetting even his hunger for the time; and it was received with the deepest and tenderest sympathy by the gentle little maids. But when he got down to his latest experiences and they learned how long he had been without food, they cut him short and hurried him away to the farmhouse to find a breakfast for him.

The king was cheerful and happy now and said to himself, "When I am come to mine own again, I will always honor little children, remembering how that these trusted me and believed in me in my time of trouble, whilst they that were older and thought themselves wiser mocked at me and held me for a liar."

The children's mother received the king kindly and was full of pity, for his forlorn condition and apparently crazed intellect touched her womanly heart. She was a widow and rather poor; consequently she had seen trouble enough to enable her to feel for the unfortunate. She imagined that the demented boy had wandered away from his friends or keepers, so she tried to find out whence he had come in order that she might take measures to return him; but all her references to neighboring towns and villages, and all her inquiries in the same line, went for nothing: the boy's face, and his answers too, showed that the things she was talking of were not familiar to him. He spoke earnestly and simply about court matters and broke down more than once when speaking of the late king "his father"; but whenever the conversation changed to baser topics, he lost interest and became silent.

The woman was mightily puzzled, but she did not give up. As she proceeded with her cooking, she set herself to contriving devices to surprise the boy into betraying his real secret. She talked about cattle—he showed no concern; then about sheep—the same result, so her guess that he had been a shepherd boy was an error; she talked about mills; and about weavers, tinkers, smiths, trades, and tradesmen of all sorts; and about Bedlam, and jails, and charitable retreats; but no matter, she was baffled at all points. Not altogether, either, for she argued that she had narrowed the thing down to domestic service. Yes, she was sure she was on the right track now; he must have been a house servant. So she led up to that. But the result was discouraging. The subject of sweeping appeared to weary him; firebuilding failed to stir him; scrubbing and scouring awoke no enthusiasm. Then the goodwife touched, with a perishing hope, and rather as a matter of form, upon the subject of cooking. To her surprise and her vast delight, the king's face lighted at once! Ah, she had hunted him down at last, she thought; and she was right proud too of the devious shrewdness and tact which had accomplished it.

Her tired tongue got a chance to rest now, for the king's, inspired by gnawing hunger and the fragrant smells that came from the sputtering pots and pans, turned itself loose and delivered itself up to such an eloquent dissertation upon certain toothsome dishes that within three minutes the woman said to herself, "Of a truth I was right—he hath holpen in a kitchen!" Then he broadened his bill of fare, and discussed it with such appreciation and

animation that the goodwife said to herself, "Good lack!
How can he know so many dishes, and so fine ones
withal? For these belong only upon the tables of the rich
and great. Ah, now I see! Ragged outcast as he is, he
must have served in the palace before his reason went
astray; yes, he must have helped in the very kitchen of the
king himself! I will test him."

Full of eagerness to prove her sagacity, she told the
king to mind the cooking a moment, hinting that he
might manufacture and add a dish or two if he chose; then
she went out of the room and gave her children a sign to
follow after. The king muttered, "Another English king
had a commission like to this in a bygone time; it is nothing against my dignity to undertake an office which the
great Alfred stooped to assume. But I will try to better
serve my trust than he, for he let the cakes burn."

The intent was good, but the performance was not
answerable to it; for this king, like the other one, soon
fell into deep thinkings concerning his vast affairs, and
the same calamity resulted—the cookery got burned. The
woman returned in time to save the breakfast from entire
destruction, and she promptly brought the king out of
his dreams with a brisk and cordial tongue-lashing. Then,
seeing how troubled he was over his violated trust, she
softened at once and was all goodness and gentleness toward him.

The boy made a hearty and satisfying meal, and was
greatly refreshed and gladdened by it. It was a meal which
was distinguished by this curious feature, that rank was
waived on both sides; yet neither recipient of the favor
was aware that it had been extended. The goodwife had
intended to feed this young tramp with broken victuals in
a corner like any other tramp or like a dog, but she was
so remorseful for the scolding she had given him that she
did what she could to atone for it by allowing him to
sit at the family table and eat with his betters, on ostensible terms of equality with them; and the king, on his side,
was so remorseful for having broken his trust after the
family had been so kind to him that he forced himself
to atone for it by humbling himself to the family level,
instead of requiring the woman and her children to stand
and wait upon him while he occupied their table in the
solitary state due his birth and dignity. It does us all good

to unbend sometimes. This good woman was made happy all the day long by the applauses which she got out of herself for her magnanimous condescension to a tramp, and the king was just as self-complacent over his gracious humility toward a humble peasant woman.

When breakfast was over, the housewife told the king to wash up the dishes. This command was a staggerer for a moment, and the king came near rebelling; but then he said to himself, "Alfred the Great watched the cakes; doubtless he would have washed the dishes too; therefore will I essay it."

He made a sufficiently poor job of it; and to his surprise too, for the cleaning of wooden spoons and trenchers had seemed an easy thing to do. It was a tedious and trouble-some piece of work, but he finished it at last. He was be-coming impatient to get away on his journey now; however, he was not to lose this thrifty dame's society so easily. She furnished him some little odds and ends of employment, which he got through with after a fair fash-ion and with some credit. Then she set him and the little girl to paring some winter apples, but he was so awkward at this service that she retired him from it and gave him a butcher knife to grind. Afterward she kept him carding wool until he began to think he had laid the good king Alfred about far enough in the shade for the present in the matter of showy menial heroisms that would read picturesquely in storybooks and histories, and so he was half minded to resign. And when, just after the noonday dinner, the goodwife gave him a basket of kittens to drown, he did resign. At least he was just going to re-sign—for he felt that he must draw the line somewhere, and it seemed to him that to draw it at kitten drowning was about the right thing—when there was an interrup-tion. The interruption was John Canty, with a peddler's pack on his back, and Hugo!

The king discovered these rascals approaching the front gate before they had had a chance to see him; so he said nothing about drawing the line, but took up his basket of kittens and stepped quietly out the back way, without a word. He left the creatures in an outhouse and hurried on into a narrow lane at the rear.

20 THE PRINCE AND THE HERMIT

The high hedge hid him from the house now, and so under the impulse of a deadly fright he let out all his forces and sped toward a wood in the distance. He never looked back until he had almost gained the shelter of the forest; then he turned and descried two figures in the distance. That was sufficient; he did not wait to scan them critically, but hurried on, and never abated his pace till he was far within the twilight depths of the wood. Then he stopped, being persuaded that he was now tolerably safe. He listened intently, but the stillness was profound and solemn—awful, even, and depressing to the spirits. At wide intervals his straining ear did detect sounds, but they were so remote, and hollow, and mysterious that they seemed not to be real sounds, but only the moaning and complaining ghosts of departed ones. So the sounds were yet more dreary than the silence which they interrupted.

It was his purpose, in the beginning, to stay where he was the rest of the day; but a chill soon invaded his perspiring body, and he was at last obliged to resume movement in order to get warm. He struck straight through the forest, hoping to pierce to a road presently, but he was disappointed in this. He traveled on and on, but the farther he went, the denser the wood became apparently. The gloom began to thicken by and by, and the king realized that the night was coming on. It made him shudder to think of spending it in such an uncanny place; so he tried to hurry faster, but he only made the less speed, for he could not now see well enough to choose his steps judiciously; consequently he kept tripping over roots and tangling himself in vines and briers.

And how glad he was when at last he caught the glimmer of a light! He approached it warily, stopping often

to look about him and listen. It came from an unglazed
window opening in a shabby little hut. He heard a voice
now and felt a disposition to run and hide; but he changed
his mind at once, for this voice was praying evidently. He
glided to the one window of the hut, raised himself on
tiptoes, and stole a glance within. The room was small;
its floor was the natural earth, beaten hard by use; in a
corner was a bed of rushes and a ragged blanket or two;
near it was a pail, a cup, a basin, and two or three pots
and pans; there was a short bench and a three-legged
stool; on the hearth the remains of a fagot fire were
smoldering; before a shrine, which was lighted by a single
candle, knelt an aged man; and on an old wooden box at
his side lay an open book and a human skull. The man
was of large, bony frame; his hair and whiskers were very
long and snowy white; he was clothed in a robe of sheep-
skins which reached from his neck to his heels.

"A holy hermit!" said the king to himself. "Now am I
indeed fortunate."

The hermit rose from his knees; the king knocked. A
deep voice responded, "Enter! But leave sin behind, for
the ground whereon thou shalt stand is holy!"

The king entered and paused. The hermit turned a pair
of gleaming, unrestful eyes upon him and said, "Who art
thou?"

"I am the king," came the answer, with placid simplicity.

"Welcome, king!" cried the hermit with enthusiasm.
Then, bustling about with feverish activity and constantly
saying "Welcome, welcome," he arranged his bench,
seated the king on it, by the hearth, threw some fagots
on the fire, and finally fell to pacing the floor with a
nervous stride.

"Welcome! Many have sought sanctuary here, but
they were not worthy, and were turned away. But a king
who casts his crown away, and despises the vain splendors
of his office, and clothes his body in rags to devote his
life to holiness and the mortification of the flesh—he
is worthy, he is welcome! Here shall he abide all his days
till death come." The king hastened to interrupt and explain, but the hermit paid no attention to him, did not
even hear him apparently, but went right on with his
talk with a raised voice and a growing energy. "And

thou shalt be at peace here. None shall find out thy refuge to disquiet thee with supplications to return to that empty and foolish life which God hath moved thee to abandon. Thou shalt pray here; thou shalt study the Book; thou shalt meditate upon the follies and delusions of this world, and upon the sublimities of the world to come; thou shalt feed upon crusts and herbs, and scourge thy body with whips daily to the purifying of thy soul. Thou shalt wear a hair shirt next thy skin; thou shalt drink water only; and thou shalt be at peace, yes, wholly at peace, for whoso comes to seek thee shall go his way again, baffled; he shall not find thee, he shall not molest thee."

The old man, still pacing back and forth, ceased to speak aloud and began to mutter. The king seized this opportunity to state his case, and he did it with an eloquence inspired by uneasiness and apprehension. But the hermit went on muttering and gave no heed. And still muttering, he approached the king and said impressively, "Sh! I will tell you a secret!" He bent down to impart it, but checked himself and assumed a listening attitude. After a moment or two he went on tiptoe to the window opening, put his head out and peered around in the gloaming, then came tiptoeing back again, put his face close down to the king's, and whispered, "I am an archangel!"

The king started violently and said to himself, "Would God I were with the outlaws again; for lo, now am I the prisoner of a madman!" His apprehensions were heightened, and they showed plainly in his face.

In a low, excited voice the hermit continued, "I see you feel my atmosphere! There's awe in your face! None may be in this atmosphere and not be thus affected, for it is the very atmosphere of heaven. I go thither and return in the twinkling of an eye. I was made an archangel on this very spot, it is five years ago, by angels sent from heaven to confer that awful dignity. Their presence filled this place with an intolerable brightness. And they knelt to me, king! Yes, they knelt to me! For I was greater than they. I have walked in the courts of heaven and held speech with the patriarchs. Touch my hand—be not afraid —touch it. There, now thou hast touched a hand which has been clasped by Abraham and Isaac and Jacob! For I have walked in the golden courts, I have seen the Deity face to face!" He paused to give this speech effect; then his face suddenly changed, and he started to his feet again, saying with angry energy, "Yes, I am an archangel, *a mere archangel!* I that might have been pope! It is verily true. I was told it from heaven in a dream twenty years ago; ah, yes, I was to be pope! And I *should* have been pope, for heaven had said it, but the king dissolved my religious house, and I, poor, obscure, unfriended monk, was cast homeless upon the world, robbed of my mighty destiny!" Here he began to mumble again and beat his forehead in futile rage with his fist, now and then articulating a venomous curse, and now and then a pathetic, "Wherefore I am nought but an archangel—I that should have been pope!"

So he went on for an hour, whilst the poor little king sat and suffered. Then all at once the old man's frenzy departed and he became all gentleness. His voice softened, he came down out of his clouds and fell to prattling along so simply and so humanly that he soon won the king's heart completely. The old devotee moved the boy nearer to the fire and made him comfortable, doctored his small bruises and abrasions with a deft and tender hand, and then set about preparing and cooking a supper, chatting pleasantly all the time and occasionally stroking the lad's cheek or patting his head in such a gently caressing way that in a little while all the fear and repulsion inspired by the archangel were changed to reverence and affection for the man.

This happy state of things continued while the two ate the supper; then, after a prayer before the shrine, the hermit put the boy to bed in a small adjoining room, tucking him in as snugly and lovingly as a mother might; and so, with a parting caress, left him and sat down by the fire and began to poke the brands about in an absent and aimless way. Presently he paused, then tapped his forehead several times with his fingers as if trying to recall some thought which had escaped from his mind. Apparently he was unsuccessful. Now he started quickly up and entered his guest's room and said, "Thou art king?"

"Yes," was the response drowsily uttered.

"What king?"

"Of England."

"Of England! Then Henry is gone!"

"Alack, it is so. I am his son."

A black frown settled down upon the hermit's face, and he clenched his bony hands with a vindictive energy. He stood a few moments, breathing fast and swallowing repeatedly, then said in a husky voice, "Dost know it was he that turned us out into the world houseless and homeless?"

There was no response. The old man bent down and scanned the boy's reposeful face and listened to his placid breathing. "He sleeps—sleeps soundly"; and the frown vanished away and gave place to an expression of evil satisfaction. A smile flitted across the dreaming boy's features. The hermit muttered, "So, his heart is happy," and he turned away. He went stealthily about the place, seeking here and there for something, now and then halting to listen, now and then jerking his head around and casting a quick glance toward the bed, and always muttering, always mumbling to himself. At last he found what he seemed to want—a rusty old butcher knife and a whetstone. Then he crept to his place by the fire, sat himself down, and began to whet the knife softly on the stone, still muttering, mumbling, ejaculating. The winds sighed around the lonely place, the mysterious voices of the night floated by out of the distances. The shining eyes of venturesome mice and rats peered out at the old man from cracks and coverts, but he went on with his work, rapt absorbed, and noted none of these things.

At long intervals he drew his thumb along the edge of his knife and nodded his head with satisfaction. "It grows sharper," he said; "yes, it grows sharper."

He took no note of the flight of time, but worked tranquilly on, entertaining himself with his thoughts, which broke out occasionally in articulate speech: "His father wrought us evil, he destroyed us—and is gone down into the eternal fires! Yes, down into the eternal fires! He escaped us, but it was God's will, yes, it was God's will, we must not repine. But he hath not escaped the fires! No, he hath not escaped the fires, the consuming, unpitying, remorseless fires—and *they* are everlasting!"

And so he wrought, and still wrought, mumbling—chuckling a low rasping chuckle at times, and at times breaking again into words: "It was his father that did it all. I am but an archangel; but for him, I should be pope!"

The king stirred. The hermit sprang noiselessly to the bedside and went down upon his knees, bending over the prostrate form with his knife uplifted. The boy stirred again; his eyes came open for an instant, but there was no speculation in them, they saw nothing; the next moment his tranquil breathing showed that his sleep was sound once more.

The hermit watched and listened for a time, keeping his position and scarcely breathing; then he slowly lowered his arm and presently crept away, saying, "It is long past midnight; it is not best that he should cry out, lest by accident someone be passing."

He glided about his hovel, gathering a rag here, a thong there, and another one yonder; then he returned, and by careful and gentle handling he managed to tie the king's ankles together without waking him. Next he essayed to tie the wrists; he made several attempts to cross them, but the boy always drew one hand or the other away just as the cord was ready to be applied; but at last, when the archangel was almost ready to despair, the boy crossed his hands himself, and the next moment they were bound. Now a bandage was passed under the sleeper's chin and brought up over his head and tied fast; and so softly, so gradually, and so deftly were the knots drawn together and compacted that the boy slept peacefully through it all without stirring.

21 HENDON TO THE RESCUE

The old man glided away, stooping, stealthy, catlike, and brought the low bench. He seated himself upon it, half his body in the dim and flickering light and the other half in shadow; and so, with his craving eyes bent upon the slumbering boy, he kept his patient vigil there, heedless of the drift of time, and softly whetted his knife and mumbled and chuckled; and in aspect and attitude he resembled nothing so much as a grisly, monstrous spider gloating over some hapless insect that lay bound and helpless in his web.

After a long while the old man, who was still gazing, yet not seeing, his mind having settled into a dreamy abstraction, observed on a sudden that the boy's eyes were open—wide open and staring, staring up in frozen horror at the knife! The smile of a gratified devil crept over the old man's face, and he said, without changing his attitude or his occupation, "Son of Henry the Eighth, hast thou prayed?"

The boy struggled helplessly in his bonds and at the same time forced a smothered sound through his closed jaws, which the hermit chose to interpret as an affirmative answer to his question.

"Then pray again. Pray the prayer for the dying!"

A shudder shook the boy's frame, and his face blenched. Then he struggled again to free himself, turning and twisting himself this way and that, tugging frantically, fiercely, desperately—but uselessly—to burst his fetters; and all the while, the old ogre smiled down upon him, and nodded his head, and placidly whetted his knife, mumbling from time to time. "The moments are precious; they are few and precious; pray the prayer for the dying!"

The boy uttered a despairing groan and ceased from his struggles, panting. The tears came then and trickled, one after the other, down his face; but this piteous sight wrought no softening effect upon the savage old man.

The dawn was coming now; the hermit observed it and spoke up sharply with a touch of nervous apprehension in his voice, "I may not indulge this ecstasy longer! The night is already gone. It seems but a moment, only a moment; would it had endured a year! Seed of the Church's spoiler, close thy perishing eyes, an' thou fearest to look upon—"

The rest was lost in inarticulate mutterings. The old man sunk upon his knees, his knife in his hand, and bent himself over the moaning boy.

Hark! There was a sound of voices near the cabin; the knife dropped from the hermit's hand; he cast a sheepskin over the boy and started up, trembling. The sounds increased, and presently the voices became rough and angry; then came blows, and cries for help; then a clatter of swift footsteps retreating. Immediately came a succession of thundering knocks upon the cabin door, followed by, "Hullo-o-o! Open! And dispatch, in the name of all the devils!"

Oh, this was the blessedest sound that had ever made music in the king's ears, for it was Miles Hendon's voice!

The hermit, grinding his teeth in impotent rage, moved swiftly out of the bedchamber, closing the door behind him; and straightway the king heard a talk to this effect proceeding from the "chapel":

"Homage and greeting, reverend sir! Where is the boy —*my* boy?"

"What boy, friend?"

"What boy! Lie me no lies, sir priest, play me no deceptions! I am not in the humor for it. Near to this place I caught the scoundrels who I judged did steal him from me, and I made them confess; they said he was at large again, and they had tracked him to your door. They showed me his very footprints. Now palter no more; for look you, holy sir, an' thou produce him not— Where is the boy?"

"Oh, good sir, peradventure you mean the ragged regal vagrant that tarried here the night. If such as you take interest in such as he, know then that I have sent him of an errand. He will be back anon."

"How soon? How soon? Come, waste not the time; cannot I overtake him? How soon will he be back?"

"Thou needst not stir; he will return quickly."

"So be it then. I will try to wait. But stop! *You* sent him of an errand? You! Verily this is a lie—he would not go. He would pull thy old beard, an' thou didst offer him such an insolence. Thou hast lied, friend; thou hast surely lied! He would not go for thee nor for any man."

"For any *man*, no; haply not. But I am not a man."

"*What!* Now o' God's name what art thou then?"

"It is a secret; mark thou reveal it not. I am an arch-angel!"

There was a tremendous ejaculation from Miles Hendon—not altogether unprofane—followed by, "This doth well and truly account for his complaisance! Right well I knew he would budge nor hand nor foot in the menial service of any mortal; but lord, even a king must obey when an archangel gives the word o' command! Let me—sh! What noise was that?"

All this while the little king had been yonder, alternately quaking with terror and trembling with hope; and all the while too he had thrown all the strength he could into his anguished moanings, constantly expecting them to reach Hendon's ear but always realizing, with bitterness, that they failed, or at least made no impression. So this last remark of his servant came as comes a reviving breath from fresh fields to the dying; and he exerted himself once more, and with all his energy, just as the hermit was saying, "Noise? I hear only the wind."

"Mayhap it was. Yes, doubtless that was it. I have been hearing it faintly all the— There it is again! It is not the wind! What an odd sound! Come, we will hunt it out!"

Now the king's joy was nearly insupportable. His tired lungs did their utmost—and hopefully, too—but the sealed jaws and the muffling sheepskin sadly crippled the effort. Then the poor fellow's heart sank to hear the hermit say, "Ah, it came from without—I think from the copse yonder. Come, I will lead the way."

The king heard the two pass out, talking; heard their footsteps die quickly away; then he was alone with a boding, brooding, awful silence.

It seemed an age till he heard the steps and voices ap-

proaching again, and this time he heard an added sound
—the trampling of hoofs apparently. Then he heard Hendon say, "I will not wait longer. I *cannot* wait longer. He
has lost his way in this thick wood. Which direction took
he? Quick, point it out to me."

"He— But wait; I will go with thee."

"Good—good! Why, truly thou art better than thy
looks. Marry I do not think there's not another archangel
with so right a heart as thine. Wilt ride? Wilt take the
wee donkey that's for my boy, or wilt thou fork thy holy
legs over this ill-conditioned slave of a mule that I have
provided for myself? And had been cheated in too, had he
cost but the indifferent sum of a month's usury on a brass
farthing let to a tinker out of work."

"No, ride thy mule and lead thine ass; I am surer on
mine own feet and will walk."

"Then prithee mind the little beast for me while I take
my life in my hands and make what success I may toward mounting the big one."

Then followed a confusion of kicks, cuffs, tramplings,
and plungings, accompanied by a thunderous intermingling of volleyed curses, and finally a bitter apostrophe to
the mule, which must have broken its spirit, for hostilities
seemed to cease from that moment.

With unutterable misery the fettered little king heard
the voices and footsteps fade away and die out. All hope
forsook him now for the moment, and a dull despair settled down upon his heart. "My only friend is deceived
and got rid of," he said; "the hermit will return and—"
He finished with a gasp, and at once fell to struggling so
frantically with his bonds again that he shook off the
smothering sheepskin.

And now he heard the door open! The sound chilled
him to the marrow; already he seemed to feel the knife at
his throat. Horror made him close his eyes; horror made
him open them again—and before him stood John Canty
and Hugo!

He would have said, "Thank God!" if his jaws had
been free.

A moment or two later his limbs were at liberty, and
his captors, each gripping him by an arm, were hurrying
him with all speed through the forest.

22 A VICTIM OF TREACHERY

Once more "King Foo-foo the First" was roving with the tramps and outlaws, a butt for their coarse jests and dull-witted railleries, and sometimes the victim of small spitefulnesses at the hands of Canty and Hugo when the Ruffler's back was turned. None but Canty and Hugo really disliked him. Some of the others liked him, and all admired his pluck and spirit. During two or three days, Hugo, in whose ward and charge the king was, did what he covertly could to make the boy uncomfortable; and at night, during the customary orgies, he amused the company by putting small indignities upon him—always as if by accident. Twice he stepped upon the king's toes—accidentally—and the king, as became his royalty, was contemptuously unconscious of it and indifferent to it; but the third time Hugo entertained himself in that way, the king felled him to the ground with a cudgel, to the prodigious delight of the tribe. Hugo, consumed with anger and shame, sprang up, seized a cudgel, and came at his small adversary in a fury. Instantly a ring was formed around the gladiators, and the betting and cheering began. But poor Hugo stood no chance whatever. His frantic and lubberly 'prenticework found but a poor market for itself when pitted against an arm which had been trained by the first masters of Europe in single-stick, quarter-staff, and every art and trick of swordmanship. The little king stood, alert but at graceful ease, and caught and turned aside the thick rain of blows with a facility and precision which set the motley onlookers wild with admiration; and every now and then, when his practiced eye detected an opening, and a lightning-swift rap upon Hugo's head followed as a result, the storm of cheers and laughter that swept the place was something wonderful to hear. At the end of fifteen minutes, Hugo, all

battered, bruised, and the target for a pitiless bombard-
ment of ridicule, slunk from the field; and the unscathed
hero of the fight was seized and borne aloft upon the shoulders of the joyous rabble to the place of honor beside the
Ruffler, where with vast ceremony he was crowned king
of the Gamecocks, his meaner title being at the same
time solemnly canceled and annulled, and a decree of
banishment from the gang pronounced against any who
should thenceforth utter it.

All attempts to make the king serviceable to the troop
had failed. He had stubbornly refused to act; moreover,
he was always trying to escape. He had been thrust into
an unwatched kitchen the first day of his return; he not
only came forth empty-handed, but tried to rouse the
housemates. He was sent out with a tinker to help him at
his work; he would not work; moreover, he threatened
the tinker with his own soldering iron; and finally both
Hugo and the tinker found their hands full with the mere
matter of keeping him from getting away. He delivered
the thunders of his royalty upon the heads of all who
hampered his liberties or tried to force him to service. He
was sent out, in Hugo's charge, in company with a slatternly woman and a diseased baby to beg; but the result
was not encouraging: he declined to plead for the mendicants or be a party to their cause in any way.

Thus several days went by; and the miseries of this
tramping life, and the weariness and sordidness and mean-
ness and vulgarity of it, became gradually and steadily
so intolerable to the captive that he began at last to feel
that his release from the hermit's knife must prove only a
temporary respite from death at best.

But at night, in his dreams, these things were forgotten,
and he was on his throne, and master again. This, of
course, intensified the sufferings of the awakening, so the
mortifications of each succeeding morning of the few that
passed between his return to bondage and the combat
with Hugo grew bitterer and bitterer, and harder and
harder to bear.

The morning after that combat, Hugo got up with a
heart filled with vengeful purposes against the king. He
had two plans in particular. One was to inflict upon the
lad what would be, to his proud spirit and "imagined"
royalty, a peculiar humiliation; and if he failed to ac-

complish this, his other plan was to put a crime of some kind upon the king and then betray him into the implacable clutches of the law.

In pursuance of the first plan, he purposed to put a "clime" upon the king's leg, rightly judging that that would mortify him to the last and perfect degree; and as soon as the clime should operate, he meant to get Canty's help, and *force* the king to expose his leg in the highway and beg for alms. "Clime" was the cant term for a sore artificially created. To make a clime, the operator made a paste or poultice of unslaked lime, soap, and the rust of old iron, and spread it upon a piece of leather, which was then bound tightly upon the leg. This would presently fret off the skin and make the flesh raw and angry looking; blood was then rubbed upon the limb, which, being fully dried, took on a dark and repulsive color. Then a bandage of soiled rags was put on in a cleverly careless way which would allow the hideous ulcer to be seen and move the compassion of the passerby.*

Hugo got the help of the tinker whom the king had cowed with the soldering iron; they took the boy on a tinkering tramp, and as soon as they were out of sight of the camp they threw him down and the tinker held him while Hugo bound the poultice tight and fast upon his leg.

The king raged and stormed and promised to hang the two the moment the scepter was in his hand again, but they kept a firm grip upon him and enjoyed his impotent struggling and jeered at his threats. This continued until the poultice began to bite, and in no long time its work would have been perfected if there had been no interruption. But there was, for about this time the "slave" who had made the speech denouncing England's laws appeared on the scene and put an end to the enterprise and stripped off the poultice and bandage.

The king wanted to borrow his deliverer's cudgel and warm the jackets of the two rascals on the spot; but the man said no, it would bring trouble—leave the matter till night; the whole tribe being together then, the outside world would not venture to interfere or interrupt. He marched the party back to camp and reported the affair to the Ruffler, who listened, pondered, and then decided

* From *The English Rogue;* London, 1665.

that the king should not be again detailed to beg, since it was plain he was worthy of something higher and better, wherefore, on the spot he promoted him from the mendicant rank and appointed him to steal!

Hugo was overjoyed. He had already tried to make the king steal and failed, but there would be no more trouble of that sort now, for of course the king would not dream of defying a distinct command delivered directly from headquarters. So he planned a raid for that very afternoon, purposing to get the king in the law's grip in the course of it; and to do it, too, with such ingenious strategy that it should seem to be accidental and unintentional, for the king of the Gamecocks was popular now, and the gang might not deal overgently with an unpopular member who played so serious a treachery upon him as the delivering him over to the common enemy, the law.

Very well. All in good time Hugo strolled off to a neighboring village with his prey; and the two drifted slowly up and down one street after another, the one watching sharply for a sure chance to achieve his evil purpose, and the other watching as sharply for a chance to dart away and get free of his infamous captivity forever.

Both threw away some tolerably fair-looking opportunities; for both, in their secret hearts, were resolved to make absolutely sure work this time, and neither meant to allow his fevered desires to seduce him into any venture that had much uncertainty about it.

Hugo's chance came first. For at last a woman approached who carried a fat package of some sort in a basket. Hugo's eyes sparkled with sinful pleasure as he said to himself, "Breath o' my life an' I can but put *that* upon him, 'tis good-den and God keep thee, king of the Gamecocks!" He waited and watched, outwardly patient but inwardly consuming with excitement, till the woman had passed by and the time was ripe; then said in a low voice, "Tarry here till I come again," and darted stealthily after the prey.

The king's heart was filled with joy: he could make his escape now if Hugo's quest only carried him far enough away.

But he was to have no such luck. Hugo crept behind the woman, snatched the package, and came running back, wrapping it in an old piece of blanket which he carried on his arm. The hue and cry was raised in a moment by the woman, who knew her loss by the lightening of her burden, although she had not seen the pilfering done. Hugo thrust the bundle into the king's hands without halting, saying, "Now speed ye after me with the rest, and cry 'Stop, thief!' but mind ye lead them astray!"

The next moment Hugo turned a corner and darted down a crooked alley, and in another moment or two he lounged into view again, looking innocent and indifferent, and took up a position behind a post to watch results.

The insulted king threw the bundle on the ground, and the blanket fell away from it just as the woman arrived with an augmenting crowd at her heels; she seized the king's wrist with one hand, snatched up her bundle with the other, and began to pour out a tirade of abuse upon the boy while he struggled, without success, to free himself from her grip.

Hugo had seen enough—his enemy was captured and the law would get him now—so he slipped away, jubilant and chuckling, and wended campwards, framing a judicious version of the matter to give to the Ruffler's crew as he strode along.

The king continued to struggle in the woman's strong grasp, and now and then cried out in vexation, "Unhand me, thou foolish creature; it was not I that bereaved thee of thy paltry goods."

The crowd closed around, threatening the king and calling him names; a brawny blacksmith in leather apron and sleeves rolled to his elbows made a reach for him, saying he would trounce him well for a lesson; but just then a long sword flashed in the air and fell with convincing force upon the man's arm, flat side down, the fantastic owner of it remarking pleasantly at the same time, "Marry, good souls, let us proceed gently, not with ill blood and uncharitable words. This is a matter for the law's consideration, not private and unofficial handling. Loose thy hold from the boy, goodwife."

The blacksmith averaged the stalwart soldier with a glance, then went muttering away, rubbing his arm; the woman released the boy's wrist reluctantly; the crowd eyed the stranger unlovingly, but prudently closed their mouths. The king sprang to his deliverer's side, with flushed cheeks and sparkling eyes, exclaiming, "Thou hast lagged sorely, but thou comest in good season now, Sir Miles; carve me this rabble to rags!"

23 THE PRINCE A PRISONER

Hendon forced back a smile and bent down and whispered in the king's ear, "Softly, softly, my prince; wag thy tongue warily; nay, suffer it not to wag at all. Trust in me—all shall go well in the end." Then he added to himself: "*Sir* Miles! Bless me, I had totally forgot I was a knight! Lord how marvelous a thing it is, the grip his memory doth take upon his quaint and crazy fancies! An empty and foolish title is mine, and yet it is something to have deserved it, for I think it is more honor to be held worthy to be a specter-knight in his Kingdom of Dreams and Shadows, than to be held base enough to be an earl in some of the *real* kingdoms of this world."

The crowd fell apart to admit a constable, who approached and was about to lay his hand upon the king's shoulder when Hendon said, "Gently, good friend, withhold your hand; he shall go peaceably; I am responsible for that. Lead on, we will follow."

The officer led, with the woman and her bundle; Miles and the king followed after, with the crowd at their heels. The king was inclined to rebel, but Hendon said to him in a low voice, "Reflect, sire; your laws are the wholesome breath of your own royalty; shall their source resist them, yet require the branches to respect them? Apparently one of these laws has been broken; when the king is on his throne again, can it ever grieve him to remember that when he was seemingly a private person he loyally sunk the king in the citizen and submitted to its authority?"

"Thou art right; say no more; thou shalt see that whatsoever the king of England requires a subject to suffer under the law, he will himself suffer while he holdeth the station of a subject."

When the woman was called upon to testify before the justice of the peace, she swore that the small prisoner at the bar was the person who had committed the theft; there was none able to show the contrary, so the king stood convicted. The bundle was now unrolled, and when the contents proved to be a plump little dressed pig, the judge looked troubled, whilst Hendon turned pale, and his body was thrilled with an electric shiver of dismay; but the king remained unmoved, protected by his ignorance. The judge meditated during an ominous pause, then turned to the woman with the question, "What dost thou hold this property to be worth?"

The woman courtesied and replied, "Three shillings and eightpence, your worship; I could not abate a penny and set forth the value honestly."

The justice glanced around uncomfortably upon the crowd, then nodded to the constable and said, "Clear the court and close the doors."

It was done. None remained but the two officials, the accused, the accuser, and Miles Hendon. This latter was rigid and colorless, and on his forehead big drops of cold sweat gathered, broke and blended together, and trickled down his face. The judge turned to the woman again and said in a compassionate voice, " 'Tis a poor ignorant lad, and mayhap was driven hard by hunger, for these be grievous times for the unfortunate; mark you, he hath not an evil face, but when hunger driveth— Good woman! Dost know that when one steals a thing above the value of thirteen pence ha'penny the law saith he shall *hang* for it!"

The little king started, wide-eyed with consternation, but controlled himself and held his peace; but not so the woman. She sprang to her feet, shaking with fright, and cried out, "Oh, good lack, what have I done! God-a-mercy, I would not hang the poor thing for the whole world! Ah, save me from this, your worship; what shall I do, what *can* I do?"

The justice maintained his judicial composure and simply said, "Doubtless it is allowable to revise the value, since it is not yet writ upon the record."

"Then in God's name call the pig eightpence, and heaven bless the day that freed my conscience of this awesome thing!"

Miles Hendon forgot all decorum in his delight, and surprised the king and wounded his dignity by throwing his arms around him and hugging him. The woman made her grateful adieux and started away with her pig; and when the constable opened the door for her, he followed her out into the narrow hall. The justice proceeded to write in his record book. Hendon, always alert, thought he would like to know why the officer followed the woman out; so he slipped softly into the dusky hall and listened. He heard a conversation to this effect:

"It is a fat pig and promises good eating; I will buy it of thee; here is the eightpence."

"Eightpence, indeed! Thou'lt do no such thing. It cost me three shillings and eightpence, good honest coin of the last reign, that old Harry that's just dead ne'er touched nor tampered with. A fig for thy eightpence!"

"Stands the wind in that quarter? Thou wast under oath, and so swore falsely when thou saidst the value was but eightpence. Come straightway back with me before his worship and answer for the crime! And then the lad will hang."

"There, there, dear heart, say no more, I am content. Give me the eightpence, and hold thy peace about the matter."

The woman went off crying; Hendon slipped back into the courtroom, and the constable presently followed, after hiding his prize in some convenient place. The justice wrote a while longer, then read the king a wise and kindly lecture and sentenced him to a short imprisonment in the common jail, to be followed by a public flogging. The astounded king opened his mouth and was probably going to order the good judge to be beheaded on the spot, but he caught a warning sign from Hendon and succeeded in closing his mouth again before he lost anything out of it. Hendon took him by the hand now, made reverence to the justice, and the two departed in the wake of the constable toward the jail. The moment the street was reached, the inflamed monarch halted, snatched away his hand, and exclaimed, "Idiot, dost imagine I will enter a common jail *alive?*"

Hendon bent down and said somewhat sharply, *"Will* you trust in me? Peace! And forbear to worsen our chances with dangerous speech. What God wills, will happen; thou canst not hurry it, thou canst not alter it; therefore wait, and be patient; 'twill be time enow to rail or rejoice when what is to happen has happened." *

24 THE ESCAPE

The short winter day was nearly ended. The streets were deserted save for a few random stragglers, and these hurried straight along, with the intent look of people who were only anxious to accomplish their errands as quickly as possible and then snugly house themselves from the rising wind and the gathering twilight. They looked neither to the right nor to the left; they paid no attention to our party; they did not even seem to see them. Edward the Sixth wondered if the spectacle of a king on his way to jail had ever encountered such marvelous indifference before. By and by the constable arrived at a deserted market square and proceeded to cross it. When he had reached the middle of it, Hendon laid his hand upon his arm and said in a low voice, "Bide a moment, good sir; there is none in hearing, and I would say a word to thee."

"My duty forbids it, sir; prithee hinder me not; the night comes on."

"Stay, nevertheless, for the matter concerns thee nearly. Turn thy back a moment and seem not to see: *let this poor lad escape.*"

"This to me, sir! I arrest thee in——"

"Nay, be not too hasty. See thou be careful and commit no foolish error"—then he shut his voice down to a whisper and said in the man's ear—"the pig thou hast purchased for eightpence may cost thee thy neck, man!"

The poor constable, taken by surprise, was speechless at first, then found his tongue and fell to blustering and threatening; but Hendon was tranquil and waited with patience till his breath was spent; then said, "I have a liking to thee, friend, and would not willingly see thee come to harm. Observe, I heard it all—every word. I will prove it to thee." Then he repeated the conversa-

tion which the officer and the woman had had together in
the hall, word for word, and ended with, "There, have I
set it forth correctly? Should not I be able to set it forth
correctly before the judge, if occasion required?"

The man was dumb with fear and distress for a moment;
then he rallied and said with forced lightness, " 'Tis making
a mighty matter indeed out of a jest; I but plagued the
woman for mine amusement."

"Kept you the woman's pig for amusement?"

The man answered sharply, "Nought else, good sir. I
tell thee 'twas but a jest."

"I do begin to believe thee," said Hendon with a perplexing mixture of mockery and half conviction in his
tone; "but tarry thou here a moment whilst I run and ask
his worship, for nathless, he being a man experienced
in law, in jests, in——"

He was moving away, still talking; the constable hesitated, fidgeted, spat out an oath or two, then cried out,
"Hold, hold, good sir; prithee wait a little—the judge!
Why, man, he hath no more sympathy with a jest than
hath a dead corpse! Come, and we will speak further. Ods
body! I seem to be in evil case, and all for an innocent and thoughtless pleasantry. I am a man of family;
and my wife and little ones— List to reason, good your
worship; what wouldst thou of me?"

"Only that thou be blind and dumb and paralytic whilst
one may count a hundred thousand, counting slowly,"
said Hendon with the expression of a man who asks but
a reasonable favor, and that a very little one.

"It is my destruction!" said the constable despairingly.
"Ah, be reasonable, good sir; only look at this matter on
all its sides, and see how mere a jest it is—how manifestly and how plainly it is so. And even if one granted
it were not a jest, it is a fault so small that e'en the
grimmest penalty it could call forth would be but a rebuke
and warning from the judge's lips."

Hendon replied with a solemnity which chilled the air
about him, "This jest of thine hath a name in law; wot
you what it is?"

"I knew it not! Peradventure I have been unwise. I
never dreamed it had a name; as, sweet heaven, I thought
it was original."

"Yes, it hath a name. In the law this crime is called

Non compos mentis lex talionis sic transit gloria mundi."

"Ah, my God!"

"And the penalty is death!"

"God be merciful to me, a sinner!"

"By advantage taken of one in fault, in dire peril, and at thy mercy, thou hast seized goods above thirteen pence ha'penny, paying but a trifle for the same; and this, in the eye of the law, is constructive barratry, misprision of treason, malfeasance in office, *ad hominem expurgatis in statu quo*—and the penalty is death by the halter, without ransom, commutation, or benefit of clergy."

"Bear me up, bear me up, sweet sir, my legs do fail me! Be thou merciful; spare me this doom, and I will turn my back and see nought that shall happen."

"Good! Now thou'rt wise and reasonable. And thou'lt restore the pig?"

"I will, I will indeed, nor ever touch another, though heaven send it and an archangel fetch it. Go—I am blind for thy sake—I see nothing. I will say thou didst break in and wrest the prisoner from my hands by force. It is but a crazy, ancient door; I will batter it down myself betwixt midnight and the morning."

"Do it, good soul; no harm will come of it; the judge hath a loving charity for this poor lad and will shed no tears and break no jailer's bones for his escape."

25 HENDON HALL

As soon as Hendon and the king were out of sight of the constable, his Majesty was instructed to hurry to a certain place outside the town and wait there whilst Hendon should go to the inn and settle his account. Half an hour later the two friends were blithely jogging eastward on Hendon's sorry steeds. The king was warm and comfortable now, for he had cast his rags and clothed himself in the secondhand suit which Hendon had bought on London Bridge.

Hendon wished to guard against overfatiguing the boy; he judged that hard journeys, irregular meals, and illiberal measures of sleep would be bad for his crazed mind, whilst rest, regularity, and moderate exercise would be pretty sure to hasten its cure; he longed to see the stricken intellect made well again and its diseased visions driven out of the tormented little head; therefore he resolved to move by easy stages toward the home whence he had so long been banished, instead of obeying the impulse of his impatience and hurrying along night and day.

When he and the king had journeyed about ten miles, they reached a considerable village and halted there for the night at a good inn. The former relations were resumed; Hendon stood behind the king's chair while he dined, and waited upon him; undressed him when he was ready for bed; then took the floor for his own quarters and slept athwart the door rolled up in a blanket.

The next day, and the day after, they jogged lazily along talking over the adventures they had met since their separation, and mightily enjoying each other's narratives. Hendon detailed all his wide wanderings in search of the king and described how the archangel had led him a fool's journey all over the forest and taken him back to the hut finally when he found he could not get rid of him.

Then, he said, the old man went into the bedchamber and came staggering back looking brokenhearted and saying he had expected to find that the boy had returned and lain down in there to rest, but it was not so. Hendon had waited at the hut all day; hope of the king's return died out then, and he departed upon the quest again.

"And old Sanctum Sanctorum *was* truly sorry your Highness came not back," said Hendon; "I saw it in his face."

"Marry I will never doubt *that!*" said the king; and then told his own story, after which Hendon was sorry he had not destroyed the archangel.

During the last day of the trip Hendon's spirits were soaring. His tongue ran constantly. He talked about his old father and his brother Arthur, and told of many things which illustrated their high and generous characters; he went into loving frenzies over his Edith, and was so gladhearted that he was even able to say some gentle and brotherly things about Hugh. He dwelt a deal on the coming meeting at Hendon Hall; what a surprise it would be to everybody, and what an outburst of thanksgiving and delight there would be.

It was a fair region, dotted with cottages and orchards, and the road led through broad pasturelands whose receding expanses, marked with gentle elevations and depressions, suggested the swelling and subsiding undulations of the sea. In the afternoon the returning prodigal made constant deflections from his course to see if by ascending some hillock he might not pierce the distance and catch a glimpse of his home. At last he was successful and cried out excitedly, "There is the village, my prince, and there is the Hall close by! You may see the towers from here; and that wood there—that is my father's park. Ah, *now* thou'lt know what state and grandeur be! A house with seventy rooms—think of that!—and seven and twenty servants! A brave lodging for such as we, is it not so? Come, let us speed; my impatience will not brook further delay."

All possible hurry was made; still, it was after three o'clock before the village was reached. The travelers scampered through it, Hendon's tongue going all the time. "Here is the church—covered with the same ivy, none gone, none added." "Yonder is the inn, the old

Red Lion; and yonder is the marketplace." "Here is the Maypole, and here the pump; nothing is altered—nothing but the people, at any rate; ten years make a change in people; some of these I seem to know, but none know me." So his chat ran on. The end of the village was soon reached; then the travelers struck into a crooked, narrow road, walled in with tall hedges, and hurried briskly along it for a half mile, then passed into a vast flower garden through an imposing gateway whose huge stone pillars bore sculptured armorial devices. A noble mansion was before them.

"Welcome to Hendon Hall, my king!" exclaimed Miles. "Ah, 'tis a great day! My father and my brother, and the lady Edith will be so mad with joy that they will have eyes and tongue for none but me in the first transports of the meeting, and so thou'lt seem but coldly welcomed; but mind it not; 'twill soon seem otherwise, for when I say thou art my ward and tell them how costly is my love for thee, thou'lt see them take thee to their breasts for Miles Hendon's sake and make their house and hearts thy home forever after!"

The next moment Hendon sprang to the ground before the great door, helped the king down, then took him by the hand and rushed within. A few steps brought him to a spacious apartment; he entered, seated the king with more hurry than ceremony, then ran toward a young man who sat at a writing table in front of a generous fire of logs.

"Embrace me, Hugh," he cried, "and say thou'rt glad I am come again! And call our father, for home is not home till I shall touch his hand, and see his face, and hear his voice once more!"

But Hugh only drew back, after betraying a momentary surprise, and bent a grave stare upon the intruder—a stare which indicated somewhat of offended dignity at first, then changed, in response to some inward thought or purpose, to an expression of marveling curiosity mixed with a real or assumed compassion. Presently he said in a mild voice, "Thy wits seem touched, poor stranger; doubtless thou hast suffered privations and rude buffetings at the world's hands; thy looks and dress betoken it. Whom dost thou take me to be?"

"Take thee? Prithee for whom else than whom thou art?

I take thee to be Hugh Hendon," said Miles sharply.

The other continued in the same soft tone, "And whom dost thou imagine thyself to be?"

"Imagination hath nought to do with it! Dost thou pretend thou knowest me not for thy brother Miles Hendon?"

An expression of pleased surprise flitted across Hugh's face, and he exclaimed, "What! Thou art not jesting? Can the dead come to life? God be praised if it be so! Our poor lost boy restored to our arms after all these cruel years! Ah, it seems too good to be true, it *is* too good to be true; I charge thee, have pity, do not trifle with me! Quick, come to the light—let me scan thee well!"

He seized Miles by the arm, dragged him to the window, and began to devour him from head to foot with his eyes, turning him this way and that and stepping briskly around him and about him to prove him from all points of view, whilst the returned prodigal, all aglow with gladness, smiled, laughed, and kept nodding his head and saying, "Go on, brother, go on, and fear not; thou'lt find nor limb nor feature that cannot bide the test. Scour and scan me to thy content, my good old Hugh. I am indeed thy old Miles, thy same old Miles, thy lost brother, is't not so? Ah, 'tis a great day—I *said* 'twas a great day! Give me thy hand, give me thy cheek; lord, I am like to die of very joy!"

He was about to throw himself upon his brother, but Hugh put up his hand in dissent, then dropped his chin mournfully upon his breast, saying with emotion, "Ah, God of his mercy give me strength to bear this grievous disappointment!"

Miles, amazed, could not speak for a moment; then he found his tongue and cried out, "*What* disappointment? Am I not thy brother?"

Hugh shook his head sadly and said, "I pray heaven it may prove so, and that other eyes may find the resemblances that are hid from mine. Alack, I fear me the letter spoke but too truly."

"What letter?"

"One that came from over sea, some six or seven years ago. It said my brother died in battle."

"It was a lie! Call thy father; he will know me."

"One may not call the dead."

"Dead?" Miles's voice was subdued, and his lips trembled. "My father dead! Oh, this is heavy news. Half my new joy is withered now. Prithee let me see my brother Arthur; he will know me; he will know me and console me."

"He also is dead."

"God be merciful to me, a stricken man! Gone, both gone—the worthy taken and the worthless spared, in me! Ah! I crave your mercy! Do not say the lady Edith——"

"Is dead? No, she lives."

"Then, God be praised, my joy is whole again! Speed thee, brother, let her come to me! An' *she* say I am not myself, but she will not; no, no, *she* will know me; I were a fool to doubt it. Bring her, bring the old servants; they too will know me."

"All are gone but five—Peter, Halsey, David, Bernard, and Margaret."

So saying, Hugh left the room. Miles stood musing a while, then began to walk the floor, muttering, "The five arch villains have survived the two and twenty leal and honest—'tis an odd thing."

He continued walking back and forth, muttering to himself; he had forgotten the king entirely. By and by his Majesty said gravely, and with a touch of genuine compassion, though the words themselves were capable of being interpreted ironically, "Mind not thy mischance, good man; there be others in the world whose identity is denied and whose claims are derided. Thou hast company."

"Ah, my king," cried Hendon, coloring slightly, "do not thou condemn me; wait, and thou shalt see. I am no impostor; she will say it; you shall hear it from the sweetest lips in England. I an impostor? Why, I know this old hall, these pictures of my ancestors, and all things that are about us as a child knoweth its own nursery. Here was I born and bred, my lord; I speak the truth; I would not deceive thee; and should none else believe, I pray thee do not *thou* doubt me; I could not bear it."

"I do not doubt thee," said the king with a childlike simplicity and faith.

"I thank thee out of my heart!" exclaimed Hendon with a fervency which showed that he was touched.

The king added, with the same gentle simplicity, "Dost thou doubt *me?*"

A guilty confusion seized upon Hendon, and he was grateful that the door opened to admit Hugh at that moment and saved him the necessity of replying.

A beautiful lady, richly clothed, followed Hugh, and after her came several liveried servants. The lady walked slowly, with her head bowed and her eyes fixed upon the floor. The face was unspeakably sad. Miles Hendon sprang forward, crying out, "Oh, my Edith, my darling"—

But Hugh waved him back gravely and said to the lady, "Look upon him. Do you know him?"

At the sound of Miles's voice the woman had started slightly and her cheeks had flushed; she was trembling now. She stood still during an impressive pause of several moments, then slowly lifted up her head and looked into Hendon's eyes with a stony and frightened gaze; the blood sank out of her face, drop by drop, till nothing remained but the gray pallor of death; then she said, in a voice as dead as the face, "I know him not!" and turned, with a moan and a stifled sob, and tottered out of the room.

Miles Hendon sank into a chair and covered his face with his hands. After a pause, his brother said to the servants, "You have observed him. Do you know him?"

They shook their heads; then the master said, "The servants know you not, sir. I fear there is some mistake. You have seen that my wife knew you not."

"Thy *wife!*" In an instant Hugh was pinned to the wall with an iron grip about his throat. "Oh, thou fox-hearted slave, I see it all! Thou'st writ the lying letter thyself, and my stolen bride and goods are its fruit. There, now get thee gone, lest I shame mine honorable soldiership with the slaying of so pitiful a manikin!"

Hugh, red-faced and almost suffocated, reeled to the nearest chair and commanded the servants to seize and bind the murderous stranger. They hesitated, and one of them said, "He is armed, Sir Hugh, and we are weaponless."

"Armed? What of it, and ye so many? Upon him, I say!"

But Miles warned them to be careful what they did, and added, "Ye know me of old—I have not changed; come on, an' it like you."

This reminder did not hearten the servants much; they held back.

"Then go, ye paltry cowards, and arm yourselves and guard the doors, whilst I send one to fetch the watch," said Hugh. He turned at the threshold and said to Miles, "You'll find it to your advantage to offend not with useless endeavors at escape."

"Escape? Spare thyself discomfort, an' that is all that troubles thee. For Miles Hendon is master of Hendon Hall and all its belongings. He will remain; doubt it not."

The king sat musing a few moments, then looked up and said, " 'Tis strange—most strange. I cannot account for it."

"No, it is not strange, my liege. I know him, and this conduct is but natural. He was a rascal from his birth."

"Oh, I spake not of *him,* Sir Miles."

"Not of him? Then of what? What is it that is strange?"

"That the king is not missed."

"How? Which? I doubt I do not understand."

"Indeed? Doth it not strike you as being passing strange that the land is not filled with couriers and proclamations describing my person and making search for me? Is it no matter for commotion and distress that the head of the state is gone, that I am vanished away and lost?"

"Most true, my king, I had forgot." Then Hendon sighed and muttered to himself, "Poor ruined mind—still busy with its pathetic dream."

"But I have a plan that shall right us both. I will write a paper in three tongues—Latin, Greek and English—and thou shalt haste away with it to London in the morning. Give it to none but my uncle the lord Hertford; when he shall see it, he will know and say I wrote it. Then he will send for me."

"Might it not be best, my prince, that we wait here until I prove myself and make my rights secure to my domains? I should be so much the better able then to——"

The king interrupted him imperiously, "Peace! What are thy paltry domains, thy trivial interests, contrasted with matters which concern the weal of a nation and the integrity of a throne!" Then he added in a gentle voice, as if he were sorry for his severity, "Obey, and have no fear; I will right thee, I will make thee whole—yes, more than whole. I shall remember, and requite."

So saying, he took the pen and set himself to work. Hendon contemplated him lovingly awhile, then said to himself, "An' it were dark, I should think it *was* a king that spoke; there's no denying it, when the humor's upon him he doth thunder and lighten like your true king; now where got he that trick? See him scribble and scratch away contentedly at his meaningless pothooks, fancying them to be Latin and Greek; and except my wit shall serve me with a lucky device for diverting him from his purpose, I shall be forced to pretend to post away tomorrow on this wild errand he hath invented for me."

The next moment Sir Miles's thoughts had gone back to the recent episode. So absorbed was he in his musings that when the king presently handed him the paper which he had been writing, he received it and pocketed it without being conscious of the act. "How marvelous strange she acted," he muttered. "I think she knew me, and I think she did *not* know me. These opinions do conflict, I perceive it plainly; I cannot reconcile them; neither can I by argument dismiss either of the two or even persuade one to outweigh the other. The matter standeth simply thus: she *must* have known my face, my figure, my voice, for how could it be otherwise? Yet she *said* she knew me not, and that is proof perfect, for she cannot lie. But stop —I think I begin to see. Peradventure he hath influenced her—commanded her—compelled her to lie. That is the solution! The riddle is unriddled. She seemed dead with fear; yes, she was under his compulsion. I will seek her; I will find her; now that he is away, she will speak her true mind. She will remember the old times when we were little playfellows together, and this will soften her heart, and she will no more betray me, but will confess me. There is no treacherous blood in her; no, she was always honest and true. She has loved me in those old days; this is my security, for whom one has loved one cannot betray."

He stepped eagerly toward the door; at that moment it opened, and the lady Edith entered. She was very pale, but she walked with a firm step, and her carriage was full of grace and gentle dignity. Her face was sad as before.

Miles sprang forward with a happy confidence to meet her, but she checked him with a hardly perceptible gesture, and he stopped where he was. She seated herself and asked him to do likewise. Thus simply did she take the sense of old comradeship out of him and transform him into stranger and a guest. The surprise of it, the bewildering unexpectedness of it, made him begin to question, for a moment, if he *was* the person he was pretending to be after all.

The lady Edith said, "Sir, I have come to warn you. The mad cannot be persuaded out of their delusions, perchance; but doubtless they may be persuaded to avoid perils. I think this dream of yours hath the seeming of honest truth to you, and therefore is not criminal; but do not tarry here with it, for here it is dangerous." She looked steadily into Miles's face a moment, then added impressively, "It is the more dangerous for that you *are* much like what our lost lad must have grown to be if he had lived."

"Heavens, madam, but I *am* he!"

"I truly think you think it, sir. I question not your honesty in that; I but warn you, that is all. My husband is master in this region; his power hath hardly any limit; the people prosper or starve as he wills. If you resembled not the man whom you profess to be, my husband might bid you pleasure yourself with your dream in peace; but trust me, I know him well, I know what he will do; he will say to all that you are but a mad impostor, and straightway all will echo him." She bent upon Miles that same steady look once more and added, "If you *were* Miles Hendon, and he knew it and all the region knew it —consider what I am saying, weigh it well—you would stand in the same peril, your punishment would be no less sure; he would deny you and denounce you, and none would be bold enough to give you countenance."

"Most truly I believe it," said Miles bitterly. "The power that can command one lifelong friend to betray and disown another be obeyed, may well look to be obeyed in quarters where bread and life are on the stake and no cobweb ties of loyalty and honor are concerned."

A faint tinge appeared for a moment in the lady's cheek, and she dropped her eyes to the floor; but her voice betrayed no emotion which she proceeded, "I have warned you, I must still warn you, to go hence. This man will destroy you, else. He is a tyrant who knows no pity. I, who am his fettered slave, know this. Poor Miles, and

Arthur, and my dear guardian, Sir Richard, are free of him and at rest; better that you were with them than that you bide here in the clutches of this miscreant. Your pretensions are a menace to his title and possessions; you have assaulted him in his own house; you are ruined if you stay. Go—do not hesitate. If you lack money, take this purse, I beg of you, and bribe the servants to let you pass. Oh, be warned, poor soul, and escape while you may."

Miles declined the purse with a gesture and rose up and stood before her.

"Grant me one thing," he said. "Let your eyes rest upon mine so that I may see if they be steady. There, now answer me. Am I Miles Hendon?"

"No. I know you not."

"Swear it!"

The answer was low but distinct, "I swear."

"Oh, this passes belief!"

"Fly! Why will you waste the precious time? Fly, and save yourself."

At that moment the officers burst into the room, and a violent struggle began; but Hendon was soon over-powered and dragged away. The king was taken also, and both were bound and led to prison.

27 IN PRISON

      The cells were all crowded, so the two friends were chained in a large room where persons charged with trifling offenses were commonly kept. They had company, for there were some twenty manacled and fettered prisoners here, of both sexes and of varying ages —an obscene and noisy gang. The king chafed bitterly over the stupendous indignity thus put upon his royalty, but Hendon was moody and taciturn. He was pretty thoroughly bewildered. He had come home a jubilant prodigal expecting to find everybody wild with joy over his return, and instead had got the cold shoulder and a jail. The promise and the fulfillment differed so widely that the effect was stunning; he could not decide whether it was most tragic or most grotesque. He felt much as a man might who had danced blithely out to enjoy a rainbow and got struck by lightning.

But gradually his confused and tormenting thoughts settled down into some sort of order, and then his mind centered itself upon Edith. He turned her conduct over and examined it in all lights, but he could not make anything satisfactory out of it. Did she know him? Or didn't she know him? It was a perplexing puzzle and occupied him a long time, but he ended finally with the conviction that she did know him and had repudiated him for interested reasons. He wanted to load her name with curses now, but this name had so long been sacred to him that he found he could not bring his tongue to profane it.

Wrapped in prison blankets of a soiled and tattered condition, Hendon and the king passed a troubled night. For a bribe the jailer had furnished liquor to some of the prisoners; singing of ribald songs, fighting, shouting, and carousing was the natural consequence. At last, a while after midnight, a man attacked a woman and nearly killed

her by beating her over the head with his manacles before
the jailer could come to the rescue. The jailer restored
peace by giving the man a sound clubbing about the head
and shoulders; then the carousing ceased, and after that
all had an opportunity to sleep who did not mind the
annoyance of the moanings and groanings of the two
wounded people.

During the ensuing week, the days and nights were of
a monotonous sameness as to events; men whose faces
Hendon remembered more or less distinctly came by day
to gaze at the "impostor" and repudiate and insult him;
and by night the carousing and brawling went on with
symmetrical regularity.

However, there was a change of incident at last. The
jailer brought in an old man and said to him, "The villain
is in this room; cast thy old eyes about and see if thou
canst say which is he."

Hendon glanced up and experienced a pleasant sensation for the first time since he had been in the jail. He
said to himself, "This is Blake Andrews, a servant all
his life in my father's family—a good honest soul, with
a right heart in his breast. That is, formerly. But none
are true now; all are liars. This man will know me—
and will deny me too, like the rest."

The old man gazed around the room, glanced at
each face in turn, and finally said, "I see none here but
paltry knaves, scum o' the streets. Which is he?"

The jailer laughed.

"Here," he said; "scan this big animal, and grant me
an opinion."

The old man approached and looked Hendon over
long and earnestly, then shook his head and said, "Marry,
this is no Hendon—nor ever was!"

"Right! Thy old eyes are sound yet. An' I were Sir
Hugh, I would take the shabby carl and—"

The jailer finished by lifting himself atiptoe with an
imaginary halter, at the same time making a gurgling
noise in his throat suggestive of suffocation. The old man
said vindictively, "Let him bless God an' he fare no
worse. An' *I* had the handling o' the villain, he should
roast, or I am no true man!"

The jailer laughed a pleasant hyena laugh and said,

"Give him a piece of thy mind, old man; they all do it. Thou'lt find it good diversion."

Then he sauntered toward his anteroom and disappeared. The old man dropped upon his knees and whispered, "God be thanked, thou'rt come again, my master! I believed thou wert dead these seven years, and lo, here thou art alive! I knew thee the moment I saw thee; and main hard work it was to keep a stony countenance and seem to see none here but tuppenny knaves and rubbish o' the streets. I am old and poor, Sir Miles; but say the word and I will go forth and proclaim the truth, though I be strangled for it."

"No," said Hendon; "thou shalt not. It would ruin thee, and yet help but little in my cause. But I thank thee, for thou hast given me back somewhat of my lost faith in my kind."

The old servant became very valuable to Hendon and the king, for he dropped in several times a day to "abuse" the former and always smuggled in a few delicacies to help out the prison bill of fare; he also furnished the current news. Hendon reserved the dainties for the king; without them his Majesty might not have survived, for he was not able to eat the coarse and wretched food provided by the jailer. Andrews was obliged to confine himself to brief visits in order to avoid suspicion, but he managed to impart a fair degree of information each time—information delivered in a low voice for Hendon's benefit, and interlarded with insulting epithets delivered in a louder voice for the benefit of other hearers.

So little by little the story of the family came out. Arthur had been dead six years. This loss, with the absence of news from Hendon, impaired the father's health; he believed he was going to die, and he wished to see Hugh and Edith settled in life before he passed away; but Edith begged hard for delay, hoping for Miles's return; then the letter came which brought the news of Miles's death; the shock prostrated Sir Richard; he believed his end was very near, and he and Hugh insisted upon the marriage; Edith begged for and obtained a month's respite; then another and finally a third; the marriage then took place by the deathbed of Sir Richard. It had not proved a happy one. It was whispered about the country that shortly after the nuptials the bride found among her husband's papers several rough and incomplete drafts of the fatal letter and had accused him of precipitating the marriage, and Sir Richard's death too, by a wicked forgery. Tales of cruelty to the lady Edith and the servants were to be heard on all hands; and since the father's death Sir Hugh had thrown off all soft disguises and become a pitiless master toward all who in any way depended upon him and his domains for bread.

There was a bit of Andrews' gossip which the king listened to with a lively interest, "There is rumor that the king is mad. But in charity forbear to say *I* mentioned it, for 'tis death to speak of it, they say."

His Majesty glared at the old man and said, "The king is *not* mad, good man, and thou'lt find it to thy advantage to busy thyself with matters that nearer concern thee than this seditious prattle."

"What doth the lad mean?" said Andrews, surprised at this brisk assault from an unexpected quarter. Hendon gave a sign, and he did not pursue his question, but went on with his budget, "The late king is to be buried at Windsor in a day or two—the sixteenth of the month— and the new king will be crowned at Westminster the twentieth."

"Methinks they must needs find him first," muttered his Majesty; then added confidently, "but they will look to that—and also shall I."

"In the name of—"

But the old man got no further: a warning sign from Hendon checked his remark. He resumed the thread of his gossip, "Sir Hugh goeth to the coronation, and with grand hopes. He confidently looketh to come back a peer, for he is high in favor with the Lord Protector."

"What Lord Protector?" asked his Majesty.

"His grace the Duke of Somerset."

"What Duke of Somerset?"

"Marry, there is but one—Seymour, Earl of Hertford."

The king asked sharply, "Since when is *he* a duke, and Lord Protector?"

"Since the last day of January."

"And prithee who made him so?"

"Himself and the Great Council, with help of the king."

His Majesty started violently. "The *king!*" he cried. *"What* king, good sir?"

"What king, indeed! (God-a-mercy, what aileth the boy?) Sith we have but one, 'tis not difficult to answer—his most sacred Majesty King Edward the Sixth, whom God preserve! Yea, and a dear and gracious little urchin is he too; and whether he be mad or no—and they say he mendeth daily—his praises are on all men's lips; and all bless him, likewise, and offer prayers that he may be spared to reign long in England, for he began humanely, with saving the old Duke of Norfolk's life, and now is he bent on destroying the cruelest of the laws that harry and oppress the people."

This news struck his Majesty dumb with amazement and plunged him into so deep dismal a reverie that he heard no more of the old man's gossip. He wondered if the "little urchin" was the beggar boy whom he left dressed in his own garments in the palace. It did not seem possible that this could be, for surely his manners and speech would betray him if he pretended to be the Prince of Wales; then he would be driven out, and search made for the true prince. Could it be that the court had set up some sprig of the nobility in his place? No, for his uncle would not allow that; he was all-powerful and could and would crush such a movement, of course. The boy's musings profited him nothing; the more he tried to unriddle the mystery, the more perplexed he became, the more his head ached, and the worse he slept. His impatience to get to London grew hourly, and his captivity became almost unendurable.

Hendon's arts all failed with the king—he could not be comforted; but a couple of women who were chained near him succeeded better. Under their gentle ministrations he found peace and learned a degree of patience. He was very grateful and came to love them dearly and to delight in the sweet and soothing influence of their presence. He asked them why they were in prison, and when they said they were Baptists, he smiled and inquired, "Is that a crime to be shut up for, in a prison? Now I grieve, for I shall lose ye—they will not keep ye long for such a little thing."

They did not answer, and something in their faces made him uneasy. He said eagerly, "You do not speak; be good to me and tell me—there will be no other punishment? Prithee tell me there is no fear of that."

They tried to change the topic, but his fears were

aroused, and he pursued it, "Will they scourge thee? No, no, they would not be so cruel! Say they would not. Come, they *will* not, will they?"

The women betrayed confusion and distress, but there was no avoiding an answer, so one of them said in a voice choked with emotion, "Oh, thou'lt break our hearts, thou gentle spirit! God will help us to bear our——"

"It is a confession!" the king broke in. "Then they *will* scourge thee, the stonyhearted wretches! But oh, thou must not weep; I cannot bear it. Keep up thy courage; I shall come to my own in time to save thee from this bitter thing, and I will do it!"

When the king awoke in the morning, the women were gone.

"They are saved!" he said, joyfully; then added despondently, "but woe is me, for they were my comforters."

Each of them had left a shred of ribbon pinned to his clothing in token of remembrance. He said he would keep these things always and that soon he would seek out these dear good friends of his and take them under his protection.

Just then the jailer came in with some subordinates and commanded that the prisoners be conducted to the jailyard. The king was overjoyed: it would be a blessed thing to see the blue sky and breathe the fresh air once more. He fretted and chafed at the slowness of the officers, but his turn came at last and he was released from his staple and ordered to follow the other prisoners, with Hendon.

The court, or quadrangle, was stone-paved and open to the sky. The prisoners entered it through a massive archway of masonry, and were placed in file, standing with their backs against the wall. A rope was stretched in front of them, and they were also guarded by their officers. It was a chill and lowering morning, and light snow which had fallen during the night whitened the great empty space and added to the general dismalness of its aspect. Now and then a wintry wind shivered through the place and sent the snow eddying hither and thither.

In the center of the court stood two women, chained to posts. A glance showed the king that these were his good friends. He shuddered and said to himself, "Alack, they are not gone free, as I had thought. To think that such as these should know the lash! In England! Aye, there's the shame of it—not in Heathenesse, but Christian England! They will be scourged; and I, whom they have comforted and kindly entreated, must look on and see the great wrong done; it is strange, so strange, that I, the very source of power in this broad realm, am helpless to protect them. But let these miscreants look well to themselves, for there is a day coming when I will require of them a heavy reckoning for this work. For every blow they strike now they shall feel a hundred then."

A great gate swung open and a crowd of citizens poured in. They flocked around the two women and hid them from the king's view. A clergyman entered and passed through the crowd, and he also was hidden. The king now heard talking back and forth as if questions were being asked and answered, but he could not make out what was said. Next there was a deal of bustle and preparation, and much passing and repassing of officials through that part of the crowd that stood on the further side of the women; and whilst this proceeded a deep hush gradually fell upon the people.

Now, by command, the masses parted and fell aside, and the king saw a spectacle that froze the marrow in his bones. Fagots had been piled about the two women, and a kneeling man was lighting them!

The women bowed their heads and covered their faces with their hands; the yellow flames began to climb upward among the snapping and crackling fagots, and wreaths of blue smoke to stream away on the wind; the clergyman lifted his hands and began a prayer; just then two young girls came flying through the great gate uttering piercing screams and threw themselves upon the women at the stake. Instantly they were torn away by officers, and one of them was kept in a tight grip, but the other broke loose, saying she would die with her mother; and before she could be stopped she had flung her arms about her mother's neck again. She was torn away once more, and with her gown on fire. Two of three men held her, and the burning portion of her gown was snatched off and thrown flaming aside, she struggling all the while to free herself, and saying she would be alone in the world now, and begging to be allowed to die with her mother. Both the girls screamed continually and fought for freedom, but suddenly this tumult was drowned under a volley of heart-piercing shrieks of mortal agony; the king glanced from the frantic girls to the stake, then turned away and leaned his ashen face against the wall, and looked no more. He said, "That which I have seen in that one little moment will never go out from my memory, but will abide there; and I shall see it all the days, and dream of it all the nights, till I die. Would God I had been blind!"

Hendon was watching the king. He said to himself with satisfaction, "His disorder mendeth, he hath changed, and groweth gentler. If he had followed his wont, he would have stormed at these varlets, and said he was king, and commanded that the women be turned loose unscathed. Soon his delusion will pass away and be forgotten, and his poor mind will be whole again. God speed the day!"

That same day several prisoners were brought in to remain overnight, who were being conveyed under guard to various places in the kingdom to undergo punishment for crimes committed. The king conversed with these—he had made it a point from the beginning to instruct himself for the kingly office by questioning prisoners whenever the opportunity offered—and the tale of their woes wrung his heart. One of them was a poor half-witted woman who had stolen a yard or two of cloth from a weaver; she was to be hanged for it. Another was a man accused of stealing a horse; he said the proof had failed, and he had imagined that he was safe from the halter; but no, he was hardly free before he was arraigned for killing a deer in the king's park; this was proved against him, and now he was on his way to the gallows. There was a tradesman's apprentice whose case particularly distressed the king; this youth said he found a hawk one evening that had escaped from its owner, and he took it home with him, imagining himself entitled to it; but the court convicted him of stealing it and sentenced him to death.

The king was furious over these inhumanities and wanted Hendon to break jail and fly with him to Westminster so that he could mount his throne and hold out his scepter in mercy over these unfortunate people and save their lives. "Poor child," sighed Hendon, "these woeful tales have brought his malady upon him again;

alack, but for this evil hap, he would have been well in a little time."

Among these prisoners was an old lawyer—a man with a strong face and a dauntless mien. Three years past he had written a pamphlet against the Lord Chancellor, accusing him of injustice, and had been punished for it by the loss of his ears in the pillory and degradation from the bar, and in addition had been fined £3,000 and sentenced to imprisonment for life. Lately he had repeated his offense; and in consequence was now under sentence to lose *what remained of his ears,* pay a fine of £5,000, be branded on both cheeks, and remain in prison for life.

"These be honorable scars," he said, and turned back his gray hair and showed the mutilated stubs of what had once been his ears.

The king's eye burned with passion. He said, "None believe in me; neither wilt thou. But no matter; within the compass of a month thou shalt be free; and more, the laws that have dishonored thee and shamed the English name shall be swept from the statute books. The world is made wrong; kings should go to school to their own laws at times, and so learn mercy."*

* See Notes to Chapter 27 at end of volume.

28 THE SACRIFICE

Meantime Miles was growing sufficiently tired of confinement and inaction. But now his trial came on, to his great gratification, and he thought he could welcome any sentence provided a further imprisonment should not be a part of it. But he was mistaken about that. He was in a fine fury when he found himself described as a "sturdy vagabond" and sentenced to sit two hours in the pillory for bearing that character and for assaulting the master of Hendon Hall. His pretensions as to brothership with his prosecutor, and rightful heirship to the Hendon honors and estates, were left contemptuously unnoticed as being not even worth examination.

He raged and threatened on his way to punishment, but it did no good; he was snatched roughly along by the officers and got an occasional cuff besides for his unreverent conduct.

The king could not pierce through the rabble that swarmed behind, so he was obliged to follow in the rear, remote from his good friend and servant. The king had been nearly condemned to the stocks himself for being in such bad company, but had been let off with a lecture and a warning in consideration of his youth. When the crowd at last halted, he flitted feverishly from point to point around its outer rim hunting a place to get through, and at last, after a deal of difficulty and delay, succeeded. There sat his poor henchman in the degrading stocks, the sport and butt of a dirty mob—he the body servant of the king of England! Edward had heard the sentence pronounced, but he had not realized the half that it meant. His anger began to rise as the sense of this new indignity which had been put upon him sank home; it jumped to summer heat the next moment, when he saw an egg sail through the air and crush itself against Hendon's cheek, and heard the crowd roar its enjoyment of the episode. He sprang across the open circle and confronted the officer in charge, crying, "For shame! This is my servant; set him free! I am the——"

"Oh, peace!" exclaimed Hendon in a panic. "Thou'lt destroy thyself. Mind him not, officer, he is mad."

"Give thyself no trouble as to the matter of minding him, good man; I have small mind to mind him; but as to teaching him somewhat, to that I am well inclined." He turned to a subordinate and said, "Give the little fool a taste or two of the lash, to mend his manners."

"Half a dozen will better serve his turn," suggested Sir Hugh, who had ridden up a moment before to take a passing glance at the proceedings.

The king was seized. He did not even struggle, so paralyzed was he with the mere thought of the monstrous outrage that was proposed to be inflicted upon his sacred person. History was already defiled with the record of the scourging of an English king with whips; it was an intolerable reflection that he must furnish a duplicate of that shameful page. He was in the toils; there was no help for him: he must either take this punishment or beg for its remission. Hard conditions; he would take the stripes—a king might do that, but a king could not beg.

But meantime Miles Hendon was resolving the difficulty. "Let the child go," said he; "ye heartless dogs, do ye not see how young and frail he is? Let him go; I will take his lashes."

"Marry, a good thought, and thanks for it," said Sir Hugh, his face lighting with a sardonic satisfaction. "Let the little beggar go, and give this fellow a dozen in his place—an honest dozen, well laid on." The king was in the act of entering a fierce protest, but Sir Hugh silenced him with the potent remark, "Yes, speak up, do, and free thy mind; only, mark ye, that for each word you utter he shall get six strokes the more."

Hendon was removed from the stocks and his back laid bare, and whilst the lash was applied the poor little king turned away his face and allowed unroyal tears to channel his cheeks unchecked. "Ah, brave good heart," he said to himself, "this loyal deed shall never perish out of my memory. I will not forget it; and neither shall *they!*" he added with passion. Whilst he mused, his appreciation of Hendon's magnanimous conduct grew to greater and still greater dimensions in his mind, and so also did his gratefulness for it. Presently he said to himself, "Who saves his prince from wounds and possible death—and this he did for me—performs high service; but it is little—it is nothing, oh, less than nothing!—when 'tis weighed against the act of him who saves his prince from shame!"

Hendon made no outcry under the scourge, but bore the heavy blows with soldierly fortitude. This, together with his redeeming the boy by taking his stripes for him, compelled the respect of even that forlorn and degraded mob that was gathered there; and its gibes and hootings died away, and no sound remained but the sound of the falling blows. The stillness that pervaded the place when Hendon found himself once more in the stocks was in strong contrast with the insulting clamor which had prevailed there so little a while before. The king came softly to Hendon's side and whispered in his ear, "Kings cannot ennoble thee, thou good, great soul, for One who is higher than kings hath done that for thee; but a king can confirm thy nobility to men." He picked up the scourge from the ground, touched Hendon's bleeding shoulders lightly with it, and whispered, "Edward of England dubs thee earl!"

Hendon was touched. The water welled to his eyes, yet at the same time the grisly humor of the situation and circumstances so undermined his gravity that it was all he could do to keep some sight of his inward mirth from showing outside. To be suddenly hoisted, naked and gory, from the common stocks to the Alpine altitude and splendor of an earldom seemed to him the last possibility in the line of the grotesque. He said to himself, "Now am I finely tinseled indeed! The specter knight of the Kingdom of Dreams and Shadows is become a specter earl! A dizzy flight for a callow wing! An' this go on, I shall presently be hung like a very maypole with fantastic gauds and make-believe honors. But I shall value them, all valueless as they are, for the love that doth bestow them. Better these poor mock dignities of mine, that come unasked from a clean hand and a right spirit, than real ones bought by servility from grudging and interested power."

The dreaded Sir Hugh wheeled his horse about, and as he spurred away, the living wall divided silently to let him

pression which had settled down upon his spirits lifted and
blew away, and he raised his head and looked about him.
He was surprised to see how far he had come; the village
was away behind him. The king was jogging along in his
wake with his head bowed, for he too was deep in plans
and thinkings. A sorrowful misgiving clouded Hendon's
newborn cheerfulness: would the boy be willing to go again
to a city where, during all his brief life, he had never
known anything but ill usage and pinching want? But the
question must be asked; it could not be avoided; so Hendon reined up and called out, "I had forgotten to inquire
whither we are bound. Thy commands, my liege!"

"To London!"

Hendon moved on again, mightily contented with the
answer, but astounded at it too.

The whole journey was made without an adventure of
importance. But it ended with one. About ten o'clock on
the night of the nineteenth of February, they stepped upon
London Bridge in the midst of a writhing, struggling jam
of howling and hurrahing people whose beer-jolly faces
stood out strongly in the glare from manifold torches; and
at that instant the decaying head of some former duke or
other grandee tumbled down between them, striking Hendon on the elbow and then bounding off among the hurrying confusion of feet. So evanescent and unstable are
men's works in this world! The late good king is but three
weeks dead and three days in his grave, and already the
adornments which he took such pains to select from prominent people for his noble bridge are falling. A citizen
stumbled over that head and drove his own head into the
back of somebody in front of him, who turned and knocked
down the first person that came handy, and was promptly
laid out himself by that person's friend. It was the right
ripe time for a free fight, for the festivities of the morrow—
Coronation Day—were already beginning; everybody was
full of strong drink and patriotism; within five minutes the
free fight was occupying a good deal of ground; within
ten or twelve it covered an acre or so and was become a
riot. By this time Hendon and the king were hopelessly
separated from each other and lost in the rush and turmoil
of the roaring masses of humanity. And so we leave them.

30 TOM'S PROGRESS

Whilst the true king wandered about the land poorly clad, poorly fed, cuffed and derided by tramps one while, herding with thieves and murderers in a jail another, and called idiot and impostor by all impartially, the mock king, Tom Canty, enjoyed a quite different experience.

When we saw him last, royalty was just beginning to have a bright side for him. This bright side went on brightening more and more every day; in a very little while it was become almost all sunshine and delightfulness. He lost his fears; his misgivings faded out and died; his embarrassments departed and gave place to an easy and confident bearing. He worked the whipping boy mine to ever-increasing profit.

He ordered my lady Elizabeth and my lady Jane Grey into his presence when he wanted to play or talk, and dismissed them when he was done with them, with the air of one familiarly accustomed to such performances. It no longer confused him to have these lofty personages kiss his hand at parting.

He came to enjoy being conducted to bed in state at night and dressed with intricate and solemn ceremony in the morning. It came to be a proud pleasure to march to dinner attended by a glittering procession of officers of state and gentlemen-at-arms; insomuch, indeed, that he doubled his guard of gentlemen-at-arms and made them a hundred. He liked to hear the bugles sounding down the long corridors and the distant voices responding, "Way for the king!"

He even learned to enjoy sitting in throned state in council and seeming to be something more than the Lord Protector's mouthpiece. He liked to receive great ambassadors and their gorgeous trains and listen to the affectionate messages they brought from illustrious monarchs who called him "brother." O happy Tom Canty, late of Offal Court!

He enjoyed his splendid clothes and ordered more; he found his four hundred servants too few for his proper grandeur and trebled them. The adulation of salaaming courtiers came to be sweet music to his ears. He remained kind and gentle and a sturdy and determined champion of all that were oppressed, and he made tireless war upon unjust laws; yet upon occasion, being offended, he could turn upon an earl, or even a duke, and give him a look that would make him tremble. Once, when his royal "sister" the grimly holy lady Mary set herself to reason with him against the wisdom of his course in pardoning so many people who would otherwise be jailed, or hanged, or burned, and reminded him that their august late father's prisons had sometimes contained as high as sixty thousand convicts at one time and that during his admirable reign he had delivered seventy-two thousand thieves and robbers over to death by the executioner,* the boy was filled with generous indignation and commanded her to go to her closet, and beseech God to take away the stone that was in her breast and give her a human heart.

Did Tom Canty never feel troubled about the poor little rightful prince, who had treated him so kindly and flown out with such hot zeal to avenge him upon the insolent sentinel at the palace gate? Yes; his first royal days and nights were pretty well sprinkled with painful thoughts about the lost prince, and with sincere longings for his return, and happy restoration to his native rights and splendors. But as time wore on, and the prince did not come, Tom's mind became more and more occupied with his new and enchanting experiences, and by little and little the vanished monarch faded almost out of his thoughts; and finally, when he did intrude upon them at intervals, he was become an unwelcome specter, for he made Tom feel guilty and ashamed.

Tom's poor mother and sisters traveled the same road out of his mind. At first he pined for them, sorrowed for them, longed to see them, but later the thought of their coming some day in their rags and dirt, and betraying

* Hume's *England*.

him with their kisses, and pulling him down from his lofty place, and dragging him back to penury and degradation and the slums made him shudder. At last they ceased to trouble his thoughts almost wholly. And he was content, even glad; for whenever their mournful and accusing faces did rise before him now, they made him feel more despicable than the worms that crawl.

At midnight of the nineteenth of February Tom Canty was sinking to sleep in his rich bed in the palace, guarded by his loyal vassals and surrounded by the pomps of royalty, a happy boy, for tomorrow was the day appointed for his solemn crowning as king of England. At that same hour Edward, the true king, hungry and thirsty, soiled and draggled, worn with travel, and clothed in rags and shreds—his share of the results of the riot—was wedged in among a crowd of people who were watching with deep interest hurrying gangs of workmen who streamed in and out of Westminster Abbey, busy as ants: they were making the last preparation for the royal coronation.

31 THE RECOGNITION PROCESSION

When Tom Canty awoke the next morning, the air was heavy with a thunderous murmur; all the distances were charged with it. It was music to him, for it meant that the English world was out in its strength to give loyal welcome to the great day.

Presently Tom found himself once more the chief figure in a wonderful floating pageant on the Thames, for by ancient custom the "recognition procession" through London must start from the Tower, and he was bound thither.

When he arrived there, the sides of the venerable fortress seemed suddenly rent in a thousand places, and from every rent leaped a red tongue of flame and a white gush of smoke; a deafening explosion followed, which drowned the shoutings of the multitude and made the ground tremble; the flame jets, the smoke, and the explosions were repeated over and over again with marvelous celerity, so that in a few moments the old Tower disappeared in the vast fog of its own smoke, all but the very top of the tall pile called the White Tower: this, with its banners, stood out above the dense bank of vapor as a mountain peak projects above a cloud rack.

Tom Canty, splendidly arrayed, mounted a prancing war steed, whose rich trappings almost reached to the ground; his "uncle" the Lord Protector Somerset, similarly mounted, took place in his rear; the king's guard formed in single ranks on either side, clad in burnished armor; after the Protector followed a seemingly interminable procession of resplendent nobles attended by their vassals; after these came the Lord Mayor and the aldermanic body, in crimson-velvet robes and with their gold chains across their breasts; and after these the officers and members of all the guilds of London, in rich raiment and bearing the showy banners of the several corporations. Also in the procession, as a special guard of honor through the city, was the Ancient and Honorable Artillery Company, an organization already three hundred years old at that time, and the only military body in England possessing the privilege (which it still possesses in our day) of holding itself independent of the commands of Parliament. It was a brilliant spectacle, and was hailed with acclamations all along the line as it took its stately way through the packed multitudes of citizens. The chronicler says, "The king, as he entered the city, was received by the people with prayers, welcomings, cries, and tender words, and all signs which argue an earnest love of subjects toward their sovereign; and the king, by holding up his glad countenance to such as stood afar off, and most tender language to those that stood nigh his Grace, showed himself no less thankful to receive the people's goodwill than they to offer it. To all that wished him well, he gave thanks. To such as bade 'God save his Grace,' he said in return, 'God save you all!' and added that he thanked them with all his heart. Wonderfully transported were the people with the loving answers and gestures of their king."

In Fenchurch Street a "fair child, in costly apparel," stood on a stage to welcome his Majesty to the city. The last verse of his greeting was in these words:

> Welcome, O king, as much as hearts can think;
>   Welcome again, as much as tongue can tell;
> Welcome to joyous tongues, and hearts that will
>   not shrink:
>   God thee preserve, we pray, and wish thee
>   ever well.

The people burst forth in a glad shout, repeating with one voice what the child had said. Tom Canty gazed abroad over the surging sea of eager faces, and his heart swelled with exultation and he felt that the one thing worth living for in this world was to be a king, and a nation's idol. Presently he caught sight, at a distance, of a couple of his ragged Offal Court comrades—one of them the Lord High Admiral in his late mimic court, the other the First Lord of the Bedchamber in the same pretentious fiction; and his pride swelled higher than ever.

Oh, if they could only recognize him now! What unspeakable glory it would be if they could recognize him and realize that the derided mock king of the slums and back alleys was become a real king, with illustrious dukes and princes for his humble menials and the English world at his feet! But he had to deny himself and choke down his desire, for such a recognition might cost more than it would come to; so he turned away his head and left the two soiled lads to go on with their shoutings and glad adulations, unsuspicious of whom it was they were lavishing them upon.

Every now and then rose the cry, "A largess! A largess!" and Tom responded by scattering a handful of bright new coins abroad for the multitude to scramble for.

The chronicler says, "At the upper end of Gracechurch Street, before the sign of the Eagle, the city had erected a gorgeous arch, beneath which was a stage which stretched from one side of the street to the other. This was a historical pageant, representing the king's immediate progenitors. There sat Elizabeth of York in the midst of an immense white rose whose petals formed elaborate furbelows around her; by her side was Henry VII, issuing out of a vast red rose, disposed in the same manner; the hands of the royal pair were locked together, and the wedding ring ostentatiously displayed. From the red and white roses proceeded a stem which reached up to a second stage, occupied by Henry VIII, issuing from a red-and-white rose, with the effigy of the new king's mother, Jane Seymour, represented by his side. One branch sprang from this pair, which mounted to a third stage, where sat the effigy of Edward VI himself, enthroned in royal majesty; and the whole pageant was framed with wreaths of roses, red and white."

This quaint and gaudy spectacle so wrought upon the rejoicing people that their acclamations utterly smothered the small voice of the child whose business it was to explain the thing in eulogistic rhymes. But Tom Canty was not sorry, for this loyal uproar was sweeter music to him than any poetry, no matter what its quality might be. Whithersoever Tom turned his happy young face, the people recognized the exactness of his effigy's likeness to

himself, the flesh and blood counterpart, and new whirl-
winds of applause burst forth.

The great pageant moved on, and still on, under one
triumphal arch after another, and past a bewildering succession of spectacular and symbolical tableaux, each of
which typified and exalted some virtue, or talent, or merit
of the little king's. "Throughout the whole of Cheapside,
from every penthouse and window, hung banners and
streamers; and the richest carpets, stuffs, and cloth of gold
tapestried the streets—specimens of the great wealth of the
stores within; and the splendor of this thoroughfare was
equaled in the other streets, and in some even surpassed."

"And all these wonders and these marvels are to welcome me—me!" murmured Tom Canty.

The mock king's cheeks were flushed with excitement,
his eyes were flashing, his senses swam in a delirium of
pleasure. At this point, just as he was raising his hand to
fling another rich largess, he caught sight of a pale, astounded face which was strained forward out of the second
rank of the crowd, its intense eyes riveted upon him. A
sickening consternation struck through him; he recognized
his mother! And up flew his hand, palm outward, before
his eyes—that old involuntary gesture born of a forgotten
episode and perpetuated by habit. In an instant more she
had torn her way out of the press, and past the guards,
and was at his side. She embraced his leg, she covered it
with kisses, she cried, "O my child, my darling!" lifting
toward him a face that was transfigured with joy and love.
The same instant an officer of the king's guard snatched
her away with a curse and sent her reeling back whence
she came with a vigorous impulse from his strong arm.
The words "I do not know you, woman!" were falling
from Tom Canty's lips when this piteous thing occurred,
but it smote him to the heart to see her treated so; and as
she turned for a last glimpse of him, whilst the crowd was
swallowing her from his sight, she seemed so wounded, so
brokenhearted, that a shame fell upon him which consumed his pride to ashes and withered his stolen royalty.
His grandeurs were stricken valueless; they seemed to fall
away from him like rotten rags.

The procession moved on, and still on, through ever-
augmenting splendors and ever-augmenting tempests of
welcome, but to Tom Canty they were as if they had not

been. He neither saw nor heard. Royalty had lost its grace and sweetness; its pomps were become a reproach. Remorse was eating his heart out. He said, "Would God I were free of my captivity!"

He had unconsciously dropped back into the phraseology of the first days of his compulsory greatness.

The shining pageant still went winding like a radiant and interminable serpent down the crooked lanes of the quaint old city, and through the huzzahing hosts; but still the king rode with bowed head and vacant eyes, seeing only his mother's face and that wounded look in it.

"Largess, largess!" The cry fell upon an unheeding ear.

"Long live Edward of England!" It seemed as if the earth shook with the explosion, but there was no response from the king. He heard it only as one hears the thunder of the surf when it is blown to the ear out of a great distance, for it was smothered under another sound which was still nearer, in his own breast, in his accusing conscience—a voice which kept repeating those shameful words, "I do not know you, woman!"

The words smote upon the king's soul as the strokes of a funeral bell smite upon the soul of a surviving friend when they remind him of secret treacheries suffered at his hands by him that is gone.

New glories were unfolded at every turning; new wonders, new marvels, sprung into view; the pent clamors of waiting batteries were released; new raptures poured from the throats of the waiting multitudes; but the king gave no sign, and the accusing voice that went moaning through his comfortless breast was all the sound he heard.

By and by the gladness in the faces of the populace changed a little and became touched with a something like solicitude or anxiety; an abatement in the volume of applause was observable too. The Lord Protector was quick to notice these things; he was as quick to detect the cause. He spurred to the king's side, bent low in his saddle, uncovered, and said, "My liege, it is an ill time for dreaming. The people observe thy downcast head, thy clouded mien, and they take it for an omen. Be advised; unveil the sun of royalty and let it shine upon these boding vapors and disperse them. Lift up thy face and smile upon the people."

So saying, the duke scattered a handful of coins to right

and left, then retired to his place. The mock king did mechanically as he had been bidden. His smile had no heart in it, but few eyes were near enough or sharp enough to detect that. The noddings of his plumed head as he saluted his subjects were full of grace and graciousness; the largess which he delivered from his hand was royally liberal, so the people's anxiety vanished and the acclamations burst forth again in as mighty a volume as before.

Still once more, a little before the progress was ended, the duke was obliged to ride forward and make remonstrance. He whispered, "O dread sovereign! Shake off these fatal humors; the eyes of the world are upon thee." Then he added with sharp annoyance, "Perdition catch that crazy pauper! 'Twas she that hath disturbed your Highness."

The gorgeous figure turned a lusterless eye upon the duke and said in a dead voice, "She was my mother!"

"My God!" groaned the Protector as he reigned his horse backward to his post. "The omen was pregnant with prophecy. He is gone mad again!"

32 CORONATION DAY

Let us go backward a few hours and place ourselves in Westminster Abbey at four o'clock in the morning of this memorable Coronation Day. We are not without company, for although it is still night, we find the torchlighted galleries already filling up with people who are well content to sit still and wait seven or eight hours till the time shall come for them to see what they may not hope to see twice in their lives—the coronation of a king. Yes, London and Westminster have been astir ever since the warning guns boomed at three o'clock, and already crowds of untitled rich folk who have bought the privilege of trying to find sitting room in the galleries are flocking in at the entrances reserved for their sort.

The hours drag along tediously enough. All stir has ceased for some time, for every gallery has long ago been packed. We may sit now and look and think at our leisure. We have glimpses, here and there and yonder, through the dim cathedral twilight, of portions of many galleries and balconies wedged full with people, the other portions of these galleries and balconies being cut off from sight by intervening pillars and architectural projections. We have in view the whole of the great north transept—empty and waiting for England's privileged ones. We see also the ample area or platform, carpeted with rich stuffs, whereon the throne stands. The throne occupies the center of the platform, and is raised above it upon an elevation of four steps. Within the seat of the throne is enclosed a rough, flat rock—the stone of Scone —which many generations of Scottish kings sat on to be crowned, and so it in time became holy enough to answer a like purpose for English monarchs. Both the throne and its footstool are covered with cloth of gold.

Stillness reigns, the torches blink dully, the time drags heavily. But at last the lagging daylight asserts itself, the torches are extinguished, and a mellow radiance suffuses the great spaces. All features of the noble building are distinct now, but soft and dreamy, for the sun is lightly veiled with clouds.

At seven o'clock the first break in the drowsy monotony occurs, for on the stroke of this hour the first peeress enters the transept, clothed like Solomon for splendor, and is conducted to her appointed place by an official clad in satins and velvets, whilst a duplicate of him gathers up the lady's long train, follows after, and when the lady is seated, arranges the train across her lap for her. He then places her footstool according to her desire, after which he puts her coronet where it will be convenient to her hand when the time for the simultaneous coroneting of the nobles shall arrive.

By this time the peeresses are flowing in in a glittering stream, and the satin-clad officials are flitting and glinting everywhere, seating them and making them comfortable. The scene is animated enough now. There is stir and life, and shifting color everywhere. After a time, quiet reigns again, for the peeresses are all come and are all in their places—a solid acre, or such a matter, of human flowers, resplendent in variegated colors and frosted like a Milky Way with diamonds. There are all ages here: brown, wrinkled, white-haired dowagers who are able to go back, and still back, down the stream of time and recall the crowning of Richard III and the troublous days of that old forgotten age; and there are handsome middle-aged dames; and lovely and gracious young matrons; and gentle and beautiful young girls with beaming eyes and fresh complexions who may possibly put on their jeweled coronets awkwardly when the great time comes, for the matter will be new to them and their excitement will be a sore hindrance. Still, this may not happen, for the hair of all these ladies has been arranged with a special view to the swift and successful lodging of the crown in its place when the signal comes.

We have seen that this massed array of peeresses is sown thick with diamonds, and we also see that it is a marvelous spectacle, but now we are about to be astonished in earnest. About nine the clouds suddenly break away and a shaft of sunshine cleaves the mellow atmosphere and drifts slowly along the ranks of ladies, and every rank it touches flames into a dazzling splendor of many-colored fires, and we tingle to our fingertips with the electric thrill that is shot through us by the surprise and the beauty of the spectacle! Presently a special envoy from some distant corner of the Orient, marching with the general body of foreign ambassadors, crosses this bar of sunshine, and we catch our breath, the glory that streams and flashes and palpitates about him is so overpowering, for he is crusted from head to heel with gems, and his slightest movement showers a dancing radiance all around him.

Let us change the tense for convenience. The time drifted along—one hour—two hours—two hours and a half; then the deep booming of artillery told that the king and his grand procession had arrived at last, so the waiting multitude rejoiced. All knew that a further delay must follow, for the king must be prepared and robed for the solemn ceremony; but this delay would be pleasantly occupied by the assembling of the peers of the realm in their stately robes. These were conducted ceremoniously to their seats and their coronets placed conveniently at hand; and meanwhile the multitude in the galleries were alive with interest, for most of them were beholding for the first time dukes, earls, and barons, whose names had been historical for five hundred years. When all were finally seated, the spectacle from the galleries and all coigns of vantage was complete—a gorgeous one to look upon and to remember.

Now the robed and mitered great heads of the church and their attendants filed in upon the platform and took their appointed places; these were followed by the Lord Protector and other great officials, and these again by a steel-clad detachment of the guard.

There was a waiting pause; then, at a signal, a triumphant peal of music burst forth, and Tom Canty, clothed in a long robe of cloth of gold, appeared at a door and stepped upon the platform. The entire multitude rose, and the ceremony of the Recognition ensued.

Then a noble anthem swept the Abbey with its rich

waves of sound; and thus heralded and welcomed, Tom Canty was conducted to the throne. The ancient ceremonies went on with impressive solemnity, whilst the audience gazed; and as they drew nearer and nearer to completion, Tom Canty grew pale, and still paler, and a deep and steadily deepening woe and despondency settled down upon his spirits and upon his remorseful heart.

At last the final act was at hand. The Archbishop of Canterbury lifted up the crown of England from its cushion and held it out over the trembling mock king's head. In the same instant a rainbow radiance flashed along the spacious transept, for with one impulse every individual in the great concourse of nobles lifted a coronet and poised it over his or her head—and paused in that attitude.

A deep hush pervaded the Abbey. At this impressive moment a startling apparition intruded upon the scene—an apparition observed by none in the absorbed multitude until it suddenly appeared, moving up the great central aisle. It was a boy, bareheaded, ill-shod, and clothed in coarse plebeian garments that were falling to rags. He raised his hand with a solemnity which ill comported with his soiled and sorry aspect and delivered this note of warning, "I forbid you to set the crown of England upon that forfeited head. *I* am the king!"

In an instant several indignant hands were laid upon the boy; but in the same instant Tom Canty, in his regal vestments, made a swift step forward and cried out in a ringing voice, "Loose him and forbear! He *is* the king!"

A sort of panic of astonishment swept the assemblage, and they partly rose in their places and stared in a bewildered way at one another and at the chief figures in this scene, like persons who wondered whether they were awake and in their senses or asleep and dreaming. The Lord Protector was as amazed as the rest, but quickly recovered himself and exclaimed in a voice of authority, "Mind not his Majesty, his malady is upon him again; seize the vagabond!"

He would have been obeyed, but the mock king stamped his foot and cried out, "On your peril! Touch him not; he is the king!"

The hands were withheld; a paralysis fell upon the house; no one moved, no one spoke; indeed no one knew how to act or what to say in so strange and surprising an emergency. While all minds were struggling to right themselves, the boy still moved steadily forward, with high port and confident mien; he had never halted from the beginning; and while the tangled minds still floundered helplessly, he stepped upon the platform, and the mock king ran with a glad face to meet him and fell on his knees before him and said, "Oh, my lord the king, let poor Tom Canty be first to swear fealty to thee and say, 'Put on thy crown and enter into thine own again!'"

The Lord Protector's eye fell sternly upon the newcomer's face, but straightway the sternness vanished away and gave place to an expression of wondering surprise. This thing happened also to the other great officers. They glanced at each other and retreated a step by a common and unconscious impulse. The thought in each mind was the same: "What a strange resemblance!"

The Lord Protector reflected a moment or two in perplexity; then he said with grave respectfulness, "By your favor, sir, I desire to ask certain questions which——"

"I will answer them, my lord."

The duke asked him many questions about the court, the late king, the prince, the princesses; the boy answered them correctly and without hesitating. He described the rooms of state in the palace, the late king's apartments, and those of the Prince of Wales.

It was strange, it was wonderful; yes, it was unaccountable—so all said that heard it. The tide was beginning to turn, and Tom Canty's hopes to run high, when the Lord Protector shook his head and said, "It is true it is most wonderful, but it is no more than our lord the king likewise can do." This remark and this reference to himself as still the king saddened Tom Canty, and he felt his hopes crumbling from under him. "These are not *proofs*," added the Protector.

The tide was turning very fast now, very fast indeed, but in the wrong direction; it was leaving poor Tom Canty stranded on the throne and sweeping the other out to sea. The Lord Protector communed with himself—shook his head—the thought forced itself upon him, "It is perilous to the state and to us all to entertain so fateful a riddle as this; it could divide the nation and undermine the throne." He turned and said, "Sir Thomas, arrest this—

No, hold!" His face lighted, and he confronted the ragged candidate with this question, "Where lieth the Great Seal? Answer me this truly, and the riddle is unriddled, for only he that was Prince of Wales *can* so answer. On so trivial a thing hang a throne and a dynasty!"

It was a lucky thought, a happy thought. That it was so considered by the great officials was manifested by the silent applause that shot from eye to eye around their circle in the form of bright, approving glances. Yes, none but the true prince could dissolve the stubborn mystery of the vanished Great Seal; this forlorn little impostor had been taught his lesson well, but here his teachings must fail, for his teacher himself could not answer *that* question —ah, very good, very good indeed; now we shall be rid of this troublesome and perilous business in short order! And so they nodded invisibly, and smiled inwardly with satisfaction, and looked to see this foolish lad stricken with a palsy of guilty confusion. How surprised they were, then, to see nothing of the sort happen—how they marveled to hear him answer up promptly, in a confident and untroubled voice, and say, "There is nought in this riddle that is difficult." Then, without so much as a by-your-leave to anybody, he turned and gave this command, with the easy manner of one accustomed to doing such things: "My lord St. John, go you to my private cabinet in the palace—for none knoweth the place better than you— and, close down to the floor, in the left corner remotest from the door that opens from the antechamber, you shall find in the wall a brazen nailhead; press upon it and a little jewel closet will fly open which not even you do know of—no, nor any soul else in all the world but me and the trusty artisan that did contrive it for me. The first thing that falleth under your eye will be the Great Seal; fetch it hither."

All the company wondered at this speech, and wondered still more to see the little mendicant pick out this peer without hesitancy or apparent fear of mistake, and call him by name with such a placidly convincing air of having known him all his life. The peer was almost surprised into obeying. He even made a movement as if to go, but quickly recovered his tranquil attitude and confessed his blunder with a blush. Tom Canty turned upon him and said sharply, "Why dost thou hesitate? Hast not heard the king's command? Go!"

The lord St. John made a deep obeisance—and it was observed that it was a significantly cautious and non-committal one, it not being delivered at either of the kings, but at the neutral ground about halfway between the two—and took his leave.

Now began a movement of the gorgeous particles of that official group which was slow, scarcely perceptible, and yet steady and persistent—a movement such as is observed in a kaleidoscope that is turned slowly, whereby the components of one splendid cluster fall away and join themselves to another; a movement which little by little, in the present case, dissolved the glittering crowd that stood about Tom Canty and clustered it together again in the neighborhood of the newcomer. Tom Canty stood almost alone. Now ensued a brief season of deep suspense and waiting, during which even the few fainthearts still remaining near Tom Canty gradually scraped together courage enough to glide, one by one, over to the majority. So at last Tom Canty, in his royal robes and jewels, stood wholly alone and isolated from the world, a conspicuous figure occupying an eloquent vacancy.

Now the lord St. John was seen returning. As he advanced up the mid-aisle the interest was so intense that the low murmur of conversation in the great assemblage died out and was succeeded by a profound hush, a breathless stillness, through which his footfalls pulsed with a dull and distant sound. Every eye was fastened upon him as he moved along. He reached the platform, paused a moment, then moved toward Tom Canty with a deep obeisance and said, "Sire, the Seal is not there!"

A mob does not melt away from the presence of a plague patient with more haste than the band of pallid and terrified courtiers melted away from the presence of the shabby little claimant of the crown. In a moment he stood all alone, without friend or supporter, a target upon which was concentrated a bitter fire of scornful and angry looks.

The Lord Protector called out fiercely, "Cast the beggar into the street and scourge him through the town; the paltry knave is worth no more consideration!"

Officers of the guard sprang forward to obey, but Tom

Canty waved them off and said, "Back! Whoso touches him perils his life!"

The Lord Protector was perplexed in the last degree. He said to the lord St. John, "Searched you well? But it boots not to ask that. It doth seem passing strange. Little things, trifles, slip out of one's ken, and one does not think it matter for surprise; but how a so bulky thing as the Seal of England can vanish away and no man be able to get track of it again—a massy golden disk—"

Tom Canty, with beaming eyes, sprang forward and shouted, "Hold, that is enough. Was it round? And thick? And had it letters and devices graved upon it? Yes? Oh, *now* I know what this Great Seal is that there's been such worry and pother about! An' ye had described it to me, ye could have had it three weeks ago. Right well I know where it lies, but it was not I that put it there—first."

"Who, then, my liege?" asked the Lord Protector.

"He that stands there—the rightful king of England. And he shall tell you himself where it lies; then you will believe he knew it of his own knowledge. Bethink thee, my king—spur thy memory—it was the last, the very *last* thing thou didst that day before thou didst rush forth from the palace, clothed in my rags, to punish the soldier that insulted me."

A silence ensued, undisturbed by a movement or a whisper, and all eyes were fixed upon the newcomer, who stood, with bent head and corrugated brow, groping in his memory among a thronging multitude of valueless recollections for one single little elusive fact, which, found, would seat him upon a throne—unfound, would leave him as he was, for good and all, a pauper and an outcast. Moment after moment passed—the moments built themselves into minutes—still the boy struggled silently on, and gave no sign. But at last he heaved a sigh, shook his head slowly, and said with a trembling lip and in a despondent voice, "I call the scene back—all of it—but the Seal hath no place in it." He paused, then looked up and said with gentle dignity, "My lords and gentlemen, if ye will rob your rightful sovereign of his own for lack of this evidence which he is not able to furnish, I may not stay ye, being powerless. But——"

"Oh, folly, Oh, madness, my king!" cried Tom Canty in a panic. "Wait! Think! Do not give up! The cause is not lost! Nor *shall* be, neither! List to what I say—follow every word; I am going to bring that morning back again, every hap just as it happened. We talked; I told you of my sisters, Nan and Bet—ah, yes, you remember that; and about mine old grandam, and the rough games of the lads of Offal Court—yes, you remember these things also; very well, follow me still; you shall recall everything. You gave me food and drink, and did with princely courtesy send away the servant so that my low breeding might not shame me before them—ah, yes, this also you remember."

As Tom checked off his details, and the other boy nodded his head in recognition of them, the great audience and the officials stared in puzzled wonderment; the tale sounded like true history, yet how could this impossible conjunction between a prince and a beggar boy have come about? Never was a company of people so perplexed, so interested, and so stupefied before.

"For a jest, my prince, we did exchange garments. Then we stood before a mirror; and so alike were we that both said it seemed as if there had been no change made—yes, you remember that. Then you noticed that the soldier had hurt my hand. Look! Here it is; I cannot yet even write with it, the fingers are so stiff. At this your Highness sprang up, vowing vengeance upon that soldier, and ran toward the door; you passed a table; that thing you call the Seal lay on that table; you snatched it up and looked eagerly about, as if for a place to hide it; your eye caught sight of——"

"There, 'tis sufficient! And the dear God be thanked!" exclaimed the ragged claimant in a mighty excitement. "Go, my good St. John; in an armpiece of the Milanese armor that hangs on the wall thou'lt find the Seal!"

"Right, my king! Right!" cried Tom Canty. "*Now* the scepter of England is thine own; and it were better for him that would dispute it that he had been born dumb! Go, my lord St. John; give thy feet wings!"

The whole assemblage was on its feet now and well nigh out of its mind with uneasiness, apprehension, and consuming excitement. On the floor and on the platform a deafening buzz of frantic conversation burst forth, and for some time nobody knew anything or heard anything or was interested in anything but what his neighbor was shouting into his ear or he was shouting into his neighbor's ear. Time—nobody knew how much of it—swept by unheeded and unnoted. At last a sudden hush fell upon the house, and in the same moment St. John appeared upon the platform and held the Great Seal aloft in his hand. Then such a shout went up!

"Long live the true king!"

For five minutes the air quaked with shouts and the crash of musical instruments, and was white with a storm of waving handkerchiefs; and through it all a ragged lad, the most conspicuous figure in England, stood flushed and happy and proud in the center of the spacious platform with the great vassals of the kingdom kneeling around him.

Then all rose, and Tom Canty cried out, "Now, O my king, take these regal garments back and give poor Tom, thy servant, his shreds and remnants again."

The Lord Protector spoke up, "Let the small varlet be stripped and flung into the Tower."

But the new king, the true king, said, "I will not have it so. But for him I had not got my crown again; none shall lay a hand upon him to harm him. And as for thee, my good uncle, my Lord Protector, this conduct of thine is not grateful toward this poor lad, for I hear he hath made thee a duke"—the Protector blushed—"yet he was not a king; wherefore, what is thy fine title worth now? Tomorrow you shall sue to me, *through him,* for its confirmation, else no duke, but a simple earl, shalt thou remain."

Under this rebuke his grace the Duke of Somerset retired a little from the front for the moment. The king turned to Tom and said kindly, "My poor boy, how was it that you could remember where I hid the Seal when I could not remember it myself?"

"Ah, my king, that was easy, since I used it divers days."

"Used it, yet could not explain where it was?"

"I did not know it was *that* they wanted. They did not describe it, your Majesty."

"Then how used you it?"

The red blood began to steal up into Tom's cheeks, and he dropped his eyes and was silent.

"Speak up, good lad, and fear nothing," said the king. "How used you the Great Seal of England?"

Tom stammered a moment in a pathetic confusion, then got it out, "To crack nuts with!"

Poor child, the avalanche of laughter that greeted this nearly swept him off his feet. But if a doubt remained in any mind that Tom Canty was not the king of England and familiar with the august appurtenances of royalty, this reply disposed of it utterly.

Meantime the sumptuous robe of state had been removed from Tom's shoulders to the king's, whose rags were effectually hidden from sight under it. Then the coronation ceremonies were resumed; the true king was anointed and the crown set upon his head, whilst cannon thundered the news to the city, and all London seemed to rock with applause.

Miles Hendon was picturesque enough before he got into the riot on London Bridge; he was more so when he got out of it. He had but little money when he got in, none at all when he got out. The pickpockets had stripped him of his last farthing.

But no matter, so he found his boy. Being a soldier, he did not go at his task in a random way, but set to work first of all to arrange his campaign.

What would the boy naturally do? Where would he naturally go? Well, argued Miles, he would naturally go to his former haunts, for that is the instinct of unsound minds when homeless and forsaken, as well as of sound ones. Whereabouts were his former haunts? His rags, taken together with the low villain who seemed to know him and who even claimed to be his father, indicated that his home was in one or another of the poorest and meanest districts of London. Would the search for him be difficult or long? No, it was likely to be easy and brief. He would not hunt for the boy, he would hunt for a crowd; in the center of a big crowd or a little one, sooner or later, he should find his poor little friend, sure; and the mangy mob would be entertaining itself with pestering and aggravating the boy, who would be proclaiming himself king, as usual. Then Miles Hendon would cripple some of those people, and carry off his little ward, and comfort and cheer him with loving words, and the two would never be separated any more.

So Miles started on his quest. Hour after hour he tramped through back alleys and squalid streets seeking groups and crowds, and finding no end of them, but never any sign of the boy. This greatly surprised him but did not discourage him. To his notion there was nothing the matter with his plan of campaign; the only miscalculation about it was that the campaign was becoming a lengthy one, whereas he had expected it to be short.

When daylight arrived at last, he had made many a mile and canvassed many a crowd, but the only result was that he was tolerably tired, rather hungry, and very sleepy. He wanted some breakfast, but there was no way to get it. To beg for it did not occur to him; as to pawning his sword, he would as soon have thought of parting with his honor; he could spare some of his clothes—yes, but one could as easily find a customer for a disease as for such clothes.

At noon he was still tramping—among the rabble which followed after the royal procession now, for he argued that this regal display would attract his little lunatic powerfully. He followed the pageant through all its devious windings about London and all the way to Westminster and the Abbey. He drifted here and there amongst the multitudes that were massed in the vicinity for a weary long time, baffled and perplexed, and finally wandered off thinking and trying to contrive some way to better his plan of campaign. By and by, when he came to himself out of his musings, he discovered that the town was far behind him and that the day was growing old. He was near the river and in the country; it was a region of fine rural seats—not the sort of district to welcome clothes like his.

It was not at all cold, so he stretched himself on the ground in the lee of a hedge to rest and think. Drowsiness presently began to settle upon his senses; the faint and far-off boom of cannon was wafted to his ear, and he said to himself, "The new king is crowned," and straightway fell asleep. He had not slept or rested before for more than thirty hours. He did not wake again until near the middle of the next morning.

He got up lame, stiff, and half famished, washed himself in the river, stayed his stomach with a pint or two of water, and trudged off toward Westminister grumbling at himself for having wasted so much time. Hunger helped him to a new plan now; he would try to get speech with old Sir Humphrey Marlow and borrow a few marks, and —but that was enough of a plan for the present; it would be time enough to enlarge it when this first stage should be accomplished.

Toward eleven o'clock he approached the palace; and although a host of showy people were about him, moving in the same direction, he was not inconspicuous—his costume took care of that. He watched these people's faces narrowly, hoping to find a charitable one whose possessor might be willing to carry his name to the old lieutenant; as to trying to get into the palace himself, that was simply out of the question.

Presently our whipping boy passed him, then wheeled about and scanned his figure well, saying to himself, "An' that is not the very vagabond his Majesty is in such a worry about, then am I an ass—though belike I was that before. He answereth the description to a rag; that God should make two such would be to cheapen miracles by wasteful repetition. I would I could contrive an excuse to speak with him."

Miles Hendon saved him the trouble, for he turned about then as a man generally will when somebody mesmerizes him by gazing hard at him from behind; and observing a strong interest in the boy's eyes, he stepped toward him and said, "You have just come out from the palace; do you belong there?"

"Yes, your worship."

"Know you Sir Humphrey Marlow?"

The boy started and said to himself, "Lord! Mine old departed father!" Then he answered aloud, "Right well, your worship."

"Good; is he within?"

"Yes," said the boy; and added to himself, "Within his grave."

"Might I crave your favor to carry my name to him and say I beg to say a word in his ear?"

"I will dispatch the business right willingly, fair sir."

"Then say Miles Hendon, son of Sir Richard, is here without; I shall be greatly bounden to you, my good lad."

The boy looked disappointed; "The king did not name him so," he said to himself, "but it mattereth not; this is his twin brother and can give his Majesty news of t'other Sir-Odds-and-Ends, I warrant." So he said to Miles, "Step in there a moment, good sir, and wait till I bring you word."

Hendon retired to the place indicated; it was a recess sunk in the palace wall, with a stone bench in it—a shelter for sentinels in bad weather. He had hardly seated himself when some halberdiers in charge of an officer passed by. The officer saw him, halted his men, and commanded Hendon to come forth. He obeyed, and was promptly arrested as a suspicious character prowling within the precincts of the palace. Things began to look ugly. Poor Miles was going to explain, but the officer roughly silenced him and ordered his men to disarm him and search him.

"God of his mercy grant that they find somewhat," said poor Miles; "I have searched enow and failed, yet is my need greater than theirs."

Nothing was found but a document. The officer tore it open, and Hendon smiled when he recognized the "pot-hooks" made by his lost little friend that black day at Hendon Hall. The officer's face grew dark as he read the English paragraph, and Miles blenched to the opposite color as he listened.

"Another new claimant of the crown!" cried the officer. "Verily they breed like rabbits today. Seize the rascal, men, and see ye keep him fast whilst I convey this precious paper within and send it to the king."

He hurried away, leaving the prisoner in the grip of the halberdiers.

"Now is my evil luck ended at last," muttered Hendon, "for I shall dangle at a rope's end for a certainty, by reason of that bit of writing. And what will become of my poor lad! Ah, only the good God knoweth."

By and by he saw the officer coming again in a great hurry, so he plucked his courage together, purposing to meet his trouble as became a man. The officer ordered the men to loose the prisoner and return his sword to him, then bowed respectfully and said, "Please you sir, to follow me."

Hendon followed, saying to himself, "An' I were not traveling to death and judgment, and so must needs economize in sin, I would throttle this knave for his mock courtesy."

The two traversed a populous court and arrived at the grand entrance of the palace, where the officer, with another bow, delivered Hendon into the hands of a gorgeous official, who received him with profound respect and led him forward through a great hall lined on both sides with rows of splendid flunkies (who made reverential obeisance

as the two passed along, but fell into death throes of
silent laughter at our stately scarecrow the moment his
back was turned) and up a broad staircase, among flocks
of fine folk, and finally conducted him into a vast room,
clove a passage for him through the assembled nobility
of England, then made a bow, reminded him to take
his hat off, and left him standing in the middle of the
room, a mark for all eyes, for plenty of indignant frowns,
and for a sufficiency of amused and derisive smiles.

Miles Hendon was entirely bewildered. There sat the
young king under a canopy of state five steps away, with
his head bent down and aside, speaking with a sort of
human bird of paradise—a duke, maybe; Hendon observed to himself that it was hard enough to be sentenced
to death in the full vigor of life without having this peculiarly public humiliation added. He wished the king would
hurry about it; some of the gaudy people nearby were becoming offensive. At this moment the king raised his head
slightly and Hendon caught a good view of his face. The
sight nearly took his breath away! He stood gazing at the
fair young face like one transfixed, then presently ejaculated, "Lo, the lord of the Kingdom of Dreams and
Shadows on his throne!"

He muttered some broken sentences, still gazing and
marveling, then turned his eyes around and about, scan-
ning the gorgeous throng and the splendid saloon, murmuring, "But these are *real*—verily these are *real*—surely
it is not a dream."

He stared at the king again and thought, "*Is* it a dream?
Or *is* he the veritable sovereign of England, and not the
friendless poor Tom o' Bedlam I took him for? Who shall
solve me this riddle?"

A sudden idea flashed in his eye, and he strode to the
wall, gathered up a chair, brought it back, planted it on
the floor, and sat down in it!

A buzz of indignation broke out, a rough hand was laid
upon him, and a voice exclaimed, "Up, thou mannerless
clown! Wouldst sit in the presence of the king?"

The disturbance attracted his Majesty's attention, who
stretched forth his hand and cried out, "Touch him not;
it is his right!"

The throng fell back, stupefied. The king went on,
"Learn ye all, ladies, lords and gentlemen, that this is

my trusty and well-beloved servant Miles Hendon, who interposed his good sword and saved his prince from bodily harm and possible death; and for this he is a knight, by the king's voice. Also learn that for a higher service, in that he saved his sovereign stripes and shame, taking these upon himself, he is a peer of England, Earl of Kent, and shall have gold and lands meet for the dignity. More— the privilege which he hath just exercised is his by royal grant, for we have ordained that the chiefs of his line shall have and hold the right to sit in the presence of the Majesty of England henceforth, age after age, so long as the crown shall endure. Molest him not."

Two persons who, through delay, had only arrived from the country during this morning and had now been in this room only five minutes stood listening to these words and looking at the king, then at the scarecrow, then at the king again, in a sort of torpid bewilderment. These were Sir Hugh and the lady Edith. But the new earl did not see them. He was still staring at the monarch in a dazed way and muttering, "Oh, body o' me! *This* my pauper! This my lunatic! This is he whom *I* would show what grandeur was in my house of seventy rooms and seven and twenty servants! This is he who had never known aught but rags for raiment, kicks for comfort, and offal for diet! This is he whom *I* adopted and would make respectable! Would God I had a bag to hide my head in!"

Then his manners suddenly came back to him, and he dropped upon his knees, with his hands between the king's and swore allegiance and did homage for his lands and titles. Then he rose and stood respectfully aside, a mark still for all eyes—and much envy too.

Now the king discovered Sir Hugh and spoke out with wrathful voice and kindling eye, "Strip this robber of his false show and stolen estates and put him under lock and key till I have need of him."

The late Sir Hugh was led away.

There was a stir at the other end of the room now; the assemblage fell apart, and Tom Canty, quaintly but richly clothed, marched down between these living walls, preceded by an usher. He knelt before the king, who said, "I have learned the story of these past few weeks and am well pleased with thee. Thou hast governed the realm with right royal gentleness and mercy. Thou hast found thy mother and thy sisters again? Good; they shall be cared for, and thy father shall hang if thou desire it and the law consent. Know, all ye that hear my voice, that from this day they that abide in the shelter of Christ's Hospital and share the king's bounty shall have their minds and hearts fed, as well as their baser parts; and this boy shall dwell there, and hold the chief place in its honorable body of governors during life. And for that he hath been a king, it is meet that other than common observance shall be his due; wherefore, note this his dress of state, for by it he shall be known, and none shall copy it; and wheresoever he shall come, it shall remind the people that he hath been royal in his time, and none shall deny him his due of reverence or fail to give him salutation. He hath the throne's protection, he hath the Crown's support, he shall be known and called by the honorable title of the King's Ward."

The proud and happy Tom Canty rose and kissed the king's hand, and was conducted from the presence. He did not waste any time, but flew to his mother to tell her and Nan and Bet all about it and get them to help him enjoy the great news.*

* See Notes to Chapter 33 at end of volume.

CONCLUSION

JUSTICE AND RETRIBUTION

When the mysteries were all cleared up, it came out by confession of Hugh Hendon that his wife had repudiated Miles by his command that day at Hendon Hall—a command assisted and supported by the perfectly trustworthy promise that if she did not deny that he was Miles Hendon and stand firmly to it, he would have her life; whereupon she said take it, she did not value it—and she would not repudiate Miles; then the husband said he would spare her life but have Miles assassinated! This was a different matter, so she gave her word and kept it.

Hugh was not prosecuted for his threats or for stealing his brother's estates and title because the wife and brother would not testify against him, and the former would not have been allowed to do it even if she had wanted to. Hugh deserted his wife and went over to the Continent, where he presently died; and by and by the Earl of Kent married his relict. There were grand times and rejoicings at Hendon village when the couple paid their first visit to the Hall.

Tom Canty's father was never heard of again.

The king sought out the farmer who had been branded and sold as a slave, and reclaimed him from his evil life with the Ruffler's gang, and put him in the way of a comfortable livelihood.

He also took that old lawyer out of prison and remitted his fine. He provided good homes for the daughters of the two Baptist women whom he saw burned at the stake, and roundly punished the official who laid the undeserved stripes upon Miles Hendon's back.

He saved from the gallows the boy who had captured

the stray falcon, and also the woman who had stolen a remnant of cloth from a weaver; but he was too late to save the man who had been convicted of killing a deer in the royal forest.

He showed favor to the justice who had pitied him when he was supposed to have stolen a pig, and he had the gratification of seeing him grow in the public esteem and become a great and honored man.

As long as the king lived he was fond of telling the story of his adventures, all through, from the hour that the sentinel cuffed him away from the palace gate till the final midnight when he deftly mixed himself into a gang of hurrying workmen and so slipped into the Abbey and climbed up and hid himself in the Confessor's tomb, and then slept so long next day that he came within one of missing the coronation altogether. He said that the frequent rehearsing of the precious lesson kept him strong in his purpose to make its teachings yield benefits to his people; and so, whilst his life was spared he should continue to tell the story, and thus keep its sorrowful spectacles fresh in his memory and the springs of pity replenished in his heart.

Miles Hendon and Tom Canty were favorites of the king all through his brief reign, and his sincere mourners when he died. The good Earl of Kent had too much sense to abuse his peculiar privilege, but he exercised it twice after the instance we have seen of it before he was called from the world—once at the accession of Queen Mary, and once at the accession of Queen Elizabeth. A descendant of his exercised it at the accession of James I. Before this one's son chose to use the privilege, near a quarter of a century had elapsed, and the "privilege of the Kents" had faded out of most people's memories; so when the Kent of that day appeared before Charles I and his court and sat down in the sovereign's presence to assert and perpetuate the right of his house, there was a fine stir indeed! But the matter was soon explained, and the right confirmed. The last earl of the line fell in the wars of the commonwealth fighting for the king, and the odd privilege ended with him.

Tom Canty lived to be a very old man, a handsome, white-haired old fellow of grave and benignant aspect. As enced, for his striking and peculiar costume kept the people reminded that "in his time he had been royal"; so wherever he appeared the crowd fell apart, making way for him and whispering, one to another, "Doff thy hat, it is the King's Ward!" And so they saluted and got his kindly smile in return, and they valued it too, for his was an honorable history.

Yes, King Edward VI lived only a few years, poor boy, but he lived them worthily. More than once when some great dignitary, some gilded vassal of the crown, made argument against his leniency and urged that some law which he was bent upon amending was gentle enough for its purpose and wrought no suffering or oppression which anyone need mightily mind, the young king turned the mournful eloquence of his great compassionate eyes upon him and answered, "What dost *thou* know of suffering and oppression? I and my people know, but not thou."

The reign of Edward VI was a singularly merciful one for those harsh times. Now that we are taking leave of him, let us try to keep this in our minds, to his credit.

NOTES

Note 1—Page 27

Christ's Hospital Costume

It is most reasonable to regard the dress as copied from the costume of the citizens of London of that period, when long blue coats were the common habit of apprentices and servingmen, and yellow stockings were generally worn; the coat fits closely to the body but has loose sleeves, and beneath is worn a sleeveless yellow undercoat; around the waist is a red leathern girdle; a clerical band around the neck; and a small flat black cap about the size of a saucer completes the costume.—Timbs's *Curiosities of London*

Note 2—Page 29

It appears that Christ's Hospital was not originally founded as a *school;* its object was to rescue children from the streets, to shelter, feed, clothe them, etc.—Timbs's *Curiosities of London*

Note 3—Page 36

The Duke of Norfolk's Condemnation Commanded

The king was now approaching fast towards his end, and fearing lest Norfolk should escape him, he sent a message to the Commons, by which he desired them to hasten the bill, on pretence that Norfolk enjoyed the dignity of earl marshal, and it was necessary to appoint another, who might officiate at the ensuing ceremony of installing his son, Prince of Wales. —Hume, vol. iii., p. 307

Note 4—Page 46

It was not till the end of this reign [Henry VIII] that any salads, carrots, turnips, or other edible roots were produced in England. The little of these vegetables that was used was formerly imported from Holland and Flanders. Queen Catherine, when she wanted a salad, was obliged to dispatch a messenger thither on purpose.—Hume's *History of England,* vol. iii, p. 314

Note 5—Page 51

Attainder of Norfolk

THE house of peers, without examining the prisoner, without trial or evidence, passed a bill of attainder against him and sent it down to the Commons.... The obsequious Commons obeyed his [the king's] directions; and the king, having affixed the royal assent to the bill by commissioners, issued orders for the execution of Norfolk on the morning of the twenty-ninth of January [the next day].—Hume's *England,* vol. iii, p. 306

Note 6—Page 61

The Loving Cup

THE loving cup, and the peculiar ceremonies observed in drinking from it, are older than English history. It is thought that both are Danish importations. As far back as knowledge goes, the loving cup has always been drunk at English banquets. Tradition explains the ceremonies in this way: in the rude ancient times it was deemed a wise precaution to have both hands of both drinkers employed, lest while the pledger pledged his love and fidelity to the pledgee, the pledgee take that opportunity to slip a dirk into him!

Note 7—Page 67

The Duke of Norfolk's Narrow Escape

HAD Henry VIII survived a few hours longer, his order for the duke's execution would have been carried into effect. "But news being carried to the Tower that the king himself had expired that night, the lieutenant deferred obeying the warrant; and it was not thought advisable by the council to begin a new reign by the death of the greatest nobleman in the kingdom, who had been condemned by a sentence so unjust and tyrannical."—Hume's *England,* vol. iii, p. 307

Note 8—Page 90

The Whipping Boy

JAMES I and Charles II had whipping boys, when they were little fellows, to take their punishment for them when they fell short in their lessons; so I have ventured to furnish my small prince with one, for my own purposes.

Notes to Chapter 15—Page 102

Character of Hertford

THE young king discovered an extreme attachment to his uncle, who was, in the main, a man of moderation and probity. —Hume's *England,* vol. iii, p. 324

But if he [the Protector] gave offense by assuming too much state, he deserves great praise on account of the laws passed this session, by which the rigor of former statutes was much mitigated and some security given to the freedom of the constitution. All laws were repealed which extended the crime of treason beyond the statute of the twenty-fifth of Edward III; all laws enacted during the late reign extending the crime of felony; all the former laws against Lollardy, or heresy, together with the statute of the Six Articles. None were to be accused for words, but within a month after they were spoken. By these repeals several of the most rigorous laws that ever had passed in England were annulled; and some dawn, both of civil and religious liberty, began to appear to the people. A repeal also passed of that law, the destruction of all laws, by which the king's proclamation was made of equal force with a statute.—*Ibid.,* vol. iii, p. 339

Boiling to Death

IN the reign of Henry VIII poisoners were by act of Parliament condemned to be boiled to death. This act was repealed in the following reign.

In Germany, even in the seventeenth century, this horrible punishment was inflicted on coiners and counterfeiters. Taylor, the Water Poet, describes an execution he witnessed in Hamburg in 1616. The judgment pronounced against a coiner of false money was that he should "be boiled to death in oil; not thrown into the vessel at once, but with a pulley or rope to be hanged under the armpits and then let down into the oil by degrees; first the feet, and next the legs, and so to boil his flesh from his bones alive." —Dr. J. Hammond Trumbull's *Blue Laws, True and False,* p. 13

The Famous Stocking Case

A WOMAN and her daughter nine years old were hanged in

Huntingdon for selling their souls to the devil and raising a storm by pulling off their stockings!—*Ibid.*, p. 20

Note 10—Page 112

Enslaving

So young a king and so ignorant a peasant were likely to make mistakes, and this is an instance in point. This peasant was suffering from this law *by anticipation;* the king was venting his indignation against a law which was not yet in existence, for this hideous statute was to have birth in this little king's own reign. However, we know from the humanity of his character that it could never have been suggested by him.

Notes to Chapter 23—Page 146

Death for Trifling Larcenies

WHEN Connecticut and New Haven were framing their first codes, larceny above the value of twelvepence was a capital crime in England, as it had been since the time of Henry I.—Dr. J. Hammond Trumbull's *Blue Laws, True and False*, p. 17

The curious old book called *The English Rogue* makes the limit thirteen pence ha'penny, death being the portion of any who steal a thing "above the value of thirteen pence ha'penny."

Notes to Chapter 27—Page 169

FROM many descriptions of larceny, the law expressly took away the benefit of clergy; to steal a horse, or a hawk, or woolen cloth from the weaver was a hanging matter. So it was, to kill a deer from the king's forest or to export sheep from the kingdom.—Dr. J. Hammond Trumbull's *Blue Laws, True and False*, p. 13

William Prynne, a learned barrister, was sentenced [long after Edward the Sixth's time] to lose both his ears in the pillory, to degradation from the bar, a fine of £3,000, and imprisonment for life. Three years afterwards he gave new offense to Laud by publishing a pamphlet against the hierarchy. He was again prosecuted and was sentenced to lose what remained of his ears, to pay a fine of £5,000, to be branded on both his cheeks with the letters S. L. (for Seditious Libeler), and to remain in prison for life. The severity of this sentence was equaled by the savage rigor of its execution.—*Ibid.*, p. 12

Notes to Chapter 33—Page 202

Christ's Hospital, or Blue Coat School, "the Noblest Institution in the World"

THE ground on which the priory of the Grey Friars stood was conferred by Henry the Eighth on the Corporation of London [who caused the institution there of a home for poor boys and girls]. Subsequently Edward the Sixth caused the old priory to be properly repaired, and founded within it that noble establishment called the Blue Coat School, or Christ's Hospital, for the education and maintenance of orphans and the children of indigent persons.... Edward would not let him [Bishop Ridley] depart till the letter was written [to the Lord Mayor], and then charged him to deliver it himself, and sign his special request and commandment that no time might be lost in proposing what was convenient, and apprising him of the proceedings. The work was zealously undertaken, Ridley himself engaging in it; and the result was the founding of Christ's Hospital for the Education of Poor Children. [The king endowed several other charities at the same time.] "Lord God," said he, "I yield thee most hearty thanks that thou hast given me life thus long to finish this work to the glory of thy name!" That innocent and most exemplary life was drawing rapidly to its close, and in a few days he rendered up his spirit to his Creator, praying God to defend the realm from papistry.—J. Heneage Jesse's *London, Its Celebrated Characters and Places*

In the Great Hall hangs a large picture of King Edward VI seated on his throne in a scarlet and ermined robe, holding the scepter in his left hand and presenting with the other the charter to the kneeling Lord Mayor. By his side stands the Chancellor, holding the seals, and next to him are other officers of state. Bishop Ridley kneels before him with uplifted hands as if supplicating a blessing on the event; whilst the aldermen, etc., with the Lord Mayor, kneel on both sides, occupying the middle ground of the picture; and lastly, in front are a double row of boys on one side and girls on the other, from the master and matron down to the boy and girl who have stepped forward from their respective rows and kneel with raised hands before the king.—Timbs's *Curiosities of London*, p. 98

Christ's Hospital, by ancient custom, possesses the privilege of addressing the sovereign on the occasion of his or her coming into the city to partake of the hospitality of the Corporation of London.—*Ibid*.

The Dining Hall, with its lobby and organ gallery, occupies the entire story, which is 187 feet long, 51 feet wide, and 47 feet high; it is lit by nine large windows, filled with stained glass on the south side; and is, next to Westminster Hall, the noblest room in the metropolis. Here the boys, now about eight hundred in number, dine; and here are held the "Suppings in Public," to

which visitors are admitted by tickets, issued by the treasurer
and by the governors of Christ's Hospital. The tables are laid
with cheese in wooden bowls; beer in wooden piggins, poured
from leathern jacks; and bread brought in large baskets. The
official company enter; the Lord Mayor, or President, takes his
seat in a state chair, made of oak from St. Catherine's Church,
by the Tower; a hymn is sung, accompanied by the organ; a
"Grecian," or head boy, reads the prayers from the pulpit,
silence being enforced by three drops of a wooden hammer.
After prayer the supper commences, and the visitors walk
between the tables. At its close, the "trade boys" take up the
baskets, bowls, jacks, piggins, and candlesticks and pass in procession, the bowing to the governors being curiously formal.
This spectacle was witnessed by Queen Victoria and Prince
Albert in 1845.

Among the more eminent Blue Coat Boys are Joshua Barnes,
editor of Anacreon and Euripides; Jeremiah Markland, the
eminent critic, particularly in Greek literature; Camden, the
antiquary; Bishop Stillingfleet; Samuel Richardson, the novelist;
Thomas Mitchell, the translator of Aristophanes; Thomas Barnes,
many years editor of the London *Times;* Coleridge, Charles Lamb,
and Leigh Hunt.

No boy is admitted before he is seven years old or after he
is nine; and no boy can remain in the school after he is fifteen,
king's boys and "Grecians" alone excepted. There are about
five hundred governors, at the head of whom are the sovereign
and the Prince of Wales. The qualification for a governor is
payment of £500.—*Ibid.*

GENERAL NOTE

ONE hears much about the "hideous blue laws of Connecticut," and is accustomed to shudder piously when they are mentioned. There are people in America—and even in England!—
who imagine that they were a very monument of malignity,
pitilessness, and inhumanity, whereas in reality they were about
the first *sweeping departure from judicial atrocity* which the "civilized" world had seen. This humane and kindly Blue-Law code,
of two hundred and forty years ago, stands all by itself, with ages
of bloody law on the further side of it, and a century and three
quarters of bloody English law on this side of it.

There has never been a time—under the blue laws or any
other—when above *fourteen* crimes were punishable by death in
Connecticut. But in England, within the memory of men who are
still hale in body and mind, *two hundred and twenty-three* crimes
were punishable by death!* These facts are worth knowing—and
worth thinking about, too.

* See Dr. J. Hammond Trumbull's *Blue Laws, True and False,*
p. 11

A CONNECTICUT YANKEE IN KING ARTHUR'S COURT

A NOTE ON THE TEXT

The text of this edition of *A Connecticut Yankee in King Arthur's Court* is that of the first edition of the book, published by the American Publishing Company at Hartford, Connecticut, in 1889. The spelling and punctuation have been brought into conformity with modern American usage.

Contents

CONTENTS

CONTENTS

Preface

The ungentle laws and customs touched upon in this tale are historical, and the episodes which are used to illustrate them are also historical. It is not pretended that these laws and customs existed in England in the sixth century; no, it is only pretended that inasmuch as they existed in the English and other civilizations of far later times, it is safe to consider that it is no libel upon the sixth century to suppose them to have been in practice in that day also. One is quite justified in inferring that wherever one of these laws or customs was lacking in that remote time, its place was competently filled by a worse one.

The question as to whether there is such a thing as divine right of kings is not settled in this book. It was found too difficult. That the executive head of a nation should be a person of lofty character and extraordinary ability was manifest and indisputable; that none but the Deity could select that head unerringly was also manifest and indisputable; that the Deity ought to make that selection, then, was likewise manifest and indisputable; consequently, that He does make it, as claimed, was an unavoidable deduction. I mean, until the author of this book encountered the Pompadour and Lady Castlemaine and some other executive heads of that kind; these were found so difficult to work into the scheme that it was judged better to take the other tack in this book (which must be issued this fall) and then go into training and settle the question in another book. It is of course a thing which ought to be settled, and I am not going to have anything particular to do next winter anyway.

MARK TWAIN

HARTFORD, July 21, 1889

A Word of Explanation

IT WAS IN Warwick Castle that I came across the curious stranger whom I am going to talk about. He attracted me by three things: his candid simplicity, his
marvelous familiarity with ancient armor, and the
restfulness of his company—for he did all the talking.
We fell together, as modest people will, in the tail of the
herd that was being shown through, and he at once began
to say things which interested me. As he talked along,
softly, pleasantly, flowingly, he seemed to drift away imperceptibly out of this world and time, and into some
remote era and old forgotten country; and so he gradually wove such a spell about me that I seemed to move
among the specters and shadows and dust and mold of a
gray antiquity, holding speech with a relic of it! Exactly
as I would speak of my nearest personal friends or
enemies, or my most familiar neighbors, he spoke of
Sir Bedivere, Sir Bors de Ganis, Sir Launcelot of the
Lake, Sir Galahad, and all the other great names of the
Table Round—and how old, old, unspeakably old and
faded and dry and musty and ancient he came to look
as he went on! Presently he turned to me and said, just
as one might speak of the weather or any other common
matter—

"You know about transmigration of souls; do you
know about transposition of epochs—and bodies?"

I said I had not heard of it. He was so little interested
—just as when people speak of the weather—that he did
not notice whether I made him any answer or not. There

11

was half a moment of silence, immediately interrupted by the droning voice of the salaried cicerone:

"Ancient hauberk, date of the sixth century, time of King Arthur and the Round Table; said to have belonged to the knight Sir Sagramore le Desirous; observe the round hole through the chain-mail in the left breast; can't be accounted for; supposed to have been done with a bullet since invention of firearms—perhaps maliciously by Cromwell's soldiers."

My acquaintance smiled—not a modern smile, but one that must have gone out of general use many, many centuries ago—and muttered apparently to himself:

"Wit ye well, *I saw it done*." Then, after a pause, added: "I did it myself."

By the time I had recovered from the electric surprise of this remark, he was gone.

All that evening I sat by my fire at the Warwick Arms, steeped in a dream of the olden time, while the rain beat upon the windows, and the wind roared about the eaves and corners. From time to time I dipped into old Sir Thomas Malory's enchanting book and fed at its rich feast of prodigies and adventures, breathed-in the fragrance of its obsolete names, and dreamed again. Midnight being come at length, I read another tale, for a nightcap—this which here follows, to wit:

HOW SIR LAUNCELOT SLEW TWO GIANTS, AND MADE A CASTLE FREE.

Anon withal came there upon him two great giants, well armed, all save the heads, with two horrible clubs in their hands. Sir Launcelot put his shield afore him, and put the stroke away of the one giant, and with his sword he clave his head asunder. When his fellow saw that, he ran away as he were wood,* for fear of the horrible strokes, and Sir Launcelot after him with all his might, and smote him on the shoulder, and clave him to the middle. Then Sir Launcelot went into the hall, and there came afore him three score ladies and damsels, and all kneeled unto him, and thanked God and him of their deliverance. For, sir, said they, the most part of us have been here this seven year their prisoners, and we

* Demented.

have worked all manner of silk works for our meat, and we are all great gentlewomen born, and blessed be the time, knight, that ever thou wert born; for thou hast done the most worship that ever did knight in the world, that will we bear record, and we all pray you to tell us your name, that we may tell our friends who delivered us out of prison. Fair damsels, he said, my name is Sir Launcelot du Lake. And so he departed from them and betaught them unto God. And then he mounted upon his horse, and rode into many strange and wild countries, and through many waters and valleys, and evil was he lodged. And at the last by fortune him happened against a night to come to a fair courtelage, and therein he found an old gentlewoman that lodged him with a good will, and there he had good cheer for him and his horse. And when time was, his host brought him into a fair garret over the gate to his bed. There Sir Launcelot unarmed him, and set his harness by him, and went to bed, and anon he fell on sleep. So, soon after there came one on horseback, and knocked at the gate in great haste. And when Sir Launcelot heard this he arose up, and looked out at the window, and saw by the moon-light three knights come riding after that one man, and all three lashed on him at once with swords, and that one knight turned on them knightly again and defended him. Truly, said Sir Launcelot, yonder one knight shall I help, for it were shame for me to see three knights on one, and if he be slain I am partner of his death. And therewith he took his harness and went out at a window by a sheet down to the four knights, and then Sir Launcelot said on high, Turn you knights unto me, and leave your fighting with that knight. And then they all three left Sir Kay, and turned unto Sir Launcelot, and there began great battle, for they alight all three, and strake many strokes at Sir Launcelot, and assailed him on every side. Then Sir Kay dressed him for to have holpen Sir Launcelot. Nay, sir, said he, I will none of your help, therefore as ye will have my help let me alone with them. Sir Kay for the pleasure of the knight suffered him for to do his will, and so stood aside. And then anon within six strokes Sir Launcelot had stricken them to the earth.

And then they all three cried, Sir knight, we yield us unto you as man of might matchless. As to that, said Sir Launcelot, I will not take your yielding unto me, but so that ye yield you unto Sir Kay the seneschal, on that covenant I will save your lives and else not. Fair knight, said they, that were we loth to do; for as for Sir Kay we chased him hither, and had overcome him had ye not been; therefore, to yield us unto him it were no reason. Well, as to that, said Sir Launcelot, advise you well, for ye may choose whether ye will die or live, for an ye be yielden, it shall be unto Sir Kay. Fair knight, then they said, in saving our lives we will do as thou commandest us. Then shall ye, said Sir Launcelot, on Whitsunday next coming go unto the court of King Arthur, and there shall ye yield you unto Queen Guenever, and put you all three in her grace and mercy, and say that Sir Kay sent you thither to be her prisoners. On the morn Sir Launcelot arose early, and left Sir Kay sleeping: and Sir Launcelot took Sir Kay's armour and his shield and armed him, and so he went to the stable and took his horse, and took his leave of his host, and so he departed. Then soon after arose Sir Kay and missed Sir Launcelot: and then he espied that he had his armour and his horse. Now by my faith I know well that he will grieve some of the court of King Arthur: for on him knights will be bold, and deem that it is I, and that will beguile them; and because of his armour and shield I am sure I shall ride in peace. And then soon after departed Sir Kay, and thanked his host.

As I laid the book down there was a knock at the door, and my stranger came in. I gave him a pipe and a chair and made him welcome. I also comforted him with a hot Scotch whiskey; gave him another one; then still another—hoping always for his story. After a fourth persuader, he drifted into it himself, in a quite simple and natural way:

THE STRANGER'S HISTORY.

I am an American. I was born and reared in Hartford, in the State of Connecticut—anyway, just over the river, in the country. So I am a Yankee of the Yankees—and practical; yes, and nearly barren of sentiment, I suppose—or poetry, in other words. My father was a blacksmith, my uncle was a horse doctor, and I was both, along at first. Then I went over to the great arms factory and learned my real trade; learned all there was to it; learned to make everything; guns, revolvers, cannon, boilers, engines, all sorts of labor-saving machinery. Why, I could make anything a body wanted—anything in the world, it didn't make any difference what; and if there wasn't any quick new-fangled way to make a thing, I could invent one—and do it as easy as rolling off a log. I became head superintendent; had a couple of thousand men under me.

Well, a man like that is a man that is full of fight—that goes without saying. With a couple of thousand rough men under one, one has plenty of that sort of amusement. I had, anyway. At last I met my match, and I got my dose. It was during a misunderstanding conducted with crowbars with a fellow we used to call Hercules. He laid me out with a crusher alongside the head that made everything crack, and seemed to spring every joint in my skull and make it overlap its neighbor. Then the world went out in darkness, and I didn't feel anything more, and didn't know anything at all—at least for a while.

When I came to again, I was sitting under an oak tree, on the grass, with a whole beautiful and broad country landscape all to myself—nearly. Not entirely; for there was a fellow on a horse, looking down at me—a fellow fresh out of a picture book. He was in old-time iron armor from head to heel, with a helmet on his head the shape of a nail keg with slits in it; and he had a shield, and a sword, and a prodigious spear; and his horse had armor on, too, and a steel horn projecting from his forehead, and gorgeous red and green silk trappings that hung down all around him like a bed quilt, nearly to the ground.

"Fair sir, will ye just?" said this fellow.

"Will I which?"

"Will ye try a passage of arms for land or lady or for—"

"What are you giving me?" I said. "Get along back to your circus, or I'll report you."

Now what does this man do but fall back a couple of hundred yards and then come rushing at me as hard as he could tear, with his nail keg bent down nearly to his horse's neck and his long spear pointed straight ahead.

I saw he meant business, so I was up the tree when he arrived.

He allowed that I was his property, the captive of his spear. There was argument on his side—and the bulk of the advantage—so I judged it best to humor him. We fixed up an agreement whereby I was to go with him and he was not to hurt me. I came down, and we started away, I walking by the side of his horse. We marched comfortably along, through glades and over brooks which I could not remember to have seen before—which puzzled me and made me wonder—and yet we did not come to any circus or sign of a circus. So I gave up the idea of a circus, and concluded he was from an asylum. But we never came to any asylum—so I was up a stump, as you may say. I asked him how far we were from Hartford. He said he had never heard of the place; which I took to be a lie, but allowed it to go at that. At the end of an hour we saw a faraway town sleeping in a valley by a winding river; and beyond it on a hill, a vast gray fortress, with towers and turrets, the first I had ever seen out of a picture.

"Bridgeport?" said I, pointing.

"Camelot," said he.

My stranger had been showing signs of sleepiness. He caught himself nodding, now, and smiled one of those pathetic, obsolete smiles of his, and said:

"I find I can't go on; but come with me, I've got it all written out, and you can read it if you like."

In his chamber, he said: "First, I kept a journal; then by and by, after years, I took the journal and turned it into a book. How long ago that was!"

He handed me his manuscript, and pointed out the place where I should begin:

"Begin here—I've already told you what goes before." He was steeped in drowsiness by this time. As I went out at his door I heard him murmur sleepily: "Give you good den, fair sir."

I sat down by my fire and examined my treasure. The first part of it—the great bulk of it—was parchment, and yellow with age. I scanned a leaf particularly and saw that it was a palimpsest. Under the old dim writing of the Yankee historian appeared traces of a penmanship which was older and dimmer still—Latin words and sentences: fragments from old monkish legends, evidently. I turned to the place indicated by my stranger and began to read—as follows.

{ CHAPTER I }

Camelot

"CAMELOT—Camelot," said I to myself. "I don't seem to remember hearing of it before. Name of the asylum, likely."

It was a soft, reposeful summer landscape, as lovely as a dream, and as lonesome as Sunday. The air was full of the smell of flowers, and the buzzing of insects, and the twittering of birds, and there were no people, no wagons, there was no stir of life, nothing going on. The road was mainly a winding path with hoofprints in it, and now and then a faint trace of wheels on either side in the grass—wheels that apparently had a tire as broad as one's hand.

Presently a fair slip of a girl, about ten years old, with a cataract of golden hair streaming down over her shoulders, came along. Around her head she wore a hoop of flame-red poppies. It was as sweet an outfit as ever I saw, what there was of it. She walked indolently along, with a mind at rest, its peace reflected in her innocent face. The circus man paid no attention to her; didn't even seem to see her. And she—she was no more startled at his fantastic makeup than if she was used to his like every day of her life. She was going by as indifferently as she might have gone by a couple of cows; but when she happened to notice me, *then* there was a change! Up went her hands, and she was turned to stone; her mouth dropped open, her eyes stared wide and timorously, she was the picture of astonished curiosity

19

touched with fear. And there she stood gazing, in a sort of stupefied fascination, till we turned a corner of the wood and were lost to her view. That she should be startled at me instead of at the other man, was too many for me; I couldn't make head or tail of it. And that she should seem to consider me a spectacle, and totally overlook her own merits in that respect, was another puzzling thing, and a display of magnanimity, too, that was surprising in one so young. There was food for thought here. I moved along as one in a dream.

As we approached the town, signs of life began to appear. At intervals we passed a wretched cabin, with a thatched roof, and about it small fields and garden patches in an indifferent state of cultivation. There were people, too; brawny men, with long, coarse, uncombed hair that hung down over their faces and made them look like animals. They and the women, as a rule, wore a coarse tow-linen robe that came well below the knee, and a rude sort of sandals, and many wore an iron collar. The small boys and girls were always naked; but nobody seemed to know it. All of these people stared at me, talked about me, ran into the huts and fetched out their families to gape at me; but nobody ever noticed that other fellow, except to make him humble salutation and get no response for their pains.

In the town were some substantial windowless houses of stone scattered among a wilderness of thatched cabins; the streets were mere crooked alleys, and unpaved; troops of dogs and nude children played in the sun and made life and noise; hogs roamed and rooted contentedly about, and one of them lay in a reeking wallow in the middle of the main thoroughfare and suckled her family. Presently there was a distant blare of military music; it came nearer, still nearer, and soon a noble cavalcade wound into view, glorious with plumed helmets and flashing mail and flaunting banners and rich doublets and horsecloths and gilded spearheads; and through the muck and swine, and naked brats, and joyous dogs, and shabby huts it took its gallant way, and in its wake we followed. Followed through one winding alley and then another— and climbing, always climbing—till at last we gained the breezy height where the huge castle stood. There was an exchange of bugle blasts; then a parley from the walls, where men-at-arms, in hauberk and morion marched back and forth with halberd at shoulder under flapping banners with the rude figure of a dragon displayed upon them; and then the great gates were flung open, the draw-bridge was lowered, and the head of the cavalcade swept forward under the frowning arches; and we, following, soon found ourselves in a great paved court, with towers and turrets stretching up into the blue air on all the four sides; and all about us the dismount was going on, and much greeting and ceremony, and running to-and-fro, and a gay display of moving and intermingling colors, and an altogether pleasant stir and noise and confusion.

〖 CHAPTER II 〗

King Arthur's Court

THE MOMENT I got a chance I slipped aside privately and touched an ancient common looking man on the shoulder and said, in an insinuating, confidential way—

"Friend, do me a kindness. Do you belong to the asylum, or are you just here on a visit or something like that?"

He looked me over stupidly, and said—

"Marry, fair, sir, me seemeth—"

"That will do," I said; "I reckon you are a patient."

I moved away, cogitating, and at the same time keep-ing an eye out for any chance passenger in his right mind that might come along and give me some light. I judged I had found one, presently; so I drew him aside and said in his ear—

"If I could see the head keeper a minute—only just a minute—"

"Prithee do not let me."

"Let you what?"

"Hinder me, then, if the word please thee better." Then he went on to say he was an undercook and could not stop to gossip, though he would like it another time; for it would comfort his very liver to know where I got my clothes. As he started away he pointed and said yonder was one who was idle enough for my purpose, and was seeking me besides, no doubt. This was an airy slim boy in shrimp-colored tights that made him look like a forked carrot; the rest of his gear was blue silk and dainty laces and ruffles; and he had long yellow curls, and wore a plumed pink satin cap tilted complacently over his ear. By his look, he was good-natured; by his gait, he was satisfied with himself. He was pretty enough to frame. He arrived, looked me over with a smiling and impudent curiosity; said he had come for me, and informed me that he was a page.

"Go 'long," I said; "you ain't more than a paragraph."

It was pretty severe, but I was nettled. However, it never phazed him; he didn't appear to know he was hurt. He began to talk and laugh, in happy, thoughtless, boyish fashion, as we walked along, and made himself old friends with me at once; asked me all sorts of questions about myself and about my clothes, but never waited for an answer—always chattered straight ahead, as if he didn't know he had asked a question and wasn't expecting any reply, until at last he happened to mention that he was born in the beginning of the year 513.

It made the cold chills creep over me! I stopped, and said, a little faintly:

"Maybe I didn't hear you just right. Say it again—and say it slow. What year was it?"

"Five thirteen."

"Five thirteen! You don't look it! Come, my boy, I am a stranger and friendless: be honest and honorable with me. Are you in your right mind?"

He said he was.

"Are these other people in their right minds?"

He said they were.

"And this isn't an asylum? I mean, it isn't a place where they cure crazy people?"

He said it wasn't.

"Well, then," I said, "either I am a lunatic, or something just as awful has happened. Now tell me, honest and true, where am I?"

"IN KING ARTHUR'S COURT."

I waited a minute, to let that idea shudder its way home, and then said:

"And according to your notions, what year is it now?"

"Five twenty-eight—nineteenth of June."

I felt a mournful sinking at the heart, and muttered: "I shall never see my friends again—never, never again. They will not be born for more than thirteen hundred years yet."

I seemed to believe the boy, I didn't know why. *Something* in me seemed to believe him—my consciousness, as you may say; but my reason didn't. My reason straightway began to clamor; that was natural. I didn't know how to go about satisfying it, because I knew that the testimony of men wouldn't serve—my reason would say they were lunatics, and throw out their evidence. But all of a sudden I stumbled on the very thing, just by luck. I knew that the only total eclipse of the sun in the first half of the sixth century occurred on the twenty-first of June, A.D. 528 o. s., and began at three minutes after twelve noon. I also knew that no total eclipse of the sun was due in what to *me* was the present year—*i.e.*, 1879. So, if I could keep my anxiety and curiosity from eating the heart out of me for forty-eight hours, I should then find out for certain whether this boy was telling me the truth or not.

Wherefore, being a practical Connecticut man, I now shoved this whole problem clear out of my mind till its appointed day and hour should come, in order that I might turn all my attention to the circumstances of the present moment, and be alert and ready to make the most out of them that could be made. One thing at a time, is my motto—and just play that thing for all it is worth, even if it's only two pair and a jack. I made up my mind to two things; if it was still the nineteenth century and I was among lunatics and couldn't get away, I would presently boss that asylum or know the reason why; and if on the other hand it was really the sixth century, all right, I didn't want any softer thing: I would boss the whole country inside of three months; for I judged I would have the start of the best-educated man in the kingdom by a matter of thirteen hundred years and upwards. I'm not a man to waste time after my mind's made up and there's work on hand; so I said to the page—

"Now, Clarence, my boy—if that might happen to be your name—I'll get you to post me up a little if you don't mind. What is the name of that apparition that brought me here?"

"My master and thine? That is the good knight and great lord Sir Kay the Seneschal, foster brother to our liege the king."

"Very good; go on, tell me everything."

He made a long story of it; but the part that had immediate interest for me was this. He said I was Sir Kay's prisoner, and that in the due course of custom I would be flung into a dungeon and left there on scant commons until my friends ransomed me—unless I chanced to rot, first. I saw that the last chance had the best show, but I didn't waste any bother about that; time was too precious. The page said, further, that dinner was about ended in the great hall by this time, and that as soon as the sociability and the heavy drinking should begin, Sir Kay would have me in and exhibit me before King Arthur and his illustrious knights seated at the Table Round, and would brag about his exploit in capturing me, and would probably exaggerate the facts a little, but it wouldn't be good form for me to correct him, and not over safe, either; and when I was done being exhibited, then ho for the dungeon; but he, Clarence, would find a way to come and see me every now and then, and cheer me up, and help me get word to my friends.

Get word to my friends! I thanked him; I couldn't do less; and about this time a lackey came to say I was wanted; so Clarence led me in and took me off to one side and sat down by me.

Well, it was a curious kind of spectacle, and interesting. It was an immense place, and rather naked—yes, and full of loud contrasts. It was very, very lofty; so lofty that the banners depending from the arched beams and girders away up there floated in a sort of twilight; there was a stone-railed gallery at each end, high up, with musicians in the one, and women, clothed in stunning colors, in the other. The floor was of big stone flags laid in black and white squares, rather battered by age and use, and needing repair. As to ornament, there wasn't any, strictly speaking; though on the walls hung some huge tapestries which were probably taxed as works of art; battle pieces, they were, with horses shaped like those which children cut out of paper or create in ginger-bread; with men on them in scale armor whose scales are represented by round holes—so that the man's coat looks as if it had been done with a biscuit punch. There was a fireplace big enough to camp in; and its projecting sides and hood, of carved and pillared stonework, had the look of a cathedral door. Along the walls stood men-at-arms, in breastplate and morion, with halberds for their only weapon—rigid as statues; and that is what they looked like.

In the middle of this groined and vaulted public square was an oaken table which they called the Table Round. It was as large as a circus ring; and around it sat a great company of men dressed in such various and splendid colors that it hurt one's eyes to look at them. They wore their plumed hats, right along, except that when-ever one addressed himself directly to the king, he lifted his hat a trifle just as he was beginning his remark.

Mainly they were drinking—from entire ox horns; but a few were still munching bread or gnawing beef bones. There was about an average of two dogs to one man; and these sat in expectant attitudes till a spent bone was flung to them, and then they went for it by brigades and divisions, with a rush, and there ensued a fight which filled the prospect with a tumultuous chaos of plunging heads and bodies and flashing tails, and the storm of howlings and barkings deafened all speech for the time; but that was no matter, for the dogfight was always a bigger interest anyway; the men rose, sometimes, to ob-serve it the better and bet on it, and the ladies and the musicians stretched themselves out over their balusters with the same object; and all broke into delighted ejacu-lations from time to time. In the end, the winning dog stretched himself out comfortably with his bone between his paws, and proceeded to growl over it, and gnaw it, and grease the floor with it, just as fifty others were already doing; and the rest of the court resumed their previous industries and entertainments.

As a rule the speech and behavior of these people were gracious and courtly; and I noticed that they were good and serious listeners when anybody was telling anything —I mean in a dogfightless interval. And plainly, too, they were a childlike and innocent lot; telling lies of the stateliest pattern with a most gentle and winning naïvety, and ready and willing to listen to anybody else's lie, and believe it, too. It was hard to associate them with anything cruel or dreadful; and yet they dealt in tales of blood and suffering with a guileless relish that made me almost forget to shudder.

I was not the only prisoner present. There were twenty or more. Poor devils, many of them were maimed, hacked, carved, in a frightful way; and their hair, their faces, their clothing, were caked with black and stiffened drenchings of blood. They were suffering sharp physical pain, of course; and weariness, and hunger and thirst, no doubt; and at least none had given them the comfort of a wash, or even the poor charity of a lotion for their wounds; yet you never heard them utter a moan or a groan, or saw them show any sign of restlessness, or any disposition to complain. The thought was forced upon me: "The rascals—*they* have served other people so in their day; it being their own turn, now, they were not expecting any better treatment than this; so their philosophical bearing is not an outcome of mental training, intellectual fortitude, reasoning; it is mere animal training; they are white Indians."

⟦ CHAPTER III ⟧

Knights of the Table Round

MAINLY THE Round Table talk was monologues—narrative accounts of the adventures in which these prisoners were captured and their friends and backers killed and

stripped of their steeds and armor. As a general thing—
as far as I could make out—these murderous adventures
were not forays undertaken to avenge injuries, nor to
settle old disputes or sudden fallings out; no, as a rule
they were simple duels between strangers—duels between
people who had never even been introduced to each
other, and between whom existed no cause of offense
whatever. Many a time I had seen a couple of boys, strangers, meet by chance, and say simultaneously, "I can lick
you," and go at it on the spot; but I had always imagined
until now, that that sort of thing belonged to children
only, and was a sign and mark of childhood; but here
were these big boobies sticking to it and taking pride in it
clear up into full age and beyond. Yet there was something very engaging about these great simplehearted creatures, something attractive and lovable. There did not
seem to be brains enough in the entire nursery, so to
speak, to bait a fishhook with; but you didn't seem to
mind that, after a little, because you soon saw that
brains were not needed in a society like that, and, indeed would have marred it, hindered it, spoiled its sym-
metry—perhaps rendered its existence impossible.

There was a fine manliness observable in almost every
face; and in some a certain loftiness and sweetness
that rebuked your belittling criticisms and stilled them.
A most noble benignity and purity reposed in the countenance of him they called Sir Galahad, and likewise in
the king's also; and there was majesty and greatness in
the giant frame and high bearing of Sir Launcelot of
the Lake.

There was presently an incident which centered the
general interest upon this Sir Launcelot. At a sign from a
sort of master of ceremonies, six or eight of the prisoners
rose and came forward in a body and knelt on the floor
and lifted up their hands toward the ladies' gallery and
begged the grace of a word with the queen. The most
conspicuously situated lady in that massed flower bed of
feminine show and finery inclined her head by way of
assent, and then the spokesman of the prisoners delivered
himself and his fellows into her hands for free pardon,
ransom, captivity or death, as she in her good pleasure might elect; and this, as he said, he was doing by

command of Sir Kay the Seneschal, whose prisoners they
were, he having vanquished them by his single might and
prowess in sturdy conflict in the field.

Surprise and astonishment flashed from face to face
all over the house; the queen's gratified smile faded out
at the name of Sir Kay, and she looked disappointed;
and the page whispered in my ear with an accent and
manner expressive of extravagant derision—

"Sir *Kay,* forsooth! Oh, call me pet names, dearest, call
me a marine! In twice a thousand years shall the unholy
invention of man labor at odds to beget the fellow to this
majestic lie!"

Every eye was fastened with severe inquiry upon Sir
Kay. But he was equal to the occasion. He got up and
played his hand like a major—and took every trick. He
said he would state the case, exactly according to the
facts; he would tell the simple straightforward tale, without comment of his own; "and then," said he, "if ye find
glory and honor due, ye will give it unto him who is the
mightiest man of his hands that ever bare shield or strake
with sword in the ranks of Christian battle—even him that
sitteth there!" and he pointed to Sir Launcelot. Ah, he
fetched them; it was a rattling good stroke. Then he went
on and told how Sir Launcelot, seeking adventures, some
brief time gone by, killed seven giants at one sweep of
his sword, and set a hundred and forty-two captive
maidens free; and then went further, still seeking adventures, and found him (Sir Kay) fighting a desperate fight
against nine foreign knights, and straightway took the battle solely into his own hands, and conquered the nine;
and that night Sir Launcelot rose quietly, and dressed him
in Sir Kay's armor and took Sir Kay's horse and gat him
away into distant lands, and vanquished sixteen knights
in one pitched battle and thirty-four in another; and all
these and the former nine he made to swear that about
Whitsuntide they would ride to Arthur's court and yield
them to Queen Guenever's hands as captives of Sir Kay
the Seneschal, spoil of his knightly prowess; and now
here were these half dozen, and the rest would be along
as soon as they might be healed of their desperate
wounds.

Well, it was touching to see the queen blush and smile,

and look embarrassed and happy, and fling furtive glances at Sir Launcelot that would have got him shot in Arkansas, to a dead certainty.

Everybody praised the valor and magnanimity of Sir Launcelot; and as for me, I was perfectly amazed, that one man, all by himself, should have been able to beat down and capture such battalions of practiced fighters. I said as much to Clarence; but this mocking featherhead only said—

"An Sir Kay had had time to get another skin of sour wine into him, ye had seen the accompt doubled."

I looked at the boy in sorrow; and as I looked I saw the cloud of a deep despondency settle upon his counte-nance. I followed the direction of his eye, and saw that a very old and white-bearded man, clothed in a flowing black gown, had risen and was standing at the table upon unsteady legs, and feebly swaying his ancient head and surveying the company with his watery and wandering eye. The same suffering look that was in the page's face was observable in all the faces around—the look of dumb creatures who know that they must endure and make no moan.

"Marry, we shall have it again," sighed the boy; "that same old weary tale that he hath told a thousand times in the same words, and that he *will* tell till he dieth, every time he hath gotten his barrel full and feeleth his exag-geration-mill a-working. Would God I had died or I saw this day!"

"Who is it?"

"Merlin, the mighty liar and magician, perdition singe him for the weariness he worketh with his one tale! But that men fear him for that he hath the storms and the lightnings and all the devils that be in hell at his beck and call, they would have dug his entrails out these many years ago to get at that tale and squelch it. He telleth it always in the third person, making believe he is too modest to glorify himself—maledictions light upon him, misfortune be his dole! Good friend, prithee call me for evensong."

The boy nestled himself upon my shoulder and pre-tended to go to sleep. The old man began his tale; and

presently the lad was asleep in reality; so also were the
dogs, and the court, the lackeys, and the files of men-
at-arms. The droning voice droned on; a soft snoring
arose on all sides and supported it like a deep and subdued accompaniment of wind instruments. Some heads
were bowed upon folded arms, some lay back with open
mouths that issued unconscious music; the flies buzzed
and bit, unmolested, the rats swarmed softly out from a
hundred holes, and pattered about, and made themselves
at home everywhere; and one of them sat up like a squirrel on the king's head and held a bit of cheese in its hands
and nibbled it, and dribbled the crumbs in the king's
face with naïve and impudent irreverence. It was a tranquil scene, and restful to the weary eye and the jaded
spirit.

This was the old man's tale. He said:

"Right so the king and Merlin departed, and went until
an hermit that was a good man and a great leech. So the
hermit searched all his wounds and gave him good
salves; so the king was there three days, and then were
his wounds well amended that he might ride and go, and
so departed. And as they rode, Arthur said, I have no
sword. No force,* said Merlin, hereby is a sword that
shall be yours and I may. So they rode till they came to a
lake, the which was a fair water and broad, and in the
midst of the lake Arthur was ware of an arm clothed in
white samite, that held a fair sword in that hand. Lo, said
Merlin, yonder is that sword that I spake of. With that
they saw a damsel going upon the lake. What damsel is
that? said Arthur. That is the Lady of the lake, said Merlin;
and within that lake is a rock, and therein is as fair a
place as any on earth, and richly beseen, and this damsel
will come to you anon, and then speak ye fair to her that
she will give you that sword. Anon withal came the damsel unto Arthur and saluted him, and he her again. Damsel, said Arthur, what sword is that, that yonder the arm
holdeth above the water? I would it were mine, for I have
no sword. Sir Arthur King, said the damsel, that sword
is mine, and if ye will give me a gift when I ask it you, ye
shall have it. By my faith, said Arthur, I will give you

* No matter.

what gift ye will ask. Well, said the damsel, go ye into yonder barge and row yourself to the sword, and take it and the scabbard with you, and I will ask my gift when I see my time. So Sir Arthur and Merlin alight, and tied their horses to two trees, and so they went into the ship, and when they came to the sword that the hand held, Sir Arthur took it up by the handles, and took it with him. And the arm and the hand went under the water; and so they came into the land and rode forth. And then Sir Arthur saw a rich pavilion. What signifieth yonder pavilion? It is the knight's pavilion, said Merlin, that ye fought with last, Sir Pellinore, but he is out, he is not there; he hath ado with a knight of yours, that hight Egglame, and they have fought together, but at the last Egglame fled, and else he had been dead, and he hath chased him even to Carlion, and we shall meet with him anon in the highway. That is well said, said Arthur, now have I a sword, now will I wage battle with him, and be avenged on him. Sir, ye shall not so, said Merlin, for the knight is weary of fighting and chasing, so that ye shall have no worship to have ado with him; also, he will not lightly be matched of one knight living; and therefore it is my counsel, let him pass, for he shall do you good service in short time, and his sons, after his days. Also ye shall see that day in short space ye shall be right glad to give him your sister to wed. When I see him, I will do as ye advise me, said Arthur. Then Sir Arthur looked on the sword, and liked it passing well. Whether liketh you better, said Merlin, the sword or the scabbard? Me liketh better the sword, said Arthur. Ye are more unwise, said Merlin, for the scabbard is worth ten of the sword, for while ye have the scabbard upon you ye shall never lose no blood, be ye never so sore wounded; therefore, keep well the scabbard always with you. So they rode unto Carlion, and by the way they met with Sir Pellinore; but Merlin had done such a craft that Pellinore saw not Arthur, and he passed by without any words. I marvel, said Arthur, that the knight would not speak. Sir, said Merlin, he saw you not; for and he had seen you ye had not lightly departed. So they came unto Carlion, whereof his knights were passing glad. And when

they heard of his adventures they marveled that he
would jeopard his person so alone. But all men of worship
said it was merry to be under such a chieftain that would
put his person in adventure as other poor knights did."

⟦ CHAPTER IV ⟧

Sir Dinadan the Humorist

IT SEEMED to me that this quaint lie was most simply
and beautifully told; but then I had heard it only once,
and that makes a difference; it was pleasant to the others
when it was fresh, no doubt.

Sir Dinadan the Humorist was the first to awake, and
he soon roused the rest with a practical joke of a sufficiently poor quality. He tied some metal mugs to a dog's
tail and turned him loose, and he tore around and
around the place in a frenzy of fright, with all the other
dogs bellowing after him and battering and crashing
against everything that came in their way and making altogether a chaos of confusion and a most deafening din
and turmoil; at which every man and woman of the
multitude laughed till the tears flowed, and some fell out
of their chairs and wallowed on the floor in ecstasy. It
was just like so many children. Sir Dinadan was so
proud of his exploit that he could not keep from telling
over and over again, to weariness, how the immortal idea
happened to occur to him; and as is the way with humorists of his breed, he was still laughing at it after everybody else had got through. He was so set up that he
concluded to make a speech—of course a humorous
speech. I think I never heard so many old played out
jokes strung together in my life. He was worse than the
minstrels, worse than the clown in the circus. It seemed
peculiarly sad to sit here, thirteen hundred years before
I was born and listen again to poor, flat, worm-eaten
jokes that had given me the dry gripes when I was a boy
thirteen hundred years afterwards. It about convinced me

that there isn't any such thing as a new joke possible. Everybody laughed at these antiquities—but then they always do; I had noticed that, centuries later. However, of course the scoffer didn't laugh—I mean the boy. No, he scoffed; there wasn't anything he wouldn't scoff at. He said the most of Sir Dinadan's jokes were rotten and the rest were petrified. I said "petrified" was good; as I believed, myself, that the only right way to classify the majestic ages of some of those jokes was by geologic periods. But that neat idea hit the boy in a blank place, for geology hadn't been invented yet. However, I made a note of the remark, and calculated to educate the commonwealth up to it if I pulled through. It is no use to throw a good thing away merely because the market isn't ripe yet.

Now Sir Kay arose and began to fire up on his history-mill, with me for fuel. It was time for me to feel serious, and I did. Sir Kay told how he had encountered me in a far land of barbarians, who all wore the same ridiculous garb that I did—a garb that was a work of enchantment, and intended to make the wearer secure from hurt by human hands. However, he had nullified the force of the enchantment by prayer, and had killed my thirteen knights in a three-hours' battle, and taken me prisoner, sparing my life in order that so strange a curiosity as I was might be exhibited to the wonder and admiration of the king and the court. He spoke of me all the time, in the blandest way, as "this prodigious giant," and "this horrible sky-towering monster," and "this tusked and taloned man-devouring ogre;" and everybody took in all this bosh in the naïvest way, and never smiled or seemed to notice that there was any discrepancy between these watered statistics and me. He said that in trying to escape from him I sprang into the top of a tree two hundred cubits high at a single bound, but he dislodged me with a stone the size of a cow, which "all-to brast" the most of my bones, and then swore me to appear at Arthur's court for sentence. He ended by condemning me to die at noon on the twenty-first; and was so little concerned about it that he stopped to yawn before he named the date.

I was in a dismal state by this time; indeed, I was

hardly enough in my right mind to keep the run of a
dispute that sprung up as to how I had better be killed,
the possibility of the killing being doubted by some, because of the enchantment in my clothes. And yet it was
nothing but an ordinary suit of fifteen-dollar slopshops.
Still, I was sane enough to notice this detail, to wit: many
of the terms used in the most matter-of-fact way by this
great assemblage of the first ladies and gentlemen in the
land would have made a Comanche blush. Indelicacy is
too mild a term to convey the idea. However, I had read
"Tom Jones" and "Roderick Random," and other books
of that kind, and knew that the highest and first ladies
and gentlemen in England had remained little or no cleaner
in their talk, and in the morals and conduct which such
talk implies, clear up to a hundred years ago; in fact
clear into our own nineteenth century—in which century,
broadly speaking, the earliest samples of the real lady
and real gentleman discoverable in English history—or in
European history, for that matter—may be said to have
made their appearance. Suppose Sir Walter, instead of
putting the conversation into the mouths of his characters, had allowed the characters to speak for themselves? We should have had talk from Rachel and Ivanhoe
and the soft lady Rowena which would embarrass a tramp
in our day. However, to the unconsciously indelicate all
things are delicate. King Arthur's people were not aware
that they were indecent, and I had presence of mind
enough not to mention it.

They were so troubled about my enchanted clothes
that they were mightily relieved, at last, when old Merlin
swept the difficulty away for them with a commonsense
hint. He asked them why they were so dull—why didn't it
occur to them to strip me. In half a minute I was as
naked as a pair of tongs! And dear, dear, to think of it: I
was the only embarrassed person there. Everybody discussed me; and did it as unconcernedly as if I had been a
cabbage. Queen Guenever was as naïvely interested as
the rest, and said she had never seen anybody with
legs just like mine before. It was the only compliment I
got—if it was a compliment.

Finally I was carried off in one direction, and my

perilous clothes in another. I was shoved into a dark and narrow cell in a dungeon, with some scant remnants for dinner, some moldy straw for a bed, and no end of rats for company.

{ CHAPTER V }

An Inspiration

I WAS SO TIRED that even my fears were not able to keep me awake long.

When I next came to myself, I seemed to have been asleep a very long time. My first thought was, "Well, what an astonishing dream I've had! I reckon I've waked only just in time to keep from being hanged or drowned or burned, or something. . . . I'll nap again till the whistle blows, and then I'll go down to the arms factory and have it out with Hercules."

But just then I heard the harsh music of rusty chains and bolts, a light flashed in my eyes, and that butterfly, Clarence, stood before me! I gasped with surprise; my breath almost got away from me.

"What!" I said, "you here yet? Go along with the rest of the dream! scatter!"

But he only laughed, in his lighthearted way, and fell to making fun of my sorry plight.

"All right," I said resignedly, "let the dream go on; I'm in no hurry."

"Prithee what dream?"

"What dream? Why, the dream that I am in Arthur's court—a person who never existed; and that I am talking to you, who are nothing but a work of the imagination."

"Oh, la, indeed! And is it a dream that you're to be burned tomorrow? Ho-ho—answer me that!"

The shock that went through me was distressing. I now began to reason that my situation was in the last degree serious, dream or no dream; for I knew by past experience of the lifelike intensity of dreams, that to be burned to death, even in a dream, would be very far from being a jest, and was a thing to be avoided, by any means, fair or foul, that I could contrive. So I said beseechingly:

"Ah, Clarence, good boy, only friend I've got—for you *are* my friend, aren't you—don't fail me; help me to devise some way of escaping from this place!"

"Now do but hear thyself! Escape? Why, man, the corridors are in guard and keep of men-at-arms."

"No doubt, no doubt. But how many, Clarence? Not many, I hope?"

"Full a score. One may not hope to escape." After a pause—hesitatingly: "and there be other reasons—and weightier."

"Other ones? What are they?"

"Well, they say—oh, but I daren't, indeed I daren't!"

"Why, poor lad, what is the matter? Why do you blench? Why do you tremble so?"

"Oh, in sooth, there is need! I do want to tell you, but—"

"Come, come, be brave, be a man—speak out, there's a good lad!"

He hesitated, pulled one way by desire, the other way by fear; then he stole to the door and peeped out, listening; and finally crept close to me and put his mouth to my ear and told me his fearful news in a whisper, and with all the cowering apprehension of one who was venturing upon awful ground and speaking of things whose very mention might be freighted with death.

"Merlin, in his malice, has woven a spell about this dungeon, and there bides not the man in these kingdoms that would be desperate enough to essay to cross its lines with you! Now God pity me, I have told it! Ah, be kind to me, be merciful to a poor boy who means thee well; for an thou betray me I am lost!"

I laughed the only really refreshing laugh I had had for some time; and shouted—

"Merlin has wrought a spell! *Merlin*, forsooth! That cheap old humbug, that maundering old ass? Bosh, pure bosh, the silliest bosh in the world! Why, it does seem to me that of all the childish, idiotic, chuckleheaded, chicken-livered superstitions that ev—oh, damn Merlin!"

But Clarence had slumped to his knees before I had

half finished, and he was like to go out of his mind with fright.

"Oh, beware! These are awful words! Any moment these walls may crumble upon us if you say such things. Oh call them back before it is too late!"

Now this strange exhibition gave me a good idea and set me to thinking. If everybody about here was so honestly and sincerely afraid of Merlin's pretended magic as Clarence was, certainly a superior man like me ought to be shrewd enough to contrive some way to take advantage of such a state of things. I went on thinking, and worked out a plan. Then I said:

"Get up. Pull yourself together; look me in the eye. Do you know why I laughed?"

"No—but for our blessed Lady's sake, do it no more."

"Well, I'll tell you why I laughed. Because I'm a magician myself."

"Thou!" The boy recoiled a step, and caught his breath, for the thing hit him rather sudden; but the aspect which he took on was very, very respectful. I took quick note of that; it indicated that a humbug didn't need to have a reputation in this asylum; people stood ready to take him at his word, without that. I resumed:

"I've known Merlin seven hundred years, and he—"

"Seven hun—"

"Don't interrupt me. He has died and come alive again thirteen times, and traveled under a new name every time: Smith, Jones, Robinson, Jackson, Peters, Haskins, Merlin—a new alias every time he turns up. I knew him in Egypt three hundred years ago; I knew him in India five hundred years ago—he is always blethering around in my way, everywhere I go; he makes me tired. He don't amount to shucks, as a magician; knows some of the old common tricks, but has never got beyond the rudiments, and never will. He is well enough for the provinces—one-night stands and that sort of thing, you know—but dear me, *he* oughtn't to set up for an expert—anyway not where there's a real artist. Now look here, Clarence, I am going to stand your friend, right along, and in return you must be mine. I want you to do me a favor. I want you to get word to the king that I am a magician myself—and the Supreme Grand High-yu-Muckamuck and head of the tribe, at that; and I want him to be made to understand that I am just quietly arranging a little calamity here that will make the fur fly in these realms if Sir Kay's project is carried out and any harm comes to me. Will you get that to the king for me?"

The poor boy was in such a state that he could hardly answer me. It was pitiful to see a creature so terrified, so unnerved, so demoralized. But he promised everything; and on my side he made me promise over and over again that I would remain his friend, and never turn against him or cast any enchantments upon him. Then he worked his way out, staying himself with his hand along the wall, like a sick person.

Presently this thought occurred to me: how heedless I have been! When the boy gets calm, he will wonder why a great magician like me should have begged a boy like him to help me get out of this place; he will put this and that together, and will see that I am a humbug.

I worried over that heedless blunder for an hour, and called myself a great many hard names, meantime. But finally it occurred to me all of a sudden that these animals didn't reason; that *they* never put this and that together; that all their talk showed that they didn't know a discrepancy when they saw it. I was at rest, then.

But as soon as one is at rest, in this world, off he goes on something else to worry about. It occurred to me that I had made another blunder: I had sent the boy off to alarm his betters with a threat—I intending to invent a calamity at my leisure; now the people who are the readiest and eagerest and willingest to swallow miracles are the very ones who are the hungriest to see you perform them; suppose I should be called on for a sample? Suppose I should be asked to name my calamity? Yes, I had made a blunder; I ought to have invented my calamity first. "What shall I do? what can I say, to gain a little time?" I was in trouble again; in the deepest kind of trouble: . . . "There's a footstep—they're coming! If I had only just a moment to think. . . . Good, I've got it. I'm all right."

You see, it was the eclipse. It came into my mind, in the nick of time, how Columbus, or Cortez, or one of those people, played an eclipse as a saving trump once, on some savages, and I saw my chance. I could play it myself, now; and it wouldn't be any plagiarism, either, because I should get it in nearly a thousand years ahead of those parties.

Clarence came in, subdued, distressed, and said:

"I hasted the message to our liege the king, and straightway he had me to his presence. He was frighted even to the marrow, and was minded to give order for your instant enlargement, and that you be clothed in fine raiment and lodged as befitted one so great; but then came Merlin and spoiled all; for he persuaded the king that you are mad, and know not whereof you speak; and said your threat is but foolishness and idle vaporing. They disputed long, but in the end, Merlin, scoffing, said, 'Wherefore hath he not *named* his brave calamity? Verily it is because he cannot.' This thrust did in a most sudden sort close the king's mouth, and he could offer naught to turn the argument; and so, reluctant, and full loth to do you the discourtesy, he yet prayeth you to consider his perplexed case, as noting how the matter stands, and name the calamity—if so be you have determined the nature of it and the time of its coming. Oh, prithee delay not; to delay at such a time were to double and treble the perils that already compass thee about. Oh, be thou wise—name the calamity!"

I allowed silence to accumulate while I got my impressiveness together, and then said:

"How long have I been shut up in this hole?"

"Ye were shut up when yesterday was well spent. It is nine of the morning now."

"No! Then I have slept well, sure enough. Nine in the morning now! And yet it is the very complexion of midnight, to a shade. This is the 20th, then?"

"The 20th—yes."

"And I am to be burned alive tomorrow." The boy shuddered.

"At what hour?"

"At high noon."

"Now then, I will tell you what to say." I paused, and stood over that cowering lad a whole minute in awful silence; then in a voice deep, measured, charged with doom, I began, and rose by dramatically graded stages to my colossal climax, which I delivered in as sublime and noble a way as ever I did such a thing in my life: "Go back and tell the king that at that hour I will smother the whole world in the dead blackness of midnight; I will blot out the sun, and he shall never shine again; the fruits of the earth shall rot for lack of light and warmth, and the peoples of the earth shall famish and die, to the last man!"

I had to carry the boy out myself, he sunk into such a collapse. I handed him over to the soldiers, and went back.

❲ CHAPTER VI ❳

The Eclipse

IN THE STILLNESS and the darkness, realization soon began to supplement knowledge. The mere knowledge of a fact is pale; but when you come to *realize* your fact, it takes on color. It is all the difference between hearing of a man being stabbed to the heart, and seeing it done. In the stillness and the darkness, the knowledge that I was in deadly danger took to itself deeper and deeper meaning all the time; a something which was realization crept inch by inch through my veins and turned me cold.

But it is a blessed provision of nature that at times like these, as soon as a man's mercury has got down to a certain point there comes a revulsion, and he rallies. Hope springs up, and cheerfulness along with it, and then he is in good shape to do something for himself, if anything can be done. When my rally came, it came with a bound. I said to myself that my eclipse would be sure to save me, and make me the greatest man in the kingdom besides; and straightway my mercury went up to the top of the tube, and my solicitudes all vanished. I was as happy a man as there was in the world. I was even impatient for tomorrow to come, I so wanted to gather in that great triumph and be the center of all the nation's wonder and reverence. Besides, in a business way it would be the making of me; I knew that.

Meantime there was one thing which had got pushed into the background of my mind. That was the half conviction that when the nature of my proposed calamity should be reported to those superstitious people, it would have such an effect that they would want to compromise. So, by and by when I heard footsteps coming, that thought was recalled to me, and I said to myself, "As sure as anything, it's the compromise. Well, if it is good, all right, I will accept; but if it isn't, I mean to stand my ground and play my hand for all it is worth."

The door opened, and some men-at-arms appeared. The leader said—

"The stake is ready. Come!"

The stake! The strength went out of me, and I almost fell down. It is hard to get one's breath at such a time, such lumps come into one's throat, and such gaspings, but as soon as I could speak, I said:

"But this is a mistake—the execution is tomorrow."

"Order changed; been set forward a day. Haste thee!"

I was lost. There was no help for me. I was dazed, stupefied; I had no command over myself; I only wandered purposelessly about, like one out of his mind; so the soldiers took hold of me, and pulled me along with them, out of the cell and along the maze of underground corridors, and finally into the fierce glare of daylight and the upper world. As we stepped into the vast inclosed court of the castle I got a shock; for the first thing I saw was the stake, standing in the center, and near it the piled fagots and a monk. On all four sides of the court the seated multitudes rose rank above rank, forming sloping terraces that were rich with color. The king and the queen sat in their thrones, the most conspicuous figures there, of course.

To note all this, occupied but a second. The next second Clarence had slipped from some place of concealment and was pouring news into my ear, his eyes beaming with triumph and gladness. He said:

" 'Tis through *me* the change was wrought! And main hard have I worked to do it, too. But when I revealed to them the calamity in store, and saw how mighty was the terror it did engender, then saw I also that this was the time to strike! Wherefore I diligently pretended, unto this and that and the other one, that your power against the sun could not reach its full until the morrow; and so if any would save the sun and the world, you must be slain today, whilst your enchantments are but in the weaving and lack potency. Odsbodikins, it was but a dull lie, a most indifferent invention, but you should have seen them seize it and swallow it, in the frenzy of their fright, as it were salvation sent from heaven; and all the while was I laughing in my sleeve the one moment, to see them so cheaply deceived, and glorifying God the next, that He was content to let the meanest of His creatures be His instrument to the saving of thy life. Ah, how happy has the matter sped! You will not need to do the sun a *real* hurt—ah, forget not that, on your soul forget it not! Only make a little darkness—only the littlest little darkness, mind, and cease with that. It will be sufficient. They will see that I spoke falsely,—being ignorant, as they will fancy—and with the falling of the first shadow of that darkness you shall see them go mad with fear; and they will set you free and make you great! Go to thy triumph, now! But remember—ah, good friend, I implore thee remember my supplication, and do the blessed sun no hurt. For *my* sake, thy true friend."

I choked out some words through my grief and misery; as much as to say I would spare the sun; for which the lad's eyes paid me back with such deep and loving gratitude that I had not the heart to tell him his good-hearted foolishness had ruined me and sent me to my death.

As the soldiers assisted me across the court the stillness was so profound that if I had been blindfold I should have supposed I was in a solitude instead of walled in by four thousand people. There was not a movement perceptible in those masses of humanity; they were as rigid as stone images, and as pale; and dread sat upon every countenance. This hush continued while I was being chained to the stake; it still continued while the fagots were carefully and tediously piled about my ankles, my knees, my thighs, my body. Then there was a pause, and a deeper hush, if possible, and a man knelt down at my feet with a blazing torch; the multitude strained forward, gazing, and parting slightly from their seats without knowing it; the monk raised his hands above my head, and his eyes toward the blue sky, and began some words in Latin; in this attitude he droned on and on, a little while, and then stopped. I waited two or three moments: then looked up; he was standing there petrified. With a common impulse the multitude rose slowly up and stared into the sky. I followed their eyes; as sure as guns, there was my eclipse beginning! The life went boiling through my veins; I was a new man! The rim of black spread slowly into the sun's disk, my heart beat higher and higher, and still the assemblage and the priest stared into the sky, motionless. I knew that this gaze would be turned upon me, next. When it was, I was ready. I was in one of the most grand attitudes I ever struck, with my arm stretched up pointing to the sun. It was a noble effect. You could *see* the shudder sweep the mass like a wave. Two shouts rang out, one close upon the heels of the other:

"Apply the torch!"

"I forbid it!"

The one was from Merlin, the other from the king. Merlin started from his place—to apply the torch himself, I judged. I said:

"Stay where you are. If any man moves—even the king—before I give him leave, I will blast him with thunder, I will consume him with lightnings!"

The multitude sank meekly into their seats, and I was just expecting they would. Merlin hesitated a moment or two, and I was on pins and needles during that little while. Then he sat down, and I took a good breath; for I knew I was master of the situation now. The king said:

"Be merciful, fair sir, and essay no further in this perilous matter, lest disaster follow. It was reported to us that your powers could not attain unto their full strength until the morrow; but"—

"Your Majesty thinks the report may have been a lie? It *was* a lie."

That made an immense effect; up went appealing hands everywhere, and the king was assailed with a storm of supplications that I might be bought off at any price, and the calamity stayed. The king was eager to comply. He said:

"Name any terms, reverend sir, even to the halving of my kingdom; but banish this calamity, spare the sun!"

My fortune was made. I would have taken him up in a minute, but *I* couldn't stop an eclipse; the thing was out of the question. So I asked time to consider. The king said—

"How long—ah, how long, good sir? Be merciful; look, it groweth darker, moment by moment. Prithee how long?"

"Not long. Half an hour—maybe an hour."

There were a thousand pathetic protests, but I couldn't shorten up any, for I couldn't remember how long a total eclipse lasts. I was in a puzzled condition, anyway, and wanted to think. Something was wrong about that eclipse, and the fact was very unsettling. If this wasn't the one I was after, how was I to tell whether this was the sixth century, or nothing but a dream? Dear me, if I could only prove it was the latter! Here was a glad new hope. If the boy was right about the date, and this was surely the twentieth, it *wasn't* the sixth century. I reached for the monk's sleeve, in considerable excitement, and asked him what day of the month it was.

Hang him, he said it was the *twenty-first!* It made me turn cold to hear him. I begged him not to make any mistake about it; but he was sure; he knew it was the twenty-first. So, that featherheaded boy had botched things again! The time of the day was right for the eclipse; I had seen that for myself, in the beginning, by the dial that was nearby. Yes, I *was* in King Arthur's court, and I might as well make the most out of it I could.

The darkness was steadily growing, the people becoming more and more distressed. I now said:

"I have reflected, Sir King. For a lesson, I will let this darkness proceed, and spread night in the world; but whether I blot out the sun for good, or restore it, shall rest with you. These are the terms, to wit: You shall remain king over all your dominions, and receive all the glories and honors that belong to the kingship; but you shall appoint me your perpetual minister and executive, and give me for my services one per cent of such actual increase of revenue over and above its present amount as I may succeed in creating for the state. If I can't live on that, I shan't ask anybody to give me a lift. Is it satisfactory?"

There was a prodigious roar of applause, and out of the midst of it the king's voice rose, saying:

"Away with his bonds, and set him free! and do him homage, high and low, rich and poor, for he is become the king's right hand, is clothed with power and authority, and his seat is upon the highest step of the throne! Now sweep away this creeping night, and bring the light and cheer again, that all the world may bless thee."

But I said:

"That a common man should be shamed before the world, is nothing; but it were dishonor to the *king* if any that saw his minister naked should not also see him delivered from his shame. If I might ask that my clothes be brought again—"

"They are not meet," the king broke in. "Fetch raiment of another sort; clothe him like a prince!"

My idea worked. I wanted to keep things as they were till the eclipse was total, otherwise they would be trying again to get me to dismiss the darkness, and of course I couldn't do it. Sending for the clothes gained some delay, but not enough. So I had to make another excuse. I said it would be but natural if the king should change his mind and repent to some extent of what he had done under excitement; therefore I would let the darkness grow a while, and if at the end of a reasonable time the king had kept his mind the same, the darkness should be dismissed. Neither the king nor anybody else was satisfied with that arrangement, but I had to stick to my point.

It grew darker and darker and blacker and blacker, while I struggled with those awkward sixth-century clothes. It got to be pitch dark, at last, and the multitude groaned with horror to feel the cold uncanny night breezes fan through the place and see the stars come out and twinkle in the sky. At last the eclipse was total, and I was very glad of it, but everybody else was in misery; which was quite natural. I said:

"The king, by his silence, still stands to the terms."

Then I lifted up my hands—stood just so a moment—
then I said, with the most awful solemnity: "Let the enchantment dissolve and pass harmless away!"

There was no response, for a moment, in that deep
darkness and that graveyard hush. But when the silver
rim of the sun pushed itself out a moment or two later,
the assemblage broke loose with a vast shout and came
pouring down like a deluge to smother me with blessings
and gratitude; and Clarence was not the last of the wash,
be sure.

⟦ CHAPTER VII ⟧

Merlin's Tower

INASMUCH as I was now the second personage in the
Kingdom, as far as political power and authority were
concerned, much was made of me. My raiment was of
silks and velvets and cloth of gold, and by consequence
was very showy, also uncomfortable. But habit would
soon reconcile me to my clothes; I was aware of that. I
was given the choicest suite of apartments in the castle, after the king's. They were aglow with loud-colored
silken hangings, but the stone floors had nothing but
rushes on them for a carpet, and they were misfit rushes
at that, being not all of one breed. As for conveniences,
properly speaking, there weren't any. I mean *little* conveniences; it is the little conveniences that make the real
comfort of life. The big oaken chairs, graced with rude
carvings, were well enough, but that was the stopping
place. There was no soap, no matches, no looking glass
—except a metal one, about as powerful as a pail of
water. And not a chromo. I had been used to chromos
for years, and I saw now that without my suspecting it a
passion for art had got worked into the fabric of my
being, and was become a part of me. It made me home-
sick to look around over this proud and gaudy but heartless barrenness and remember that in our house in East

Hartford, all unpretending as it was, you couldn't go into a room but you would find an insurance chromo, or at least a three-color God-Bless-Our-Home over the door; and in the parlor we had nine. But here, even in my grand room of state, there wasn't anything in the nature of a picture except a thing the size of a bed quilt, which was either woven or knitted (it had darned places in it), and nothing in it was the right color or the right shape; and as for proportions, even Raphael himself couldn't have botched them more formidably, after all his practice on those nightmares they call his "celebrated Hampton Court cartoons." Raphael was a bird. We had several of his chromos; one was his "Miraculous Draught of Fishes," where he puts in a miracle of his own—puts three men into a canoe which wouldn't have held a dog without upsetting. I always admired to study R.'s art, it was so fresh and unconventional.

There wasn't even a bell or a speaking tube in the castle. I had a great many servants, and those that were on duty lolled in the anteroom; and when I wanted one of them I had to go and call for him. There was no gas, there were no candles; a bronze dish half full of boarding-house butter with a blazing rag floating in it was the thing that produced what was regarded as light. A lot of these hung along the walls and modified the dark, just toned it down enough to make it dismal. If you went out at night, your servants carried torches. There were no books, pens, paper, or ink, and no glass in the openings they believed to be windows. It is a little thing—glass is —until it is absent, then it becomes a big thing. But perhaps the worst of all was, that there wasn't any sugar, coffee, tea, or tobacco. I saw that I was just another Robinson Crusoe cast away on an uninhabited island, with no society but some more or less tame animals, and if I wanted to make life bearable I must do as he did— invent, contrive, create, reorganize things; set brain and hand to work, and keep them busy. Well, that was in my line.

One thing troubled me along at first—the immense interest which people took in me. Apparently the whole nation wanted a look at me. It soon transpired that the eclipse had scared the British world almost to death:

that while it lasted the whole country, from one end
to the other, was in a pitiable state of panic, and the
churches, hermitages, and monkeries overflowed with
praying and weeping poor creatures who thought the
end of the world was come. Then had followed the news
that the producer of this awful event was a stranger, a
mighty magician at Arthur's court; that he could have
blown out the sun like a candle, and was just going to
do it when his mercy was purchased, and he then dissolved his enchantments, and was now recognized and
honored as the man who had by his unaided might saved
the globe from destruction and its peoples from extinc-
tion. Now if you consider that everybody believed that,
and not only believed it but never even dreamed of
doubting it, you will easily understand that there was not
a person in all Britain that would not have walked fifty
miles to get a sight of me. Of course I was all the talk—
all other subjects were dropped; even the king became
suddenly a person of minor interest and notoriety. Within
twenty-four hours the delegations began to arrive, and
from that time onward for a fortnight they kept coming.
The village was crowded, and all the countryside. I had
to go out a dozen times a day and show myself to these
reverent and awestricken multitudes. It came to be a
great burden, as to time and trouble, but of course it
was at the same time compensatingly agreeable to be so
celebrated and such a center of homage. It turned Brer
Merlin green with envy and spite, which was a great satisfaction to me. But there was one thing I couldn't understand; nobody had asked for an autograph. I spoke to
Clarence about it. By George, I had to explain to him
what it was. Then he said nobody in the country could
read or write but a few dozen priests. Land! think of
that.

There was another thing that troubled me a little.
Those multitudes presently began to agitate for another
miracle. That was natural. To be able to carry back to
their far homes the boast that they had seen the man
who could command the sun, riding in the heavens, and
be obeyed, would make them great in the eyes of their
neighbors, and envied by them all; but to be able to also
say they had seen him work a miracle themselves—why,

people would come a distance to see *them*. The pressure got to be pretty strong. There was going to be an eclipse of the moon, and I knew the date and hour, but it was too far away. Two years. I would have given a good deal for license to hurry it up and use it now when there was a big market for it. It seemed a great pity to have it wasted so, and come lagging along at a time when a body wouldn't have any use for it as like as not. If it had been booked for only a month away, I could have sold it short; but as matters stood, I couldn't seem to cipher out any way to make it do me any good, so I gave up trying. Next, Clarence found that old Merlin was making himself busy on the sly among those people. He was spreading a report that I was a humbug, and that the reason I didn't accommodate the people with a miracle was because I couldn't. I saw that I must do something. I presently thought out a plan.

By my authority as executive I threw Merlin into prison—the same cell I had occupied myself. Then I gave public notice by herald and trumpet that I should be busy with affairs of state for a fortnight, but about the end of that time I would take a moment's leisure and blow up Merlin's stone tower by fires from heaven; in the meantime, whoso listened to evil reports about me, let him beware. Furthermore, I would perform but this one miracle at this time, and no more; if it failed to satisfy and any murmured, I would turn the murmurers into horses, and make them useful. Quiet ensued.

I took Clarence into my confidence, to a certain degree, and we went to work privately. I told him that this was a sort of miracle that required a trifle of preparation; and that it would be sudden death to ever talk about these preparations to anybody. That made his mouth safe enough. Clandestinely we made a few bushels of first-rate blasting powder, and I superintended my armorers while they constructed a lightning rod and some wires. This old stone tower was very massive—and rather ruinous, too, for it was Roman, and four hundred years old. Yes, and handsome, after a rude fashion, and clothed with ivy from base to summit, as with a shirt of scale mail. It stood on a lonely eminence, in good view from the castle, and about half a mile away.

Working by night, we stowed the powder in the tower
—dug stones out, on the inside, and buried the powder
in the walls themselves, which were fifteen feet thick at
the base. We put in a peck at a time, in a dozen places.
We could have blown up the Tower of London with
these charges. When the thirteenth night was come we
put up our lightning rod, bedded it in one of the batches
of powder, and ran wires from it to the other batches.
Everybody had shunned that locality from the day of
my proclamation, but on the morning of the fourteenth
I thought best to warn the people, through the heralds, to
keep clear away—a quarter of a mile away. Then added,
by command, that at some time during the twenty-four
hours I would consummate the miracle, but would first
give a brief notice; by flags on the castle towers, if in the
daytime, by torch baskets in the same places if at night.

Thundershowers had been tolerably frequent, of late,
and I was not much afraid of a failure; still, I shouldn't
have cared for a delay of a day or two; I should have
explained that I was busy with affairs of state, yet, and
the people must wait.

Of course we had a blazing sunny day—almost the
first one without a cloud for three weeks; things always
happen so. I kept secluded, and watched the weather.
Clarence dropped in from time to time and said the public excitement was growing and growing all the time, and
the whole country filling up with human masses as far
as one could see from the battlements. At last the wind
sprang up and a cloud appeared—in the right quarter,
too, and just at nightfall. For a little while I watched that
distant cloud spread and blacken, then I judged it was
time for me to appear. I ordered the torch baskets to be
lit, and Merlin liberated and sent to me. A quarter of
an hour later I ascended the parapet and there found
the king and the court assembled and gazing off in the
darkness toward Merlin's tower. Already the darkness
was so heavy that one could not see far; these people,
and the old turrets, being partly in deep shadow and
partly in the red glow from the great torch baskets overhead, made a good deal of a picture.

Merlin arrived in a gloomy mood. I said:

"You wanted to burn me alive when I had not done

you any harm, and latterly you have been trying to injure my professional reputation. Therefore I am going to call down fire and blow up your tower, but it is only fair to give you a chance; now if you think you can break my enchantments and ward off the fires, step to the bat, it's your innings."

"I can, fair sir, and I will. Doubt it not."

He drew an imaginary circle on the stones of the roof, and burnt a pinch of powder in it which sent up a small cloud of aromatic smoke, whereat everybody fell back, and began to cross themselves and get uncomfortable. Then he began to mutter and make passes in the air with his hands. He worked himself up slowly and gradually into a sort of frenzy, and got to thrashing around with his arms like the sails of a windmill. By this time the storm had about reached us; the gusts of wind were flaring the torches and making the shadows swash about, the first heavy drops of rain were falling, the world abroad was black as pitch, the lightning began to wink fitfully. Of course my rod would be loading itself now. In fact, things were imminent. So I said:

"You have had time enough. I have given you every advantage, and not interfered. It is plain your magic is weak. It is only fair that I begin now."

I made about three passes in the air, and then there was an awful crash and that old tower leaped into the sky in chunks, along with a vast volcanic fountain of fire that turned night to noonday, and showed a thousand acres of human beings groveling on the ground in a general collapse of consternation. Well, it rained mortar and masonry the rest of the week. This was the report; but probably the facts would have modified it.

It was an effective miracle. The great bothersome temporary population vanished. There were a good many thousand tracks in the mud the next morning, but they were all outward bound. If I had advertised another miracle I couldn't have raised an audience with a sheriff.

Merlin's stock was flat. The king wanted to stop his wages; he even wanted to banish him, but I interfered. I said he would be useful to work the weather, and attend to small matters like that, and I would give him a lift now and then when his poor little parlor magic soured

on him. There wasn't a rag of his tower left, but I had
the government rebuild it for him, and advised him to
take boarders; but he was too high-toned for that. And
as for being grateful, he never even said thank-you. He
was a rather hard lot, take him how you might; but
then you couldn't fairly expect a man to be sweet that had
been set back so.

[CHAPTER VIII]

The Boss

TO BE VESTED with enormous authority is a fine thing; but
to have the onlooking world consent to it is a finer. The
tower episode solidified my power, and made it impreg-
nable. If any were perchance disposed to be jealous and
critical before that, they experienced a change of heart,
now. There was not anyone in the kingdom who would
have considered it good judgment to meddle with my
matters.

I was fast getting adjusted to my situation and circumstances. For a time, I used to wake up, mornings, and
smile at my "dream," and listen for the Colt's factory
whistle; but that sort of thing played itself out, gradually,
and at last I was fully able to realize that I was actually
living in the sixth century, and in Arthur's court, not a
lunatic asylum. After that, I was just as much at home in
that century as I could have been in any other; and as
for preference, I wouldn't have traded it for the twentieth. Look at the opportunities here for a man of knowledge, brains, pluck, and enterprise to sail in and grow up
with the country. The grandest field that ever was; and
all my own; not a competitor; not a man who wasn't a
baby to me in acquirements and capacities; whereas, what
would I amount to in the twentieth century? I should be
foreman of a factory, that is about all; and could drag a
seine downstreet any day and catch a hundred better
men than myself.

What a jump I had made! I couldn't keep from thinking about it, and contemplating it, just as one does who has struck oil. There was nothing back of me that could approach it, unless it might be Joseph's case; and Joseph's only approached it, it didn't equal it, quite. For it stands to reason that as Joseph's splendid financial ingenuities advantaged nobody but the king, the general public must have regarded him with a good deal of disfavor, whereas I had done my entire public a kindness in sparing the sun, and was popular by reason of it.

I was no shadow of a king; I was the substance; the king himself was the shadow. My power was colossal; and it was not a mere name, as such things have generally been, it was the genuine article. I stood here, at the very spring and source of the second great period of the world's history; and could see the trickling stream of that history gather, and deepen and broaden, and roll its mighty tides down the far centuries; and I could note the upspringing of adventurers like myself in the shelter of its long array of thrones: De Montforts, Gavestons, Mortimers, Villierses; the war-making, campaign-directing wantons of France, and Charles the Second's scepter-wielding drabs; but nowhere in the procession was my full-sized fellow visible. I was a Unique; and glad to know that that fact could not be dislodged or challenged for thirteen centuries and a half, for sure.

Yes, in power I was equal to the king. At the same time there was another power that was a trifle stronger than both of us put together. That was the Church. I do not wish to disguise that fact. I couldn't, if I wanted to. But never mind about that, now; it will show up, in its proper place, later on. It didn't cause me any trouble in the beginning—at least any of consequence.

Well, it was a curious country, and full of interest. And the people! They were the quaintest and simplest and trustingest race; why, they were nothing but rabbits. It was pitiful for a person born in a wholesome free atmosphere to listen to their humble and hearty outpourings of loyalty toward their king and Church and nobility; as if they had any more occasion to love and honor king and Church and noble than a slave has to love and honor the lash, or a dog has to love and honor the stranger that kicks him! Why, dear me, *any* kind of royalty, howsoever modified, *any* kind of aristocracy, howsoever prunced, is rightly an insult; but if you are born and brought up under that sort of arrangement you probably never find it out for yourself, and don't believe it when somebody else tells you. It is enough to make a body ashamed of his race to think of the sort of froth that has always occupied its thrones without shadow of right or reason, and the seventh-rate people that have always figured as its aristocracies—a company of monarchs and nobles who, as a rule, would have achieved only poverty and obscurity if left, like their betters, to their own exertions.

The most of King Arthur's British nation were slaves, pure and simple, and bore that name, and wore the iron collar on their necks; and the rest were slaves in fact, but without the name; they imagined themselves men and freemen, and called themselves so. The truth was, the nation as a body was in the world for one object, and one only: to grovel before king and Church and noble; to slave for them, sweat blood for them, starve that they might be fed, work that they might play, drink misery to the dregs that they might be happy, go naked that they might wear silks and jewels, pay taxes that they might be spared from paying them, be familiar all their lives with the degrading language and postures of adulation that they might walk in pride and think themselves the gods of this world. And for all this, the thanks they got were cuffs and contempt; and so poor-spirited were they that they took even this sort of attention as an honor.

Inherited ideas are a curious thing, and interesting to observe and examine. I had mine, the king and his people had theirs. In both cases they flowed in ruts worn deep by time and habit, and the man who should have proposed to divert them by reason and argument would have had a long contract on his hands. For instance, those people had inherited the idea that all men without title and a long pedigree, whether they had great natural gifts and acquirements or hadn't, were creatures of no more consideration than so y animals, bugs, insects; whereas I had inherited the that human daws who can consent to masquer-

ade in the peacock-shams of inherited dignities and unearned titles, are of no good but to be laughed at. The
way I was looked upon was odd, but it was natural. You
know how the keeper and the public regard the elephant
in the menagerie: well, that is the idea. They are full of
admiration of his vast bulk and his prodigious strength;
they speak with pride of the fact that he can do a hundred
marvels which are far and away beyond their own powers;
and they speak with the same pride of the fact that in his
wrath he is able to drive a thousand men before him.
But does that make him one of *them?* No; the raggedest
tramp in the pit would smile at the idea. He couldn't
comprehend it; couldn't take it in; couldn't in any remote way conceive of it. Well, to the king, the nobles,
and all the nation, down to the very slaves and tramps, I
was just that kind of an elephant, and nothing more. I
was admired, also feared; but it was as an animal is admired and feared. The animal is not reverenced, neither
was I; I was not even respected. I had no pedigree, no inherited title; so in the king's and nobles' eyes I was mere
dirt; the people regarded me with wonder and awe, but
there was no reverence mixed with it; through the force
of inherited ideas they were not able to conceive of
anything being entitled to that except pedigree and lordship. There you see the hand of that awful power, the
Roman Catholic Church. In two or three little centuries
it had converted a nation of men to a nation of worms.
Before the day of the Church's supremacy in the world,
men were men, and held their heads up, and had a man's
pride and spirit and independence; and what of greatness
and position a person got, he got mainly by achievement,
not by birth. But then the Church came to the front, with
an ax to grind; and she was wise, subtle, and knew more
than one way to skin a cat—or a nation; she invented
"divine right of kings," and propped it all around, brick
by brick, with the Beatitudes—wrenching them from
their good purpose to make them fortify an evil one; she
preached (to the commoner) humility, obedience to superiors, the beauty of self-sacrifice; she preached (to the
commoner) meekness under insult; preached (still to
the commoner, always to the commoner) patience, mean-
ness of spirit, nonresistance under oppression; and she in-

troduced heritable ranks and aristocracies, and taught all
the Christian populations of the earth to bow down to
them and worship them. Even down to my birth century
that poison was still in the blood of Christendom, and the
best of English commoners was still content to see his in-
feriors impudently continuing to hold a number of positions, such as lordships and the throne, to which the grotesque laws of his country did not allow him to aspire;
in fact he was not merely contented with this strange condition of things, he was even able to persuade himself
that he was proud of it. It seems to show that there isn't
anything you can't stand, if you are only born and bred
to it. Of course that taint, that reverence for rank and
title, had been in our American blood, too—I know that;
but when I left America it had disappeared—at least to
all intents and purposes. The remnant of it was restricted to the dudes and dudesses. When a disease has
worked its way down to that level, it may fairly be said
to be out of the system.

But to return to my anomalous position in King
Arthur's kingdom. Here I was, a giant among pigmies, a
man among children, a master intelligence among intellectual moles: by all rational measurement the one and
only actually great man in that whole British world; and
yet there and then, just as in the remote England of my
birth time, the sheep-witted earl who could claim long descent from a king's leman, acquired at secondhand from
the slums of London, was a better man than I was. Such a
personage was fawned upon in Arthur's realm and reverently looked up to by everybody, even though his dis-
positions were as mean as his intelligence, and his morals
as base as his lineage. There were times when *he* could
sit down in the king's presence, but I couldn't. I could
have got a title easily enough, and that would have raised
me a large step in everybody's eyes; even in the king's,
the giver of it. But I didn't ask for it; and I declined it
when it was offered. I couldn't have enjoyed such a thing
with my notions; and it wouldn't have been fair, anyway,
because as far back as I could go, our tribe had always
been short of the bar sinister. I couldn't have felt really
and satisfactorily fine and proud and set up over any
title except one that should come from the nation itself,

the only legitimate source; and such an one I hoped to win; and in the course of years of honest and honorable endeavor, I did win it and did wear it with a high and clean pride. This title fell casually from the lips of a blacksmith, one day, in a village, was caught up as a happy thought and tossed from mouth to mouth with a laugh and an affirmative vote; in ten days it had swept the kingdom, and was become as familiar as the king's name. I was never known by any other designation afterward, whether in the nation's talk or in grave debate upon matters of state at the council board of the sovereign. This title, translated into modern speech, would be THE BOSS. Elected by the nation. That suited me. And it was a pretty high title. There were very few THE'S, and I was one of them. If you spoke of the duke, or the earl, or the bishop, how could anybody tell which one you meant? But if you spoke of The King or The Queen or The Boss, it was different.

Well, I liked the king, and *as* king I respected him—respected the office; at least respected it as much as I was capable of respecting any unearned supremacy; but as *men* I looked down upon him and his nobles—privately. And he and they liked me, and respected my office; but as an animal, without birth or sham title, they looked down upon me—and were not particularly private about it, either. I didn't charge for my opinion about them, and they didn't charge for their opinion about me: the account was square, the books balanced, everybody was satisfied.

CHAPTER IX

The Tournament

THEY WERE always having grand tournaments there at Camelot; and very stirring and picturesque and ridiculous human bullfights they were, too, but just a little wearisome to the practical mind. However, I was generally on hand—for two reasons: a man must not hold himself

aloof from the things which his friends and his community have at heart if he would be liked—especially as a
statesman; and both as business man and statesman I
wanted to study the tournament and see if I couldn't invent an improvement on it. That reminds me to remark,
in passing, that the very first official thing I did, in my administration—and it was on the very first day of it, too—
was to start a patent office; for I knew that a country
without a patent office and good patent laws was just a
crab, and couldn't travel any way but sideways or backwards.

Things ran along, a tournament nearly every week; and
now and then the boys used to want me to take a hand—
I mean Sir Launcelot and the rest—but I said I would
by and by; no hurry yet, and too much government machinery to oil up and set to rights and start a-going.

We had one tournament which was continued from day
to day during more than a week, and as many as five
hundred knights took part in it, from first to last. They
were weeks gathering. They came on horseback from
everywhere; from the very ends of the country, and even
from beyond the sea; and many brought ladies and all
brought squires, and troops of servants. It was a most
gaudy and gorgeous crowd, as to costumery, and very
characteristic of the country and the time, in the way of
high animal spirits, innocent indecencies of language, and
happy-hearted indifference to morals. It was fight or look
on, all day and every day; and sing, gamble, dance, ca-
rouse, half the night every night. They had a most noble
good time. You never saw such people. Those banks of
beautiful ladies, shining in their barbaric splendors, would
see a knight sprawl from his horse in the lists with a
lance shaft the thickness of your ankle clean through him
and the blood spouting, and instead of fainting they would
clap their hands and crowd each other for a better view;
only sometimes one would dive into her handkerchief, and
look ostentatiously brokenhearted, and then you could
lay two to one that there was a scandal there somewhere
and she was afraid the public hadn't found it out.

The noise at night would have been annoying to me
ordinarily, but I didn't mind it in the present circumstances, because it kept me from hearing the quacks de-

taching legs and arms from the day's cripples. They ruined an uncommon good old crosscut saw for me, and broke the sawbuck, too, but I let it pass. And as for my ax— well, I made up my mind that the next time I lent an ax to a surgeon I would pick my century.

I not only watched this tournament from day to day, but detailed an intelligent priest from my Department of Public Morals and Agriculture, and ordered him to report it; for it was my purpose by and by, when I should have gotten the people along far enough, to start a newspaper. The first thing you want in a new country, is a patent office; then work up your school system; and after that, out with your paper. A newspaper has its faults, and plenty of them, but no matter, it's hark from the tomb for a dead nation, and don't you forget it. You can't resurrect a dead nation without it; there isn't any way. So I wanted to sample things, and be finding out what sort of reporter material I might be able to rake together out of the sixth century when I should come to need it.

Well, the priest did very well, considering. He got in all the details, and that is a good thing in a local item: you see he had kept books for the undertaker department of his church when he was younger, and there, you know, the money's in the details; the more details, the more swag: bearers, mutes, candles, prayers—everything counts; and if the bereaved don't buy prayers enough you mark up your candles with a forked pencil, and your bill shows up all right. And he had a good knack at getting in the complimentary thing here and there about a knight that was likely to advertise—no, I mean a knight that had influence; and he also had a neat gift of exaggeration, for in his time he had kept door for a pious hermit who lived in a sty and worked miracles.

Of course this novice's report lacked whoop and crash and lurid description, and therefore wanted the true ring; but its antique wording was quaint and sweet and simple, and full of the fragrances and flavors of the time, and these little merits made up in a measure for its more important lacks. Here is an extract from it:

Then Sir Brian de les Isles and Grummore Grummorsum, knights of the castle, encountered with Sir Aglovale

and Sir Tor, and Sir Tor smote down Sir Grummore
Grummorsum to the earth. Then came in Sir Carados
of the dolorous tower, and Sir Turquine, knights of the
castle, and there encountered with them Sir Percivale de
Galis and Sir Lamorak de Galis, that were two brethren,
and there encountered Sir Percivale with Sir Carados,
and either brake their spears unto their hands, and then
Sir Turquine with Sir Lamorak, and either of them smote
down other, horse and all, to the earth, and either
parties rescued other and horsed them again. And Sir
Arnold, and Sir Gauter, knights of the castle, encountered with Sir Brandiles and Sir Kay, and these four
knights encountered mightily, and brake their spears to
their hands. Then came Sir Pertolope from the castle,
and there encountered with him Sir Lionel, and there
Sir Pertolope the green knight smote down Sir Lionel,
brother to Sir Launcelot. All this was marked by noble
heralds, who bare him best, and their names. Then Sir
Bleobaris brake his spear upon Sir Gareth, but of that
stroke Sir Bleobaris fell to the earth. When Sir Galihodin
saw that, he bad Sir Gareth keep him, and Sir Gareth
smote him to the earth. Then Sir Galihud gat a spear
to avenge his brother, and in the same wise Sir Gareth
served him, and Sir Dinadan and his brother La Cote
Male Taile, and Sir Sagramor le Desirous, and Sir Dodi-
nas le Savage; all these he bare down with one spear.
When King Agwisance of Ireland saw Sir Gareth fare so
he marvelled what he might be, that one time seemed
green, and another time, at his again coming, he seemed
blue. And thus at every course that he rode to and fro
he changed his color, so that there might neither king
nor knight have ready cognizance of him. Then Sir
Agwisance the King of Ireland encountered with Sir
Gareth, and there Sir Gareth smote him from his horse,
saddle and all. And then came King Carados of Scotland, and Sir Gareth smote him down horse and man.
And in the same wise he served King Uriens of the land
of Gore. And then there came in Sir Bagdemagus, and
Sir Gareth smote him down horse and man to the earth.
And Bagdemagus's son Meliganus brake a spear upon Sir
Gareth mightily and knightly. And then Sir Galahault
the noble prince cried on high, Knight with the many
colors, well hast thou justed; now make thee ready that
I may just with thee. Sir Gareth heard him, and he gat a
       r, and so they encountered together, and there
       brake his spear; but Sir Gareth smote him

upon the left side of the helm, that he reeled here and
there, and he had fallen down had not his men recovered him. Truly said King Arthur, that knight with the
many colors is a good knight. Wherefore the king called
unto him Sir Launcelot, and prayed him to encounter with
that knight. Sir, said Launcelot, I may as well find in my
heart for to forbear him at this time, for he hath had
travail enough this day, and when a good knight doth
so well upon some day, it is no good knight's part to
let him of his worship, and, namely, when he seeth a
knight hath done so great labour: for peradventure, said
Sir Launcelot, his quarrel is here this day, and peradventure he is best beloved with this lady of all that be
here, for I see well he paineth himself and enforceth him
to do great deeds, and therefore, said Sir Launcelot, as
for me, this day he shall have the honour; though it lay
in my power to put him from it, I would not.

There was an unpleasant little episode that day, which
for reasons of state I struck out of my priest's report.
You will have noticed that Garry was doing some great
fighting in the engagement. When I say Garry I mean Sir
Gareth. Garry was my private pet name for him; it suggests
that I had a deep affection for him, and that was the case.
But it was a private pet name only, and never spoken
aloud to any one, much less to him; being a noble, he
would not have endured a familiarity like that from me.
Well, to proceed: I sat in the private box set apart for
me as the king's minister. While Sir Dinadan was waiting
for his turn to enter the lists, he came in there and sat
down and began to talk; for he was always making up to
me, because I was a stranger and he liked to have a
fresh market for his jokes, the most of them having
reached that stage of wear where the teller has to do the
laughing himself while the other person looks sick. I had
always responded to his efforts as well as I could, and
felt a very deep and real kindness for him, too, for the
reason that if by malice of fate he knew the one particular anecdote which I had heard oftenest and had most
hated and most loathed all my life, he had at least spared
it me. It was one which I had heard attributed to every
humorous person who had ever stood on American soil,
from Columbus down to Artemus Ward. It was about a

humorous lecturer who flooded an ignorant audience with the killingest jokes for an hour and never got a laugh; and then when he was leaving, some gray simpletons wrung him gratefully by the hand and said it had been the funniest thing they had ever heard, and "it was all they could do to keep from laughin' right out in meetin'." That anecdote never saw the day that it was worth the telling; and yet I had sat under the telling of it hundreds and thousands and millions and billions of times, and cried and cursed all the way through. Then who can hope to know what my feelings were, to hear this armorplated ass start on it again, in the murky twilight of tradition, before the dawn of history, while even Lactantius might be referred to as "the late Lactantius," and the Crusades wouldn't be born for five hundred years yet? Just as he finished, the call boy came; so, haw-hawing like a demon, he went rattling and clanking out like a crate of loose castings, and I knew nothing more. It was some minutes before I came to, and then I opened my eyes just in time to see Sir Gareth fetch him an awful welt, and I unconsciously out with the prayer, "I hope to gracious he's killed!" But by ill luck, before I had got half through with the words, Sir Gareth crashed into Sir Sagramor le Desirous and sent him thundering over his horse's crupper, and Sir Sagramor caught my remark and thought I meant it for *him*.

Well, whenever one of those people got a thing into his head, there was no getting it out again. I knew that, so I saved my breath, and offered no explanations. As soon as Sir Sagramor got well, he notified me that there was a little account to settle between us, and he named a day three or four years in the future; place of settlement, the lists where the offense had been given. I said I would be ready when he got back. You see, he was going for the Holy Grail. The boys all took a flier at the Holy Grail now and then. It was several years' cruise. They always put in the long absence snooping around, in the most conscientious way, though none of them had any idea where the Holy Grail really was, and I don't think any of them actually expected to find it, or would have known what to do with it if he *had* run across it. You see, it was just the Northwest Passage of that day, as you may say;

that was all. Every year expeditions went out holy grailing, and next year relief expeditions went out to hunt for *them*. There was worlds of reputation in it, but no money. Why, they actually wanted *me* to put in! Well, I should smile.

⟦ CHAPTER X ⟧

Beginnings of Civilization

THE ROUND TABLE soon heard of the challenge, and of course it was a good deal discussed, for such things interested the boys. The king thought I ought now to set forth in quest of adventures, so that I might gain renown and be the more worthy to meet Sir Sagramor when the several years should have rolled away. I excused myself for the present; I said it would take me three or four years yet to get things well fixed up and going smoothly; then I should be ready; all the chances were that at the end of that time Sir Sagramor would still be out grailing, so no valuable time would be lost by the postponement; I should then have been in office six or seven years, and I believed my system and machinery would be so well developed that I could take a holiday without its working any harm.

I was pretty well satisfied with what I had already accomplished. In various quiet nooks and corners I had the beginnings of all sorts of industries under way—nuclei of future vast factories, the iron and steel missionaries of my future civilization. In these were gathered together the brightest young minds I could find, and I kept agents out raking the country for more, all the time. I was training a crowd of ignorant folk into experts—experts in every sort of handiwork and scientific calling. These nurseries of mine went smoothly and privately along undisturbed in their obscure country retreats, for nobody was allowed to come into their precincts without a special permit—for I was afraid of the Church.

I had started a teacher factory and a lot of Sunday schools the first thing; as a result, I now had an admirable system of graded schools in full blast in those places, and also a complete variety of Protestant congregations all in a prosperous and growing condition. Everybody could be any kind of a Christian he wanted to; there was perfect freedom in that matter. But I confined public religious teaching to the churches and the Sunday schools, permitting nothing of it in my other educational buildings. I could have given my own sect the preference and made everybody a Presbyterian without any trouble, but that would have been to affront a law of human nature: spiritual wants and instincts are as various in the human family as are physical appetites, complexions, and features, and a man is only at his best, morally, when he is equipped with the religious garment whose color and shape and size most nicely accommodate themselves to the spiritual complexion, angularities, and stature of the individual who wears it; and besides I was afraid of a united Church; it makes a mighty power, the mightiest conceivable, and then when it by and by gets into selfish hands, as it is always bound to do, it means death to human liberty, and paralysis to human thought.

All mines were royal property, and there were a good many of them. They had formerly been worked as savages always work mines—holes grubbed in the earth and the mineral brought up in sacks of hide by hand, at the rate of a ton a day; but I had begun to put the mining on a scientific basis as early as I could.

Yes, I had made pretty handsome progress when Sir Sagramor's challenge struck me.

Four years rolled by—and then! Well, you would never imagine it in the world. Unlimited power *is* the ideal thing when it is in safe hands. The despotism of heaven is the one absolutely perfect government. An earthly despotism would be the absolutely perfect earthly government, if the conditions were the same, namely, the despot the perfectest individual of the human race, and his lease of life perpetual. But as a perishable perfect man must die, and leave his despotism in the hands of an imperfect successor, an earthly despotism is not merely a bad form of government, it is the worst form that is possible.

My works showed what a despot could do with the resources of a kingdom at his command. Unsuspected by this dark land, I had the civilization of the nineteenth century booming under its very nose! It was fenced away from the public view, but there it was, a gigantic and unassailable fact—and to be heard from, yet, if I lived and had luck. There it was, as sure a fact, and as substantial a fact as any serene volcano, standing innocent with its smokeless summit in the blue sky and giving no sign of the rising hell in its bowels. My schools and churches were children four years before; they were grownup, now; my shops of that day were vast factories, now; where I had a dozen trained men then, I had a thousand, now; where I had one brilliant expert then, I had fifty now. I stood with my hand on the cock, so to speak, ready to turn it on and flood the midnight world with light at any moment. But I was not going to do the thing in that sudden way. It was not my policy. The people could not have stood it; and moreover I should have had the Established Roman Catholic Church on my back in a minute.

No, I had been going cautiously all the while. I had had confidential agents trickling through the country some time, whose office was to undermine knighthood by imperceptible degrees, and to gnaw a little at this and that and the other superstition, and so prepare the way gradually for a better order of things. I was turning on my light one candlepower at a time, and meant to continue to do so.

I had scattered some branch schools secretly about the kingdom, and they were doing very well. I meant to work this racket more and more, as time wore on, if nothing occurred to frighten me. One of my deepest secrets was my West Point—my military academy. I kept that most jealously out of sight; and I did the same with my naval academy which I had established at a remote seaport. Both were prospering to my satisfaction.

Clarence was twenty-two now, and was my head executive, my right hand. He was a darling; he was equal to anything; there wasn't anything he couldn't turn his hand to. Of late I had been training him for journalism, for the time seemed about right for a start in the newspaper line; nothing big, but just a small weekly for experimental circulation in my civilization-nurseries. He took to it like a duck; there was an editor concealed in him, sure. Already he had doubled himself in one way; he talked sixth century and wrote nineteenth. His journalistic style was climbing, steadily; it was already up to the back settlement Alabama mark, and couldn't be told from the editorial output of that region either by matter or flavor.

We had another large departure on hand, too. This was a telegraph and a telephone; our first venture in this line. These wires were for private service only, as yet, and must be kept private until a riper day should come. We had a gang of men on the road, working mainly by night. They were stringing ground wires; we were afraid to put up poles, for they would attract too much inquiry. Ground wires were good enough, in both instances, for my wires were protected by an insulation of my own invention which was perfect. My men had orders to strike across country, avoiding roads, and establishing connection with any considerable towns whose lights betrayed their presence, and leaving experts in charge. Nobody could tell you how to find any place in the kingdom, for nobody ever went intentionally to any place, but only struck it by accident in his wanderings, and then generally left it without thinking to inquire what its name was. At one time and another we had sent out topographical expeditions to survey and map the kingdom, but the priests had always interfered and raised trouble. So we had given the thing up, for the present; it would be poor wisdom to antagonize the Church.

As for the general condition of the country, it was as it had been when I arrived in it, to all intents and purposes. I had made changes, but they were necessarily slight, and they were not noticeable. Thus far, I had not even meddled with taxation, outside of the taxes which provided the royal revenues. I had systematized those, and put the service on an effective and righteous basis. As a result, these revenues were already quadrupled, and yet the burden was so much more equally distributed than before, that all the kingdom felt a sense of relief, and the praises of my administration were hearty and general.

Personally, I struck an interruption, now, but I did not mind it, it could not have happened at a better time. Earlier it could have annoyed me, but now everything was in good hands and swimming right along. The king had reminded me several times, of late, that the postponement I had asked for, four years before, had about run out, now. It was a hint that I ought to be starting out to seek adventures and get up a reputation of a size to make me worthy of the honor of breaking a lance with Sir Sagramor, who was still out grailing, but was being hunted for by various relief expeditions, and might be found any year, now. So you see I was expecting this interruption; it did not take me by surprise.

[CHAPTER XI]

The Yankee in Search of Adventures

THERE NEVER was such a country for wandering liars; and they were of both sexes. Hardly a month went by without one of these tramps arriving; and generally loaded with a tale about some princess or other wanting help to get her out of some faraway castle where she was held in captivity by a lawless scoundrel, usually a giant. Now you would think that the first thing the king would do after listening to such a novelette from an entire stranger, would be to ask for credentials—yes, and a pointer or two as to locality of castle, best route to it, and so on. But nobody ever thought of so simple and commonsense a thing as that. No, everybody swallowed these people's lies whole, and never asked a question of any sort or about anything. Well, one day when I was not around, one of these people came along—it was a she one, this time—and told a tale of the usual pattern. Her mistress was a captive in a vast and gloomy castle, along with forty-four other young and beautiful girls, pretty much all of them princesses; they had been languishing in that cruel captivity for twenty-six years; the masters of the castle were three stupendous brothers, each with four arms and one eye—the eye in the center of the forehead, and as big as a fruit. Sort of fruit not mentioned; their usual slovenliness in statistics.

Would you believe it? The king and the whole Round Table were in raptures over this preposterous opportunity for adventure. Every knight of the Table jumped for the chance, and begged for it; but to their vexation and chagrin the king conferred it upon me, who had not asked for it at all.

By an effort, I contained my joy when Clarence brought me the news. But he—he could not contain his. His mouth gushed delight and gratitude in a steady discharge—delight in my good fortune, gratitude to the king for this splendid mark of his favor for me. He could keep neither his legs nor his body still, but pirouetted about the place in an airy ecstasy of happiness.

On my side, I could have cursed the kindness that conferred upon me this benefaction, but I kept my vexation under the surface for policy's sake, and did what I could to let on to be glad. Indeed, I *said* I was glad. And in a way it was true; I was as glad as a person is when he is scalped.

Well, one must make the best of things, and not waste time with useless fretting, but get down to business and see what can be done. In all lies there is wheat among the chaff; I must get at the wheat in this case: so I sent for the girl and she came. She was a comely enough creature, and soft and modest, but if signs went for anything, she didn't know as much as a lady's watch. I said—

"My dear, have you been questioned as to particulars?"

She said she hadn't.

"Well, I didn't expect you had, but I thought I would ask to make sure; it's the way I've been raised. Now you mustn't take it unkindly if I remind you that as we don't know you, we must go a little slow. You may be all right, of course, and we'll hope that you are; but to take it for granted isn't business. *You* understand that. I'm obliged to ask you a few questions; just answer up fair and square, and don't be afraid. Where do you live, when you are at home?"

"In the land of Moder, fair sir."

"Land of Moder. I don't remember hearing of it before. Parents living?"

"As to that, I know not if they be yet on live, sith it is many years that I have lain shut up in the castle."

"Your name, please?"

"I hight the Demoiselle Alisande la Carteloise, an it please you."

"Do you know anybody here who can identify you?"

"That were not likely, fair lord, I being come hither now for the first time."

"Have you brought any letters—any documents—any proofs that you are trustworthy and truthful?"

"Of a surety, no; and wherefore should I? Have I not a tongue, and cannot I say all that myself?"

"But *your* saying it, you know, and somebody else's saying it, is different."

"Different? How might that be? I fear me I do not understand."

"Don't *understand?* Land of—why, you see—you see— why, great Scott, can't you understand a little thing like that? Can't you understand the difference between your— *why* do you look so innocent and idiotic!"

"I? In truth I know not, but an it were the will of God."

"Yes, yes, I reckon that's about the size of it. Don't mind my seeming excited; I'm not. Let us change the subject. Now as to this castle, with forty-five princesses in it, and three ogres at the head of it, tell me—where is this harem?"

"Harem?"

"The *castle,* you understand; where is the castle?"

"Oh, as to that, it is great, and strong, and well beseen, and lieth in a far country. Yes, it is many leagues."

"*How* many?"

"Ah, fair sir, it were woundily hard to tell, they are so many, and do so lap the one upon the other, and being made all in the same image and tincted with the same color, one may not know the one league from its fellow, nor how to count them except they be taken apart, and ye wit well it were God's work to do that, being not within man's capacity; for ye will note—"

"Hold on, hold on, never mind about the distance; *whereabouts* does the castle lie? What's the direction from here?"

"Ah, please you sir, it hath no direction from here; by reason that the road lieth not straight, but turneth evermore; wherefore the direction of its place abideth not, but is sometime under the one sky and anon under another, whereso if ye be minded that it is in the east, and wend thitherward, ye shall observe that the way of the road doth yet again turn upon itself by the space of half a circle, and this marvel happing again and yet again and still again, it will grieve you that you had thought by vanities of the mind to thwart and bring to naught the will of Him that giveth not a castle a direction from a place except it pleaseth Him, and if it please Him not, will the rather that even all castles and all directions thereunto vanish out of the earth, leaving the places wherein they tarried desolate and vacant, so warning His creatures that where He will He will, and where He will not He—"

"Oh, that's all right, that's all right, give us a rest; never mind about the direction, *hang* the direction—I beg pardon, I beg a thousand pardons, I am not well today; pay no attention when I soliloquize, it is an old habit, an old, bad habit, and hard to get rid of when one's digestion is all disordered with eating food that was raised forever and ever before he was born; good land! a man can't keep his functions regular on spring chickens thirteen hundred years old. But come—never mind about that; let's—have you got such a thing as a map of that region about you? Now a good map—"

"Is it peradventure that manner of thing which of late the unbelievers have brought from over the great seas, which, being boiled in oil, and an onion and salt added thereto, doth—"

"What, a map? What are you talking about? Don't you know what a map is? There, there, never mind, don't explain, I hate explanations; they fog a thing up so that you can't tell anything about it. Run along, dear; goodday; show her the way, Clarence."

Oh, well, it was reasonably plain, now, why these donkeys didn't prospect these liars for details. It may be that this girl had a fact in her somewhere, but I don't believe you could have sluiced it out with a hydraulic; nor got it with the earlier forms of blasting, even; it was a case for dynamite. Why, she was a perfect ass; and yet the king and his knights had listened to her as if she had been a leaf out of the gospel. It kind of sizes up the whole party. And think of the simple ways of this court: this wandering wench hadn't any more trouble to get access to the king in his palace than she would have had to get into the poorhouse in my day and country. In fact he was glad to see her, glad to hear her tale; with that adventure of hers to offer, she was as welcome as a corpse is to a coroner.

Just as I was ending up these reflections, Clarence came back. I remarked upon the barren result of my efforts with the girl; hadn't got hold of a single point that could help me to find the castle. The youth looked a little surprised, or puzzled, or something, and intimated that he had been wondering to himself what I had wanted to ask the girl all those questions for.

"Why, great guns," I said, "don't I want to find the castle? And how else would I go about it?"

"La, sweet your worship, one may lightly answer that, I ween. She will go with thee. They always do. She will ride with thee."

"Ride with me? Nonsense!"

"But of a truth she will. She will ride with thee. Thou shalt see."

"What? She browse around the hills and scour the woods with me—alone—and I as good as engaged to be married? Why, it's scandalous. Think how it would look."

My, the dear face that rose before me! The boy was eager to know all about this tender matter. I swore him to secrecy and then whispered her name—"Puss Flanagan." He looked disappointed, and said he didn't remember the countess. How natural it was for the little courtier to give her a rank. He asked me where she lived.

"In East Har—" I came to myself and stopped, a little confused; then I said, "Never mind, now; I'll tell you sometime."

And might he see her? Would I let him see her some day?

It was but a little thing to promise—thirteen hundred years or so—and he so eager; so I said Yes. But I sighed; I couldn't help it. And yet there was no sense in sighing, for she wasn't born yet. But that is the way we are made: we don't reason, where we feel; we just feel.

My expedition was all the talk that day and that night, and the boys were very good to me, and made much of me, and seemed to have forgotten their vexation and disappointment, and come to be as anxious for me to hive those ogres and set those ripe old virgins loose as if it were themselves that had the contract. Well, they *were* good children—but just children, that is all. And they gave me no end of points about how to scout for giants, and how to scoop them in; and they told me all sorts of charms against enchantments, and gave me salves and other rubbish to put on my wounds. But it never occurred to one of them to reflect that if I was such a wonderful necromancer as I was pretending to be, I ought not to need salves or instructions, or charms against enchantments, and least of all, arms and armor, on a foray of any kind—even against fire-spouting dragons, and devils hot from perdition, let alone such poor adversaries as these I was after, these commonplace ogres of the back settlements.

I was to have an early breakfast, and start at dawn, for that was the usual way; but I had the demon's own time with my armor, and this delayed me a little. It is troublesome to get into, and there is so much detail. First you wrap a layer or two of blanket around your body, for a sort of cushion and to keep off the cold iron; then you put on your sleeves and shirt of chain mail—these are made of small steel links woven together, and they form a fabric so flexible that if you toss your shirt onto the floor, it slumps into a pile like a peck of wet fishnet; it is very heavy and is nearly the uncomfortablest material in the world for a nightshirt, yet plenty used it for that—tax collectors, and reformers, and one-horse kings with a defective title, and those sorts of people; then you put on your shoes—flatboats roofed over with interleaving bands of steel—and screw your clumsy spurs into the heels. Next you buckle your greaves on your legs, and your cuisses on your thighs; then come your backplate and your breastplate, and you begin to feel crowded; then you hitch onto the breastplate and the half-petticoat of broad overlapping bands of steel which hangs down in front but is scalloped out behind so you can sit down, and isn't any real improvement on an inverted coal scuttle, either for looks or for wear, or to wipe your hands on; next you belt on your sword; then you put your stovepipe joints onto your arms, your iron gauntlets onto your hands, your iron rattrap onto your head, with a rag of steel web hitched onto it to hang over the back of your neck—and there you are, snug as a candle in a candle mold. This is no time to dance. Well, a man that is packed away like that, is a nut that isn't worth the cracking, there is so little of the meat, when you get down to it, by comparison with the shell.

The boys helped me, or I never could have got in. Just as we finished, Sir Bedivere happened in, and I saw that as like as not I hadn't chosen the most convenient outfit for a long trip. How stately he looked; and tall and broad and grand. He had on his head a conical steel casque that only came down to his ears, and for visor had only a narrow steel bar that extended down to his upper lip and protected his nose; and all the rest of him, from neck to heel, was flexible chain mail, trousers and all. But pretty much all of him was hidden under his outside garment, which of course was of chain mail, as I said, and hung straight from his shoulders to his ankles; and from his middle to the bottom, both before and behind, was divided, so that he could ride and let the skirts hang down on each side. He was going grailing, and it was just the outfit for it, too. I would have given a good deal for that ulster, but it was too late now to be fooling around. The sun was just up, the king and the court were all on hand to see me off and wish me luck; so it wouldn't be etiquette for me to tarry. You don't get on your horse yourself; no, if you tried it you would get disappointed. They carry you out, just as they carry a sunstruck man to the drug store, and put you on, and help get you to rights, and fix your feet in the

stirrups; and all the while you do feel so strange and
stuffy and like somebody else—like somebody that has
been married on a sudden, or struck by lightning, or
something like that, and hasn't quite fetched around,
yet, and is sort of numb, and can't just get his bearings.
Then they stood up the mast they called a spear, in its
socket by my left foot, and I gripped it with my hand;
lastly they hung my shield around my neck, and I was
all complete and ready to up anchor and get to sea.
Everybody was as good to me as they could be, and a
maid of honor gave me the stirrup cup her own self.
There was nothing more to do, now, but for that damsel
to get up behind me on a pillion, which she did, and put
an arm or so around me to hold on.

And so we started; and everybody gave us a good-bye
and waved their handkerchiefs or helmets. And everybody we met, going down the hill and through the village was respectful to us, except some shabby little boys
on the outskirts. They said—

"Oh, what a guy!" And hove clods at us.

In my experience boys are the same in all ages. They
don't respect anything, they don't care for anything or
anybody. They say "Go up, baldhead" to the prophet
going his unoffending way in the gray of antiquity; they
sass me in the holy gloom of the Middle Ages; and I
had seen them act the same way in Buchanan's administration; I remember, because I was there and helped.
The prophet had his bears and settled with his boys; and
I wanted to get down and settle with mine, but it
wouldn't answer, because I couldn't have got up again.
I hate a country without a derrick.

[CHAPTER XII]

Slow Torture

STRAIGHT OFF, we were in the country. It was most lovely
and pleasant in those sylvan solitudes in the early cool

morning in the first freshness of autumn. From hilltops we saw fair green valleys lying spread out below, with streams winding through them, and island groves of trees here and there, and huge lonely oaks scattered about and casting black blots of shade; and beyond the valleys we saw the ranges of hills, blue with haze, stretching away in billowy perspective to the horizon, with at wide intervals a dim fleck of white or gray on a wave summit, which we knew was a castle. We crossed broad natural lawns sparkling with dew, and we moved like spirits, the cushioned turf giving out no sound of footfall; we dreamed along through glades in a mist of green light that got its tint from the sundrenched roof of leaves overhead, and by our feet the clearest and coldest of runlets went frisking and gossiping over its reefs and making a sort of whispering music comfortable to hear; and at times we left the world behind and entered into the solemn great deeps and rich gloom of the forest, where furtive wild things whisked and scurried by and were gone before you could even get your eye on the place where the noise was; and where only the earliest birds were turning out and getting to business with a song here and a quarrel yonder and a mysterious far-off hammering and drumming for worms on a tree trunk away somewhere in the impenetrable remotenesses of the woods. And by and by out we would swing again into the glare.

About the third or fourth or fifth time that we swung out into the glare—it was along there somewhere, a couple of hours or so after sunup—it wasn't as pleasant as it had been. It was beginning to get hot. This was quite noticeable. We had a very long pull, after that, without any shade. Now it is curious how progressively little frets grow and multiply after they once get a start. Things which I didn't mind at all, at first, I began to mind now—and more and more, too, all the time. The first ten or fifteen times I wanted my handkerchief I didn't seem to care; I got along, and said never mind, it isn't any matter, and dropped it out of my mind. But now it was different; I wanted it all the time; it was nag, nag, nag, right along, and no rest; I couldn't get it out of my mind; and so at last I lost my temper and said hang a man that would make a suit of armor without any pockets in it. You see I had my handkerchief in my helmet; and some other things; but it was that kind of a helmet that you can't take off by yourself. That hadn't occurred to me when I put it there; and in fact I didn't know it. I supposed it would be particularly convenient there. And so now, the thought of its being there, so handy and close by, and yet not get-at-able, made it all the worse and the harder to bear. Yes, the thing that you can't get is the thing that you want, mainly; everyone has noticed that. Well, it took my mind off from everything else; took it clear off, and centered it in my helmet; and mile after mile, there it stayed, imagining the handkerchief, picturing the handkerchief; and it was bitter and aggravating to have the salt sweat keep trickling down into my eyes, and I couldn't get at it. It seems like a little thing, on paper, but it was not a little thing at all; it was the most real kind of misery. I would not say it if it was not so. I made up my mind that I would carry along a reticule next time, let it look how it might, and people say what they would. Of course these iron dudes of the Round Table would think it was scandalous, and maybe raise Sheol about it, but as for me, give me comfort first, and style afterwards. So we jogged along, and now and then we struck a stretch of dust, and it would tumble up in clouds and get into my nose and make me sneeze and cry; and of course I said things I oughtn't to have said, I don't deny that. I am not better than others. We couldn't seem to meet anybody in this lonesome Britain, not even an ogre; and in the mood I was in then, it was well for the ogre; that is, an ogre with a handkerchief. Most knights would have thought of nothing but getting his armor; but so I got his bandanna, he could keep his hardware, for all me.

Meantime it was getting hotter and hotter in there. You see, the sun was beating down and warming up the iron more and more all the time. Well, when you are hot, that way, every little thing irritates you. When I trotted, I rattled like a crate of dishes, and that annoyed me; and mooreover I couldn't seem to stand that shield slatting and banging, now about my breast, now around my back; and if I dropped into a walk my joints creaked and screeched in that wearisome way that a wheelbarrow does, and as we didn't create any breeze at that gait, I was like to get fried in that stove; and besides, the quieter you went the heavier the iron settled down on you and the more and more tons you seemed to weigh every minute. And you had to be always changing hands, and passing your spear over to the other foot, it got so irksome for one hand to hold it long at a time.

Well, you know, when you perspire that way, in rivers, there comes a time when you—when you—well, when you itch. You are inside, your hands are outside; so there you are; nothing but iron between. It is not a light thing, let it sound as it may. First it is one place; then another; then some more; and it goes on spreading and spreading, and at last the territory is all occupied, and nobody can imagine what you feel like, nor how unpleasant it is. And when it had got to the worst, and it seemed to me that I could not stand anything more, a fly got in through the bars and settled on my nose, and the bars were stuck and wouldn't work, and I couldn't get the visor up; and I could only shake my head, which was baking hot by this time, and the fly—well, you know how a fly acts when he has got a certainty—he only minded the shaking long enough to change from nose to lip, and lip to ear, and buzz and buzz all around in there, and keep on lighting and biting, in a way that a person already so distressed as I was, simply could not stand. So I gave in, and got Alisande to unship the helmet and relieve me of it. Then she emptied the conveniences out of it and fetched it full of water, and I drank and then stood up and she poured the rest down inside the armor. One cannot think how refreshing it was. She continued to fetch and pour until I was well soaked and thoroughly comfortable.

It was good to have a rest—and peace. But nothing is quite perfect in this life, at any time. I had made a pipe a while back, and also some pretty fair tobacco; not the real thing, but what some of the Indians use: the inside bark of the willow, dried. These comforts had been in the helmet, and now I had them again, but no matches.

Gradually, as the time wore along, one annoying fact was borne in upon my understanding—that we were

weather-bound. An armed novice cannot mount his horse
without help and plenty of it. Sandy was not enough;
not enough for me, anyway. We had to wait until somebody should come along. Waiting, in silence, would have
been agreeable enough, for I was full of matter for reflection, and wanted to give it a chance to work. I
wanted to try and think out how it was that rational or
even half-rational men could ever have learned to wear
armor, considering its inconveniences; and how they
had managed to keep up such a fashion for generations
when it was plain that what I had suffered today they
had had to suffer all the days of their lives. I wanted
to think that out; and moreover I wanted to think out
some way to reform this evil and persuade the people
to let the foolish fashion die out; but thinking was out of
the question in the circumstances. You couldn't think,
where Sandy was. She was a quite biddable creature and
good-hearted, but she had a flow of talk that was as
steady as a mill, and made your head sore like the drays
and wagons in a city. If she had had a cork she would
have been a comfort. But you can't cork that kind; they
would die. Her clack was going all day, and you would
think something would surely happen to her works, by
and by; but no, they never got out of order; and she
never had to slack up for words. She could grind, and
pump, and churn and buzz by the week, and never stop
to oil up or blow out. And yet the result was just
nothing but wind. She never had any ideas, any more
than a fog has. She was a perfect blatherskite; I mean
for jaw, jaw, jaw, talk, talk, talk, jabber, jabber, jabber;
but just as good as she could be. I hadn't minded her
mill that morning, on account of having that hornet's
nest of other troubles; but more than once in the afternoon I had to say—

"Take a rest, child; the way you are using up all the
domestic air, the kingdom will have to go to importing it
by tomorrow, and it's a low enough treasury without that."

[CHAPTER XIII]

Freemen!

YES, IT IS STRANGE how little a while at a time a person can be contented. Only a little while back, when I was riding and suffering, what a heaven this peace, this rest, this sweet serenity in this secluded shady nook by this purling stream would have seemed, where I could keep perfectly comfortable all the time by pouring a dipper of water into my armor now and then; yet already I was getting dissatisfied; partly because I could not light my pipe—for although I had long ago started a match factory, I had forgotten to bring matches with me—and partly because we had nothing to eat. Here was another illustration of the childlike improvidence of this age and people. A man in armor always trusted to chance for his food on a journey, and would have been scandalized at the idea of hanging a basket of sandwiches on his spear. There was probably not a knight of all the Round Table combination who would not rather have died than been caught carrying such a thing as that on his flagstaff. And yet there could not be anything more sensible. It had been my intention to smuggle a couple of sandwiches into my helmet, but I was interrupted in the act, and had to make an excuse and lay them aside, and a dog got them.

Night approached, and with it a storm. The darkness came on fast. We must camp, of course. I found a good shelter for the demoiselle under a rock, and went off and found another for myself. But I was obliged to remain in my armor, because I could not get it off by myself and yet could not allow Alisande to help, because it would have seemed so like undressing before folk. It would not have amounted to that in reality, because I had clothes on underneath; but the prejudices of one's breeding are not gotten rid of just at a jump, and I knew

79

that when it came to stripping off that bobtailed iron petticoat I should be embarrassed.

With the storm came a change of weather; and the stronger the wind blew, and the wilder the rain lashed around, the colder and colder it got. Pretty soon, various kinds of bugs and ants and worms and things began to flock in out of the wet and crawl down inside my armor to get warm; and while some of them behaved well enough, and snuggled up among my clothes and got quiet, the majority were of a restless, uncomfortable sort, and never stayed still, but went on prowling and hunting for they did not know what; especially the ants, which went tickling along in wearisome procession from one end of me to the other by the hour, and are a kind of creatures which I never wish to sleep with again. It would be my advice to persons situated in this way, to not roll or thrash around, because this excites the interest of all the different sorts of animals and makes every last one of them want to turn out and see what is going on, and this makes things worse than they were before, and of course makes you objurgate harder, too, if you can. Still, if one did not roll and thrash around he would die; so perhaps it is as well to do one way as the other, there is no real choice. Even after I was frozen solid I could still distinguish that tickling, just as a corpse does when he is taking electric treatment. I said I would never wear armor after this trip.

All those trying hours whilst I was frozen and yet was in a living fire, as you may say, on account of that swarm of crawlers, that same unanswerable question kept circling and circling through my tired head: How do people stand this miserable armor? How have they managed to stand it all these generations? How can they sleep at night for dreading the tortures of next day?

When the morning came at last, I was in a bad enough plight: seedy, drowsy, fagged, from want of sleep; weary from thrashing around, famished from long fasting; pining for a bath, and to get rid of the animals; and crippled with rheumatism. And how had it fared with the nobly born, the titled aristocrat, the Demoiselle Alisande la Carteloise? Why, she was as fresh as a squirrel; she had slept like the dead; and as for a bath, probably neither she nor any other noble in the land had ever had one, and so she was not missing it. Measured by modern standards, they were merely modified savages, those people. This noble lady showed no impatience to get to breakfast—and that smacks of the savage, too. On their journeys those Britons were used to long fasts, and knew how to bear them; and also how to freight up against probable fasts before starting, after the style of the Indian and the anaconda. As like as not, Sandy was loaded for a three-day stretch.

We were off before sunrise, Sandy riding and I limping along behind. In half an hour we came upon a group of ragged poor creatures who had assembled to mend the thing which was regarded as a road. They were as humble as animals to me; and when I proposed to breakfast with them, they were so flattered, so overwhelmed by this extraordinary condescension of mine that at first they were not able to believe that I was in earnest. My lady put up her scornful lip and withdrew to one side; she said in their hearing that she would as soon think of eating with the other cattle—a remark which embarrassed these poor devils merely because it referred to them, and not because it insulted or offended them, for it didn't. And yet they were not slaves, not chattels. By a sarcasm of law and phrase they were freemen. Seven-tenths of the free population of the country were of just their class and degree: small "independent" farmers, artisans, etc.; which is to say, they were the nation, the actual Nation; they were about all of it that was useful, or worth saving, or really respectworthy; and to subtract them would have been to subtract the Nation and leave behind some dregs, some refuse, in the shape of a king, nobility and gentry, idle, unproductive, acquainted mainly with the arts of wasting and destroying, and of no sort of use or value in any rationally constructed world. And yet, by ingenious contrivance, this gilded minority, instead of being in the tail of the procession where it belonged, was marching head up and banners flying, at the other end of it; had elected itself to be the Nation, and these innumerable clams had permitted it so long that they had come at last to accept it as a truth; and not only that, but to believe it right and as it should be. The priests had told

their fathers and themselves that this ironical state of
things was ordained of God; and so, not reflecting upon
how unlike God it would be to amuse himself with sar-
casms, and especially such poor transparent ones as this,
they had dropped the matter there and become respectfully quiet.

The talk of these meek people had a strange enough
sound in a formerly American ear. They were freemen,
but they could not leave the estates of their lord or their
bishop without his permission; they could not prepare their
own bread, but must have their corn ground and their
bread baked at his mill and his bakery, and pay roundly
for the same; they could not sell a piece of their own
property without paying him a handsome percentage of
the proceeds, nor buy a piece of somebody else's without
remembering him in cash for the privilege; they had to
harvest his grain for him gratis, and be ready to come
at a moment's notice, leaving their own crop to destruction by the threatened storm; they had to let him plant
fruit trees in their fields, and then keep their indignation
to themselves when his heedless fruit gatherers trampled
the grain around the trees; they had to smother their
anger when his hunting parties galloped through their
fields laying waste the result of their patient toil; they
were not allowed to keep doves themselves, and when
the swarms from my lord's dovecote settled on their
crops they must not lose their temper and kill a bird, for
awful would the penalty be; when the harvest was at last
gathered, then came the procession of robbers to levy
their blackmail upon it: first the Church carted off its
fat tenth, then the king's commissioner took his twentieth,
then my lord's people made a mighty inroad upon the
remainder; after which, the skinned freeman had liberty
to bestow the remnant in his barn, in case it was worth
the trouble; there were taxes, and taxes, and taxes, and
more taxes, and taxes again, and yet other taxes—upon
this free and independent pauper, but none upon his lord
the baron or the bishop, none upon the wasteful nobility
or the all-devouring Church; if the baron would sleep un-
vexed, the freeman must sit up all night after his day's
work and whip the ponds to keep the frogs quiet; if the
freeman's daughter—but no, that last infamy of monar-

chical government is unprintable; and finally, if the freeman, grown desperate with his tortures, found his life
unendurable under such conditions, and sacrificed it and
fled to death for mercy and refuge, the gentle Church
condemned him to eternal fire, the gentle law buried him
at midnight at the crossroads with a stake through his
back, and his master the baron or the bishop confiscated
all his property and turned his widow and his orphans
out of doors.

And here were these freemen assembled in the early
morning to work on their lord the bishop's road three
days each—gratis; every head of a family, and every son
of a family, three days each, gratis, and a day or so
added for their servants. Why, it was like reading about
France and the French, before the ever-memorable and
blessed Revolution, which swept a thousand years of such
villany away in one swift tidal wave of blood—one: a
settlement of that hoary debt in the proportion of half a
drop of blood for each hogshead of it that had been
pressed by slow tortures out of that people in the weary
stretch of ten centuries of wrong and shame and misery
the like of which was not to be mated but in hell. There
were two "Reigns of Terror," if we would but remember
it and consider it; the one wrought murder in hot passion, the other in heartless cold blood; the one lasted
mere months, the other had lasted a thousand years; the
one inflicted death upon ten thousand persons, the other
upon a hundred millions; but our shudders are all for the
"horrors" of the minor Terror, the momentary Terror,
so to speak; whereas, what is the horror of swift death
by the ax, compared with lifelong death from hunger,
cold, insult, cruelty, and heartbreak? What is swift death
by lightning compared with death by slow fire at the
stake? A city cemetery could contain the coffins filled
by that brief Terror which we have all been so diligently
taught to shiver at and mourn over; but all France could
hardly contain the coffins filled by that older and real
Terror—that unspeakably bitter and awful Terror which
none of us has been taught to see in its vastness or pity
as it deserves.

These poor ostensible freemen who were sharing their
breakfast and their talk with me, were as full of humble

reverence for their king and Church and nobility as their
worst enemy could desire. There was something pitifully
ludicrous about it. I asked them if they supposed a nation
of people ever existed, who, with a free vote in every
man's hand, would elect that a single family and its
descendants should reign over it forever, whether gifted
or boobies, to the exclusion of all other families—including the voter's; and would also elect that a certain hundred families should be raised to dizzy summits of rank,
and clothed on with offensive transmissible glories and
privileges to the exclusion of the rest of the nation's
families—*including his own.*

They all looked unhit, and said they didn't know; that
they had never thought about it before, and it hadn't ever
occurred to them that a nation could be so situated that
every man *could* have a say in the government. I said
I had seen one—and that it would last until it had an
Established Church. Again they were all unhit—at first.
But presently one man looked up and asked me to state
that proposition again; and state it slowly, so it could
soak into his understanding. I did it; and after a little he
had the idea, and he brought his fist down and said *he*
didn't believe a nation where every man had a vote would
voluntarily get down in the mud and dirt in any such
way; and that to steal from a nation its will and preference must be a crime and the first of all crimes.

I said to myself:

"This one's a man. If I were backed by enough of his
sort, I would make a strike for the welfare of this country, and try to prove myself its loyalest citizen by making
a wholesome change in its system of government."

You see my kind of loyalty was loyalty to one's country, not to its institutions or its officeholders. The country
is the real thing, the substantial thing, the eternal thing;
it is the thing to watch over, and care for, and be loyal
to; institutions are extraneous, they are its mere clothing, and clothing can wear out, become ragged, cease to
be comfortable, cease to protect the body from winter,
disease, and death. To be loyal to rags, to shout for rags,
to worship rags, to die for rags—that is a loyalty of
unreason, it is pure animal; it belongs to monarchy, was
invented by monarchy; let monarchy keep it. I was from

Connecticut, whose Constitution declares "that all political power is inherent in the people, and all free governments are founded on their authority and instituted for their benefit; and that they have *at all times* an undeniable and indefeasible right to *alter their form of government* in such a manner as they may think expedient."

Under that gospel, the citizen who thinks he sees that the commonwealth's political clothes are worn out, and yet holds his peace and does not agitate for a new suit, is disloyal; he is a traitor. That he may be the only one who thinks he sees this decay, does not excuse him; it is his duty to agitate any way, and it is the duty of the others to vote him down if they do not see the matter as he does.

And now here I was, in a country where a right to say how the country should be governed was restricted to six persons in each thousand of its population. For the nine hundred and ninety-four to express dissatisfaction with the regnant system and propose to change it, would have made the whole six shudder as one man, it would have been so disloyal, so dishonorable, such putrid black treason. So to speak, I was become a stockholder in a corporation where nine hundred and ninety-four of the members furnished all the money and did all the work, and the other six elected themselves a permanent board of direction and took all the dividends. It seemed to me that what the nine hundred and ninety-four dupes needed was a new deal. The thing that would have best suited the circus side of my nature would have been to resign the Boss-ship and get up an insurrection and turn it into a revolution; but I knew that the Jack Cade or the Wat Tyler who tries such a thing without first educating his materials up to revolution grade is almost absolutely certain to get left. I had never been accustomed to getting left, even if I do say it myself. Wherefore, the "deal" which had been for some time working into shape in my mind was of a quite different pattern from the Cade-Tyler sort.

So I did not talk blood and insurrection to that man there who sat munching black bread with that abused and mistaught herd of human sheep, but took him aside and talked matter of another sort to him. After I had finished,

I got him to lend me a little ink from his veins; and with this and a sliver I wrote on a piece of bark—

   Put him in the Man Factory—

and gave it to him, and said—

"Take it to the palace at Camelot and give it into the hands of Amyas le Poulet, whom I call Clarence, and he will understand."

"He is a priest, then," said the man, and some of the enthusiasm went out of his face.

"How—a priest? Didn't I tell you that no chattel of the Church, no bondslave of pope or bishop can enter my Man Factory? Didn't I tell you that *you* couldn't enter unless your religion, whatever it might be, was your own free property?"

"Marry, it is so, and for that I was glad; wherefore it liked me not, and bred in me a cold doubt, to hear of this priest being there."

"But he isn't a priest, I tell you."

The man looked far from satisfied. He said:

"He is not a priest, and yet can read?"

"He is not a priest and yet can read—yes, and write, too, for that matter. I taught him myself." The man's face cleared. "And it is the first thing that you yourself will be taught in that Factory—"

"I? I would give blood out of my heart to know that art. Why, I will be your slave, your—"

"No you won't, you won't be anybody's slave. Take your family and go along. Your lord the bishop will confiscate your small property, but no matter, Clarence will fix you all right."

⟦ CHAPTER XIV ⟧

"Defend thee, Lord!"

I PAID THREE pennies for my breakfast, and a most extravagant price it was, too, seeing that one could have breakfasted a dozen persons for that money; but I was

feeling good by this time, and I had always been a kind
of spendthrift any way; and then these people had wanted
to give me the food for nothing, scant as their provision
was, and so it was a grateful pleasure to emphasize my
appreciation and sincere thankfulness with a good big
financial lift where the money would do so much more
good than it would in my helmet, where, these pennies
being made of iron and not stinted in weight, my half
dollar's worth was a good deal of a burden to me. I
spent money rather too freely in those days, it is true;
but one reason for it was that I hadn't got the proportions
of things entirely adjusted, even yet, after so long a so-
journ in Britain—hadn't got along to where I was able to
absolutely realize that a penny in Arthur's land and a
couple of dollars in Connecticut were about one and the
same thing: just twins, as you may say, in purchasing
power. If my start from Camelot could have been delayed
a very few days I could have paid these people in beautiful new coins from our own mint, and that would have
pleased me; and them, too, not less. I had adopted the
American values exclusively. In a week or two now, cents,
nickels, dimes, quarters and half dollars, and also a trifle
of gold, would be trickling in thin but steady streams all
through the commercial veins of the kingdom, and I
looked to see this new blood freshen up its life.

The farmers were bound to throw in something, to sort
of offset my liberality, whether I would or no; so I let
them give me a flint and steel; and as soon as they had
comfortably bestowed Sandy and me on our horse, I lit
my pipe. When the first blast of smoke shot out through
the bars of my helmet, all those people broke for the
woods, and Sandy went over backwards and struck the
ground with a dull thud. They thought I was one of those
fire-belching dragons they had heard so much about
from knights and other professional liars. I had infinite
trouble to persuade those people to venture back within
explaining distance. Then I told them that this was only a
bit of enchantment which would work harm to none but
my enemies. And I promised, with my hand on my heart,
that if all who felt no enmity toward me would come
forward and pass before me they should see that only
those who remained behind would be struck dead. The

procession moved with a good deal of promptness. There were no casualties to report, for nobody had curiosity enough to remain behind to see what would happen.

I lost some time, now, for these big children, their fears gone, became so ravished with wonder over my awe-compelling fireworks that I had to stay there and smoke a couple of pipes out before they would let me go. Still the delay was not wholly unproductive, for it took all that time to get Sandy thoroughly wonted to the new thing, she being so close to it, you know. It plugged up her conversation-mill, too, for a considerable while, and that was a gain. But above all other benefits accruing, I had learned something. I was ready for any giant or any ogre that might come along, now.

We tarried with a holy hermit, that night, and my opportunity came about the middle of the next afternoon. We were crossing a vast meadow by way of shortcut, and I was musing absently, hearing nothing, seeing nothing, when Sandy suddenly interrupted a remark which she had begun that morning, with the cry—

"Defend thee, lord—peril of life is toward!"

And she slipped down from the horse and ran a little way and stood. I looked up and saw, far off in the shade of a tree, half a dozen armed knights and their squires; and straightway there was bustle among them and tightening of saddle girths for the mount. My pipe was ready and would have been lit, if I had not been lost in thinking about how to banish oppression from this land and restore to all its people their stolen rights and manhood without disobliging anybody. I lit up at once, and by the time I had got a good head of reserved steam on, here they came. All together, too; none of those chivalrous magnanimities which one reads so much about—one courtly rascal at a time, and the rest standing by to see fair play. No, they came in a body, they came with a whirr and a rush, they came like a volley from a battery; came with heads low down, plumes streaming out behind, lances advanced at a level. It was a handsome sight, a beautiful sight—for a man up a tree. I laid my lance in rest and waited, with my heart beating, till the iron wave was just ready to break over me, then spouted a column of white smoke through the bars of my helmet. You

should have seen the wave go to pieces and scatter! This
was a finer sight than the other one.

But these people stopped, two or three hundred yards
away, and this troubled me. My satisfaction collapsed,
and fear came; I judged I was a lost man. But Sandy was
radiant; and was going to be eloquent, but I stopped her,
and told her my magic had miscarried, somehow or other,
and she must mount, with all dispatch, and we must ride
for life. No, she wouldn't. She said that my enchantment
had disabled those knights; they were not riding on, because they couldn't; wait, they would drop out of their
saddles presently, and we would get their horses and
harness. I could not deceive such trusting simplicity, so I
said it was a mistake; that when my fireworks killed at
all, they killed instantly; no, the men would not die, there
was something wrong about my apparatus, I couldn't tell
what; but we must hurry and get away, for those people
would attack us again, in a minute. Sandy laughed, and
said—

"Lackaday, sir, they be not of that breed! Sir Launcelot
will give battle to dragons, and will abide by them, and
will assail them again, and yet again, and still again, until
he do conquer and destroy them; and so likewise will Sir
Pellinore and Sir Aglovale and Sir Carados, and mayhap
others, but there be none else that will venture it, let the
idle say what the idle will. And, la, as to yonder base
rufflers, think ye they have not their fill, but yet desire
more?"

"Well, then, what are they waiting, for? Why don't
they leave? Nobody's hindering. Good land, I'm willing to
let bygones be bygones, I'm sure."

"Leave, is it? Oh, give thyself easement as to that.
They dream not of it, no, not they. They wait to yield
them."

"Come—really, is that 'sooth'—as you people say? If
they want to, why don't they?"

"It would like them much; but an ye wot how dragons
are esteemed, ye would not hold them blamable. They
fear to come."

"Well, then, suppose I go to them instead, and——"

"Ah, wit ye well they would not abide your coming. I
will go."

And she did. She was a handy person to have along on a raid. I would have considered this a doubtful errand, myself. I presently saw the knights riding away, and Sandy coming back. That was a relief. I judged she had somehow failed to get the first innings—I mean in the conversation; otherwise the interview wouldn't have been so short. But it turned out that she had managed the business well; in fact admirably. She said that when she told those people I was The Boss, it hit them where they lived: "smote them sore with fear and dread" was her word; and then they were ready to put up with anything she might require. So she swore them to appear at Arthur's court within two days and yield them, with horse and harness, and be my knights henceforth, and subject to my command. How much better she managed that thing than I should have done it myself! She was a daisy.

⟦ CHAPTER XV ⟧

Sandy's Tale

"AND so I'm proprietor of some knights," said I, as we rode off. "Who would ever have supposed that I should live to list up assets of that sort. I shan't know what to do with them; unless I raffle them off. How many of them are there, Sandy?"

"Seven, please you, sir, and their squires."

"It is a good haul. Who are they? Where do they hang out?"

"Where do they hang out?"

"Yes, where do they live?"

"Ah, I understood thee not. That will I tell thee eftsoons." Then she said musingly, and softly, turning the words daintily over her tongue: "Hang they out— hang they out—where hang—where do they hang out; eh, right so; where do they hang out. Of a truth the phrase hath a fair and winsome grace, and is prettily worded withal. I will repeat it anon and anon in mine idlesse, whereby I may peradventure learn it. Where do they hang out. Even so! Already it falleth trippingly from my tongue, and forasmuch as—"

"Don't forget the cowboys, Sandy."

"Cowboys?"

"Yes; the knights, you know: You were going to tell me about them. A while back, you remember. Figuratively speaking, game's called."

"Game—"

"Yes, yes, yes! Go to the bat. I mean, get to work on your statistics, and don't burn so much kindling getting your fire started. Tell me about the knights."

"I will well, and lightly will begin. So they two departed and rode into a great forest. And—"

"Great Scott!"

You see, I recognized my mistake at once. I had set her works agoing; it was my own fault; she would be thirty days getting down to those facts. And she generally began without a preface and finished without a result. If you interrupted her she would either go right along without noticing, or answer with a couple of words, and go back and say the sentence over again. So, interruptions only did harm; and yet I had to interrupt, and interrupt pretty frequently, too, in order to save my life; a person would die if he let her monotony drip on him right along all day.

"Great Scott!" I said in my distress. She went right back and began over again:

"So they two departed and rode into a great forest. And——"

"*Which* two?"

"Sir Gawaine and Sir Uwaine. And so they came to an abbey of monks, and there were well lodged. So on the morn they heard their masses in the abbey, and so they rode forth till they came to a great forest; then was Sir Gawaine ware in a valley by a turret, of twelve fair damsels, and two knights armed on great horses, and the damsels went to and fro by a tree. And then was Sir Gawaine ware how there hung a white shield on that tree, and ever as the damsels came by it they spit upon it, and some threw mire upon the shield—"

"Now, if I hadn't seen the like myself in this country,

Sandy, I wouldn't believe it. But I've seen it, and I can just see those creatures now, parading before that shield and acting like that. The women here do certainly act like all possessed. Yes, and I mean your best, too, society's very choicest brands. The humblest hello-girl along ten thousand miles of wire could teach gentleness, patience, modesty, manners, to the highest duchess in Arthur's land."

"Hello-girl?"

"Yes, but don't you ask me to explain; it's a new kind of girl; they don't have them here; one often speaks sharply to them when they are not the least in fault, and he can't get over feeling sorry for it and ashamed of himself in thirteen hundred years, it's such shabby mean conduct and so unprovoked; the fact is, no gentleman ever does it—though I—well, I myself, if I've got to confess—"

"Peradventure she—"

"Never mind her; never mind her; I tell you I couldn't ever explain her so you would understand."

"Even so be it, sith ye are so minded. Then Sir Gawaine and Sir Uwaine went and saluted them, and asked them why they did that despite to the shield. Sirs, said the damsels, we shall tell you. There is a knight in this country that owneth this white shield, and he is a passing good man of his hands, but he hateth all ladies and gentlewomen, and therefore we do all this despite to the shield. I will say you, said Sir Gawaine, it beseemeth evil a good knight to despise all ladies and gentlewomen, and peradventure though he hate you he hath some cause, and peradventure he loveth in some other places ladies and gentlewomen, and to be loved again, and he such a man of prowess as ye speak of"—

"Man of prowess—yes, that is the man to please them, Sandy. Man of brains—that is a thing they never think of. Tom Sayers—John Heenan—John L. Sullivan—pity but you could be here. You would have your legs under the Round Table and a Sir in front of your names within the twenty-four hours; and you could bring about a new distribution of the married princesses and duchesses of the Court in another twenty-four. The fact is, it is just a sort of polished up court of Comanches, and there isn't a squaw in it who doesn't stand ready at the dropping of a hat to desert to the buck with the biggest string of scalps at his belt."

——"and he be such a man of prowess as ye speak of, said Sir Gawaine. Now what is his name? Sir, said they, his name is Marhaus the king's son of Ireland."

"Son of the king of Ireland, you mean; the other form doesn't mean anything. And look out and hold on tight, now, we must jump this gully. . . . There, we are all right now. This horse belongs in the circus; he is born before his time."

"I know him well, said Sir Uwaine, he is a passing good knight as any is on live."

"*On live.* If you've got a fault in the world, Sandy, it is that you are a shade too archaic. But it isn't any matter."

——" for I saw him once proved at a justs where many knights were gathered, and that time there might no man withstand him. Ah, said Sir Gawaine, damsels, methinketh ye are to blame, for it is to suppose he that hung that shield there will not be long therefrom, and then may those knights match him on horseback, and that is more your worship than thus; for I will abide no longer to see a knight's shield dishonored. And therewith Sir Uwaine and Sir Gawaine departed a little from them, and then were they ware where Sir Marhaus came riding on a great horse straight toward them. And when the twelve damsels saw Sir Marhaus they fled into the turret as they were wild, so that some of them fell by the way. Then the one of the knights of the tower dressed his shield, and said on high, Sir Marhaus defend thee. And so they ran together that the knight brake his spear on Marhaus, and Sir Marhaus smote him so hard that he brake his neck and the horse's back—"

"Well, that is just the trouble about this state of things, it ruins so many horses."

"That saw the other knight of the turret, and dressed him toward Marhaus, and they went so eagerly together, that the knight of the turret was soon smitten down, horse and man, stark dead—"

"*Another* horse gone; I tell you it is a custom that

ought to be broken up. I don't see how people with any
feeling can applaud and support it."

"So these two knights came together with great random"—

I saw that I had been asleep and missed a chapter,
but I didn't say anything. I judged that the Irish knight
was in trouble with the visitors by this time, and this
turned out to be the case.

—"that Sir Uwaine smote Sir Marhaus that his spear
brast in pieces on the shield, and Sir Marhaus smote him
so sore that horse and man he bare to the earth, and
hurt Sir Uwaine on the left side—"

"The truth is, Alisande, these archaics are a little *too*
simple; the vocabulary is too limited, and so, by consequence, descriptions suffer in the matter of variety; they
run too much to level Saharas of fact, and not enough
to picturesque detail; this throws about them a certain
air of the monotonous; in fact the fights are all alike:
a couple of people come together with great random—
random is a good word, and so is exegesis, for that
matter, and so is holocaust, and defalcation, and usufruct
and a hundred others, but land! a body ought to dis-
criminate—they come together with great random, and a
spear is brast, and one party brake his shield and the
other one goes down, horse and man, over his horsetail
and brake his neck, and then the next candidate comes
randoming in, and brast *his* spear, and the other
man brast his shield, and down *he* goes, horse and man,
over his horsetail, and brake *his* neck, and then there's
another elected, and another and another and still another, till the material is all used up; and when you
come to figure up results, you can't tell one fight from
another, nor who whipped; and as a *picture,* of living,
raging, roaring battle, sho! why, it's pale and noiseless—
just ghosts scuffling in a fog. Dear me, what would this
barren vocabulary get out of the mightiest spectacle—
the burning of Rome in Nero's time, for instance? Why,
it would merely say, 'Town burned down; no insurance;
boy brast a window, fireman brake his neck!' Why, *that*
ain't a picture!"

It was a good deal of a lecture, I thought, but it

didn't disturb Sandy, didn't turn a feather; her steam soared steadily up again, the minute I took off the lid:

"Then Sir Marhaus turned his horse and rode toward Gawaine with his spear. And when Sir Gawaine saw that, he dressed his shield, and they aventred their spears, and they came together with all the might of their horses, that either knight smote other so hard in the midst of their shields, but Sir Gawaine's spear brake"—

"I knew it would."

—"but Sir Marhaus's spear held; and therewith Sir Gawaine and his horse rushed down to the earth"—

"Just so—and brake his back."

—"and lightly Sir Gawaine rose upon his feet and pulled out his sword, and dressed him toward Sir Marhaus on foot, and therewith either came unto other eagerly, and smote together with their swords, that their shields flew in cantles, and they bruised their helms and their hauberks, and wounded either other. But Sir Gawaine, fro it passed nine of the clock, waxed by the space of three hours ever stronger and stronger, and thrice his might was increased. All this espied Sir Marhaus, and had great wonder how his might increased, and so they wounded other passing sore; and then when it was come noon"—

The pelting singsong of it carried me forward to scenes and sounds of my boyhood days:

"N-e-e-ew Haven! ten minutes for refreshments— knductr 'll strike the gong-bell two minutes before train leaves—passengers for the Shore-line please take seats in the rear k'yar, this k'yar don't go no furder—*ahh*-pls, *aw*-rnjz, b'*nan*ners, *s-a-n-d'*ches, p——*op*-corn!"

—"and waxed past noon and drew towards evensong. Sir Gawaine's strength feebled and waxed passing faint, that unnethes he might dure any longer, and Sir Marhaus was then bigger and bigger"—

"Which strained his armor, of course; and yet little would one of these people mind a small thing like that."

—"and so, Sir Knight, said Sir Marhaus, I have well felt that ye are a passing good knight, and a marvelous man of might as ever I felt any, while it lasteth, and our quarrels are not great, and therefore it were a pity to do you hurt, for I feel you are passing feeble. Ah, said Sir Gawaine, gentle knight, ye say the word that I should say. And therewith they took off their helms and either kissed other, and there they swore together either to love other as brethren"—

But I lost the thread there, and dozed off to slumber, thinking about what a pity it was that men with such superb strength—strength enabling them to stand up cased in cruelly burdensome iron and drenched with perspiration, and hack and batter and bang each other for six hours on a stretch—should not have been born at a time when they could put it to some useful purpose. Take a jackass, for instance: a jackass has that kind of strength, and puts it to a useful purpose, and is valuable to this world because he *is* a jackass; but a nobleman is not valuable because he is a jackass. It is a mixture that is always ineffectual, and should never have been attempted in the first place. And yet, once you start a mistake, the trouble is done and you never know what is going to come of it.

When I came to myself again and began to listen, I perceived that I had lost another chapter, and that Alisande had wandered a long way off with her people.

"And so they rode and came into a deep valley full of stones, and thereby they saw a fair stream of water; above thereby was the head of the stream, a fair fountain, and three damsels sitting thereby. In this country, said Sir Marhaus, came never knight since it was christened, but he found strange adventures"—

"This is not good form, Alisande. Sir Marhaus the king's son of Ireland talks like all the rest; you ought to give him a brogue, or at least a characteristic expletive; by this means one would recognize him as soon as he spoke, without his ever being named. It is a common literary device with the great authors. You should make him say, 'In this country, be jabers, came never knight since it was christened, but he found strange adventures, be jabers.' You see how much better that sounds."

—"came never knight but he found strange adventures, be jabers. Of a truth it doth indeed, fair lord, albeit 'tis passing hard to say, though peradventure that will not tarry but better speed with usage. And then they rode to the damsels, and either saluted other, and the eldest had a garland of gold about her head, and she was threescore winter of age or more"—

"The *damsel* was?"

"Even so, dear lord—and her hair was white under the garland"—

"Celluloid teeth, nine dollars a set, as like as not— the loose-fit kind, that go up and down like a portcullis when you eat, and fall out when you laugh."

"The second damsel was of thirty winter of age, with a circlet of gold about her head. The third damsel was but fifteen year of age"—

Billows of thought came rolling over my soul, and the voice faded out of my hearing!

Fifteen! Break—my heart! Oh, my lost darling! Just her age who was so gentle, and lovely, and all the world to me, and whom I shall never see again! How the thought of her carries me back over wide seas of memory to a vague dim time, a happy time, so many, many centuries hence, when I used to wake in the soft summer mornings, out of sweet dreams of her, and say "Hello, Central!" just to hear her dear voice come melting back to me with a "Hello, Hank!" that was music of the spheres to my enchanted ear. She got three dollars a week, but she was worth it.

I could not follow Alisande's further explanation of who our captured knights were, now—I mean in case she should ever get to explaining who they were. My interest was gone, my thoughts were far away, and sad. By fitful glimpses of the drifting tale, caught here and there and now and then, I merely noted in a vague way that each of these three knights took one of these three damsels up behind him on his horse, and one rode north, another east, the other south, to seek adventures, and meet again and lie, after year and day. Year and day— and without baggage. It was of a piece with the general simplicity of the country.

The sun was now setting. It was about three in the afternoon when Alisande had begun to tell me who the cowboys were; so she had made pretty good progress with it—for her. She would arrive some time or other, no doubt, but she was not a person who could be hurried.

We were approaching a castle which stood on high
ground: a huge, strong, venerable structure, whose gray
towers and battlements were charmingly draped with ivy,
and whose whole majestic mass was drenched with splendors flung from the sinking sun. It was the largest castle
we had seen, and so I thought it might be the one we
were after, but Sandy said no. She did not know who
owned it; she said she had passed it without calling,
when she went down to Camelot.

<h1>{ CHAPTER XVI }</h1>

Morgan Le Fay

IF knights-errant were to be believed, not all castles
were desirable places to seek hospitality in. As a matter
of fact, knights-errant were *not* persons to be believed—
that is, measured by modern standards of veracity; yet,
measured by the standards of their own time, and scaled
accordingly, you got the truth. It was very simple: you
discounted a statement ninety-seven percent; the rest was
fact. Now after making this allowance, the truth remained
that if I could find out something about a castle before
ringing the doorbell—I mean hailing the warders—it was
the sensible thing to do. So I was pleased when I saw
in the distance a horseman making the bottom turn of
the road that wound down from this castle.

As we approached each other, I saw that he wore a
plumed helmet, and seemed to be otherwise clothed in
steel, but bore a curious addition also—a stiff square
garment like a herald's tabard. However, I had to smile
at my own forgetfulness when I got nearer and read
this sign on his tabard:

"*Persimmon's Soap—All the Prime-Donne Use It.*"

That was a little idea of my own, and had several
wholesome purposes in view toward the civilizing and
uplifting of this nation. In the first place, it was a furtive,

underhand blow at this nonsense of knight errantry, though nobody suspected that but me. I had started a number of these people out—the bravest knights I could get—each sandwiched between bulletin boards bearing one device or another, and I judged that by and by when they got to be numerous enough they would begin to look ridiculous; and then, even the steel-clad ass that *hadn't* any board would himself begin to look ridiculous because he was out of the fashion.

Secondly, these missionaries would gradually, and without creating suspicion or exciting alarm, introduce a rudimentary cleanliness among the nobility, and from them it would work down to the people, if the priests could be kept quiet. This would undermine the Church. I mean would be a step toward that. Next, education—next, freedom—and then she would begin to crumble. It being my conviction that any Established Church is an established crime, an established slave pen, I had no scruples, but was willing to assail it in any way or with any weapon that promised to hurt it. Why, in my own former day— in remote centuries not yet stirring in the womb of time —there were old Englishmen who imagined that they had been born in a free country: a "free" country with the Corporation Act and the Test still in force in it— timbers propped against men's liberties and dishonored consciences to shore up an Established Anachronism with.

My missionaries were taught to spell out the gilt signs on their tabards—the showy gilding was a neat idea, I could have got the king to wear a bulletin board for the sake of that barbaric splendor—they were to spell out these signs and then explain to the lords and ladies what soap was; and if the lords and ladies were afraid of it, get them to try it on a dog. The missionary's next move was to get the family together and try it on himself; he was to stop at no experiment, however desperate, that could convince the nobility that soap was harmless; if any final doubt remained, he must catch a hermit—the woods were full of them; saints they called themselves, and saints they were believed to be. They were unspeakably holy, and worked miracles, and everybody stood in awe of them. If a hermit could survive a wash, and that failed to convince a duke, give him up, let him alone.

Whenever my missionaries overcame a knight errant on the road they washed him, and when he got well they swore him to go and get a bulletin board and disseminate soap and civilization the rest of his days. As a consequence the workers in the field were increasing by degrees, and the reform was steadily spreading. My soap factory felt the strain early. At first I had only two hands; but before I had left home I was already employing fifteen, and running night and day; and the atmospheric result was getting so pronounced that the king went sort of fainting and gasping around and said he did not believe he could stand it much longer, and Sir Launcelot got so that he did hardly anything but walk up and down the roof and swear, although I told him it was worse up there than anywhere else, but he said he wanted plenty of air; and he was always complaining that a palace was no place for a soap factory, anyway, and said if a man was to start one in his house he would be damned if he wouldn't strangle him. There were ladies present, too, but much these people ever cared for that; they would swear before children, if the wind was their way when the factory was going.

This missionary knight's name was La Cote Male Taile, and he said that this castle was the abode of Morgan le Fay, sister of King Arthur, and wife of King Uriens, monarch of a realm about as big as the District of Columbia —you could stand in the middle of it and throw bricks into the next kingdom. "Kings" and "Kingdoms" were as thick in Britain as they had been in little Palestine in Joshua's time, when people had to sleep with their knees pulled up because they couldn't stretch out without a passport.

La Cote was much depressed, for he had scored here the worst failure of his campaign. He had not worked off a cake; yet he had tried all the tricks of the trade, even to the washing of a hermit; but the hermit died. This was indeed a bad failure, for this animal would now be dubbed a martyr, and would take his place among the saints of the Roman calendar. Thus made he his moan, this poor Sir La Cote Male Taile, and sorrowed passing sore. And so my heart bled for him, and

I was moved to comfort and stay him. Wherefore I said—

"Forbear to grieve, fair knight, for this is not a defeat. We have brains, you and I; and for such as have brains there are no defeats, but only victories. Observe how we will turn this seeming disaster into an advertisement; an advertisement for our soap; and the biggest one, to draw, that was ever thought of; an advertisement that will transform that Mount Washington defeat into a Matterhorn victory. We will put on your bulletin board, *'Patronized by the Elect.'* How does that strike you?"

"Verily, it is wonderly bethought!"

"Well, a body is bound to admit that for just a modest little one-line ad, it's a corker."

So the poor colporteur's griefs vanished away. He was a brave fellow, and had done mighty feats of arms in his time. His chief celebrity rested upon the events of an excursion like this one of mine, which he had once made with a damsel named Maledisant, who was as handy with her tongue as was Sandy, though in a different way, for her tongue churned forth only railings and insult, whereas Sandy's music was of a kindlier sort. I knew his story well, and so I knew how to interpret the compassion that was in his face when he bade me farewell. He supposed I was having a bitter hard time of it.

Sandy and I discussed his story, as we rode along, and she said that La Cote's bad luck had begun with the very beginning of that trip; for the king's fool had overthrown him on the first day, and in such cases it was customary for the girl to desert to the conqueror, but Maledisant didn't do it; and also persisted afterward in sticking to him, after all his defeats. But, said I, suppose the victor should decline to accept his spoil? She said that that wouldn't answer—he must. He couldn't decline; it wouldn't be regular. I made a note of that. If Sandy's music got to be too burdensome, sometime I would let a knight defeat me, on the chance that she would desert to him.

In due time we were challenged by the warders, from the castle walls, and after a parley admitted. I have nothing pleasant to tell about that visit. But it was not a disappointment, for I knew Mrs. le Fay by reputation, and was not expecting anything pleasant. She was held in awe by the whole realm, for she had made everybody believe she was a great sorceress. All her ways were wicked, all her instincts devilish. She was loaded to the eyelids with cold malice. All her history was black with crime; and among her crimes murder was common. I was most curious to see her; as curious as I could have been to see Satan. To my surprise she was beautiful; black thoughts had failed to make her expression repulsive, age had failed to wrinkle her satin skin or mar its bloomy freshness. She could have passed for old Uriens's granddaughter, she could have been mistaken for sister to her own son.

As soon as we were fairly within the castle gates we were ordered into her presence. King Uriens was there, a kind-faced old man with a subdued look; and also the son, Sir Uwaine le Blanchemains, in whom I was of course interested on account of the tradition that he had once done battle with thirty knights, and also on account of his trip with Sir Gawaine and Sir Marhaus, which Sandy had been aging me with. But Morgan was the main attraction, the conspicuous personality here; she was head chief of this household, that was plain. She caused us to be seated, and then she began, with all manner of pretty graces and graciousnesses, to ask me questions. Dear me, it was like a bird or a flute, or something, talking. I felt persuaded that this woman must have been misrepresented, lied about. She trilled along, and trilled along, and presently a handsome young page, clothed like the rainbow, and as easy and undulatory of movement as a wave, came with something on a golden salver, and kneeling to present it to her, overdid his graces and lost his balance, and so fell lightly against her knee. She slipped a dirk into him in as matter-of-course a way as another person would have harpooned a rat!

Poor child, he slumped to the floor, twisted his silken limbs in one great straining contortion of pain, and was dead. Out of the old king was wrung an involuntary "O-h!" of compassion. The look he got, made him cut it suddenly short and not put any more hyphens in it. Sir Uwaine, at a sign from his mother, went to the anteroom and called some servants, and meanwhile madame went rippling sweetly along with her talk.

I saw that she was a good housekeeper, for while she talked she kept a corner of her eye on the servants to see that they made no balks in handling the body and getting it out; when they came with fresh clean towels, she sent back for the other kind; and when they had finished wiping the floor and were going, she indicated a crimson fleck the size of a tear which their duller eyes had overlooked. It was plain to me that La Cote Male Taile had failed to see the mistress of the house. Often, how louder and clearer than any tongue, does dumb circumstantial evidence speak.

Morgan le Fay rippled along as musically as ever. Marvelous woman. And what a glance she had: when it fell in reproof upon those servants, they shrunk and quailed as timid people do when the lightning flashes out of a cloud. I could have got the habit myself. It was the same with that poor old Brer Uriens; he was always on the ragged edge of apprehension; she could not even turn towards him but he winced.

In the midst of the talk I let drop a complimentary word about King Arthur, forgetting for the moment how this woman hated her brother. That one little compliment was enough. She clouded up like a storm; she called for her guards, and said—

"Hale me these varlets to the dungeons!"

That struck cold on my ears, for her dungeons had a reputation. Nothing occurred to me to say—or do. But not so with Sandy. As the guard laid a hand upon me, she piped up with the tranquilest confidence, and said—

"God's wownds, dost thou covet destruction, thou maniac? It is The Boss!"

Now what a happy idea that was—and so simple; yet it would never have occurred to me. I was born modest; not all over, but in spots; and this was one of the spots.

The effect upon madame was electrical. It cleared her countenance and brought back her smiles and all her persuasive graces and blandishments; but nevertheless she was not able to entirely cover up with them the fact that she was in a ghastly fright. She said:

"La, but do list to thine handmaid! As if one gifted

with powers like to mine might say the thing which I
have said unto one who has vanquished Merlin, and not
be jesting. By mine enchantments I foresaw your coming, and by them I knew you when you entered here. I
did but play this little jest with hope to surprise you
into some display of your art, as not doubting you would
blast the guards with occult fires, consuming them to
ashes on the spot, a marvel much beyond mine own
ability, yet one which I have long been childishly curious
to see."

The guards were less curious, and got out as soon
as they got permission.

⟦ CHAPTER XVII ⟧

A Royal Banquet

MADAME, SEEING me pacific and unresentful, no doubt
judged that I was deceived by her excuse; for her fright
dissolved away, and she was soon so importunate to have
me give an exhibition and kill somebody, that the thing
grew to be embarrassing. However, to my relief she was
presently interrupted by the call to prayers. I will say
this much for the nobility: that, tyrannical, murderous,
rapacious and morally rotten as they were, they were
deeply and enthusiastically religious. Nothing could divert them from the regular and faithful performance of
the pieties enjoined by the Church. More than once I
had seen a noble who had gotten his enemy at a disad-
vantage, stop to pray before cutting his throat; more than
once I had seen a noble, after ambushing and dispatching
his enemy, retire to the nearest wayside shrine and
humbly give thanks, without even waiting to rob the body.
There was to be nothing finer or sweeter in the life of
even Benvenuto Cellini, that roughhewn saint, ten centuries later. All the nobles of Britain, with their families,
attended divine service morning and night daily, in their
private chapels, and even the worst of them had family

worship five or six times a day besides. The credit of this belonged entirely to the Church. Although I was no friend to that Catholic Church, I was obliged to admit this. And often, in spite of me, I found myself saying, "What would this country be without the Church?"

After prayers we had dinner in a great banqueting hall which was lighted by hundreds of grease jets, and everything was as fine and lavish and rudely splendid as might become the royal degree of the hosts. At the head of the hall, on a dais, was the table of the king, queen, and their son, Prince Uwaine. Stretching down the hall from this, was the general table, on the floor. At this, above the salt, sat the visiting nobles and the grown members of their families, of both sexes—the resident Court, in effect—sixty-one persons; below the salt sat minor officers of the household, with their principal subordinates: altogether a hundred and eighteen persons sitting, and about as many liveried servants standing behind their chairs, or serving in one capacity or another. It was a very fine show. In a gallery a band with cymbals, horns, harps, and other horrors opened the proceedings with what seemed to be the crude first draft or original agony of the wail known to later centuries as "In the Sweet Bye and Bye." It was new, and ought to have been rehearsed a little more. For some reason or other the queen had the composer hanged, after dinner.

After this music, the priest who stood behind the royal table said a noble long grace in ostensible Latin. Then the battalion of waiters broke away from their posts, and darted, rushed, flew, fetched, and carried, and the mighty feeding began; no words anywhere, but absorbing attention to business. The rows of chops opened and shut in vast unison, and the sound of it was like to the muffled burr of subterranean machinery.

The havoc continued an hour and a half, and unimaginable was the destruction of substantials. Of the chief feature of the feast—the huge wild boar that lay stretched out so portly and imposing at the start—nothing was left but the semblance of a hoopskirt; and he was but the type and symbol of what had happened to all the other dishes.

With the pastries and so on, the heavy drinking began

—and the talk. Gallon after gallon of wine and mead disappeared, and everybody got comfortable, then happy, then sparklingly joyous—both sexes—and by and by pretty noisy. Men told anecdotes that were terrific to hear, but nobody blushed; and when the nub was sprung, the assemblage let go with a horselaugh that shook the fortress. Ladies answered back with historiettes that would almost have made Queen Margaret of Navarre or even the great Elizabeth of England hide behind a handkerchief, but nobody hid here, but only laughed— howled, you may say. In pretty much all of these dreadful stories, ecclesiastics were the hardy heroes, but that didn't worry the chaplain any, he had his laugh with the rest; more than that, upon invitation he roared out a song which was of as daring a sort as any that was sung that night.

By midnight everybody was fagged out, and sore with laughing; and as a rule, drunk: some weepingly, some affectionately, some hilariously, some quarrelsomely, some dead and under the table. Of the ladies, the worst spectacle was a lovely young duchess, whose wedding eve this was; and indeed she was a spectacle, sure enough. Just as she was she could have sat in advance for the portrait of the young daughter of the Regent d'Orleans, at the famous dinner whence she was carried, foulmouthed, intoxicated, and helpless, to her bed, in the lost and lamented days of the Ancient Regime.

Suddenly, even while the priest was lifting his hands, and all conscious heads were bowed in reverent expectation of the coming blessing, there appeared under the arch of the far-off door at the bottom of the hall, an old and bent and white-haired lady, leaning upon a crutchstick; and she lifted the stick and pointed it toward the queen and cried out—

"The wrath and curse of God fall upon you, woman without pity, who have slain mine innocent grandchild and made desolate this old heart that had nor chick nor friend nor stay nor comfort in all this world but him!"

Everybody crossed himself in a grisly fright, for a curse was an awful thing to those people; but the queen rose up majestic, with the death light in her eye, and flung back this ruthless command:

"Lay hands on her! To the stake with her!"

The guards left their posts to obey. It was a shame; it was a cruel thing to see. What could be done? Sandy gave me a look; I knew she had another inspiration. I said—

"Do what you choose."

She was up and facing toward the queen in a moment. She indicated me, and said:

"Madame, *he* saith this may not be. Recall the commandment, or he will dissolve the castle and it shall vanish away like the instable fabric of a dream!"

Confound it, what a crazy contract to pledge a person to! What if the queen—

But my consternation subsided there, and my panic passed off; for the queen, all in a collapse, made no show of resistance but gave a countermanding sign and sunk into her seat. When she reached it she was sober. So were many of the others. The assemblage rose, whiffed ceremony to the winds, and rushed for the door like a mob, overturning chairs, smashing crockery, tugging, struggling, shouldering, crowding—anything to get out before I should change my mind and puff the castle into the measureless dim vacancies of space. Well, well, well, they *were* a superstitious lot. It is all a body can do to conceive of it.

The poor queen was so scared and humbled that she was even afraid to hang the composer without first consulting me. I was very sorry for her—indeed any one would have been, for she was really suffering; so I was willing to do anything that was reasonable, and had no desire to carry things to wanton extremities. I therefore considered the matter thoughtfully, and ended by having the musicians ordered into our presence to play that Sweet Bye and Bye again, which they did. Then I saw that she was right, and gave her permission to hang the whole band. This little relaxation of sternness had a good effect upon the queen. A statesman gains little by the arbitrary exercise of ironclad authority upon all occasions that offer, for this wounds the just pride of his subordinates, and thus tends to undermine his strength. A little concession, now and then, where it can do no harm, is the wiser policy.

Now that the queen was at ease in her mind once more, and measurably happy, her wine naturally began to assert itself again, and it got a little the start of her. I mean it set her music going—her silver bell of a tongue. Dear me, she was a master talker. It would not become me to suggest that it was pretty late and that I was a tired man and very sleepy. I wished I had gone off to bed when I had the chance. Now I must stick it out; there was no other way. So she tinkled along and along, in the otherwise profound and ghostly hush of the sleeping castle, until by and by there came, as if from deep down under us, a faraway sound, as of a muffled shriek —with an expression of agony about it that made my flesh crawl. The queen stopped, and her eyes lighted with pleasure; she tilted her graceful head as a bird does when it listens. The sound bored its way up through the stillness again.

"What is it?" I said.

"It is truly a stubborn soul, and endureth long. It is many hours now."

"Endureth what?"

"The rack. Come—ye shall see a blithe sight. An he yield not his secret now, ye shall see him torn asunder."

What a silky smooth hellion she was; and so composed and serene, when the cords all down my legs were hurting in sympathy with that man's pain. Conducted by mailed guards bearing flaring torches, we tramped along echoing corridors, and down stone stairways dank and dripping, and smelling of mold and ages of imprisoned night—a chill, uncanny journey and a long one, and not made the shorter or the cheerier by the sorceress' talk, which was about this sufferer and his crime. He had been accused by an anonymous informer, of having killed a stag in the royal preserves. I said—

"Anonymous testimony isn't just the right thing, your Highness. It were fairer to confront the accused with the accuser."

"I had not thought of that, it being but of small consequence. But an I would, I could not, for that the accuser came masked by night, and told the forester, and straightway got him hence again, and so the forester knoweth him not."

"Then is this Unknown the only person who saw the stag killed?"

"Marry, *no man saw* the killing, but this Unknown saw this hardy wretch near to the spot where the stag lay, and came with right loyal zeal and betrayed him to the forester."

"So the Unknown was near the dead stag, too? Isn't it just possible that he did the killing himself? His loyal zeal—in a mask—looks just a shade suspicious. But what is your Highness' idea for racking the prisoner? Where is the profit?"

"He will not confess, else; and then were his soul lost. For his crime his life is forfeited by the law—and of a surety will I see that he payeth it—but it were peril to my own soul to let him die unconfessed and unabsolved. Nay, I were a fool to fling me into hell for *his* accommodation."

"But, your Highness, suppose he has nothing to confess?"

"As to that, we shall see, anon. An I rack him to death and he confess not, it will peradventure show that he had indeed naught to confess—ye will grant that that is sooth? Then shall I not be damned for an unconfessed man that had naught to confess—wherefore, I shall be safe."

It was the stubborn unreasoning of the time. It was useless to argue with her. Arguments have no chance against petrified training; they wear it as little as the waves wear a cliff. And her training was everybody's. The brightest intellect in the land would not have been able to see that her position was defective.

As we entered the rack cell I caught a picture that will not go from me; I wish it would. A native young giant of thirty or thereabouts, lay stretched upon the frame on his back, with his wrists and ankles tied to ropes which led over windlasses at either end. There was no color in him; his features were contorted and set, and sweat drops stood upon his forehead. A priest bent over him on each side; the executioner stood by; guards were on duty; smoking torches stood in sockets along the walls; in a corner crouched a poor young creature, her face drawn with anguish, a half-wild and hunted look in her eyes, and in her lap lay a little child asleep. Just as we stepped across the threshold the executioner gave his machine a slight turn, which wrung a cry from both the prisoner and the woman; but I shouted and the executioner released the strain without waiting to see who spoke. I could not let this horror go on; it would have killed me to see it. I asked the queen to let me clear the place and speak to the prisoner privately; and when she was going to object I spoke in a low voice and said I did not want to make a scene before her servants, but I must have my way; for I was King Arthur's representative, and was speaking in his name. She saw she had to yield. I asked her to endorse me to these people, and then leave me. It was not pleasant for her, but she took the pill; and even went further than I was meaning to require. I only wanted the backing of her own authority; but she said—

"Ye will do in all things as this lord shall command. It is The Boss."

It was certainly a good word to conjure with: you could see it by the squirming of these rats. The queen's guards fell into line, and she and they marched away, with their torchbearers, and woke the echoes of the cavernous tunnels with the measured beat of their retreating footfalls. I had the prisoner taken from the rack and placed upon his bed, and medicaments applied to his hurts, and wine given him to drink. The woman crept near and looked on, eagerly, lovingly, but timorously—like one who fears a repulse; indeed, she tried furtively to touch the man's forehead, and jumped back, the picture of fright, when I turned unconsciously toward her. It was pitiful to see.

"Lord," I said, "stroke him, lass, if you want to. Do anything you're a mind to; don't mind me."

Why, her eyes were as grateful as an animal's, when you do it a kindness that it understands. The baby was out of her way and she had her cheek against the man's in a minute, and her hands fondling his hair, and her happy tears running down. The man revived, and caressed his wife with his eyes, which was all he could do. I judged I might clear the den, now, and I did; cleared it of all but the family and myself. Then I said—

"Now my friend, tell me your side of this matter; I know the other side."

The man moved his head in sign of refusal. But the woman looked pleased—as it seemed to me—pleased with my suggestion. I went on:

"You know of me?"

"Yes. All do, in Arthur's realms."

"If my reputation has come to you right and straight, you should not be afraid to speak."

The woman broke in, eagerly:

"Ah, fair my lord, do thou persuade him! Thou canst an thou wilt. Ah, he suffereth so; and it is for me—for *me!* And how can I bear it? I would I might see him die —a sweet, swift death; oh, my Hugo, I cannot bear this one!"

And she fell to sobbing and groveling about my feet, and still imploring. Imploring what? The man's death? I could not quite get the bearings of the thing. But Hugo interrupted her and said—

"Peace! Ye wit not what ye ask. Shall I starve whom I love, to win a gentle death? I wend thou knewest me better."

"Well," I said, "I can't quite make this out. It is a puzzle. Now—"

"Ah, dear my lord, an ye will but persuade him! Consider how these his tortures wound me! Oh, and he will not speak—whereas, the healing, the solace that lie in a blessed swift death—"

"What *are* you maundering about? He's going out from here a free man and whole—he's not going to die."

The man's white face lit up, and the woman flung herself at me in a most surprising explosion of joy, and cried out—

"He is saved—for it is the King's word by the mouth of the king's servant—Arthur, the king whose word is gold!"

"Well, then you do believe I can be trusted, after all. Why didn't you before?"

"Who doubted? Not I, indeed; and not she."

"Well, why wouldn't you tell me your story, then?"

"Ye had made no promise; else had it been otherwise."

"I see, I see. . . . And yet I believe I don't quite see,

after all. You stood the torture and refused to confess; which shows plain enough to even the dullest understanding that you had nothing to confess—"

"*I*, my lord? How so? It was I that killed the deer!"

"You *did?* Oh, dear, this is the most mixed-up business that ever—"

"Dear Lord, I begged him on my knees to confess, but—"

"You *did!* It gets thicker and thicker. What did you want him to do that for?"

"Sith it would bring him a quick death and save him all this cruel pain."

"Well—yes, there is reason in that. But *he* didn't want the quick death."

"He? Why, of a surety he *did*."

"Well, then, why in the world didn't he confess?"

"Ah, sweet sir, and leave my wife and chick without bread and shelter?"

"Oh, heart of gold, now I see it! The bitter law takes the convicted man's estate and beggars his widow and his orphans. They could torture you to death, but without conviction or confession they could not rob your wife and baby. You stood by them like a man; and *you* —true wife and true woman that you are—you would have bought him release from torture at cost to yourself of slow starvation and death—well, it humbles a body to think what your sex can do when it comes to self-sacrifice. I'll book you both for my colony; you'll like it there; it's a Factory where I'm going to turn groping and grubbing automata into *men*."

CHAPTER XVIII

In the Queen's Dungeons

WELL, I ARRANGED all that; and I had the man sent to his home. I had a great desire to rack the executioner; not because he was a good, painstaking and paingiving official,—for surely it was not to his discredit that he performed his functions well—but to pay him back for wantonly cuffing and otherwise distressing that young woman. The priests told me about this, and were generously hot to have him punished. Something of this disagreeable sort was turning up every now and then. I mean, episodes that showed that not all priests were frauds and self-seekers, but that many, even the great majority, of these that were down on the ground among the common people, were sincere and right-hearted, and devoted to the alleviation of human troubles and sufferings. Well, it was a thing which could not be helped, so I seldom fretted about it, and never many minutes at a time; it has never been my way to bother much about things which you can't cure. But I did not like it, for it was just the sort of thing to keep people reconciled to an Established Church. We *must* have a religion—it goes without saying—but my idea is, to have it cut up into forty free sects, so that they will police each other, as had been the case in the United States in my time. Concentration of power in a political machine is bad; and an Established Church is only a political machine; it was invented for that; it is nursed, cradled, preserved for that; it is an enemy to human liberty, and does no good which it could not better do in a split-up and scattered condition. That wasn't law; it wasn't gospel: it was only an opinion—my opinion, and I was only a man, one man: so it wasn't worth any more than the Pope's—or any less, for that matter.

Well, I couldn't rack the executioner, neither would I overlook the just complaint of the priests. The man must be punished some how or other, so I degraded him from his office and made him leader of the band—the new one that was to be started. He begged hard, and said he couldn't play—a plausible excuse, but too thin; there wasn't a musician in the country that could.

The queen was a good deal outraged, next morning, when she found she was going to have neither Hugo's life nor his property. But I told her she must bear this cross; that while by law and custom she certainly was entitled to both the man's life and his property, there were extenuating circumstances, and so in Arthur the

king's name I had pardoned him. The deer was ravaging
the man's fields, and he had killed it in sudden passion,
and not for gain; and he had carried it into the royal
forest in the hope that that might make detection of the
misdoer impossible. Confound her, I couldn't make her
see that sudden passion is an extenuating circumstance in
the killing of venison—or of a person—so I gave it up
and let her sulk it out. I *did* think I was going to make
her see it by remarking that her own sudden passion in
the case of the page modified that crime.

"Crime!" she exclaimed. "How thou talkest! Crime,
forsooth! Man, I am going to *pay* for him!"

Oh, it was no use to waste sense on her. Training—
training is everything; training is all there is *to* a person.
We speak of nature; it is folly; there is no such thing as
nature; what we call by that misleading name is merely
heredity and training. We have no thoughts of our own,
no opinions of our own; they are transmitted to us,
trained into us. All that is original in us, and therefore
fairly creditable or discreditable to us, can be covered up
and hidden by the point of a cambric needle, all the rest
being atoms contributed by, and inherited from, a procession of ancestors that stretches back a billion years to
the Adam-clam or grasshopper or monkey from whom our
race has been so tediously and ostentatiously and un-
profitably developed. And as for me, all that I think
about in this plodding sad pilgrimage, this pathetic drift
between the eternities, is to look out and humbly
live a pure and high and blameless life, and save that one
microscopic atom in me that is truly *me:* the rest may
land in Sheol and welcome for all I care.

No, confound her, her intellect was good, she had
brains enough, but her training made her an ass—that is,
from a many-centuries-later point of view. To kill the
page was no crime—it was her right; and upon her right
she stood, serenely and unconscious of offense. She was
a result of generations of training in the unexamined and
unassailed belief that the law which permitted her to kill
a subject when she chose was a perfectly right and
righteous one.

Well, we must give even Satan his due. She deserved
a compliment for one thing; and I tried to pay it, but the

words stuck in my throat. She had a right to kill the boy, but she was in no wise obliged to pay for him. That was law for some other people, but not for her. She knew quite well that she was doing a large and generous thing to pay for that lad, and that I ought in common fairness to come out with something handsome about it, but I couldn't—my mouth refused. I couldn't help seeing, in my fancy, that poor old grandam with the broken heart, and that fair young creature lying butchered, his little silken pomps and vanities laced with his golden blood. How could she *pay* for him? *Whom* could she pay? And so, well knowing that this woman, trained as she had been, deserved praise, even adulation, I was yet not able to utter it, trained as *I* had been. The best I could do was to fish up a compliment from outside, so to speak —and the pity of it was, that it was true:

"Madame, your people will adore you for this."

Quite true, but I meant to hang her for it some day, if I lived. Some of those laws were too bad, altogether too bad. A master might kill his slave for nothing: for mere spite, malice, or to pass the time—just as we have seen that the crowned head could do it with *his* slave, that is to say, anybody. A gentleman could kill a free commoner, and pay for him—cash or garden truck. A noble could kill a noble without expense, as far as the law was concerned, but reprisals in kind were to be expected. *Any*body could kill *some*body, except the commoner and the slave; these had no privileges. If they killed, it was murder, and the law wouldn't stand murder. It made short work of the experimenter—and of his family too, if he murdered somebody who belonged up among the ornamental ranks. If a commoner gave a noble even so much as a Damiens-scratch which didn't kill or even hurt, he got Damiens's dose for it just the same; they pulled him to rags and tatters with horses, and all the world came to see the show, and crack jokes, and have a good time; and some of the performances of the best people present were as tough, and as properly unprintable, as any that have been printed by the pleasant Casanova in his chapter about the dismemberment of Louis XV's poor awkward enemy.

I had had enough of this grisly place by this time, and

wanted to leave, but I couldn't, because I had something
on my mind that my conscience kept prodding me about,
and wouldn't let me forget. If I had the remaking of man,
he wouldn't have any conscience. It is one of the most
disagreeable things connected with a person; and although
it certainly does a great deal of good, it cannot be said
to pay, in the long run; it would be much better to have
less good and more comfort. Still, this is only my opinion,
and I am only one man; others, with less experience, may
think differently. They have a right to their view. I only
stand to this: I have noticed my conscience for many
years, and I know it is more trouble and bother to me
than anything else I started with. I suppose that in the
beginning I prized it, because we prize anything that is
ours; and yet how foolish it was to think so. If we look
at it in another way, we see how absurd it is: if I had an
anvil in me would I prize it? Of course not. And yet
when you come to think, there is no real difference between a conscience and an anvil—I mean for comfort. I
have noticed it a thousand times. And you could dissolve
an anvil with acids, when you couldn't stand it any longer;
but there isn't any way that you can work off a conscience—at least so it will stay worked off; not that I
know of, anyway.

There was something I wanted to do before leaving,
but it was a disagreeable matter, and I hated to go at it.
Well, it bothered me all the morning. I could have mentioned it to the old king, but what would be the use—he
was but an extinct volcano; he had been active in his
time, but his fire was out, this good while, he was only a
stately ash pile, now; gentle enough, and kindly enough
for my purpose, without doubt, but not usable. He was
nothing, this so-called king: the queen was the only power
there. And she was a Vesuvius. As a favor, she might
consent to warm a flock of sparrows for you, but then she
might take that very opportunity to turn herself loose
and bury a city. However, I reflected that as often as
any other way, when you are expecting the worst, you get
something that is not so bad, after all.

So I braced up and placed my matter before her royal
Highness. I said I had been having a general jail delivery
at Camelot and among neighboring castles, and with her

permission I would like to examine her collection, her bric-a-brac—that is to say, her prisoners. She resisted; but I was expecting that. But she finally consented. I was expecting that, too, but not so soon. That about ended my discomfort. She called her guards and torches, and we went down into the dungeons. These were down under the castle's foundations, and mainly were small cells hollowed out of the living rock. Some of these cells had no light at all. In one of them was a woman, in foul rags, who sat on the ground, and would not answer a question, or speak a word, but only looked up at us once or twice, through a cobweb of tangled hair, as if to see what casual thing it might be that was disturbing with sound and light the meaningless dull dream that was become her life; after that, she sat bowed, with her dirt-caked fingers idly interlocked in her lap, and gave no further sign. This poor rack of bones was a woman of middle age, apparently; but only apparently; she had been there nine years, and was eighteen when she entered. She was a commoner, and had been sent here on her bridal night by Sir Breuse Sance Pité, a neighboring lord whose vassal her father was, and to which said lord she had refused what has since been called *le droit du Seigneur;* and moreover, had opposed violence to violence and spilt half a gill of his almost sacred blood. The young husband had interfered at that point, believing the bride's life in danger, and had flung the noble out into the midst of the humble and trembling wedding guests, in the parlor, and left him there astonished at this strange treatment, and implacably embittered against both bride and groom. The said lord being cramped for dungeon room had asked the queen to accommodate his two criminals, and here in her bastille they had been ever since; hither indeed, they had come before their crime was an hour old, and had never seen each other since. Here they were, kerneled like toads in the same rock; they had passed nine pitch dark years within fifty feet of each other, yet neither knew whether the other was alive or not. All the first years, their only question had been—asked with beseechings and tears that might have moved stones, in time, perhaps, but hearts are not stones: "Is he alive?" "Is she alive?" But they had never got an answer; and at last that question was not asked any more—or any other.

I wanted to see the man, after hearing all this. He was thirty-four years old, and looked sixty. He sat upon a squared block of stone, with his head bent down, his forearms resting on his knees, his long hair hanging like a fringe before his face, and he was muttering to himself. He raised his chin and looked us slowly over, in a listless dull way, blinking with the distress of the torchlight, then dropped his head and fell to muttering again and took no further notice of us. There were some pathetically suggestive dumb witnesses present. On his wrists and ankles were cicatrices, old smooth scars, and fastened to the stone on which he sat was a chain with manacles and fetters attached; but this apparatus lay idle on the ground, and was thick with rust. Chains cease to be needed after the spirit has gone out of a prisoner.

I could not rouse the man; so I said we would take him to her, and see—to the bride who was the fairest thing in the earth to him, once—roses, pearls, and dew made flesh, for him; a wonderwork, the masterwork of nature: with eyes like no other eyes, and voice like no other voice, and a freshness, and lithe young grace, and beauty that belonged properly to the creatures of dreams —as he thought—and to no other. The sight of her would set his stagnant blood leaping; the sight of her—

But it was a disappointment. They sat together on the ground and looked dimly wondering into each other's faces awhile, with a sort of weak animal curiosity; then forgot each other's presence, and dropped their eyes, and you saw that they were away again and wandering in some far land of dreams and shadows that we know nothing about.

I had them taken out and sent to their friends. The queen did not like it much. Not that she felt any personal interest in the matter, but she thought it disrespectful to Sir Breuse Sance Pité. However, I assured her that if he found he couldn't stand it I would fix him so that he could.

I set forty-seven prisoners loose out of those awful ratholes, and left only one in captivity. He was a lord, and had killed another lord, a sort of kinsman of the queen.

That other lord had ambushed him to assassinate him, but this fellow had got the best of him and cut his throat. However, it was not for that that I left him jailed, but for maliciously destroying the only public well in one of his wretched villages. The queen was bound to hang him for killing her kinsman, but I would not allow it: it was no crime to kill an assassin. But I said I was willing to let her hang him for destroying the well; so she concluded to put up with that, as it was better than nothing.

Dear me, for what trifling offenses the most of those forty-seven men and women were shut up there! Indeed some were there for no distinct offense at all, but only to gratify somebody's spite; and not always the queen's by any means, but a friend's. The newest prisoner's crime was a mere remark which he had made. He said he believed that men were about all alike, and one man as good as another, barring clothes. He said he believed that if you were to strip the nation naked and send a stranger through the crowd, he couldn't tell the king from a quack doctor, nor a duke from a hotel clerk. Apparently here was a man whose brains had not been reduced to an ineffectual mush by idiotic training. I set him loose and sent him to the Factory.

Some of the cells carved in the living rock were just behind the face of the precipice, and in each of these an arrow-slit had been pierced outward to the daylight, and so the captive had a thin ray from the blessed sun for his comfort. The case of one of these poor fellows was particularly hard. From his dusky swallow's hole high up in that vast wall of native rock he could peer out through the arrow-slit and see his own home off yonder in the valley; and for twenty-two years he had watched it, with heartache and longing, through that crack. He could see the lights shine there at night, and in the daytime he could see figures go in and come out—his wife and children, some of them, no doubt, though he could not make out, at that distance. In the course of years he noted festivities there, and tried to rejoice, and wondered if they were weddings or what they might be. And he noted funerals; and they wrung his heart. He could make out the coffin, but he could not determine its size, and so could not tell whether it was wife or child. He could see the procession form, with priests and mourners, and move solemnly away, bearing the secret with them. He had left behind him five children and a wife; and in nineteen years he had seen five funerals issue, and none of them humble enough in pomp to denote a servant. So he had lost five of his treasures; there must still be one remaining —one now infinitely, unspeakably precious—but *which* one? Wife, or child? That was the question that tortured him, by night and by day, asleep and awake. Well, to have an interest of some sort, and half a ray of light, when you are in a dungeon, is a great support to the body and preserver of the intellect. This man was in pretty good condition yet. By the time he had finished telling me his distressful tale, I was in the same state of mind that you would have been in yourself, if you have got average human curiosity: that is to say, I was as burning up as he was, to find out which member of the family it was that was left. So I took him over home myself; and an amazing kind of a surprise party it was, too— typhoons and cyclones of frantic joy, and whole Niagaras of happy tears; and by George we found the aforetime young matron graying toward the imminent verge of her half century, and the babies all men and women, and some of them married and experimenting familywise themselves—for not a soul of the tribe was dead! Conceive of the ingenious devilishness of that queen: she had a special hatred for this prisoner, and she had *invented* all those funerals herself, to scorch his heart with; and the sublimest stroke of genius of the whole thing was leaving the family invoice a funeral *short*, so as to let him wear his poor old soul out guessing.

But for me, he never would have got out. Morgan le Fay hated him with her whole heart, and she never would have softened toward him. And yet his crime was committed more in thoughtlessness than deliberate depravity. He had said she had red hair. Well, she had; but that was no way to speak of it. When red-headed people are above a certain social grade, their hair is auburn.

Consider it: among these forty-seven captives, there were five whose names, offenses and dates of incarceration were no longer known! One woman and four men— all bent, and wrinkled, and mind-extinguished patriarchs.

They themselves had long ago forgotten these details; at any rate they had mere vague theories about them, nothing definite and nothing that they repeated twice in the same way. The succession of priests whose office it had been to pray daily with the captives and remind them that God had put them there, for some wise purpose or other, and teach them that patience, humbleness, and submission to oppression was what He loved to see in parties of a subordinate rank, had traditions about these poor old human ruins, but nothing more. These traditions went but little way, for they concerned the length of the incarceration only, and not the names or the offenses. And even by the help of tradition the only thing that could be proven was that none of the five had seen daylight for thirty-five years: how much longer this privation had lasted was not guessable. The king and the queen knew nothing about these poor creatures, except that they were heirlooms, assets inherited, along with the throne, from the former firm. Nothing of their history had been transmitted with their persons, and so the inheriting owners had considered them of no value, and had felt no interest in them. I said to the queen—

"Then why in the world didn't you set them free?"

The question was a puzzler. She didn't know *why* she hadn't; the thing had never come up in her mind. So here she was, forecasting the veritable history of future prisoners of the castle d'If, without knowing it. It seemed plain to me now, that with her training, those inherited prisoners were merely property—nothing more, nothing less. Well, when we inherit property, it does not occur to us to throw it away, even when we do not value it.

When I brought my procession of human bats up into the open world and the glare of the afternoon sun—previously blind-folding them, in charity for eyes so long untortured by light—they were a spectacle to look at. Skeletons, scarecrows, goblins, pathetic frights, every one: legitimatest possible children of Monarchy by the Grace of God and the Established Church. I muttered absently—

"I *wish* I could photograph them!"

You have seen that kind of people who will never let on that they don't know the meaning of a new big word.

The more ignorant they are, the more pitifully certain they are to pretend you haven't shot over their heads. The queen was just one of that sort, and was always making the stupidest blunders by reason of it. She hesitated a moment; then her face brightened up with sudden comprehension, and she said she would do it for me.

I thought to myself: She? why what can she know about photography? But it was a poor time to be thinking. When I looked around, she was moving on the procession with an ax!

Well, she certainly was a curious one, was Morgan le Fay. I have seen a good many kinds of women in my time, but she laid over them all, for variety. And how sharply characteristic of her this episode was. She had no more idea than a horse of how to photograph a procession; but being in doubt, it was just like her to try to do it with an ax.

⟦ CHAPTER XIX ⟧

Knight–Errantry as a Trade

SANDY AND I were on the road again, next morning, bright and early. It was *so* good to open up one's lungs and take in whole luscious barrelfuls of the blessed God's untainted, dew-freshened, woodland-scented air once more, after suffocating body and mind for two days and nights in the moral and physical stenches of that intolerable old buzzard roost! I mean, for me: of course the place was all right and agreeable enough for Sandy, for she had been used to high life all her days.

Poor girl, her jaws had had a wearisome rest, now for a while, and I was expecting to get the consequences. I was right; but she had stood by me most helpfully in the castle, and had mightily supported and reinforced me with gigantic foolishnesses which were worth more for the occasion than wisdoms double their size; so I thought she had earned a right to work her mill for a while, if she wanted to, and I felt not a pang when she started it up:

"Now turn we unto Sir Marhaus that rode with the damsel of thirty winter of age southward"—

"Are you going to see if you can work up another half-stretch on the trail of the cowboys, Sandy?"

"Even so, fair my lord."

"Go ahead, then. I won't interrupt this time, if I can help it. Begin over again; start fair, and shake out all your reefs, and I will load my pipe and give good attention."

"Now turn we unto Sir Marhaus that rode with the damsel of thirty winter of age southward. And so they came into a deep forest, and by fortune they were nighted, and rode along in a deep way, and at the last they came into a courtelage where abode the duke of South Marches, and there they asked harbor. And on the morn the duke sent unto Sir Marhaus, and bad him make him ready. And so Sir Marhaus arose and armed him, and there was a mass sung afore him, and he brake his fast, and so mounted on horseback in the court of the castle, there they should do the battle. So there was the duke already on horseback, clean armed, and his six sons by him, and every each had a spear in his hand, and so they encountered, whereas the duke and his two sons brake their spears upon him, but Sir Marhaus held up his spear and touched none of them. Then came the four sons by couples, and two of them brake their spears, and so did the other two. And all this while Sir Marhaus touched them not. Then Sir Marhaus ran to the duke, and smote him with his spear that horse and man fell to the earth. And so he served his sons. And then Sir Marhaus alight down, and bad the duke yield him or else he would slay him. And then some of his sons recovered, and would have set upon Sir Marhaus. Then Sir Marhaus said to the duke, Cease thy sons, or else I will do the uttermost to you all. When the duke saw he might not escape the death, he cried to his sons, and charged them to yield them to Sir Marhaus. And they kneeled all down and put the pommels of their swords to the knight, and so he received them. And then they holp up their father, and so by their common assent promised unto Sir Marhaus never to be foes unto King Arthur, and thereupon at Whitsuntide after, to come he and his sons, and put them in the king's grace.*

"Even so standeth the history, fair Sir Boss. Now ye shall wit that that very duke and his six sons are they whom but few days past you also did overcome and send to Arthur's court!"

"Why, Sandy, you can't mean it!"

"An I speak not sooth, let it be the worse for me."

"Well, well, well—now who would ever have thought it? One whole duke and six dukelets; why, Sandy, it was an elegant haul. Knight-errantry is a most chuckle-headed trade, and it is tedious hard work, too, but I begin to see that there *is* money in it, after all, if you have luck. Not that I would ever engage in it as a business; for I wouldn't. No sound and legitimate business can be established on a basis of speculation. A successful whirl in the knight-errantry line—now what is it when you blow away the nonsense and come down to the cold facts? It's just a corner in pork, that's all, and you can't make anything else out of it. You're rich—yes—suddenly rich— for about a day, maybe a week: then somebody corners the market on *you*, and down goes your bucket shop; ain't that so, Sandy?"

"Whethersoever it be that my mind miscarrieth, be-wraying simple language in such sort that the words do seem to come endlong and overthwart—"

"There's no use in beating about the bush and trying to get around it that way, Sandy, it's *so*, just as I say. I *know* it's so. And, moreover, when you come right down to the bedrock, knight-errantry is *worse* than pork; for whatever happens, the pork's left, and so somebody's benefited, anyway; but when the market breaks, in a knight-errantry whirl, and every knight in the pool passes in his checks, what have you got for assets? Just a rub-bish pile of battered corpses and a barrel or two of busted hardware. Can you call *those* assets? Give me pork, every time. Am I right?"

"Ah, peradventure my head being distraught by the manifold matters whereunto the confusions of these but

---

* The story is borrowed, language and all, from the *Morte d' Arthur.*—M. T.

late adventured haps and fortunings whereby not I alone
nor you alone, but every each of us, meseemeth——"

"No, it's not your head, Sandy. Your head's all right,
as far as it goes, but you don't know business; that's
where the trouble is. It unfits you to argue about business,
and you're wrong to be always trying. However, that
aside, it was a good haul, anyway, and will breed a handsome crop of reputation in Arthur's court. And speaking
of the cowboys, what a curious country this is for women
and men that never get old. Now there's Morgan le Fay,
as fresh and young as a Vassar pullet, to all appearances,
and here is this old duke of the South Marches still
slashing away with sword and lance at his time of life,
after raising such a family as he has raised. As I understand it, Sir Gawaine killed seven of his sons, and still he
had six left for Sir Marhaus and me to take into camp.
And then there was that damsel of sixty winter of age
still excursioning around in her frosty bloom—— How
old are you, Sandy?"

It was the first time I ever struck a still place in her.
The mill had shut down for repairs, or something.

❲ CHAPTER XX ❳

The Ogre's Castle

BETWEEN SIX and nine we made ten miles, which was
plenty for a horse carrying triple—man, woman, and
armor; then we stopped for a long nooning, under some
trees by a limpid brook.

Right so came by and by a knight riding; and as he
drew near he made dolorous moan, and by the words of
it I perceived that he was cursing and swearing; yet
nevertheless was I glad of his coming, for that I saw he
bore a bulletin board whereon in letters all of shining
gold was writ—

"USE PETERSON'S PROPHYLACTIC TOOTHBRUSH
—ALL THE GO."

I was glad of his coming, for even by this token I knew him for knight of mine. It was Sir Madok de la Montaine, a burly great fellow whose chief distinction was that he had come within an ace of sending Sir Launcelot down over his horsetail once. He was never long in a stranger's presence without finding some pretext or other to let out that great fact. But there was other fact of nearly the same size, which he never pushed upon anybody unasked, and yet never withheld when asked: that was, that the reason he didn't quite succeed was, that he was interrupted and sent down over horsetail himself. This innocent vast lubber did not see any particular difference between the two facts. I liked him, for he was earnest in his work, and very valuable. And he was so fine to look at, with his broad mailed shoulders, and the grand leonine set of his plumed head, and his big shield with its quaint device of a gauntleted hand clutching a prophylactic toothbrush, with motto: *"Try Noyoudont."* This was a toothwash that I was introducing.

He was aweary, he said, and indeed he looked it; but he would not alight. He said he was after the stove-polish man; and with this he broke out cursing and swearing anew. The bulletin boarder referred to was Sir Ossaise of Surluse, a brave knight, and of considerable celebrity on account of his having tried conclusions in a tournament, once, with no less a Mogul than Sir Gaheris himself—although not successfully. He was of a light and laughing disposition, and to him nothing in this world was serious. It was for this reason that I had chosen him to work up a stove-polish sentiment. There were no stoves yet, and so there could be nothing serious about stove polish. All that the agent needed to do was to deftly and by degrees prepare the public for the great change, and have them established in predilections toward neatness against the time when the stove should appear upon the stage.

Sir Madok was very bitter, and brake out anew with cursings. He said he had cursed his soul to rags; and yet he would not get down from his horse, neither would he take any rest, or listen to any comfort, until he should have found Sir Ossaise and settled this account. It appeared, by what I could piece together of the unprofane fragments of his statement, that he had chanced upon Sir Ossaise at dawn of the morning, and been told that if he would make a shortcut across the fields and swamps and broken hills and glades, he could head off a company of travelers who would be rare customers for prophylactics and toothwash. With characteristic zeal Sir Madok had plunged away at once upon this quest, and after three hours of awful crosslot riding had overhauled his game. And behold, it was the five patriarchs that had been released from the dungeons the evening before! Poor old creatures, it was all of twenty years since any one of them had known what it was to be equipped with any remaining snag or remnant of a tooth.

"Blank-blank-blank him," said Sir Madok, "an I do not stove polish him an I may find him, leave it to me; for never no knight that hight Ossaise or aught else may do me this disservice and bide on live, an I may find him, the which I have thereunto sworn a great oath this day."

And with these words, and others, he lightly took his spear and gat him thence. In the middle of the afternoon we came upon one of those very patriarchs ourselves, in the edge of a poor village. He was basking in the love of relatives and friends whom he had not seen for fifty years; and about him and caressing him were also descendants of his own body whom he had never seen at all till now; but to him these were all strangers, his memory was gone, his mind was stagnant. It seemed incredible that a man could outlast half a century shut up in a dark hole like a rat, but here were his old wife and some old comrades to testify to it. They could remember him as he was in the freshness and strength of his young manhood, when he kissed his child and delivered it to its mother's hands and went away into that long oblivion. The people at the castle could not tell within half a generation the length of time the man had been shut up there for his unrecorded and forgotten offense; but this old wife knew; and so did her old child, who stood there among her married sons and daughters trying to realize a father who had been to her a name, a thought, a formless image, a tradition, all her life, and now was suddenly concreted into actual flesh and blood and set before her face.

It was a curious situation; yet it is not on that account that I have made room for it here, but on account of a thing which seemed to me still more curious. To wit, that this dreadful matter brought from these downtrodden people no outburst of rage against their oppressors. They had been heritors and subjects of cruelty and outrage so long that nothing could have startled them but a kindness. Yes, here was a curious revelation indeed, of the depth to which this people had been sunk in slavery. Their entire being was reduced to a monotonous dead level of patience, resignation, dumb uncomplaining acceptance of whatever might befall them in this life. Their very imagination was dead. When you can say that of a man, he has struck bottom, I reckon; there is no lower deep for him.

I rather wished I had gone some other road. This was not the sort of experience for a statesman to encounter who was planning out a peaceful revolution in his mind. For it could not help bringing up the un-get-aroundable fact that, all gentle cant and philosophising to the contrary notwithstanding, no people in the world ever did achieve their freedom by goody-goody talk and moral suasion: it being immutable law that all revolutions that will succeed, must *begin* in blood, whatever may answer afterward. If history teaches anything, it teaches that. What this folk needed, then, was a Reign of Terror and a guillotine, and I was the wrong man for them.

Two days later, toward noon, Sandy began to show signs of excitement and feverish expectancy. She said we were approaching the ogre's castle. I was surprised into an uncomfortable shock. The object of our quest had gradually dropped out of my mind; this sudden resurrection of it made it seem quite a real and startling thing, for a moment, and roused up in me a smart interest. Sandy's excitement increased every moment; and so did mine, for that sort of thing is catching. My heart got to thumping. You can't reason with your heart; it has its own laws, and thumps about things which the intellect scorns. Presently, when Sandy slid from the horse, motioned me to stop, and went creeping stealthily, with her head bent nearly to her knees, toward a row of bushes that bordered a declivity, the thumpings grew stronger and quicker. And they kept it up while she was gaining her ambush and getting her glimpse over the declivity and also while I was creeping to her side on my knees. Her eyes were burning, now, as she pointed with her finger, and said in a panting whisper—

"The castle! The castle! Lo, where it looms!"

What a welcome disappointment I experienced! I said—

"Castle? It is nothing but a pigsty; a pigsty with a wattled fence around it."

She looked surprised and distressed. The animation faded out of her face, and during many moments she was lost in thought and silent. Then—

"It was not enchanted aforetime," she said in a musing fashion, as if to herself. "And how strange is this marvel, and how awful—that to the one perception it is enchanted and dight in a base and shameful aspect; yet to the perception of the other it is not enchanted, hath suffered no change, but stands firm and stately still, girt with its moat and waving its banners in the blue air from its towers. And God shield us, how it pricks the heart to see again these gracious captives, and the sorrow deepened in their sweet faces! We have tarried long, and are to blame."

I saw my cue. The castle was enchanted to *me*, not to her. It would be wasted time to try to argue her out of her delusion, it couldn't be done; I must just humor it. So I said—

"This is a common case—the enchanting of a thing to one eye and leaving it in its proper form to another. You have heard of it before, Sandy, though you haven't happened to experience it. But no harm is done. In fact it is lucky the way it is. If these ladies were hogs to everybody and to themselves, it would be necessary to break the enchantment, and that might be impossible if one failed to find out the particular process of the enchantment. And hazardous, too; for in attempting a disenchantment without the true key, you are liable to err, and turn your hogs into dogs, and the dogs into cats, the cats into rats, and so on, and end by reducing your materials to nothing, finally, or to an odorless gas which you can't follow—which of course amounts to the same thing. But here, by good luck, no one's eyes but mine are under the enchantment, and so it is of no consequence to dissolve it. These ladies remain ladies to you, and to themselves, and to everybody else; and at the same time they will suffer in no way from my delusion, for when I know that an ostensible hog is a lady, that is enough for me, I know how to treat her."

"Thanks, oh sweet my lord, thou talkest like an angel. And I know that thou wilt deliver them, for that thou art minded to great deeds and art as strong a knight of your hands and as brave to will and to do, as any that is on live."

"I will not leave a princess in the sty, Sandy. Are those three yonder that to my disordered eyes are starveling swineherds"—

"The ogres? Are *they* changed also? It is most wonderful. Now am I fearful; for how canst thou strike with sure aim when five of their nine cubits of stature are to thee invisible? Ah, go warily, fair sir; this is a mightier emprise than I wend."

"You be easy, Sandy. All I need to know is, how *much* of an ogre is invisible; then I know how to locate his vitals. Don't you be afraid, I will make short work of these bunco steerers. Stay where you are."

I left Sandy kneeling there, corpse-faced but plucky and hopeful, and rode down to the pigsty, and struck up a trade with the swineherds. I won their gratitude by buying out all the hogs at the lump sum of sixteen pennies, which was rather above latest quotations. I was just in time; for the Church, the lord of the manor, and the rest of the tax gatherers would have been along next day and swept off pretty much all the stock, leaving the swineherds very short of hogs and Sandy out of princesses. But now the tax people could be paid in cash, and there would be a stake left besides. One of the men had ten children; and he said that last year when a priest came and of his ten pigs took the fattest one for tithes, the

wife burst out upon him, and offered him a child and
said—

"Thou beast without bowels of mercy, why leave me
my child, yet rob me of the wherewithal to feed it?"

How curious. The same thing had happened in the
Wales of my day, under this same old Established Church,
which was supposed by many to have changed its nature
when it changed its disguise.

I sent the three men away, and then opened the sty
gate and beckoned Sandy to come—which she did; and
not leisurely, but with the rush of a prairie fire. And when
I saw her fling herself upon those hogs, with tears of
joy running down her cheeks, and strain them to her
heart, and kiss them, and caress them, and call them
reverently by grand princely names, I was ashamed of
her, ashamed of the human race.

We had to drive those hogs home—ten miles; and no
ladies were ever more fickle-minded or contrary. They
would stay in no road, no path; they broke out through
the brush on all sides, and flowed away in all directions,
over rocks, and hills, and the roughest places they could
find. And they must not be struck, or roughly accosted;
Sandy could not bear to see them treated in ways unbe-
coming their rank. The troublesomest old sow of the lot
had to be called my Lady, and your Highness, like the
rest. It is annoying and difficult to scour around after
hogs, in armor. There was one small countess, with an
iron ring in her snout and hardly any hair on her back,
that was the devil for perversity. She gave me a race of
an hour, over all sorts of country, and then we were right
where we had started from, having made not a rod of
real progress. I seized her at last by the tail, and brought
her along, squealing. When I overtook Sandy, she was
horrified, and said it was in the last degree indelicate to
drag a countess by her train.

We got the hogs home just at dark—most of them.
The princess Nerovens de Morganore was missing, and
two of her ladies in waiting: namely, Miss Angela Bohun,
and the Demoiselle Elaine Courtemains, the former of
these two being a young black sow with a white star in
her forehead, and the latter a brown one with thin legs
and a slight limp in the forward shank on the starboard

side—a couple of the tryingest blisters to drive, that I ever saw. Also among the missing were several mere baronesses—and I wanted them to stay missing; but no, all that sausage meat had to be found; so, servants were sent out with torches to scour the woods and hills to that end.

Of course the whole drove was housed in the house, and great guns—well, I never saw anything like it! Nor ever heard anything like it. And never smelt anything like it. It was like an insurrection in a gasometer.

〖 CHAPTER XXI 〗

The Pilgrims

WHEN I did get to bed at last I was unspeakably tired; the stretching out, and the relaxing of the long-tense muscles, how luxurious, how delicious! but that was as far as I could get—sleep was out of the question, for the present. The ripping and tearing and squealing of the nobility up and down the halls and corridors was pandemonium come again and kept me broad awake. Being awake, my thoughts were busy, of course, and mainly they busied themselves with Sandy's curious delusion. Here she was, as sane a person as the kingdom could produce, and yet, from my point of view she was acting like a crazy woman. My land, the power of training! Of influence! Of education! It can bring a body up to believe anything. I had to put myself in Sandy's place to realize that she was not a lunatic. Yes, and put her in mine, to demonstrate how easy it is to seem a lunatic to a person who has not been taught as you have been taught. If I had told Sandy I had seen a wagon, uninfluenced by enchantment, spin along fifty miles an hour; had seen a man, unequipped with magic powers, get into a basket and soar out of sight among the clouds; and had listened, without any necromancer's help, to the conversation of a person who was several hundred miles away, Sandy would not merely have supposed me to be crazy, she would have thought she knew it. Everybody around her believed in enchantments; nobody had any doubts; to doubt that a castle could be turned into a sty, and its occupants into hogs, would have been the same as my doubting, among Connecticut people, the actuality of the telephone and its wonders—and in both cases would be absolute proof of a diseased mind, an unsettled reason. Yes, Sandy was sane; that must be admitted. If I also would be sane—to Sandy—I must keep my superstitions about unenchanted and unmiraculous locomotives, balloons, and telephones to myself. Also, I believed that the world was not flat, and hadn't pillars under it to support it, nor a canopy over it to turn off a universe of water that occupied all space above: but as I was the only person in the kingdom afflicted with such impious and criminal opinions, I recognized that it would be good wisdom to keep quiet about this matter, too, if I did not wish to be suddenly shunned and forsaken by everybody as a madman.

The next morning Sandy assembled the swine in the dining room and gave them their breakfast, waiting upon them personally and manifesting in every way the deep reverence which the natives of her island, ancient and modern, have always felt for rank, let its outward casket and the mental and moral contents be what they may. I could have eaten with the hogs if I had had birth approaching my lofty official rank; but I hadn't, and so accepted the unavoidable slight and made no complaint. Sandy and I had our breakfast at the second table. The family were not at home. I said:

"How many are in the family, Sandy, and where do they keep themselves?"

"Family?"

"Yes."

"Which family, good my lord?"

"Why, this family; your own family."

"Sooth to say, I understand you not. I have no family."

"No family? Why, Sandy, isn't this your home?"

"Now how indeed might that be? I have no home."

"Well, then, whose house is this?"

"Ah, wit you well I would tell you an I knew myself."

"Come—you don't even know these people? Then who invited us here?"

"None invited us. We but came; that is all."

"Why, woman, this is a most extraordinary performance. The effrontery of it is beyond admiration. We blandly march into a man's house, and cram it full of the only really valuable nobility the sun has yet discovered in the earth, and then it turns out that we don't even know the man's name. How did you ever venture to take this extravagant liberty? I supposed, of course, it was your home. What will the man say?"

"What will he say? Forsooth what can he say but give thanks?"

"Thanks for what?"

Her face was filled with a puzzled surprise:

"Verily, thou troublest mine understanding with strange words. Do ye dream that one of his estate is like to have the honor twice in his life to entertain company such as we have brought to grace his house withal?"

"Well, no—when you come to that. No, it's an even bet that this is the first time he has had a treat like this."

"Then let him be thankful, and manifest the same by grateful speech and due humility; he were a dog, else, and the heir and ancestor of dogs."

To my mind, the situation was uncomfortable. It might become more so. It might be a good idea to muster the hogs and move on. So I said:

"The day is wasting, Sandy. It is time to get the nobility together and be moving."

"Wherefore, fair sir and Boss?"

"We want to take them to their home, don't we?"

"La, but list to him! They be of all the regions of the earth! Each must hie to her own home; wend you we might do all these journeys in one so brief life as He hath appointed that created life, and thereto death likewise with help of Adam, who by sin done through persuasion of his helpmeet, she being wrought upon and bewrayed by the beguilements of the great enemy of man, that serpent hight Satan, aforetime consecrated and set apart unto that evil work by overmastering spite and envy begotten in his heart through fell ambitions that did blight and mildew a nature erst so white and pure whenso it hove with the shining multitudes its brethren-born in glade and shade of that fair heaven wherein all such as native be to that rich estate and——"

"Great Scott!"

"My lord?"

"Well, you know we haven't got time for this sort of thing. Don't you see, we could distribute these people around the earth in less time than it is going to take you to explain that we can't. We mustn't talk now, we must act. You want to be careful; you mustn't let your mill get the start of you that way, at a time like this. To business, now—and sharp's the word. Who is to take the aristocracy home?"

"Even their friends. These will come for them from the far parts of the earth."

This was lightning from a clear sky, for unexpectedness; and the relief of it was like pardon to a prisoner. She would remain to deliver the goods, of course.

"Well, then, Sandy, as our enterprise is handsomely and successfully ended, I will go home and report; and if ever another one——"

"I also am ready; I will go with thee."

This was recalling the pardon.

"How? You will go with me? Why should you?"

"Will I be traitor to my knight, dost think? That were dishonor. I may not part from thee until in knightly encounter in the field some overmatching champion shall fairly win and fairly wear me. I were to blame an I thought that that might ever hap."

"Elected for the long term," I sighed to myself. "I may as well make the best of it." So then I spoke up and said:

"All right; let us make a start."

While she was gone to cry her farewells over the pork, I gave that whole peerage away to the servants. And I asked them to take a duster and dust around a little where the nobilities had mainly lodged and promenaded, but they considered that that would be hardly worth-while, and would moreover be a rather grave departure from custom, and therefore likely to make talk. A departure from custom—that settled it; it was a nation capable of committing any crime but that. The servants said they would follow the fashion, a fashion grown sacred through immemorial observance: they would scatter fresh rushes in all the rooms and halls, and then the evidence of the aristocratic visitation would be no longer visible. It was a kind of satire on Nature; it was the scientific method, the geologic method; it deposited the history of the family in a stratified record; and the antiquary could dig through it and tell by the remains of each period what changes of diet the family had introduced successively for a hundred years.

The first thing we struck that day was a procession of pilgrims. It was not going our way, but we joined it nevertheless; for it was hourly being borne in upon me, now, that if I would govern this country wisely, I must be posted in the details of its life, and not at second hand but by personal observation and scrutiny.

This company of pilgrims resembled Chaucer's in this: that it had in it a sample of about all the upper occupations and professions the country could show, and a corresponding variety of costume. There were young men and old men, young women and old women, lively folk and grave folk. They rode upon mules and horses, and there was not a sidesaddle in the party; for this specialty was to remain unknown in England for nine hundred years yet.

It was a pleasant, friendly, sociable herd; pious, happy, merry, and full of unconscious coarsenesses and innocent indecencies. What they regarded as the merry tale went the continual round and caused no more embarrassment than it would have caused in the best English society twelve centuries later. Practical jokes worthy of the English wits of the first quarter of the far-off nineteenth century were sprung here and there and yonder along the line, and compelled the delightedest applause; and sometimes when a bright remark was made at one end of the procession and started on its travels toward the other, you could note its progress all the way by the sparkling spray of laughter it threw off from its bows as it plowed along; and also by the blushes of the mules in its wake.

Sandy knew the goal and purpose of this pilgrimage and she posted me. She said:

"They journey to the Valley of Holiness, for to be blessed of the godly hermits and drink of the miraculous waters and be cleansed from sin."

"Where is this watering place?"

"It lieth a two day journey hence, by the borders of the land that hight the Cuckoo Kingdom."

"Tell me about it. Is it a celebrated place?"

"Oh, of a truth, yes. There be none more so. Of old time there lived there an abbot and his monks. Belike were none in the world more holy than these; for they gave themselves to study of pious books, and spoke not the one to the other, or indeed to any, and ate decayed herbs and naught thereto, and slept hard, and prayed much, and washed never; also they wore the same garment until it fell from their bodies through age and decay. Right so came they to be known of all the world by reason of these holy austerities, and visited by rich and poor, and reverenced."

"Proceed."

"But always there was lack of water there. Whereas, upon a time, the holy abbot prayed, and for answer a great stream of clear water burst forth by miracle in a desert place. Now were the fickle monks tempted of the Fiend, and they wrought with their abbot unceasingly by beggings and beseechings that he would construct a bath; and when he was become aweary and might not resist more, he said have ye your will, then, and granted that they asked. Now mark thou what 'tis to forsake the ways of purity the which He loveth, and wanton with such as be worldly and an offense. These monks did enter into the bath and come thence washed as white as snow; and lo, in that moment His sign appeared, in miraculous rebuke! for His insulted waters ceased to flow, and utterly vanished away."

"They fared mildly, Sandy, considering how that kind of crime is regarded in this country."

"Belike; but it was their first sin; and they had been of perfect life for long, and differing in naught from the angels. Prayers, tears, torturings of the flesh, all was vain to beguile that water to flow again. Even processions;

even burnt offerings; even votive candles to the Virgin,
did fail every each of them; and all in the land did
marvel."

"How odd to find that even this industry has its financial panics, and at times sees its assignats and greenbacks
languish to zero, and everything come to a standstill.
Go on, Sandy."

"And so upon a time, after year and day, the good
abbot made humble surrender and destroyed the bath.
And behold, His anger was in that moment appeased,
and the waters gushed richly forth again, and even unto
this day they have not ceased to flow in that generous
measure."

"Then I take it nobody has washed since."

"He that would essay it could have his halter free;
yea, and swiftly would he need it, too."

"The community has prospered since?"

"Even from that very day. The fame of the miracle
went abroad into all lands. From every land came monks
to join; they came even as the fishes come, in shoals;
and the monastery added building to building, and yet
others to these, and so spread wide its arms and took
them in. And nuns came, also; and more again, and yet
more; and built over against the monastery on the yon
side of the vale, and added building to building, until
mighty was that nunnery. And these were friendly unto
those, and they joined their loving labors together, and
together they built a fair great foundling asylum midway
of the valley between."

"You spoke of some hermits, Sandy."

"These have gathered there from the ends of the earth.
A hermit thriveth best where there be multitudes of pilgrims. Ye shall not find no hermit of no sort wanting.
If any shall mention a hermit of a kind he thinketh new
and not to be found but in some far strange land, let
him but scratch among the holes and caves and swamps
that line that Valley of Holiness, and whatsoever be his
breed, it skills not, he shall find a sample of it there."

I closed up alongside of a burly fellow with a fat good-
humored face, purposing to make myself agreeable and
pick up some further crumbs of fact; but I had hardly
more than scraped acquaintance with him when he began

eagerly and awkwardly to lead up, in the immemorial way, to that same old anecdote—the one Sir Dinadan told me, what time I got into trouble with Sir Sagramor and was challenged of him on account of it. I excused myself and dropped to the rear of the procession, sad at heart, willing to go hence from this troubled life, this vale of tears, this brief day of broken rest, of cloud and storm, of weary struggle and monotonous defeat; and yet shrinking from the change, as remembering how long eternity is, and how many have wended thither who know that anecdote.

Early in the afternoon we overtook another procession of pilgrims; but in this one was no merriment, no jokes, no laughter, no playful ways, nor any happy giddiness, whether of youth or age. Yet both were here, both age and youth: gray old men and women, strong men and women of middle age, young husbands, young wives, little boys and girls, and three babies at the breast. Even the children were smileless; there was not a face among all these half a hundred people but was cast down and bore that set expression of hopelessness which is bred of long and hard trials and old acquaintance with despair. They were slaves. Chains led from their fettered feet and their manacled hands to a sole-leather belt about their waists; and all except the children were also linked together in a file, six feet apart, by a single chain which led from collar to collar all down the line. They were on foot, and had tramped three hundred miles in eighteen days, upon the cheapest odds and ends of food, and stingy rations of that. They had slept in these chains every night, bundled together like swine. They had upon their bodies some poor rags, but they could not be said to be clothed. Their irons had chafed the skin from their ankles and made sores which were ulcerated and wormy. Their naked feet were torn, and none walked without a limp. Originally there had been a hundred of these unfortunates, but about half had been sold on the trip. The trader in charge of them rode a horse and carried a whip with a short handle and a long heavy lash divided into several knotted tails at the end. With this whip he cut the shoulders of any that tottered from weariness and pain, and straightened them up. He did not speak;

the whip conveyed his desire without that. None of these poor creatures looked up as we rode along by; they showed no consciousness of our presence. And they made no sound but one; that was the dull and awful clank of their chains from end to end of the long file, as forty-three burdened feet rose and fell in unison. The file moved in a cloud of its own making.

All these faces were gray with a coating of dust. One has seen the like of this coating upon furniture in unoccupied houses, and has written his idle thought in it with his finger. I was reminded of this when I noticed the faces of some of those women, young mothers carrying babes that were near to death and freedom, how a something in their hearts was written in the dust upon their faces, plain to see, and lord how plain to read! For it was the track of tears. One of these young mothers was but a girl, and it hurt me to the heart to read that writing, and reflect that it was come up out of the breast of such a child, a breast that ought not to know trouble yet, but only the gladness of the morning of life; and no doubt—

She reeled just then, giddy with fatigue, and down came the lash and flicked a flake of skin from her naked shoulder. It stung me as if I had been hit instead. The master halted the file and jumped from his horse. He stormed and swore at this girl, and said she had made annoyance enough with her laziness, and as this was the last chance he should have, he would settle the account now. She dropped on her knees and put up her hands and began to beg and cry and implore, in a passion of terror, but the master gave no attention. He snatched the child from her, and then made the men slaves who were chained before and behind her throw her on the ground and hold her there and expose her body; and then he laid on with his lash like a madman till her back was flayed, she shrieking and struggling the while, piteously. One of the men who was holding her turned away his face, and for this humanity he was reviled and flogged.

All our pilgrims looked on and commented—on the expert way in which the whip was handled. They were too much hardened by lifelong everyday familiarity with slavery to notice that there was anything else in the exhibition that invited comment. This was what slavery could do, in the way of ossifying what one may call the superior lobe of human feeling; for these pilgrims were kindhearted people, and they would not have allowed that man to treat a horse like that.

I wanted to stop the whole thing and set the slaves free, but that would not do. I must not interfere too much and get myself a name for riding over the country's laws and the citizen's rights roughshod. If I lived and prospered I would be the death of slavery, that I was resolved upon; but I would try to fix it so that when I became its executioner it should be by command of the nation.

Just here was the wayside shop of a smith; and now arrived a landed proprietor who had bought this girl a few miles back, deliverable here where her irons could be taken off. They were removed; then there was a squabble between the gentleman and the dealer as to which should pay the blacksmith. The moment the girl was delivered from her irons, she flung herself, all tears and frantic sobbings, into the arms of the slave who had turned away his face when she was whipped. He strained her to his breast, and smothered her face and the child's with kisses, and washed them with the rain of his tears. I suspected. I inquired. Yes, I was right: it was husband and wife. They had to be torn apart by force; the girl had to be dragged away, and she struggled and fought and shrieked like one gone mad till a turn of the road hid her from sight; and even after that, we could still make out the fading plaint of those receding shrieks. And the husband and father, with his wife and child gone, never to be seen by him again in life—well, the look of him one might not bear at all, and so I turned away; but I knew I should never get his picture out of my mind again, and there it is to this day, to wring my heartstrings whenever I think of it.

We put up at the inn in a village just at nightfall, and when I rose next morning and looked abroad, I was ware where a knight came riding in the golden glory of the new day, and recognized him for knight of mine —Sir Ozana le Cure Hardy. He was in the gentlemen's furnishing line, and his missionarying speciality was plug hats. He was clothed all in steel, in the beautifulest armor of the time—up to where his helmet ought to have been; but he hadn't any helmet, he wore a shiny stovepipe hat, and was as ridiculous a spectacle as one might want to see. It was another of my surreptitious schemes for extinguishing knighthood by making it grotesque and absurd. Sir Ozana's saddle was hung about with leather hatboxes, and every time he overcame a wandering knight he swore him into my service and fitted him with a plug and made him wear it. I dressed and ran down to welcome Sir Ozana and get his news.

"How is trade?" I asked.

"Ye will note that I have but these four left; yet were they sixteen whenas I got me from Camelot."

"Why, you have certainly done nobly, Sir Ozana. Where have you been foraging of late?"

"I am but now come from the Valley of Holiness, please you sir."

"I am pointed for that place myself. Is there anything stirring in the monkery, more than common?"

"By the mass ye may not question it! . . . Give him good feed, boy, and stint it not, an thou valuest thy crown; so get ye lightly to the stable and do even as I bid. . . . Sir, it is parlous news I bring, and—be these pilgrims? Then ye may not do better, good folk, than gather and hear the tale I have to tell, sith it concerneth you, forasmuch as ye go to find that ye will not find, and seek that ye will seek in vain, my life being hostage for my word, and my word and message being these, namely: That a hap has happened whereof the like has not been seen no more but once this two hundred years, which was the first and last time that that said misfortune strake the holy valley in that form by commandment of the Most High whereto by reasons just and causes thereunto contributing, wherein the matter—"

"The miraculous fount hath ceased to flow!" This shout burst from twenty pilgrim mouths at once.

"Ye say well, good people. I was verging to it, even when ye spake."

"Has somebody been washing again?"

"Nay, it is suspected, but none believe it. It is thought to be some other sin, but none wit what."

"How are they feeling about the calamity?"

"None may describe it in words. The fount is these nine days dry. The prayers that did begin then, and the lamentations in sackcloth and ashes, and the holy processions, none of these have ceased nor night nor day; and so the monks and the nuns and the foundlings be all exhausted, and do hang up prayers writ upon parchment, sith that no strength is left in man to lift up voice. And at last they sent for thee, Sir Boss, to try magic and enchantment; and if you could not come, then was the messenger to fetch Merlin, and he is there these three days, now, and saith he will fetch that water though he burst the globe and wreck its kingdoms to accomplish it; and right bravely doth he work his magic and call upon his hellions to hie them hither and help, but not a whiff of moisture hath he started yet, even so much as might qualify as mist upon a copper mirror an ye count not the barrel of sweat he sweateth betwixt sun and sun over the dire labors of his task; and if ye——"

Breakfast was ready. As soon as it was over I showed to Sir Ozana these words which I had written on the inside of his hat: *"Chemical Department, Laboratory extension, Section G. Pxxp. Send two of first size, two of No. 3 and six of No. 4, together with the proper complementary details—and two of my trained assistants."* And I said:

"Now get you to Camelot as fast as you can fly, brave knight, and show the writing to Clarence, and tell him to have these required matters in the Valley of Holiness with all possible dispatch."

"I will well, Sir Boss," and he was off.

〔 CHAPTER XXII 〕

The Holy Fountain

THE PILGRIMS were human beings. Otherwise they would have acted differently. They had come a long and difficult journey, and now when the journey was nearly finished, and they learned that the main thing they had come for had ceased to exist, they didn't do as horses or cats or angleworms would probably have done—turn back and get at something profitable—no, anxious as they had before been to see the miraculous fountain, they were as much as forty times as anxious now to see the place where it had used to be. There is no accounting for human beings.

We made good time, and a couple of hours before sunset we stood upon the high confines of the Valley of Holiness and our eyes swept it from end to end and noted its features. That is, its large features. These were the three masses of buildings. They were distant and isolated temporalities shrunken to toy constructions in the lonely waste of what seemed a desert—and was. Such a scene is always mournful, it is so impressively still, and looks so steeped in death. But there was a sound here which interrupted the stillness only to add to its mournfulness; this was the faint far sound of tolling bells which floated fitfully to us on the passing breeze, and so faintly, so softly, that we hardly knew whether we heard it with our ears or with our spirits.

We reached the monastery before dark, and there the males were given lodging, but the women were sent over to the nunnery. The bells were close at hand, now, and their solemn booming smote upon the ear like a message of doom. A superstitious despair possessed the heart of every monk and published itself in his ghastly face. Everywhere, these black-robed, soft-sandled, tallow-visaged specters appeared, flitted about, and disappeared, noiseless as the creatures of a troubled dream, and as uncanny.

The old abbot's joy to see me was pathetic. Even to tears; but he did the shedding himself. He said:

"Delay not, son, but get to thy saving work. An we bring not the water back again, and soon, we are ruined, and the good work of two hundred years must end. And see thou do it with enchantments that be holy, for the Church will not endure that work in her cause be done by devil's magic."

"When I work, Father, be sure there will be no devil's

work connected with it. I shall use no arts that come of the devil, and no elements not created by the hand of God. But is Merlin working strictly on pious lines?"

"Ah, he said he would, my son, he said he would, and took oath to make his promise good."

"Well, in that case, let him proceed."

"But surely you will not sit idle by, but help?"

"It will not answer to mix methods, Father; neither would it be professional courtesy. Two of a trade must not underbid each other. We might as well cut rates and be done with it; it would arrive at that in the end. Merlin has the contract; no other magician can touch it till he throws it up."

"But I will take it from him; it is a terrible emergency and the act is thereby justified. And if it were not so, who will give law to the Church? The Church giveth law to all; and what she wills to do, that she may do, hurt whom it may. I will take it from him; you shall begin upon the moment."

"It may not be, Father. No doubt, as you say, where power is supreme, one can do as one likes and suffer no injury; but we poor magicians are not so situated. Merlin is a very good magician in a small way, and has quite a neat provincial reputation. He is struggling along, doing the best he can, and it would not be etiquette for me to take his job until he himself abandons it."

The abbot's face lighted.

"Ah, that is simple. There are ways to persuade him to abandon it."

"No-no, Father, it skills not, as these people say. If he were persuaded against his will, he would load that well with a malicious enchantment which would balk me until I found out its secret. It might take a month. I could set up a little enchantment of mine which I call the telephone, and he could not find out its secret in a hundred years. Yes, you perceive, he might block me for a month. Would you like to risk a month in a dry time like this?"

"A month! The mere thought of it maketh me to shudder. Have it thy way, my son. But my heart is heavy with this disappointment. Leave me, and let me wear my spirit with weariness and waiting, even as I have done these ten long days, counterfeiting thus the thing that is called rest, the prone body making outward sign of repose where inwardly is none."

Of course it would have been best, all round, for Merlin to waive etiquette and quit and call it half a day, since he would never be able to start that water, for he was a true magician of the time: which is to say, the big miracles, the ones that gave him his reputation, always had the luck to be performed when nobody but Merlin was present; he couldn't start this well with all this crowd around to see; a crowd was as bad for a magician's miracle in that day as it was for a spiritualist's miracle in mine: there was sure to be some skeptic on hand to turn up the gas at the crucial moment and spoil everything. But I did not want Merlin to retire from the job until I was ready to take hold of it effectively myself; and I could not do that until I got my things from Camelot, and that would take two or three days.

My presence gave the monks hope, and cheered them up a good deal; insomuch that they ate a square meal that night for the first time in ten days. As soon as their stomachs had been properly reinforced with food, their spirits began to rise fast; when the mead began to go round they rose faster. By the time everybody was half-seas over, the holy community was in good shape to make a night of it; so we stayed by the board and put it through on that line. Matters got to be very jolly. Good old questionable stories were told that made the tears run down and cavernous mouths stand wide and the round bellies shake with laughter; and questionable songs were bellowed out in a mighty chorus that drowned the boom of the tolling bells.

At last I ventured a story myself; and vast was the success of it. Not right off, of course, for the native of those islands does not as a rule dissolve upon the early applications of a humorous thing; but the fifth time I told it, they began to crack, in places; the eighth time I told it, they began to crumble; at the twelfth repetition they fell apart in chunks; and at the fifteenth they disintegrated, and I got a broom and swept them up. This language is figurative. Those islanders—well, they are slow pay, at first, in the matter of return for your in-

vestment of effort, but in the end they make the pay of
all other nations poor and small by contrast.

I was at the well next day betimes. Merlin was there,
enchanting away like a beaver, but not raising the moisture. He was not in a pleasant humor; and every time
I hinted that perhaps this contract was a shade too hefty
for a novice he unlimbered his tongue and cursed like a
bishop—French bishop of the Regency days, I mean.

Matters were about as I expected to find them. The
"fountain" was an ordinary well, it had been dug in the
ordinary way, and stoned up in the ordinary way. There
was no miracle about it. Even the lie that had created
its reputation was not miraculous; I could have told it
myself, with one hand tied behind me. The well was in a
dark chamber which stood in the center of a cut-stone
chapel, whose walls were hung with pious pictures of a
workmanship that would have made a chromo feel good;
pictures historically commemorative of curative miracles
which had been achieved by the waters when nobody was
looking. That is, nobody but angels: they are always on
deck when there is a miracle to the fore—so as to get
put in the picture, perhaps. Angels are as fond of that
as a fire company; look at the old masters.

The well chamber was dimly lighted by lamps; the
water was drawn with a windlass and chain, by monks,
and poured into troughs which delivered it into stone
reservoirs outside, in the chapel—when there was water
to draw, I mean—and none but monks could enter the
well chamber. I entered it, for I had temporary authority
to do so, by courtesy of my professional brother and
subordinate. But he hadn't entered it himself. He did
everything by incantations; he never worked his intellect.
If he had stepped in there and used his eyes, instead of
his disordered mind, he could have cured the well by
natural means, and then turned it into a miracle in the
customary way; but no, he was an old numskull, a magician who believed in his own magic; and no magician
can thrive who is handicapped with a superstition like
that.

I had an idea that the well had sprung a leak; that
some of the wall stones near the bottom had fallen and
exposed fissures that allowed the water to escape. I

measured the chain—ninety-eight feet. Then I called in a couple of monks, locked the door, took a candle, and made them lower me in the bucket. When the chain was all paid out, the candle confirmed my suspicion; a considerable section of the wall was gone, exposing a good big fissure.

I almost regretted that my theory about the well's trouble was correct, because I had another one that had a showy point or two about it for a miracle. I remembered that in America, many centuries later, when an oil well ceased to flow, they used to blast it out with a dynamite torpedo. If I should find this well dry, and no explanation of it, I could astonish these people most nobly by having a person of no especial value drop a dynamite bomb into it. It was my idea to appoint Merlin. However, it was plain that there was no occasion for the bomb. One cannot have everything the way he would like it. A man has no business to be depressed by a disappointment, anyway; he ought to make up his mind to get even. That is what I did. I said to myself, I am in no hurry, I can wait; that bomb will come good, yet. And it did, too.

When I was above ground again, I turned out the monks, and let down a fishline: the well was a hundred and fifty feet deep, and there was forty-one feet of water in it! I called in a monk and asked:

"How deep is the well?"

"That, sir, I wit not, having never been told."

"How does the water usually stand in it?"

"Near to the top, these two centuries, as the testimony goeth, brought down to us through our predecessors."

It was true—as to recent times at least—for there was witness to it, and better witness than a monk: only about twenty or thirty feet of the chain showed wear and use, the rest of it was unworn and rusty. What had happened when the well gave out that other time? Without doubt some practical person had come along and mended the leak, and then had come up and told the abbot he had discovered by divination that if the sinful bath were destroyed the well would flow again. The leak had befallen again, now, and these children would have prayed, and processioned, and tolled their bells for heavenly succor till they all dried up and blew away, and no innocent of them all would ever have thought to drop a fishline into the well or go down in it and find out what was really the matter. Old habit of mind is one of the toughest things to get away from in the world. It transmits itself like physical form and feature; and for a man, in those days, to have had an idea that his ancestors hadn't had, would have brought him under suspicion of being illegitimate. I said to the monk:

"It is a difficult miracle to restore water in a dry well, but we will try, if my brother Merlin fails. Brother Merlin is a very passable artist, but only in the parlor magic line, and he may not succeed; in fact is not likely to succeed. But that should be nothing to his discredit; the man that can do *this* kind of miracle knows enough to keep hotel."

"Hotel? I mind not to have heard——"

"Of hotel? It's what you call hostel. The man that can do this miracle can keep hostel. I can do this miracle; I shall do this miracle; yet I do not try to conceal from you that it is a miracle to tax the occult powers to the last strain."

"None knoweth that truth better than the brotherhood, indeed; for it is of record that aforetime it was parlous difficult and took a year. Natheless, God send you good success, and to that end will we pray."

As a matter of business it was a good idea to get the notion around that the thing was difficult. Many a small thing has been made large by the right kind of advertising. That monk was filled up with the difficulty of this enterprise; he would fill up the others. In two days the solicitude would be booming.

On my way home at noon, I met Sandy. She had been sampling the hermits. I said:

"I would like to do that, myself. This is Wednesday. Is there a matinèe?"

"A which, please you, sir?"

"Matinèe. Do they keep open, afternoons?"

"Who?"

"The hermits, of course."

"Keep open?"

"Yes, keep open. Isn't that plain enough? Do they knock off at noon."

"Knock off?"

"Knock off—yes, knock off. What is the matter with knock off? I never saw such a dunderhead; can't you understand anything at all? In plain terms, do they shut up shop, draw the game, bank the fires—"

"Shut up shop, draw—"

"There, never mind, let it go. You make me tired. You can't seem to understand the simplest thing."

"I would I might please thee, sir, and it is to me dole and sorrow that I fail, albeit sith I am but a simple damsel and taught of none, being from the cradle unbaptized in those deep waters of learning that do anoint with a sovereignty him that partaketh of that most noble sacrament, investing him with reverend state to the mental eye of the humble mortal who, by bar and lack of that great consecration seeth in his own unlearned estate but a symbol of that other sort of lack and loss which men do publish to the pitying eye with sackcloth trappings whereon the ashes of grief do lie bepowdered and bestrewn, and so, when such shall in the darkness of his mind encounter these golden phrases of high mystery, these shut-up-shops, and draw-the-game, and bank-the-fires, it is but by the grace of God that he burst not for envy of the mind that can beget, and tongue that can deliver so great and mellow-sounding miracles of speech, and if there do ensue confusion in that humbler mind, and failure to divine the meanings of these wonders, then if so be this miscomprehension is not vain but sooth and true, wit ye well it is the very substance of worshipful dear homage and may not lightly be misprized, nor had been, an ye had noted this complexion of my mood and mind and understood that that I would I could not, and that I could not I might not, nor yet nor might *nor* could, nor might-not nor could-not, might be by advantage turned to the desired *would*, and so I pray you mercy of my fault, and that ye will of your kindness and your charity forgive it, good my master and most dear lord."

I couldn't make it all out—that is, the details—but I got the general idea; and enough of it, too, to be ashamed. It was not fair to spring those nineteenth century technicalities upon the untutored infant of the sixth and then rail at her because she couldn't get their drift; and when she was making the honest best drive at it she could, too, and no fault of hers that she couldn't fetch the home plate; and so I apologized. Then we meandered pleasantly away toward the hermit holes in sociable converse together, and better friends than ever.

I was gradually coming to have a mysterious and shuddery reverence for this girl; for nowadays whenever she pulled out from the station and got her train fairly started on one of those horizonless transcontinental sentences of hers, it was borne in upon me that I was standing in the awful presence of the Mother of the German Language. I was so impressed with this, that sometimes when she began to empty one of these sentences on me I unconsciously took the very attitude of reverence, and stood uncovered; and if words had been water, I had been drowned, sure. She had exactly the German way: whatever was in her mind to be delivered, whether a mere remark, or a sermon, or a cyclopedia, or the history of a war, she would get it into a single sentence or die. Whenever the literary German dives into a sentence, that is the last you are going to see of him till he emerges on the other side of his Atlantic with his verb in his mouth.

We drifted from hermit to hermit all the afternoon. It was a most strange menagerie. The chief emulation among them seemed to be, to see which could manage to be the uncleanest and most prosperous with vermin. Their manner and attitudes were the last expression of complacent self-righteousness. It was one anchorite's pride to lie naked in the mud and let the insects bite him and blister him unmolested; it was another's to lean against a rock, all day long, conspicuous to the admiration of the throng of pilgrims, and pray; it was another's to go naked, and crawl around on all fours; it was another's to drag about with him, year in and year out, eighty pounds of iron; it was another's to never lie down when he slept, but to stand among the thornbushes and snore when there were pilgrims around to look; a woman, who had the white hair of age, and no other apparel, was black from crown to heel with forty-seven years of holy abstinence from water. Groups of gazing pilgrims stood around all and every of these strange objects, lost in reverent wonder, and envious of the fleckless sanctity which these pious austerities had won for them from an exacting heaven.

By and by we went to see one of the supremely great ones. He was a mighty celebrity; his fame had penetrated all Christendom; the noble and the renowned journeyed from the remotest lands on the globe to pay him reverence. His stand was in the center of the widest part of the valley; and it took all that space to hold his crowds.

His stand was a pillar sixty feet high, with a broad platform on the top of it. He was now doing what he had been doing every day for twenty years up there—bowing his body ceaselessly and rapidly almost to his feet. It was his way of praying. I timed him with a stopwatch, and he made twelve hundred and forty-four revolutions in twenty-four minutes and forty-six seconds. It seemed a pity to have all this power going to waste. It was one of the most useful motions in mechanics, the pedal movement; so I made a note in my memorandum book, purposing some day to apply a system of elastic cords to him and run a sewing machine with it. I afterwards carried out that scheme, and got five years' good service out of him; in which time he turned out upwards of eighteen thousand first-rate tow-linen shirts, which was ten a day. I worked him Sundays and all; he was going Sundays the same as weekdays, and it was no use to waste the power. These shirts cost me nothing but just the mere trifle for the materials—I furnished those myself, it would not have been right to make him do that—and they sold like smoke to pilgrims at a dollar and a half apiece, which was the price of fifty cows or a blooded racehorse in Arthurdom. They were regarded as a perfect protection against sin, and advertised as such by my knights everywhere, with the paintpot and stencil plate; insomuch that there was not a cliff or a boulder or a dead wall in England but you could read on it at a mile distance:

"*Buy the only genuine St. Stylite; patronized by the Nobility. Patent applied for.*"

There was more money in the business than one knew what to do with. As it extended, I brought out a line of goods suitable for kings, and a nobby thing for duchesses and that sort, with ruffles down the fore hatch and the running gear clewed up with a featherstitch to leeward and then hauled aft with a backstay and triced up with a half-turn in the standing rigging forward of the weather gaskets. Yes, it was a daisy.

But about that time I noticed that the motive power had taken to standing on one leg, and I found that there was something the matter with the other one; so I stocked the business and unloaded, taking Sir Bors de Ganis into camp financially along with certain of his friends: for the works stopped within a year, and the good saint got him to his rest. But he had earned it. I can say that for him.

When I saw him that first time—however, his personal condition will not quite bear description here. You can read it in the Lives of the Saints.*

⟦ CHAPTER XXIII ⟧

Restoration of the Fountain

SATURDAY NOON I went to the well and looked on a while. Merlin was still burning smoke powders, and pawing the air, and muttering gibberish as hard as ever, but looking pretty downhearted, for of course he had not started even a perspiration in that well yet. Finally I said:

"How does the thing promise by this time, partner?"

"Behold, I am even now busied with trial of the powerfulest enchantment known to the princes of the occult arts in the lands of the East; an it fail me, naught can avail. Peace, until I finish."

He raised a smoke this time that darkened all the region, and must have made matters uncomfortable for the hermits, for the wind was their way, and it rolled down over

* All the details concerning the hermits, in this chapter, are from Lecky—but greatly modified. This book not being a history but only a tale, the majority of the historian's frank details were too strong for reproduction in it.—EDITOR.

their dens in a dense and billowy fog. He poured out volumes of speech to match, and contorted his body and sawed the air with his hands in a most extraordinary way. At the end of twenty minutes he dropped down panting, and about exhausted. Now arrived the abbot and several hundred monks and nuns, and behind them a multitude of pilgrims and a couple of acres of foundlings, all drawn by the prodigious smoke, and all in a grand state of excitement. The abbot inquired anxiously for results. Merlin said:

"If any labor of mortal might break the spell that binds these waters, this which I have but just essayed had done it. It has failed; whereby I do now know that that which I had feared is a truth established: the sign of this failure is, that the most potent spirit known to the magicians of the East, and whose name none may utter and live, has laid his spell upon this well. The mortal does not breathe, nor ever will, who can penetrate the secret of that spell, and without that secret none can break it. The water will flow no more forever, good Father. I have done what man could. Suffer me to go."

Of course this threw the abbot into a good deal of a consternation. He turned to me with the signs of it in his face, and said:

"Ye have heard him. Is it true?"

"Part of it is."

"Not all, then, not all! What part is true?"

"That that spirit with the Russian name has put his spell upon the well."

"God's wownds, then are we ruined!"

"Possibly."

"But not certainly? Ye mean, not certainly?"

"That is it."

"Wherefore, ye also mean that when he saith none can break the spell—"

"Yes, when he says that, he says what isn't necessarily true. There are conditions under which an effort to break it may have some chance—that is, some small, some trifling chance—of success."

"The conditions—"

"Oh, they are nothing difficult. Only these: I want the well and the surroundings for the space of half a mile, entirely to myself from sunset today until I remove the ban—and nobody allowed to cross the ground but by my authority."

"Are these all?"

"Yes."

"And you have no fear to try?"

"Oh, none. One may fail, of course; and one may also succeed. One can try, and I am ready to chance it. I have my conditions?"

"These and all others ye may name. I will issue commandment to that effect."

"Wait," said Merlin, with an evil smile. "Ye wit that he that would break this spell must know that spirit's name?"

"Yes, I know his name."

"And wit you also that to know it skills not of itself, but ye must likewise pronounce it? Ha-ha! Knew ye that?"

"Yes, I knew that, too."

"You have that knowledge! Art a fool? Are ye minded to utter that name and die?"

"Utter it? Why certainly. I would utter it if it was Welsh."

"Ye are even a dead man, then; and I go to tell Arthur."

"That's all right. Take your gripsack and get along. The thing for *you* to do is to go home and work the weather, John W. Merlin."

It was a home shot, and it made him wince; for he was the worst weather-failure in the kingdom. Whenever he ordered up the danger signals along the coast there was a week's dead calm, sure, and every time he prophesied fair weather it rained brickbats. But I kept him in the weather bureau right along, to undermine his reputation. However, that shot raised his bile, and instead of starting home to report my death, he said he would remain and enjoy it.

My two experts arrived in the evening, and pretty well fagged, for they had traveled double tides. They had pack mules along, and had brought everything I needed—tools, pump, lead pipe, Greek fire, sheaves of big rockets, roman candles, colored-fire sprays, electric apparatus, and a lot of sundries—everything necessary for the stateliest kind of a miracle. They got their supper and a nap, and about midnight we sallied out through a solitude so wholly vacant and complete that it quite over-passed the required conditions. We took possession of the well and its surroundings. My boys were experts in all sorts of things, from the stoning up of a well to the constructing of a mathematical instrument. An hour before sunrise we had that leak mended in shipshape fashion, and the water began to rise. Then we stowed our fireworks in the chapel, locked up the place, and went home to bed.

Before the noon mass was over, we were at the well again; for there was a deal to do, yet, and I was determined to spring the miracle before midnight, for business reasons: for whereas a miracle worked for the Church on a weekday is worth a good deal, it is worth six times as much if you get it in on a Sunday. In nine hours the water had risen to its customary level, that is to say, it was within twenty-three feet of the top. We put in a little iron pump, one of the first turned out by my works near the capital; we bored into a stone reservoir which stood against the outer wall of the well chamber and inserted a section of lead pipe that was long enough to reach to the door of the chapel and project beyond the threshold, where the gushing water would be visible to the two hundred and fifty acres of people I was intending should be present on the flat plain in front of this little holy hillock at the proper time.

We knocked the head out of an empty hogshead and hoisted this hogshead to the flat roof of the chapel, where we clamped it down fast, poured in gunpowder till it lay loosely an inch deep on the bottom, then we stood up rockets in the hogshead as thick as they could loosely stand, all the different breeds of rockets there are; and they made a portly and imposing sheaf, I can tell you. We grounded the wire of a pocket electrical battery in that powder, we placed a whole magazine of Greek fire on each corner of the roof—blue on one corner, green on another, red on another, and purple on the last, and grounded a wire in each.

About two hundred yards off, in the flat, we built a

pen of scantlings, about four feet high, and laid planks on it, and so made a platform. We covered it with swell tapestries borrowed for the occasion, and topped it off with the abbot's own throne. When you are going to do a miracle for an ignorant race, you want to get in every detail that will count; you want to make all the properties impressive to the public eye; you want to make matters comfortable for your head guest; then you can turn yourself loose and play your effects for all they are worth. I know the value of these things, for I know human nature. You can't throw too much style into a miracle. It costs trouble, and work, and sometimes money; but it pays in the end. Well, we brought the wires to the ground at the chapel, and then brought them under the ground to the platform, and hid the batteries there. We put a rope fence a hundred feet square around the platform to keep off the common multitude, and that finished the work. My idea was, doors open at ten thirty, performance to begin at eleven twenty-five sharp. I wished I could charge admission, but of course that wouldn't answer. I instructed my boys to be in the chapel as early as ten, before anybody was around, and be ready to man the pumps at the proper time, and make the fur fly. Then we went home to supper.

The news of the disaster to the well had traveled far, by this time; and now for two or three days a steady avalanche of people had been pouring into the valley. The lower end of the valley was become one huge camp; we should have a good house, no question about that. Criers went the rounds early in the evening and announced the coming attempt, which put every pulse up to fever heat. They gave notice that the abbot and his official suite would move in state and occupy the platform at ten thirty, up to which time all the region which was under my ban must be clear; the bells would then cease from tolling, and this sign should be permission to the multitudes to close in and take their places.

I was at the platform and all ready to do the honors when the abbot's solemn procession hove in sight—which it did not do till it was nearly to the rope fence, because it was a starless black night and no torches permitted. With it came Merlin, and took a front seat on the platform; he was as good as his word, for once. One could not see the multitudes banked together beyond the ban, but they were there, just the same. The moment the bells stopped, those banked masses broke and poured over the line like a vast black wave, and for as much as a half hour it continued to flow, and then it solidified itself, and you could have walked upon a pavement of human heads to—well, miles.

We had a solemn stage wait, now, for about twenty minutes—a thing I had counted on for effect; it is always good to let your audience have a chance to work up its expectancy. At length, out of the silence a noble Latin chant—men's voices—broke and swelled up and rolled away into the night, a majestic tide of melody. I had put that up, too, and it was one of the best effects I ever invented. When it was finished I stood up on the platform and extended my hands abroad, for two minutes, with my face uplifted—that always produces a dead hush —and then slowly pronounced this ghastly word with a kind of awfulness which caused hundreds to tremble, and many women to faint:

"𝕮onstantinopolitanischerdudelsackspfeifenmachersgesellschafft!"

Just as I was moaning out the closing hunks of that word, I touched off one of my electric connections, and all that murky world of people stood revealed in a hideous blue glare! It was immense—that effect! Lots of people shrieked, women curled up and quit in every direction, foundlings collapsed by platoons. The abbot and the monks crossed themselves nimbly and their lips fluttered with agitated prayers. Merlin held his grip, but he was astonished clear down to his corns; he had never seen anything to begin with that, before. Now was the time to pile in the effects. I lifted my hands and groaned out this word—as it were in agony—

"𝕹ihilistendynamittheaterkaestchenssprengungsatten-taetsversuchungen!"

—and turned on the red fire! You should have heard that Atlantic of people moan and howl when that crimson hell joined the blue! After sixty seconds I shouted—

"Transbaaltruppentropentransporttrampelthiertr-
eibertrauungsthraenentragoedie!"

—and lit up the green fire! After waiting only forty seconds, this time, I spread my arms abroad and thundered
out the devastating syllables of this word of words—

**Mekkamuselmannenmassenmenchenmoe-
rdermohrenmuttermarmormonumentenmac-
her!"**

—and whirled on the purple glare! There they were, all
going at once, red, blue, green, purple! Four furious vol-
canoes pouring vast clouds of radiant smoke aloft, and
spreading a blinding rainbowed noonday to the furthest
confines of that valley. In the distance one could see that
fellow on the pillar standing rigid against the background
of sky, his seesaw stopped for the first time in twenty
years. I knew the boys were at the pump, now, and
ready. So I said to the abbot:

"The time is come, Father. I am about to pronounce
the dread name and command the spell to dissolve. You
want to brace up and take hold of something." Then I
shouted to the people: "Behold, in another minute the
spell will be broken, or no mortal can break it. If it
break, all will know it, for you will see the sacred water
gush from the chapel door!"

I stood a few moments, to let the hearers have a
chance to spread my announcement to those who
couldn't hear, and so convey it to the furthest ranks, then
I made a grand exhibition of extra posturing and gestur-
ing, and shouted:

"Lo, I command the fell spirit that possesses the holy
fountain to now disgorge into the skies all the infernal
fires that still remain in him, and straightway dissolve
his spell and flee hence to the pit, there to lie bound a
thousand years. By his own dread name I command it—
BGWJJILLIGKKK!"

Then I touched off the hogshead of rockets, and a vast
fountain of dazzling lances of fire vomited itself toward
the zenith with a hissing rush, and burst in mid-sky into a

storm of flashing jewels! One mighty groan of terror
started up from the massed people—then suddenly
broke into a wild hosannah of joy—for there, fair and
plain in the uncanny glare, they saw the freed water leaping forth! The old abbot could not speak a word, for
tears and the chokings in his throat; without utterance of
any sort, he folded me in his arms and mashed me. It
was more eloquent than speech. And harder to get over,
too, in a country where there were really no doctors that
were worth a damaged nickel.

You should have seen those acres of people throw
themselves down in that water and kiss it; kiss it, and
pet it, and fondle it, and talk to it as if it were alive, and
welcome it back with the dear names they gave their
darlings, just as if it had been a friend who was long
gone away and lost, and was come home again. Yes, it
was pretty to see, and made me think more of them
than I had done before.

I sent Merlin home on a shutter. He had caved in and
gone down like a landslide when I pronounced that
fearful name, and had never come to since. He never had
heard that name before—neither had I—but to him it
was the right one; any jumble would have been the right
one. He admitted, afterward, that that spirit's own mother
could not have pronounced that name better than I did.
He never could understand how I survived it, and I didn't
tell him. It is only young magicians that give away a
secret like that. Merlin spent three months working enchantments to try to find out the deep trick of how
to pronounce that name and outlive it. But he didn't
arrive.

When I started to the chapel, the populace uncovered
and fell back reverently to make a wide way for me, as if
I had been some kind of a superior being—and I was. I
was aware of that. I took along a night shift of monks,
and taught them the mystery of the pump, and set them
to work, for it was plain that a good part of the people
out there were going to sit up with the water all night,
consequently it was but right that they should have all
they wanted of it. To those monks that pump was a good
deal of a miracle itself, and they were full of wonder over

it; and of admiration, too, of the exceeding effectiveness of its performance.

It was a great night, an immense night. There was reputation in it. I could hardly get to sleep for glorying over it.

CHAPTER XXIV

A Rival Magician

MY INFLUENCE in the Valley of Holiness was something prodigious now. It seemed worthwhile to try to turn it to some valuable account. The thought came to me the next morning and was suggested by my seeing one of my knights who was in the soap line come riding in. According to history, the monks of this place two centuries before, had been worldly minded enough to want to wash. It might be that there was a leaven of this unrighteousness still remaining. So I sounded a Brother:

"Wouldn't you like a bath?"

He shuddered at the thought—the thought of the peril of it to the well—but he said with feeling—

"One needs not to ask that of a poor body who has not known that blessed refreshment sith that he was a boy. Would God I might wash me! But it may not be, fair sir, tempt me not; it is forbidden."

And then he sighed in such a sorrowful way that I was resolved he should have at least one layer of his real estate removed, if it sized up my whole influence and bankrupted the pile. So I went to the abbot and asked for a permit for this Brother. He blenched at the idea—I don't mean that you could see him blench, for of course you couldn't see it without you scraped him, and I didn't care enough about it to scrape him, but I knew the blench was there, just the same, and within a book cover's thickness of the surface, too—blenched, and trembled. He said:

"Ah, son, ask aught else thou wilt, and it is thine, and

freely granted out of a grateful heart—but this, oh, this! Would you drive away the blessed water again?"

"No, Father, I will not drive it away. I have mysterious knowledge which teaches me that there was an error that other time when it was thought the institution of the bath banished the fountain." A large interest began to show up in the old man's face. "My knowledge informs me that the bath was innocent of that misfortune, which was caused by quite another sort of sin."

"These are brave words—but—but right welcome, if they be true."

"They are true, indeed. Let me build the bath again, Father. Let me build it again, and the fountain shall flow forever."

"You promise this—you promise it? Say the word—say you promise it!"

"I do promise it."

"Then will I have the first bath myself! Go—get ye to your work. Tarry not, tarry not, but go."

I and my boys were at work, straight off. The ruins of the old bath were there yet, in the basement of the monastery, not a stone missing. They had been left just so, all these lifetimes, and avoided with a pious fear, as things accursed. In two days we had it all done and the water in—a spacious pool of clear pure water that a body could swim in. It was running water, too. It came in and went out through the ancient pipes. The old abbot kept his word and was the first to try it. He went down black and shaky, leaving the whole black community above troubled and worried and full of bodings; but he came back white and joyful, and the game was made! Another triumph scored.

It was a good campaign that we made in that Valley of Holiness, and I was very well satisfied, and ready to move on, now, but I struck a disappointment. I caught a heavy cold, and it started up an old lurking rheumatism of mine. Of course the rheumatism hunted up my weakest place and located itself there. This was the place where the abbot put his arms about me and mashed me, what time he was moved to testify his gratitude to me with an embrace.

When at last I got out, I was a shadow. But everybody was full of attentions and kindnesses, and these brought cheer back into my life and were the right medicine to help a convalescent swiftly up toward health and strength again; so I gained fast.

Sandy was worn out with nursing, so I made up my mind to turn out and go a cruise alone, leaving her at the nunnery to rest up. My idea was to disguise myself as a freeman of peasant degree and wander through the country a week or two on foot. This would give me a chance to eat and lodge with the lowliest and poorest class of free citizens on equal terms. There was no other way to inform myself perfectly of their everyday life and the operation of the laws upon it. If I went among them as a gentleman, there would be restraints and conventionalities which would shut me out from their private joys and troubles, and I should get no further than the outside shell.

One morning I was out on a long walk to get up muscle for my trip and had climbed the ridge which bordered the northern extremity of the valley, when I came upon an artificial opening in the face of a low precipice, and recognized it by its location as a hermitage which had often been pointed out to me from a distance, as the den of a hermit of high renown for dirt and austerity. I knew he had lately been offered a situation in the Great Sahara, where lions and sandflies made the hermit life peculiarly attractive and difficult, and had gone to Africa to take possession, so I thought I would look in and see how the atmosphere of this den agreed with its reputation.

My surprise was great: the place was newly swept and scoured. Then there was another surprise. Back in the gloom of the cavern I heard the clink of a little bell, and then this exclamation:

"*Hello, Central! Is this you, Camelot?* ——Behold, thou mayst glad thy heart an thou hast faith to believe the wonderful when that it cometh in unexpected guise and maketh itself manifest in impossible places—here standeth in the flesh his mightiness The Boss, and with thine own ears shall ye hear him speak!"

Now what a radical reversal of things this was; what a jumbling together of extravagant incongruities; what a

fantastic conjunction of opposites and irreconcilables—
the home of the bogus miracle become the home of a
real one, the den of a medieval hermit turned into a telephone office!

The telephone clerk stepped into the light, and I recognized one of my young fellows. I said:

"How long has this office been established here,
Ulfius?"

"But since midnight, fair Sir Boss, an it please you. We
saw many lights in the valley, and so judged it well to
make a station, for that where so many lights be needs
must they indicate a town of goodly size."

"Quite right. It isn't a town in the customary sense,
but it's a good stand, anyway. Do you know where you
are?"

"Of that I have had no time to make inquiry; for whenas my comradeship moved hence upon their labors, leaving me in charge, I got me to needed rest, purposing to
inquire when I waked, and report the place's name to
Camelot for record."

"Well, this is the Valley of Holiness."

It didn't take; I mean, he didn't start at the name, as
I had supposed he would. He merely said—

"I will so report it."

"Why, the surrounding regions are filled with the noise
of late wonders that have happened here! You don't
hear of them?"

"Ah, ye will remember we move by night, and avoid
speech with all. We learn naught but that we get by the
telephone from Camelot."

"Why *they* know all about this thing. Haven't they
told you anything about the great miracle of the restoration of a holy fountain?"

"Oh, *that?* Indeed yes. But the name of *this* valley
doth woundily differ from the name of *that* one; indeed
to differ wider were not pos—"

"What was that name, then?"

"The Valley of Hellishness."

"*That* explains it. Confound a telephone, anyway. It
is the very demon for conveying similarities of sound
that are miracles of divergence from similarity of sense.

But no matter, you know the name of the place now. Call up Camelot."

He did it, and had Clarence sent for. It was good to hear my boy's voice again. It was like being home. After some affectionate interchanges and some account of my late illness, I said:

"What is new?"

"The king and queen and many of the court do start even in this hour, to go to your Valley to pay pious homage to the waters ye have restored, and cleanse themselves of sin, and see the place where the infernal spirit spouted true hell flames to the clouds—an ye listen sharply ye may hear me wink and hear me likewise smile a smile, sith 'twas I that made selection of those flames from out our stock and sent them by your order."

"Does the king know the way to this place?"

"The king? No, nor to any other in his realms, mayhap; but the lads that holp you with your miracle will be his guide and lead the way, and appoint the places for rests at noons and sleeps at night."

"This will bring them here—when?"

"Midafternoon, or later, the third day."

"Anything else in the way of news?"

"The king hath begun the raising of the standing army ye suggested to him; one regiment is complete and officered."

"The mischief! I wanted a main hand in that, myself. There is only one body of men in the kingdom that are fitted to officer a regular army."

"Yes—and now ye will marvel to know there's not so much as one West Pointer in that regiment."

"What are you talking about? Are you in earnest?"

"It is truly as I have said."

"Why, this makes me uneasy. Who were chosen, and what was the method? Competitive examination?"

"Indeed I know naught of the method. I but know this—these officers be all of noble family, and are born— what is it you call it—chuckleheads."

"There's something wrong, Clarence."

"Comfort yourself, then; for two candidates for a lieutenancy do travel hence with the king—young nobles both—and if you but wait where you are you will hear them questioned."

"That is news to the purpose. I will get one West Pointer in, anyway. Mount a man and send him to that school with a message; let him kill horses, if necessary, but he must be there before sunset tonight and say—"

"There is no need. I have laid a ground wire to the school. Prithee let me connect you with it."

It sounded good! In this atmosphere of telephones and lightning communication with distant regions, I was breathing the breath of life again after long suffocation. I realized, then, what a creepy, dull, inanimate horror this land had been to me all these years, and how I had been in such a stifled condition of mind as to have grown used to it almost beyond the power to notice it.

I gave my order to the superintendent of the Academy personally. I also asked him to bring me some paper and a fountain pen and a box or so of safety matches. I was getting tired of doing without these conveniences. I could have them, now, as I wasn't going to wear armor any more at present, and therefore could get at my pockets.

When I got back to the monastery, I found a thing of interest going on. The abbot and his monks were assembled in the great hall, observing with childish wonder and faith the performances of a new magician, a fresh arrival. His dress was the extreme of the fantastic; as showy and foolish as the sort of thing an Indian medicine man wears. He was mowing, and mumbling, and gesticulating, and drawing mystical figures in the air and on the floor—the regular thing, you know. He was a celebrity from Asia—so he said, and that was enough. That sort of evidence was as good as gold, and passed current everywhere.

How easy and cheap it was to be a great magician on this fellow's terms. His specialty was to tell you what any individual on the face of the globe was doing at the moment; and what he had done at any time in the past, and what he would do at any time in the future. He asked if any would like to know what the Emperor of the East was doing now? The sparkling eyes and the delighted rubbing of hands made eloquent answer—this reverend crowd *would* like to know what that monarch was at, just at this moment. The fraud went through some more mummery, and then made grave announcement:

"The high and mighty Emperor of the East doth at this moment put money in the palm of a holy begging friar— one, two, three pieces, and they be all of silver."

A buzz of admiring exclamations broke out, all around:

"It is marvelous!" "Wonderful!" "What study, what labor, to have acquired a so amazing power as this!"

Would they like to know what the Supreme Lord of Inde was doing? Yes. He told them what the Supreme Lord of Inde was doing. Then he told them what the Sultan of Egypt was at; also what the King of the Remote Seas was about. And so on and so on; and with each new marvel the astonishment at his accuracy rose higher and higher. They thought he must surely strike an uncertain place sometime; but no, he never had to hesitate, he always knew, and always with unerring precision. I saw that if this thing went on I should lose my supremacy, this fellow would capture my following, I should be left out in the cold. I must put a cog in his wheel, and do it right away, too. I said:

"If I might ask, I should very greatly like to know what a certain person is doing."

"Speak, and freely. I will tell you."

"It will be difficult—perhaps impossible."

"My art knoweth not that word. The more difficult it is, the more certainly will I reveal it to you."

You see, I was working up the interest. It was getting pretty high, too; you could see that by the craning necks all around, and the half suspended breathing. So now I climaxed it:

"If you make no mistake—if you tell me truly what I want to know—I will give you two hundred silver pennies."

"The fortune is mine! I will tell you what you would know."

"Then tell me what I am doing with my right hand."

"Ah-h!" There was a general gasp of surprise. It had not occurred to anybody in the crowd—that simple trick of inquiring about somebody who wasn't ten thousand miles away. The magician was hit hard; it was an emergency that had never happened in his experience before, and it corked him; he didn't know how to meet it. He looked stunned, confused; he couldn't say a word. "Come," I said, "what are you waiting for? Is it possible you can answer up, right off, and tell what anybody on the other side of the earth is doing, and yet can't tell what a person is doing who isn't three yards from you? Persons behind me know what I am doing with my right hand—they will endorse you if you tell correctly." He was still dumb. "Very well, I'll tell you why you don't speak up and tell; it is because you don't know. *You* a magician! Good friends, this tramp is a mere fraud and liar."

This distressed the monks and terrified them. They were not used to hearing these awful beings called names, and they did not know what might be the consequence. There was a dead silence, now; superstitious bodings were in every mind. The magician began to pull his wits together, and when he presently smiled an easy, nonchalant smile, it spread a mighty relief around; for it indicated that his mood was not destructive. He said:

"It hath struck me speechless, the frivolity of this person's speech. Let all know, if perchance there be any who know it not, that enchanters of my degree deign not to concern themselves with the doings of any but Kings, Princes, Emperors, them that be born in the purple and them only. Had ye asked me what Arthur the great king is doing, it were another matter, and I had told ye; but the doings of a subject interest me not."

"Oh, I misunderstood you. I thought you said 'anybody,' and so I supposed 'anybody' included—well, anybody; that is, everybody."

"It doth—anybody that is of lofty birth; and the better if he be royal."

"That, it meseemeth, might well be," said the abbot, who saw his opportunity to smooth things and avert disaster, "for it were not likely that so wonderful a gift as this would be conferred for the revelation of the concerns of lesser beings than such as be born near to the summits of greatness. Our Arthur the king—"

"Would you know of him?" broke in the enchanter.

"Most gladly, yea, and gratefully."

Everybody was full of awe and interest again, right away, the incorrigible idiots. They watched the incantations absorbingly, and looked at me with a "There, now, what can you say to that?" air, when the announcement came:

"The king is weary with the chase, and lieth in his palace these two hours sleeping a dreamless sleep."

"God's benison upon him!" said the abbot, and crossed himself; "may that sleep be to the refreshment of his body and his soul."

"And so it might be, if he were sleeping," I said, "but the king is not sleeping, the king rides."

Here was trouble again—a conflict of authority. Nobody knew which of us to believe; I still had some reputation left. The magician's scorn was stirred, and he said:

"Lo, I have seen many wonderful soothsayers and prophets and magicians in my life days, but none before that could sit idle and see to the heart of things with never an incantation to help."

"You have lived in the woods and lost much by it. I use incantations myself, as this good brotherhood are aware—but only on occasions of moment."

When it comes to sarcasaming, I reckon I know how to keep my end up. That jab made this fellow squirm. The abbot inquired after the queen and the court, and got this information:

"They be all on sleep, being overcome by fatigue, like as to the king."

I said:

"That is merely another lie. Half of them are about their amusements, the queen and the other half are not sleeping, they ride. Now perhaps you can spread yourself a little, and tell us where the king and queen and all that are this moment riding with them are going?"

"They sleep now, as I said; but on the morrow they will ride, for they go a journey toward the sea."

"And where will they be the day after tomorrow at vespers?"

"Far to the north of Camelot, and half their journey will be done."

"That is another lie, by the space of a hundred and

fifty miles. Their journey will not be merely half done, it will be all done, and they will be *here*, in this valley."

That was a noble shot! It set the abbot and the monks in a whirl of excitement, and it rocked the enchanter to his base. I followed the thing right up:

"If the king does not arrive, I will have myself ridden on a rail; if he does I will ride you on a rail instead."

Next day I went up to the telephone office and found that the king had passed through two towns that were on the line. I spotted his progress on the succeeding day in the same way. I kept these matters to myself. The third day's reports showed that if he kept up his gait he would arrive by four in the afternoon. There was still no sign anywhere of interest in his coming; there seemed to be no preparations making to receive him in state; a strange thing, truly. Only one thing could explain this: that other magician had been cutting under me, sure. This was true. I asked a friend of mine, a monk, about it, and he said, yes, the magician had tried some further enchantments and found out that the court had concluded to make no journey at all, but stay at home. Think of that! Observe how much a reputation was worth in such a country. These people had seen me do the very showiest bit of magic in history, and the only one within their memory that had a positive value, and yet here they were, ready to take up with an adventurer who could offer no evidence of his powers but his mere unproven word.

However, it was not good politics to let the king come without any fuss and feathers at all, so I went down and drummed up a procession of pilgrims and smoked out a batch of hermits and started them out at two o'clock to meet him. And that was the sort of state he arrived in. The abbot was helpess with rage and humiliation when I brought him out on a balcony and showed him the head of the state marching in and never a monk on hand to offer him welcome, and no stir of life or clang of joy bell to glad his spirit. He took one look and then flew to rouse out his forces. The next minute the bells were dinning furiously, and the various buildings were vomiting monks and nuns, who went swarming in a rush toward the coming procession; and with them went that magician—and

he was on a rail, too, by the abbot's order; and his reputation was in the mud, and mine was in the sky again.
Yes, a man can keep his trademark current in such a
country, but he can't sit around and do it; he has got to
be on deck and attending to business, right along.

[CHAPTER XXV]

A Competitive Examination

WHEN THE KING traveled for change of air, or made a
progress, or visited a distant noble whom he wished to
bankrupt with the cost of his keep, part of the administration moved with him. It was a fashion of the time. The
Commission charged with the examination of candidates
for posts in the army came with the king to the Valley,
whereas they could have transacted their business just as
well at home. And although this expedition was strictly
a holiday excursion for the king, he kept some of his
business functions going, just the same. He touched for
the evil, as usual; he held court in the gate at sunrise and tried cases, for he was himself Chief Justice of
the King's Bench.

He shone very well in this latter office. He was a wise
and humane judge, and he clearly did his honest best
and fairest—according to his lights. That is a large reser-
vation. His lights—I mean his rearing—often colored his
decisions. Whenever there was a dispute between a noble
or gentleman and a person of lower degree, the king's
leanings and sympathies were for the former class always,
whether he suspected it or not. It was impossible that this
should be otherwise. The blunting effects of slavery upon
the slaveholder's moral perceptions are known and con-
ceded, the world over, and a privileged class, an aristocracy, is but a band of slaveholders under another
name. This has a harsh sound and yet should not be offensive to any—even to the noble himself—unless the fact
itself be an offense: for the statement simply formulates

a fact. The repulsive feature of slavery is the *thing*, not its name. One needs but to hear an aristocrat speak of the classes that are below him to recognize—and in but indifferently modified measure—the very air and tone of the actual slaveholder; and behind these are the slaveholder's spirit, the slaveholder's blunted feeling. They are the result of the same cause in both cases: the possessor's old and inbred custom of regarding himself as a superior being. The king's judgment wrought frequent injustices, but it was merely the fault of his training, his natural and unalterable sympathies. He was as unfitted for a judgeship as would be the average mother for the position of milk-distributor to starving children in famine time; her own children would fare a shade better than the rest.

One very curious case came before the king. A young girl, an orphan, who had a considerable estate, married a fine young fellow who had nothing. The girl's property was within a seignory held by the Church. The bishop of the diocese, an arrogant scion of the great nobility, claimed the girl's estate on the ground that she had married privately, and thus had cheated the Church out of one of its rights as lord of the seignory—the one heretofore referred to as *le droit du seigneur*. The penalty of refusal or avoidance was confiscation. The girl's defense was that the lordship of the seignory was vested in the bishop, and the particular right here involved was not transferable, but must be exercised by the lord himself or stand vacated; and that an older law of the Church itself strictly barred the bishop from exercising it. It was a very odd case, indeed.

It reminded me of something I had read in my youth about the ingenious way in which the aldermen of London raised the money that built the Mansion House. A person who had not taken the Sacrament according to the Anglican rite, could not stand as a candidate for sheriff of London. Thus Dissenters were ineligible; they could not run if asked, they could not serve if elected. The aldermen, who without any question were Yankees in disguise, hit upon this neat device: they passed a bylaw imposing a fine of £400 upon any one who should refuse to be a candidate for sheriff, and a fine of £600 upon any person who, after being elected sheriff, refused to serve. Then they went to work and elected a lot of Dissenters, one after another, and kept it up until they had collected £15,000 in fines; and there stands the stately Mansion House to this day, to keep the blushing citizen in mind of a long past and lamented day when a band of Yankees slipped into London and played games of the sort that has given their race a unique and shady reputation among all truly good and holy peoples that be in the earth.

The girl's case seemed strong to me; the bishop's case was just as strong. I did not see how the king was going to get out of this hole. But he got out. I append his decision:

"Truly I find small difficulty here, the matter being even a child's affair for simpleness. An the young bride had conveyed notice, as in duty bound, to her feudal lord and proper master and protector the bishop, she had suffered no loss, for the said bishop could have got a dispensation making him, for temporary conveniency, eligible to the exercise of his said right, and thus would she have kept all she had. Whereas, failing in her first duty, she hath by that failure failed in all; for whoso, clinging to a rope, severeth it above his hands, must fall; it being no defense to claim that the rest of the rope is sound, neither any deliverance from his peril, as he shall find. Pardy, the woman's case is rotten at the source. It is the decree of the Court that she forfeit to the said lord bishop all her goods, even to the last farthing that she doth possess, and be thereto mulcted in the costs. Next!"

Here was a tragic end to a beautiful honeymoon not yet three months old. Poor young creatures! They had lived these three months lapped to the lips in worldly comforts. These clothes and trinkets they were wearing were as fine and dainty as the shrewdest stretch of the sumptuary laws allowed to people of their degree; and in these pretty clothes, she crying on his shoulder, and he trying to comfort her with hopeful words set to the music of despair, they went from the judgment seat out into the world homeless, bedless, breadless; why, the very beggars by the roadsides were not so poor as they.

Well, the king was out of the hole; and on terms satisfactory to the Church and the rest of the aristocracy, no doubt. Men write many fine and plausible arguments in support of monarchy, but the fact remains that where every man in a State has a vote, brutal laws are impossible. Arthur's people were of course poor material for a republic, because they had been debased so long by monarchy, and yet even they would have been intelligent enough to make short work of that law which the king had just been administering if it had been submitted to their full and free vote. There is a phrase which has grown so common in the world's mouth that it has come to seem to have sense and meaning—the sense and meaning implied when it is used—that is, the phrase which refers to this or that or the other nation as possibly being "capable of self-government"; and the implied sense of it is, that there has been a nation somewhere, sometime or other which *wasn't* capable of it—wasn't as able to govern itself as some self-appointed specialists were or would be to govern it. The master minds of all nations, in all ages, have sprung in affluent multitude from the mass of the nation, and from the mass of the nation only—not from its privileged classes; and so, no matter what the nation's intellectual grade was, whether high or low, the bulk of its ability was in the long ranks of its nameless and its poor, and so it never saw the day that it had not the material in abundance whereby to govern itself. Which is to assert an always self-proven fact: that even the best governed and most free and most enlightened monarchy is still behind the best condition attainable by its people; and that the same is true of kindred governments of lower grades, all the way down to the lowest.

King Arthur had hurried up the army business altogether beyond my calculations. I had not supposed he would move in the matter while I was away; and so I had not mapped out a scheme for determining the merits of officers; I had only remarked that it would be wise to submit every candidate to a sharp and searching examination; and privately I meant to put together a list of military qualifications that nobody could answer to but my West Pointers. That ought to have been attended to before I left; for the king was so taken with the idea of a standing army that he couldn't wait but must get about it at once, and get up as good a scheme of examination as he could invent out of his own head.

I was impatient to see what this was; and to show, too, how much more admirable was the one which I should display to the Examining Board. I intimated this, gently, to the king, and it fired his curiosity. When the Board was assembled, I followed him in, and behind us came the candidates. One of these candidates was a bright young West Pointer of mine, and with him were a couple of my West Point professors.

When I saw the Board, I did not know whether to cry or to laugh. The head of it was the officer known to later centuries as Norroy King-at-Arms! The two other members were chiefs of bureaus in his department; and all three were priests, of course; all officials who had to know how to read and write were priests.

My candidate was called first, out of courtesy to me, and the head of the Board opened on him with official solemnity:

"Name?"

"Mal-ease."

"Son of?"

"Webster."

"Webster—Webster. Hm—I—my memory faileth to recall the name. Condition?"

"Weaver."

"Weaver—God keep us!"

The king was staggered, from his summit to his foundations; one clerk fainted, and the others came near it. The chairman pulled himself together, and said indignantly:

"It is sufficient. Get you hence."

But I appealed to the king. I begged that my candidate might be examined. The king was willing, but the Board, who were all well-born folk, implored the king to spare them the indignity of examining the weaver's son. I knew they didn't know enough to examine him anyway, so I joined my prayers to theirs and the king turned the duty over to my professors. I had had a blackboard prepared, and it was put up now, and the circus began. It was beautiful to hear the lad lay out the science of war, and wallow in details of battle and siege, of supply, transportation, mining and countermining, grand tactics, big strategy and little strategy, signal service, infantry, cavalry, artillery, and all about siege guns, field guns, gatling guns, rifled guns, smooth bores, musket practice, revolver practice—and not a solitary word of it all could these catfish make head or tail of, you understand—and it was handsome to see him chalk off mathematical nightmares on the blackboard that would stump the angels themselves, and do it like nothing, too—all about eclipses, and comets, and solstices, and constellations, and mean time, and sidereal time, and dinner time, and bedtime, and every other imaginable thing above the clouds or under them that you could harry or bullyrag an enemy with and make him wish he hadn't come—and when the boy made his military salute and stood aside at last, I was proud enough to hug him, and all those other people were so dazed they looked partly petrified, partly drunk, and wholly caught out and snowed under. I judged that the cake was ours, and by a large majority.

Education is a great thing. This was the same youth who had come to West Point so ignorant that when I asked him, "If a general officer should have a horse shot under him on the field of battle, what ought he to do?" answered up naïvely and said:

"Get up and brush himself."

One of the young nobles was called up, now. I thought I would question him a little myself. I said:

"Can your lordship read?"

His face flushed indignantly, and he fired this at me:

"Takest me for a clerk? I trow I am not of a blood that"—

"Answer the question!"

He crowded his wrath down and made out to answer "No."

"Can you write?"

He wanted to resent this, too, but I said:

"You will confine yourself to the questions, and make no comments. You are not here to air your blood or your graces, and nothing of the sort will be permitted. Can you write?"

"No."

"Do you know the multiplication table?"

"I wit not what ye refer to."

"How much is nine times six?"

"It is a mystery that is hidden from me by reason that the emergency requiring the fathoming of it hath not in my life-days occurred, and so, not having no need to know this thing, I abide barren of the knowledge."

"If A trade a barrel of onions to B, worth twopence the bushel, in exchange for a sheep worth fourpence and a dog worth a penny, and C kill the dog before delivery, because bitten by the same, who mistook him for D, what sum is still due to A from B, and which party pays for the dog, C or D, and who gets the money? If A, is the penny sufficient, or may he claim consequential damages in the form of additional money to represent the possible profit which might have inured from the dog, and classifiable as earned increment, that is to say, usufruct?"

"Verily, in the all-wise and unknowable providence of God, who moveth in mysterious ways his wonders to perform, have I never heard the fellow to this question for confusion of the mind and congestion of the ducts of thought. Wherefore I beseech you let the dog and the onions and these people of the strange and godless names work out their several salvations from their piteous and wonderful difficulties without help of mine, for indeed their trouble is sufficient as it is, whereas an I tried to help I should but damage their cause the more and yet mayhap not live myself to see the desolation wrought."

"What do you know of the laws of attraction and gravitation?"

"If there be such, mayhap his grace the king did promulgate them whilst that I lay sick about the beginning of the year and thereby failed to hear his proclamation."

"What do you know of the science of optics?"

"I know of governors of places, and seneschals of castles, and sheriffs of counties, and many like small offices and titles of honor, but him you call the Science of Optics I have not heard of before; peradventure it is a new dignity."

"Yes, in this country."

Try to conceive of this mollusk gravely applying for an official position, of any kind under the sun! Why, he had all the earmarks of a typewriter copyist, if you leave out the disposition to contribute uninvited emendations of your grammar and punctuation. It was unaccountable that he didn't attempt a little help of that sort out of his majestic supply of incapacity for the job. But that didn't prove that he hadn't material in him for the disposition, it only proved that he wasn't a typewriter copyist yet. After nagging him a little more, I let the professors loose on him and they turned him inside out, on the line of scientific war, and found him empty, of course. He knew somewhat about the warfare of the time—bushwhacking around for ogres, and bullfights in the tournament ring, and such things—but otherwise he was empty and useless. Then we took the other young noble in hand, and he was the first one's twin, for ignorance and incapacity. I delivered them into the hands of the chairman of the board with the comfortable consciousness that their cake was dough. They were examined in the previous order of precedence.

"Name, so please you?"

"Pertipole, son of Sir Pertipole, Baron of Barley Mash."

"Grandfather?"

"Also Sir Pertipole, Baron of Barley Mash."

"Great-grandfather?"

"The same name and title."

"Great-great-grandfather?"

"We had none, worshipful sir, the line failing before it had reached so far back."

"It mattereth not. It is a good four generations, and fulfilleth the requirements of the rule."

"Fulfills what rule?" I asked.

"The rule requiring four generations of nobility or else the candidate is not eligible."

"A man not eligible for a lieutenancy in the army unless he can prove four generations of noble descent?"

"Even so; neither lieutenant nor any other officer may be commissioned without that qualification."

"Oh come, this is an astonishing thing. What good is such a qualification as that?"

"What good? It is a hardy question, fair sir and Boss, since it doth go far to impugn the wisdom of even our holy Mother Church herself."

"As how?"

"For that she hath established the self-same rule regarding saints. By her law none may be canonized until he hath lain dead four generations."

"I see, I see—it is the same thing. It is wonderful. In the one case a man lies dead-alive four generations—mummified in ignorance and sloth—and that qualifies him to command live people, and take their weal and woe into his impotent hands; and in the other case, a man lies bedded with death and worms four generations, and that qualifies him for office in the celestial camp. Does the king's grace approve of this strange law?"

The king said:

"Why, truly I see naught about it that is strange. All places of honor and of profit do belong, by natural right, to them that be of noble blood, and so these dignities in the army are their property and would be so without this or any rule. The rule is but to mark a limit. Its purpose is to keep out too recent blood, which would bring into contempt these offices, and men of lofty lineage would turn their backs and scorn to take them. I were to blame an I permitted this calamity. *You* can permit it an you are minded so to do, for you have the delegated authority, but that the king should do it were a most strange madness and not comprehensible to any."

"I yield. Proceed, sir Chief of the Herald's College."

The chairman resumed as follows:

"By what illustrious achievement for the honor of the Throne and State did the founder of your great line lift himself to the sacred dignity of the British nobility?"

"He built a brewery."

"Sire, the Board finds this candidate perfect in all the requirements and qualifications for military command, and doth hold his case open for decision after due examination of his competitor."

The competitor came forward and proved exactly four generations of nobility himself. So there was a tie in military qualifications that far.

He stood aside, a moment, and Sir Pertipole was questioned further:

"Of what condition was the wife of the founder of your line?"

"She came of the highest landed gentry, yet she was not

noble; she was gracious and pure and charitable, of a blameless life and character, insomuch that in these regards was she peer of the best lady in the land."

"That will do. Stand down." He called up the competing lordling again, and asked: "What was the rank and condition of the great-grandmother who conferred British nobility upon your great house?"

"She was a king's leman and did climb to that splendid eminence by her own unholpen merit from the sewer where she was born."

"Ah, this indeed is true nobility, this is the right and perfect intermixture. The lieutenancy is yours, fair lord. Hold not in contempt; it is the humble step which will lead to grandeurs more worthy of the splendor of an origin like to thine."

I was down in the bottomless pit of humiliation. I had promised myself an easy and zenith-scouring triumph, and this was the outcome!

I was almost ashamed to look my poor disappointed cadet in the face. I told him to go home and be patient, this wasn't the end.

I had a private audience with the king, and made a proposition. I said it was quite right to officer that regiment with nobilities, and he couldn't have done a wiser thing. It would also be a good idea to add five hundred officers to it; in fact, add as many officers as there were nobles and relatives of nobles in the country, even if there should finally be five times as many officers as privates in it, and thus make it the crack regiment, the envied regiment, the King's Own regiment, and entitled to fight on its own hook and in its own way, and go whither it would and come when it pleased, in time of war, and be utterly swell and independent. This would make that regiment the heart's desire of all the nobility, and they would all be satisfied and happy. Then we would make up the rest of the standing army out of commonplace materials, and officer it with nobodies, as was proper—nobodies selected on a basis of mere efficiency—and we would make this regiment toe the line, allow it no aristocratic freedom from restraint, and force it to do all the work and persistent hammering, to the end that whenever the King's Own was tired and wanted to go off for a change and rummage around amongst ogres and have a good time, it could go without uneasiness, knowing that matters were in safe hands behind it, and business going to be continued at the old stand, same as usual. The king was charmed with the idea.

When I noticed that, it gave me a valuable notion. I thought I saw my way out of an old and stubborn difficulty at last. You see, the royalties of the Pendragon stock were a long-lived race and very fruitful. Whenever a child was born to any of these—and it was pretty often—there was wild joy in the nation's mouth, and piteous sorrow in the nation's heart. The joy was questionable, but the grief was honest. Because the event meant another call for a Royal Grant. Long was the list of these royalties, and they were a heavy and steadily increasing burden upon the treasury and a menace to the crown. Yet Arthur could not believe this latter fact, and he would not listen to any of my various projects for substituting something in the place of the royal grants. If I could have persuaded him to now and then provide a support for one of these outlying scions from his own pocket, I could have made a grand to-do over it, and it would have had a good effect with the nation; but no, he wouldn't hear of such a thing. He had something like a religious passion for a royal grant; he seemed to look upon it as a sort of sacred swag, and one could not irritate him in any way so quickly and so surely as by an attack upon that venerable institution. If I ventured to cautiously hint that there was not another respectable family in England that would humble itself to hold out the hat —however, that is as far as I ever got; he always cut me short, there, and peremptorily, too.

But I believed I saw my chance at last. I would form this crack regiment out of officers alone—not a single private. Half of it should consist of nobles, who should fill all the places up to Major General, and serve gratis and pay their own expenses; and they would be glad to do this when they should learn that the rest of the regiment would consist exclusively of princes of the blood. These princes of the blood should range in ranks from Lieutenant General up to Field Marshal, and be gorgeously salaried and equipped and fed by the state. Moreover—and this was the master stroke—it should be decreed that these princely grandees should be always addressed by a stunningly gaudy and awe-compelling title (which I would presently invent) and they and they only in all England should be so addressed. Finally, all princes of the blood should have free choice: join that regiment, get that great title, and renounce the royal grant, or stay out and receive a grant. Neatest touch of all: unborn but imminent princes of the blood could be *born* into the regiment, and start fair, with good wages and a permanent situation, upon due notice from the parents.

All the boys would join, I was sure of that; so all existing grants would be relinquished; that the newly born would always join was equally certain. Within sixty days that quaint and bizarre anomaly, the Royal Grant, would cease to be a living fact, and take its place among the curiosities of the past.

〚 CHAPTER XXVI 〛

The First Newspaper

WHEN I told the king I was going out disguised as a petty freeman to scour the country and familiarize myself with the humbler life of the people, he was all afire with the novelty of the thing in a minute, and was bound to take a chance in the adventure himself—nothing should stop him—he would drop everything and go along—it was the prettiest idea he had run across for many a day. He wanted to glide out the back way and start at once; but I showed him that that wouldn't answer. You see, he was billed for the king's-evil—to touch for it, I mean—and it wouldn't be right to disappoint the house; and it wouldn't make a delay worth considering, anyway, it was only a one-night stand. And I thought he ought to tell the queen he was going away. He clouded up at that, and looked sad. I was sorry I had spoken, especially when he said mournfully:

"Thou forgettest that Launcelot is here; and where Launcelot is, she noteth not the going forth of the king, nor what day he returneth."

Of course I changed the subject. Yes, Guenever was beautiful, it is true, but take her all around she was pretty slack. I never meddled in these matters, they weren't my affair, but I did hate to see the way things were going on, and I don't mind saying that much. Many's the time she had asked me, "Sir Boss, hast seen Sir Launcelot about?" but if ever she went fretting around for the king I didn't happen to be around at the time.

There was a very good layout for the king's-evil business—very tidy and creditable. The king sat under a canopy of state, about him were clustered a large body of the clergy in full canonicals. Conspicuous, both for location and personal outfit, stood Marinel, a hermit of the quack-doctor species, to introduce the sick. All abroad over the spacious floor, and clear down to the doors, in a thick jumble, lay or sat the scrofulous, under a strong light. It was as good as a tableau; in fact it had all the look of being gotten up for that, though it wasn't. There were eight hundred sick people present. The work was slow; it lacked the interest of novelty for me, because I had seen the ceremonies before; the thing soon became tedious, but the proprieties required me to stick it out. The doctor was there for the reason that in all such crowds there were many people who only imagined something was the matter with them, and many who were consciously sound but wanted the immortal honor of fleshly contact with a king, and yet others who pretended to illness in order to get the piece of coin that went with the touch. Up to this time this coin had been a wee little gold piece worth about a third of a dollar. When you consider how much that amount of money would buy, in that age and country, and how usual it was to be scrofulous, when not dead, you will understand that the annual king's-evil appropriation was just the River and Harbor bill of that government for the grip it took on the treasury and the chance it afforded for skinning the surplus. So I had privately concluded to touch the treasury itself for the king's-evil. I covered sixth-sevenths of the appropriation into the treasury a week before starting from Camelot on my adventures, and ordered that the other seventh be inflated into five-cent nickels and delivered into the hands of the head clerk of the King's Evil Department; a nickel to take the place of each gold coin, you see, and do its work for it. It might strain the nickel some, but I judged it could stand it. As a rule, I do not approve of watering stock, but I considered it square enough in this case, for it was just a gift, anyway. Of course you can water a gift as much as you want to; and I generally do. The old gold and silver coins of the country were of ancient and unknown origin, as a rule, but some of them were Roman; they were ill-shapen, and seldom rounder than a moon that is a week past the full; they were hammered, not minted, and they were so worn with use that the devices upon them were as illegible as blisters, and looked like them. I judged that a sharp, bright new nickel, with a first-rate likeness of the king on one side of it and Guenever on the other, and a blooming pious motto, would take the tuck out of scrofula as handy as a nobler coin and please the scrofulous fancy more; and I was right. This batch was the first it was tried on, and it worked to a charm. The saving in expense was a notable economy. You will see that by these figures: We touched a trifle over seven hundred of the eight hundred patients; at former rates, this would have cost the government about two hundred forty dollars; at the new rate we pulled through for about thirty-five dollars, thus saving upward of two hundred dollars at one swoop. To appreciate the full magnitude of this stroke, consider these other figures: the annual expenses of a national government amount to the equivalent of a contribution of three days' average wages of every individual of the population, counting every individual as if he were a man. If you take a nation of sixty million where average wages are two dollars per day, three days' wages taken from each individual will provide three hundred sixty million dollars and pay the government's expenses. In my day, in my own country, this money was collected from imposts, and the citizen imagined that the foreign importer paid it, and it made him comfortable to think so; whereas, in fact, it was paid by the American people, and was so equally and exactly distributed among them that the annual cost to the one hundred millionaire and the annual cost to the sucking child of the day laborer was precisely the same —each paid six dollars. Nothing could be equaler than that, I reckon. Well, Scotland and Ireland were tributary to Arthur, and the united populations of the British Islands amounted to something less than one million. A mechanic's average wage was three cents a day, when he paid his own keep. By this rule, the national government's expenses were ninety thousand dollars a year, or about two hundred fifty dollars a day. Thus, by the substitution of nickels for gold on a king's-evil day, I not only injured no one, dissatisfied no one, but pleased all concerned and saved four-fifths of that day's national expense into the bargain—a saving which would have been the equivalent of eight hundred thousand dollars in my day in America. In making this substitution I had drawn upon the wisdom of a very remote source—the wisdom of my boyhood—for the true statesman does not despise any wisdom, howsoever lowly may be its origin: in my boyhood I had always saved my pennies and contributed buttons to the foreign missionary cause. The buttons would answer the ignorant savage as well as the coin, the coin would answer me better than the buttons; all hands were happy and nobody hurt.

Marinel took the patients as they came. He examined the candidate; if he couldn't qualify he was warned off; if he could he was passed along to the king. A priest pronounced the words, "They shall lay their hands on the sick, and they shall recover." Then the king stroked the ulcers, while the reading continued; finally, the patient graduated and got his nickel—the king hanging it around his neck himself—and was dismissed. Would you think that that would cure? It certainly did. Any mummery will cure if the patient's faith is strong in it. Up by Astolat there was a chapel where the Virgin had once appeared to a girl who used to herd geese around there— the girl said so herself—and they built the chapel upon that spot and hung a picture in it representing the occurrence—a picture which you would think it dangerous for a sick person to approach; whereas, on the contrary, thousands of the lame and the sick came and prayed

before it every year and went away whole and sound,
and even the well could look upon it and live. Of course
when I was told these things I did not believe them; but
when I went there and saw them I had to succumb. I
saw the cures effected myself, and they were real cures
and not questionable. I saw cripples whom I had seen
around Camelot for years on crutches, arrive and pray
before that picture, and put down their crutches and
walk off without a limp. There were piles of crutches
there which had been left by such people as a testimony.

In other places people operated on a patient's mind,
without saying a word to him, and cured him. In others,
experts assembled patients in a room and prayed over
them, and appealed to their faith, and those patients
went away cured. Wherever you find a king who can't
cure the king's-evil you can be sure that the most valuable superstition that supports his throne—the subject's
belief in the divine appointment of his sovereign—has
passed away. In my youth the monarchs of England had
ceased to touch for the evil, but there was no occasion
for this diffidence: they could have cured it forty-nine
times in fifty.

Well, when the priest had been droning for three hours,
and the good king polishing the evidences, and the sick
were still pressing forward as plenty as ever, I got to
feeling intolerably bored. I was sitting by an open window
not far from the canopy of state. For the five hundredth
time a patient stood forward to have his repulsivenesses
stroked; again those words were being droned out: "they
shall lay their hands on the sick"—when outside there
rang clear as a clarion a note that enchanted my soul
and tumbled thirteen worthless centuries about my ears:
"Camelot *Weekly Hosannah and Literary Volcano*—
latest irruption—only two cents—all about the big miracle in the Valley of Holiness!" One greater than kings had
arrived—the newsboy. But I was the only person in all
that throng who knew the meaning of this mighty birth
and what this imperial magician was come into the world
to do.

I dropped a nickel out of the window and got my
paper; the Adam-newsboy of the world went around the
corner to get my change; is around the corner yet. It was

delicious to see a newspaper again, yet I was conscious
of a secret shock when my eye fell upon the first batch
of display headlines. I had lived in a clammy atmosphere
of reverence, respect, deference, so long, that they sent
a quivery little cold wave through me:

HIGH TIMES IN THE VALLEY
OF HOLINESS!

THE WATER-WORKS CORKED!

BRER MERLIN WORKS HIS ARTS, BUT GETS
LEFT!

But the Boss scores on his first Innings!

The Miraculous Well Uncorked amid
awful outbursts of
INFERNAL FIRE AND SMOKE
ANDTHUNDER!

THE BUZZARD-ROOST ASTONISHED!

UNPARALLELED REJOIBINGS!

—and so on and so on. Yes, it was too loud. Once I could
have enjoyed it and seen nothing out of the way about it,
but now its note was discordant. It was good Arkansas
journalism, but this was not Arkansas. Moreover, the
next to the last line was calculated to give offense to
the hermits, and perhaps lose us their advertising. Indeed,
there was too lightsome a tone of flippancy all through
the paper. It was plain I had undergone a considerable
change without noticing it. I found myself unpleasantly
affected by pert little irreverencies which would have
seemed but proper and airy graces of speech at an

earlier period of my life. There was an abundance of the following breed of items, and they discomforted me:

Local Smoke and Cinders.

Sir Launce[o] met up with old King Vgrivance of Ireland unexpectedly last week over on the moor south of Sir Balmoral le Merveilleuse's hog dasture. The widow has been notified.

Expedition No. 3 will start adout the first of next month on a search for Sir Sagramour le Desirous. It is in command of the renowned Knight of the Red Lawns, assissted by Sir Persant of Inde, who is competegt. intelligent, courteous, and in every way a brick, and furtuer assisted by Sir Palamides the Saracen, who is no huckleberry himself. This is no pic-nic, these boys mean busine&s.

The readers of the Hosannah will regict to learn that the hadndsome and popular Sir Charolais of Gaul, who during his four weeks' stay at the Bull and Halibut, this city, has won every heart by his polished manners and elegant c¶nversation, will pull out to-day for home. Give us another call, Charley!

The bdsiness end of the funeral of the late Sir Dalliance the duke's son of Cornwall, killed in an encounter with the Giant of the Knotted Bludgeon last.

Tuesday on the borders of the Plain of
Enchantment was in the hands of the
ever affable and euycient Mumble,
prince of unzertakers, than whom there
exists none by whom it were a more
satisfying pieasure to have the last sad
offices performed. Give him a trial.

The corvial thanks of the Hosannah
office are due, from editor down to
devil, to the ever courteous and thoughtful Lord High Steward of the Palace's
Thrid Assistant V— t for several sau-
certs of ice cream a quality calculated
to make the ey— of the recipients hu-
mid with gr— ude; and it done it.
When this administration wants to
chalk up a desirable name for early
promotion, the Hosannah would like a
chance to sudgest.

The Demoiselle Irene uewlap, of
South Astolat, is visiting her uncle, the
popular host of the Cattlemen's Board-
ing Ho&se, Liver Lane, this city.

Young Barker the bellows-mender is
hoMe again, and looks much improved
by his vacauon round-up among the
out-lying smithies. See his ad.

Of course it was good enough journalism for a beginning; I knew that quite well, and yet it was somehow
disappointing. The "Court Circular" pleased me better;
indeed its simple and dignified respectfulness was a distinct refreshment to me after all those disgraceful fa-
miliarities. But even it could have been improved. Do
what one may, there is no getting an air of variety into
a court circular, I acknowledge that. There is a profound
monotonousness about its facts that baffles and defeats
one's sincerest efforts to make them sparkle and enthuse.
The best way to manage—in fact, the only sensible way

—is to disguise repetitiousness of fact under variety of form: skin your fact each time and lay on a new cuticle of words. It deceives the eye; you think it is a new fact; it gives you the idea that the court is carrying on like everything; this excites you, and you drain the whole column, with a good appetite, and perhaps never notice that it's a barrel of soup made out of a single bean. Clarence's way was good, it was simple, it was dignified, it was direct and businesslike; all I say is, it was not the best way:

Court Circular.

On Monday, the King rode in the park.

"	Tuesday,	"	"	"
"	Wendesday	"	"	"
"	Thursday	"	"	"
"	Friday,	"	"	"
"	Saturday	"	"	"
"	Sunday,	"	"	"

However, take the paper by and large, I was vastly pleased with it. Little crudities of a mechanical sort were observable here and there, but there were not enough of them to amount to anything, and it was good enough Arkansas proofreading, anyhow, and better than was needed in Arthur's day and realm. As a rule, the grammar was leaky and the construction more or less lame; but I did not much mind these things. They are common defects of my own, and one mustn't criticize other people on grounds where he can't stand perpendicular himself.

I was hungry enough for literature to want to take down the whole paper at this one meal, but I got only a few bites, and then had to postpone, because the monks around me besieged me so with eager questions: What is this curious thing? What is it for? Is it a handkerchief—saddle blanket—part of a shirt? What is it made of? How thin it is, and how dainty and frail, and how it rattles. Will it wear, do you think, and won't the rain injure it? Is it writing that appears on it, or is it only ornamentation? They suspected it was writing, because those among them who knew how to read Latin and had a smattering of Greek, recognized some of the letters, but they could make nothing out of the result as a whole. I put my information in the simplest form I could:

"It is a public journal; I will explain what that is, another time. It is not cloth, it is made of paper; sometime I will explain what paper is. The lines on it are reading matter; and not written by hand, but printed; by and by I will explain what printing is. A thousand of these sheets have been made, all exactly like this, in every minute detail—they can't be told apart." Then they all broke out with exclamations of surprise and admiration:

"A thousand! Verily a mighty work—a year's work for many men."

"No—merely a day's work for a man and a boy."

They crossed themselves and whiffed out a protective prayer or two.

"Ah-h—a miracle, a wonder! Dark work of enchantment."

I let it go at that. Then I read in a low voice, to as many as could crowd their shaven heads within hearing distance, part of the account of the miracle of the restoration of the well, and was accompanied by astonished and reverent ejaculations all through: "Ah-h-h!" "How true!" "Amazing, amazing!" "These be the very haps as they happened, in marvelous exactness!" And might they take this strange thing in their hands and feel of it and examine it—they would be very careful. Yes. So they took it, handling it as cautiously and devoutly as if it had been some holy thing come from some supernatural region; and gently felt of its texture, caressed its pleasant smooth surface with lingering touch, and scanned the mysterious characters with fascinated eyes. These grouped bent heads, these charmed faces, these speaking eyes—how beautiful to me! For was not this my darling, and was not all this mute wonder and interest and homage a most eloquent tribute and unforced compliment to it? I knew, then, how a mother feels when women, whether strangers or friends, take her new baby, and close themselves about it with one eager impulse, and bend their heads over it in a tranced adoration that

makes all the rest of the universe vanish out of their
consciousness and be as if it were not, for that time. I
knew how she feels, and that there is no other satisfied
ambition, whether of king, conqueror, or poet, that
ever reaches half way to that serene far summit or
yields half so divine a contentment.

During all the rest of the séance my paper traveled
from group to group all up and down and about that huge
hall, and my happy eye was upon it always, and I sat
motionless, steeped in satisfaction, drunk with enjoyment.
Yes, this was heaven; I was tasting it once, if I might
never taste it more.

⟦ CHAPTER XXVII ⟧

The Yankee and the King Travel Incognito

ABOUT BEDTIME I took the king to my private quarters
to cut his hair and help him get the hang of the lowly
raiment he was to wear. The high classes wore their hair
banged across the forehead but hanging to the shoulders
the rest of the way around, whereas the lowest ranks
of commoners were banged fore and aft both; the slaves
were bangless, and allowed their hair free growth. So I
inverted a bowl over his head and cut away all the locks
that hung below it. I also trimmed his whiskers and
moustache until they were only about a half inch long;
and tried to do it inartistically, and succeeded. It was a
villainous disfigurement. When he got his lubberly sandals on, and his long robe of coarse brown linen cloth,
which hung straight from his neck to his anklebones, he
was no longer the comeliest man in his kingdom, but one
of the unhandsomest and most commonplace and unat-
tractive. We were dressed and barbered alike, and could
pass for small farmers, or farm bailiffs, or shepherds, or
carters; yes, or for village artisans, if we chose, our
costume being in effect universal among the poor, because of its strength and cheapness. I don't mean that it

was really cheap to a very poor person, but I do mean that it was the cheapest material there was for male attire—manufactured material, you understand.

We slipped away an hour before dawn, and by broad sunup had made eight or ten miles, and were in the midst of a sparsely settled country. I had a pretty heavy knapsack; it was laden with provisions—provisions for the king to taper down on, till he could take to the course fare of the country without damage.

I found a comfortable seat for the king by the road-side, and then gave him a morsel or two to stay his stomach with. Then I said I would find some water for him, and strolled away. Part of my project was to get out of sight and sit down and rest a little myself. It had always been my custom to stand, when in his presence; even at the council board, except upon those rare occa-sions when the sitting was a very long one, extending over hours; then I had a trifling little backless thing which was like a reversed culvert and was as comforta-ble as the toothache. I didn't want to break him in sud-denly, but do it by degrees. We should have to sit to-gether now when in company, or people would notice; but it would not be good politics for me to be playing equality with him when there was no necessity for it.

I found the water, some three hundred yards away, and had been resting about twenty minutes, when I heard voices. That is all right, I thought—peasants going to work; nobody else likely to be stirring this early. But the next moment these comers jingled into sight around a turn of the road—smartly clad people of quality, with luggage-mules and servants in their train! I was off like a shot, through the bushes, by the shortest cut. For a while it did seem that these people would pass the king before I could get to him; but desperation gives you wings, you know, and I canted my body forward, inflated my breast, and held my breath and flew. I arrived. And in plenty good enough time, too.

"Pardon, my king, but it's no time for ceremony—jump! Jump to your feet—some quality are coming!"

"Is that a marvel? Let them come."

"But my liege! You must not be seen sitting. Rise—and

stand in humble posture while they pass! You are a peasant, you know."

"True—I had forgot it, so lost was I in planning of a
huge war with Gaul"—he was up by this time, but a farm
could have got up quicker, if there was any kind of a
boom in real estate—"and right-so a thought came randoming overthwart this majestic dream the which—"

"A humbler attitude, my lord the king—and quick!
Duck your head—more—still more—droop it!"

He did his honest best, but lord it was not great things.
He looked as humble as the leaning tower at Pisa. It is
the most you could say of it. Indeed it was such a
thundering poor success that it raised wondering scowls
all along the line, and a gorgeous flunkey at the tail end
of it raised his whip; but I jumped in time and was
under it when it fell; and under cover of the volley of
coarse laughter which followed, I spoke up sharply and
warned the king to take no notice. He mastered himself for the moment, but it was a sore tax; he wanted to
eat up the procession. I said:

"It would end our adventures at the very start; and
we, being without weapons, could do nothing with that
armed gang. If we are going to succeed in our emprise,
we must not only look the peasant but act the peasant."

"It is wisdom; none can gainsay it. Let us go on, Sir
Boss. I will take note and learn, and do the best I may."

He kept his word. He did the best he could, but I've
seen better. If you have ever seen an active, heedless,
enterprising child going diligently out of one mischief and
into another all day long, and an anxious mother at its
heels all the while, and just saving it by a hair from
drowning itself or breaking its neck with each new experiment, you've seen the king and me.

If I could have foreseen what the thing was going to
be like, I should have said, No, if anybody wants to
make his living exhibiting a king as a peasant, let him take
the layout; I can do better with a menagerie, and last
longer. And yet, during the first three days I never allowed him to enter a hut or other dwelling. If he could
pass muster anywhere, during his early novitiate, it
would be in small inns and on the road; so to these
places we confined ourselves. Yes, he certainly did the

best he could, but what of that? He didn't improve a bit that I could see.

He was always frightening me, always breaking out with fresh astonishers, in new and unexpected places. Toward evening on the second day, what does he do but blandly fetch out a dirk from inside his robe!

"Great guns, my liege, where did you get that?"

"From a smuggler at the inn, yester eve."

"What in the world possessed you to buy it?"

"We have escaped divers dangers by wit—thy wit—but I have bethought me that it were but prudence if I bore a weapon, too. Thine might fail thee in some pinch."

"But people of our condition are not allowed to carry arms. What would a lord say—yes, or any other person of whatever condition—if he caught an upstart peasant with a dagger on his person?"

It was a lucky thing for us that nobody came along just then. I persuaded him to throw the dirk away; and it was as easy as persuading a child to give up some bright fresh new way of killing itself. We walked along, silent and thinking. Finally the king said:

"When ye know that I meditate a thing inconvenient, or that hath a peril in it, why do you not warn me to cease from that project?"

It was a startling question, and a puzzler. I didn't quite know how to take hold of it, or what to say, and so of course I ended by saying the natural thing:

"But sire, how can *I* know what your thoughts are?"

The king stopped dead in his tracks, and stared at me.

"I believed thou wert greater than Merlin; and truly in magic thou art. But prophecy is greater than magic. Merlin is a prophet."

I saw I had made a blunder. I must get back my lost ground. After deep reflection and careful planning, I said:

"Sire, I have been misunderstood. I will explain. There are two kinds of prophecy. One is the gift to foretell things that are but a little way off, the other is the gift to foretell things that are whole ages and centuries away. Which is the mightier gift, do you think?"

"Oh, the last, most surely!"

"True. Does Merlin possess it?"

"Partly, yes. He foretold mysteries about my birth and future kingship that were twenty years away."

"Has he ever gone beyond that?"

"He would not claim more, I think."

"It is probably his limit. All prophets have their limit. The limit of some of the great prophets has been a hundred years."

"These are few, I ween."

"There have been two still greater ones, whose limit was four hundred and six hundred years, and one whose limit compassed even seven hundred and twenty."

"Gramercy, it is marvelous!"

"But what are these in comparison with me? They are nothing."

"What? Canst thou truly look beyond even so vast a stretch of time as—"

"Seven hundred years? My liege, as clear as the vision of an eagle does my prophetic eye penetrate and lay bare the future of this world for nearly thirteen centuries and a half!"

My land, you should have seen the king's eyes spread slowly open, and lift the earth's entire atmosphere as much as an inch! That settled Brer Merlin. One never had any occasion to prove his facts, with these people; all he had to do was state them. It never occurred to anybody to doubt the statement.

"Now, then," I continued, "I *could* work both kinds of prophecy—the long and the short—if I chose to take the trouble to keep in practice; but I seldom exercise any but the long kind, because the other is beneath my dignity. It is properer to Merlin's sort—stump-tail prophets, as we call them in the profession. Of course I whet up now and then and flirt out a minor prophecy, but not often—hardly ever, in fact. You will remember that there was great talk, when you reached the Valley of Holiness, about my having prophesied your coming and the very hour of your arrival, two or three days beforehand."

"Indeed, yes, I mind it now."

"Well, I could have done it as much as forty times easier, and piled on a thousand times more detail into the bargain, if it had been five hundred years away instead of two or three days."

"How amazing that it should be so!"

"Yes, a genuine expert can always foretell a thing that is five hundred years away easier than he can a thing that's only five hundred seconds off."

"And yet in reason it should clearly be the other way: it should be five hundred times as easy to foretell the last as the first, for indeed it is so close by that one uninspired might almost see it. In truth the law of prophecy doth contradict the likelihoods, most strangely making the difficult easy, and the easy difficult."

It was a wise head. A peasant's cap was no safe disguise for it; you could know it for a king's, under a diving bell, if you could hear it work its intellect.

I had a new trade, now, and plenty of business in it. The king was as hungry to find out everything that was going to happen during the next thirteen centuries as if he were expecting to live in them. From that time out, I prophesied myself bald-headed trying to supply the demand. I have done some indiscreet things in my day, but this thing of playing myself for a prophet was the worst. Still, it had its ameliorations. A prophet doesn't have to have any brains. They are good to have, of course, for the ordinary exigencies of life, but they are no use in professional work. It is the restfulest vocation there is. When the spirit of prophecy comes upon you, you merely take your intellect and lay it off in a cool place for a rest, and unship your jaw and leave it alone; it will work itself: the result is prophecy.

Everyday a knight-errant or so came along, and the sight of them fired the king's martial spirit every time. He would have forgotten himself, sure, and said something to them in a style a suspicious shade or so above his ostensible degree, and so I always got him well out of the road in time. Then he would stand, and look with all his eyes; and a proud light would flash from them, and his nostrils would inflate like a war-horse's, and I knew he was longing for a brush with them. But about noon of the third day I had stopped in the road to take a precaution which had been suggested by the whip stroke that had fallen to my share two days before; a precaution which I had afterward decided to leave untaken, I was so loath to institute it; but now I had just had a fresh reminder: while striding heedlessly along, with jaw spread and intellect at rest, for I was prophesying, I stubbed my toe and fell sprawling. I was so pale I couldn't think, for a moment; then I got softly and carefully up and unstrapped my knapsack. I had that dynamite bomb in it, done up in wool, in a box. It was a good thing to have along; the time would come when I could do a valuable miracle with it, maybe, but it was a nervous thing to have about me, and I didn't like to ask the king to carry it. Yet I must either throw it away or think up some safe way to get along with its society. I got it out and slipped it into my scrip, and just then, here came a couple of knights. The king stood, stately as a statue, gazing toward them—had forgotten himself again, of course—and before I could get a word of warning out, it was time for him to skip, and well that he did it, too. He supposed they would turn aside. Turn aside to avoid trampling peasant dirt under foot? When had he ever turned aside himself—or ever had the chance to do it, if a peasant saw him or any other noble knight in time to judiciously save him the trouble? The knights paid no attention to the king at all; it was his place to look out himself, and if he hadn't skipped he would have been placidly ridden down, and laughed at besides.

The king was in a flaming fury, and launched out his challenge and epithets with a most royal vigor. The knights were some little distance by, now. They halted, greatly surprised, and turned in their saddles and looked back, as if wondering if it might be worth while to bother with such scum as we. Then they wheeled and started for us. Not a moment must be lost. I started for *them*. I passed them at a rattling gait, and as I went by I flung out a hair-lifting soul-scorching thirteen-jointed insult which made the king's effort poor and cheap by comparison. I got it out of the nineteenth century where they know how. They had such headway that they were nearly to the king before they could check up; then, frantic with rage, they stood up their horses on their hind hoofs and whirled them around, and the next moment here they came, breast to breast. I was seventy yards off,

then, and scrambling up a great boulder at the roadside.
When they were within thirty yards of me they let their
long lances droop to a level, depressed their mailed
heads, and so, with their horsehair plumes streaming
straight out behind, most gallant to see, this lightning
express came tearing for me! When they were within
fifteen yards, I sent that bomb with a sure aim, and it
struck the ground just under the horses' noses.

Yes, it was a neat thing, very neat and pretty to see.
It resembled a steamboat explosion on the Mississippi;
and during the next fifteen minutes we stood under a
steady drizzle of microscopic fragments of knights and
hardware and horseflesh. I say we, for the king joined
the audience, of course, as soon as he had got his breath
again. There was a hole there which would afford steady
work for all the people in that region for some years to
come—in trying to explain it, I mean; as for filling it up,
that service would be comparatively prompt, and would
fall to the lot of a select few—peasants of that siegnory,
and they wouldn't get anything for it, either.

But I explained it to the king myself. I said it was
done with a dynamite bomb. This information did him
no damage, because it left him as intelligent as he was
before. However, it was a noble miracle, in his eyes,
and was another settler for Merlin. I thought it well
enough to explain that this was a miracle of so rare a
sort that it couldn't be done except when the atmospheric conditions were just right. Otherwise he would
be encoring it every time we had a good subject, and
that would be inconvenient, because I hadn't any more
bombs along.

[[CHAPTER XXVIII]]

Drilling the King

ON THE MORNING of the fourth day, when it was just
sunrise, and we had been tramping an hour in the chill

dawn, I came to a resolution: the king *must* be drilled; things could not go on so, he must be taken in hand and deliberately and conscientiously drilled, or wc couldn't ever venture to enter a dwelling; the very cats would know this masquerader for a humbug and no peasant. So I called a halt and said:

"Sire, as between clothes and countenance, you are all right, there is no discrepancy; but as between your clothes and your bearing, you are all wrong, there is a most noticeable discrepancy. Your soldierly stride, your lordly port—these will not do. You stand too straight, your looks are too high, too confident. The cares of a kingdom do not stoop the shoulders, they do not droop the chin, they do not depress the high level of the eye glance, they do not put doubt and fear in the heart and hang out the signs of them in slouching body and unsure step. It is the sordid cares of the lowly born that do these things. You must learn the trick; you must imitate the trademarks of poverty, misery, oppression, insult, and the other several and common inhumanities that sap the manliness out of a man and make him a loyal and proper and approved subject and a satisfaction to his masters, or the very infants will know you for better than your disguise, and we shall go to pieces at the first hut we stop at. Pray try to walk like this."

The king took careful note, and then tried an imitation.

"Pretty fair—pretty fair. Chin a little lower, please— there, very good. Eyes too high; pray don't look at the horizon, look at the ground, ten steps in front of you. Ah—that is better, that is very good. Wait, please; you betray too much vigor, too much decision; you want more of a shamble. Look at me, please—this is what I mean. . . . Now you are getting it; that is the idea—at least, it sort of approaches it. . . . Yes, that is pretty fair. *But!* There is a great big something wanting, I don't quite know what it is. Please walk thirty yards, so that I can get a perspective on the thing. . . . Now, then—your head's right, speed's right, shoulders right, eyes right, chin right, gait, carriage, general style right—everything's right! And yet the fact remains, the aggregate's wrong.

The account don't balance. Do it again, please . . . *now* I think I begin to see what it is. Yes, I've struck it. You see, the genuine spiritlessness is wanting; that's what's the trouble. It's all *amateur*—mechanical details all right, almost to a hair; everything about the delusion perfect, except that it don't delude."

"What, then, must one do to prevail?"

"Let me think . . . I can't seem to quite get at it. In fact there isn't anything that can right the matter but practice. This is a good place for it: roots and stony ground to break up your stately gait, a region not liable to interruption, only one field and one hut in sight, and they so far away that nobody could see us from there. It will be well to move a little off the road and put in the whole day drilling you, sire."

After the drill had gone on a little while, I said:

"Now, sire, imagine that we are at the door of the hut yonder, and the family are before us. Proceed, please— accost the head of the house."

The king unconsciously straightened up like a monument and said, with frozen austerity:

"Varlet, bring a seat; and serve to me what cheer ye have."

"Ah, your grace, that is not well done."

"In what lacketh it?"

"These people do not call *each other* varlets."

"Nay, is that true?"

"Yes; only those above them call them so."

"Then must I try again. I will call him villein."

"No-no; for he may be a freeman."

"Ah—so. Then peradventure I should call him goodman."

"That would answer, your grace, but it would be still better if you said friend, or brother."

"Brother! To dirt like that?"

"Ah, but *we* are pretending to be dirt like that, too."

"It is even true. I will say it. Brother, bring a seat, and thereto what cheer ye have, withal. *Now* 'tis right."

"Not quite, not wholly right. You have asked for one, not *us*—for one, not both; food for one, a seat for one."

The king looked puzzled—he wasn't a very heavy weight, intellectually. His head was an hourglass; it could stow an idea, but it had to do it a grain at a time, not the whole idea at once.

"Would *you* have a seat also—and sit?"

"If I did not sit, the man would perceive that we were only pretending to be equals—and playing the deception pretty poorly, too."

"It is well and truly said! How wonderful is truth, come it in whatsoever unexpected form it may! Yes, he must bring out seats and food for both, and in serving us present not ewer and napkin with more show of respect to the one than to the other."

"And there is even yet a detail that needs correcting. He must bring nothing outside—we will go in—in among the dirt, and possibly other repulsive things—and take the food with the household, and after the fashion of the house, and all on equal terms, except the man be of the serf class; and finally, there will be no ewer and no napkin, whether he be serf or free. Please walk again, my liege. There—it is better—it is the best yet; but not perfect. The shoulders have known no ignobler burden than iron mail, and they will not stoop."

"Give me, then, the bag. I will learn the spirit that goeth with burdens that have not honor. It is the spirit that stoopeth the shoulders, I ween, and not the weight; for armor is heavy, yet it is a proud burden, and a man standeth straight in it. . . . Nay, but me no buts, offer me no objections. I will have the thing. Strap it upon my back."

He was complete, now, with that knapsack on, and looked as little like a king as any man I had ever seen. But it was an obstinate pair of shoulders; they could not seem to learn the trick of stooping with any sort of deceptive naturalness. The drill went on, I prompting and correcting:

"Now, make believe you are in debt, and eaten up by relentless creditors; you are out of work—which is horse-shoeing, let us say—and can get none; and your wife is sick, your children are crying because they are hungry—"

And so on, and so on. I drilled him as representing in turn, all sorts of people out of luck and suffering dire privations and misfortunes. But lord it was only just words, words—they meant nothing in the world to him,

I might just as well have whistled. Words realize nothing, vivify nothing to you, unless you have suffered in your own person the thing which the words try to describe. There are wise people who talk ever so knowingly and complacently about "the working classes," and satisfy themselves that a day's hard intellectual work is very much harder than a day's hard manual toil, and is righteously entitled to much bigger pay. Why, they really think that, you know, because they know all about the one, but haven't tried the other. But I know all about both; and so far as I am concerned, there isn't money enough in the universe to hire me to swing a pickax thirty days, but I will do the hardest kind of intellectual work for just as near nothing as you can cipher it down —and I will be satisfied, too.

Intellectual "work" is misnamed; it is a pleasure, a dissipation, and is its own highest reward. The poorest paid architect, engineer, general, author, sculptor, painter, lecturer, advocate, legislator, actor, preacher, singer is constructively in heaven when he is at work; and as for the magician with the fiddle bow in his hand who sits in the midst of a great orchestra with the ebbing and flowing tides of divine sound washing over him—why, certainly, he is at work, if you wish to call it that, but lord, it's a sarcasm just the same. The law of work does seem utterly unfair—but there it is: and nothing can change it: the higher the pay in enjoyment the worker gets out of it, the higher shall be his pay in cash, also. And it's also the very law of those transparent swindles, transmissible nobility and kingship.

⟦ CHAPTER XXIX ⟧

The Smallpox Hut

WHEN WE arrived at that hut at midafternoon, we saw no signs of life about it. The field near by had been denuded of its crop some time before, and had a skinned

look, so exhaustively had it been harvested and gleaned.
Fences, sheds, everything had a ruined look, and were
eloquent of poverty. No animal was around anywhere, no
living thing in sight. The stillness was awful, it was like the
stillness of death. The cabin was a one-story one, whose
thatch was black with age, and ragged from lack of repair.

The door stood a trifle ajar. We approached it
stealthily—on tiptoe and at half breath—for that is the
way one's feeling makes him do, at such a time. The
king knocked. We waited. No answer. Knocked again.
No answer. I pushed the door softly open and looked in.
I made out some dim forms, and a woman started up
from the ground and stared at me, as one does who is
wakened from sleep. Presently she found her voice—

"Have mercy!" she pleaded. "All is taken, nothing is
left."

"I have not come to take anything, poor woman."

"You are not a priest?"

"No."

"Nor come not from the lord of the manor?"

"No, I am a stranger."

"Oh, then, for the fear of God, who visits with misery
and death such as be harmless, tarry not here, but fly!
This place is under his curse—and his Church's."

"Let me come in and help you—you are sick and in
trouble."

I was better used to the dim light, now. I could see her
hollow eyes fixed upon me. I could see how emaciated
she was.

"I tell you the place is under the Church's ban. Save
yourself—and go, before some straggler see thee here,
and report it."

"Give yourself no trouble about me; I don't care anything for the Church's curse. Let me help you."

"Now all good spirits—if there be any such—bless
thee for that word. Would God I had a sup of water—
but hold, hold, forget I said it, and fly; for there is that
here that even he that feareth not the Church must fear:
this disease whereof we die. Leave us, thou brave, good
stranger, and take with thee such whole and sincere blessing as them that be accursed can give."

But before this I had picked up a wooden bowl and

was rushing past the king on my way to the brook. It was ten yards away. When I got back and entered, the king was within, and was opening the shutter that closed the window hole, to let in air and light. The place was full of a foul stench. I put the bowl to the woman's lips, and as she gripped it with her eager talons the shutter came open and a strong light flooded her face. Smallpox!

I sprang to the king, and said in his ear:

"Out of the door on the instant, sire! the woman is dying of that disease that wasted the skirts of Camelot two years ago."

He did not budge.

"Of a truth I shall remain—and likewise help."

I whispered again:

"King, it must not be. You must go."

"Ye mean well, and ye speak not unwisely. But it were shame that a king should know fear, and shame that belted knight should withhold his hand where be such as need succor. Peace, I will not go. It is you who must go. The Church's ban is not upon me, but it forbiddeth you to be here, and she will deal with you with a heavy hand an word come to her of your trespass."

It was a desperate place for him to be in, and might cost him his life, but it was no use to argue with him. If he considered his knightly honor at stake here, that was the end of argument; he would stay, and nothing could prevent it; I was aware of that. And so I dropped the subject. The woman spoke:

"Fair sir, of your kindness will ye climb the ladder there, and bring me news of what ye find? Be not afraid to report, for times can come when even a mother's heart is past breaking—being already broke."

"Abide," said the king, "and give the woman to eat. I will go." And he put down the knapsack.

I turned to start but the king had already started. He halted, and looked down upon a man who lay in a dim light, and had not noticed us, thus far, or spoken.

"Is it your husband?" the king asked.

"Yes."

"Is he asleep?"

"God be thanked for that one charity, yes—these three hours. Where shall I pay to the full, my gratitude! For my heart is bursting with it for that sleep he sleepeth now."

I said:

"We will be careful. We will not wake him."

"Ah, no, that ye will not, for he is dead."

"Dead?"

"Yes, what triumph it is to know it! None can harm him, none insult him more. He is in heaven, now, and happy; or if not there, he bides in hell and is content; for in that place he will find neither abbot nor yet bishop. We were boy and girl together; we were man and wife these five and twenty years, and never separated till this day. Think how long that is, to love and suffer together. This morning was he out of his mind, and in his fancy we were boy and girl again and wandering in the happy fields; and so in that innocent glad converse wandered he far and farther, still lightly gossiping, and entered into those other fields we know not of, and was shut away from mortal sight. And so there was no parting, for in his fancy I went with him; he knew not but I went with him, my hand in his—my young soft hand, not this withered claw. Ah, yes, to go, and know it not; to separate and know it not; how could one go peacefuler than that? It was his reward for a cruel life patiently borne."

There was a slight noise from the direction of the dim corner where the ladder was. It was the king, descending. I could see that he was bearing something in one arm, and assisting himself with the other. He came forward into the light; upon his breast lay a slender girl of fifteen. She was but half conscious; she was dying of smallpox. Here was heroism at its last and loftiest possibility, its utmost summit; this was challenging death in the open field unarmed, with all the odds against the challenger, no reward set upon the contest, and no admiring world in silks and cloth of gold to gaze and applaud; and yet the king's bearing was as serenely brave as it had always been in those cheaper contests where knight meets knight in equal fight and clothed in protecting steel. He was great, now; sublimely great. The rude statues of his ancestors in his palace should have an addition—I would see to that; and it would not be a mailed king killing a giant or a dragon, like the rest, it would be a king in commoner's garb bearing death in his arms that a peasant mother might look her last upon her child and be comforted.

He laid the girl down by her mother, who poured out endearments and caresses from an overflowing heart, and one could detect a flickering faint light of response in the child's eyes, but that was all. The mother hung over her, kissing her, petting her, and imploring her to speak, but the lips only moved and no sound came. I snatched my liquor flask from my knapsack, but the woman forbade me, and said:

"No—she does not suffer; it is better so. It might bring her back to life. None that be so good and kind as ye are, would do her that cruel hurt. For look you—what is left to live for? Her brothers are gone, her father is gone, her mother goeth, the Church's curse is upon her, and none may shelter or befriend her even though she lay perishing in the road. She is desolate. I have not asked you, good heart, if her sister be still on live, here overhead; I had no need; ye had gone back, else, and not left the poor thing forsaken—"

"She lieth at peace," interrupted the king, in a subdued voice.

"I would not change it. How rich is this day in happiness! Ah, my Annis, thou shalt join thy sister soon—thou'rt on thy way, and these be merciful friends, that will not hinder."

And so she fell to murmuring and cooing over the girl again, and softly stroking her face and hair, and kissing her and calling her by endearing names; but there was scarcely sign of response, now, in the glazing eyes. I saw tears well from the king's eyes, and trickle down his face. The woman noticed them, too, and said:

"Ah, I know that sign: thou'st a wife at home, poor soul, and you and she have gone hungry to bed, many's the time, that the little ones might have your crust; you know what poverty is, and the daily insults of your betters, and the heavy hand of the Church and the king."

The king winced under this accidental home shot, but kept still; he was learning his part; and he was playing it well, too, for a pretty dull beginner. I struck up a diversion. I offered the woman food and liquor, but she re-

fused both. She would allow nothing to come between
her and the release of death. Then I slipped away and
brought the dead child from aloft, and laid it by her.
This broke her down again, and there was another scene
that was full of heartbreak. By and by I made another
diversion, and beguiled her to sketch her story.

"Ye know it well, yourselves, having suffered it—for
truly none of our condition in Britain escape it. It is the
old, weary tale. We fought and struggled and succeeded;
meaning by success, that we lived and did not die; more
than that is not to be claimed. No troubles came that we
could not outlive, till this year brought them; then came
they all at once, as one might say, and overwhelmed us.
Years ago the lord of the manor planted certain fruit
trees on our farm; in the best part of it, too—a grievous
wrong and shame"—

"But it was his right," interrupted the king.

"None denieth that, indeed; an the law mean anything,
what is the lord's is his, and what is mine is his also. Our
farm was ours by lease, therefore 'twas likewise his, to do
with it as he would. Some little time ago, three of those
trees were found hewn down. Our three grown sons ran
frightened to report the crime. Well, in his lordship's
dungeon there they lie, who saith there shall they lie and
rot till they confess. They have naught to confess, being
innocent, wherefore there will they remain until they die.
Ye know that right well, I ween. Think how this left
us: a man, a woman, and two children, to gather a crop
that was planted by so much greater force, yes, and protect it night and day from pigeons and prowling animals
that be sacred and must not be hurt by any of our sort.
When my lord's crop was nearly ready for the harvest,
so also was ours; when his bell rang to call us to his
fields to harvest his crops for nothing, he would not allow that I and my two girls should count for our three
captive sons, but for only two of them; so, for the
lacking one were we daily fined. All this time our own
crop was perishing through neglect; and so both the priest
and his lordship fined us because their shares of it were
suffering through damage. In the end the fines ate up
our crop—and they took it all; they took it all and made
us harvest it for them, without pay or food, and we starv-

ing. Then the worst came when I, being out of my mind with hunger and loss of my boys, and grief to see my husband and my little maids in rags and misery and despair, uttered a deep blasphemy—oh, a thousand of them—against the Church and the Church's ways. It was ten days ago. I had fallen sick with this disease, and it was to the priest I said the words, for he was come to chide me for lack of due humility under the chastening hand of God. He carried my trespass to his betters; I was stubborn; wherefore, presently upon my head and upon all heads that were dear to me, fell the curse of Rome.

"Since that day, we are avoided, shunned with horror. None has come near this hut to know whether we live or not. The rest of us were taken down. Then I roused me and got up, as wife and mother will. It was little they could have eaten in any case; it was less than little they had to eat. But there was water, and I gave them that. How they craved it! And how they blessed it! But the end came yesterday; my strength broke down. Yesterday was the last time I ever saw my husband and this youngest child alive. I have lain here all these hours—these ages, ye may say—listening, listening, for any sound up there that—"

She gave a sharp quick glance at her eldest daughter, then cried out, "Oh, my darling!" and feebly gathered the stiffening form to her sheltering arms. She had recognized the death rattle.

⟦ CHAPTER XXX ⟧

The Tragedy of the Manor House

AT MIDNIGHT all was over, and we sat in the presence of four corpses. We covered them with such rags as we could find, and started away, fastening the door behind us. Their home must be these people's grave, for they could not have Christian burial, or be admitted to consecrated ground. They were as dogs, wild beasts, lepers, and no soul that valued its hope of eternal life would throw it away by meddling in any sort with these rebuked and smitten outcasts.

We had not moved four steps when I caught a sound as of footsteps upon gravel. My heart flew to my throat. We must not be seen coming from that house. I plucked at the king's robe and we drew back and took shelter behind the corner of the cabin.

"Now we are safe," I said, "but it was a close call—so to speak. If the night had been lighter he might have seen us, no doubt, he seemed to be so near."

"Mayhap it is but a beast and not a man at all."

"True. But man or beast, it will be wise to stay here a minute and let it get by and out of the way."

"Hark! It cometh hither."

True again. The step was coming toward us—straight toward the hut. It must be a beast, then, and we might as well have saved our trepidation. I was going to step out, but the king laid his hand upon my arm. There was a moment of silence, then we heard a soft knock on the cabin door. It made me shiver. Presently the knock was repeated, and then we heard these words in a guarded voice:

"Mother! Father! Open—we have got free, and we bring news to pale your cheeks but glad your hearts; and we may not tarry, but must fly! And—but they answer not. Mother! Father! ——"

I drew the king toward the other end of the hut and whispered:

"Come—now we can get to the road."

The king hesitated, was going to demur; but just then we heard the door give way, and knew that those desolate men were in the presence of their dead.

"Come, my liege! in a moment they will strike a light, and then will follow that which it would break your heart to hear."

He did not hesitate this time. The moment we were in the road, I ran; and after a moment he threw dignity aside and followed. I did not want to think of what was happening in the hut—I couldn't bear it; I wanted to drive it out of my mind; so I struck into the first subject that lay under that one in my mind:

"I have had the disease those people died of, and so have nothing to fear; but if you have not had it also—"

He broke in upon me to say he was in trouble, and it was his conscience that was troubling him:

"These young men have got free, they say—but *how?* It is not likely that their lord hath set them free."

"Oh, no, I make no doubt they escaped."

"That is my trouble; I have a fear that this is so, and your suspicion doth confirm it, you having the same fear."

"I should not call it by that name though. I do suspect that they escaped, but if they did, I am not sorry, certainly."

"I am not sorry, I *think*—but—"

"What is it? What is there for one to be troubled about?"

"*If* they did escape, then are we bound in duty to lay hands upon them and deliver them again to their lord; for it is not seemly that one of his quality should suffer a so insolent and high-handed outrage from persons of their base degree."

There it was, again. He could see only one side of it. He was born so, educated so, his veins were full of ancestral blood that was rotten with this sort of unconscious brutality, brought down by inheritance from a long procession of hearts that had each done its share toward poisoning the stream. To imprison these men without proof, and starve their kindred, was no harm, for they were merely peasants and subject to the will and pleasure of their lord, no matter what fearful form it might take; but for these men to break out of unjust captivity was insult and outrage, and a thing not to be countenanced by any conscientious person who knew his duty to his sacred caste.

I worked more than half an hour before I got him to change the subject—and even then an outside matter did it for me. This was a something which caught our eyes as we struck the summit of a small hill—a red glow, a good way off.

"That's a fire," said I.

Fires interested me considerably, because I was getting a good deal of an insurance business started, and was also training some horses and building some steam fire engines, with an eye to a paid fire department by and by. The priests opposed both my fire and life insurance, on the ground that it was an insolent attempt to hinder the decrees of God; and if you pointed out that they did not hinder the decrees in the least, but only modified the hard consequences of them if you took out policies and had luck, they retorted that that was gambling against the decrees of God, and was just as bad. So they managed to damage those industries more or less, but I got even on my Accident business. As a rule, a knight is a lummux, and sometimes even a labrick, and hence open to pretty poor arguments when they come glibly from a superstition monger, but even *he* could see the practical side of a thing once in a while; and so of late you couldn't clean up a tournament and pile the result without finding one of my accident-tickets in every helmet.

We stood there awhile, in the thick darkness and stillness, looking toward the red blur in the distance and trying to make out the meaning of a far away murmur that rose and fell fitfully on the night. Sometimes it swelled up and for a moment seemed less remote; but when we were hopefully expecting it to betray its cause and nature, it dulled and sank again, carrying its mystery with it. We started down the hill in its direction, and the winding road plunged us at once into almost solid darkness— darkness that was packed and crammed in between two tall forest walls. We groped along down for half a mile, perhaps, that murmur growing more and more distinct all the time, the coming storm threatening more and more, with now and then a little shiver of wind, a faint show of lightning, and dull grumblings of distant thunder. I was in the lead. I ran against something—a soft heavy something which gave, slightly, to the impulse of my weight; at the same moment the lightning glared out, and within a foot of my face was the writhing face of a man who was hanging from the limb of a tree! That is, it seemed to be writhing, but it was not. It was a gruesome sight. Straightway there was an earsplitting explosion of thunder, and the bottom of heaven fell out; the rain poured down in a deluge. No matter, we must try to cut this man down, on the chance that there might be life in him yet, mustn't we? The lightning came quick and sharp, now, and the place was alternately noonday and midnight. One moment the man would be hanging before me in an intense light, and the next he was blotted out again in the darkness. I told the king we must cut him down. The king at once objected.

"If he hanged himself, he was willing to lose his property to his lord; so let him be. If others hanged him, belike they had the right—let him hang."

"But"—

"But me no buts, but even leave him as he is. And for yet another reason. When the lightning cometh again—there, look abroad."

Two others hanging, within fifty yards of us!

"It is not weather meet for doing useless courtesies unto dead folk. They are past thanking you. Come—it is unprofitable to tarry here."

There was reason in what he said, so we moved on. Within the next mile we counted six more hanging forms by the blaze of the lightning, and altogether it was a grisly excursion. That murmur was a murmur no longer, it was a roar; a roar of men's voices. A man came flying by, now, dimly through the darkness, and other men chasing him. They disappeared. Presently another case of the kind occurred, and then another and another. Then a sudden turn of the road brought us in sight of that fire—it was a large manor house, and little or nothing was left of it—and everywhere men were flying and other men raging after them in pursuit.

I warned the king that this was not a safe place for strangers. We would better get away from the light, until matters should improve. We stepped back a little, and hid in the edge of the wood. From this hiding place we saw both men and women hunted by the mob. The fearful work went on until nearly dawn. Then, the fire being out and the storm spent, the voices and flying footsteps presently ceased, and darkness and stillness reigned again.

We ventured out, and hurried cautiously away; and although we were worn out and sleepy, we kept on until we had put this place some miles behind us. Then we asked hospitality at the hut of a charcoal burner, and got what was to be had. A woman was up and about, but the man was still asleep, on a straw shakedown, on the clay floor.

The woman seemed uneasy until I explained that we were travelers and had lost our way and been wandering in the woods all night. She became talkative, then, and asked if we had heard of the terrible goings-on at the manor house of Abblasoure. Yes, we had heard of them, but what we wanted now, was rest and sleep. The king broke in:

"Sell us the house and take yourselves away, for we be perilous company, being but late come from people that died of the Spotted Death."

It was good of him, but unnecessary. One of the commonest decorations of the nation was the waffle-iron face. I had early noticed that the woman and her husband were both so decorated. She made us entirely welcome, and had no fears; and plainly she was immensely impressed by the king's proposition; for of course it was a good deal of an event in her life to run across a person of the king's humble appearance who was ready to buy a man's house for the sake of a night's lodging. It gave her a large respect for us, and she strained the lean possibilities of her hovel to their utmost to make us comfortable.

We slept till far into the afternoon, and then got up hungry enough to make cotter fare quite palatable to the king, the more particularly as it was scant in quantity. And also in variety; it consisted solely of onions, salt, and the national black bread—made out of horse feed. The woman told us about the affair of the evening before. At ten or eleven at night, when everybody was in bed, the manor house burst into flames. The countryside swarmed to the rescue, and the family were saved, with one exception, the master. He did not appear. Everybody was frantic over this loss, and two brave yeomen sacrificed their lives in ransacking the burning house seeking that valuable personage. But after a while he was found —what was left of him—which was his corpse. It was in a copse three hundred yards away, bound, gagged, stabbed in a dozen places.

Who had done this? Suspicion fell upon a humble family in the neighborhood who had been lately treated with peculiar harshness by the baron; and from these people the suspicion easily extended itself to their relatives and

familiars. A suspicion was enough; my lord's liveried re-
tainers proclaimed an instant crusade against these people, and were promptly joined by the community in general. The woman's husband had been active with the mob,
and had not returned home until nearly dawn. He was
gone, now, to find out what the general result had been.
While we were still talking, he came back from his quest.
His report was revolting enough. Eighteen persons hanged
or butchered, and two yeomen and thirteen prisoners lost
in the fire.

"And how many prisoners were there altogether, in
the vaults?"

"Thirteen."

"Then every one of them was lost."

"Yes, all."

"But the people arrived in time to save the family; how
is it they could save none of the prisoners?"

The man looked puzzled, and said:

"Would one unlock the vaults at such a time? Marry,
some would have escaped."

"Then you mean that nobody *did* unlock them?"

"None went near them, either to lock or unlock. It
standeth to reason that the bolts were fast; wherefore it
was only needful to establish a watch, so that if any
broke the bonds he might not escape, but be taken. None
were taken."

"Natheless, three did escape," said the king, "and ye will
do well to publish it and set justice upon their track, for
these murthered the baron and fired the house."

I was just expecting he would come out with that. For
a moment the man and his wife showed an eager interest
in this news and an impatience to go out and spread it;
then a sudden something else betrayed itself in their
faces, and they began to ask questions. I answered the
questions myself, and narrowly watched the effects produced. I was soon satisfied that the knowledge of who
these three prisoners were, had somehow changed the
atmosphere; that our hosts' continued eagerness to go
and spread the news was now only pretended and not
real. The king did not notice the change, and I was glad
of that. I worked the conversation around toward other de-

tails of the night's proceedings, and noted that these people were relieved to have it take that direction.

The painful thing observable about all this business was, the alacrity with which this oppressed community had turned their cruel hands against their own class in the interest of the common oppressor. This man and woman seemed to feel that in a quarrel between a person of their own class and his lord, it was the natural and proper and rightful thing for that poor devil's whole caste to side with the master and fight his battle for him, without ever stopping to inquire into the rights or wrongs of the matter. This man had been out helping to hang his neighbors, and had done his work with zeal, and yet was aware that there was nothing against them but a mere suspicion, with nothing back of it describable as evidence, still neither he nor his wife seemed to see anything horrible about it.

This was depressing—to a man with the dream of a republic in his head. It reminded me of a time thirteen centuries away, when the "poor whites" of our South who were always despised and frequently insulted, by the slave-lords around them, and who owed their base condition simply to the presence of slavery in their midst, were yet pusillanimously ready to side with slave-lords in all political moves for the upholding and perpetuating of slavery, and did also finally shoulder their muskets and pour out their lives in an effort to prevent the destruction of that very institution which degraded them. And there was only one redeeming feature connected with that pitiful piece of history; and that was, that secretly the "poor white" did detest the slave-lord, and did feel his own shame. That feeling was not brought to the surface, but the fact that it was there and could have been brought out, under favoring circumstances, was something—in fact it was enough; for it showed that a man is at bottom a man, after all, even if it doesn't show on the outside.

Well, as it turned out, this charcoal burner was just the twin of the Southern "poor white" of the far future. The king presently showed impatience, and said:

"An ye prattle here all the day, justice will miscarry. Think ye the criminals will abide in their father's house?

They are fleeing, they are not waiting. You should look to it that a party of horse be set upon their track."

The woman paled slightly, but quite perceptibly, and the man looked flustered and irresolute. I said:

"Come, friend, I will walk a little way with you, and explain which direction I think they would try to take. If they were merely resisters of the gabelle or some kindred absurdity I would try to protect them from capture; but when men murder a person of high degree and likewise burn his house, that is another matter."

The last remark was for the king—to quiet him. On the road the man pulled his resolution together, and began the march with a steady gait, but there was no eagerness in it. By and by I said:

"What relation were these men to you—cousins?"

He turned as white as his layer of charcoal would let him, and stopped, trembling.

"Ah, my God, how knew you that?"

"I didn't know it; it was a chance guess."

"Poor lads, they are lost. And good lads they were, too."

"Were you actually going yonder to tell on them?"

He didn't quite know how to take that; but he said, hesitatingly:

"Ye-s."

"Then I think you are a damned scoundrel!"

It made him as glad as if I had called him an angel.

"Say the good words again, brother! For surely ye mean that ye would not betray me an I failed of my duty."

"Duty? There is no duty in the matter, except the duty to keep still and let those men get away. They've done a righteous deed."

He looked pleased; pleased, and touched with apprehension at the same time. He looked up and down the road to see that no one was coming, and then said in a cautious voice:

"From what land come you, brother, that you speak such perilous words, and seem not to be afraid?"

"They are not perilous words when spoken to one of my own caste, I take it. You would not tell anybody I said them?"

"I? I would be drawn asunder by wild horses first."

"Well, then, let me say my say. I have no fears of your repeating it. I think devil's work has been done last night upon those innocent poor people. That old baron got only what he deserved. If I had my way, all his kind should have the same luck."

Fear and depression vanished from the man's manner, and gratefulness and a brave animation took their place:

"Even though you be a spy, and your words a trap for my undoing, yet are they such refreshment that to hear them again and others like to them, I would go to the gallows happy, as having had one good feast at least in a starved life. And I will say my say, now, and ye may report it if ye be so minded. I helped to hang my neighbors for that it were peril to my own life to show lack of zeal in the master's cause; the others helped for none other reason. All rejoice today that he is dead, but all do go about seemingly sorrowing, and shedding the hypocrite's tear, for in that lies safety. I have said the words. I have said the words! the only ones that have ever tasted good in my mouth, and the reward of that taste is sufficient. Lead on, an ye will, be it even to the scaffold, for I am ready."

There it was, you see. A man *is* a man, at bottom. Whole ages of abuse and oppression cannot crush the manhood clear out of him. Whoever thinks it a mistake, is himself mistaken. Yes, there is plenty good enough material for a republic in the most degraded people that ever existed— even the Russians; plenty of manhood in them—even in the Germans—if one could but force it out of its timid and suspicious privacy, to overthrow and trample in the mud any throne that ever was set up and any nobility that ever supported it. We should see certain things yet, let us hope and believe. First, a modified monarchy, till Arthur's days were done, then the destruction of the throne, nobility abolished, every member of it bound out to some useful trade, universal suffrage instituted, and the whole government placed in the hands of the men and women of the nation there to remain. Yes, there was no occasion to give up my dream yet awhile.

❴ CHAPTER XXXI ❵

Marco

WE STROLLED along in a sufficiently indolent fashion, now, and talked. We must dispose of about the amount of time it ought to take to go to the little hamlet of Abblasoure and put justice on the track of those murderers and get back home again. And meantime I had an auxiliary interest which had never paled yet, never lost its novelty for me, since I had been in Arthur's kingdom: the behavior—born of nice and exact subdivisions of caste—of chance passersby toward each other. Toward the shaven monk who trudged along with his cowl tilted back and the sweat washing down his fat jowls, the coal burner was deeply reverent; to the gentleman he was abject; with the small farmer and the free mechanic he was cordial and gossipy; and when a slave passed by with a countenance respectfully lowered, this chap's nose was in the air—he couldn't even see him. Well, there are times when one would like to hang the whole human race and finish the farce.

Presently we struck an incident. A small mob of half naked boys and girls came tearing out of the woods, scared and shrieking. The eldest among them were not more than twelve or fourteen years old. They implored help, but they were so beside themselves that we couldn't make out what the matter was. However, we plunged into the wood, they scurrying in the lead, and the trouble was quickly revealed: they had hanged a little fellow with a bark rope, and he was kicking and struggling, in the process of choking to death. We rescued him, and fetched him around. It was some more human nature; the admiring little folk imitating their elders; they were playing mob, and had achieved a success which promised to be a good deal more serious than they had bargained for.

It was not a dull excursion for me. I managed to put

in the time very well. I made various acquaintanceships, and in my quality of stranger was able to ask as many questions as I wanted to. A thing which naturally interested me, as a statesman, was the matter of wages. I picked up what I could under that head during the afternoon. A man who hasn't had much experience, and doesn't think, is apt to measure a nation's prosperity or lack of prosperity by the mere size of the prevailing wages: if the wages be high, the nation is prosperous; if low, it isn't. Which is an error. It isn't what sum you get, it's how much you can buy with it that's the important thing; and it's that that tells whether your wages are high in fact or only high in name. I could remember how it was in the time of our great civil war in the nineteenth century. In the North a carpenter got three dollars a day, gold valuation; in the South he got fifty—payable in Confederate shinplasters worth a dollar a bushel. In the North a suit of overalls cost three dollars—a day's wages; in the South it cost seventy-five—which was two days' wages. Other things were in proportion. Consequently, wages were twice as high in the North as they were in the South, because the one wage had that much more purchasing power than the other had.

Yes, I made various acquaintances in the hamlet, and a thing that gratified me a good deal was to find our new coins in circulation—lots of milrays, lots of mills, lots of cents, a good many nickels, and some silver; all this among the artisans and commonalty generally; yes, and even some gold—but that was at the bank, that is to say, the goldsmith's. I dropped in there while Marco the son of Marco was haggling with a shopkeeper over a quarter of a pound of salt, and asked for change for a twenty dollar gold piece. They furnished it—that is, after they had chewed the piece, and rung it on the counter, and tried acid on it, and asked me where I got it, and who I was, and where I was from, and where I was going to, and when I expected to get there, and perhaps a couple of hundred more questions; and when they got aground, I went right on and furnished them a lot of information voluntarily: told them I owned a dog, and his name was Watch, and my first wife was a Free Will Baptist, and her grandfather was a Prohibitionist, and I used to know a man who had two thumbs on each hand and a wart on the inside of his upper lip, and died in the hope of a glorious resurrection and so on and so on and so on till even that hungry village questioner began to look satisfied, and also a shade put out; but he had to respect a man of my financial strength, and so he didn't give me any lip, but I noticed he took it out of his underlings, which was a perfectly natural thing to do. Yes, they changed my twenty, but I judged it strained the bank a little, which was a thing to be expected, for it was the same as walking into a paltry village store in the nineteenth century and requiring the boss of it to change a two-thousand dollar bill for you all of a sudden. He could do it, maybe; but at the same time he would wonder how a small farmer happened to be carrying so much money around in his pocket; which was probably this goldsmith's thought, too; for he followed me to the door and stood there gazing after me with reverent admiration.

Our new money was not only handsomely circulating, but its language was already glibly in use; that is to say, people had dropped the names of the former moneys, and spoke of things as being worth so many dollars or cents or mills or milrays, now. It was very gratifying. We were progressing, that was sure.

I got to know several master mechanics, but about the most interesting fellow among them was the blacksmith, Dowley. He was a live man and a brisk talker, and had two journeymen and three apprentices, and was doing a raging business. In fact, he was getting rich, hand over fist, and was vastly respected. Marco was very proud of having such a man for a friend. He had taken me there ostensibly to let me see the big establishment which bought so much of his charcoal, but really to let me see what easy and almost familiar terms he was on with this great man. Dowley and I fraternized at once; I had had just such picked men, splendid fellows, under me in the Colt Arms Factory. I was bound to see more of him, so I invited him to come out to Marco's, Sunday, and dine with us. Marco was appalled, and held his breath; and when the grandee accepted, he was so grateful that he almost forgot to be astonished at the condescension.

Marco's joy was exuberant—but only for a moment;

then he grew thoughtful, then sad; and when he heard me
tell Dowley I should have Dickon the boss mason, and
Smug the boss wheelwright out there, too, the coal dust
on his face turned to chalk, and he lost his grip. But I
knew what was the matter with him; it was the expense.
He saw ruin before him; he judged that his financial days
were numbered. However, on our way to invite the others,
I said:

"You must allow me to have these friends come, and
you must also allow me to pay the costs."

His face cleared, and he said with spirit:

"But not all of it, not all of it. Ye cannot well bear a
burden like to this alone."

I stopped him, and said:

"Now let's understand each other on the spot, old
friend. I am only a farm bailiff, it is true; but I am not
poor, nevertheless. I have been very fortunate this year
—you would be astonished to know how I have thriven.
I tell you the honest truth when I say I could squander
away as many as a dozen feasts like this and never care
that for the expense!" And I snapped my fingers. I could
see myself rise a foot at a time in Marco's estimation, and
when I fetched out those last words I was become a very
tower, for style and altitude. "So you see, you must let
me have my way. You can't contribute a cent to this
orgy, that's *settled*."

"It's grand and good of you—"

"No, it isn't. You've opened your house to Jones and
me in the most generous way; Jones was remarking upon
it today, just before you came back from the village; for
although he wouldn't be likely to say such a thing to you,
—because Jones isn't a talker, and is diffident in society—
he has a good heart and a grateful, and knows how to
appreciate it when he is well treated; yes, you and your
wife have been very hospitable toward us—"

"Ah, brother, 'tis nothing—*such* hospitality!"

"But it *is* something; the best a man has, freely given,
is always something, and is as good as a prince can do,
and ranks right along beside it—for even a prince can
but do his best. And so we'll shop around and get up this
layout, now, and don't you worry about the expense. I'm
one of the worst spendthrifts that ever was born. Why, do

you know, sometimes in a single week I spend—but never mind about that—you'd never believe it anyway."

And so we went gadding along, dropping in here and there, pricing things, and gossiping with the shopkeepers about the riot, and now and then running across pathetic reminders of it, in the persons of shunned and tearful and houseless remnants of families whose homes had been taken from them and their parents butchered or hanged. The raiment of Marco and his wife was of coarse tow linen and linsey-woolsey respectively, and resembled township maps, it being made up pretty exclusively of patches which had been added, township by township, in the course of five or six years, until hardly a handbreadth of the original garments was surviving and present. Now I wanted to fit these people out with new suits, on account of that swell company, and I didn't know just how to get at it with delicacy, until at last it struck me that as I had already been liberal in inventing wordy gratitude for the king, it would be just the thing to back it up with evidence of a substantial sort; so I said:

"And Marco, there's another thing which you must permit—out of kindness for Jones—because you wouldn't want to offend him. He was very anxious to testify his appreciation in some way, but he is so diffident he couldn't venture it himself, and so he begged me to buy some little things and give them to you and Dame Phyllis and let him pay for them without your ever knowing they came from him—you know how a delicate person feels about that sort of thing—and so I said I would, and we would keep mum. Well, his idea was, a new outfit of clothes for you both—"

"Oh, it is wastefulness! It may not be, brother, it may not be. Consider the vastness of the sum—"

"Hang the vastness of the sum! Try to keep quiet for a moment, and see how it would seem; a body can't get in a word edgeways, you talk so much. You ought to cure that, Marco; it isn't good form, you know, and it will grow on you if you don't check it. Yes, we'll step in here, now, and price this man's stuff—and don't forget to remember to not let on to Jones that you know he had anything to do with it. You can't think how curiously sensitive and proud he is. He's a farmer—pretty fairly well-to-do farmer—and I'm his bailiff; *but*—the imagination of that man! Why, sometimes when he forgets himself and gets to blowing off, you'd think he was one of the swells of the earth; and you might listen to him a hundred years and never take him for a farmer—especially if he talked agriculture. He *thinks* he's a Sheol of a farmer; thinks he's old Grayback from Wayback; but between you and me privately he don't know as much about farming as he does about running a kingdom—still, whatever he talks about, you want to drop your underjaw and listen, the same as if you had never heard such incredible wisdom in all your life before, and were afraid you might die before you got enough of it. That will please Jones."

It tickled Marco to the marrow to hear about such an odd character; but it also prepared him for accidents; and in my experience when you travel with a king who is letting on to be something else and can't remember it more than about half the time, you can't take too many precautions.

This was the best store we had come across yet; it had everything in it, in small quantities, from anvils and dry goods all the way down to fish and pinchbeck jewelry. I concluded I would bunch my whole invoice right here, and not go pricing around any more. So I got rid of Marco, by sending him off to invite the mason and the wheelwright, which left the field free to me. For I never care to do a thing in a quiet way; it's got to be theatrical or I don't take any interest in it. I showed up money enough, in a careless way, to corral the shopkeeper's respect, and then I wrote down a list of the things I wanted, and handed it to him to see if he could read it. He could, and was proud to show that he could. He said he had been educated by a priest, and could read and write both. He ran it through, and remarked with satisfaction that it was a pretty heavy bill. Well, and so it was, for a little concern like that. I was not only providing a swell dinner, but some odds and ends of extras. I ordered that the things be carted out and delivered at the dwelling of Marco the son of Marco by Saturday evening, and send me the bill at dinner time Sunday. He said I could depend upon his promptness and exactitude, it was the rule of the house. He also observed that he would throw in a couple of miller-guns for the Marcos, gratis—that everybody was using them now. He had a mighty opinion of that clever device. I said:

"And please fill them up to the middle mark, too; and add that to the bill."

He would, with pleasure. He filled them, and I took them with me. I couldn't venture to tell him that the miller-gun was a little invention of my own, and that I had officially ordered that every shopkeeper in the kingdom keep them on hand and sell them at government price—which was the merest trifle, and the shopkeeper got that, not the government. We furnished them for nothing.

The king had hardly missed us when we got back at nightfall. He had early dropped again into his dream of a grand invasion of Gaul with the whole strength of his kingdom at his back, and the afternoon had slipped away without his ever coming to himself again.

CHAPTER XXXII

Dowley's Humiliation

WELL, WHEN that cargo arrived, toward sunset, Saturday afternoon, I had my hands full to keep the Marcos from fainting. They were sure Jones and I were ruined past help, and they blamed themselves as accessories to this bankruptcy. You see, in addition to the dinner materials, which called for a sufficiently round sum, I had bought a lot of extras for the future comfort of the family: for instance, a big lot of wheat, a delicacy as rare to the tables of their class as was ice cream to a hermit's; also a sizable deal dinner table; also two entire pounds of salt, which was another piece of extravagance in those people's eyes; also crockery, stools, the clothes, a small cask of beer, and so on. I instructed the Marcos to keep quiet about this sumptuousness, so as to give me a chance to surprise the guests and show off a little. Concerning the new clothes, the simple couple were like children; they were up and down, all night, to see if it wasn't nearly daylight, so that they could put them on, and they were into them at last as much as an hour before dawn was due. Then their pleasure—not to say delirium—was so fresh and novel and inspiring that the sight of it paid me well for the interruptions which my sleep had suffered. The king had slept just as usual —like the dead. The Marcos could not thank him for their clothes, that being forbidden; but they tried every way they could think of to make him see how grateful they were. Which all went for nothing: he didn't notice any change.

It turned out to be one of those rich and rare fall days which is just a June day toned down to a degree where it is heaven to be out of doors. Toward noon the guests arrived and we assembled under a great tree and were soon as sociable as old acquaintances. Even the king's reserve melted a little, though it was some little trouble to him to adjust himself to the name of Jones along at first. I had asked him to try to not forget that he was a farmer; but I had also considered it prudent to ask him to let the thing stand at that, and not elaborate it any. Because he was just the kind of person you could depend on to spoil a little thing like that if you didn't warn him, his tongue was so handy, and his spirit so willing, and his information so uncertain.

Dowley was in fine feather, and I early got him started, and then adroitly worked him around onto his own history for a text and himself for a hero, and then it was good to sit there and hear him hum. Self-made man, you know. They know how to talk. They do deserve more credit than any other breed of men, yes, that is true; and they are among the very first to find it out, too. He told how he had begun life an orphan lad without money and without friends able to help him; how he had lived as the slaves of the meanest master lived; how his day's work was from sixteen to eighteen hours long, and yielded him only enough black bread to keep him in a half-fed condition; how his faithful endeavors finally attracted the attention of a good blacksmith, who came near knocking him dead with kindness by suddenly offering, when he was totally unprepared, to take him as his bound apprentice for nine years and give him board and clothes and teach him the trade—or "mystery" as Dowley called it. That was his first great rise, his first gorgeous stroke of fortune; and you saw that he couldn't yet speak of it without a sort of eloquent wonder and delight that such a gilded promotion should have fallen to the lot of a common human being. He got no new clothing during his apprenticeship, but on his graduation day his master tricked him out in spang-new tow linens and made him feel unspeakably rich and fine.

"I remember me of that day!" the wheelwright sang out, with enthusiasm.

"And I likewise!" cried the mason. "I would not believe they were thine own; in faith I could not."

"Nor others!" shouted Dowley, with sparkling eyes. "I was like to lose my character, the neighbors wending I had mayhap been stealing. It was a great day, a great day; one forgetteth not days like that."

Yes, and his master was a fine man, and prosperous, and always had a great feast of meat twice in the year, and with it white bread, true wheaten bread; in fact, lived like a lord, so to speak. And in time Dowley succeeded to the business and married the daughter.

"And now consider what is come to pass," said he, impressively. "Two times in every month there is fresh meat upon my table." He made a pause here, to let that fact sink home, then added—"and eight times, salt meat."

"It is even true," said the wheelwright, with bated breath.

"I know it of mine own knowledge," said the mason, in the same reverent fashion.

"On my table appeareth white bread every Sunday in the year," added the master smith, with solemnity. "I leave it to your own consciences, friends, if this is not also true?"

"By my head, yes!" cried the mason.

"I can testify it—and I do," said the wheelwright.

"And as to furniture, ye shall say yourselves what mine equipment is." He waved his hand in fine gesture of granting frank and unhampered freedom of speech, and added: "Speak as ye are moved; speak as ye would speak an I were not here."

"Ye have five stools, and of the sweetest workmanship at that, albeit your family is but three," said the wheelwright, with deep respect.

"And six wooden goblets, and six platters of wood and two of pewter to eat and drink from withal," said the mason, impressively. "And I say it as knowing God is my judge, and we tarry not here alway, but must answer at the last day for the things said in the body, be they false or be they sooth."

"Now ye know what manner of man I am, brother Jones," said the smith, with a fine and friendly condescension, "and doubtless ye would look to find me a man jealous of his due of respect and but sparing of outgo to strangers till their rating and quality be assured, but trouble yourself not, as concerning that; wit ye well ye shall find me a man that regardeth not these matters but is willing to receive any he as his fellow and equal that carrieth a right heart in his body, be his worldly estate howsoever modest. And in token of it, here is my hand; and I say with my own mouth we are equals—equals"—and he smiled around on the company with the satisfaction of a god who is doing the handsome and gracious thing and is quite well aware of it.

The king took the hand with a poorly disguised reluctance, and let go of it as willingly as a lady lets go of a fish; all of which had a good effect, for it was mistaken for an embarrassment natural to one who was being beamed upon by greatness.

The dame brought out the table, now, and set it under the tree. It caused a visible stir of surprise, it being brand new and a sumptuous article of deal. But the surprise rose higher still, when the dame, with a body oozing easy indifference at every pore, but eyes that gave it all away by absolutely flaming with vanity, slowly unfolded an actual simon-pure tablecloth and spread it. That was a notch above even the blacksmith's domestic grandeurs, and it hit him hard; you could see it. But Marco was in Paradise; you could see that, too. Then the dame brought two fine new stools—whew! That was a sensation; it was visible in the eyes of every guest. Then she brought two more—as calmly as she could. Sensation again—with awed murmurs. Again she brought two—walking on air, she was so proud. The guests were petrified, and the mason muttered:

"There is that about earthly pomps which doth ever move to reverence."

As the dame turned away, Marco couldn't help slapping on the climax while the thing was hot; so he said with what was meant for a languid composure but was a poor imitation of it:

"These suffice; leave the rest."

So there were more yet! It was a fine effect. I couldn't have played the hand better myself.

From this out, the madame piled up the surprises with a rush that fired the general astonishment up to a hundred and fifty in the shade, and at the same time paralyzed expression of it down to gasped "Oh's" and "Ah's" and mute upliftings of hands and eyes. She fetched crockery—new, and plenty of it; new wooden goblets and other table furniture; and beer, fish, chicken, a goose, eggs, roast beef, roast mutton, a ham, a small roast pig, and a wealth of genuine white wheaten bread. Take it by and large, that spread laid everything far and away in the shade that ever that crowd had seen before. And while they sat there just simply stupefied with wonder and awe, I sort of waved my hand as if by accident, and the store-keeper's son emerged from space and said he had come to collect.

"That's all right," I said, indifferently. "What is the amount? Give us the items."

Then he read off this bill, while those three amazed men listened, and serene waves of satisfaction rolled over my soul and alternate waves of terror and admiration surged over Marco's:

2 pounds salt	200
8 dozen pints beer, in the wood	800
3 bushels wheat	2,700
2 pounds fish	100
3 hens	400
1 goose	400
3 dozen eggs	150
1 roast of beef	450

1 " " mutton	400
1 ham	800
1 sucking pig	500
2 crockery dinner sets	6,000
2 men's suits and underwear	2,800
1 stuff and 1 linsey-woolsey gown and underwear	1,600
8 wooden goblets	800
Various table furniture	10,000
1 deal table	3,000
8 stools	4,000
2 miller-guns, loaded	3,000

He ceased. There was a pale and awful silence. Not a limb stirred. Not a nostril betrayed the passage of breath.

"Is that all?" I asked, in a voice of the most perfect calmness.

"All, fair sir, save that certain matters of light moment are placed together under a head hight sundries. If it would like you, I will sepa—"

"It is of no consequence," I said, accompanying the words with a gesture of the most utter indifference; "give me the grand total, please."

The clerk leaned against the tree to stay himself, and said:

"Thirty-nine thousand one hundred and fifty milrays!"

The wheelwright fell off his stool, the others grabbed the table to save themselves, and there was a deep and general ejaculation of—

"God be with us in the day of disaster!"

The clerk hastened to say:

"My father chargeth me to say he cannot honorably require you to pay it all at this time, and therefore only prayeth you—"

I paid no more heed than if it were the idle breeze, but with an air of indifference amounting almost to weariness, got out my money and tossed four dollars onto the table. Ah, you should have seen them stare!

The clerk was astonished and charmed. He asked me to retain one of the dollars as security, until he could go to town and—I interrupted:

"What, and fetch back nine cents? Nonsense. Take the whole. Keep the change."

There was an amazed murmur to this effect:

"Verily this being is *made* of money! He throweth it away even as it were dirt."

The blacksmith was a crushed man.

The clerk took his money and reeled away drunk with fortune. I said to Marco and his wife:

"Good folk, here is a little trifle for you"—handing the miller-guns as if it were a matter of no consequence though each of them contained fifteen cents in solid cash; and while the poor creatures went to pieces with astonishment and gratitude, I turned to the others and said as calmly as one would ask the time of day:

"Well, if we are all ready, I judge the dinner is. Come, fall to."

Ah, well, it was immense; yes, it was a daisy. I don't know that I ever put a situation together better, or got happier spectacular effects out of the materials available. The blacksmith—well, he was simply mashed. Land! I wouldn't have felt what that man was feeling, for anything in the world. Here he had been blowing and bragging about his grand meat-feast twice a year, and his fresh meat twice a month, and his salt meat twice a week, and his white bread every Sunday the year round—all for a family of three: the entire cost for the year not above 69.2.6 (sixty-nine cents, two mills, and six milrays), and all of a sudden here comes along a man who slashes out nearly four dollars on a single blowout; and not only that, but acts as if it made him tired to handle such small sums. Yes, Dowley was a good deal wilted, and shrunk up and collapsed; he had the aspect of a bladder balloon that's been stepped on by a cow.

[CHAPTER XXXIII]

Sixth-Century Political Economy

HOWEVER, I made a dead set at him, and before the first third of the dinner was reached, I had him happy again. It was easy to do—in a country of ranks and castes.

You see, in a country where they have ranks and castes, a man isn't ever a man, he is only part of a man, he can't ever get his full growth. You prove your superiority over him in station, or rank, or fortune and that's the end of it—he knuckles down. You can't insult him after that. No, I don't mean quite that; of course you *can* insult him, I only mean it's difficult; and so, unless you've got a lot of useless time on your hands it doesn't pay to try. I had the smith's reverence, now, because I was apparently immensely prosperous and rich; I could have had his adoration if I had had some little gimcrack title of nobility. And not only his, but any commoner's in the land, though he were the mightiest production of all the ages, in intellect, worth, and character, and I bankrupt in all three. This was to remain so, as long as England should exist in the earth. With the spirit of prophecy upon me, I could look into the future and see her erect statues and monuments to her unspeakable Georges and other royal and noble clotheshorses, and leave unhonored the creators of this world—after God—Gutenberg, Watt, Arkwright, Whitney, Morse, Stephenson, Bell.

The king got his cargo aboard, and then, the talk not turning upon battle, conquest, or ironclad duel, he dulled down to drowsiness and went off to take a nap. Mrs. Marco cleared the table, placed the beer keg handy, and went away to eat her dinner of leavings in humble privacy, and the rest of us soon drifted into matters near and dear to the hearts of our sort—business and wages, of course. At a first glance, things appeared to be exceeding prosperous in this little tributary kingdom—whose lord was King Bagdemagus—as compared with the state of things in my own region. They had the "protection" system in full force here, whereas we were working along down towards free trade, by easy stages, and were now about half way. Before long, Dowley and I were doing all the talking, the others hungrily listening. Dowley warmed to his work, snuffed an advantage in the air, and began to put questions which he considered pretty awkward ones for me, and they did have something of that look:

"In your country, brother, what is the wage of a master bailiff, master hind, carter, shepherd, swineherd?"

"Twenty-five milrays a day; that is to say, a quarter of a cent."

The smith's face beamed with joy. He said:

"With us they are allowed the double of it! And what may a mechanic get—carpenter, dauber, mason, painter, blacksmith, wheelwright, and the like?"

"On the average, fifty milrays; half a cent a day."

"Ho-ho! With us they are allowed a hundred! With us any good mechanic is allowed a cent a day! I count out the tailor, but not the others—they are all allowed a cent a day, and in driving times they get more—yes, up to a hundred and ten and even fifteen milrays a day. I've paid a hundred and fifteen myself, within the week. 'Rah for protection—to Sheol with free trade!"

And his face shone upon the company like a sunburst. But I didn't scare at all. I rigged up my pile driver, and allowed myself fifteen minutes to drive him into the earth—drive him *all* in—drive him in till not even the curve of his skull should show above ground. Here is the way I started in on him. I asked:

"What do you pay a pound for salt?"

"A hundred milrays."

"We pay forty. What do you pay for beef and mutton—when you buy it?" That was a neat hit; it made the color come.

"It varieth somewhat, but not much; one may say seventy-five milrays the pound."

"*We* pay thirty-three. What do you pay for eggs?"

"Fifty milrays the dozen."

"We pay twenty. What do you pay for beer?"

"It costeth us eight and one half milrays the pint."

"We get it for four; twenty-five bottles for a cent. What do you pay for wheat?"

"At the rate of nine hundred milrays the bushel."

"We pay four hundred. What do you pay for a man's tow-linen suit?"

"Thirteen cents."

"We pay six. What do you pay for a stuff gown for the wife of the laborer or the mechanic?"

"We pay eight cents and four mills."

"Well, observe the difference: you pay eight cents and four mills, we pay only four cents." I prepared, now, to sock it to him. I said: "Look here, dear friend, *what's become of your high wages you were bragging so about, a few minutes ago?*" And I looked around on the company with placid satisfaction, for I had slipped up on him gradually and tied him hand and foot, you see, without his ever noticing that he was being tied at all. "What's become of those noble high wages of yours? I seem to have knocked the stuffing all out of them, it appears to me."

But if you will believe me, he merely looked surprised, that is all! He didn't grasp the situation at all, didn't know he had walked into a trap, didn't discover that he was *in* a trap. I could have shot him, from sheer vexation. With cloudy eye and a struggling intellect, he fetched this out:

"Marry, I seem not to understand. It is *proved* that our wages be double thine; how then may it be that thou'st knocked therefrom the stuffing—an I miscall not the wonderly word, this being the first time under grace and providence of God it hath been granted me to hear it."

Well, I was stunned; partly with this unlooked-for stupidity on his part, and partly because his fellows so manifestly sided with him and were of his mind—if you might call it mind. My position was simple enough, plain enough; how could it ever be simplified more? However, I must try:

"Why, look here, brother Dowley, don't you see? Your wages are merely higher than ours in *name*, not in *fact*."

"Hear him! They are the *double*—ye have confessed it yourself."

"Yes-yes, I don't deny that at all. But that's got nothing to do with it; the *amount* of the wages in mere coins, with meaningless names attached to them to know them by, has got nothing to do with it. The thing is, how much can you *buy* with your wages? That's the idea. While it is true that with you a good mechanic is allowed about three dollars and a half a year, and with us only about a dollar and seventy-five—"

"There—ye're confessing it again, ye're confessing it again!"

"Confound it, I've never denied it I tell you! What I say is this. With us *half* a dollar buys more than a *dollar* buys with you—and *therefore* it stands to reason and the commonest kind of common sense, that our wages are *higher* than yours."

He looked dazed, and said, despairingly:

"Verily, I cannot make it out. Ye've just *said* ours are the higher, and with the same breath ye take it back."

"Oh, great Scott, isn't it possible to get such a simple thing through your head? Now look here—let me illustrate. We pay four cents for a woman's stuff gown, you pay eight cents and four mills which is four mills more than *double*. What do you allow a laboring woman who works on a farm?"

"Two mills a day."

"Very good; we allow but half as much; we pay her only a tenth of a cent a day; and—"

"Again ye're conf—"

"Wait! Now, you see, the thing is very simple; this time you'll understand it. For instance, it takes your woman forty-two days to earn her gown, at two mills a day—seven weeks' work; but ours earns hers in forty days—two days *short* of seven weeks. Your woman has a gown, and her whole seven weeks' wages are gone; ours has a gown, and two days' wages left, to buy something else with. There—*now* you understand it!"

He looked—well, he merely looked dubious, it's the most I can say; so did the others. I waited—to let the the thing work. Dowley spoke at last—and betrayed the fact that he actually hadn't gotten away from his rooted and grounded superstitions yet. He said, with a trifle of hesitancy:

"But—but—ye cannot fail to grant that two mills a day is better than one."

Shucks! Well, of course I hated to give it up. So I chanced another flyer:

"Let us suppose a case. Suppose one of your journeymen goes out and buys the following articles:

"1   pound of salt;
1   dozen eggs;
1   dozen pints of beer;
1   bushel of wheat;

1 tow-linen suit;
5 pounds of beef;
5 pounds of mutton.

"The lot will cost him thirty-two cents. It takes him thirty-two working days to earn the money—five weeks and two days. Let him come to us and work thirty-two days at *half* the wages; he can buy all those things for a shade under fourteen and one half cents; they will cost him a shade under twenty-nine days' work, and he will have about half a week's wages over. Carry it through the year; he would save nearly a week's wages every two months, *your* man nothing; thus saving five or six weeks' wages in a year, your man not a cent. *Now* I reckon you understand that 'high wages' and 'low wages' are phrases that don't mean anything in the world until you find out which of them will *buy* the most!"

It was a crusher.

But alas, it didn't crush. No, I had to give it up. What those people valued was *high wages;* it didn't seem to be a matter of any consequence to them whether the high wages would buy anything or not. They stood for "protection," and swore by it, which was reasonable enough, because interested parties had gulled them into the notion that it was protection which had created their high wages. I proved to them that in a quarter of a century their wages had advanced but thirty per cent, while the cost of living had gone up one hundred; and that with us, in a shorter time, wages had advanced forty per cent, while the cost of living had gone steadily down. But it didn't do any good. Nothing could unseat their strange beliefs.

Well, I was smarting under a sense of defeat. Undeserved defeat, but what of that? That didn't soften the smart any. And to think of the circumstances! The first statesman of the age, the capablest man, the best-informed man in the entire world, the loftiest uncrowned head that had moved through the clouds of any political firmament for centuries, sitting here apparently defeated in argument by an ignorant country blacksmith! And I could see that those others were sorry for me—which made me blush till I could smell my whiskers scorching.

Put yourself in my place; feel as mean as I did, as ashamed as I felt—wouldn't *you* have struck below the belt to get even? Yes, you would; it is simply human nature. Well, that is what I did. I am not trying to justify it; I'm only saying that I was mad, and *anybody* would have done it.

Well, when I make up my mind to hit a man, I don't plan out a love tap; no, that isn't my way; as long as I'm going to hit him at all, I'm going to hit him a lifter. And I don't jump at him all of a sudden, and risk making a blundering halfway business of it; no, I get away off yonder to one side, and work up on him gradually, so that he never suspects that I'm going to hit him at all; and by and by, all in a flash, he's flat of his back, and he can't tell for the life of him how it all happened. That is the way I went for brother Dowley. I started to talking lazy and comfortable, as if I was just talking to pass the time; and the oldest man in the world couldn't have taken the bearings of my starting place and guessed where I was going to fetch up:

"Boys, there's a good many curious things about law, and custom, and usage, and all that sort of thing, when you come to look at it; yes, and about the drift and progress of human opinion and movement, too. There are written laws—they perish; but there are also unwritten laws—*they* are eternal. Take the unwritten law of wages: it says they've got to advance, little by little, straight through the centuries. And notice how it works. We know what wages are now, here and there and yonder; we strike an average, and say that's the wages of today. We know what the wages were a hundred years ago, and what they were two hundred years ago; that's as far back as we can get, but it suffices to give us the law of progress, the measure and rate of the periodical augmentation; and so, without a document to help us, we can come pretty close to determining what the wages were three and four and five hundred years ago. Good, so far. Do we stop there? No. We stop looking backward; we face around and apply the law to the future. My friends, I can tell you what people's wages are going to be at any date in the future you want to know, for hundreds and hundreds of years."

"What, goodman, what!"

"Yes. In seven hundred years wages will have risen to six times what they are now, here in your region, and farm hands will be allowed three cents a day, and mechanics six."

"I would I might die now and live then!" interrupted Smug the mason, with a fine avaricious glow in his eye.

"And that isn't all; they'll get their board besides— such as it is: it won't bloat them. Two hundred and fifty years later—pay attention, now—a mechanic's wages will be—mind you, this is law, not guesswork; a mechanic's wages will then be *twenty* cents a day!"

There was a general gasp of awed astonishment. Dickon the wheelwright murmured, with raised eyes and hands:

"More than three weeks' pay for one day's work!"

"Riches—of a truth, yes, riches!" muttered Marco, his breath coming quick and short, with excitement.

"Wages will keep on rising, little by little, little by little, as steadily as a tree grows, and at the end of three hundred and forty years more there'll be at least *one* country where the mechanic's average wage will be *two hundred* cents a day!"

It knocked them absolutely dumb! Not a man of them could get his breath for upwards of two minutes. Then the coal burner said prayerfully:

"Might I but live to see it!"

"It is the income of an earl!" said Smug.

"An earl, say ye?" said Dowley; "ye could say more than that and speak no lie; there's no earl in the realm of Bagdemagus that hath an income like to that. Income of an earl—mf! It's the income of an angel!"

"Now then, that is what is going to happen as regards wages. In that remote day, that man will earn, with *one* week's work, that bill of goods which it takes you upwards of *five* weeks to earn now. Some other pretty surprising things are going to happen, too. Brother Dowley, who is it that determines, every spring, what the particular wage of each kind of mechanic, laborer, and servant shall be for that year?"

"Sometimes the courts, sometimes the town council; but most of all, the magistrate. Ye may say, in general terms, it is the magistrate that fixes the wages."

"Doesn't ask any of those poor devils to *help* him fix their wages for them, does he?"

"Hm! That *were* an idea! The master that's to pay him the money is the one that's rightly concerned in that matter, ye will notice."

"Yes—but I thought the other man might have some little trifle at stake in it, too; and even his wife and children, poor creatures. The masters are these: nobles, rich men, the prosperous generally. These few, who do no work, determine what pay the vast hive shall have who *do* work. You see? They're a 'combine'—a trade union, to coin a new phrase—who band themselves together to force their lowly brother to take what they choose to give. Thirteen hundred years hence—so says the unwritten law—the 'combine' will be the other way, and then how these fine people's posterity will fume and fret and grit their teeth over the insolent tyranny of trade unions! Yes indeed! the magistrate will tranquilly arrange the wages from now clear away down into the nineteenth century; and then all of a sudden the wage earner will consider that a couple of thousand years or so is enough of this one-sided sort of thing; and he will rise up and take a hand in fixing his wages himself. Ah, he will have a long and bitter account of wrong and humiliation to settle."

"Do ye believe—"

"That he actually will help to fix his own wages? Yes, indeed. And he will be strong and able, then."

"Brave times, brave times, of a truth!" sneered the prosperous smith.

"Oh—and there's another detail. In that day, a master may hire a man for only just one day, or one week, or one month at a time, if he wants to."

"What?"

"It's true. Moreover, a magistrate won't be able to force a man to work for a master a whole year on a stretch whether the man wants to or not."

"Will there be *no* law or sense in that day?"

"Both of them, Dowley. In that day a man will be his own property, not the property of magistrate and master. And he can leave town whenever he wants to, if the wages don't suit him—and they can't put him in the pillory for it!"

"Perdition catch such an age!" shouted Dowley, in strong indignation. "An age of dogs, an age barren of reverence for superiors and respect for authority! The pillory—"

"Oh, wait, brother; say no good word for that institution. *I* think the pillory ought to be abolished."

"A most strange idea. Why?"

"Well, I'll tell you why. Is a man ever put in the pillory for a capital crime?"

"No."

"Is it right to condemn a man to a slight punishment for a small offense and then kill him?"

There was no answer. I had scored my first point! For the first time, the smith wasn't up and ready. The company noticed it. Good effect.

"You don't answer, brother. You were about to glorify the pillory a while ago, and shed some pity on a future age that isn't going to use it. *I* think the pillory ought to be abolished. What usually happens when a poor fellow is put in the pillory for some little offense that didn't amount to anything in the world? The mob try to have some fun with him, don't they?"

"Yes."

"They begin by clodding him; and they laugh themselves to pieces to see him try to dodge one clod and get hit with another?"

"Yes."

"Then they throw dead cats at him, don't they?"

"Yes."

"Well, then, suppose he has a few personal enemies in that mob—and here and there a man or a woman with a secret grudge against him—and suppose especially, that he is unpopular in the community, for his pride, or his prosperity, or one thing or another—stones and bricks take the place of clods and cats presently, don't they?"

"There is no doubt of it."

"As a rule he is crippled for life, isn't he—jaws broken, teeth smashed out—or legs mutilated, gangrened, presently cut off—or an eye knocked out, maybe both eyes?"

"It is true, God knoweth it."

"And if he is unpopular he can depend on *dying,* right there in the stocks, can't he?"

"He surely can! One may not deny it."

"I take it none of *you* are unpopular—by reason of pride or insolence, or conspicuous prosperity, or any of those things that excite envy and malice among the base scum of a village? *You* wouldn't think it much of a risk to take a chance in the stocks?"

Dowley winced, visibly. I judged he was hit. But he didn't betray it by any spoken word. As for the others, they spoke out plainly, and with strong feeling. They said they had seen enough of the stocks to know what a man's chance in them was, and they would never consent to enter them if they could compromise on a quick death by hanging.

"Well, to change the subject—for I think I've established my point that the stocks ought to be abolished. I think some of our laws are pretty unfair. For instance, if I do a thing which ought to deliver me to the stocks, and you know I did it and yet keep still and don't report me, *you* will get the stocks if anybody informs on you."

"Ah, but that would serve you but right," said Dowley, "for you *must* inform. So saith the law."

The others coincided.

"Well, all right, let it go, since you vote me down. But there's one thing which certainly isn't fair. The magistrate fixes a mechanic's wage at one cent a day, for instance. The law says that if any master shall venture even under utmost press of business, to pay anything *over* that cent a day, even for a single day, he shall be both fined and pilloried for it; and whoever knows he did it and doesn't inform, they also shall be fined and pilloried. Now it seems to me unfair, Dowley, and a deadly peril to all of us, that because you thoughtlessly confessed, a while ago, that within a week you have paid a cent and fifteen mil—"

Oh, I tell *you* it was a smasher! You ought to have seen them go to pieces, the whole gang. I had just slipped up on poor smiling and complacent Dowley so nice and easy and softly, that he never suspected anything was going to happen till the blow came crashing down and knocked him all to rags.

A fine effect. In fact as fine as any I ever produced, with so little time to work it up in.

But I saw in a moment that I had overdone the thing a little. I was expecting to scare them, but I wasn't expecting to scare them to death. They were mighty near it, though. You see they had been a whole lifetime learning to appreciate the pillory; and to have that thing staring them in the face, and every one of them distinctly at the mercy of me, a stranger, if I chose to go and report— well, it was awful, and they couldn't seem to recover from the shock, they couldn't seem to pull themselves together. Pale, shaky, dumb, pitiful? Why, they weren't any better than so many dead men. It was very uncomfortable. Of course I thought they would appeal to me to keep mum, and then we would shake hands, and take a drink all round, and laugh it off, and there an end. But no; you see I was an unknown person, among a cruelly oppressed and suspicious people, a people always accustomed to having advantage taken of their helplessness, and never expecting just or kind treatment from any but their own families and very closest intimates. Appeal to *me* to be gentle, to be fair, to be generous? Of course they wanted to, but they couldn't dare.

CHAPTER XXXIV

The Yankee and the King Sold as Slaves

WELL, WHAT had I better do? Nothing in a hurry, sure. I must get up a diversion; anything to employ me while I could think, and while these poor fellows could have a chance to come to life again. There sat Marco, petrified in the act of trying to get the hang of his miller-gun— turned to stone, just in the attitude he was in when my pile driver fell, the toy still gripped in his unconscious fingers. So I took it from him and proposed to explain its mystery. Mystery! a simple little thing like that; and yet it was mystery enough, for that race and that age.

I never saw such an awkward people, with machinery;
you see, they were totally unused to it. The miller-gun was
a little double-barreled tube of toughened glass, with a
neat little trick of a spring to it, which upon pressure
would let a shot escape. But the shot wouldn't hurt anybody, it would only drop into your hand. In the gun were
two sizes—wee mustard-seed shot, and another sort that
were several times larger. They were money. The mustard-
seed shot represented milrays, the larger ones mills. So
the gun was a purse; and very handy, too; you could
pay out money in the dark with it, with accuracy; and
you could carry it in your mouth; or in your vest pocket,
if you had one. I made them of several sizes—one size
so large that it would carry the equivalent of a dollar.
Using shot for money was a good thing for the government; the metal cost nothing, and the money couldn't be
counterfeited, for I was the only person in the kingdom who knew how to manage a shot tower. "Paying the
shot" soon came to be a common phrase. Yes, and I knew
it would still be passing men's lips, away down in the
nineteenth century, yet none would suspect how and when
it originated.

The king joined us, about this time, mightily refreshed
by his nap, and feeling good. Anything could make me
nervous now, I was so uneasy—for our lives were in danger; and so it worried me to detect a complacent something in the king's eye which seemed to indicate that he
had been loading himself up for a performance of some
kind or other; confound it, why must he go and choose
such a time as this?

I was right. He began, straight off, in the most innocently artful, and transparent, and lubberly way, to
lead up to the subject of agriculture. The cold sweat broke
out all over me. I wanted to whisper in his ear, "Man,
we are in awful danger! Every moment is worth a principality till we get back these men's confidence; *don't*
waste any of this golden time." But of course I couldn't
do it. Whisper to him? It would look as if we were
conspiring. So I had to sit there and look calm and pleasant while the king stood over that dynamite mine and
mooned along about his damned onions and things. At
first the tumult of my own thoughts, summoned by the

danger signal and swarming to the rescue from every quarter of my skull, kept up such a hurrah and confusion and fifing and drumming that I couldn't take in a word; but presently when my mob of gathering plans began to crystallize and fall into position and form line of battle, a sort of order and quiet ensued and I caught the boom of the king's batteries, as if out of remote distance:

—"were not the best way, methinks, albeit it is not to be denied that authorities differ as concerning this point, some contending that the onion is but an unwholesome berry when stricken early from the tree"—

The audience showed signs of life, and sought each other's eyes in a surprised and troubled way.

—"whileas others do yet maintain, with much show of reason, that this is not of necessity the case, instancing that plums and other like cereals do be always dug in the unripe state"—

The audience exhibited distinct distress; yes, and also fear.

—"yet are they clearly wholesome, the more especially when one doth assuage the asperities of their nature by admixture of the tranquilizing juice of the wayward cabbage"—

The wild light of terror began to glow in these men's eyes, and one of them muttered, "These be errors, every one—God hath surely smitten the mind of this farmer." I was in miserable apprehension; I sat upon thorns.

—"and further instancing the known truth that in the case of animals, the young, which may be called the green fruit of the creature, is the better, all confessing that when a goat is ripe, his fur doth heat and sore engame his flesh, the which defect, taken in connection with his several rancid habits, and fulsome appetites, and godless attitudes of mind, and bilious quality of morals"—

They rose and went for him! With a fierce shout, "The one would betray us, the other is mad! Kill them! Kill them!" they flung themselves upon us. What joy flamed up in the king's eye! He might be lame in agriculture, but this kind of thing was just in his line. He had been fasting long, he was hungry for a fight. He hit the blacksmith a crack under the jaw that lifted him clear off his feet and stretched him flat of his back. "St. George for Britain!" And he downed the wheelwright. The mason was big, but I laid him out like nothing. The three gathered themselves up and came again; went down again; came again; and kept on repeating this, with native British pluck, until they were battered to jelly, reeling with exhaustion, and so blind that they couldn't tell us from each other; and yet they kept right on, hammering away with what might was left in them. Hammering each other—for we stepped aside and looked on while they rolled, and struggled, and gouged, and pounded, and bit, with the strict and wordless attention to business of so many bulldogs. We looked on without apprehension, for they were fast getting past ability to go for help against us, and the arena was far enough from the public road to be safe from intrusion.

Well, while they were gradually playing out, it suddenly occurred to me to wonder what had become of Marco. I looked around; he was nowhere to be seen. Oh, but this was ominous! I pulled the king's sleeve, and we glided away and rushed for the hut. No Marco there, no Phyllis there! They had gone to the road for help, sure. I told the king to give his heels wings, and I would explain later. We made good time across the open ground, and as we darted into the shelter of the wood I glanced back and saw a mob of excited peasants swarm into view, with Marco and his wife at their head. They were making a world of noise, but that couldn't hurt anybody; the wood was dense, and as soon as we were well into its depths we would take to a tree and let them whistle. Ah, but then came another sound—dogs! Yes, that was quite another matter. It magnified our contract—we must find running water.

We tore along at a good gait, and soon left the sounds far behind and modified to a murmur. We struck a stream and darted into it. We waded swiftly down it, in the dim forest light, for as much as three hundred yards, and then came across an oak with a great bough sticking out over the water. We climbed up on this bough, and began to work our way along it to the body of the tree; now we began to hear those sounds more plainly; so the mob had struck our trail. For a while the sounds approached pretty fast. And then for another while they didn't. No doubt the dogs had found the place where we had entered the stream, and were now waltzing up and down the shores trying to pick up the trail again.

When we were snugly lodged in the tree and curtained with foliage, the king was satisfied, but I was doubtful. I believed we could crawl along a branch and get into the next tree, and I judged it worth while to try. We tried it, and made a success of it, though the king slipped, at the junction, and came near failing to connect. We got comfortable lodgment and satisfactory concealment among the foliage, and then we had nothing to do but listen to the hunt.

Presently we heard it coming—and coming on the jump, too; yes, and down both sides of the stream. Louder—louder—next minute it swelled swiftly up into a roar of shoutings, barkings, tramplings, and swept by like a cyclone.

"I was afraid that the overhanging branch would suggest something to them," said I, "but I don't mind the disappointment. Come, my liege, it were well that we make good use of our time. We've flanked them. Dark is coming on, presently. If we can cross the stream and get a good start, and borrow a couple of horses from somebody's pasture to use for a few hours, we shall be safe enough."

We started down, and got nearly to the lowest limb, when we seemed to hear the hunt returning. We stopped to listen.

"Yes," said I, "they're baffled, they've given it up, they're on their way home. We will climb back to our roost again, and let them go by."

So we climbed back. The king listened a moment and said:

"They still search—I wit the sign. We did best to abide."

He was right. He knew more about hunting than I did. The noise approached steadily, but not with a rush. The king said:

"They reason that we were advantaged by no parlous start of them, and being on foot are as yet no mighty way from where we took the water."

"Yes, sire, that is about it, I am afraid, though I was hoping better things."

The noise drew nearer and nearer, and soon the van was drifting under us, on both sides of the water. A voice called a halt from the other bank, and said:

"An they were so minded, they could get to yon tree by this branch that overhangs, and yet not touch ground. Ye will do well to send a man up it."

"Marry, that will we do!"

I was obliged to admire my cuteness in foreseeing this very thing and swapping trees to beat it. But don't you know, there are some things that can beat smartness and foresight? Awkwardness and stupidity can. The best swordsman in the world doesn't need to fear the second best swordsman in the world; no, the person for him to be afraid of is some ignorant antagonist who has never had a sword in his hand before; he doesn't do the thing he ought to do, and so the expert isn't prepared for him; he does the thing he ought not to do: and often it catches the expert out and ends him on the spot. Well, how could I, with all my gifts, make any valuable preparation against a nearsighted, cross-eyed, puddingheaded clown who would aim himself at the wrong tree and hit the right one? And that is what he did. He went for the wrong tree, which was of course the right one by mistake, and up he started.

Matters were serious, now. We remained still and awaited developments. The peasant toiled his difficult way up. The king raised himself up and stood; he made a leg ready, and when the comer's head arrived in reach of it there was a dull thud, and down went the man floundering to the ground. There was a wild outbreak of anger, below, and the mob swarmed in from all around, and there we were treed, and prisoners. Another man started up; the bridging bough was detected, and a volunteer started up the tree that furnished the bridge. The king ordered me to play Horatius and keep the bridge. For a while the enemy came thick and fast; but no matter, the head man of each procession always got a buffet that dislodged him as soon as he came in reach. The king's spirits rose, his joy was limitless. He said that if nothing occurred to mar the prospect we should have a beautiful night, for on this line of tactics we could hold the tree against the whole countryside.

However, the mob soon came to that conclusion themselves; wherefore they called off the assault and began to debate other plans. They had no weapons, but there were plenty of stones, and stones might answer. We had no objections. A stone might possibly penetrate to us once in a while, but it wasn't very likely; we were well protected by boughs and foliage, and were not visible from any good aiming point. If they would but waste half an hour in stone throwing, the dark would come to our help. We were feeling very well satisfied. We could smile; almost laugh.

But we didn't; which was just as well, for we should have been interrupted. Before the stones had been raging through the leaves and bouncing from the boughs fifteen minutes, we began to notice a smell. A couple of sniffs of it was enough of an explanation: it was smoke! Our game was up at last. We recognized that. When smoke invites you, you have to come. They raised their pile of dry brush and damp weeds higher and higher, and when they saw the thick cloud begin to roll up and smother the tree, they broke out in a storm of joy-clamors. I got enough breath to say:

"Proceed, my liege; after you is manners."

The king gasped:

"Follow me down, and then back thyself against one side of the trunk, and leave me the other. Then will we fight. Let each pile his dead according to his own fashion and taste."

Then he descended barking and coughing, and I followed. I struck the ground an instant after him; we sprang to our appointed places, and began to give and take with all our might. The powwow and racket were prodigious; it was a tempest of riot and confusion and thick-falling blows. Suddenly some horsemen tore into the midst of the crowd, and a voice shouted:

"Hold—or ye are dead men!"

How good it sounded! The owner of the voice bore all the marks of a gentleman: picturesque and costly raiment, the aspect of command, a hard countenance with complexion and features marred by dissipation. The mob fell humbly back, like so many spaniels. The gentleman inspected us critically, then said sharply to the peasants:

"What are ye doing to these people?"

"They be madmen, worshipful sir, that have come wandering we know not whence, and—"

"Ye know not whence? Do ye pretend ye know them not?"

"Most honored sir, we speak but the truth. They are strangers and unknown to any in this region; and they be the most violent and bloodthirsty madmen that ever—"

"Peace! Ye know not what ye say. They are not mad. Who are ye? And whence are ye? Explain."

"We are but peaceful strangers, sir," I said, "and traveling upon our own concerns. We are from a far country, and unacquainted here. We have purposed no harm; and yet but for your brave interference and protection these people would have killed us. As you have divined, sir, we are not mad; neither are we violent or bloodthirsty."

The gentleman turned to his retinue and said calmly:

"Lash me these animals to their kennels!"

The mob vanished in an instant; and after them plunged the horsemen, laying about them with their whips and pitilessly riding down such as were witless enough to keep the road instead of taking to the bush. The shrieks and supplications presently died away in the distance, and soon the horsemen began to straggle back. Meantime the gentleman had been questioning us more closely, but had dug no particulars out of us. We were lavish of recognition of the service he was doing us, but we revealed nothing more than that we were friendless strangers from a far country. When the escort were all returned, the gentleman said to one of his servants:

"Bring the led horses and mount these people."

"Yes, my lord."

We were placed toward the rear, among the servants. We traveled pretty fast, and finally drew rein some time after dark at a roadside inn some ten or twelve miles from the scene of our troubles. My lord went immediately to his room, after ordering his supper, and we saw no more of him. At dawn in the morning we breakfasted and made ready to start.

My lord's chief attendant sauntered forward at that moment with indolent grace, and said:

"Ye have said ye should continue upon this road, which is our direction likewise; wherefore my lord, the earl Grip, hath given commandment that ye retain the horses and ride, and that certain of us ride with ye a twenty mile to a fair town that hight Cambenet, whenso ye shall be out of peril."

We could do nothing less than express our thanks and accept the offer. We jogged along, six in the party, at a moderate and comfortable gait, and in conversation learned that my lord Grip was a very great personage in his own region, which lay a day's journey beyond Cambenet. We loitered to such a degree that it was near the middle of the forenoon when we entered the market square of the town. We dismounted, and left our thanks once more for my lord, and then approached a crowd assembled in the center of the square, to see what might be the object of interest. It was the remnant of that old peregrinating band of slaves! So they had been dragging their chains about, all this weary time. That poor husband was gone, and also many others; and some few purchases had been added to the gang. The king was not interested, and wanted to move along, but I was absorbed, and full of pity. I could not take my eyes away from these worn and wasted wrecks of humanity. There they sat, grouped upon the ground, silent, uncomplaining, with bowed heads, a pathetic sight. And by hideous contrast, a redundant orator was making a speech to another gathering not thirty steps away, in fulsome laudation of "our glorious British liberties!"

I was boiling. I had forgotten I was a plebeian, I was remembering I was a man. Cost what it might, I would mount that rostrum and—

Click! the king and I were handcuffed together! Our companions, those servants, had done it; my lord Grip stood looking on. The king burst out in a fury, and said:

"What meaneth this ill-mannered jest?"

My lord merely said to his head miscreant, coolly:

"Put up the slaves and sell them!"

Slaves! The word had a new sound—and how unspeakably awful! The king lifted his manacles and brought them down with a deadly force; but my lord was out of the way when they arrived. A dozen of the rascal's servants sprang forward, and in a moment we were helpless, with our hands bound behind us. We so loudly and so earnestly proclaimed ourselves freemen, that we got the interested attention of that liberty-mouthing orator and his patriotic crowd, and they gathered about us and assumed a very determined attitude. The orator said:

"If indeed ye are freemen, ye have nought to fear—the God-given liberties of Britain are about ye for your shield and shelter! (Applause.) Ye shall soon see. Bring forth your proofs."

"What proofs?"

"Proof that ye are freemen."

Ah—I remembered! I came to myself; I said nothing. But the king stormed out:

"Thou'rt insane, man. It were better, and more in reason, that this thief and scoundrel here prove that we are *not* freemen."

You see, he knew his own laws just as other people so often know the laws: by words, not by effects. They take a *meaning*, and get to be very vivid, when you come to apply them to yourself.

All hands shook their heads and looked disappointed; some turned away, no longer interested. The orator said —and this time in the tones of business, not of sentiment:

"An ye do not know your country's laws, it were time ye learned them. Ye are strangers to us; ye will not deny that. Ye may be freemen, we do not deny that; but also ye may be slaves. The law is clear: it doth not require the claimant to prove ye are slaves, it requireth you to prove ye are *not*."

I said:

"Dear sir, give us only time to send to Astolat; or give us only time to send to the Valley of Holiness—"

"Peace, good man, these are extraordinary requests, and you may not hope to have them granted. It would cost much time, and would unwarrantably inconvenience your master—"

"*Master,* idiot!" stormed the king. "I have no master, I myself am the m——"

"Silence, for God's sake!"

I got the words out in time to stop the king. We were in trouble enough already; it could not help us any to give these people the notion that we were lunatics.

There is no use in stringing out the details. The earl put us up and sold us at auction. This same infernal law had existed in our own South in my own time, more than thirteen hundred years later, and under it hundreds of freemen who could not prove that they were freemen had been sold into lifelong slavery without the circumstance making any particular impression upon me; but the minute law and the auction block came into my personal experience, a thing which had been merely improper before became suddenly hellish. Well, that's the way we are made.

Yes, we were sold at auction, like swine. In a big town and an active market we should have brought a good price; but this place was utterly stagnant and so we sold at a figure which makes me ashamed, every time I think of it. The King of England brought seven dollars, and his prime minister nine; whereas the king was easily worth twelve dollars and I as easily worth fifteen. But that is the way things always go; if you force a sale on a dull market, I don't care what the property is, you are going to make a poor business of it, and you can make up your mind to it. If the earl had had wit enough to—

However, there is no occasion for my working my sympathies up on his account. Let him go, for the present: I took his number, so to speak.

The slave dealer bought us both, and hitched us onto that long chain of his, and we constituted the rear of his procession. We took up our line of march and passed out of Cambenet at noon; and it seemed to me unaccountably strange and odd that the King of England and his chief minister, marching manacled and fettered and yoked, in a slave convoy, could move by all manner of idle men and women, and under windows where sat the sweet and the lovely, and yet never attract a curious eye, never provoke a single remark. Dear, dear, it only shows that there is nothing diviner about a king than there is about a tramp, after all. He is just a cheap and hollow artificiality when you don't know he is a king. But reveal his quality, and dear me it takes your very breath away to look at him. I reckon we are all fools. Born so, no doubt.

CHAPTER XXXV

A Pitiful Incident

IT'S A WORLD of surprises. The king brooded; this was natural. What would he brood about, should you say? Why, about the prodigious nature of his fall, of course— from the loftiest place in the world to the lowest; from the most illustrious station in the world to the obscurest; from the grandest vocation among men to the basest. No, I take my oath that the thing that graveled him most, to start with, was not this, but the price he had fetched! He couldn't seem to get over that seven dollars. Well, it stunned me so, when I first found it out, that I couldn't believe it; it didn't seem natural. But as soon as my mental sight cleared and I got a right focus on it, I saw I was mistaken: it *was* natural. For this reason: a king is a mere artificiality, and so a king's feelings, like the impulses of an automatic doll, are mere artificialities; but as a man, he is a reality, and his feelings, as a man, are real, not phantoms. It shames the average man to be valued below his own estimate of his worth; and the king certainly wasn't anything more than an average man, if he was up that high.

Confound him, he wearied me with arguments to show that in anything like a fair market he would have fetched twenty-five dollars, sure—a thing which was plainly nonsense, and full of the baldest conceit; I wasn't worth it myself. But it was tender ground for me to argue on. In fact I had to simply shirk argument and do the diplomatic instead. I had to throw conscience aside, and brazenly concede that he ought to have brought twenty-five dollars; whereas I was quite well aware that in all the ages, the world had never seen a king that was worth half the money, and during the next thirteen centuries wouldn't see one that was worth the fourth of it. Yes, he tired me. If he began to talk about the crops, or about the recent weather, or about the condition of politics, or about dogs, or cats, or morals, or theology—no matter what—I sighed, for I knew what was coming: he was going to get out of it a palliation of that tiresome seven-dollar sale. Wherever we halted, where there was a crowd, he would give me a look which said, plainly: "if that thing could be tried over again, now, with this kind of folk, you would see a different result." Well, when he was first sold, it secretly tickled me to see him go for seven dollars; but before he was done with his sweating and worrying I wished he had fetched a hundred. The thing never got a chance to die, for every day, at one place or another, possible purchasers looked us over, and as often as any other way, their comment on the king was something like this:

"Here's a two-dollar-and-a-half chump with a thirty-dollar style. Pity but style was marketable."

At last this sort of remark produced an evil result. Our owner was a practical person and he perceived that this defect must be mended if he hoped to find a purchaser for the king. So he went to work to take the style out of his sacred majesty. I could have given the man some valuable advice, but I didn't; you mustn't volunteer advice to a slave driver unless you want to damage the cause you are arguing for. I had found it a sufficiently difficult job to reduce the king's style to a peasant's style, even when he was a willing and anxious pupil; now then, to undertake to reduce the king's style to a slave's style—and by force—go to! It was a stately contract. Never mind the details—it will save me trouble to let you imagine them. I will only remark that at the end of a week there was plenty of evidence that lash and club and fist had done their work well; the king's body was a sight to see—and to weep over; but his spirit—why, it wasn't even phased. Even that dull clod of a slave driver was able to see that there can be such a thing as a slave who will remain a man till he dies; whose bones you can break, but whose manhood you can't. This man found that from his first effort down to his latest, he couldn't ever come within reach of the king but the king was ready to plunge for him, and did it. So he gave up, at last, and left the king in possession of his style unimpaired. The fact is, the king was a good deal more than a king, he was a man; and when a man is a man, you can't knock it out of him.

We had a rough time for a month, tramping to and fro in the earth, and suffering. And what Englishman was the most interested in the slavery question by that time? His grace the king! Yes; from being the most indifferent, he was become the most interested. He was become the bitterest hater of the institution I had ever heard talk. And so I ventured to ask once more a question which I had asked years before and had gotten such a sharp answer that I had not thought it prudent to meddle in the matter further. Would he abolish slavery?

His answer was as sharp as before, but it was music this time; I shouldn't ever wish to hear pleasanter, though the profanity was not good, being awkwardly put together, and with the crash word almost in the middle instead of at the end, where of course it ought to have been.

I was ready and willing to get free, now; I hadn't wanted to get free any sooner. No, I cannot quite say that. I had wanted to, but I had not been willing to take desperate chances, and had always dissuaded the king from them. But now—ah, it was a new atmosphere! Liberty would be worth any cost that might be put upon it now. I set about a plan, and was straightway charmed with it. It would require time, yes, and patience, too, a great deal of both. One could invent quicker ways, and fully as sure ones; but none that would be as picturesque as this; none that could be made so dramatic. And so I was not going to give this one up. It might delay us months, but no matter, I would carry it out or break something.

Now and then we had an adventure. One night we were overtaken by a snowstorm while still a mile from the village we were making for. Almost instantly we were shut up as in a fog, the driving snow was so thick. You couldn't see a thing, and we were soon lost. The slave driver lashed us desperately, for he saw ruin before him, but his lashings only made matters worse, for they drove us further from the road and from likelihood of succor. So we had to stop, at last, and slump down in the snow where we were. The storm continued until toward midnight, then ceased. By this time two of our feebler men and three of our women were dead, and others past moving and threatened with death. Our master was nearly beside himself. He stirred up the living and made us stand, jump, slap ourselves, to restore our circulation, and he helped as well as he could with his whip.

Now came a diversion. We heard shrieks and yells, and soon a woman came running, and crying; and seeing our group, she flung herself into our midst and begged for protection. A mob of people came tearing after her, some with torches, and they said she was a witch who had caused several cows to die by a strange disease, and practiced her arts by help of a devil in the form of a black cat. This poor woman had been stoned until she hardly looked human, she was so battered and bloody. The mob wanted to burn her.

Well, now, what do you suppose our master did? When we closed around this poor creature to shelter her, he saw his chance. He said, burn her here, or they shouldn't have her at all. Imagine that! They were willing. They fastened her to a post; they brought wood and piled it about her; they applied the torch while she shrieked and pleaded and strained her two young daughters to her breast; and our brute, with a heart solely for business, lashed us into position about the stake and warmed us into life and commercial value by the same fire which took away the innocent life of that poor harmless mother. That was the sort of master we had. I took *his* number. That snowstorm cost him nine of his flock; and he was more brutal to us than ever, after that, for many days together, he was so enraged over his loss.

We had adventures, all along. One day we ran into a procession. And such a procession! All the riffraff of the kingdom seemed to be comprehended in it; and all drunk at that. In the van was a cart with a coffin in it, and on the coffin sat a comely young girl of about eighteen suckling a baby, which she squeezed to her breast in a passion of love every little while, and every little while wiped from its face the tears which her eyes rained down upon it; and always the foolish little thing smiled up at her, happy and content, kneading her breast with its dimpled fat hand, which she patted and fondled right over her breaking heart.

Men and women, boys and girls, trotted along beside or after the cart, hooting, shouting profane and ribald remarks, singing snatches of foul song, skipping, dancing —a very holiday of hellions, a sickening sight. We had struck a suburb of London, outside the walls, and this was a sample of one sort of London society. Our master secured a good place for us near the gallows. A priest was in attendance, and he helped the girl climb up, and said comforting words to her, and made the undersheriff provide a stool for her. Then he stood there by her on the gallows, and for a moment looked down upon the mass of upturned faces at his feet, then out over the solid pavement of heads that stretched away on every side occupying the vacancies far and near, and then began to tell the story of the case. And there was pity in his voice—how seldom a sound that was in that ignorant and savage land! I remember every detail of what he said, except the words he said it in; and so I change it into my own words:

"Law is intended to mete out justice. Sometimes it fails. This cannot be helped. We can only grieve, and be resigned, and pray for the soul of him who falls unfairly by the arm of the law, and that his fellows may be few. A law sends this poor young thing to death—and it is right. But another law had placed her where she must commit her crime or starve, with her child—and before God that law is responsible for both her crime and her ignominious death!

"A little while ago this young thing, this child of eighteen years, was as happy a wife and mother as any in England; and her lips were blithe with song, which is the native speech of glad and innocent hearts. Her young husband was as happy as she; for he was doing his whole duty, he worked early and late at his handicraft, his bread was honest bread well and fairly earned, he was prospering, he was furnishing shelter and sustenance to his family, he was adding his mite to the wealth of the nation. By consent of a treacherous law, instant destruction fell upon this holy home and swept it away! That young husband was waylaid and impressed, and sent to sea. The wife knew nothing of it. She sought him everywhere, she moved the hardest hearts with the supplications of her tears, the broken eloquence of her despair. Weeks dragged by, she watching, waiting, hoping, her mind going slowly to wreck under the burden of her misery. Little by little all her small possessions went for food. When she could no longer pay her rent, they turned her out of doors. She begged, while she had strength; when she was starving, at last, and her milk failing, she stole a piece of linen cloth of the value of a fourth part of a cent, thinking to sell it and save her child. But she was seen by the owner of the cloth. She was put in jail and brought to trial. The man testified to the facts. A plea was made for her, and her sorrowful story was told in her behalf. She spoke, too, by permission, and said she did steal the cloth, but that her mind was so disordered of late, by trouble, that when she was overborne with hunger all acts, criminal or other, swam meaningless through her brain and she knew nothing rightly, except that she was *so* hungry! For a moment all were touched, and there was disposition to deal mercifully with her, seeing that she was so young and friendless, and her case so piteous, and the law that robbed her of her support to blame as being the first and only cause of her transgression; but the prosecuting officer replied that whereas these things were all true, and most pitiful as well, still there was much small theft in these days, and mistimed mercy here would be a danger to property—oh, my God, is there no property in ruined homes, and orphaned babes, and broken hearts that British law holds precious—and so he must require sentence.

"When the judge put on his black cap, the owner of the stolen linen rose trembling up, his lip quivering, his face as gray as ashes; and when the awful words came, he cried out, 'Oh, poor child, poor child, I did not know it was death!' and fell as a tree falls. When they lifted him up his reason was gone; before the sun was set, he had taken his own life. A kindly man; a man whose heart was right, at bottom; add his murder to this that is to be now done here; and charge them both where they belong—to the rulers and the bitter laws of Britain. The time is come, my child; let me pray over thee—not *for* thee, dear abused poor heart and innocent, but for them that be guilty of thy ruin and death, who need it more."

After his prayer they put the noose around the young girl's neck, and they had great trouble to adjust the knot under her ear, because she was devouring the baby all the time, wildly kissing it, and snatching it to her face and her breast, and drenching it with tears, and half moaning, half shrieking all the while, and the baby crowing, and laughing, and kicking its feet with delight over what it took for romp and play. Even the hangman couldn't stand it, but turned away. When all was ready the priest gently pulled and tugged and forced the child out of the mother's arms, and stepped quickly out of her reach; but she clasped her hands, and made a wild spring toward him, with a shriek; but the rope—and the undersheriff—held her short. Then she went on her knees and stretched out her hands and cried:

"One more kiss—Oh, my God, one more, one more— it is the dying that begs it!"

She got it; she almost smothered the little thing. And when they got it away again, she cried out:

"Oh, my child, my darling, it will die! It has no home, it has no father, no friend, no mother—"

"It has them all!" said that good priest. "All these will I be to it till I die."

You should have seen her face then! Gratitude? Lord, what do you want with words to express that? Words are only painted fire; a look is the fire itself. She gave that look, and carried it away to the treasury of heaven, where all things that are divine belong.

【 CHAPTER XXXVI 】

An Encounter in the Dark

LONDON—to a slave—was a sufficiently interesting place. It was merely a great big village; and mainly mud and thatch. The streets were muddy, crooked, unpaved. The populace was an ever flocking and drifting swarm of rags and splendors, of nodding plumes and shining armor. The king had a palace there; he saw the outside of it. It made him sigh; yes, and swear a little, in a poor juvenile sixth-century way. We saw knights and grandees whom we knew, but they didn't know us in our rags and dirt and raw welts and bruises, and wouldn't have recognized us if we had hailed them, nor stopped to answer, either, it being unlawful to speak with slaves on a chain. Sandy passed within ten yards of me on a mule—hunting for me, I imagined. But the thing which clean broke my heart was something which happened in front of our old barrack in a square, while we were enduring the spectacle of a man being boiled to death in oil for counterfeiting pennies. It was the sight of a newsboy—and I couldn't get at him! Still, I had one comfort; here was proof that Clarence was still alive and banging away. I meant to be with him before long; the thought was full of cheer.

I had one little glimpse of another thing, one day, which gave me a great uplift. It was a wire stretching from housetop to housetop. Telegraph or telephone, sure. I did very much wish I had a little piece of it. It was just what I needed, in order to carry out my project of escape. My idea was, to get loose some night, along with the king, then gag and bind our master, change clothes with him, batter him into the aspect of a stranger, hitch him to the slave chain, assume possession of the property, march to Camelot, and—

But you get my idea; you see what a stunning dramatic surprise I would wind up with at the palace. It was all feasible, if I could only get hold of a slender piece of iron which I could shape into a lockpick. I could then undo the lumbering padlocks with which our chains were fastened, whenever I might choose. But I never had any luck; no such thing ever happened to fall in my way. However, my chance came at last. A gentleman who had come twice before to dicker for me, without result, or indeed any approach to a result, came again. I was far from expecting ever to belong to him, for the price asked for me from the time I was first enslaved was exorbitant, and always provoked either anger or derision, yet my master stuck stubbornly to it—twenty-two dollars. He wouldn't bate a cent. The king was greatly admired, because of his grand physique, but his kingly style was against him, and he wasn't salable; nobody wanted that kind of a slave. I considered myself safe from parting from him because of my extravagant price. No, I was not expecting to ever belong to this gentleman whom I have spoken of, but he had something which I expected would belong to me eventually, if he would but visit us often enough. It was a steel thing with a long pin to it, with which his long cloth outside garment was fastened together in front. There were three of them. He had disappointed me twice, because he did not come quite close enough to me to make my project entirely safe; but this time I succeeded; I captured the lower clasp of the three, and when he missed it he thought he had lost it on the way.

I had a chance to be glad about a minute, then straightway a chance to be sad again. For when the purchase was about to fail, as usual, the master suddenly spoke up and said what would be worded thus—in modern English:

"I'll tell you what I'll do. I'm tired supporting these two for no good. Give me twenty-two dollars for this one, and I'll throw the other one in."

The king couldn't get his breath, he was in such a fury. He began to choke and gag, and meantime the master and the gentleman moved away, discussing.

"An ye will keep the offer open—"

" 'Tis open till the morrow at this hour."

"Then will I answer you at that time," said the gentleman and disappeared, the master following him.

I had a time of it to cool the king down, but I managed it. I whispered in his ear, to this effect:

"Your grace *will* go for nothing, but after another fashion. And so shall I. Tonight we shall both be free."

"Ah! How is that?"

"With this thing which I have stolen, I will unlock these locks and cast off these chains tonight. When he comes about nine-thirty to inspect us for the night, we will seize him, gag him, batter him, and early in the morning we will march out of this town, proprietors of this caravan of slaves."

That was as far as I went, but the king was charmed and satisfied. That evening we waited patiently for our fellow slaves to get to sleep and signify it by the usual sign, for you must not take many chances on those poor fellows if you can avoid it. It is best to keep your own secrets. No doubt they fidgeted only about as usual, but it didn't seem so to me. It seemed to me that they were going to be forever getting down to their regular snoring. As the time dragged on I got nervously afraid we shouldn't have enough of it left for our needs; so I made several premature attempts, and merely delayed things by it; for I couldn't seem to touch a padlock, there in the dark, without starting a rattle out of it which interrupted somebody's sleep and made him turn over and wake some more of the gang.

But finally I did get my last iron off, and was a free man once more. I took a good breath of relief, and reached for the king's irons. Too late! in comes the master, with a light in one hand and his heavy walking staff in the other. I snuggled close among the wallow of snorers, to conceal as nearly as possible that I was naked of irons; and I kept a sharp lookout and prepared to spring for my man the moment he should bend over me.

But he didn't approach. He stopped, gazed absently toward our dusky mass a minute, evidently thinking about something else; then set down his light, moved musingly toward the door, and before a body could imagine what he was going to do, he was out of the door and had closed it behind him.

"Quick!" said the king. "Fetch him back!"

Of course it was the thing to do, and I was up and out in a moment. But dear me, there were no lamps in those days, and it was a dark night. But I glimpsed a dim figure a few steps away. I darted for it, threw myself upon it, and then there was a state of things and lively! We fought and scuffled and struggled, and drew a crowd in no time. They took an immense interest in the fight and encouraged us all they could, and in fact couldn't have been pleasanter or more cordial if it had been their own fight. Then a tremendous row broke out behind us, and as much as half of our audience left us, with a rush, to invest some sympathy in that. Lanterns began to swing in all directions; it was the watch, gathering from far and near. Presently a halberd fell across my back, as a reminder, and I knew what it meant. I was in custody. So was my adversary. We were marched off toward prison, one on each side of the watchman. Here was disaster, here was a fine scheme gone to sudden destruction! I tried to imagine what would happen when the master should discover that it was I who had been fighting him; and what would happen if they jailed us together in the general apartment for brawlers and petty law breakers, as was the custom; and what might—

Just then my antagonist turned his face around in my direction, the freckled light from the watchman's tin lantern fell on it, and by George he was the wrong man!

CHAPTER XXXVII

An Awful Predicament

SLEEP? It was impossible. It would naturally have been impossible in that noisome cavern of a jail, with its mangy crowd of drunken, quarrelsome and song-singing rapscallions. But the thing that made sleep all the more a thing not to be dreamed of, was my racking impatience to get out of this place and find out the whole size of what might have happened yonder in the slave quarters in consequence of that intolerable miscarriage of mine.

It was a long night but the morning got around at last. I made a full and frank explanation to the court. I said I was a slave, the property of the great Earl Grip, who had arrived just after dark at the Tabard inn in the village on the other side of the water, and had stopped there over night, by compulsion, he being taken deadly sick with a strange and sudden disorder. I had been ordered to cross to the city in all haste and bring the best physician; I was doing my best; naturally I was running with all my might; the night was dark, I ran against this common person here, who seized me by the throat and began to pummel me, although I told him my errand and implored him, for the sake of the great earl my master's mortal peril—

The common person interrupted and said it was a lie; and was going to explain how I rushed upon him and attacked him without a word—

"Silence, sirrah!" from the court. "Take him hence and give him a few stripes whereby to teach him how to treat the servant of a nobleman after a different fashion another time. Go!"

Then the court begged my pardon, and hoped I would not fail to tell his lordship it was in no wise the court's fault that this high-handed thing had happened. I said I would make it all right, and so took my leave. Took it just in time, too; he was starting to ask me why I didn't fetch out these facts the moment I was arrested. I said I would if I had thought of it—which was true—but that I was so battered by that man that all my wit was knocked out of me—and so forth and so on, and got myself away, still mumbling.

I didn't wait for breakfast. No grass grew under my feet. I was soon at the slave quarters. Empty—everybody gone! That is, everybody except one body—the slave master's. It lay there all battered to pulp; and all about were the evidences of a terrific fight. There was a rude board coffin on a cart at the door, and workmen, assisted by the police, were thinning a road through the gaping crowd in order that they might bring it in.

I picked out a man humble enough in life to condescend to talk with one so shabby as I, and got his account of the matter.

"There were sixteen slaves here. They rose against their master in the night, and thou seest how it ended."

"Yes. How did it begin?"

"There was no witness but the slaves. They said the slave that was most valuable got free of his bonds and escaped in some strange way—by magic arts 'twas thought, by reason that he had no key, and the locks were neither broke nor in any wise injured. When the master discovered his loss, he was mad with despair, and threw himself upon his people with his heavy stick, who resisted and brake his back and in other and divers ways did give him hurts that brought him swiftly to his end."

"This is dreadful. It will go hard with the slaves, no doubt, upon the trial."

"Marry, the trial is over."

"Over!"

"Would they be a week, think you—and the matter so simple? They were not the half of a quarter of an hour at it."

"Why, I don't see how they could determine which were the guilty ones in so short a time."

"*Which* ones? Indeed they considered not particulars like to that. They condemned them in a body. Wit ye not the law—which men say the Romans left behind them here when they went—that if one slave killeth his master all the slaves of that man must die for it."

"True. I had forgotten. And when will these die?"

"Belike within a four and twenty hours; albeit some say they will wait a pair of days more, if peradventure they may find the missing one meantime."

The missing one! It made me feel uncomfortable.

"Is it likely they will find him?"

"Before the day is spent—yes. They seek him everywhere. They stand at the gates of the town, with certain of the slaves who will discover him to them if he cometh, and none can pass out but he will be first examined."

"Might one see the place where the rest are confined?"

"The outside of it—yes. The inside of it—but ye will not want to see that."

I took the address of that prison, for future reference,

and then sauntered off. At the first secondhand clothing shop I came to, up a back street, I got a rough rig suitable for a common seaman who might be going on a cold voyage, and bound up my face with a liberal bandage, saying I had a toothache. This concealed my worst bruises. It was a transformation. I no longer resembled my former self. Then I struck out for that wire, found it and followed it to its den. It was a little room over a butcher's shop—which meant that business wasn't very brisk in the telegraphic line. The young chap in charge was drowsing at his table. I locked the door and put the vast key in my bosom. This alarmed the young fellow, and he was going to make a noise; but I said:

"Save your wind; if you open your mouth you are dead, sure. Tackle your instrument. Lively, now! Call Camelot."

"This doth amaze me! How should such as you know aught of such matters as—"

"Call Camelot! I am a desperate man. Call Camelot, or get away from the instrument and I will do it myself."

"What—you?"

"Yes—certainly. Stop gabbling. Call the palace." He made the call.

"Now then, call Clarence."

"Clarence *who?*"

"Never mind Clarence who. Say you want Clarence; you'll get an answer."

He did so. We waited five nerve-straining minutes—ten minutes—how long it did seem!—and then came a click that was as familiar to me as a human voice; for Clarence had been my own pupil.

"Now, my lad, vacate! They wouldn't have known *my* touch, maybe, and so your call was surest; but I'm all right, now."

He vacated the place and cocked his ear to listen—but it didn't win. I used a cipher. I didn't waste any time in sociabilities with Clarence, but squared away for business, straight off—thus:

"The king is here and in danger. We were captured and brought here as slaves. We should not be able to prove our identity—and the fact is, I am not in a position to try. Send a telegram for the palace here which will carry conviction with it."

His answer came straight back:

"They don't know anything about the telegraph; they haven't had any experience yet, the line to London is so new. Better not venture that. They might hang you. Think up something else."

Might hang us! Little he knew how closely he was crowding the facts. I couldn't think up anything for the moment. Then an idea struck me, and I started it along:

"Send five hundred picked knights with Launcelot in the lead; and send them on the jump. Let them enter by the southwest gate, and look out for the man with a white cloth around his right arm."

The answer was prompt:

"They shall start in half an hour."

"All right, Clarence; now tell this lad here that I'm a friend of yours and a deadhead; and that he must be discreet and say nothing about this visit of mine."

The instrument began to talk to the youth and I hurried away. I fell to ciphering. In half an hour it would be nine o'clock. Knights and horses in heavy armor couldn't travel very fast. These would make the best time they could, and now that the ground was in good condition, and no snow or mud, they would probably make a seven-mile gait; they would have to change horses a couple of times; they would arrive about six, or a little after; it would still be plenty light enough; they would see the white cloth which I should tie around my right arm, and I would take command. We would surround that prison and have the king out in no time. It would be showy and picturesque enough, all things considered, though I would have preferred noonday, on account of the more theatrical aspect the thing would have.

Now then, in order to increase the strings to my bow, I thought I would look up some of those people whom I had formerly recognized, and make myself known. That would help us out of our scrape, without the knights. But I must proceed cautiously, for it was a risky business. I must get into sumptuous raiment, and it wouldn't do to run and jump into it. No, I must work up to it by degrees, buying suit after suit of clothes, in shops wide apart, and getting a little finer article with each change, until I should finally reach silk and velvet, and be ready for my project. So I started.

But the scheme fell through like scat! The first corner I turned, I came plump upon one of our slaves, snooping around with a watchman. I coughed, at the moment, and he gave me a sudden look that bit right into my marrow. I judge he thought he had heard that cough before. I turned immediately into a shop and worked along down the counter, pricing things and watching out of the corner of my eye. Those people had stopped, and were talking together and looking in at the door. I made up my mind to get out the back way, if there was a back way, and I asked the shopwoman if I could step out there and look for the escaped slave, who was believed to be in hiding back there somewhere, and said I was an officer in disguise, and my pard was yonder at the door with one of the murderers in charge, and would she be good enough to step there and tell him he needn't wait, but had better go at once to the further end of the back alley and be ready to head him off when I rousted him out.

She was blazing with eagerness to see one of those already celebrated murderers, and she started on the errand at once. I slipped out the back way, locked the door behind me, put the key in my pocket and started off, chuckling to myself and comfortable.

Well, I had gone and spoiled it again, made another mistake. A double one, in fact. There were plenty of ways to get rid of that officer by some simple and plausible device, but no, I must pick out a picturesque one; it is the crying defect of my character. And then, I had ordered my procedure upon what the officer, being human, would *naturally* do; whereas when you are least expecting it, a man will now and then go and do the very thing which it's *not* natural for him to do. The natural thing for the officer to do, in this case, was to follow straight on my heels; he would find a stout oaken door, securely locked, between him and me; before he could break it down, I should be far away and engaged in slipping into a succession of baffling disguises which would soon get me into a sort of raiment which was a surer protection from meddling law dogs in Britain than any amount of mere innocence and purity of character. But instead of doing the natural thing, the officer took me at my word, and followed my instructions. And so, as I came trotting out of that cul-de-sac, full of satisfaction with my own cleverness, he turned the corner and I walked right into his handcuffs. If I had known it was a cul-de-sac—however, there isn't any excusing a blunder like that, let it go. Charge it up to profit and loss.

Of course I was indignant, and swore I had just come ashore from a long voyage, and all that sort of thing—just to see, you know, if it would deceive that slave. But it didn't. He knew me. Then I reproached him for betraying me. He was more surprised than hurt. He stretched his eyes wide, and said:

"What, wouldst have me let thee, of all men, escape and not hang with us, when thou'rt the very *cause* of our hanging? Go to!"

"Go to" was their way of saying "I should smile!" or "I like that!" Queer talkers, those people.

Well, there was a sort of bastard justice in his view of the case, and so I dropped the matter. When you can't cure a disaster by argument, what is the use to argue? It isn't my way. So I only said:

"You're not going to be hanged. None of us are."

Both men laughed, and the slave said:

"Ye have not ranked as a fool—before. You might better keep your reputation, seeing the strain would not be for long."

"It will stand it, I reckon. Before tomorrow we shall be out of prison, and free to go where we will, besides."

The witty officer lifted at his left ear with his thumb, made a rasping noise in his throat, and said:

"Out of prison—yes—ye say true. And free likewise to go where ye will, so ye wander not out of his grace the Devil's sultry realm."

I kept my temper, and said, indifferently:

"Now I suppose you really think we are going to hang within a day or two."

"I thought it not many minutes ago, for so the thing was decided and proclaimed."

"Ah, then you've changed your mind, is that it?"

"Even that. I only *thought,* then; I *know,* now."

I felt sarcastical, so I said:

"Oh, sapient servant of the law, condescend to tell us, then, what you *know*."

"That ye will all be hanged *today*, at midafternoon! Oho! that shot hit home! Lean upon me."

The fact is I did need to lean upon somebody. My knights couldn't arrive in time. They would be as much as three hours too late. Nothing in the world could save the King of England; nor me, which was more important. More important, not merely to me, but to the nation—the only nation on earth standing ready to blossom into civilization. I was sick. I said no more, there wasn't anything to say. I knew what the man meant; that if the missing slave was found, the postponement would be revoked, the execution take place today. Well, the missing slave was found.

[CHAPTER XXXVIII]

Sir Launcelot and Knights to the Rescue

NEARING four in the afternoon. The scene was just outside the walls of London. A cool, comfortable, superb day, with a brilliant sun; the kind of day to make one want to live, not die. The multitude was prodigious and far-reaching; and yet we fifteen poor devils hadn't a friend in it. There was something painful in that thought, look at it how you might. There we sat, on our tall scaffold, the butt of the hate and mockery of all those enemies. We were being made a holiday spectacle. They had built a sort of grandstand for the nobility and gentry, and these were there in full force, with their ladies. We recognized a good many of them.

The crowd got a brief and unexpected dash of diversion out of the king. The moment we were freed of our bonds he sprang up, in his fantastic rags, with face bruised out of all recognition, and proclaimed himself Arthur, King of Britain, and denounced the awful penalties of treason upon every soul there present if hair of his

sacred head were touched. It startled and surprised him
to hear them break into a vast roar of laughter. It
wounded his dignity, and he locked himself up in silence,
then, although the crowd begged him to go on, and tried
to provoke him to it by catcalls, jeers, and shouts of:

"Let him speak! The king! The king! his humble subjects
hunger and thirst for words of wisdom out of the mouth
of their master his Serene and Sacred Raggedness!"

But it went for nothing. He put on all his majesty and
sat under this rain of contempt and insult unmoved. He
certainly was great in his way. Absently, I had taken off
my white bandage and wound it about my right arm. When
the crowd noticed this, they began upon me. They said:

"Doubtless this sailorman is his minister—observe his
costly badge of office!"

I let them go on until they got tired, and then I said:

"Yes, I am his minister, The Boss; and tomorrow you
will hear that from Camelot which—"

I got no further. They drowned me out with joyous derision. But presently there was silence; for the sheriffs of
London, in their official robes, with their subordinates,
began to make a stir which indicated that business was
about to begin. In the hush which followed, our crime
was recited, the death warrant read, then everybody uncovered while a priest uttered a prayer.

Then a slave was blindfolded, the hangman unslung his
rope. There lay the smooth road below us, we upon one
side of it, the banked multitude walling its other side—
a good clear road, and kept free by the police—how good
it would be to see my five hundred horsemen come tearing down it! But, no, it was out of the possibilities. I followed its receding thread out into the distance—not a
horseman on it, or sign of one.

There was a jerk, and the slave hung dangling; dangling and hideously squirming, for his limbs were not
tied.

A second rope was unslung, in a moment another slave
was dangling.

In a minute a third slave was struggling in the air. It
was dreadful. I turned away my head a moment, and
when I turned back I missed the king! They were blind-
folding him! I was paralyzed; I couldn't move, I was chok-

ing, my tongue was petrified. They finished blindfolding him, they led him under the rope. I couldn't shake off that clinging impotence. But when I saw them put the noose around his neck, then everything let go in me and I made a spring to the rescue—and as I made it I shot one more glance abroad—by George, here they came, atilting—five hundred mailed and belted knights on bicycles!

The grandest sight that ever was seen. Lord, how the plumes streamed, how the sun flamed and flashed from the endless procession of webby wheels!

I waved my right arm as Launcelot swept in—he reoognized my rag—I tore away noose and bandage, and shouted:

"On your knees, every rascal of you, and salute the king! Who fails shall sup in hell tonight!"

I always use that high style when I'm climaxing an effect. Well, it was noble to see Launcelot and the boys swarm up onto that scaffold and heave sheriffs and such overboard. And it was fine to see that astonished multitude go down on their knees and beg their lives of the king they had just been deriding and insulting. And as he stood apart, there, receiving this homage in his rags, I thought to myself, well really there *is* something peculiarly grand about the gait and bearing of a king, after all.

I was immensely satisfied. Take the whole situation all around, it was one of the gaudiest effects I ever instigated.

And presently up comes Clarence, his own self! And winks, and says, very modernly:

"Good deal of a surprise, wasn't it? I knew you'd like it. I've had the boys practicing, this long time, privately; and just hungry for a chance to show off."

CHAPTER XXXIX

The Yankee's Fight with the Knights

HOME AGAIN, at Camelot. A morning or two later I found the paper, damp from the press, by my plate at the breakfast table. I turned to the advertising columns, knowing I should find something of personal interest to me there. It was this:

DE PAR LE ROI.

ʏnow that the great lord and illustrious kni8ht ƨIR SAGRAMOUR LE
DESIЯOUS having condescended to
meet the King'ᵴ Minister, Hank Morgan, the which is surnamed The Boss,
for satisfgction of offence anciently given,

these wiLL engage ın the ʟists
by Camelot about the fourtL
hour oʃ the morning oɪ the
sixteenth day oƒ this next succeeding month. The battle
wiil be à l'outrance, sith the
said offence was of a deadly
sort, admitting no com-
Position.

DE PAK ˙E ЯOI

273

Clarence's editorial reference to this affair was to this effect:

ndrew.
work maintained
there since, soon
listic have with
cked interest
upon the ea...
ve been m...d
by the ar...,s,
ent out ch...y by
yterian B..., and
c some y...ng men
of our unde...he
i guidance of the
for a...in a...known
he great enterprise
of making pure;
esent
movement had its
origin in preven-
has ever been a
sions in our
on of Wis-
ether one
ospel,
by-
e
The
he same
co represent
zed thirty of
deeds and hear-
which years ago!
resgn was organ-
ing, the missions,
sso that both had
o withdraw' and
much to their
grief,

It will be observed, by a glance at our advertising columns, that the community is to be favored with a treat of unusual interest in the tournament line. The names of the artists are warrant of good entertainment. The box-office will be open at noon of the 13th; admission 3 cents, reserved seats 5; proceeds to go to the hospital fund. The royal pair and all the Court will be present. With these exceptions, and the press and the clergy, the free list is strictly suspended. Parties are hereby warned against buying tickets of speculators; they will not be good at the door. Everybody knows and likes The Boss, everybody knows and likes Sir Sag.; come, let us give the lads a good send-off. ReMember, the proceeds go to a great and free charity, and one whose broad benevolence stretches out its helping hand, warm with the blood of a loving heart, to all that suffer, regardless of race, creed, condition or color—the only charity yet established in the earth which has no politico-religious stopcock on its compassion, but says Here flows the stream: let *all* come and drink! Turn out, all hands! fetch along your doughnuts and your gum-drops and have a good time. Pie for sale on the grounds, and rocks to crack it with; also circus-lemonade—three drops of lime juice to a barrel of water.

N. B. *This is the first tournament under the new law, which allows each combatant to use any weapon he may prefer.* You want to make a note of that.

our disappointn.
dromptly and...
two of their felo
erlain, and oth
ers have already
spoken, yon...
furnished for
their use,...
make and
the kind
letters
o introa
duction wh
they are un...
ing friends to us
ried, and... leave the
thot kind words...
which you, m, joy
hind; and it is a
home matter of b
it is our durp
direct them to
now under the...
g fields as an...
These young men
are warm-hearte...
azirl. regions bet...
not to "build...
ond,', and the
der instructi
ons of our
another man
founhati's on.
ociety, which
They go un-
say tyat "inr
ionaries to mon
say sending miss

Up to the day set, there was no talk in all Britain of anything but this combat. All other topics sank into insignificance and passed out of men's thoughts and interest. It was not because a tournament was a great matter; it was not because Sir Sagramor had found the Holy Grail, for he had not, but had failed; it was not because the second (official) personage in the kingdom was one of the duelists; no, all these features were commonplace. Yet there was abundant reason for the extraordinary interest which this coming fight was creating. It was born of the fact that all the nation knew that this was not to be a duel between mere men, so to speak, but a duel between two mighty magicians; a duel not of muscle but of mind, not of human skill but of superhuman art and craft; a final struggle for supremacy between the two master enchanters of the age. It was realized that the most prodigious achievements of the most renowned knights could not be worthy of comparison with a spectacle like this; they could be but child's play, contrasted with this mysterious and awful battle of the gods. Yes, all the world knew it was going to be in reality a duel between Merlin and me, a measuring of his magic powers against mine. It was known that Merlin had been busy whole days and nights together, imbuing Sir Sagramor's arms and armor with supernal powers of offense and defense, and that he had procured for him from the spirits of the air a fleecy veil which would render the wearer invisible to his antagonist while still visible to other men. Against Sir Sagramor, so weaponed and protected, a thousand knights could accomplish nothing; against him no known enchantments could prevail. These facts were sure; regarding them there was no doubt, no reason for doubt. There was but one question: might there be still other enchantments, *unknown* to Merlin, which could render Sir Sagramor's veil transparent to me, and make his enchanted mail vulnerable to my weapons? This was the one thing to be decided in the lists. Until then the world must remain in suspense.

So the world thought there was a vast matter at stake here, and the world was right, but it was not the one they had in their minds. No, a far vaster one was upon the cast of this die: *the life of knight-errantry.* I was a champion, it was true, but not the champion of the frivolous black arts, I was the champion of hard unsentimental common sense and reason. I was entering the lists to either destroy knight-errantry or be its victim.

Vast as the showgrounds were, there were no vacant spaces in them outside of the lists, at ten o'clock on the morning of the 16th. The mammoth grandstand was clothed in flags, streamers, and rich tapestries, and packed with several acres of small-fry tributary kings, their suites, and the British aristocracy; with our own royal gang in the chief place, and each and every individual a flashing prism of gaudy silks and velvets—well, I never saw anything to begin with it but a fight between an Upper Mississippi sunset and the aurora borealis. The huge camp of beflagged and gay-colored tents at one end of the lists, with a stiff-standing sentinel at every door and a shining shield hanging by him for challenge, was another fine sight. You see, every knight was there who had any ambition or any caste feeling; for my feeling toward their order was not much of a secret, and so here was their chance. If I won my fight with Sir Sagramor, others would have the right to call me out as long as I might be willing to respond.

Down at our end there were but two tents; one for me, and another for my servants. At the appointed hour the king made a sign, and the heralds, in their tabards, appeared and made proclamation, naming the combatants and stating the cause of quarrel. There was a pause, then a ringing bugle blast, which was the signal for us to come forth. All the multitude caught their breath, and an eager curiosity flashed into every face.

Out from his tent rode great Sir Sagramor, an imposing tower of iron, stately and rigid, his huge spear standing upright in its socket and grasped in his strong hand, his grand horse's face and breast cased in steel, his body clothed in rich trappings that almost dragged the ground —oh, a most noble picture. A great shout went up, of welcome and admiration.

And then out I came. But I didn't get any shout. There was a wondering and eloquent silence, for a moment, then a great wave of laughter began to sweep along that human sea, but a warning bugle blast cut its career short. I was in the simplest and comfortablest of gymnast costumes—flesh-colored tights from neck to heel, with blue silk puffings about my loins, and bareheaded. My horse was not above medium size, but he was alert, slender-limbed, muscled with watch springs, and just a greyhound to go. He was a beauty, glossy as silk, and naked as he was when he was born, except for bridle and ranger saddle.

The iron tower and the gorgeous bed quilt came cumbrously but gracefully pirouetting down the lists, and we tripped lightly up to meet them. We halted; the tower saluted, I responded; then we wheeled and rode side by side to the grandstand and faced our king and queen, to whom we made obeisance. The queen exclaimed:

"Alack, Sir Boss, wilt fight naked, and without lance or sword or—"

But the king checked her and made her understand, with a polite phrase or two, that this was none of her business. The bugles rang again; and we separated and rode to the ends of the lists, and took position. Now old Merlin stepped into view and cast a dainty web of gossamer threads over Sir Sagramor which turned him into Hamlet's ghost; the king made a sign, the bugles blew, Sir Sagramor laid his great lance in rest, and the next moment here he came thundering down the course with his veil flying out behind, and I went whistling through the air like an arrow to meet him—cocking my ear, the while, as if noting the invisible knight's position and progress by hearing, not sight. A chorus of encouraging shouts burst out for him, and one brave voice flung out a heartening word for me—said:

"Go it, slim Jim!"

It was an even bet that Clarence had procured that favor for me—and furnished the language, too. When that formidable lance point was within a yard and a half of my breast I twitched my horse aside without an effort and the big knight swept by, scoring a blank. I got plenty of applause that time. We turned, braced up, and down we came again. Another blank for the knight, a roar of applause for me. This same thing was repeated once more; and it fetched such a whirlwind of applause that Sir Sagramor lost his temper, and at once changed his tactics and set himself the task of chasing me down. Why, he hadn't any show in the world at that; it was a game of tag, with all the advantage on my side; I whirled out of his path with ease whenever I chose, and once I slapped him on the back as I went to the rear. Finally I took the chase into my own hands; and after that, turn, or twist, or do what he would, he was never able to get behind me again; he found himself always in front, at the end of his maneuver. So he gave up that business and retired to his end of the lists. His temper was clear gone, now, and he forgot himself and flung an insult at me which disposed of mine. I slipped my lasso from the horn of my saddle, and grasped the coil in my right hand. This time you should have seen him come! It was a business trip, sure; by his gait there was blood in his eye. I was sitting my horse at ease, and swinging the great loop of my lasso in wide circles about my head; the moment he was under way, I started for him; when the space between us had narrowed to forty feet, I sent the snaky spirals of the rope a-cleaving through the air, then darted aside and faced about and brought my trained animal to a halt with all his feet braced under him for a surge. The next moment the rope sprang taut and yanked Sir Sagramor out of the saddle! Great Scott, but there was a sensation!

Unquestionably the popular thing in this world is novelty. These people had never seen anything of that cowboy business before, and it carried them clear off their feet with delight. From all around and everywhere, the shout went up—

"Encore! encore!"

I wondered where they got the word, but there was no time to cipher on philological matters, because the whole knight-errantry hive was just humming, now, and my prospect for trade couldn't have been better. The moment my lasso was released and Sir Sagramor had been assisted to his tent, I hauled in the slack, took my station and began to swing my loop around my head again. I was sure to have use for it as soon as they could elect a successor for Sir Sagramor, and that couldn't take long where there were so many hungry candidates. Indeed, they elected one straight off—Sir Hervis de Revel.

Bzz! Here he came, like a house afire; I dodged; he passed like a flash, with my horsehair coils settling around his neck; a second or so later, *fst!* his saddle was empty.

I got another encore; and another, and another, and still another. When I had snaked five men out, things began to look serious to the ironclads, and they stopped and consulted together. As a result, they decided that it was time to waive etiquette and send their greatest and best against me. To the astonishment of that little world, I lassoed Sir Lamorak de Galis, and after him Sir Galahad. So you see there was simply nothing to be done, now, but play their right bower—bring out the superbest of the superb, the mightiest of the mighty, the great Sir Launcelot himself!

A proud moment for me? I should think so. Yonder was Arthur, King of Britain; yonder was Guenever; yes, and whole tribes of little provincial kings and kinglets; and in the tented camp yonder, renowned knights from many lands; and likewise the selectest body known to chivalry, the Knights of the Table Round, the most illustrious in Christendom; and biggest fact of all, the very sun of their shining system was yonder couching his lance, the focal point of forty thousand adoring eyes; and all by myself, here was I laying for him. Across my mind flitted the dear image of a certain hello-girl of West Hartford, and I wished she could see me now. In that moment, down came the Invincible, with the rush of a whirlwind—the courtly world rose to its feet and bent forward—the fateful coils went circling through the air, and before you could wink I was towing Sir Launcelot across the field on his back, and kissing my hand to the storm of waving kerchiefs and the thundercrash of applause that greeted me!

Said I to myself, as I coiled my lariat and hung it on my saddle horn, and sat there drunk with glory, "The victory is perfect—no other will venture against me—knight-errantry is dead." Now imagine my astonishment—and everybody else's too—to hear the peculiar bugle call which announces that another competitor is about to enter the lists! There was a mystery here; I couldn't account for this thing. Next, I noticed Merlin gliding away from me; and then I noticed that my lasso was gone! The old sleight-of-hand expert had stolen it, sure, and slipped it under his robe.

The bugle blew again. I looked, and down came Sagramor riding again, with his dust brushed off and his veil nicely rearranged. I trotted up to meet him, and pretended to find him by the sound of his horse's hoofs. He said:

"Thou'rt quick of ear, but it will not save thee from this!" and he touched the hilt of his great sword. "An ye are not able to see it, because of the influence of the veil, know that it is no cumbrous lance, but a sword— and I ween ye will not be able to avoid it."

His visor was up; there was death in his smile. I should never be able to dodge his sword, that was plain. Somebody was going to die, this time. If he got the drop on me, I could name the corpse. We rode forward together, and saluted the royalties. This time the king was disturbed. He said:

"Where is thy strange weapon?"

"It is stolen, sire."

"Hast another at hand?"

"No, sire, I brought only the one."

Then Merlin mixed in:

"He brought but the one because there was but the one to bring. There exists none other but that one. It belongeth to the king of the Demons of the Sea. This man is a pretender, and ignorant; else he had known that that weapon can be used in but eight bouts only, and then it vanisheth away to its home under the sea."

"Then is he weaponless," said the king. "Sir Sagramor, ye will grant him leave to borrow."

"And I will lend!" said Sir Launcelot, limping up. "He is as brave a knight of his hands as any that be on live, and he shall have mine."

He put his hand on his sword to draw it, but Sir Sagramor said:

"Stay, it may not be. He shall fight with his own weapons; it was his privilege to choose them and bring them. If he has erred, on his head be it."

"Knight!" said the king. "Thou'rt overwrought with passion; it disorders thy mind. Wouldst kill a naked man?"

"An he do it, he shall answer it to me," said Sir Launcelot.

"I will answer it to any he that desireth!" retorted Sir Sagramor hotly.

Merlin broke in, rubbing his hands and smiling his lowdownest smile of malicious gratification:

" 'Tis well said, right well said! And 'tis enough of parleying, let my lord the king deliver the battle signal."

The king had to yield. The bugle made proclamation, and we turned apart and rode to our stations. There we stood, a hundred yards apart, facing each other, rigid and motionless, like horsed statues. And so we remained, in a soundless hush, as much as a full minute, everybody gazing, nobody stirring. It seemed as if the king could not take heart to give the signal. But at last he lifted his hand, the clear note of the bugle followed, Sir Sagramor's long blade described a flashing curve in the air, and it was superb to see him come. I sat still. On he came. I did not move. People got so excited that they shouted to me:

"Fly, fly! Save thyself! This is murther!"

I never budged so much as an inch, till that thundering apparition had got within fifteen paces of me; then I snatched a dragoon revolver out of my holster, there was a flash and a roar, and the revolver was back in the holster before anybody could tell what had happened.

Here was a riderless horse plunging by, and yonder lay Sir Sagramor, stone dead.

The people that ran to him were stricken dumb to find that the life was actually gone out of the man and no reason for it visible, no hurt upon his body, nothing like a wound. There was a hole through the breast of his chain mail, but they attached no importance to a little thing like that; and as a bullet wound there produces but little blood, none came in sight because of the clothing and swaddlings under the armor. The body was dragged over to let the king and the swells look down upon it. They were stupefied with astonishment, naturally. I was requested to come and explain the miracle. But I remained in my tracks, like a statue, and said:

"If it is a command, I will come, but my lord the king knows that I am where the laws of combat require me to remain while any desire to come against me."

I waited. Nobody challenged. Then I said:

"If there are any who doubt that this field is well and

fairly won, I do not wait for them to challenge me, I challenge them."

"It is a gallant offer," said the king, "and well beseems you. Whom will you name, first?"

"I name none, I challenge all! Here I stand, and dare the chivalry of England to come against me—not by individuals, but in mass!"

"What!" shouted a score of knights.

"You have heard the challenge. Take it, or I proclaim you recreant knights and vanquished, every one!"

It was a "bluff" you know. At such a time it is sound judgment to put on a bold face and play your hand for a hundred times what it is worth; forty-nine times out of fifty nobody dares to "call," and you rake in the chips. But just this once—well, things looked squally! In just no time, five hundred knights were scrambling into their saddles, and before you could wink a widely scattering drove were under way and clattering down upon me. I snatched both revolvers from the holsters and began to measure distances and calculate chances.

Bang! One saddle empty. Bang! another one. Bang—bang! and I bagged two. Well it was nip and tuck with us, and I knew it. If I spent the eleventh shot without convincing these people, the twelfth man would kill me, sure.

And so I never did feel so happy as I did when my ninth downed its man and I detected the wavering in the crowd which is premonitory of panic. An instant lost now, could knock out my last chance. But I didn't lose it. I raised both revolvers and pointed them—the halted host stood their ground just about one good square moment, then broke and fled.

The day was mine. Knight-errantry was a doomed institution. The march of civilization was begun. How did I feel? Ah, you never could imagine it.

And Brer Merlin? His stock was flat again. Somehow, every time the magic of folderol tried conclusions with the magic of science, the magic of folderol got left.

[CHAPTER XL]

Three Years Later

WHEN I broke the back of knight-errantry that time, I no longer felt obliged to work in secret. So, the very next day I exposed my hidden schools, my mines, and my vast system of clandestine factories and workshops to an astonished world. That is to say, I exposed the nineteenth century to the inspection of the sixth.

Well it is always a good plan to follow up an advantage promptly. The knights were temporarily down, but if I would keep them so I must just simply paralyze them— nothing short of that would answer. You see, I was "bluffing" that last time, in the field; it would be natural for them to work around to that conclusion, if I gave them a chance. So I must not give them time: and I didn't.

I renewed my challenge, engraved it on brass, posted it up where any priest could read it to them, and also kept it standing, in the advertising columns of the paper.

I not only renewed it, but added to its proportions. I said, name the day, and I would take fifty assistants and stand up *against the massed chivalry of the whole earth and destroy it.*

I was not bluffing this time. I meant what I said; I could do what I promised. There wasn't any way to misunderstand the language of that challenge. Even the dullest of the chivalry perceived that this was a plain case of "put up, or shut up." They were wise and did the latter. In all the next three years they gave me no trouble worth mentioning.

Consider the three years sped. Now look around on England. A happy and prosperous country, and strangely altered. Schools everywhere, and several colleges; a number of pretty good newspapers. Even authorship was taking a start; Sir Dinadan the Humorist was first in the field, with a volume of gray-headed jokes which I had been familiar with during thirteen centuries. If he had left out that old rancid one about the lecturer I wouldn't have said anything; but I couldn't stand that one. I suppressed the book and hanged the author.

Slavery was dead and gone; all men were equal before the law; taxation had been equalized. The telegraph, the telephone, the phonograph, the typewriter, the sewing machine, and all the thousand willing and handy servants of steam and electricity were working their way into favor. We had a steamboat or two on the Thames, we had steam warships, and the beginnings of a steam commercial marine; I was getting ready to send out an expedition to discover America.

We were building several lines of railway, and our line from Camelot to London was already finished and in operation. I was shrewd enough to make all offices connected with the passenger service places of high and distinguished honor. My idea was to attract the chivalry and nobility, and make them useful and keep them out of mischief. The plan worked very well, the competition for the places was hot. The conductor of the 4:33 express was a duke, there wasn't a passenger conductor on the line below the degree of earl. They were good men, every one, but they had two defects which I couldn't cure, and so had to wink at: they wouldn't lay aside their armor, and they would "knock down" fares—I mean rob the company.

There was hardly a knight in all the land who wasn't in some useful employment. They were going from end to end of the country in all manner of useful missionary capacities; their penchant for wandering, and their experience in it, made them altogether the most effective spreaders of civilization we had. They went clothed in steel and equipped with sword and lance and battle-ax, and if they couldn't persuade a person to try a sewing machine on the installment plan, or a melodeon, or a barbed wire fence, or a prohibition journal, or any of the other thousand and one things they canvassed for, they removed him and passed on.

I was very happy. Things were working steadily toward a secretly longed-for point. You see, I had two schemes in my head which were the vastest of all my projects. The one was, to overthrow the Catholic Church and set up the Protestant faith on its ruins—not as an Established Church, but a go-as-you-please one; and the other project was, to get a decree issued by and by, commanding that upon Arthur's death unlimited suffrage should be introduced, and given to men and women alike—at any rate to all men, wise or unwise, and to all mothers who at middle age should be found to know nearly as much as their sons at twenty-one. Arthur was good for thirty years yet, he being about my own age—that is to say, forty—and I believed that in that time I could easily have the active part of the population of that day ready and eager for an event which should be the first of its kind in the history of the world—a rounded and complete governmental revolution without bloodshed. The result to be a republic. Well, I may as well confess, though I do feel ashamed when I think of it: I was beginning to have a base hankering to be its first president myself. Yes, there was more or less human nature in me; I found that out.

Clarence was with me as concerned the revolution, but in a modified way. His idea was a republic, without privileged orders but with a hereditary royal family at the head of it instead of an elective chief magistrate. He believed that no nation that had ever known the joy of worshiping a royal family could ever be robbed of it and not fade away and die of melancholy. I urged that kings were dangerous. He said, then have cats. He was sure that a royal family of cats would answer every purpose. They would be as useful as any other royal family, they would know as much, they would have the same virtues and the same treacheries, the same disposition to get up shindies with other royal cats, they would be laughably vain and absurd and never know it, they would be wholly inexpensive; finally, they would have as sound a divine right as any other royal house, and "Tom VII, or Tom XI, or Tom XIV by the grace of God King," would sound as well as it would when applied to the ordinary royal tomcat with tights on. "And as a rule," said he, in his neat modern English, "the character of these cats would be considerably above the character of the average king, and this would be an immense moral advantage to the

nation, for the reason that a nation always models its
morals after its monarch's. The worship of royalty being
founded in unreason, these graceful and harmless cats
would easily become as sacred as any other royalties,
and indeed more so, because it would presently be noticed that they hanged nobody, beheaded nobody, imprisoned nobody, inflicted no cruelties or injustices of
any sort, and so must be worthy of a deeper love and
reverence than the customary human king, and would
certainly get it. The eyes of the whole harried world
would soon be fixed upon this humane and gentle system,
and royal butchers would presently begin to disappear;
their subjects would fill the vacancies with catlings from
our own royal house; we should become a factory; we
should supply the thrones of the world; within forty years
all Europe would be governed by cats, and we should
furnish the cats. The reign of universal peace would begin
then, to end no more forever. . . . *Me-e-e-yow-ow-ow-ow
—fzt—wow!"*

Hang him, I supposed he was in earnest, and was beginning to be persuaded by him, until he exploded that cat-
howl and startled me almost out of my clothes. But he
never could be in earnest. He didn't know what it was.
He had pictured a distinct and perfectly rational and
feasible improvement upon constitutional monarchy, but
he was too featherheaded to know it, or care anything
about it, either. I was going to give him a scolding, but
Sandy came flying in at that moment, wild with terror,
and so choked with sobs that for a minute she could not
get her voice. I ran and took her in my arms, and lavished
caresses upon her and said, beseechingly:

"Speak, darling, speak! What is it?"

Her head fell limp upon my bosom, and she gasped,
almost inaudibly:

"HELLO-CENTRAL!"

"Quick!" I shouted to Clarence; "telephone the
king's homeopath to come!"

In two minutes I was kneeling by the child's crib, and
Sandy was dispatching servants here, there, and everywhere,
all over the palace. I took in the situation almost at a glance
—membranous croup! I bent down and whispered:

"Wake up, sweetheart! Hello-Central!"

She opened her soft eyes languidly, and made out to say—
"Papa."

That was a comfort. She was far from dead, yet. I
sent for preparations of sulphur, I rousted out the croup
kettle myself; for I don't sit down and wait for doctors
when Sandy or the child is sick. I knew how to nurse both
of them, and had had experience. This little chap had
lived in my arms a good part of its small life, and often
I could soothe away its troubles and get it to laugh
through the tear-dews on its eyelashes when even its mother couldn't.

Sir Launcelot, in his richest armor, came striding along
the great hall, now, on his way to the stock board; he
was president of the stock board, and occupied the Siege
Perilous, which he had bought of Sir Galahad; for the
stock board consisted of the Knights of the Round Table,
and they used the Round Table for business purposes, now.
Seats at it were worth—well, you would never believe the
figure, so it is no use to state it. Sir Launcelot was a bear,
and he had put up a corner in one of the new lines, and
was just getting ready to squeeze the shorts today; but
what of that? He was the same old Launcelot, and when
he glanced in as he was passing the door and found out
that his pet was sick, that was enough for him; bulls and
bears might fight it out their own way for all him, he
would come right in here and stand by little Hello-Central for all he was worth. And that was what he did. He
shied his helmet into the corner, and in half a minute
he had a new wick in the alcohol lamp and was firing up
on the croup kettle. By this time Sandy had built a blanket canopy over the crib, and everything was ready.

Sir Launcelot got up steam, he and I loaded up the
kettle with unslaked lime and carbolic acid, with a touch
of lactic acid added thereto, then filled the thing up with
water and inserted the steam spout under the canopy.
Everything was shipshape, now, and we sat down on
either side of the crib to stand our watch. Sandy was so
grateful and so comforted that she charged a couple of
churchwardens with willowbark and sumac tobacco for
us, and told us to smoke as much as we pleased, it
couldn't get under the canopy, and she was used to
smoke, being the first lady in the land who had ever

seen a cloud blown. Well, there couldn't be a more contented or comfortable sight than Sir Launcelot in his noble armor sitting in gracious serenity at the end of a yard of snowy churchwarden. He was a beautiful man, a lovely man, and was just intended to make a wife and children happy. But of course, Guenever—however, it's no use to cry over what's done and can't be helped.

Well, he stood watch and watch with me, right straight through, for three days and nights, till the child was out of danger; then he took her up in his great arms and kissed her, with his plumes falling about her golden head, then laid her softly in Sandy's lap again and took his stately way down the vast hall, between the ranks of admiring men-at-arms and menials, and so disappeared. And no instinct warned me that I should never look upon him again in this world! Lord, what a world of heartbreak it is.

The doctors said we must take the child away, if we would coax her back to health and strength again. And she must have sea air. So we took a man-of-war, and a suite of two hundred and sixty persons, and went cruising about, and after a fortnight of this we stepped ashore on the French coast, and the doctors thought it would be a good idea to make something of a stay there. The little king of that region offered us his hospitalities, and we were glad to accept. If he had had as many conveniences as he lacked, we should have been plenty comfortable enough; even as it was, we made out very well, in his queer old castle, by the help of comforts and luxuries from the ship.

At the end of a month I sent the vessel home for fresh supplies, and for news. We expected her back in three or four days. She would bring me, along with other news, the result of a certain experiment which I had been starting. It was a project of mine to replace the tournament with something which might furnish an escape for the extra steam of the chivalry, keep those bucks entertained and out of mischief, and at the same time preserve the best thing in them, which was their hardy spirit of emulation. I had had a choice band of them in private training for some time, and the date was now arriving for their first public effort.

This experiment was baseball. In order to give the thing vogue from the start, and place it out of the reach of criticism, I chose my nines by rank, not capacity. There wasn't a knight in either team who wasn't a sceptered sovereign. As for material of this sort, there was a glut of it, always, around Arthur. You couldn't throw a brick in any direction and not cripple a king. Of course I couldn't get these people to leave off their armor; they wouldn't do that when they bathed. They consented to differentiate the armor so that a body could tell one team from the other, but that was the most they would do. So, one of the teams wore chain-mail ulsters, and the other wore plate armor made of my new Bessemer steel. Their practice in the field was the most fantastic thing I ever saw. Being ballproof, they never skipped out of the way, but stood still and took the result; when a Bessemer was at the bat and a ball hit him, it would bound a hundred and fifty yards, sometimes. And when a man was running, and threw himself on his stomach to slide to his base, it was like an ironclad coming into port. At first I appointed men of no rank to act as umpires, but I had to discontinue that. These people were no easier to please than other nines. The umpire's first decision was usually his last; they broke him in two with a bat, and his friends toted him home on a shutter. When it was noticed that no umpire ever survived a game, umpiring got to be unpopular. So I was obliged to appoint somebody whose rank and lofty position under the government would protect him.

Here are the names of the nines:

BESSEMERS.	ULSTERS.
KING ARTHUR.	EMPEROR LUCIUS.
KING LOT OF LOTHIAN.	KING LOGRIS.
KING OF NORTHGALIS.	KING MARHALT OF IRELAND.
KING MARSIL.	KING MORGANORE.
KING OF LITTLE BRITAIN.	KING MARK OF CORNWALL.
KING LABOR.	KING NENTRES OF GARLOT.
KING PELLAM OF LISTENGESE.	KING MELIODAS OF LIONES.
KING BAGDEMAGUS.	KING OF THE LAKE.
KING TOLLEME LA FEINTES.	THE SOWDAN OF SYRIA.

Umpire—CLARENCE.

The first public game would certainly draw fifty thousand people; and for solid fun would be worth going around the world to see. Everything would be favorable; it was balmy and beautiful spring weather, now, and Nature was all tailored out in her new clothes.

〚 CHAPTER XLI 〛

The Interdict

HOWEVER, my attention was suddenly snatched from such matters; our child began to lose ground again, and we had to go to sitting up with her, her case became so serious. We couldn't bear to allow anybody to help, in this service, so we two stood watch and watch, day in and day out. Ah, Sandy, what a right heart she had, how simple, and genuine, and good she was! She was a flawless wife and mother; and yet I had married her for no particular reason, except that by the customs of chivalry she was my property until some knight should win her from me in the field. She had hunted Britain over for me; had found me at the hanging-bout outside of London, and had straightway resumed her old place at my side in the placidest way and as of right. I was a New Englander, and in my opinion this sort of partnership would compromise her, sooner or later. She couldn't see how, but I cut argument short and we had a wedding.

Now I didn't know I was drawing a prize, yet that was what I did draw. Within the twelvemonth I became her worshiper; and ours was the dearest and perfectest comradeship that ever was. People talk about beautiful friendships between two persons of the same sex. What is the best of that sort, as compared with the friendship of man and wife, where the best impulses and highest ideals of both are the same? There is no place for comparison between the two friendships; the one is earthly, the other divine.

In my dreams, along at first, I still wandered thirteen

centuries away, and my unsatisfied spirit went calling and harking all up and down the unreplying vacancies of a vanished world. Many a time Sandy heard that imploring cry come from my lips in my sleep. With a grand magnanimity she saddled that cry of mine upon our child, conceiving it to be the name of some lost darling of mine. It touched me to tears, and it also nearly knocked me off my feet, too, when she smiled up in my face for an earned reward, and played her quaint and pretty surprise upon me:

"The name of one who was dear to thee is here preserved, here made holy, and the music of it will abide alway in our ears. Now thou'll kiss me, as knowing the name I have given the child."

But I didn't know it, all the same. I hadn't an idea in the world; but it would have been cruel to confess it and spoil her pretty game; so I never let on, but said:

"Yes, I know, sweetheart—how dear and good it is of you, too! But I want to hear these lips of yours, which are also mine, utter it first—then its music will be perfect."

Pleased to the marrow, she murmured—

"HELLO-CENTRAL!"

I didn't laugh—I am always thankful for that—but the strain ruptured every cartilage in me, and for weeks afterward I could hear my bones clack when I walked. She never found out her mistake. The first time she heard that form of salute used at the telephone she was surprised, and not pleased; but I told her I had given order for it: that henceforth and forever the telephone must always be invoked with that reverent formality, in perpetual honor and remembrance of my lost friend and her small namesake. This was not true. But it answered.

Well, during two weeks and a half we watched by the crib, and in our deep solicitude we were unconscious of any world outside of that sickroom. Then our reward came: the center of the universe turned the corner and began to mend. Grateful? It isn't the term. There *isn't* any term for it. You know that, yourself, if you've watched your child through the Valley of the Shadow and seen it come back to life and sweep night out of the earth with one all-illuminating smile that you could cover with your hand.

Why, we were back in this world in one instant! Then we looked the same startled thought into each other's eyes at the same moment: more than two weeks gone, and that ship not back yet!

In another minute I appeared in the presence of my train. They had been steeped in troubled bodings all this time—their faces showed it. I called an escort and we galloped five miles to a hilltop overlooking the sea. Where was my great commerce that so lately had made these glistering expanses populous and beautiful with its white-winged flocks? Vanished, every one! Not a sail, from verge to verge, not a smoke bank—just a dead and empty solitude, in place of all that brisk and breezy life.

I went swiftly back, saying not a word to anybody. I told Sandy this ghastly news. We could imagine no explanation that would begin to explain. Had there been an invasion? An earthquake? A pestilence? Had the nation been swept out of existence? But guessing was profitless. I must go—at once. I borrowed the king's navy—a "ship" no bigger than a steam launch—and was soon ready.

The parting—ah, yes, that was hard. As I was devouring the child with last kisses, it brisked up and jabbered out its vocabulary—the first time in more than two weeks, and it made fools of us for joy. The darling mispronunciations of childhood! Dear me, there's no music that can touch it; and how one grieves when it wastes away and dissolves into correctness, knowing it will never visit his bereaved ear again. Well, how good it was to be able to carry that gracious memory away with me!

I approached England the next morning, with the wide highway of salt water all to myself. There were ships in the harbor, at Dover, but they were naked as to sails, and there was no sign of life about them. It was Sunday; yet at Canterbury the streets were empty; strangest of all, there was not even a priest in sight, and no stroke of a bell fell upon my ear. The mournfulness of death was everywhere. I couldn't understand it. At last, in the further edge of that town I saw a small funeral procession—just a family and a few friends following a coffin—no priest; a funeral without bell, book, or candle; there was a church there, close at hand, but they passed it by, weeping, and did not enter it; I glanced up at the belfry, and there hung the bell, shrouded in black, and its tongue tied back. Now I knew! Now I understood the stupendous calamity that had overtaken England. Invasion? Invasion is a triviality to it. It was the INTERDICT!

I asked no questions; I didn't need to ask any. The Church had struck; the thing for me to do was to get into a disguise, and go warily. One of my servants gave me a suit of his clothes, and when we were safe beyond the town I put them on, and from that time I traveled alone; I could not risk the embarrassment of company.

A miserable journey. A desolate silence everywhere. Even in London itself. Traffic had ceased; men did not talk or laugh, or go in groups, or even in couples; they moved aimlessly about, each man by himself, with his head down, and woe and terror at his heart. The Tower showed recent war scars. Verily, much had been happening.

Of course I meant to take the train for Camelot. Train! Why, the station was as vacant as a cavern. I moved on. The journey to Camelot was a repetition of what I had already seen. The Monday and the Tuesday differed in no way from the Sunday. I arrived, far in the night. From being the best electric-lighted town in the kingdom and the most like a recumbent sun of anything you ever saw, it was become simply a blot—a blot upon darkness—that is to say, it was darker and solider than the rest of the darkness, and so you could see it a little better; it made me feel as if maybe it was symbolical— a sort of sign that the Church was going to *keep* the upper hand, now, and snuff out all my beautiful civilization just like that. I found no life stirring in the somber streets. I groped my way with a heavy heart. The vast castle loomed black upon the hilltop, not a spark visible about it. The drawbridge was down, the great gate stood wide, I entered without challenge, my own heels making the only sound I heard—and it was sepulchral enough, in those huge vacant courts.

❴ CHAPTER XLII ❵

War!

I FOUND Clarence, alone in his quarters, drowned in melancholy; and in place of the electric light, he had reinstituted the ancient rag-lamp, and sat there in a grisly twilight with all curtains drawn tight. He sprang up and rushed for me eagerly, saying:

"Oh, it's worth a billion milrays to look upon a live person again!"

He knew me as easily as if I hadn't been disguised at all. Which frightened me; one may easily believe that.

"Quick, now, tell me the meaning of this fearful disaster," I said. "How did it come about?"

"Well, if there hadn't been any Queen Guenever, it wouldn't have come so early; but it would have come, anyway. It would have come on your own account, by and by; by luck, it happened to come on the queen's."

"*And* Sir Launcelot's?"

"Just so."

"Give me the details."

"I reckon you will grant that during some years there has been only one pair of eyes in these kingdoms that has not been looking steadily askance at the queen and Sir Launcelot—"

"Yes, King Arthur's."

—"and only one heart that was without suspicion—"

"Yes—the king's; a heart that isn't capable of thinking evil of a friend."

"Well, the king might have gone on, still happy and unsuspecting, to the end of his days, but for one of your modern improvements—the stock board. When you left, three miles of the London, Canterbury and Dover were ready for the rails, and also ready and ripe for manipulation in the stock market. It was wildcat, and everybody

knew it. The stock was for sale at a giveaway. What does
Sir Launcelot do, but—"

"Yes, I know; he quietly picked up nearly all of it, for
a song; then he bought about twice as much more, deliverable upon call; and he was about to call when I
left."

"Very well, he did call. The boys couldn't deliver. Oh,
he had them—and he just settled his grip and squeezed
them. They were laughing in their sleeves over their smartness in selling stock to him at fifteen and sixteen and
along there, that wasn't worth ten. Well, when they had
laughed long enough on that side of their mouths, they
rested up that side by shifting the laugh to the other
side. That was when they compromised with the Invincible at two hundred eighty-three!"

"Good land!"

"He skinned them alive, and they deserved it—anyway, the whole kingdom rejoiced. Well, among the
flayed were Sir Agravaine and Sir Mordred, nephews
to the king. End of the first act. Act second, scene first,
an apartment in Carlisle castle, where the court had gone
for a few day's hunting. Persons present, the whole tribe
of the king's nephews. Mordred and Agravaine propose
to call the guileless Arthur's attention to Guenever and
Sir Launcelot. Sir Gawaine, Sir Gareth, and Sir Gaheris
will have nothing to do with it. A dispute ensues, with
loud talk; in the midst of it, enter the king. Mordred and
Agravaine spring their devastating tale upon him. *Tableau*. A trap is laid for Launcelot, by the king's command,
and Sir Launcelot walks into it. He made it sufficiently
uncomfortable for the ambushed witnesses—to wit, Mordred, Agravaine, and twelve knights of lesser rank, for
he killed every one of them but Mordred; but of course
that couldn't straighten matters between Launcelot and
the king, and didn't."

"Oh, dear, only one thing could result—I see that. War,
and the knights of the realm divided into a king's party
and a Sir Launcelot's party."

"Yes—that was the way of it. The king sent the queen
to the stake, proposing to purify her with fire. Launcelot
and his knights rescued her, and in doing it slew certain good old friends of yours and mine—in fact, some

of the best we ever had, to wit: Sir Belias le Orgulous,
Sir Segwarides, Sir Griflet le Fils de Dieu, Sir Brandiles, Sir
Aglovale"—

"Oh, you tear out my heartstrings."

—"wait, I'm not done yet—Sir Tor, Sir Gauter, Sir
Gillimer"—

"The very best man in my subordinate nine. What a
handy right fielder he was!"

—"Sir Reynold's three brothers, Sir Damus, Sir Pria-
mus, Sir Kay the Stranger"—

"My peerless shortstop! I've seen him catch a daisy
cutter in his teeth. Come, I can't stand this!"

—"Sir Driant, Sir Lambegus, Sir Herminde, Sir Perti-
lope, Sir Perimones, and—whom do you think?"

"Rush! Go on."

"Sir Gaheris, and Sir Gareth—both!"

"Oh, incredible! Their love for Launcelot was inde-
structible."

"Well, it was an accident. They were simply onlookers;
they were unarmed, and were merely there to witness the
queen's punishment. Sir Launcelot smote down whoever
came in the way of his blind fury, and he killed these without noticing who they were. Here is an instantaneous
photograph one of our boys got of the battle; it's for
sale on every newsstand. There—the figures nearest the
queen are Sir Launcelot with his sword up, and Sir Gareth
gasping his latest breath. You can catch the agony in
the queen's face through the curling smoke. It's a rattling
battle picture."

"Indeed it is. We must take good care of it; its historical
value is incalculable. Go on."

"Well, the rest of the tale is just war, pure and simple.
Launcelot retreated to his town and castle of Joyous Gard,
and gathered there a great following of knights. The
king, with a great host, went there, and there was desperate fighting during several days, and as a result, all the
plain around was paved with corpses and cast iron. Then
the Church patched up a peace between Arthur and
Launcelot and the queen and everybody—everybody but
Sir Gawaine. He was bitter about the slaying of his brothers, Gareth and Gaheris, and would not be appeased. He
notified Launcelot to get him thence, and make swift prep-

aration, and look to be soon attacked. So Launcelot sailed to his Duchy of Guienne, with his following, and Gawaine soon followed, with an army, and he beguiled Arthur to go with him. Arthur left the kingdom in Sir Mordred's hands until you should return—"

"Ah—a king's customary wisdom!"

"Yes. Sir Mordred set himself at once to work to make his kingship permanent. He was going to marry Guenever, as a first move; but she fled and shut herself up in the Tower of London. Mordred attacked; the Bishop of Canterbury dropped down on him with the Interdict. The king returned; Mordred fought him at Dover, at Canterbury, and again at Barham Down. Then there was talk of peace and a composition. Terms, Mordred to have Cornwall and Kent during Arthur's life, and the whole kingdom afterward."

"Well, upon my word! My dream of a republic to *be* a dream, and so remain."

"Yes. The two armies lay near Salisbury. Gawaine—Gawaine's head is at Dover Castle, he fell in the fight there—Gawaine appeared to Arthur in a dream, at least his ghost did, and warned him to refrain from conflict for a month, let the delay cost what it might. But battle was precipitated by an accident. Arthur had given order that if a sword was raised during the consultation over the proposed treaty with Mordred, sound the trumpet and fall on! for he had no confidence in Mordred. Mordred had given a similar order to *his* people. Well, by and by an adder bit a knight's heel; the knight forgot all about the order, and made a slash at the adder with his sword. Inside of half a minute those two prodigious hosts came together with a crash! They butchered away all day. Then the king—however, we have started something fresh since you left—our paper has."

"No? What is that?"

"War correspondence!"

"Why, that's good."

"Yes, the paper was booming right along, for the Interdict made no impression, got no grip, while the war lasted. I had war correspondents with both armies. I will finish that battle by reading you what one of the boys says:

Then the king looked about him, and then was he
ware of all his host and of all his good knights were
left no more on live but two knights, that was Sir
Lucan de Butlere, and his brother Sir Bedivere: and they
were full sore wounded. Jesu mercy, said the king,
where are all my noble knights becomen? Alas that ever
I should see this doleful day. For now, said Arthur, I
am come to mine end. But would to God that I wist
where were that traitor Sir Mordred, that hath caused
all this mischief. Then was King Arthur ware where Sir
Mordred leaned upon his sword among a great heap of
dead men. Now give me my spear, said Arthur unto Sir
Lucan, for yonder I have espied the traitor that all this
woe hath wrought. Sir, let him be, said Sir Lucan, for he
is unhappy; and if ye pass this unhappy day, ye shall be
right well revenged upon him. Good lord, remember ye
of your night's dream, and what the spirit of Sir Gawaine
told you this night, yet God of his great goodness hath
preserved you hitherto. Therefore, for God's sake, my
lord, leave off by this. For blessed be God ye have won
the field: for here we be three on live, and with Sir
Mordred is none on live. And if ye leave off now, this
wicked day of destiny is past. Tide me death, betide me
life, saith the king, now I see him yonder alone, he shall
never escape mine hands, for at a better avail shall I
never have him. God speed you well, said Sir Bedivere.
Then the king gat his spear in both his hands, and ran
toward Sir Mordred, crying, Traitor, now is thy death
day come. And when Sir Mordred heard Sir Arthur, he
ran until him with his sword drawn in his hand. And
then King Arthur smote Sir Mordred under the shield,
with a foin of his spear throughout the body more than
a fathom. And when Sir Mordred felt that he had his
death's wound, he thrust himself, with the might that
he had, up to the butt of King Arthur's spear. And right
so he smote his father Arthur with his sword holden
in both his hands, on the side of the head, that the sword
pierced the helmet and the brain-pan, and therewithal
Sir Mordred fell stark dead to the earth. And the noble
Arthur fell in a swoon to the earth, and there he
swooned ofttimes."

"That is a good piece of war correspondence, Clarence;
you are a first-rate newspaper man. Well—is the king all
right? Did he get well?"

"Poor soul, no. He is dead."

I was utterly stunned; it had not seemed to me that any wound could be mortal to him.

"And the queen, Clarence?"

"She is a nun, in Almesbury."

"What changes! and in such a short while. It is inconceivable. What next, I wonder?"

"I can tell you what next."

"Well?"

"Stake our lives and stand by them!"

"What do you mean by that?"

"The Church is master, now. The Interdict included you with Mordred; it is not to be removed while you remain alive. The clans are gathering. The Church has gathered all the knights that are left alive, and as soon as you are discovered we shall have business on our hands."

"Stuff! With our deadly scientific war material; with our hosts of trained—"

"Save your breath—we haven't sixty faithful left!"

"What are you saying? Our schools, our colleges, our vast workshops, our—"

"When those knights come, those establishments will empty themselves and go over to the enemy. Did you think you had educated the superstition out of those people?"

"I certainly did think it."

"Well, then, you may unthink it. They stood every strain easily—until the Interdict. Since then, they merely put on a bold outside—at heart they are quaking. Make up your mind to it—when the armies come, the mask will fall."

"It's hard news. We are lost. They will turn our own science against us."

"No they won't."

"Why?"

"Because I and a handful of the faithful have blocked that game. I'll tell you what I've done, and what moved me to it. Smart as you are, the Church was smarter. It was the Church that sent you cruising—through her servants the doctors."

"Clarence!"

"It is the truth. I know it. Every officer of your ship was the Church's picked servant, and so was every man of the crew."

"Oh, come!"

"It is just as I tell you. I did not find out these things at once, but I found them out finally. Did you send me verbal information, by the commander of the ship, to the effect that upon his return to you, with supplies, you were going to leave Cadiz"—

"Cadiz! I haven't been at Cadiz at all!"

—"going to leave Cadiz and cruise in distant seas indefinitely, for the health of your family? Did you send me that word?"

"Of course not. I would have written, wouldn't I?"

"Naturally. I was troubled and suspicious. When the commander sailed again I managed to ship a spy with him. I have never heard of vessel or spy since. I gave myself two weeks to hear from you in. Then I resolved to send a ship to Cadiz. There was a reason why I didn't."

"What was that?"

"Our navy had suddenly and mysteriously disappeared! Also as suddenly and as mysteriously, the railway and telegraph and telephone service ceased, the men all deserted, poles were cut down, the Church laid a ban upon the electric light! I had to be up and doing—and straight off. Your life was safe—nobody in these kingdoms but Merlin would venture to touch such a magician as you without ten thousand men at his back—I had nothing to think of but how to put preparations in the best trim against your coming. I felt safe myself—nobody would be anxious to touch a pet of yours. So this is what I did. From our various works I selected all the men—boys I mean—whose faithfulness under whatsoever pressure I could swear to, and I called them together secretly and gave them their instructions. There are fifty-two of them; none younger than fourteen, and none above seventeen years old."

"Why did you select boys?"

"Because all the others were born in an atmosphere of superstition and reared in it. It is in their blood and bones. We imagined we had educated it out of them; they thought so, too; the Interdict woke them up like a thunderclap! It revealed them to themselves, and it revealed them to me, too. With boys it was different. Such as have been under our training from seven to ten years have had no acquaintance with the Church's terrors, and it was among these that I found my fifty-two. As a next move, I paid a private visit to that old cave of Merlin's—not the small one—the big one—"

"Yes, the one where we secretly established our first great electric plant when I was projecting a miracle."

"Just so. And as that miracle hadn't become necessary then, I thought it might be a good idea to utilize the plant now. I've provisioned the cave for a siege—"

"A good idea, a first rate idea."

"I think so. I placed four of my boys there, as a guard—inside, and out of sight. Nobody was to be hurt—while outside; but any attempt to enter—well, we said just let anybody try it! Then I went out into the hills and uncovered and cut the secret wires which connected your bedroom with the wires that go to the dynamite deposits under all our vast factories, mills, workshops, magazines, etc., and about midnight I and my boys turned out and connected that wire with the cave, and nobody but you and I suspects where the other end of it goes to. We laid it under ground, of course, and it was all finished in a couple of hours or so. We shan't have to leave our fortress, now, when we want to blow up our civilization."

"It was the right move—and the natural one; a military necessity, in the changed condition of things. Well, what changes *have* come! We expected to be besieged in the palace some time or other, but—however, go on."

"Next, we built a wire fence."

"Wire fence?"

"Yes. You dropped the hint of it yourself, two or three years ago."

"Oh, I remember—the time the Church tried her strength against us the first time, and presently thought it wise to wait for a hopefuler season. Well, how have you arranged the fence?"

"I start twelve immensely strong wires—naked, not insulated—from a big dynamo in the cave—dynamo with no brushes except a positive and a negative one—"

"Yes, that's right."

"The wires go out from the cave and fence-in a circle of level ground a hundred yards in diameter; they make twelve independent fences, ten feet apart—that is to say, twelve circles within circles—and their ends come into the cave again."

"Right; go on."

"The fences are fastened to heavy oaken posts only three feet apart, and these posts are sunk five feet in the ground."

"That is good and strong."

"Yes. The wires have no ground connection outside of the cave. They go out from the positive brush of the dynamo; there is a ground connection through the negative brush; the other ends of the wire return to the cave, and each is grounded independently."

"No-no, that won't do!"

"Why?"

"It's too expensive—uses up force for nothing. You don't want any ground connection except the one through the negative brush. The other end of every wire must be brought back into the cave and fastened independently, and *without* any ground connection. Now, then, observe the economy of it. A cavalry charge hurls itself against the fence; you are using no power, you are spending no money, for there is only one ground connection till those horses come against the wire; the moment they touch it they form a connection with the negative brush *through the ground,* and drop dead. Don't you see—you are using no energy until it is needed; your lightning is there, and ready, like the load in a gun; but it isn't costing you a cent till you touch it off. Oh, yes, the single ground connection—"

"Of course! I don't know how I overlooked that. It's not only cheaper, but it's more effectual than the other way, for if wires break or get tangled, no harm is done."

"No, especially if we have a telltale in the cave and disconnect the broken wire. Well, go on. The gatlings?"

"Yes—that's arranged. In the center of the inner circle, on a spacious platform six feet high, I've grouped a battery of thirteen gatling guns, and provided plenty of ammunition."

"That's it. They command every approach, and when the Church's knights arrive, there's going to be music. The brow of the precipice over the cave—"

"I've got a wire fence there, and a gatling. They won't drop any rocks down on us."

"Well, and the glass-cylinder dynamite torpedoes?"

"That's attended to. It's the prettiest garden that was ever planted. It's a belt forty feet wide, and goes around the outer fence—distance between it and the fence one hundred yards—kind of neutral ground, that space is. There isn't a single square yard of that whole belt but is equipped with a torpedo. We laid them on the surface of the ground, and sprinkled a layer of sand over them. It's an innocent looking garden, but you let a man start in to hoe it once, and you'll see."

"You tested the torpedoes?"

"Well, I was going to, but—"

"But what? Why, it's an immense oversight not to apply a—"

"Test? Yes, I know; but they're all right; I laid a few in the public road beyond our lines and they've been tested."

"Oh, that alters the case. Who did it?"

"A Church committee."

"How kind!"

"Yes. They came to command us to make submission. You see they didn't really come to test the torpedoes; that was merely an incident."

"Did the committee make a report?"

"Yes, they made one. You could have heard it a mile."

"Unanimous?"

"That was the nature of it. After that I put up some signs, for the protection of future committees, and we have had no intruders since."

"Clarence, you've done a world of work, and done it perfectly."

"We had plenty of time for it; there wasn't any occasion for hurry."

We sat silent awhile, thinking. Then my mind was made up, and I said:

"Yes, everything is ready; everything is shipshape, no detail is wanting. I know what to do, now."

"So do I: sit down and wait."

"No, *sir!* rise up and *strike!*"

"Do you mean it?"

"Yes, indeed! The *de*fensive isn't in my line, and the

*off*ensive is. That is, when I hold a fair hand—two-thirds as good a hand as the enemy. Oh, yes, we'll rise up and strike; that's our game."

"A hundred to one, you are right. When does the performance begin?"

"*Now!* We'll proclaim the Republic."

"Well, that *will* precipitate things, sure enough!"

"It will make them buzz, *I* tell you! England will be a hornet's nest before noon tomorrow, if the Church's hand hasn't lost its cunning—and we know it hasn't. Now you write and I'll dictate—thus:

"PROCLAMATION.

"BE IT KNOWN UNTO ALL. Whereas the king having died and left no heir, it becomes my duty to continue the executive authority vested in me, until a government shall have been created and set in motion. The monarchy has lapsed, it no longer exists. By consequence, all political power has reverted to its original source, the people of the nation. With the monarchy, its several adjuncts died also; wherefore there is no longer a nobility, no longer a privileged class, no longer an Established Church: all men are become exactly equal, they are upon one common level, and religion is free. *A Republic is hereby proclaimed,* as being the natural estate of a nation when other authority has ceased. It is the duty of the British people to meet together immediately, and by their votes elect representatives and deliver into their hands the government."

I signed it "The Boss," and dated it from Merlin's Cave. Clarence said:

"Why, that tells where we are, and invites them to call right away."

"That is the idea. We *strike*—by the Proclamation— then it's their innings. Now have the thing set up and printed and posted, right off; that is, give the order; then, if you've got a couple of bicycles handy at the foot of the hill, ho for Merlin's Cave!"

"I shall be ready in ten minutes. What a cyclone there is going to be tomorrow when this piece of paper gets to work! . . . It's a pleasant old palace, this is; I wonder if we shall ever again—but never mind about that."

⟦ CHAPTER XLIII ⟧

The Battle of the Sand Belt

IN MERLIN'S CAVE—Clarence and I and fifty-two fresh, bright, well-educated, clean-minded young British boys. At dawn I sent an order to the factories and to all our great works to stop operations and remove all life to a safe distance, as everything was going to be blown up by secret mines, *"and no telling at what moment—therefore, vacate at once."* These people knew me, and had confidence in my word. They would clear out without waiting to part their hair, and I could take my own time about dating the explosion. You couldn't hire one of them to go back during the century, if the explosion was still impending.

We had a week of waiting. It was not dull for me, because I was writing all the time. During the first three days, I finished turning my old diary into this narrative form; it only required a chapter or so to bring it down to date. The rest of the week I took up in writing letters to my wife. It was always my habit to write to Sandy everyday, whenever we were separate, and now I kept up the habit for love of it, and of her, though I couldn't do anything with the letters, of course, after I had written them. But it put in the time, you see, and was almost like talking; it was almost as if I was saying, "Sandy, if you and Hello-Central were here in the cave, instead of only your photographs, what good times we could have!" And then, you know, I could imagine the baby goo-gooing something out in reply, with its fists in its mouth and itself stretched across its mother's lap on its back, and she a-laughing and admiring and worshiping, and now and then tickling under the baby's chin to set it cackling, and then maybe throwing in a word of answer to me herself —and so on and so on—well, don't you know, I could sit there in the cave with my pen, and keep it up, that way,

by the hour with them. Why, it was almost like having us
all together again.

I had spies out, every night, of course, to get news.
Every report made things look more and more impressive.
The hosts were gathering, gathering; down all the roads
and paths of England the knights were riding, and priests
rode with them, to hearten these original Crusaders, this
being the Church's war. All the nobilities, big and little,
were on their way, and all the gentry. This was all as was
expected. We should thin out this sort of folk to such a
degree that the people would have nothing to do but just
step to the front with their republic and——

Ah, what a donkey I was! Toward the end of the week
I began to get this large and disenchanting fact through
my head: that the mass of the nation had swung their
caps and shouted for the republic for about one day, and
there an end! The Church, the nobles, and the gentry
then turned one grand, all-disapproving frown upon them
and shriveled them into sheep! From that moment the
sheep had begun to gather to the fold—that is to say,
the camps—and offer their valueless lives and their
valuable wool to the "righteous cause." Why, even the very
men who had lately been slaves were in the "righteous
cause," and glorifying it, praying for it, sentimentally
slabbering over it, just like all the other commoners. Imagine such human muck as this; conceive of this folly!

Yes, it was now "Death to the Republic!" everywhere—
not a dissenting voice. All England was marching against
us! Truly this was more than I had bargained for.

I watched my fifty-two boys narrowly; watched their
faces, their walk, their unconscious attitudes: for all these
are a language—a language given us purposely that it
may betray us in times of emergency, when we have
secrets which we want to keep. I knew that that thought
would keep saying itself over and over again in their
minds and hearts, *All England is marching against us!* and
evermore strenuously imploring attention with each repetition, ever more sharply realizing itself to their imagina-
tions, until even in their sleep they would find no rest
from it, but hear the vague and flitting creatures of their
dreams say, *All England—*ALL ENGLAND—*is marching
against you!* I knew all this would happen; I knew that

ultimately the pressure would become so great that it would compel utterance; therefore, I must be ready with an answer at that time—an answer well chosen and tranquilizing.

I was right. The time came. They *had* to speak. Poor lads, it was pitiful to see, they were so pale, so worn, so troubled. At first their spokesman could hardly find voice or words; but he presently got both. This is what he said—and he put it in the neat modern English taught him in my schools:

"We have tried to forget what we are—English boys! We have tried to put reason before sentiment, duty before love; our minds approve, but our hearts reproach us. While apparently it was only the nobility, only the gentry, only the twenty-five or thirty thousand knights left alive out of the late wars, we were of one mind, and undisturbed by any troubling doubt; each and every one of these fifty-two lads who stand here before you, said, 'They have chosen—it is their affair.' But think—the matter is altered—*all England is marching against us!* Oh, sir, consider! Reflect! These people are our people, they are bone of our bone, flesh of our flesh, we love them—do not ask us to destroy our nation!"

Well, it shows the value of looking ahead, and being ready for a thing when it happens. If I hadn't foreseen this thing and been fixed, that boy would have had me—I couldn't have said a word. But I *was* fixed. I said:

"My boys, your hearts are in the right place, you have thought the worthy thought, you have done the worthy thing. You are English boys, you will remain English boys, and you will keep that name unsmirched. Give yourselves no further concern, let your minds be at peace. Consider this: while all England *is* marching against us, who is in the van? Who, by the commonest rules of war, will march in the front? Answer me."

"The mounted host of mailed knights."

"True. They are 30,000 strong. Acres deep, they will march. Now, observe: none but *they* will ever strike the sand belt! Then there will be an episode! Immediately after, the civilian multitude in the rear will retire, to meet business engagements elsewhere. None but nobles and gentry are knights, and *none but these* will remain to

dance to our music after that episode. It is absolutely
true that we shall have to fight nobody but these thirty
thousand knights. Now speak, and it shall be as you de-
cide. Shall we avoid the battle, retire from the field?"

"NO ! ! !"

The shout was unanimous and hearty.

"Are you—are you—well, afraid of these thirty thousand knights?"

That joke brought out a good laugh, the boys' troubles
vanished away, and they went gaily to their posts. Ah,
they were a darling fifty-two! As pretty as girls, too.

I was ready for the enemy, now. Let the approaching
big day come along—it would find us on deck.

The big day arrived on time. At dawn the sentry on
watch in the corral came into the cave and reported a
moving black mass under the horizon, and a faint sound
which he thought to be military music. Breakfast was
just ready; we sat down and ate it.

This over, I made the boys a little speech, and then
sent out a detail to man the battery, with Clarence in
command of it.

The sun rose presently and sent its unobstructed splendors over the land, and we saw a prodigious host moving
slowly toward us, with the steady drift and aligned front
of a wave of the sea. Nearer and nearer it came, and
more and more sublimely imposing became its aspect;
yes, all England were there, apparently. Soon we could
see the innumerable banners fluttering, and then the sun
struck the sea of armor and set it all a-flash. Yes, it was a
fine sight; I hadn't ever seen anything to beat it.

At last we could make out details. All the front ranks,
no telling how many acres deep, were horsemen—
plumed knights in armor. Suddenly we heard the blare
of trumpets; the slow walk burst into a gallop, and then
—well, it was wonderful to see! Down swept that vast
horseshoe wave—it approached the sand belt—my
breath stood still; nearer, nearer—the strip of green turf
beyond the yellow belt grew narrow—narrower still—
became a mere ribbon in front of the horses—then disappeared under their hoofs. Great Scott! Why, the whole
front of that host shot into the sky with a thundercrash,
and became a whirling tempest of rags and fragments;

and along the ground lay a thick wall of smoke that hid what was left of the multitude from our sight.

Time for the second step in the plan of campaign! I touched a button, and shook the bones of England loose from her spine!

In that explosion all our noble civilization-factories went up in the air and disappeared from the earth. It was a pity, but it was necessary. We could not afford to let the enemy turn our own weapons against us.

Now ensued one of the dullest quarter hours I had ever endured. We waited in a silent solitude enclosed by our circles of wire, and by a circle of heavy smoke outside of these. We couldn't see over the wall of smoke, and we couldn't see through it. But at last it began to shred away lazily, and by the end of another quarter hour the land was clear and our curiosity was enabled to satisfy itself. No living creature was in sight! We now perceived that additions had been made to our defenses. The dynamite had dug a ditch more than a hundred feet wide, all around us, and cast up an embankment some twenty-five feet high on both borders of it. As to destruction of life, it was amazing. Moreover, it was beyond estimate. Of course we could not *count* the dead, because they did not exist as individuals, but merely as homogeneous protoplasm, with alloys of iron and buttons.

No life was in sight, but necessarily there must have been some wounded in the rear ranks, who were carried off the field under cover of the wall of smoke; there would be sickness among the others—there always is, after an episode like that. But there would be no reinforcements; this was the last stand of the chivalry of England; it was all that was left of the order, after the recent annihilating wars. So I felt quite safe in believing that the utmost force that could for the future be brought against us would be but small; that is, of knights. I therefore issued a congratulatory proclamation to my army in these words:

SOLDIERS, CHAMPIONS OF HUMAN LIBERTY AND EQUALITY: Your General congratulates you! In the pride of his strength and the vanity of his renown, an arrogant enemy came against you. You were ready. The conflict was brief; on your side, glorious. This mighty victory having been achieved utterly without loss, stands without example in history. So long as the planets shall continue to move in their orbits, the BATTLE OF THE SAND BELT will not perish out of the memories of men.

THE BOSS.

I read it well, and the applause I got was very gratifying to me. I then wound up with these remarks:

"The war with the English nation, as a nation, is at an end. The nation has retired from the field and the war. Before it can be persuaded to return, war will have ceased. This campaign is the only one that is going to be fought. It will be brief—the briefest in history. Also the most destructive to life, considered from the standpoint of proportion of casualties to numbers engaged. We are done with the nation; henceforth we deal only with the knights. English knights can be killed, but they cannot be conquered. We know what is before us. While one of these men remains alive, our task is not finished, the war is not ended. We will kill them all." [Loud and long continued applause.]

I picketed the great embankments thrown up around our lines by the dynamite explosion—merely a lookout of a couple of boys to announce the enemy when he should appear again.

Next, I sent an engineer and forty men to a point just beyond our lines on the south, to turn a mountain brook that was there, and bring it within our lines and under our command, arranging it in such a way that I could make instant use of it in an emergency. The forty men were divided into two shifts of twenty each, and were to relieve each other every two hours. In ten hours the work was accomplished.

It was nightfall, now, and I withdrew my pickets. The one who had had the northern outlook reported a camp in sight, but visible with the glass only. He also reported that a few knights had been feeling their way toward us, and had driven some cattle across our lines, but that the knights themselves had not come very near. That was what I had been expecting. They were feeling us, you see; they wanted to know if we were going to play that red terror on them again. They would grow bolder in the night, perhaps. I believed I knew what project they would attempt, because it was plainly the thing I would attempt myself if I were in their places and as ignorant as they were. I mentioned it to Clarence.

"I think you are right," said he; "it is the obvious thing for them to try."

"Well, then," I said, "if they do it they are doomed."

"Certainly."

"They won't have the slightest show in the world."

"Of course they won't."

"It's dreadful, Clarence. It seems an awful pity."

The thing disturbed me so, that I couldn't get any peace of mind for thinking of it and worrying over it. So, at last, to quiet my conscience, I framed this message to the knights:

To THE HONORABLE THE COMMANDER OF THE IN-SURGENT CHIVALRY OF ENGLAND: You fight in vain. We know your strength—if one may call it by that name. We know that at the utmost you cannot bring against us above five and twenty thousand knights. Therefore, you have no chance—none whatever. Reflect: we are well equipped, well fortified, we number fifty-four. Fifty-four what? Men? No, *minds*—the capablest in the world; a force against which mere animal might may no more hope to prevail than may the idle waves of the sea hope to prevail against the granite barriers of England. Be ad-vised. We offer you your lives; for the sake of your families, do not reject the gift. We offer you this chance, and it is the last: throw down your arms; surrender un-conditionally to the Republic, and all will be forgiven.

(Signed)   THE BOSS.

I read it to Clarence, and said I proposed to send it by a flag of truce. He laughed the sarcastic laugh he was born with, and said:

"Somehow it seems impossible for you to ever fully realize what these nobilities are. Now let us save a little time and trouble. Consider me the commmander of the knights yonder. Now then, you are the flag of truce; approach and deliver me your message, and I will give you your answer."

I humored the idea. I came forward under an imaginary guard of the enemy's soldiers, produced my paper, and read it through. For answer, Clarence struck the paper out of my hand, pursed up a scornful lip and said with lofty disdain—

"Dismember me this animal, and return him in a basket to the baseborn knave who sent him; other answer have I none!"

How empty is theory in presence of fact! And this was just fact, and nothing else. It was the thing that would have happened, there was no getting around that. I tore up the paper and granted my mistimed sentimentalities a permanent rest.

Then, to business. I tested the electric signals from the gatling platform to the cave, and made sure that they were all right; I tested and retested those which commanded the fences—these were signals whereby I could break and renew the electric current in each fence independently of the others, at will. I placed the brook connection under the guard and authority of three of my best boys, who would alternate in two-hour watches all night and promptly obey my signal, if I should have occasion to give it—three revolver-shots in quick succession. Sentry duty was discarded for the night, and the corral left empty of life; I ordered that quiet be maintained in the cave, and the electric lights turned down to a glimmer.

As soon as it was good and dark, I shut off the current from all of the fences, and then groped my way out to the embankment bordering our side of the great dynamite ditch. I crept to the top of it and lay there on the slant of the muck to watch. But it was too dark to see anything. As for sounds, there were none. The stillness was deathlike. True, there were the usual nightsounds of the country—the whir of night birds, the buzzing of insects, the barking of distant dogs, the mellow lowing of far-off kine—but these didn't seem to break the stillness, they only intensified it, and added a gruesome melancholy to it into the bargain.

I presently gave up looking, the night shut down so black, but I kept my ears strained to catch the least suspicious sound, for I judged I had only to wait and I shouldn't be disappointed. However, I had to wait a long time. At last I caught what you may call indistinct glimpses of sound—dulled metallic sound. I pricked up my ears, then, and held my breath, for this was the sort of thing I had been waiting for. This sound thickened, and approached—from toward the north. Presently I heard it at my own level—the ridgetop of the opposite embankment, a hundred feet or more away. Then I seemed to see a row of black dots appear along that ridge—human heads? I couldn't tell; it mightn't be anything at all; you can't depend on your eyes when your imagination is out of focus. However, the question was soon settled. I heard that metallic noise descending into the great ditch. It augmented fast, it spread all along, and it unmistakably furnished me this fact: an armed host was taking up its quarters in the ditch. Yes, these people were arranging a little surprise party for us. We could expect entertainment about dawn, possibly earlier.

I groped my way back to the corral, now; I had seen enough. I went to the platform and signaled to turn the current onto the two inner fences. Then I went into the cave, and found everything satisfactory there—nobody awake but the working watch. I woke Clarence and told him the great ditch was filling up with men, and that I believed all the knights were coming for us in a body. It was my notion that as soon as dawn approached we could expect the ditch's ambuscaded thousands to swarm up over the embankment and make an assault, and be followed immediately by the rest of their army.

Clarence said:

"They will be wanting to send a scout or two in the dark to make preliminary observations. Why not take the lightning off the outer fences, and give them a chance?"

"I've already done it, Clarence. Did you ever know me to be inhospitable?"

"No, you are a good heart. I want to go and—"

"Be a reception committee? I will go, too."

We crossed the corral and lay down together between the two inside fences. Even the dim light of the cave had disordered our eyesight somewhat, but the focus straightway began to regulate itself and soon it was adjusted for present circumstances. We had had to feel our way before, but we could make out to see the fence posts now.

We started a whispered conversation, but suddenly Clarence broke off and said:

"What is that?"

"What is what?"

"That thing yonder?"

"What thing—where?"

"There beyond you a little piece—a dark something—a dull shape of some kind—against the second fence."

I gazed and he gazed. I said:

"Could it be a man, Clarence?"

"No, I think not. If you notice, it looks a lit—why, it *is* a man—leaning on the fence!"

"I certainly believe it is; let's us go and see."

We crept along on our hands and knees until we were pretty close, and then looked up. Yes, it was a man—a dim great figure in armor, standing erect, with both hands on the upper wire—and of course there was a smell of burning flesh. Poor fellow, dead as a doornail, and never knew what hurt him. He stood there like a statue—no motion about him, except that his plumes swished about a little in the night wind. We rose up and looked in through the bars of his visor, but couldn't make out whether we knew him or not—features too dim and shadowed.

We heard muffled sounds approaching, and we sank down to the ground where we were. We made out another knight vaguely; he was coming very stealthily, and feeling his way. He was near enough, now, for us to see him put out a hand, find an upper wire, then bend and step under it and over the lower one. Now he arrived at the first knight—and started slightly when he discovered him. He stood a moment—no doubt wondering why the other one didn't move on; then he said, in a low voice, "Why dreamest thou here, good Sir Mar—" then he laid his hand on the corpse's shoulder—and just uttered a little soft moan and sunk down dead. Killed by a dead man, you see—killed by a dead friend, in fact. There was something awful about it.

These early birds came scattering along after each other, about one every five minutes in our vicinity, during half an hour. They brought no armor of offense but their swords; as a rule they carried the sword ready in the hand, and put it forward and found the wires with it. We would now and then see a blue spark when the knight that caused it was so far away as to be invisible to us; but we knew what had happened, all the same, poor fellow; he had touched a charged wire with his sword and been elected. We had brief intervals of grim stillness, interrupted with piteous regularity by the clash made by the falling of an ironclad; and this sort of thing was going on, right along, and was very creepy, there in the dark and lonesomeness.

We concluded to make a tour between the inner fences. We elected to walk upright, for convenience sake; we argued that if discerned, we should be taken for friends rather than enemies, and in any case we should be out of reach of swords, and these gentry did not seem to have any spears along. Well, it was a curious trip. Everywhere dead men were lying outside the second fence—not plainly visible, but still visible; and we counted fifteen of those pathetic statues—dead knights standing with their hands on the upper wire.

One thing seemed to be sufficiently demonstrated: our current was so tremendous that it killed before the victim could cry out. Pretty soon we detected a muffled and heavy sound, and next moment we guessed what it was. It was a surprise in force coming! I whispered Clarence to go and wake the army, and notify it to wait in silence in the cave for further orders. He was soon back, and we stood by the inner fence and watched the silent lightning do its awful work upon that swarming host. One could make out but little of detail; but he could note that a black mass was piling itself up beyond the second fence. That swelling bulk was dead men! Our camp was enclosed with a solid wall of the dead—a bulwark, a breastwork, of corpses, you may say. One terrible thing about this thing was the absence of human voices; there were no cheers, no war cries: being intent upon a surprise, these men moved as noiselessly as they could; and always when the front rank was near enough to their goal to make it proper for them to begin to get a shout ready, of course they struck the fatal line and went down without testifying.

I sent a current through the third fence, now; and al-

most immediately through the fourth and fifth, so quickly
were the gaps filled up. I believed the time was come,
now, for my climax; I believed that that whole army was
in our trap. Anyway, it was high time to find out. So I
touched a button and set fifty electric suns aflame on
the top of our precipice.

Land, what a sight! We were enclosed in three walls
of dead men! All the other fences were pretty nearly
filled with the living, who were stealthily working their
way forward through the wires. The sudden glare paralyzed this host, petrified them, you may say, with astonishment; there was just one instant for me to utilize their
immobility in, and I didn't lose the chance. You see, in
another instant they would have recovered their faculties, then they'd have burst into a cheer and made a rush,
and my wires would have gone down before it; but that
lost instant lost them their opportunity forever; while
even that slight fragment of time was still unspent, I shot
the current through all the fences and struck the whole
host dead in their tracks! *There* was a groan you could
hear! It voiced the death pang of eleven thousand men.
It swelled out on the night with awful pathos.

A glance showed that the rest of the enemy—perhaps
ten thousand strong—were between us and the encircling
ditch, and pressing forward to the assault. Consequently
we had them *all!* and had them past help. Time for the
last act of the tragedy. I fired the three appointed revolver shots—which meant:

"Turn on the water!"

There was a sudden rush and roar, and in a minute
the mountain brook was raging through the big ditch and
creating a river a hundred feet wide and twenty-five deep.

"Stand to your guns, men! Open fire!"

The thirteen gatlings began to vomit death into the
fated ten thousand. They halted, they stood their ground
a moment against that withering deluge of fire, then
they broke, faced about and swept toward the ditch
like chaff before a gale. A full fourth part of their force
never reached the top of the lofty embankment; the
three-fourths reached it and plunged over—to death by
drowning.

Within ten short minutes after we had opened fire,

armed resistance was totally annihilated, the campaign was ended, we fifty-four were masters of England! Twenty-five thousand men lay dead around us.

But how treacherous is fortune! In a little while—say an hour—happened a thing, by my own fault, which—but I have no heart to write that. Let the record end here.

〖 CHAPTER XLIV 〗

A Postscript by Clarence

I, CLARENCE, must write it for him. He proposed that we two go out and see if any help could be afforded the wounded. I was strenuous against the project. I said that if there were many, we could do but little for them; and it would not be wise for us to trust ourselves among them, anyway. But he could seldom be turned from a purpose once formed; so we shut off the electric current from the fences, took an escort along, climbed over the enclosing ramparts of dead knights, and moved out upon the field. The first wounded man who appealed for help, was sitting with his back against a dead comrade. When the Boss bent over him and spoke to him, the man recognized him and stabbed him. That knight was Sir Meliagraunce, as I found out by tearing off his helmet. He will not ask for help any more.

We carried the Boss to the cave and gave his wound, which was not very serious, the best care we could. In this service we had the help of Merlin, though we did not know it. He was disguised as a woman, and appeared to be a simple old peasant goodwife. In this disguise, with brown-stained face and smooth-shaven, he had appeared a few days after the Boss was hurt, and offered to cook for us, saying her people had gone off to join certain new camps which the enemy were forming, and that she was starving. The Boss had been getting along very well, and had amused himself with finishing up his record.

We were glad to have this woman, for we were short-handed. We were in a trap, you see—a trap of our own making. If we stayed where we were, our dead would kill us; if we moved out of our defenses, we should no longer be invincible. We had conquered; in turn we were conquered. The Boss recognized this; we all recognized it. If we could go to one of those new camps and patch up some kind of terms with the enemy—yes, but the Boss could not go, and neither could I, for I was among the first that were made sick by the poisonous air bred by those dead thousands. Others were taken down, and still others. Tomorrow—

Tomorrow. It is here. And with it the end. About midnight I awoke, and saw that hag making curious passes in the air about the Boss's head and face, and wondered what it meant. Everybody but the dynamo-watch lay steeped in sleep; there was no sound. The woman ceased from her mysterious foolery, and started tiptoeing toward the door. I called out—

"Stop! What have you been doing?"

She halted, and said with an accent of malicious satisfaction:

"Ye were conquerors; ye are conquered! These others are perishing—you also. Ye shall all die in this place—every one—except *him*. He sleepeth, now—and shall sleep thirteen centuries. I am Merlin!"

Then such a delirium of silly laughter overtook him that he reeled about like a drunken man, and presently fetched up against one of our wires. His mouth is spread open yet; apparently he is stll laughing. I suppose the face will retain that petrified laugh until the corpse turns to dust.

The Boss has never stirred—sleeps like a stone. If he does not wake today we shall understand what kind of a sleep it is, and his body will then be borne to a place in one of the remote recesses of the cave where none will ever find it to desecrate it. As for the rest of us—well, it is agreed that if any one of us ever escapes alive from this place, he will write the fact here, and loyally hide this Manuscript with the Boss, our dear good chief, whose property it is, be he alive or dead.

END OF THE MANUSCRIPT

Final P. S. by M. T.

THE dawn was come when I laid the manuscript aside.
The rain had almost ceased, the world was gray and
sad, the exhausted storm was sighing and sobbing itself to
rest. I went to the stranger's room, and listened at his
door, which was slightly ajar. I could hear his voice, and
so I knocked. There was no answer, but I still heard the
voice. I peeped in. The man lay on his back, in bed,
talking brokenly but with spirit, and punctuating with
his arms, which he thrashed about, restlessly, as sick
people do in delirium. I slipped in softly and bent over
him. His mutterings and ejaculations went on. I spoke
—merely a word, to call his attention. His glassy eyes
and his ashy face were alight in an instant with pleasure,
gratitude, gladness, welcome:

"O, Sandy, you are come at last—how I have longed for
you! Sit by me—do not leave me—never leave me again,
Sandy, never again. Where is your hand—give it me, dear,
let me hold it—there—now all is well, all is peace, and
I am happy again—*we* are happy again, isn't it so, Sandy?
You are so dim, so vague, you are but a mist, a cloud,
but you are *here,* and that is blessedness sufficient; and I
have your hand; don't take it away—it is for only a little
while, I shall not require it long. . . . Was that the child?
. . . Hello-Central! . . . She doesn't answer. Asleep, perhaps? Bring her when she wakes, and let me touch her
hands, her face, her hair, and tell her good-bye. . . .
Sandy! . . . Yes, you are there. I lost myself a moment,

319

and I thought you were gone. . . . Have I been sick long? It must be so; it seems months to me. And such dreams! Such strange and awful dreams, Sandy! Dreams that were as real as reality—delirium, of course, but *so* real! Why, I thought the king was dead, I thought you were in Gaul and couldn't get home, I thought there was a revolution; in the fantastic frenzy of these dreams, I thought that Clarence and I and a handful of my cadets fought and exterminated the whole chivalry of England! But even that was not the strangest. I seemed to be a creature out of a remote unborn age, centuries hence, and even *that* was as real as the rest! Yes, I seemed to have flown back out of that age into this of ours, and then forward to it again, and was set down, a stranger and forlorn in that strange England, with an abyss of thirteen centuries yawning between me and you! between me and my home and my friends! between me and all that is dear to me, all that could make life worth the living! It was awful— awfuler than you can ever imagine, Sandy. Ah, watch by me, Sandy—stay by me every moment—*don't* let me go out of my mind again; death is nothing, let it come, but not with those dreams, not with the torture of those hideous dreams—I cannot endure *that* again. . . . Sandy? . . ."

He lay muttering incoherently some little time; then for a time he lay silent, and apparently sinking away toward death. Presently his fingers began to pick busily at the coverlet, and by that sign I knew that his end was at hand. With the first suggestion of the death rattle in his throat he started up slightly, and seemed to listen; then he said:

"A bugle? . . . It is the king! The drawbridge, there! Man the battlements—turn out the—"

He was getting up his last "effect"; but he never finished it.

SELECTED BIBLIOGRAPHY

Works by Mark Twain

The Celebrated Jumping Frog of Calaveras County, 1865 Story (Signet Classic CE1390)

The Innocents Abroad, 1869 Travel (Signet Classic CE1379)

Roughing It, 1872 Travel (Signet Classic CJ1216)

The Gilded Age (with Charles Dudley Warner), 1873 Novel (Signet Classic CE1375)

The Adventures of Tom Sawyer, 1876 Novel (Signet Classic CW1337)

The Facts Concerning the Recent Carnival of Crime in Connecticut, 1876 Story (Signet Classic CE1390)

A Tramp Abroad, 1880 Travel

The Prince and the Pauper, 1882 Novel (Signet Classic CE1407)

The Stolen White Elephant, 1882 Story (Signet Classic CE1390)

Life on the Mississippi, 1883 Travel (Signet Classic CQ936)

The Adventures of Huckleberry Finn, 1884 Novel (Signet Classic CE1434)

A Connecticut Yankee in King Arthur's Court, 1889 Novel (Signet Classic CW1283)

Luck, 1891 Story (Signet Classic CE1390)

The American Claimant, 1892 Novel

The £1,000,000 Bank Note, 1893 Story (Signet Classic CE1390)

The Tragedy of Pudd'nhead Wilson and the Comedy of Those Extraordinary Twins, 1894 Novel (Signet Classic CW 1229)

Personal Recollections of Joan of Arc, 1896 Novel

Tom Sawyer Abroad, Tom Sawyer, Detective, and Other Stories, 1896 Novels and Stories

How to Tell a Story and Other Essays, 1897 Essays

The Man that Corrupted Hadleyburg, 1899 Story (Signet Classic CE1390)

The Five Boons of Life, 1902 Story (Signet Classic CE1390)

Was It Heaven? Or Hell?, 1902 Story (Signet Classic CE1390)

The Mysterious Stranger, 1916 Short Novel (Signet Classic

Biography and Criticism

Anderson, Frederick, ed. *Mark Twain: The Critical Heritage.* New York: Barnes & Noble, 1971.

Anderson, Frederick, *et al.*, eds. *Mark Twain's Notebooks & Journals*. Berkeley: Univ. of California Press. *vol. II (1877–1883)*, 1975; *vol. III (1883–1891)*, 1979.

Andrews, Kenneth R. *Nook Farm: Mark Twain's Hartford Circle*. Cambridge: Harvard Univ. Press, 1950.

Asselineau, Roger. *The Literary Reputation of Mark Twain from 1910 to 1950*. Paris: Didier, 1954; repr. Westport: Greenwood Press, 1971.

Baetzhold, Howard G. *Mark Twain and John Bull: The British Connection*. Bloomington: Indiana Univ. Press, 1970.

Budd, Louis J. *Mark Twain, Social Philosopher*. Bloomington: Indiana Univ. Press, 1962.

Cox, James M. "*A Connecticut Yankee in King Arthur's Court:* The Machinery of Self-Preservation," *Yale Review* 50 (Autumn 1960), repr. in Henry Nash Smith, ed. *Mark Twain: A Collection of Critical Essays*. Englewood Cliffs: Prentice-Hall, 1963.

DeVoto, Bernard. *Mark Twain's America*. Boston: Houghton Mifflin, 1932,

Hansen, Chadwick. "The Once and Future Boss: Mark Twain's Yankee," *Nineteenth-Century Fiction* 28 (June 1973),

Howells, William Dean. *My Mark Twain: Reminiscences and Criticism*. New York & London: Harper, 1910.

Kaplan, Justin. *Mr. Clemens and Mark Twain*. New York: Simon & Schuster, 1966.

Kasson, John A. *Civilizing the Machine: Technology and Republican Values in America, 1776–1900*. New York: Grossman, 1176; Penguin, 1977.

Lynn, Kenneth S. *Mark Twain and Southwestern Humor*. Boston: Little, Brown, 1959.

Salomon, Roger B. *Twain and the Image of History*. New Haven: Yale Univ. Press, 1961.

Scott, Arthur L. "Mark Twain Looks at Europe," *South Atlantic Quarterly* 52 (1953).

————, ed. *Mark Twain: Selected Criticism*. Dallas: Southern Methodist Univ. Press, 1955.

Smith, Henry Nash. *Mark Twain: The Development of a Writer*. Cambridge: Harvard Univ. Press, 1962.

————. *Mark Twain's Fable of Progress: Political and Economic Ideas in "A Connecticut Yankee"*. New Brunswick: Rutgers Univ. Press, 1964.